THE QUEEN CITY

Happy Reading!

Tyler R. Tichelaar

THE QUEEN CITY

The Marquette Trilogy: Book Two

a novel

Tyler R. Tichelaar

Marquette Fiction
Marquette, Michigan

THE QUEEN CITY

Marquette Fiction
1202 Pine Street
Marquette, MI 49855
www.marquettefiction.com

ISBN-13: 978-0-9791790-1-3
ISBN-10: 0-9791790-1-7

Library of Congress PCN 2007932348

Publication managed by Back Channel Press
www.backchannelpress.com

To the Memory of
Lester and Grace White
My Wonderful Grandparents
Whom I Miss Everyday

"I had searched for books telling about the beauty of the country I loved, its romance, and heroism and strength of courage of its people that had been plowed into the very furrows of its soil, and I did not find them. And so I wrote *O Pioneers!*" - Willa Cather

PRINCIPAL FAMILIES IN *THE QUEEN CITY*
Note: some characters are not included so as not to give away the plots

The Whitmans

Cordelia Whitman - family matriarch, mother of Edna and the late
    Jacob Whitman
Edna Brookfield - Cordelia's married daughter who lives in Utah
Will Whitman - son of the late Jacob Whitman, brother to Clarence, Sylvia,
    and Mary
Clarence Whitman - brother to Will, Sylvia, and Mary
Mary Feake - sister to Will, Clarence, and Sylvia. She is married and lives in
    Chicago
Sylvia Cumming - sister to Mary, Will, and Clarence. Married to Harry
    Cumming
Harry Cumming - Sylvia Whitman's husband
Harry Cumming Jr. - Harry and Sylvia's oldest son
Douglas Cumming - Harry and Sylvia's son
Serena Cumming - Harry and Sylvia's daughter

The Dalrymples

Arthur Dalrymple - family patriarch, born in Nova Scotia, of Scottish descent
Charles Dalrymple - son of Arthur, a carpenter
Christina Dalrymple - Charles's wife
Margaret Dalrymple - Charles and Christina's oldest daughter
Sarah Dalrymple - Charles and Christina's daughter
Charles Dalrymple Jr. - Charles and Christina's son

The McCareys and Bergmanns

Molly Bergmann Montoni - family matriarch, and twice a widow. An Irish
    immigrant who came to Marquette in 1849 when it was founded
Kathy McCarey - daughter to Molly, wife to Patrick
Patrick McCarey - an Irish immigrant, husband of Kathy
Frank McCarey - Patrick and Kathy's oldest son
Jeremy McCarey - Patrick and Kathy's son
Michael McCarey - Patrick and Kathy's son

Beth McCarey - Patrick and Kathy's daughter
Karl Bergmann - Molly's son
Aino Nordmaki - Karl's wife
Thelma Bergmann - Karl and Aino's daughter

Other Principal Characters

Lysander Blackmore - a rich young man, later a banker
Eric Hobson - friend of Robert O'Neill, a teacher in the Marquette Schools
Mrs. Hopewell, Jessie and Lyla - the abandoned wife of a Finn and her two
    daughters
Robert O'Neill - famous local novelist born in South Carolina but raised and
    living in Marquette
Vincent Smiley - a young man, newly moved to Marquette from Sault Sainte
    Marie
Lex Weidner - a young man who works at the Huron Mountain Club
Chloe - an attractive waitress

HISTORICAL PEOPLE IN *THE QUEEN CITY*

Abbott and Costello - famous comedy team who came to Marquette to
    promote war bonds during World War II
Bishop Ablewhite - Episcopalian bishop of Marquette in 1938
Buffalo Bill (William F. Cody) - Wild West Showman who visited Marquette
    in 1902
Don H. Bottum - Dean of Men at Northern Michigan College of Education
    in 1949
Father Bucholtz - priest at St. Peter's Cathedral in 1935
Paul Bunyan - the famous logger. Karl Bergmann insists he is a real person
Warden Catlin - Warden of the Marquette Branch Prison during the
    1921 riot
Henry Ford - automobile magnate and member of the Huron Mountain Club
Bob Harper - inmate at the Marquette Branch Prison involved in the
    1921 riot
Perry Hatch - scoutmaster, organizer of the Bartlett King memorial obelisk
Daniel L. Hebard - President of the Huron Mountain Club 1926-1938
Otto Hultgren - a decorated World War II soldier from Marquette

Chief Charles Kawbawgam - last Chief of the Chippewa, who lived from 1799-1902

Bartlett King - boy scout leader and soldier who dies in World War I

Frank Krieg - owner of a gold mine in Marquette County, founder of the town of Birch

J.M. Longyear - prosperous Marquette entrepreneur, city benefactor, member of the Huron Mountain Club

Mrs. Longyear - his wife

Howard Longyear - their son who drowned in Lake Superior

David McClintock - submarine commander at Battle of Leyte Gulf in World War II

Mr. Miller - embezzler of funds from St. Paul's Episcopal Church

William Molby - World War I soldier

Mrs. Carroll Paul - member of the Huron Mountain Club, daughter of J.M. Longyear

Perry - inmate of the Marquette Branch Prison involved in the 1921 riot

Carroll Watson Rankin - local Marquette author of *Dandelion Cottage* and several other children's novels

Roberts - inmate of the Marquette Branch Prison involved in the 1921 riot

Theodore Roosevelt - U.S. President, defendant in 1913 trial at the Marquette County Courthouse

Fred Rydholm - employee at the Huron Mountain Club, later Mayor of Marquette and author of *Superior Heartland*, a history of Marquette and the Huron Mountain Club

William Howard Taft - first U.S. President to visit Marquette while in office

Henry Tape - President of Northern Michigan College of Education in 1949

John Voelker - Marquette County prosecuting attorney

Dwight D. Waldo - first President of Northern State Normal School

Dr. Luther West - head of Northern Michigan College of Education's Science Department

Lester White - a carpenter in Marquette

The Honorable Peter White - one of Marquette's founding fathers, a prosperous businessman and Marquette's greatest benefactor

William, Roland, and Frank White - three brothers who served in World War II, brothers to Lester White

Governor Williams - Governor of Michigan in 1949

Monsignor Joseph Zryd - first pastor of St. Michael's Parish

1902

"You better talk to him today. No sense in them boys carrying on with their fancy dreaming any longer."

Harry Cumming made this declaration to his wife at breakfast.

"But Clarence is going over to Grandma's house to help her pack this morning, and Will and I are taking the boys to the Wild West Show," Sylvia Cumming replied.

"No reason why you can't tell Will on the way to the show."

Harry Cumming chugged down his morning cup of coffee. Then he got up from the table to leave for work.

"Harry, isn't there any money left at all? Poor Clarence will be heartbroken."

"Can't be helped," he muttered, grabbing his lunch pail.

"I don't see why I should be the one to tell them."

"You're their sister."

"But — "

"Damn it, woman. I told you to tell them. Now you mind me, or it'll make things worse. Those boys are too lazy anyhow. Look at them; here it is a Wednesday, and Clarence is going to his Grandma's and Will's going with you to the Buffalo Bill Show. They both ought to be out working. I never saw such spoiled folks as your family. You all act as if you're royalty or something."

"Harry, you know Clarence is helping Grandma pack; you can't expect him not to help her when she's moving away. And Will is looking for work. He can't help that he was laid off from his last job."

"He can't be looking too hard if he hasn't found anything in three weeks. Now you tell them before I get home tonight, or you'll be sorry; I guarantee it."

"Sorry about what?" asked Clarence, coming into the kitchen.

"Don't butt in when I'm talking to my wife," Harry snapped. Then he offered his cheek to Sylvia for the obligatory kiss before he disappeared out the door.

Sylvia immediately turned the topic of conversation away from her husband.

"Clarence, are you sure you don't want to go to the Wild West Show with us?"

"No, I'm late now. I told Grandma I'd be there by eight."

"Don't you want me to make you breakfast?"

Before Clarence could answer, his two-year old nephew screamed in the parlor.

"I'll just take a muffin with me," Clarence hollered as Sylvia ran to see whether her child were safe.

Will came downstairs in time to bid his brother goodbye. Then he went to the stove to help cook breakfast so they would not be late for the parade. Sylvia returned to the kitchen with her little boys, Harry Jr. and Doug. Both boys were too excited about the parade to eat more than a bite. Sylvia was thankful for Will's help; the boys kept her and Will so busy she was momentarily relieved from having to tell Will the awful news. But she knew she would have to tell him before Harry returned home.

On July 16, 1902, the residents of Marquette, Michigan anticipated seeing an exhibition unparalleled in American history. The one and only Colonel William F. Cody had come to town with his famous Wild West Show. Better known as Buffalo Bill, Colonel Cody had hundreds of fans just among Marquette's young boys while fathers eagerly anticipated seeing the man who had been their boyhood hero, and even mothers willingly attended, although less interested in the colonel than in the sharp shooting prowess of Annie Oakley.

Never had the remote little Northern town expected such famous visitors. The exciting day began with a parade led by the infamous Buffalo Bill himself; every boy idolized him as the famous cowboy pranced his white horse down Washington Street. Hundreds of locals followed the procession west of town to the Toupin Farm where the show would be held. No one wanted to miss this once in a lifetime chance. People traveled from Ishpeming, Negaunee, and the surrounding farms to create a crowd of ten thousand attendants. The program would include twenty-three fabulous demonstrations, including artillery drills, Buffalo Bill rescuing covered wagons from an Indian attack, a buffalo hunt, an Indian war dance, lasso throwing, sharp shooting, and a new feature, a ship-wreck lifesaving drill.

Will Whitman, his sister Sylvia, and his two nephews cheered the parade, then joined half the city's population at the Wild West Show. In high spirits, Will effortlessly took turns carrying his nephews on his shoulders as they hiked to the show grounds. The boys adored Uncle Will who paid more attention to them than their own father. Since the sudden death of Will's father five years before, he and Clarence had made their home with Sylvia's family.

Will had been seventeen when his father died; he had then wanted to run the family farm, but his brothers-in-law had insisted such a plan was impractical; truthfully, they had wanted their wives' shares of the estate. Because Jacob Whitman had failed to make a will or appoint an executor, Harry Cumming had taken it upon himself to sell the farm and divide the estate equally between his wife, her sister Mary, and the two brothers. Mary had not even come home from Chicago for the funeral, so her share of the inheritance was sent to her. She and her husband despised Marquette and felt no ties to the area. Her contact with her siblings had since become irregular. With the farm sold, Will and Clarence had no choice but to live with Harry and Sylvia. The arrangement was far from ideal.

Sylvia had suggested her inheritance be used to purchase a larger home, but Harry had refused, so Clarence and Will were forced to share a room. Sylvia and Harry had their own room while their two boys had the third bedroom. Now Sylvia was expecting her third child, whom she insisted would be a girl. Will saw this expected family addition as reason for him and Clarence to find their own place; for Sylvia's sake, he had kept the peace these five years, but he knew his brother-in-law did not want him around.

Jacob Whitman had wanted both his sons to attend college, but his sudden death had made higher education impossible for Will. Both Will and Clarence were too young to know how to handle money without guidance. Rather than assist her younger brothers, Sylvia entrusted both her and her brothers' inheritances to her husband. During the ensuing five years, Harry was frequently out of work; as money became tight, he spent his wife's inheritance, then borrowed freely from Will, who gave from a sense of duty toward the family. Gradually, Will's savings dwindled; he did not mind terribly when he had to give up plans to attend college; he had been a good student, but he preferred working outdoors with his hands to being buried in books. Yet Will was adamant that Clarence, this spring just graduated from high school, would attend Marquette's newly established Normal School to be trained as a teacher.

At night, in the quiet of their room, the brothers would discuss their future. Neither was happy with his current situation. Will had found several odd jobs over the years ranging from logging and carpentry to cooking and pounding spikes on the railroad. Often he had been laid off or quit a job he hated, in hopes of finding something better, but something better never seemed to come. Now the brothers focused on what they would do once Clarence finished college. They agreed that wherever Clarence found a teaching job, they would move there together. They loved Sylvia and her children, but living with her family was a strain for two young men who wanted to be on their own. They had no real reason to remain in Marquette. Their parents were both gone, and their grandfather had passed away the previous winter. Grandma Whitman was their only other relative in Marquette, and now she had decided to move out West to live with her daughter, son-in-law, and sister, Great-Aunt Sophia.

Today, Will found welcomed relief from his constant brooding over his future by attending the Wild West Show. When Harry Jr. decided to practice his Indian war whoops from his uncle's shoulders, Will eagerly joined in, despite stares from onlookers.

"Will, don't encourage him," Sylvia said.

"Uncle Will, do you think we'll see any Indians get killed?" Harry Jr. asked.

"We'll see Indians, but not any getting killed," said Will. "There are only peace loving Indians in the show."

"Oh," Harry Jr. frowned. "Will there be buffaloes?"

"I don't think so," said Will.

"Well, then what is there going to be?"

"People marching and horse riding tricks and a band and some sharp shooting."

"Okay." Harry Jr. felt satisfied.

The family followed the streaming crowd into the circle of wagons that formed the stadium. They soon found seats amid the excited, good-natured spectators. Will explained to his nephews what cowboys did when they were not busy chasing Indians while Sylvia searched for her handkerchief to wipe away the perspiration from the long, warm walk.

Finally when none of the crowd could bear any longer the anticipation to see an Indian from the Wild West or an army cavalry, the band struck up the music. The Star Spangled Banner played, and Harry Jr. waved the American flag Uncle Will had bought him on the Fourth of July, and which he had insisted on bringing along.

Into the arena galloped a stream of mounted horses. INDIANS! Sioux, Arapaho, Brule, Cheyenne in war paint and feathers, waving terrible weapons and intimidating all their enemies with ferocious war whoops. Harry Jr. laughed in delight. Little Doug looked frightened until his mother whispered it was all "make-believe." Now came the U.S. Cavalry, and cowboys, and an old stagecoach — what would a Wild West Show be without a stagecoach robbery? A stage scene was set of an Indian camp, with the inhabitants going about their daily lives amid their teepees, until suddenly a group of braves rushed into camp. An attack was coming! Then appeared the hostile tribe. Fighting! Arrows flying! Scalping! Noise and confusion. Cries of terror! Shouts of victory! The crowd was aghast at such realism, marveling at the war bonnets, wishing such excitement existed in everyday life despite the bloodshed. Dozens fell to the ground, actors acting dead.

"Uncle Will, I told you we would see Indians get shot!" Harry Jr. said.

Will did not spoil the boy's fun by reminding him it was just a show.

"My word!" said Sylvia when the cowgirls rode out on their horses. Infamous Annie Oakley arrived to display her sharp shooting skills. "It ain't natural," said Sylvia, yet she was secretly exulted to see a woman do something better than a man.

Now the Buffalo Chase. Most of Marquette's citizens had never seen a buffalo. Harry Jr. shook with the thrill of the sight, and even Will was impressed by the animals' inclusion in the program.

"Those buffalo are the ugliest things I've ever seen," Sylvia said.

"They make fine coats though," Will replied.

"I wouldn't wear one."

"I would," Harry Jr. said.

"You would, would you?" Will laughed. He could not afford a buffalo coat, but he resolved to buy his nephew a cowboy hat before they left.

Even after the show ended, Harry Jr.'s enthusiasm did not wane. He insisted they go get a closer look at the animals.

Sylvia clung to her brother's arm as they passed Indians fully dressed in war bonnets. These noble warriors, well aware of how they frightened white women, smirked gleefully at Sylvia's discomfort.

"Uncle Will, do you think you could wrestle one of them Indians?" Harry Jr. asked.

"I don't know. They look awful strong," he said as they walked toward the animals.

"I think you could," replied his admiring nephew.

"I'm too thirsty to wrestle now," Will said. "How about I buy us all some lemonade?"

"Okay," said Harry Jr.

"No, Will, you spoil the boys too much," said Sylvia. He had already bought Harry the cowboy hat. His generosity made Sylvia all the more nervous about what she must tell him before supper.

Lemonades in hand, for Will would not be dissuaded, the family walked home. Will whistled tunes from the Wild West Show while Harry Jr. tried to imitate him. The whistling grated on Sylvia's nerves. She felt herself trembling with anxiety. When they reached their front yard, Sylvia caught a glimpse of her husband through the window. He was home early. She tried to steel her nerves.

"Will, I need to talk to you a minute before we go inside."

Will was surprised by her sudden seriousness when all had been gaiety a moment before.

"Uncle Will, I — "

"Harry," Sylvia told her son, "go inside and take Doug with you. I have to talk to Uncle Will."

Doug did not want to go with his brother, but when Sylvia glared at him, the little boy took his brother's hand. Will stood awkwardly while the boys went up the porch steps into the house. Then he turned to his sister, silently waiting for her to speak.

"Will," she trembled, "I know you have your heart set on Clarence going to college, and so do I. It's what Father wanted, but — "

"But what?"

"Will, please don't be angry with me."

She did not need to say more. Will guessed.

"What happened to the money? What did the bastard do with it?"

"You know how it is," Sylvia cried. "Things are hard for us with so many mouths to feed."

"I pay my and Clarence's room and board," Will said. "You had your inheritance from Pa. You don't need Clarence's. How much is gone?"

"All except maybe fifty dollars," she said.

"Why?"

She sighed. "You know what Harry's like."

"Gambling debts?" Will did not need to ask; he knew the answer.

"Among other things. He made some risky investments. We'll try to pay it back, Will. It doesn't mean Clarence can't go to college. Just maybe, he could work for a year or so, and — Will, no, don't go in yet. Don't. Wait!"

She chased her brother up the front steps. Enraged, Will had leapt onto the porch, flung open the front door, torn through the house and found his brother-in-law seated at the kitchen table.

"How was the show, Will?" Harry Cumming asked before he saw the wrath on his brother-in-law's face.

"You bastard! How could you?" Will demanded of the man he doubly detested for marrying his sister and stealing his and his siblings' inheritance.

"Now, Will, don't get your dander up! You don't understand what I — "

"Will!" Sylvia cried. Harry said no more. Before he could stand up, Will's fist had met his jaw. He fell to the floor, his chair collapsing on top of him. Will grabbed the overturned chair by its legs and prepared to batter Harry with it, but Sylvia grabbed him from behind. In thoughtless rage, Will jerked to free himself from her hold, flinging her back against the sink.

"Mama!" cried Doug, standing in the doorway.

The alarm in his nephew's voice recalled Will to his senses.

Harry Jr. had heard the screams and now stood beside his little brother in the doorway. Doug let up a torrential cry. Sylvia ran to comfort him. She would have carried him from the room, but she feared to leave her husband to her brother's mercy.

"Will, I didn't mean, I — " said Harry, despite his mean streak, cowering on the floor. Will set down the chair, disgusted by his brother-in-law's fear.

"You deserve worse than I gave you," he spat out, "but for Sylvia and the boys' sake — "

Harry bowed his head under Will's glare.

"Damn you!" Will shouted, flinging the chair to the floor. He brushed past his sister and nephews to leave the room.

"Sylvia," Harry called, but she left him lying on the floor while she rushed after her brother.

"Will!" she cried, but he did not stop until he was halfway down the front porch steps.

"I can't stand to see him ever again, Sylvia. He blew all your money, and I loaned him all of mine, and now he's stolen all of Clarence's. He's not even man enough to own up to it, but instead makes you tell me, and now I have to tell Clarence."

"We'll pay it back, Will, even if I have to work myself to do it."

"You don't owe it to us, Sylvia, he does, and that means I'll never see that money again. Just like I'll never see him again."

"What are you saying, Will? You're talking crazy." Tears streamed from her eyes. She feared his words. Could he be so cruel as to leave her alone with Harry? "Where will you go, Will?"

"I don't know. Maybe Clarence and I'll join the Wild West Show. We'll both have to work now."

"Don't talk so foolish. I couldn't bear you going away. We can work something out."

"I can't discuss it now, Sylvia. I'm sorry, but I'm about ready to blow again."

He turned toward the sidewalk.

"But where will you go?"

"I don't know. I have to talk to Clarence. I'll tell you later."

Sylvia watched his feet pound down the street. She dreaded going back inside the house, but when she heard Doug wailing, her maternal instinct conquered her fear.

"How dare you take his side? I'm your husband!" Harry roared when she returned to the kitchen. He had managed to stumble back into a chair. "I don't want that ruffian in my house from this day on. Do you hear me?"

"He won't be coming back," said Sylvia.

Her answer was not enough for Harry. His pride was wounded by the thrashing he had received; he ranted for the next half hour to assert he was king in his own home. Sylvia scarcely listened. She was in a panic that she and her children would now be alone with him.

Will worked off much of his anger as he walked to his grandmother's house. He was not by nature a violent or unreasonable man. Had it only been his money that was lost, he never would have acted as he had — he might have yelled — but never resorted to physical violence. After years of his brother-in-law's antics, however, Will had become protective toward Clarence, not taking lightly any mistreatment of his younger brother. He warned himself not to express his anger before his grandmother; she was eighty years old and troubled enough since his grandfather's recent death. Will had never enlightened his grandparents to the economic woes of his sister's family or his own resulting deprivations, and now that his grandmother was going out West to live with Aunt Edna, it was pointless to mention it.

"There you are," Cordelia smiled when Will entered her kitchen. "I was hoping you'd come over. I have a cake cooling in the pantry, and I didn't want

Clarence to eat it all, though I'm sure he would. I've never known a Whitman who didn't have a sweet tooth."

"Cake sounds wonderful, Grandma," Will replied. "Where is Clarence?"

He wanted to speak to his brother in private, but Clarence was already coming downstairs, bearing a crate of items to be shipped out West.

"Hi, Will; how was the Wild West Show?"

"Great," said Will, surprised to think only an hour ago, he had been having a pleasant day with his sister and nephews; now his head throbbed from his violent outburst.

"Was that lady sharpshooter there?" asked Cordelia.

"Yes," said Will. Despite his mental anguish, he found himself answering a dozen questions about the Wild West Show. His grandmother set slices of cake before them all and poured coffee which they all doused with cream and sugar.

"My, I hope I don't see any Indians get shot when I'm out West," said Cordelia.

"The West isn't that way anymore, Grandma," said Clarence.

"Well, you would know; you're book smart. I'm so proud to think you'll be starting college soon, and becoming a teacher of all things."

Clarence lowered his eyes and stuffed more cake in his mouth. Will's heart sank at the mention of his brother attending college.

"Your Aunt Edna is proud of you too," Cordelia said, "which reminds me — I wanted to read you boys the letter I got from her yesterday."

Neither Will nor Clarence were interested in Aunt Edna's letters. They had never met her except the two times she had briefly come home for their father and grandfather's funerals. They rather resented Aunt Edna for stealing their grandmother away, although they were too good-natured to say so; they knew Grandma was looking forward to spending her final days with her daughter's family.

"Here it is," said Cordelia, finding Edna's letter in a clutter of mail on the cupboard. She poured herself another cup of coffee, then sat down to read aloud.

> Dear Mother,
>   I'm so happy you've agreed to come live with Esau, Aunt Sophia and me now that Father has passed away. We've been so lonely since Uncle Darius died. Aunt Sophia talks constantly about your coming. She is anticipating it by telling us stories about your childhood back in New York. You were quite a mischievous girl.
>   Mother

"Not as mischievous as Sophia," Cordelia said. All her life she had striven to be a good Methodist, and she did not wish her grandsons to think ill of her.

> You will not miss those cold Upper Michigan winters once you are here and see how pleasant and warm is Utah's climate. Aunt Sophia insists she will live to be one hundred in this warm land, and with all the energy she has at eighty-two, we do not doubt it. She is becoming a bit forgetful now, but I think old age has mellowed her, and with all her money, she is delighted to be the richest citizen in the county. She rarely goes out, however, but seems content here at the ranch. She has a few church ladies who come to visit her and who do not seem to mind when she lords it over them, but I think she has given up on social prominence. At her age, she just prefers to relax. If only Uncle Darius were still alive, the three of you would have such fun, rocking away on our veranda on a warm summer day while you remembered the old days.
>
> I'm afraid we are all old folks here now that the children are grown. The boys help out on the ranch in the summers, but they are gone off to the University of Utah the rest of the year. Phillip has begun a master's degree there and Tom will be a freshman this fall. Harry looks forward to your being here for his wedding this fall. I can't believe my oldest boy is about to get married. Only Celia is at home with me now, and at fourteen, I realize it won't be long before some young man steals her away.
>
> I don't have much more to say. I will be arriving by train in Marquette on July 20th so please be packed and ready to go then. I know Jacob's boys will be helpful to you. Give my best wishes to all the family and my old friends there. I'll see you in a couple weeks.
>
> Love, Edna

Cordelia sighed as she folded up the letter. She saw the look of disinterest in her grandsons' faces. They barely knew their Aunt Edna, and they had never met their Great-Uncle Darius, Great-Aunt Sophia, or their Brookfield cousins.

"I'm so anxious to see my grandchildren in Utah," Cordelia said, "but I'll miss the ones I'm leaving here in Marquette."

She hoped she had made the right decision to go out West. She had always missed Sophia, and after Sophia's husband, Gerald, had died, and Sophia had moved to Utah, Cordelia had often wished to visit her sister and her daughter's family. Her own husband had been too frail for her to leave alone, but now that he was gone, she knew if she did not move, she would soon be too old to make the journey. She could not remain in Marquette for Sylvia and Harry's sake; she never felt welcome in their home. She would miss only Will and Clarence, but they were young men likely to leave Marquette to seek their fortunes. The warm dry climate of the West would be better for her health. Still, with all her reasoning, she found it hard to leave this town.

Cordelia had arrived in Marquette in its infancy half a century before, right after it had been established as a port on Lake Superior for shipping the newly discovered iron being mined just ten miles south of the lakeshore; here she had raised her children and watched her grandchildren be raised; here her son and daughter-in-law, husband, parents, niece and nephew were buried; she had watched Marquette grow from a village of a few unstable wooden cabins to a city of ten thousand inhabitants, the seat of the county, the Queen City of the North; as the Civil War encroached, Marquette's solitary dock had become a harbor full of ships, hauling iron ore that was poured from its magnificent pocket docks. That ore had helped to win the Civil War for the Union, and in the years that followed, despite occasional economic hardships, the town had grown and thrived with the iron industry. Cordelia's father and brother-in-law had built one of the town's first forges, her mother had been a leader in founding the Methodist church, her nephew had worked on the ore docks during the war, her sister owned one of the first stores, her husband and son had prosperously farmed the land, and she had operated one of the early boarding houses, while still raising her family.

Cordelia was proud of how Marquette had grown and prospered, and she was reluctant to leave the town that had become her home. She would miss everything here — the gorgeous view of the great blue Lake Superior, the lush green forests that surrounded the town, the sublime lakeside cliffs, the cool lake breezes, and the long yet serene winters when the snowbanks grew and grew until they towered over a person. Utah would be warm and that would be fine for her health, but the lake, the trees, and the snow had been good for Cordelia's spirit. She would miss the town as much as her grandchildren, but she could not expect them to devote their young lives to caring for her in old age, and she knew she should no longer live alone. In Utah, her sister, daughter and other grandchildren would be a comfort to her. Life was always changing — if nothing else, she had learned in her long life that she could either die or embrace change; her pioneer spirit rose up in her as she prepared for her next adventure.

"Grandma," Clarence asked. "What's Aunt Edna's last name? Didn't she marry some sort of cousin?"

"Yes, she married my brother Darius's son, Esau."

"So her married name is Brookfield?"

"Yes, same as my maiden name. She has three boys to carry on the Brookfield name. My father would have been happy to know it if he had lived long enough."

"Will and I will carry on the Whitman name," said Clarence.

"Yes, but don't forget you have Brookfield blood too."

"Whitman or Brookfield, either is better than being a Cumming," Will thought. He hated all this chitchat, this delaying of his telling his brother what a scoundrel Harry was, but he held his tongue before his grandmother.

"I have a surprise for you boys," said Cordelia when the cake was all gone. "I was going to sell this little house, but I don't really need the money, and I know you boys don't like living with Sylvia's family, so I've decided to deed it over to you."

"Grandma, that's a great idea!" said Clarence.

Will was stunned, but he managed to object, "We can't afford to buy the house, Grandma, and it wouldn't be fair to accept it as a gift."

"I can't give it to you. I have to deed it over to you so if you just pay the costs for the paperwork, we'll call it fair."

"But we don't have any money," Will replied.

"Yes, we do," said Clarence, thinking of his college savings. He felt owning a house would be a better investment than going to the Normal School where only girls went.

"No, we can't," Will repeated.

"Yes, you can," Cordelia said. "I talked to Peter White down at the bank. He said I could sell it to you boys for one dollar."

"A dollar?" Will was amazed. He could easily afford one dollar. That would mean not having to live with Harry and Sylvia anymore. It would mean he could support himself and Clarence on his wages since they would not have to pay rent. And Mr. Dalrymple had said he would have carpentry work for him next week. If he were frugal, he might still send Clarence to college.

"What do you say?" Cordelia asked.

"Yes. We say yes," said Clarence.

"Yes," Will agreed. "Now we'll have our own rooms, and the house won't be full of screaming children, not that I don't love Doug and Harry Jr., but Clarence'll need a quiet place so he can study."

Will felt the future seemed not as awful as an hour ago.

"Good. I'm glad," said Cordelia. "Let me clean up this table. Then I have something else to tell you boys before you go."

Clarence and Will carried more crates downstairs while Cordelia washed the dishes. With each trip they made downstairs, she had new directions for them. "I don't want the furniture; I'll leave it here for you boys. We'll go to the bank tomorrow to sign the papers. Would one of you mind staying with me until Edna comes next week? I don't want to be alone in case I trip over some of this mess when I get up during the night."

All this while, Will just wanted to hug his grandmother. She had solved his troubles without his telling them to her. He would still have to tell Clarence how Harry had wasted all their money, but he could wait now until after Grandma had moved out West so she would not get involved. Will was content simply not to sleep under his brother-in-law's roof any longer.

"We'll both stay with you until Aunt Edna comes," Will told his grand-mother. "We'll just move in now if it's all right."

"That's fine. You can go fetch your things while I make supper," said Cordelia, "but first I have something to give you boys before it accidentally gets packed."

She led them into the parlor where she sat down on the sofa beside a crate of china. She directed the boys' gaze to the mantle, over which hung an ancient rifle.

"My other grandsons will carry on the Brookfield name, but you boys are Brookfields too. I was always going to give that rifle to your father, but I could never quite do it. It belonged to my grandfather, and having it here always made me feel as if he were still with me. It used to hang over the mantle at my father's farm, but when he died, your Aunt Sophia snatched it up — I never understood why since she never liked our Grandpa Brookfield too much — but later she gave it to me. I feel it should go to you boys and one of you can pass it on to a son of your own someday."

"Are you sure you want us to have it, Grandma?" Will asked.

"Yes. I would have given it to you boys sooner, but — well — we both know what Harry is like. I didn't want it to end up in a pawn shop with him pocketing the money."

"Grandma!" Clarence laughed.

"I'm just being honest," said Cordelia. "At my age, I'm allowed, and it's no secret that Sylvia made a mistake when she married that man."

Will was tempted to expose Harry's latest crime against the family, but the rifle dominated the conversation.

"It was really your grandfather's?" Clarence asked.

"Yes, it belonged to your great-great grandfather, Major Esau Brookfield."

"He was a major?" Clarence repeated.

"Yes," said Cordelia. "Didn't your father tell you about him?"

"I think so," said Will, "but it was so long ago."

"Well, your father didn't like to talk about war after his own experiences fighting in the South. Anyway, my grandfather was a major during the American Revolution."

"Was he the one in the navy?" asked Clarence.

"No, that was your Grandpa Whitman's grandpa. My grandpa was in the army. He carried this rifle through the war. When I was a little girl, he used to tell me stories about the battles he was in."

"What was he like?" Will asked.

Cordelia avoided mentioning that in his old age her grandfather had been a drunkard and a bankrupt; she had long ago forgiven him for it, and she chose to remember him as the kind old man of her childhood. "He was a great man, a hero of the Revolution; he went off to fight when he was only thirteen years old."

"Thirteen!" said Clarence.

"Yes, he felt it was his duty," Cordelia said. "You boys would do the same for your country if you had to, but back then, no one was even sure the United States would be a nation — it was just an idea, a dream of freedom."

"I don't know whether I could fight in a war," said Will.

"I hope you never have to," said Cordelia, "but the Brookfields, and the Whitmans too, are made of sturdy stuff. When courage is necessary, we hold our ground."

"But why did your grandfather go to war? Couldn't his father or older brothers go instead?" asked Clarence.

"Listen, and I'll tell you the whole story," said Cordelia. "My grandfather's family lived in Vermont when the war started, not far from the Canadian border. They and their neighbors helped to capture some of the local Tories and other traitors to the Revolution who were trying to escape into Canada. The Redcoats came to punish the families for siding against the British Crown. When my great-grandpa saw the soldiers coming, he told my grandfather, Esau, to take the family silver and with his brothers and sisters, to hide in the woods and stay there until he came to let them know it was safe. Esau's mother remained at the house. She refused to leave her husband's side or to abandon her home until she was forced to it."

"Esau must have found it hard to leave his parents like that," said Clarence.

"Yes, but he knew if anything happened to them, he would have to care for his brothers and sisters. He told me that while he hid in the forest, he saw smoke rising up and knew the house was being burnt down. It was all he could do to keep from running back, but he waited until he heard the drums and knew the soldiers were leaving. Then he left his brothers and sisters in the woods and went to investigate. The house was burnt down and the crops had been torched. He found his mother sitting on the ground crying before the house's smoldering ruins. She told him the soldiers had taken his father away. His father remained a prisoner in Canada until the war was over. His mother had managed to save the barn; some wicked Indians had come with the Redcoats, and they had tried to burn the barn, but she had scared them off by throwing pots of boiling water at them."

"That was brave of her," said Will.

"Yes," said Cordelia. "I don't know how any woman could have endured it, but we Brookfields find inner strength when we need it."

"Is that when your grandpa joined the army?" asked Clarence.

"Yes, but first he escorted his mother and his siblings to a fort held by the Continental Army. My great-grandmother became the laundry woman for the fort, while her children played safely inside. She sold the family silver and used the money to feed the family, and to buy my grandpa this rifle and a uniform to fight in. The rest of the money she gave out to people like herself who had lost their homes or to widows whose husbands had been killed in the war."

"But what happened to Esau?" Clarence asked.

"He joined the army and fought in a lot of battles. I don't remember all the names of them, but he was promoted to major before the war ended. He told me he was the youngest major in the army."

"Was he ever wounded?"

"No, surprisingly not. I wish I could remember the battles he told me he was in. I guess I remember more about his mother since I can't imagine being a woman during a war like that."

"I wish I knew which battles he was in," said Clarence.

"Well, we can just be proud that he was a brave man," Cordelia said. "I like to think he passed some of that bravery on to us."

"Thank you for the rifle, Grandma," said Will. "It'll mean a lot to us."

"I want it to be a reminder to you boys of the brave people you come from. It will help you remember how much one person can matter in bringing about something as great as our nation."

"Your grandpa would be proud of you, Grandma. You're as brave as he was," said Will.

Cordelia was embarrassed, but she did not argue when he elaborated, "You came to Marquette when it was just a wilderness, and now, in your old age, you're not afraid to go West. And even if you didn't fight in a war, you spent years struggling to care for your family and run the boarding house and to set a good example for everyone."

"Well, I have tried," Cordelia said.

Only now when his grandmother was leaving did Will realize what a strength she had been to him, especially since his father's death. And here she was doing one last kind act by giving him this rifle, and a home, giving him hope and a reminder of the strong pioneer blood that flowed in his veins.

"Anyway," said Cordelia, "I figured you boys would take good care of that rifle. I'll go fix supper for us now."

Clarence returned to packing crates while Will set out for his sister's house. He hated even to enter it and see his brother-in-law again. He regretted he had lost his temper in front of his nephews; it was a shame those boys should know their father was a scoundrel and a coward, but as they grew older, they would have realized it anyway. Even now, Will felt tempted to give Harry another good thrashing, but he also felt guilty to abandon Sylvia and her children to that man.

Will approached his sister's house slowly; he hoped to find Harry Jr. outside so he could get some information regarding the state of his brother-in-law's temper. But the house was silent. Even when he stood on the front porch and listened through the screen door, he could hear no sound.

Cautiously, he opened the front door and stepped inside. He saw his sister lying on the sofa, her eyes red from an hour spent crying.

"Sylvia," he whispered, sitting down beside her.

"Will, I didn't think you'd be back so soon," she said, jumping up in mixed fright and joy at his return.

"I came to collect my stuff. Grandma is giving Clarence and me her house. We'll live there from now on."

"Oh," she said, wiping her eyes. "I'm glad, Will. I never wanted you and Clarence to live here like this. It was my mistake that I married him, not yours."

"Where is he now?" Will asked.

"He went off to the tavern for supper. He said he was in no mood to eat my slop."

She half smiled to keep from crying further.

"Where are the boys?"

"Upstairs in their room. They're too scared to make any noise."

"I'm sorry," said Will, putting his arm around her. "I didn't mean to attack him like that. I just got so angry, more for Clarence's sake than mine."

"I know," said Sylvia. "Did you tell Clarence yet?"

"No, I'll wait until Grandma leaves. I don't want to upset her."

"You're so sensitive, Will, always taking care of everyone."

"I wish I could take better care of you, Syl."

"You can't," she sighed. "I'm stuck because I married him; I don't mind so much for me; I just wish my boys had a better father."

Will knew he could say or do nothing more. He could not change the boys' father, and he could not support his sister and her children when he could barely feed himself and Clarence.

"I'll come upstairs to help you pack," said Sylvia.

Everything was quickly in a suitcase. The brothers possessed nothing more than their few clothes and a couple items they had managed to keep from their father's house — a watch, a few books, a couple old family photographs.

"Don't be a stranger, Will," Sylvia said on the front porch. "The boys adore you. I couldn't bear for us to live in the same town and not be civil to one another. Harry told me not to see you anymore, but I won't let him stop us."

"It'll all work out," said Will to make her feel better, but he had no hope for peace between him and his brother-in-law. "Someday I'll have money, Syl, and then I'll take care of you and the boys so we can be together again."

Sylvia hugged him. He had a good heart, but she had lived long enough to doubt such dreams could come true. "Give Clarence my love," she said, then let him go.

"At least they're not leaving town," she thought as she watched Will walk down the street, "or doing anything reckless like joining the Wild West Show. Maybe it will still work out."

When Karl Bergmann finally married, he did it in a big way. Had he decided otherwise, his mother would have been disappointed. She was seventy-two years old and had waited thirty years to marry off her forty-eight year old son. She insisted on a large church wedding at St. Peter's Cathedral, even though Karl lived in Calumet and his bride was from Ishpeming. Following the festivities, a reception was to be held at the Hotel Marquette, where the bride and groom would spend their wedding night before leaving on their honey-moon to Chicago.

The future couple first met at Marquette's Clifton Hotel. Karl spent a couple nights there that summer while in town on business. While Karl loved his mother, sister, brother-in-law, and three nephews, the McCarey house felt too cramped and noisy for a middle-aged bachelor. Karl had left home at nineteen, and since then his life had been spent in tents and logging camps with other lumberjacks, particularly his friend and business partner, Ben. Karl and Ben had become owners of their own logging company, growing wealthy and building a fine house in Calumet where they resided when they were not out in the woods. Then one day, while supervising a logging operation, Ben had been killed instantly by a falling tree. The tragic accident was a devastating blow to Karl. Working in the woods had been his and Ben's life, and now he could not imagine going on without his best friend. Still he did not weep for Ben; to be taken by a tree seemed the ideal death for a lumberjack, a fair reparation for the many trees he had chopped down. Karl had, however, dreaded the years of loneliness he saw stretching before him.

During this difficult time, Karl met Aino Nordmaki, a Finnish girl less than half his age. She was a housemaid at Marquette's Clifton Hotel, working to help support her large family of parents, brothers, and sisters. Aino's family was among the vast number of Finnish and Scandinavian immigrants who settled in Upper Michigan at the turn of the century. The Nordmakis lived in Ishpeming, where Aino's father and brothers worked in the iron mines. Upon arriving in the United States, Aino had attended school only long enough to learn English, then gone to work. She soon became a favorite among the hotel clientele. Unlike most of Upper Michigan's clannish Finnish immigrants, Aino realized that to get ahead in this foreign land, she must assimilate into American culture. She thought working in one of Marquette's finest hotels was a fine start compared to the jobs in the mining towns of Ishpeming and Negaunee; Marquette seemed practically a cosmopolitan city compared to the nearby little mining towns, and the Clifton Hotel was frequently visited by shipping and railroad magnates.

The morning he met Aino, Karl had slept in late at the Clifton Hotel. During the height of his logging days, he would have been up before the dawn. But Ben's death had caused him to retire to bed early to escape the monotony of empty evenings, and he rarely rose now before ten in the morning. When he did wake, he would wish to return into the slumber of oblivion. On this fated morning, Karl had only woken early enough to run to the bank before going to his sister's house for lunch. He was half-dressed, and standing in direct line with the doorway when Aino opened the door, thinking the room empty and available to be cleaned. She stood in embarrassed surprise at the magnificent sight before her.

Karl Bergmann was far from a young man, but a life spent in the woods had sculpted his muscles and developed his chest until it was a barrel of power. Aino stared at his naked torso. He stared at Aino, glad to see another human being after a long, lonely, half-sleepless night. Then, a sense of decorum intruded; Karl clutched his shirt and Aino apologized for barging into his room. He accepted the apology, yet noticed she continued to stare at him as he buttoned his shirt. He gazed back, discovering her lovely blonde Finnish hair.

When she saw how he looked at her, she became nervous and went to clean his bathroom. He grabbed his hat and coat and departed. Their first meeting had lasted less than a minute.

Karl went to the First National Bank to complete his business. He went to lunch at his sister Kathy's house. He went to a nearby lumberyard to ensure enough lumber was available for an order Charles Dalrymple had contracted to build a house. Then he returned to the Clifton and wandered up and down the stairs and through the halls, feeling like a silly schoolboy — he had no more experience than a schoolboy in what he was about to attempt. Finally, he found Aino Nordmaki in a stairwell and asked her to have supper with him. She tried to explain she could not be involved with the hotel's male clients. He persisted when her eyes betrayed her pleasure at being asked. He took her to the Hotel Marquette — known for its splendid cuisine — where no one from the Clifton would see them. Aino had never eaten in a restaurant before — she had certainly never dined alone with a man. That he was a giant of a man made her feel both nervous and safe, as if even losing her position at the hotel could not happen if he were with her. They did not talk much; neither knew what to say, but in the end, she thanked him for the meal. When they returned to the Clifton, Karl walked her to the back door. Then he walked alone to the front door to preserve her reputation.

That was the first night Karl did not dwell on his grief over Ben's loss. He had known moments of romantic inclination in the past, but he had never known how to gain a woman's interest. Ben had repeatedly stated he had no interest in marriage, and with Ben's friendship, Karl had been content and focused on his work, but now he was alone, and work and all its profits were insufficient to fill his loneliness. Lunch that day with his sister's family had made him long for his own wife and children. He had felt foolish asking Aino to dinner. It had been a silly spontaneous decision. Yet he thought they had gotten along well. She had been a bit shy, but he could see she wanted to please him. She seemed like a good girl; she had told him she was working to help support her family. He imagined her life was not easy. It dawned on Karl that marriage might be a mutual benefit to them.

When Mr. Bergmann asked her to dinner again the next night, Aino feared she was setting herself up for trouble. She said yes anyway. She might lose her position if caught with one of the hotel's clients, but somehow she guessed Mr. Bergmann would protect her against that happening. He seemed kind, like her father, even though a little older, and a lot wealthier. But it was not just his money. He was the first man not from Finland whom she thought she could trust. She felt sorry for him; he seemed so lonely. And although he had told her he was just a roughneck lumberjack, Aino thought him exotic and so American in his large size and bushy beard.

By the end of the week, they were engaged, and a wedding date set for September, just a few weeks away. Aino and the wedding preparations were left in the care of Karl's mother and sister while he returned to Calumet to settle some business and make his home suitable for his future bride. Aino's parents were unsure about the marriage, but they knew it might mean a better life for their daughter. The Nordmakis wanted a Finnish Lutheran wedding, but Aino convinced them a Catholic wedding was best — that she must adopt her husband's American ways rather than remain entrenched in her Finnish heritage. That Karl's parents had been immigrants from Germany and Ireland hardly mattered — his family had spent half a century assimilating to American ways, and consequently, Karl had become prosperous. If the Nordmakis felt they were losing their daughter, they could not help being pleased by the large wedding in the impressive St. Peter's Cathedral and the grand reception at the Hotel Marquette.

Among Karl's acquaintances, however, were those who looked down on him for marrying a foreigner. The Upper Peninsula's Finnish population was growing so rapidly that jealousy, prejudice, and discrimination against them were bound to surface. Aino was well aware of how her people were maligned. Her husband's prosperity represented how hard work leads to money and money washes away the taint of immigration. By marrying Karl, she would have money and a respectable husband, and then she would be as good as anyone whose ancestors had been in the United States since before the American Revolution. No one need even know her children were half-Finn.

Although some of Marquette County's earliest settlers did not like the newcomer Finns, Aino found herself warmly welcomed into Karl's family. His widowed mother, Molly, was so kindhearted she even won over Aino's suspicious parents. Mrs. Montoni — Molly retained her second husband's Italian surname — was respected throughout the community for her many charitable deeds. No parents could disapprove of such a saintly old woman or her son. Karl's sister, Kathy, was content to see her brother settle down, and she thought Aino such a sensible, hardworking girl that the bride and groom's vast age difference would be irrelevant. Kathy's husband, Patrick McCarey, had come to America as a fugitive from Ireland not so many years before; having found safety and love in Marquette, he was willing to stretch out his arms to welcome others into the family that had accepted him.

After the immediate family, the person most elated over the Bergmann-Nordmaki wedding was Margaret Dalrymple. Until now, Margaret had long hated the Bergmanns. Karl's mother, Mrs. Montoni, had served as midwife when Margaret was born in a boarding house. Margaret had never forgotten her inauspicious origin, and she had been ashamed when her family had several times accepted charity from Mrs. Montoni. Yet Margaret overcame her qualms when her father, a simple carpenter in Marquette, was invited to the wedding because he was one of Karl's lumber customers. Mr. Dalrymple was reluctant to attend the wedding, feeling uncomfortable among the wealthier guests, but Margaret insisted her father take her. She was a young lady of eighteen, and it was mandatory she attend such social events to scope out a prospective husband. Rather than admit her reason for wanting to attend, she cajoled her father by saying, "The city's most important men will be there. It'll be the perfect opportunity for you to make business contacts."

Margaret was always scheming to make money. Her ideas were seldom ingenious or successful, but at least she had ideas. She believed attending this prominent wedding could boost her family's social, if not financial position.

But for all Margaret's anticipation and the new dress she bought for the occasion, she was disappointed to find not one suitable young man at the reception.

"Aren't you going to dance, Maggie?" her father asked.

"Father, I'm a young lady now. Don't call me Maggie."

"Well, that's your name. What else should I call you?"

"I'm Margaret, and when you introduce me, it's as Miss Margaret."

"Miss Margaret, ain't ya gonna dance?" her father mocked.

"No," she sighed. "There's no one here to dance with."

"How about your old man?"

"I can't dance with my father." Margaret rolled her eyes.

"Margaret, what about that young man over there?" said her mother. "I think he's the bride's brother. He looks about your age."

Margaret had noticed the fellow before; he was decidedly "too Finnish looking" for her; that he be suggested as a prospective dance partner made her decide he was downright homely.

"He doesn't look pleasant," she said.

Then Frank McCarey, fourteen-year old nephew of the groom, approached.

"Would you care to dance?" he asked.

He was only a boy in Margaret's eyes.

"Go ahead, Maggie," said her father.

Margaret glared at her father; had she not just warned him about using the derivative form of her name?

"I'd be honored if you would," Frank McCarey said.

"I'm sorry. I'm not feeling well," said Margaret.

Frank went away, disappointed.

"Margaret, how could you hurt that poor boy's feelings?" asked her mother.

"Oh, Mother, he's just a boy. I'm eighteen. I'm not a child anymore."

She felt like crying. Instead, she went to get herself a glass of punch. She wondered why she could not have a father polite enough to fetch her a drink. Her grandfather would have, but he was at home, suffering from a cold.

After an uneventful hour, Margaret asked to leave.

"We just got here," said Charles Dalrymple.

"Father, it's only fashionable to put in a brief appearance; we don't want to look as if we have nothing better to do than just sit here."

Charles Dalrymple was enjoying the music, but he knew better than to argue with Maggie.

"I have to do the laundry tomorrow anyway," said Christina Dalrymple. "I'll be too tired to do any housework if I'm out all night."

It was only nine o'clock. That her mother thought laundry more important than social events annoyed Margaret, even if it gave them an additional reason to leave.

As she walked home, Margaret felt so disappointed she could not help remarking, "Don't you think Marquette is terribly lacking in handsome young bachelors?"

"I never really noticed," said her mother.

"You're just too picky," said her father.

"It's such a shame," said Margaret, "that Howard Longyear drowned. He was handsome."

"As if a Longyear would have danced with you," said her father.

The comment made Margaret's blood boil, but she managed to hold her tongue. She knew Howard Longyear never would have danced with her. She was just the daughter of a simple carpenter while the Longyears were millionaires. Yet she would not admit defeat to her parents.

"I saw Howard Longyear at the Opera House the year before he died," she said. "I thought he was so handsome, and I saw he kept looking at me. He would have come over and talked to me, only intermission ended and the orchestra started playing right then so he couldn't. I've always regretted that he never did."

"You're such a dreamer," laughed her mother.

Margaret sulked; why couldn't her family support her aspirations? She could not believe her life was so drab, so dull, so pointless.

When Margaret reached home, her grandfather was still awake; she went into his room to kiss him good night. He was the only one who understood her. "You look so pretty in that dress, Margaret," he said. "I bet you were the belle of the ball." She did not disillusion him.

Once in her room, she began to hum softly.

> Many a heart is aching,
> If you could read them all;
> Many the hopes that have vanished
> After the ball.

But Margaret's aspirations refused to accept defeat. As she turned off her bedroom light, and heard her sister Sarah snoring in the neighboring bed, she looked at the picture of Mary, Queen of Scots, which she kept beside her mirror.

"My grandfather's mother was a Stewart," she reminded herself, "and the Stewarts were the royal family of Scotland. Someday I'll live up to my heritage. I'll find a way to escape this little town. I'll show them all."

Ever since he was seventeen, Will Whitman felt his life was a perpetual state of crisis, marked by continual loss. His father's death had jolted him into adulthood; his family's farm had been sold; his and Clarence's inheritance was stolen by their brother-in-law; his grandmother had moved away; and now, he was no longer on speaking terms with his sister's family because Harry had forbidden Sylvia to contact him or Clarence. Will tried to convince himself he had reason to be thankful — he and Clarence had a roof over their heads, and so far, enough money to eat and pay Clarence's tuition at the Northern State Normal School that fall. The school was only a few buildings on land donated by the wealthy Mr. Longyear in the most northern part of Marquette, but in the three years since its establishment, the Normal School's enrollment had increased from an initial class of a couple dozen to over two-hundred fifty for the 1902-1903 school year. Clarence was one of a handful of male students, but Will believed that would make his brother all the more in demand once he received his teaching certificate. Hope for Clarence's future was all that kept Will going most days.

Christmas was especially hard that year. The brothers spent the day alone, and little money was spared for presents. By afternoon, both felt restless. Clarence finally went for a walk down to the lake, but Will sat home, sadly reminiscing upon happier Christmases spent with parents, grandparents, and siblings.

Will's spirits sunk further a few days later when he learned Chief Kawbawgam had died. Old Charles Kawbawgam had been the last Chief of the Chippewa. Rumored to have been born in 1799, he had lived in three different centuries. He was Marquette's oldest and longest resident. He had been the first to welcome the settlers to Iron Bay when the community was established in 1849. More importantly to Will, Chief Kawbawgam had befriended Will's father when Jacob Whitman was still a boy; they had fished together until Jacob's death.

Will felt obliged to attend the funeral at St. Peter's Cathedral. He mourned the chief, and the entire way of life he had represented. Will recalled when he had first met the chief, in his childhood, in a simpler time. He suspected the Chippewa had known an easier life in many ways before the white men came to devastate their land, to rip iron ore from the ground, to cut down forests, to make moneymaking their lives' purpose. Chief Kawbawgam had learned to adapt until he had become a local celebrity, well loved by his native people and the white foreigners alike; his kindness, especially in Marquette's lean infancy, would never be forgotten. Yet Will thought it odd the chief's funeral should be held in a Catholic Church, his eulogy given by a white man, Peter White, even if that man had been his friend. Following the funeral, the casket was transported by streetcar to Presque Isle for burial on the island home where Kawbawgam had spent the last years of his life. This chief, this ancient connection to the past, this father figure of the land, was gone, and the twentieth century had arrived. Will knew he had no choice but to live in the present, but he yearned for that simpler past, even if he occasionally wondered whether he did not romanticize the past into a time that had never existed. Whatever that past had been, he felt the future would be more grim.

Will was in a sour mood when he came home from the funeral. He found his brother sitting at the kitchen table, poring over a book on shipwrecks.

"How was the funeral?" Clarence asked. Will had tried to convince his brother to attend, but Clarence's mind was filled with other troubles, which today he planned to confess to Will.

"It was nice," Will replied. "It made me lonesome for Pa since he and the Chief were such good friends."

"I know," said Clarence, "but they're in a happier place; I bet they're up in Heaven fishing together right now."

"That would be no Heaven for the fish," Will smiled, trying to shake off his depression as he sat down at the table.

"Will, I have to talk to you," Clarence said. Will felt annoyed by his brother's tone. He was too tired to have a serious conversation right now.

"What?"

Clarence sensed he had picked the wrong time, but if he did not speak now, he feared his courage would fail him.

"Will, I've decided I'm not going to finish school."

"What do you mean you're not going to finish?" Will asked. He had worked so hard to send Clarence to school. Was his brother crazy?

"Now don't get angry, Will. Hear me out," said Clarence. He knew his brother would not be happy, but it was his life at stake. "It isn't fair, Will, for you to support me. You have a right to your own life."

"Don't worry about it," Will said. "You can pay me back when you find a job."

"No, that's not what I'm getting at. Listen to me, Will. You've done everything for me. No one could ask for a better brother. You're the only family I've got, and I never want there to be bad blood between us."

"Why would there be?" asked Will.

"Because I don't want to go to college anymore. I don't want to teach."

"You know Ma and Pa wanted — "

"I know," said Clarence, "but this is my life, not yours or Ma's or Pa's or anyone else's. I have to do what's best for me. Otherwise, I'll be miserable, and I'll make everyone around me miserable."

Will was too irritated to speak.

"I figure, Will, that you have as much right to go to school as me. I don't belong in college, so you should use the money for yourself. After all, Ma and Pa would have wanted you to go just as much as me."

"No, I'm not the college type," said Will. "Not that I'm any less smart than college boys, but I prefer working with my hands to sitting behind a desk and learning things with no practical purpose. I'd rather build a house; at least you know a house is needed and will be appreciated."

"That's the same," said Clarence, "as how I'd rather sail on a ship. What I'm trying to tell you is I'm going to be a sailor, just as soon as the boats start running in the spring."

Will thought it worse that his brother be a sailor than that he leave college. "Being a sailor is a hard life," he said, but he was thinking, "You mean you're going to leave me alone."

"I'm not afraid of hard work," said Clarence. "I've had my heart set on sailing ever since I can remember. I never even would have finished high school if you hadn't insisted so much. I mean, everytime I see a ship, I feel I ought to be on it. I don't belong in school. If I don't go on the boats, Will, I think I'll always regret it."

Will said nothing; his face spoke his disappointment.

"Don't be glum, Will. It's for the best. I'll be making my own money so you won't have to support me, and someday, you'll want your money so you can get married and have a family, and then you won't want me hanging around."

"You're always welcome; you know that," said Will, "and besides, I don't imagine I'll marry anytime soon."

Will thought he had seen enough of marriage from living with Harry and Sylvia that he never wanted such an entanglement. He had been too young when his mother died to remember his parents' marital happiness.

He wanted to argue, to accuse Clarence of being a dreamer, but he felt too exhausted. He weakly tried to compromise.

"Your tuition is paid for this next term, and no boats will run until spring. You finish out this school year, and that'll give you time to think more, and then you'll be halfway to finishing your teaching certificate. Then go on the boats, and if at the end of the summer, you discover you don't like being a sailor, you can take up school again."

"Fair enough," said Clarence, "but I'm warning you I won't change my mind."

"I'm going upstairs to lie down," Will replied. He lacked the energy to discuss anything more at the moment. Clarence ate alone that evening, hurting to have hurt his brother, but he felt he would hurt himself and Will far more if he were not true to himself. Meanwhile, Will lay on his bed until the sun went down and the room grew black and cold with night. He had thought he already knew what loss was, but with his brother gone, he would now have nothing.

1903

"Father, can I come with you to see the house?" Margaret asked.

Charles Dalrymple had been hired to help disassemble the Longyear Mansion, the largest house Marquette had ever seen. Margaret had ached to be inside the palatial home since she had been a girl, and now was her last chance.

"No," her father replied, "we can't have just anyone wandering about in our way, and no one is allowed inside just to satisfy curiosity."

"But I'm not just anyone, Father. You're one of the people in charge, and I'm your daughter. Surely, you can get me in."

"Maybe some other time," he tried to put her off.

"There won't be another time. I want to see the house while it still has its splendor, but the longer I wait, the more of it will be taken apart so there won't be anything for me to see."

Margaret pouted until her mother came to her defense.

"Oh, let her go, Charles. What can it hurt?"

"Well," he hesitated, "I suppose if I forgot my lunch today, you could bring it to me around noon. You would have to come inside then to find me, and maybe I could let you look around for a few minutes."

"Oh, thank you," said Margaret, kissing his cheek. "You're the best father ever!"

Charles did not blame his daughter for wanting to see the interior of the Longyear Mansion. From outside, the enormous house was intimidating, but inside, it radiated with the height of genteel Victorian splendor. Every Marquette resident grieved to see it disassembled.

When Margaret had bemoaned the death of handsome Howard Longyear, she could not have imagined how his loss would be perpetuated by the loss of the home she dreamt of living in, the most beautiful gilded palace in America, or at least, the only one she had ever seen.

Howard Longyear had drowned while canoeing on Lake Superior to the Huron Mountain Club with a friend. His parents, shaken with grief, had traversed the entire beach from Marquette to the Club in search of their son, but his body was never recovered. To console his wife, John Longyear suggested a piece of their lakeshore property be preserved as a memorial park to their son. However, the Marquette and Southwestern Railroad wanted to run its tracks over the designated area. Despite Mr. Longyear's efforts to find an alternative piece of land for the railroad line, an active promotion for the railroad was begun in Marquette. Mrs. Longyear had warned the City of Marquette that if the railroad were allowed to run over her waterfront property, she would never return to the city. To escape their grief and frustration, the Longyears traveled to Europe. There they learned their efforts to stop the railroad had failed. One day, while riding down the Champs Elysee in Paris, Mr. Longyear suggested to his wife that since she would not return to Marquette, perhaps they might move to Boston and take their beloved home with them; there they would have all the comforts of home, and their children could enjoy the cultural advantages of the East. Mrs. Longyear readily agreed, and land was purchased three miles inland from the Atlantic Ocean, where she would not have to hear the pounding waves to remind her of her son's drowning.

Marquette's residents were stunned by the decision; they already had railroads, but they had nothing to compare to the Longyear Mansion. Immediately, work began to dismantle the enormous sixty-five room house, complete with towers and an indoor bowling alley, and spanning an entire city block. When the move was completed, two trains would have pulled one hundred ninety railroad cars for thirteen hundred miles to Massachusetts. Then, in the Boston suburb of Brookline, three years would be spent reassembling the house. The Longyears would return to the Upper Peninsula for visits, usually staying at their private cottage on Ives Lake, part of the Huron Mountain Club property. But good as her word, Mrs. Longyear never again set foot within the city limits of Marquette.

Margaret felt like a grieving mother herself as she walked to the Longyear Mansion with her father's lunch. The house had long been the one bright dream of her drab life. Even when Grandpa Dalrymple had told her of Scottish castles, she had imagined the Longyear Mansion as the setting for these tales. Her grandfather had died just before Christmas, and the blow had devastated her; as the only member of the family who fully understood her, he had been her link to the family's grand Scottish heritage, a heritage her father and Swiss blooded mother, were not interested in. Grandpa would have been happy to know she had finally set foot inside the Longyear Mansion, but the visit was not to be how she had fantasized — she had always imagined one of the millionaire Longyears inviting her inside and then adopting her into the family.

She climbed the stone steps of the palatial home, then rang the doorbell. She half-expected an English butler to greet her, but the door was whipped open by a sawdust covered workman.

"Um, I'm looking for my father, Charles Dalrymple. I've brought his lunch," she said.

"I'm kind of busy right now," the workman said. "Would you mind bringing it to him yourself? He's up there at the top of the stairs."

Margaret stepped inside, and — was it her imagination? The workman was smiling at her, eyeing her actually. She told herself not to be surprised; she was eighteen now, and fully conscious of her natural beauty. She lowered her eyes in her most demure manner, but not before she noticed his handsome smile, and replied, "Thank you." She would not meet his eyes, for she would not encourage the wrong type of men, and laborers were the wrong type. Now if a Longyear man were about the house, that would be different. She started up the staircase, walking slowly so she could admire the mansion's every ornate detail.

Will Whitman closed the front door. He had smiled at Margaret only because Mr. Dalrymple had confided to him that his precocious daughter would bring him lunch so she could get a peek inside the house. Will had been watching twenty minutes for "Maggie"; he was glad when she finally came so he could get back to work.

Margaret climbed the grand staircase, marveling at the elaborate wallpaper, the finely carved wooden bannister, the etchings in the windows. She tried to pretend she was ascending to an elegant party, perhaps a royal ball at Holyrood Palace. But for once, Margaret's imagination was overshadowed by reality. Never had she dreamt elegance could reach such an epitome.

She feared her father would send her straight home once she delivered his lunch, yet she boldly stepped up to him at the top of the stairs.

Charles Dalrymple, kneeling on the floor, spotted her from the corner of his eye. "I see you made it," he said, speaking lowly so no one would overhear him. "There doesn't seem to be anyone around who would mind much, so go ahead and look around. Just don't touch anything, and be back in twenty minutes. Most of the workers will be back from lunch by then."

Margaret glowed. "Thank you, Father. Don't worry. I'll be back in time."

She had started down the upstairs hall before the words were out of her mouth. She could not see everything in the tremendous house in just twenty minutes, but she would inspect every inch possible. Walking down the corridor, she kept exclaiming "My gosh!" and "Oh wow!" in sheer wonderment. She passed from one bedroom to the next, one sitting room to another. Even with the rooms empty of furniture, the splendor of the home shone forth. She nearly burst with awe when she went downstairs and looked into the dining room; she could just imagine herself at the head of its table, a hostess and leader of society, or better yet, a visiting dignitary, a Scottish princess invited as guest of honor. The closets, even the pantry, were bigger than her bedroom; each could hold a lifetime of clothes compared to her little closet and its six dresses. The servants' quarters were so fine she would have almost been content to work here; then she could spend each day in this palatial mansion; then she could meet wealthy guests who would realize she was of such high caliber that she deserved to be married and live as mistress of an equally fine home.

Twenty minutes passed in what seemed seconds. Margaret had returned upstairs again, but by a different staircase; she tried to find her way in the third story hall, but after a minute, nothing looked familiar to her. Worried she would cause her father trouble, she tried to retrace her steps, but she could not even find the staircase she had come up a minute before.

Then she came across the young man who had met her at the front door.

She got a better look at him this time; she had thought he had a beard, but now she saw that dirt was smudged on his cheeks. He did have a handsome smile. She feared he would accost her for wandering about the house, but instead, he smiled and was about to pass her by, when she found courage to ask for his help.

"Excuse me; I seem to be lost. Could you tell me how to reach my father?"

"Oh sure, it is a rather confusing house," he said. "I'll take you to him."

"Thank you," said Margaret, following behind.

"What have you been doing since you graduated from school?" he asked.

She was surprised by the question from a stranger, but perhaps her father had told him something about her. "I just stay home and help my mother, at least for now until I have a family of my own." It was her usual response; everyone expected her to get married; she could not tell people she was holding out to marry a European count.

"Clarence is in college now you know," he replied, "at the Normal School."

"Clarence?" She did not recall the name.

"My brother," he said. "I'm sorry; you don't remember me." He offered her a sawdust-filled hand, but she would not shake hands with a strange man. "I'm Will Whitman."

"Oh!" She looked closely and giggled, then accepted his hand. "I'm sorry. I haven't seen you in years."

She remembered the last time she had spoken to Will Whitman — at the party at the Hotel Superior several years ago, held for the unveiling of the Father Marquette statue — the night she had found Mr. Whitman lying on the ground, having a stroke, and Mrs. Montoni had sent her to tell his family; Margaret and her sister, Sarah, had run to the Whitmans' house, and she herself had told Clarence of his father's passing. That was a horrible night, and poor Will had been there at the party when it happened. She remembered she had wanted to dance with him then, although she had liked Clarence better since he was in her class at school. Clarence was a step above the other boys she knew, even if his father had been a farmer and his grandparents ran a boarding house — a boarding house she regretted having been born in. Reminders of her humble beginning always irritated Margaret, but Will could not be blamed for it.

"Tell Clarence I said 'hello,'" she replied.

"Okay," said Will, as they went downstairs to the second floor.

"Maggie, where have you been?" asked her father, coming around a corner and preventing her from further conversation with Will.

As she disappeared down the hall with her father, she took one last look back at Will. "Yes," she thought, "he is handsome, even with sawdust all over him."

Despite having gained access into the Longyear Mansion, Margaret was unsatisfied. A couple days later, she deliberately went to the house half an hour before her father got off work with the pretense of walking home with him. She was irritated when he told her he would be working late, so she could go back home. She wanted to stay and look around the house again, but his stern look said he would not allow it. Will Whitman happened to witness the conversation, but he interpreted Margaret's visible displeasure as fear of walking home in the dark. It was early January, and dark by five o'clock. Will had finished his work and welcomed the chance to have company; he did not relish going home to his brother's chatter about working on the ore boats.

"Miss Dalrymple, I'd be happy to walk you home," he said.

Margaret was pleased by his polite address, but she was uncertain whether she should accept.

"I would hate for you to walk alone in the dark," Will said, "especially with it starting to snow."

"Thank you," she agreed. She did not want to be seen walking with a workman, but in the dark, no one would recognize him, and wealthier young men might think her more attractive when they saw another man with her. She failed to consider that no one would recognize her in the dark.

As Will put on his coat, he wondered what Clarence would say about him walking Margaret Dalrymple home. When he had mentioned to Clarence that he had seen Margaret the other day, Clarence had spent a second trying to remember her, then only said, "Oh, her." Will had asked whether he should say hello to Margaret for Clarence; his brother had replied, "No, don't encourage her." But Will was more charitable, or perhaps more lonely than his brother.

Will and Margaret went outside into the snowy streets, trying not to shiver at the abrupt temperature change.

After a minute, Margaret said, "Isn't it a shame the Longyear Mansion is leaving Marquette? It's just not right. It's the grandest home in the city. Whoever heard of moving a house halfway across the country?"

"I can't complain," said Will. "It gives me work, and your father too."

"But don't you think it a travesty?"

"Well, no. There are other fine homes in town," said Will.

"These are all fine homes," Margaret said as they walked through the neighborhood of Marquette's well-to-do, "but they can't compare to the Longyear Mansion."

"I've always been partial to this house," said Will, stopping before a sandstone structure which thirty years before had been Marquette's most fashionable home.

"Yes, I've always thought it quite distinctive," said Margaret.

"It is," said Will, "but I mainly like it because it belonged to my grandparents."

Margaret was astounded. "I thought your grandparents owned a boarding house?"

"My father's parents did, but this house belonged to my mother's parents, the Hennings."

"Oh," said Margaret. She looked more closely at the house, peered inside the window, over which the curtains had not yet been drawn; she saw an elegant room lit by electric light. A remarkably fastidious woman perched on a sofa; in a second, her husband sat down beside her, and she set to work adjusting his necktie.

"That's Judge Smith and his wife, isn't it?" said Margaret.

"I don't know," said Will. "I don't know who bought the house from my grandparents. The house was sold years before I was born."

"Why would anyone sell a house like that?" asked Margaret.

"My grandparents decided to move back East," Will replied. "My grandpa had a business back there I guess." He scarcely remembered his Aunt Madeleine had ever existed, much less that her death had caused his grandparents to leave the area.

"Did you ever meet your mother's parents?" asked Margaret.

"Just my grandpa — once when I was fifteen. He came to visit us, but he died soon after. My grandmother died long before I was born; my step-grandmother, who is also my Grandma Whitman's sister, lives in Utah, but I've never met her either."

"You must have inherited a fortune from them," said Margaret.

"No," said Will. "My grandpa left everything to my step-grandmother, and since she lives with my Aunt Edna, I imagine my aunt'll inherit her money. I don't keep in touch with my relatives out West, except for my Grandma Whitman."

"That's too bad," said Margaret. For a moment, she diverted her eyes from the expensive wallpaper inside Judge Smith's house and the delicate lace curtains she longed one day to have in her own parlor. She recalled her own grandfather's death. Then she remembered she had been the one to tell Will's brother of his father's death. "It's hard when you lose your family," she sympathized.

"Well, I still have Clarence," said Will, but then he admitted, "Actually I don't have him either. He's going to sign up on the ore boats."

"I thought he was going to the Normal School to become a teacher?"

"He's quitting school to become a sailor," said Will. "Then I'll be alone."

"Why would anyone want to be a sailor? Teachers are more respectable."

Will could not answer this. "We better go," he said. "It's getting cold out here."

They turned away from the cozy vision of his family's former home. He wished Grandpa and Grandma Henning still owned it. Grandma Whitman had told him his own parents had been married in that fine house. But now his brother was to be a sailor and he a carpenter. "How the mighty have fallen," he thought.

"Are you always going to be a carpenter?" asked Margaret, as if reading his mind. They turned onto Front Street, then headed north toward the Dalrymples' home on Michigan Street.

"I don't know," said Will. "I guess so."

"Don't you have ambition to be something more, like a teacher maybe?"

"No," said Will, "not a teacher anyway. I'm not interested in book learning. I'd rather work with my hands. It might sound silly, but whenever I see my grandparents' old house, it makes me want to build homes. If I can't afford to live in such a fine home, there's no reason why I can't build them for other people."

"If you could build houses like that," said Margaret, "you'd be rich; people would pay you so much money you could afford to build one for yourself."

"Maybe," said Will. He had never confided his passion for building houses to anyone before. Of course he was a carpenter, but people thought that was just his job. For Will, it was a vocation; it was why he got out of bed in the morning. His love for carpentry had begrudgingly allowed him to understand his brother's legitimate desire to be a sailor. And work kept him from loneliness, from resisting the urge to visit Sylvia's family. His grandparents' mansion reminded him of the family bonds he had known in childhood; it made him homesick for the past. If he could not have such happiness in his family, he would build beautiful homes where other families could gather, and perhaps someday, he might again have a —

"Thank you for walking me home, Will," said Margaret. It was the first time she had called him by name.

"You're welcome," he replied.

After she turned to enter her house, he walked away in deep thought.

Margaret was equally meditative. She made several more trips to the Longyear Mansion, but no longer to view its treasures. Her father thought he saw through all her little excuses to visit him at work, but Charles Dalrymple did not yet suspect a young man had replaced an extravagant home in his daughter's affections. Even Margaret was surprised by her sudden interest in Will, who was not quite as handsome as his younger brother. And he was definitely not wealthy. But something about him — perhaps she only fancied it, but she did not think so — something about him seemed so determined, so creative and capable of turning his creativity into prosperity. Margaret continually recalled his statement that he wished to build beautiful homes like the one his grandparents had owned, and she embellished his words until they took on deeper tones and meanings than a young man of twenty-two could intend when making small talk with a young lady he scarcely knew.

One February evening, Margaret Dalrymple could control her feelings no longer. Bursting into the bedroom she shared with her sister, she announced, "Sarah, I have a secret. You can't tell anyone else, not even Mother or Father. Promise?"

"What is it?" asked Sarah.

"Do you promise?"

"Of course."

Margaret was doubtful. Past experience had taught her that Sarah was not to be trusted, but she had to confide in someone. The time had come to fulfill her destiny. "Sarah," she said, "I'm going to marry Will Whitman!"

Sarah had been lying on the bed, pondering the feminine undergarments in the Sears, Roebuck catalog, but her sister's declaration made her lose all interest in bloomers. She sat up and stared.

"Will Whitman! Doesn't he work for Father?"

"Yes, but he's more than just Father's employee," said Margaret, sitting down beside her sister. Sarah flooded her with questions until it was revealed how Margaret had weighed advantages and disadvantages to make her choice. Will was not rich, but he was intelligent enough to become so. He hardly had any family, but that meant his relatives could not oppose their marriage. He came from a good family — his grandparents had been among Marquette's leading citizens, and he still had rich relatives out West. Margaret imagined Will could get back in touch with those relatives. After the wedding, perhaps she and Will would even move out West where he could make his fortune. Even if they stayed in Marquette, Will owned his own house — granted, half of it belonged to Clarence, but Clarence was going on the boats, so she and Will would have the house to themselves. How many eighteen-year old girls had their own homes? Her mother had not had a home until she was in her mid-twenties. By the time Margaret was in her mid-twenties, she imagined Will would have built her a fine mansion. Had she not thought of everything? Could she make any other decision?

"The way I see it," said Sarah, "you could marry Will, have your own home, and a husband from a respectable family fallen into genteel poverty, or you could wait for a rich man, but a rich man might never come. Better take the best you can get now than wait for better and risk settling later for someone not half so good."

The expected bride-to-be took her fourteen-year old sister's advice. From whom else could she ask counsel? Not her seven-year old brother, Charles. And she was too shy to ask her parents' advice before she got Will to propose. Everything was decided. Now she just had to inform the groom.

Will Whitman was deeply grieved by his brother's departure. But he was a practical young man. And a responsible one. While Harry Cumming considered his brother-in-law lazy, Will had worked continually since his father's death whenever he could find work; he had scrimped and saved to put aside every penny he could, only to have money slip through his fingers and into his brother-in-law's pockets. Will had always tried to get ahead in the world, but he also always tried to take care of his family, and there were always mouths to feed; he had never desired love because he did not think he could afford it. While he would miss Clarence, he realized he could now save a substantial sum by no longer funding Clarence's tuition and food. The money would become a nest egg so someday he could start his own contracting company. No longer worrying about money might bring him some happiness at last. Yet however man tries to plan his life, Life, refusing to be yoked, has a masterly way of placing the yoke onto the most cautious man by creating a mess to replace a goal.

One morning at breakfast, Clarence announced how many days remained before he would leave on an ore boat. Will left for work in a grumpy mood at the thought of his brother leaving, although he knew it would be best for both of them. His mood did not improve when he had to trudge to work in a foot of freshly fallen snow. As always by February, the snowbanks were becoming alarmingly high. Will moaned because he would have to go home to shovel off the porch and front walk after work. Clarence would help him, but next winter, Will knew he would not have any help. The ore boats did not run in winter, but Will could not count on Clarence returning to Marquette. Once his brother saw other harbor towns — Detroit, Chicago, Green Bay, Cleveland, Buffalo — all warmer than Marquette — he might decide to winter in one of them. Will was almost tempted to sign onto an ore boat just to be with his brother — but he really wanted to build houses. And as illogical as it was, he could not leave

Marquette in case Sylvia needed him, even if now they never saw one another. Other times, he reminded himself this town was where his parents, grandparents and great-grandparents were buried; his roots, all his memories were here, and here he belonged.

His thoughts were suddenly interrupted by a girl singing at the top of her lungs.

"Who's that crazy person?" he muttered.

He strained his eyes in the direction of the noise, but the morning sun's reflection off the snow blinded him until he could scarcely see where he walked, much less who was approaching.

"Hello, Will."

It was Margaret.

"Hello," he said, glad she had not heard him comment on her singing.

"Isn't it a beautiful day?" she asked.

"It would be if it would quit snowing."

"It's not snowing now. It's so sunny the snow is sparkling. I love it like this. You can't help singing when the world is as white as heaven."

"What was that you were singing?" he asked.

" 'Hie Johnny Cope.' It's an old Scottish song my grandfather taught me. A sunny day always brings the Scot out in me."

"You're Scottish?"

"Why what else do ye think the name a' Dalrymple is?" she teased. "I'm only half Scot though; my mother's Swiss. Her maiden name was Zurbrugg, but she was born in Canada. Still, my heart belongs to Scotland."

"Oh," said Will, not knowing what to say to this flood of family information.

"You seem kind of down today, Will. Sing with me. It'll lift your spirits."

"Are you going to the Longyear House?" he asked to avoid singing.

"Yes, my father's sick, so he asked me to bring the workmen his orders."

Then she launched into "In the Good Old Summertime," pausing after a few lines to explain, "Winter feels less cold when you sing about summer."

Will could not help laughing, and by the second verse, he found himself joining in the song. A passerby stared at them as if they were crazy, but Margaret whispered to Will, "She's just Judge Smith's maid so what do we care?" Had someone prominent stared, Margaret would have been embarrassed, but Will did not yet realize her social conscience. He only thought her a jolly girl, a pleasant companion for a walk or chat. He had told Clarence "Margaret's grown up since you knew her in school," but Clarence had only rolled his eyes. Will had then defended her by stating, "Maybe you never took the time to get to know her properly," but Clarence was not interested in hearing his brother had a new friend. Will did not care what Clarence thought.

This sunny, yet snowy day, Will began to feel something more than friendship for Margaret. He began to feel that with her, the dark days ahead might not be quite so dark. If she were so cheery now, perhaps she could handle greater calamities with calmness. She was right; if he had taken the time to notice, today was a beautiful day. He was glad it would take a long time to dismantle the Longyear Mansion because as long as he worked under Margaret's father, he would see her.

The next morning, Will went up the stone steps and into the Longyear Mansion to begin another day's work. In the entry hall, he found Mr. Dalrymple waiting for him.

"Are you feeling better today, sir?" he asked.

"Will, I need to talk with you," said Mr. Dalrymple. The words were cold, serious, not at all friendly in tone. Will was surprised; he looked about him for a second, trying to understand what was wrong. He noticed Margaret standing behind her father, but her face was toward the wall. She would not look at him.

"What is it, sir?" he quivered.

"Will, I've known your family for many years. They're good people. I think you're an honorable young man, but I won't take any chances with my daughter."

"Sir, I don't understand," said Will, hearing his voice shake. Of what was he being accused?

"Maggie says you and she intend to be married."

In Margaret's defense, those were not her actual words. At supper the night before, she had told her father that she had met Will and walked to the Longyear Mansion with him that morning. Then Mrs. Dalrymple had asked Sarah why she was giggling; the untrustworthy sister confessed that Margaret intended to marry Will. Margaret tried to explain; she entreated her father to listen to her. She claimed she had only fancied it; that Will had never spoken to her of love. But Mr. Dalrymple was determined to learn the truth.

"Sir, I — " Will fumbled for words.

"Do you intend to marry her?" Mr. Dalrymple demanded. "Have you asked, and has she accepted? Come, Will. I'm her father. I have a right to know."

Will looked at Margaret; she turned to look at him, as if frightened of his answer. He did not know what she had told her father, but he did not wish to expose her as a liar. He knew this was a misunderstanding. She would not try to trap him like this.

"Will, I tried to tell Father that I — " she began.

"Margaret," her father snapped, "I'm waiting for Will to answer."

"If she'll have me, sir," Will said, only half-astonished by his words.

"Why wasn't I told of this sooner? Why did you keep this from me?" he asked, but his face relaxed.

"I — well," Will fumbled.

"Father, I tried to tell you, but — " said Margaret. Then she saw Will smile at her and her face broke into a tremendous grin.

"I only just asked her yesterday," said Will. "I know I should have asked you first, but you were sick yesterday, and I was too nervous to wait any longer. I was going to tell you today. I was afraid I'd look foolish if you gave me permission and then she refused me. I guess I just wanted to be sure of how she felt before I troubled you."

"That's all right then, I guess," said Mr. Dalrymple. He patted Will on the back, and then all three of them broke into laughter. Charles had always liked Will. He had been grieved to think the young fellow might be a scoundrel. "I am pleased," he said. "Of course, Margaret's far too young to be married yet. A long engagement will be — "

"Actually, sir, my brother, Clarence," Will said, his head reeling at his sudden unexpected happiness, "I'd like him to be my best man, and he's leaving on the ore boats once the ice breaks on the lake. We thought a spring wedding — "

"Maybe early May?" Margaret added.

"I'll have to discuss it with Mrs. Dalrymple," said Charles. "She'll want to plan the wedding. She's a woman, so she's fussy about these things. But I'll see what I can do. You're smart, Margaret, not to let this young man slip through your fingers. He has brains and a good future as a carpenter, not like some of the lazy oafs who work for me. Well, I better get to work. I imagine you two would like a moment alone, but only a moment. I have a lot of work for Will to do today."

Mr. Dalrymple disappeared down one of the mansion's numerous halls.

"Do you really mean it, Will?" Margaret asked, stepping up to her betrothed.

"Yes." He felt he should take her hand, wrap his arm around her waist, kiss her. But he could only stand awkwardly.

"I know you were just covering for me, Will. It was sweet of you, but — "

"I like you, Margaret. You would make me happy."

"Oh." They were the most — the only — romantic words a man had ever said to her. That he had said he liked her, not loved her, did not matter. He thought she would make him happy. She knew she would. She would be the perfect wife. She would make their home comfortable and elegant. She would learn to be economical so they could save money and prosper. She would make certain he was successful.

"I better get to work," he said. "I'll walk you home if you come by later."

"All right," she said, "and when we reach my house, you'll come inside to meet my mother."

"Okay," he agreed, more frightened by the thought of a mother-in-law than a wife. Margaret stood on tiptoe to kiss his cheek. Before he summoned up courage to return the kiss, she disappeared out the open front door.

It was a simple wedding. Margaret knew it was not as elegant as Karl Bergmann's had been a few months before. But she was happy. If expense could not be lavished on the wedding, at least the groom was better looking than at the Bergmann wedding. For that matter, Margaret thought the bride prettier too. And just as at the Bergmann wedding, loneliness dropped away from the groom as he left the church with his bride on his arm.

1908

"Mother, you were always worried I'd never get married," said Karl Bergmann, "so I went and found a wife and look what happened. Only married five years and then she dies of the grippe. I'd have been better off staying a bachelor."

Aino had died the month before. Karl was devastated. After much soul searching, he had brought his little girl, Thelma, to visit his family in Marquette. He had made a decision, although he could scarcely explain his reasons. He wanted to leave his daughter with his sister's family.

"That's not true," said Molly. "You were happy for five years, weren't you?"

Molly sighed. More than anything, it hurt her to see her children unhappy. She had worked all her life, always for Karl and Kathy, and now she was an old lady, liable to die at anytime, and her son was still unhappy, still had no one to care for him after she was gone. Karl had always worried her — she suspected he was more capable than Kathy, but somehow less resilient to change, and Kathy had a husband to care for her. Karl's lot had always been harder than his sister's because he was older; Molly had relied on him to care for his sick father, then to protect her from her second, abusive husband, Montoni. Karl should have had an easier life; she agreed it was not fair that after only five short years, God had taken his wife.

"I was happy with Aino," Karl said, "but that only makes the pain worse. What good is happiness when it can be taken away so easily?"

"It's not our place to question God's ways," said Molly. "Maybe God sends us happy moments to give us a glimpse of the eternal happiness to come."

"Maybe," Karl mumbled. He did not want to hear his mother talk about God. He respected that her religion inspired her many charitable deeds, but try as she did to relieve others' wants, Karl thought she missed the big picture — the lonely knowledge that if God existed, He did nothing to relieve people's wants. Karl failed to see how belief in God had made his life any easier.

"You have a little girl now," Molly said. "You have to be strong for her sake. You can give her everything in the world, but she most needs your love."

"I do love her."

"I know," said Molly, "but she's only four. She can't understand why her mother is gone, and when you mope around, she thinks you're angry with her, and that only confuses and frightens her more."

"I can't help her when I can't help myself," said Karl. "That's why I need to get away for a while. Kathy will watch Thelma until I come back."

"What do you mean? Where are you going?" Molly asked. His problems would not go away by avoiding them.

"I don't know where. I just need to go away somewhere to think."

"What is there to think about? You have a daughter to look after. You can't just run off whenever you feel like it. What you ought to do is move to Marquette. Then Kathy and I can help you raise Thelma. Kathy misses you, and you know her boys idolize you — Frank would be a logger already if his mother let him."

Karl smiled. "He's about the same age I was when I first went into the woods. He's awful thin; swinging an ax would put some muscle on his bones. Maybe when I get back, I'll make a lumberjack out of him."

"Don't let Kathy hear you say that," said Molly, "but tell me where you're going."

Karl sighed. "I've worked so hard for so long, Mother. I just want a little trip. My whole life I've never been farther than Green Bay. You and Father lived in other countries and traveled over a good part of the United States before coming to Marquette. I want to see more than just the same old trees over and over."

"But where are you going?"

Karl knew his mother worried about him as if he were still her little boy; that was why he would not tell her his plan. He was relieved when his nephews burst in the front door and distracted him from his mother's questions.

"Uncle Karl! Mother told us you'd be coming today," said Frank, who at twenty was tall but thin like his father, while his seventeen-year old brother Jeremy was shorter and stocky like his uncle. Bringing up the rear was eight-year old Michael, a quiet, sensitive boy, living in his older brothers' shadows. Michael went upstairs to see Thelma, despite his grandmother's warning that his little cousin was napping.

"How are my nephews?" roared Karl, jumping up to bury the boys in bear hugs. Both boys relished the attention, even if they were too self-conscious to hug anyone else. Uncle Karl was their idol. He was strong and capable of anything.

"We're fine, Uncle Karl," said Jeremy.

"When are you going to let me come work with you?" asked Frank.

Karl frowned. "Maybe when I get back."

"Where are you going?"

"On a trip."

"Where?" asked Jeremy.

"Just on business," Karl said. He did not add it was personal business.

Kathy and Patrick now followed their children into the house. The family had just come from Sunday Mass. Molly had stayed home from church to wait for Karl to arrive that morning. Although a devout Catholic, she did not believe it a sin to miss one service, especially not when she attended daily Mass. God understood that she rarely saw her son.

After everyone said hello, Kathy and Molly went into the kitchen to put Sunday dinner on the table. Michael came downstairs with Thelma.

"Uncle Karl, will you tell us a story about Paul Bunyan?" he asked.

Jeremy laughed. "Not Paul Bunyan. I've heard those stories so many times."

"I could tell them myself," said Frank. "Uncle Karl raised us on those stories."

"Well," said Karl, "what do you expect when I've spent my life in the woods, and I worked right beside Paul Bunyan for twenty years."

"Sure, Uncle," said Frank.

"Please tell a story," Michael begged.

"All right, how about I tell — "

"I'll go help in the kitchen," said Jeremy. "I've heard them all before."

"I happen to know many stories you haven't heard yet," said Karl.

"I doubt it," Jeremy replied. Another uncle might have thought his nephew rude, but Karl understood the boy's good-natured kidding; Jeremy had inherited an Irish drollery from both his parents.

"Do you know about the Black Rocks at Presque Isle?" Karl asked.

"Of course, I've been there about a hundred times," Jeremy replied, but he sat back down, not remembering a Paul Bunyan story about the Black Rocks.

"And do you know how they came to be black?" asked Karl.

"No, but I imagine there's some geological reason."

"Oh, you believe in science then?" said Karl. "Let me tell you; all those scientists don't have one lick of sense when it comes to explaining things. I know because I was there when the Black Rocks became black."

"They've been black for about a million years," Jeremy scoffed.

"Jeremy, let him tell the story," said Patrick. "Don't spoil Michael and Thelma's fun."

"All right," said Jeremy, who actually wanted to hear the story as much as anyone else.

PAUL BUNYAN AND THE BLACK ROCKS

"This happened many years ago," Karl began, "when I first started out as a lumberjack and Ben and I had just become partners. Let me tell you, my pal Ben was about the best logger I ever saw. He had arms thick and strong as jackpines. You'd almost think he was a jackpine himself, he was so tall and sturdy. He could hack down more trees in a day than you would have time to count."

"Yes, he could," Frank said. "I remember him."

"He wasn't as strong as you though, was he, Uncle Karl?" asked Jeremy. Despite the good-natured ribbing of his uncle, Jeremy did not idolize any man as much as Uncle Karl, not even his own father.

"Well, to be honest with you," Karl said, "Ben's the only man who ever laid me flat on my back. For years we wondered who was stronger, until one day we decided to arm wrestle; we strained for a good hour until Ben slammed my arm down, clear right through the table, knocking me clean on the ground. I never would have crossed him after that, not that I ever had reason to because he was the best tempered man I ever knew."

"But what about Paul Bunyan?" asked Michael.

"Well, as I was saying, my friend Ben and I were the most successful loggers in the entire Upper Peninsula of Michigan save for Paul Bunyan. Sometimes we thought Paul would put us clean out of business, but when he realized what good folks Ben and I was, we all became friends, and he would give us hints on how to cut down trees all the faster.

"Anyway, one year about Christmas time, Ben and I were coming up here to Marquette to visit. We were riding through the woods in our sleigh on the road from L'anse when who did we happen upon but Paul Bunyan and his Big Blue Ox, Babe. They were just walking along the road although the snow was already piled up in drifts. They thought nothing about a little snow. Paul Bunyan could step over the snowbanks as you and I would step over an ant mound. Paul said he was walking to Marquette all the way from Ontonagon, a walk he could usually do in two hours because his legs were so long and his strides so big. Well, Ben and I offered him a ride, only he said he'd never fit in the sleigh, he was so big, and we didn't want to risk him breaking it, so we continued along the road and he walked beside us in his snowshoes, but even with our horses going at a swift trot, we could barely keep up with him.

"Then, a fierce blizzard sprang up, and before we knew it, we were lost in that blustery storm. Even Paul Bunyan could not walk in that nasty weather. We couldn't see an inch ahead of us, and pretty soon we didn't know where the horses were pulling the sleigh, but we figured we were off the trail. Not all the forest trees could protect us from those chilling gusts. The wind was so loud we could barely yell over it, and when Paul claimed he could hear Lake Superior's waves pounding, we got scared that we might walk plumb into the lake. Not wanting to risk the danger, we decided to stop for the night.

"We found a sturdy clump of trees all sprung up together to break the wind for us. Then Paul took his ax, and in half a minute, he had half a dozen trees chopped down and split into boards to make a lean-to. If we'd had a few nails, we could have had ourselves a real comfortable little cabin.

"So we went inside our little shelter, and tried to stay warm throughout the storm. Wasn't too hard because Paul had on two flannel shirts, so he loaned one to me and Ben to use as a blanket — he was so big his shirts could have made a tent with room left over for a pair of curtains. We weren't worried about no wild animals bothering us out in the wild 'cause Babe slept right there in the shelter with us, and that ox has a fierce temper when it's angry. Even without Babe, we wouldn't have had to worry because Paul snores just like a bear growls, only a might bit louder. But we'd had such a hard long ride from the Keweenaw in all that blinding snow that we napped right well that night, even with Paul and Babe snoring. I only remember waking up once that night, and then I peeked outside and saw nothing but sheer white. Since the storm was still raging, I cuddled back under Paul's giant shirt and went back to sleep. The next time I woke was a full day later, and again I saw the snow still pouring down, and again I went back to sleep. And the next day, the snow was still raging, only that time I could hear the wind blowing fierce, so I didn't even bother to look outside but just rolled over and kept my eyes closed."

"How'd you know how many days had passed?" asked Michael.

"Shh," Jeremy shushed his brother. "Don't interrupt."

"Well, I lost track of how many days we were actually there. But when I finally did wake up and stayed awake, a crack of light was peering into our shelter, and the snow had piled up, foot after foot all around us. We were lucky the storm stopped when it did, or we might all have been buried under the snow and not been found until spring. Why half the trees were bent over to the ground from the weight of the snow, and the drifts were so thick and wet, it was impossible to walk through them.

"'It'll be May before all this snow melts and we can travel again,' Ben said.

"'Not even our sleigh could make it through this mess,' I agreed.

"But Paul just looked about him, thinking and thinking and not saying a word.

"'I'm starving,' I said, and that's how I knew we had been there for several days. I was so hungry I could have eaten an ox.

"'But we can't stay here,' said Ben. 'We'll starve to death if we do 'cause there's nothing here to eat but snow.'

"'Not even a deer,' I replied.

"'And if there was a deer,' Ben said, 'we ain't got a gun to shoot it with.'

"But Paul was still silent. He just thought and thought, and we stared at him until we thought maybe the cold had frozen him in place. Then we noticed a little tear starting down his cheek, and in a second, it turned into a footlong icicle.

"'He's crying from fear of starvation,' Ben whispered to me.

"Neither of us could believe it. Paul Bunyan was the biggest, strongest, bravest, most courageous fellow anyone could ever meet, but here he was crying 'cause he feared starving.

"'It's all right, Paul,' I told him. 'We'll get by somehow.'

"'We can always eat the horses if we have to,' said Ben.

"But Paul just kept crying and letting those tears turn into icicles. He was such a big man he must have had a tremendous size heart, and a tender one too I guess. Maybe he pitied others who were weaker than him. I don't know. He never would have killed a deer though, even though up here is big hunting country. We figured maybe he was crying now over having to slaughter our poor horses.

"'We gotta eat, Paul,' Ben told him.

"'I know,' Paul sighed.

"'Those horses are our only chance of surviving the winter,' I said.

"'No, we won't eat the horses,' he said, wiping the icicles from his eyes. 'We'll eat Babe instead.'

"'BABE!!!' Ben and I exclaimed together. Babe was Paul's best friend. We could never consent to eating him. Paul's heart would wither away and break if we were to do such a thing.

"'Not Babe,' we told him. 'We'd rather starve, Paul.'

"But Paul was looking deep into Babe's big blue eyes now, and Babe seemed to understand what he was thinking. Babe rolled his eyes sadly at Paul. Paul scratched his ears and rubbed Babe's nose. I doubt I'll ever again see such love between a man and his beast as there was between Paul and that Big Blue Ox.

"'Paul,' Ben and I said, 'you just can't do it.'

"'It's all right,' he said, after blowing his nose. 'I know a trick an Indian medicine man taught me. I saved this medicine man once from a grizzly bear, and in exchange, he enchanted Babe. See, Babe can be eaten once, and so long as we only eat the meat and don't break the bones, then there won't be no trouble. After we're done eating, I can just say a spell and cast some snow over the bones and Babe will come back alive like new.'

"'But Paul,' said I. 'What if it don't work? What if the medicine man lied to you?'

"'He wouldn't have done that,' Paul said. 'He was grateful for my saving his life.'

"'But what if — ' Ben tried to protest, but Paul hushed us both, saying nothing else was to be done, and it would all go well. Babe didn't look so sure, but he loved Paul so well, he gladly laid down his life for his friend.

"'Now I'll do the deed,' Paul said, 'but you and Ben are going to have to cut down some trees and make a clearing where we can roast the meat.'

"Ben and I willingly left the shelter. We cut down a few trees that were not in the path of the wind so they did not shelter us. Then we dug down with our bare hands about twenty or maybe it was thirty feet — the snow was that deep — until we came to real rocky ground to build a fire on. If we had not found rock, any fire we started would have melted all the snow beneath it and started a flood. Meanwhile, Paul said goodbye to Babe, and then he lifted his ax and did the deed. When he called us back inside the tent, Babe looked as if he were just sleeping peacefully. Our hearts were aching with trouble and worry, and the only thing that kept us from crying was not wanting to make Paul cry, but we helped Paul cut up that Big Blue Ox and roast the meat over the fire. We were careful all through the process to save and pile the bones where they would not be lost. Now you might think this would be hard, especially with something as small as a toe bone, but Babe's toes were the size of a man's leg, so you see, not much chance existed of us losing any bone because it was too small.

"Now it takes a mighty long time to cook anything in the middle of winter, especially when it's forty degrees below zero, and it takes even longer to cook a Big Blue Ox. We kept the extra meat stored up in the snowbanks, and we rationed it out over weeks and weeks as one horrible storm after another pounded around us. We started to think the snow had continued clear through summer and we were into the next winter. Then just as we were about to run out of meat, the snow finally started to melt. Soon the grass started to poke up through the ground, and then Paul said it was time we find our way back to civilization. I think Paul started to worry that if he didn't bring Babe back to life pretty soon, there would be no bringing Babe back. During all that winter, we had tried to be good company to Paul, playing poker with him, and telling our lumberjack stories, but Paul sure had a fondness for that Ox, and we could see he was missing Babe sorely.

"So Ben and I, we gathered up all Babe's bones and hooked them back together. We had us quite a puzzle at times since we didn't always know which bone went where, none of us being doctors of any sort, but Paul insisted we wouldn't stop trying until we knew for certain every single piece was in the right place because he didn't want no limping ox.

"When we finally had all the pieces together, Paul sprinkled the snow over the bones and began to chant in the Ojibwa language. Suddenly a North wind sprung up, and then came a blinding flurry of snow. At first I thought it was another blizzard, and since we'd eaten all of Babe, I figured we would starve for sure this time. But then the snow stopped, and sun broke forth, and there stood Babe, big and blue as ever, and Paul threw his arms around Babe's neck.

"Even Ben and I shed a couple tears, and I ain't ashamed to mention it.

"'Now, let's find our way back to civilization,' I said.

"'Look at that,' Ben then exclaimed. 'There's water over there.' And as we watched, we saw the snow melt down to ice, and then the ice break up and fall into Lake Superior. All that winter, we had been camped just a few feet from the lakeshore. We all felt lucky we hadn't walked right into the lake when the first storm hit.

"'And look here,' I said, pointing to the ground.

"Where we had cooked ox meat all winter, the rocks had turned completely black.

"So that's how the Black Rocks came to be at Presque Isle, and they'll always stand as a monument to an animal who loved a man enough to give his life for him."

THE END

The boys chuckled when the story was over.

"I'm sure glad you didn't make it into Marquette," said Molly, who had heard most of the story from the kitchen. "I wouldn't want to have fed Paul Bunyan and that ox all winter. I never would have gotten out of the kitchen. But Karl, you definitely have your father's storytelling ability." She smiled as she remembered how her Fritz used to fill Karl's head with fairy tales from Germany.

"That's exactly what it is, a story, a tall tale," Jeremy said.

"It is rather far-fetched," Patrick laughed.

"It's as true as I'm sitting here right now," said Karl.

"If Paul Bunyan was real, whatever happened to him?" asked Jeremy.

"Well, he was such a good friend to me and Ben," said Karl, "that he knew he'd put us out of business if he kept logging here, so he went out West to cut down the trees. You've heard of the Great Plains, right? Well, they were called the Great Forests until Paul Bunyan cut all the trees down, clear from the Dakotas to Kansas. He always promised he'd return someday to visit me and Ben. Paul was never much for writing letters — all the pencils are too small for him to hold — so I don't know when he'll come, but I bet I'll see him again someday."

"Yeah, he'll return about the same time King Arthur does," said Jeremy.

"What do you mean by that?" asked Karl.

"King Arthur ain't never going to return."

"At least," Frank said, "King Arthur was a real historical person. I'm not so sure about Paul Bunyan."

"Even if he is historical, that doesn't mean he can return," said Jeremy.

"Jesus will return," said Michael, not quite eight years old, but firm in his religious beliefs.

"That's different because Jesus is God, and God can do anything," said Frank.

"And Jesus ain't returned yet either," said Jeremy.

"You watch your mouth," Kathy warned her son, stepping in from the kitchen. "I'm ashamed to hear my son say such a blasphemous thing, especially when you just went to Mass this morning."

Jeremy looked ashamed, but he doubted that if Jesus had not returned after nineteen centuries, he was ever going to return.

"Dinner's ready," Kathy said. "Hurry before the potatoes get cold."

As soon as everyone was seated and the blessing over, Karl said, "If you don't believe me that Paul Bunyan was real, you can ask Mr. Peter White. He and Paul Bunyan are great friends, so he'll set you straight."

The boys were silent then. Peter White was the most respected man in town; if their uncle dared suggest they ask him, then even if the stories were a little exaggerated, they could not doubt Paul Bunyan was a real person.

Sunday dinner was followed by a spontaneous baseball game between Karl, Patrick and the boys, a long afternoon walk that Molly vigorously joined in, a light supper, and an hour of singing around the piano, despite Jeremy's complaints that all the songs his mother played were long out of date. Perhaps the evening's highlight was when little Thelma played a simple song. She had begun to take piano lessons a few months earlier and already her teacher said she excelled most of the other pupils, even those twice her age. Thelma's dimples popped out from the enthusiastic applause that followed her performance.

"I haven't heard a little girl play like that since Agnes," said Molly.

"Who's Agnes?" asked Jeremy.

"She was the daughter of my best friend, Clara," Molly replied. "She played the piano beautifully."

"Do we know her?" Jeremy asked. "What's her last name?"

"Her maiden name was Henning. She married Jacob Whitman. She's been dead for many years now."

"Did you know her, Mother?" Michael asked.

"Yes," said Kathy. "She was a sweet lady. She died just before your father and I married. She actually taught me to play the piano."

"And you knew her way back then, Grandma?" said Michael. "She must have been really old."

"Oh no, Agnes was twenty or more years younger than me. I remember she and her husband got married a couple years after he came back from the Civil War."

"The Civil War?" said Jeremy. "That was fifty years ago!"

"Not quite," said Molly. She remembered the war days as if they were yesterday. She found it hard to believe her grandchildren did not even know the Civil War's dates. What did they teach in the schools?

"It looks as if it's bedtime for all of you," Patrick told the boys. Frank wanted to protest. At twenty, he saw no reason to go to bed if he did not want to, but he would not argue in front of his uncle.

"I think I'll go to bed too," said Molly. "It's been a happy but tiring day."

Karl got up and kissed his mother on the cheek. Then Kathy did the same and offered to help her mother to bed, but Molly refused. She climbed upstairs to her bedroom where she had taken up residence a couple years ago rather than continue to live in her own home. The boys and Thelma said goodnight to their parents, then also went upstairs.

Kathy, Karl, and Patrick stayed in the parlor for a late night chat. The two men smoked cigars and each drank a pint of whiskey. Patrick, being Irish, never went to bed without having his whiskey, and Karl was happy to join in the nightly ritual. Meanwhile, Kathy finished her row of knitting.

"Thelma looks just like her mother," Kathy said, hoping to please Karl.

"I really appreciate your letting her stay with you," he replied. "I hope she won't be any trouble."

"No, we love having her here," said Kathy. "Patrick and I always did want a little girl of our own."

Neither mentioned it, but both men knew Kathy was thinking of the two daughters who had been stillborn between Jeremy and Michael's births.

"Just where are you going, Karl?" Patrick broke the uncomfortable silence. "I wouldn't ask except if something should happen to Thelma while you're gone, we'll need to know your whereabouts."

Patrick and Kathy expected he was going to Chicago or Detroit on business, but his reply completely surprised them.

"Germany!" said Kathy. "I don't think I've ever known anyone who's gone to Europe."

"Well, I came from Europe," said Patrick, "but I certainly wouldn't go back. There's nothing there for us. That's the old world, where they follow old ways, where there are still monarchies and tyranny and injustice."

"There's injustice everywhere," said Karl.

"But why do you want to go there?" asked Kathy. "I know Father was from Germany, but why go there and not Ireland?"

"I have Ireland with me all the time," he said. "Mother is from Ireland. But Father is gone. I want to see where he came from."

"Germany's a better choice than Ireland anyway," said Patrick. "Some days I miss my homeland, but I know better than to go back even to visit. Things are probably worse there now than when I left. I count myself lucky everyday to be in America."

How lucky, Patrick would not say. Karl and Kathy, as second generation Americans who had never seen Europe, could never understand. Patrick had long ago broken ties with his Irish past, rarely even corresponding with his family. He felt it best to forget that other bittersweet world. He suspected Karl's yearning to see a country he had never known was only an attempt to escape his responsibilities in reaction to Aino's death.

Nor could Karl have explained his reasons for wanting to see Germany. He felt called to go on this journey. Aino's death had hurt him deeply, as much as Ben's death six years earlier. These losses had reawakened the pain of an even deeper childhood wound; at age thirteen, when Karl was on the verge of manhood and most needed his father, Fritz Bergmann had died and Karl's life had been invaded by a hateful stepfather.

If his father had lived, Karl thought his life might have been different. He wondered whether his strong friendship for Ben had not sprung from a half-conscious longing for a father to guide him; after all, he had always let Ben hold the reins for the business, and Ben had led him into financial independence. Sometimes, Karl felt overwhelmed by homesickness for the past. Now that he was older and had lost the youthful drive to make money, he wanted to know his father better by seeing the Fatherland.

The honeymoon was long over. Not that after five years, Margaret regretted her marriage. But after five years, she and Will still lived in his grandmother's small house. In winter when the ore boats could not run, Will and Margaret were joined by Clarence; he assisted them by buying food, but his presence was a trial for Margaret. She felt he did not approve of her, even if an ill word were never spoken between them. Clarence had been especially good about helping with the baby. Henry was three now, and all the world to Margaret, even though he had come sooner than Will and she could afford a child. Until her son's birth, ambition had fueled Margaret's life. Now motherhood filled her time. Her ambitions had been reduced to dreams of how she might give her son more than she had ever had. When she learned she was expecting a second child, she despaired that she would not achieve a better life for either child.

Financial worries filled Margaret's head today as she and little Henry walked home from visiting her parents. She was preoccupied with her thoughts when she approached the block where her sister-in-law lived. Margaret had never actually met her in-laws. Harry Cumming had forbidden Sylvia to have any contact with her brothers, and by the time Will married, he had given up trying to stay in touch with his sister. A few times, he had bumped into Sylvia downtown, but after a couple hurried words, she would rush off in fear Harry would learn she had spoken to her brother.

Margaret had never been present during these infrequent meetings; she found it bizarre to live in the same town as Sylvia and Harry, yet be uncertain whether she would recognize them on the street. But she did know where they lived, and when she heard shouting, she realized it was coming from inside their house.

"God damn it, woman!" a man bellowed. The screen door flew open and slammed against the wall. An unshaven, unpleasant looking fellow stormed down the porch steps.

"Harry, where are you going?" cried a female voice.

"None of your damn business. But you can go to Hell!" he shouted back as he turned onto the sidewalk and rudely brushed past Margaret and Henry.

Margaret stood a moment, surprised by this first sighting of her brother-in-law. She thought she heard crying from inside the house. She considered going inside to comfort the sister-in-law she did not know. Then a young boy of perhaps thirteen stepped onto the porch and looked down the street after his father.

Margaret knew the boy must be Harry Jr., Will's oldest nephew. She stepped forward to speak to him, but when he saw her staring, he said, "What the hell are you looking at?"

"Nothing," she muttered. Then she grasped Henry's hand and scurried down the street. "What vulgar people!" she thought. How could they be related to Will, who was always so good-natured?

"Why were they angry, Mama?" Henry asked.

"Shh, I don't know," she said, trying to get out of sight of the Cumming house.

Will had told her Harry Cumming was a hateful man. Still she had wondered whether someday there might be reconciliation between the two families. She pitied Sylvia, but having heard the father and oldest son's foul mouths, she had no desire to associate with any of the Cummings. She did not want her children exposed to people who made scenes on city streets. She was sure Sylvia was not at fault — men were never quite whom they pretended to be before you married them — even Will was not as ambitious or industrious as she had believed — they were barely getting by on his wages, and with another baby coming — but at least Will worked, which was more than Sylvia's husband. All Harry Cumming apparently did was spend other people's inheritances so they had to pinch every penny to get by.

Margaret resolved not to tell Will about seeing his family. He had enough worries already, and she feared her mentioning the incident would make him want to help his sister when they could not afford to do so. She wished Will were close to his sister, but she would not encourage it; associating with such people would only be detrimental to her children's social advancement.

Margaret reached home to find her sister sitting on the porch steps. When Sarah Dalrymple had graduated from school, she decided she would not lie around the house and wait for a man to marry her as Margaret had. She wanted more from life; like Margaret, she was ambitious, but she was willing to make money rather than wait to marry it. She had sought employment, and after several failed attempts to find office work for which she had no qualifications, she became housemaid to the Blackmore family. Margaret had been horrified.

"It's honest work," Sarah had protested. "Lots of girls do it, and if you weren't too proud to work, you might have some of the things you want as well."

Margaret had replied that she could not work when she had a child to watch; she knew her mother would watch Henry for her, but she could not overcome her belief that working was unladylike and beneath her. Sarah constantly informed her how much money she earned and what lovely little items she could buy for herself. The sisters had always had their spats; if either were introspective, she would have realized she was jealous of the other. Sarah wanted a husband; because Margaret had married at eighteen, and Sarah was now twenty, she felt she was less than her sister. Margaret envied Sarah her additional money, even as she despised her for working. Their silent jealousy meant they rarely confided in one another, but after her unexpected meeting with the Cummings, Margaret was bursting to talk with someone.

"Sarah, guess what just happened," she said, launching into her tale of the Cummings' awful behavior as Sarah followed her inside and she set Henry down to play with the blocks his father had cut and painted for him.

While Margaret talked, Sarah sat silently on the sofa.

"I don't think I should tell Will," Margaret said. "What do you think?"

"About what?" asked Sarah.

"About Harry. Haven't you been listening to me?"

"No," said Sarah.

"Why not? This is serious."

"I have a bigger problem of my own," Sarah replied.

Margaret sighed. She got up from the floor where she had been helping Henry build a block castle. "What's wrong now?" she asked.

"Never mind if you're going to take that tone," Sarah replied.

"Just tell me what it is," Margaret said, concerned by the distress in her sister's face.

Sarah tried to speak, but the words lodged in her throat. She was terrified by what she must say, but she had no one else to confide in.

"Margaret, please don't yell at me when I say this."

"Just tell me. It can't be that bad."

"You have no idea," Sarah quivered.

"Don't cry," said Margaret, searching for her handkerchief. "What is it?"

"You'll hate me when I tell you." Tears ran down her cheeks.

"Not anymore than usual," Margaret joked to lighten the tension.

Sarah did not smile. They often fought, but that was how they dealt with each other; both knew it meant nothing. Margaret loved her sister, and she was frightened by her tears.

"Come on, Sarah, just tell me."

"I think I'm in the family way."

The words were barely whispered, yet Margaret felt as if they had been spoken over a loudspeaker. They were shocking, ghastly words. She was so stunned that she wondered she had not fainted when she heard them; a well-bred lady would faint to learn her family was disgraced. But instead, Margaret was angry.

"What are you saying?"

"I'm going to have a baby. I haven't had my usual flow for two months."

"Sarah, are you sure? What did — when — who did this to you?"

"I can't tell you."

"You better tell. He'll have to marry you."

"No, he won't," Sarah cried. "Anyway, I don't want to marry him."

"Why not? You have to get married. Did you tell him yet?"

"No, I hate him." Sarah wiped her eyes, then twisted the handkerchief as if it were the neck of the man who had disgraced her.

"Aunt Sarah, why are you sad?" asked Henry, leaving his blocks to lean against her.

"Never mind, Henry. Go back to your playing," Margaret ordered in a tone that nearly made him cry in fear. He did as he was told.

"Who is he?" Margaret repeated.

"I can't tell you."

"What will Mother and Father say? This'll ruin our family. How could you do such a thing?"

"I didn't mean to. I told him no, but he insisted. He — oh, it was horrible."

Margaret softened when she heard Sarah had been taken advantage of against her will. She knew what her first time had been like on her wedding night. Painful. Frightening. Disgusting. It had taken a long time before she and Will had become comfortable with each other and before she could find any pleasure in it.

"Does he know?" she asked.

"Yes, I told him. I didn't know what else to do. I thought maybe he'd help me, find me a doctor, but he only told me to keep quiet or he'd make trouble for me. He said he couldn't risk helping me, and he would hurt me if I told anyone."

"The scoundrel!" said Margaret. "How can he say such a thing when it's his fault?"

Margaret knew Sarah was rebellious. She rather suspected her sister had encouraged the man, but women had to support one another at such times. Men could be such animals.

"He says a scandal will ruin his position in this town," said Sarah, "but he also said his family is better than mine, so no one will believe me anyway."

Margaret sucked in her breath. Many families in Marquette were better than her own, but she did not like to be reminded of it. "That doesn't mean our family deserves such a scandal!"

"Margaret, what should I do?"

Before Margaret could answer, Will came in the front door. Unannounced, he brought Clarence with him.

"Clarence, what are you doing here?" Margaret asked, less surprised than intent on distracting attention from her red-eyed sister.

"I just got in. My ship's docked here for the night so I came to visit my family." He picked up Henry and lifted him into the air, making the boy laugh and clutch at his uncle's sailor uniform.

"Clarence, you remember my sister, Sarah," said Margaret.

"Ye-es," said Clarence, instantly noticing her swollen eyes. "How are you?"

Then Margaret had a conniving thought. If Clarence married Sarah, scandal could be avoided.

Sarah panicked at the thought of making small talk to a man she barely knew. "I better go home," she said. "Mother expects me to help with supper."

"Okay," said Margaret, ushering her sister to the door while Will offered to get Clarence a drink.

"What am I going to do?" Sarah asked when both women were outside, safe from men's ears.

"I don't know," said Margaret, "but don't tell Mother and Father until I've had time to think." She was already plotting how she might get Clarence to marry Sarah.

"You'll think of something, Margaret. You're always so smart. I know you'll help me."

"I will, but I need time to think," said Margaret. "I better go before Will suspects anything or the neighbors notice you're upset. But don't worry. I'll talk to you tomorrow. We'll figure out something."

Sarah moped her way down the street. Margaret breathed deeply, then returned inside.

That night in their bedroom, Margaret quizzed her husband. "Did you notice how shy Sarah seemed when you came home?"

"I did think she left in rather a hurry," said Will.

"It's because she gets nervous around Clarence. Do you think there's a chance he might be interested in her?"

"Clarence? Interested in Sarah? No, she's too young for him."

"They're only four years apart, the same as us."

"I don't think Clarence has ever noticed her," said Will. "I doubt he would notice any woman, except a mermaid. Clarence's only mistress will always be the sea."

"Oh." Margaret bit her lip.

"Do you really think Sarah likes him?" Will asked.

"Yes," Margaret fibbed. She saw no harm in a little matchmaking. If Clarence could be convinced of Sarah's interest, Margaret was certain she could talk Sarah into marrying him out of necessity.

"It's too bad for Sarah then," said Will. "No woman should marry a sailor. Clarence will never be home. She should look for someone else."

"Still, Clarence would make a good husband," Margaret replied. "He must have plenty of money saved up in the bank, and he's not getting any younger. He's twenty-four now. Most men are married by that age."

She waited for a response, but Will only closed his eyes and went to sleep.

A few days after her father left for Germany, Thelma Bergmann accompanied her Aunt Kathy to the First National Bank. Thelma was not quite five years old, but she was very vocal and active. She was even more fascinated than her older cousins with her father's tall tales, and her young mind was more impressionable; she had heard so many of her father's stories that they had become real to her; she never would have conceived that her father did not tell the truth.

While Aunt Kathy completed her bank transaction with the teller, Thelma watched the other bank patrons. She did not fail to notice when the Honorable Peter White stepped into the lobby. Mr. White was such a local celebrity that even the youngest children recognized him. The instant she saw him, Thelma was off like a pistol shot across the lobby. She stopped right before Mr. White and boldly looked up into his startled face.

"Hello," he smiled.

"Hello," she said.

"How are you today?" he asked.

"Fine. I have a question," she said, standing on tiptoe to get a better look at his gray bearded face.

"Thelma, come here," Kathy called while crossing the lobby to fetch her niece. "Mr. White, I'm terribly sorry. She usually has better manners."

"It's all right. Children should be inquisitive. It shows they have a good head on their shoulders," he replied. Then he turned back to Thelma. "My dear, you look just like your aunt did when she was your age. Pretty as a button."

"I have a question," Thelma repeated.

"Well, dear, what is it?"

"Do you really know Paul Bunyan?"

Mr. White had leaned down to hear Thelma. Now he lifted his head, stepped back, and let out a roaring laugh that made the bank patrons turn and stare. "What? Do you doubt it?" he replied. "I knew Paul Bunyan when he was no bigger than you."

"Then he was a real person?"

"What do you mean 'was a real person'? He's still real. As real as you or me, and a great deal more real considering he's three times the size of the average man. Oh, I know he's gone away for a while — to Minnesota I think, but you just wait. Someday he'll be back. There are plenty of trees in these Northern woods still waiting for him to cut down. Why any day now I expect to see him come walking down Washington Street as if he never left the U.P. at all."

"Oh, good," Thelma said. "I didn't want to think my daddy was a liar."

"Oh, it's your father who's been telling you about Paul Bunyan?"

"Yes."

"Well, your father is a wise man. If anyone knows about Paul Bunyan, it's him. He used to work shoulder to shoulder in the woods with Paul."

"That's what he said," Thelma replied.

"Well then, I see no reason to doubt him."

"Come along, Thelma," said Kathy. "We've troubled Mr. White long enough."

"No trouble at all," laughed Peter. "Thelma, you let me know if you see Paul Bunyan. I've wondered for a long time what he's been up to."

"Okay," said Thelma. "Goodbye."

"Goodbye, Thelma. Good day, Mrs. McCarey."

"Good day, Mr. White."

Kathy took her niece's hand and led her out of the bank.

Compared to Thelma's bank visit, Margaret's visit that day was far less pleasant. Because Clarence had left early that morning, Margaret had been entrusted to deposit his latest paycheck in the bank for him. Clarence had an account with both his and Will's names on it, so Margaret and Will often did his banking for him. The money belonged to Clarence, but he had placed Will's name on the account, "Just in case anything ever happens to me." After five years, the money had grown into a substantial sum; Margaret was envious that a bachelor with no real expenses should have so much money when she and Will would soon have a second child to support. She and Will barely scraped by from week to week, yet Will refused to borrow a penny from the money Clarence had entrusted to him.

Margaret was short-tempered this morning; twice she had raised her voice to Henry for shuffling along as they walked downtown. Keeping Sarah's secret was hard enough, and she had barely slept from scheming how to convince Clarence to marry Sarah.

Then her plans had been thwarted at breakfast when Will had said, "Clarence, Margaret says Sarah's swooning over you."

"Ha!" Clarence had roared. "That's all we need, another Dalrymple woman in the family."

Margaret had stayed silent, but Clarence's words had bothered her all morning. She had long known Clarence did not like her, but he need not make pretentious statements to suggest his family was better than hers — even if his mother had been a Henning. Sarah might be about to disgrace the Dalrymples, but Margaret had never heard such foul mouths as those of the Cummings.

Margaret was wearing her best hat that morning; she always felt cheered when she dressed up a little, and she thought perhaps a nice hat would protect her from the shame of her sister's indiscretion. Margaret had expected poverty could drag her down, but scandal was far worse. As she reached downtown, she looked about for familiar faces, for important people to whom she might mention her husband so he could increase his business prospects. But the street was fairly empty this morning. Had she been a customer of the First National Bank, she would have seen the Honorable Peter White in the bank lobby discussing a very serious matter with a little girl. A glimpse of one of the city's most prominent leaders would have been the highlight of her day. But Margaret belonged to the bank across the street. She went inside that financial institution, marched up to the teller's window, released Henry's hand, and searched in her purse for Clarence's paycheck.

"Can I help you?" asked the teller.

"Yes, I want to deposit this check into my brother-in-law's account," she replied, sliding the check across the counter. Then she looked at the teller for the first time.

"You're Mr. Blackmore, aren't you?"

"Yes," he replied.

"I didn't know you worked here. My sister, Sarah Dalrymple, works for your parents."

"Oh," he muttered, taking the check from her.

Margaret thought him unfriendly. He was a Blackmore, and rich, but he should still be polite. Did he think himself too good to speak to the sister of his parents' housemaid? His parents did have a splendid home. Margaret wondered whether Will might do some carpentry work for them sometime.

"I'm Mrs. Will Whitman," she added. "My husband's a successful carpenter."

"Pleased to meet you," he muttered, punching keys on his adding machine. Then he pushed a receipt across the counter to her.

"Thank you," said Margaret; she waited a second for him to wish her good morning, but he said nothing further.

"I'll tell my sister I saw you," Margaret smiled.

He muttered something under his breath, then turned and went into a back room.

"How rude," Margaret thought. "Sarah said he was a pleasant young man."

"Mama, go see the ships?" asked Henry, as they stepped outside in view of the lake.

"All right. Maybe your Uncle Clarence's ship is still visible," she said, leading Henry across the street and then down the hill to the harbor. She had laundry to do, but a little fresh lake air might clear her mind.

It was a beautiful spring day, too beautiful to be indoors burdened with worries. She would like to be out riding her bicycle as she had done when a girl. Clarence's ship was on the horizon, having just sailed out of Iron Bay. She pointed it out to Henry. She envied Clarence being able to sail away like that. He had freedom — he could travel about to see the world, and he could save all his money because the ship paid his expenses. She had always wanted such freedom to travel, to have money, to visit interesting places. She had married Will to escape her parents' home and in the belief he was going places. She loved Will, but she no longer expected he would give her a better life. Now her sister's shame would make things worse. Sarah's iniquity might ruin Will's business; people would shun her family as social outcasts. She feared she and Will would not even be able to feed the baby when it came.

Money. It was the curse and blessing of mankind. It was practically the blood of life. She wished she knew why God let those who did not deserve it have so much, and those in need have so little. She was almost tempted to go back to the bank and ask how much money was in her brother-in-law's account. Clarence probably didn't know himself. If she could just borrow a little — but that teller would never let her. He was so rude. Those Blackmores had so much money they would never understand her situation. How could Sarah work for such snobs? Maybe that young man was just shy, but he had been so rude that —

"Oh!" Margaret gasped. Could that be it?

"Mama, the boat's gone," said Henry, straining his eyes.

"We won't see Uncle Clarence for a while now," she said. "Come, we better go home."

She clasped Henry's hand and nearly dragged him back up Washington Street's hill. Then they turned onto Front Street, and she dragged him up that hill. She tugged him so hard he stumbled, then fell and skinned the palm of his hand. When he started crying, Margaret felt guilty. She picked him up, kissed his booboo, and carried him to the top of the hill. She would not have tugged him so hard had she been paying attention to him. But her brain could not stop whirling.

Could it be? Why else had he been so rude when Sarah had said he was pleasant? And the Blackmores were so rich. He had just started at the bank that summer after finishing college. He would have a prosperous career before him.

He would make a fine brother-in-law. She would find out for certain, then bring about the marriage. He would marry Sarah, or she would tell all Marquette he was a scoundrel.

"Who would name their son Lysander anyway?" Margaret asked. She referred to the young Mr. Blackmore, whose name Sarah had just revealed privately to Margaret as father of her expected child. Margaret was determined Lysander would be responsible for his actions.

"He goes by Ly," said Sarah.

"That's appropriate," Margaret sneered.

"Don't insult him," Sarah cried. "He's just scared. Maybe if I talk to him again."

"I'll talk to him," said Margaret. "He'll take responsibility for what he's done."

"I won't force him to marry me," said Sarah. "That'll only make it worse. He didn't mean for this to happen, and — "

"Why are you defending him?" Margaret asked. "He forced you."

Sarah stared at the floor.

"Sarah, did you encourage him?"

"He asked whether he could kiss me and touch me. I didn't know he was going to — well, I didn't know it would hurt like that."

"So you encouraged him?"

"You would have done the same; he just has this charm about him — I couldn't resist."

"Do you love him?"

"Yes," Sarah sighed, collapsing onto Margaret's couch.

Margaret was disgusted. So what if the Blackmores had money? Money did not replace good manners and morals. Sarah had no common sense.

"He'll have to marry you," said Margaret.

"He was probably just shocked when I told him," Sarah said. "If I talk to him again, he might do the right thing. I can't blame him for being upset."

"How can you take his side?" Margaret asked. "He's disgraced us, yet you act as if he did nothing wrong."

"I can't help it. I love him. If I talk to him again, maybe he'll be reasonable."

"Go ahead and talk to him," said Margaret, "but make it clear that if he doesn't marry you, the whole town will know what he's done. I'll make sure they do, even if it ruins us as well."

❦　　　❦　　　❦

Today was Thelma's first visit to the magnificent Peter White Public Library at the top of Front Street. Built four years earlier, the building's giant white columns, like those of a Greek Temple, declared the library to be Marquette's bastion of knowledge. Thelma skipped up the library's tall stone steps while Aunt Kathy and Cousin Michael tried to keep pace with her. Michael, having visited the library many times, had promised to show Thelma where all the good books were. Kathy was pleased her son got along so well with his little cousin, although it surprised her that he preferred books to running about wildly as his older brothers had done at his age. Michael was especially fond of reading Bible Stories and lives of the saints. Patrick wanted the boy to play baseball, but Kathy wondered whether Michael had not found a better occupation for his time. Last night, Michael had told Thelma the story of Joseph and his coat of many colors, so Thelma wanted to find a book with pictures of the fabulous coat in it. Kathy intended to follow her son and niece to the children's section so they would not make too much noise in the library, but as the children made a beeline for the storybooks, Kathy overheard a librarian remark to a patron, "It's a shame he's gone, but we'll always remember him for this beautiful library he left the city."

"He died in Detroit you say?" replied the patron. "That's too bad. I imagine it will be quite a funeral."

"Excuse me," said Kathy. "Did you say Peter White died?"

"Yes, just yesterday in Detroit. He fell down dead of a heart attack right on a city street. The body is being shipped back here for the funeral."

"How awful!" said Kathy. She recalled meeting Mr. White at the bank just a few weeks before. She felt stunned and momentarily unable to breathe. Then a joyful scream from Thelma made her maternal instincts return; she went to quiet the children.

Peter White was gone. He had been the greatest politician the Upper Peninsula had ever known, although he had never held a major political office. He had fought tirelessly for the Upper Peninsula, for its railroads and mines. He was the friend of U.S. Presidents and esteemed by Michigan's successive governors. He was the grand old man of Marquette, the last of those considered to be founding fathers.

"I'll have to tell Mother," Kathy thought as the children checked out their books. She walked home, surprised to be so upset by Mr. White's death. She had barely known him other than to give a passing hello on the street. Karl knew him better, having had business dealings with him over the years. Her parents had known Peter White well during Marquette's infancy. Her mother had told her how in that first year, Kathy's father had been one of several struck with typhoid. A small hospital had been built in the wilderness settlement, and Peter White, then only eighteen, had bathed and nursed the sick back to health. Kathy's mother had often said Kathy's father would have died if not for Peter White. Kathy felt consumed with grief and the dread of telling her mother such news. She could not imagine anyone else in Marquette whose loss would effect so many. In small towns, each person's life overlaps with so many others; one person's loss can be a blow to the entire community — how much more so when the lost person is the city's greatest benefactor. Kathy reflected that she had just left the library Mr. White had established, and here on the corner was the Methodist Church he had donated money to build, and just down Ridge Street, she could glimpse the Episcopalian Church where he had funded the Morgan Chapel in memory of his own deceased son. As she turned down Front Street, rising up was the First National Bank he had helped found; in the distance were the towers of St. Peter's Cathedral; Peter White had donated money to help rebuild them after the fire that destroyed the cathedral when Kathy was a girl. She thought that if she rode on the passing streetcar, it would take her to Presque Isle, which Peter White had preserved as a park for all future generations who called Marquette home, and the road to Presque Isle he had lined with Lombardy Poplars to beautify the lakeshore. And at the Normal School, the science building was named in his honor for all his efforts to establish an institution of higher learning in Upper Michigan. Marquette would never again have such a great benefactor. Without Peter White, it would be fair to say there never would have been much to Marquette.

At home, Kathy found her mother making sandwiches.

"Mother, I told you I'd make dinner when I got home. You shouldn't trouble yourself."

"I'm not helpless yet," said Molly. She greatly feared someday being helpless when she still had so much she wished to accomplish, so many people she wished to help. "Besides, I have that Altar Society meeting this afternoon, and I didn't want to be late for it."

"I'm sorry. I forgot. Sit down and I'll quickly finish making lunch. I don't want you too tired to go to your meeting."

"You act as if I'm an old lady. I'm not even eighty yet."

Before Kathy could reply, Thelma burst into the kitchen.

"Grandma! Look at the book I got at the li-berry."

"Oh, isn't it nice," said Molly, sitting down at the table to look at the picture book. She was glad to sit, but she would not admit it. "What book did Michael get?"

Molly looked about for her grandson, but he had already gone upstairs, too intent on reading to waste time showing his book to anyone.

"More Bible stories," Kathy replied. "Mother, I have to tell you something."

"Is it bad news?" asked Molly. "Seems as if it always is at my age." But she did not mind bad news terribly; she found in it another opportunity to do God's work.

"Yes, it is," said Kathy as she buttered the bread. "Peter White has died." She kept making sandwiches, afraid to see her mother's response.

Molly felt dizzy a moment. Then, she dug out her handkerchief to wipe away a tear.

"Don't cry, Grandma," said Thelma. "The book's not that scary."

"Thelma, go upstairs with Michael," Kathy told her. "Take your book with you."

"I don't think the witch in the book is that scary," Thelma said as she trotted out of the kitchen.

"I'm surprised it hit me like that," said Molly, refolding her handkerchief. "How did it happen?"

Kathy repeated what she had heard at the library.

"I must be the last one alive now who came to Marquette its first year," said Molly. "But Peter was the best one of us. No one ever would have guessed how far he would advance when he was just a young man. We were the same age, you know."

"Were you?" said Kathy, aware of the fact, but encouraging her mother to talk and ease her pain.

"Yes. I met him the very day your father and I arrived here. There were only a couple buildings then, and maybe twenty people, not counting the boatload your father and I came on from Milwaukee. It's too bad. Peter was a good man."

"I know," said Kathy, remembering how such an important man had found time to speak to a little girl at the bank. "If Marquette had more like him, we truly would be the Queen City of the North."

"We are the Queen City," said Molly. "There isn't a finer place in the world. We've known some hard times, but people here look after their neighbors, not like in those big cities."

"No, I guess not," said Kathy. She had never been farther than Calumet, but she had heard tales of the poverty and isolation her mother had experienced in Boston and Milwaukee, so she always considered herself lucky to live in Marquette.

"I'll want to go to the funeral," said Molly. "I'll wear my best black dress."

"You look tired, Mother. After lunch, maybe you should take a nap rather than go to your meeting."

"Oh no, life goes on, and the Altar Society would be lost without me. Let me pour the milk for the children," she said, getting back on her feet. "I can't sit around and mourn for the past just because my old friends are passing. They would want me to keep working for future generations."

Kathy admired her mother's spirit, but she feared her mother would overdo it. When Molly came home from her meeting that afternoon, she did take a long nap until suppertime, and then Kathy realized Peter White's death had depressed her mother more than Molly had been willing to admit.

"That horrid woman. She's ruined everything," Sarah sobbed. She and Margaret sat on the sofa. Will had gone to make tea for his sister-in-law.

"Shh, you'll wake Henry," Margaret warned.

Sarah had knocked on the front door a couple minutes before. It was half past nine o'clock, so Margaret and Will had been surprised to have such a late visitor. Will had been even more surprised to open the door to a sobbing sister-in-law.

"Is Will going to be angry?" Sarah asked. "You'll have to tell him now."

"I don't think he'll be angry," said Margaret, although she was deeply disappointed her sister should make such a scene.

"It doesn't matter who knows now. I'll have to go away because of that horrid woman."

"But, Sarah, calm down and explain it to me. What horrid woman are you talking about?"

"Mrs. Blackmore. She walked in on me and Ly when we were kissing."

"Why on earth were you kissing him?"

"Kissing who?" asked Will, shakily carrying in the tea tray because he was not used to such women's work.

"I talked to him as I told you I would," Sarah replied, ignoring Will's remark as she sipped her tea. "He saw how upset I was, so he said he'd make it right — that he would tell his parents he loved me and we'd get married."

"That's wonderful," said Margaret, although the knots in her stomach stayed tight.

"It was," said Sarah, "until his parents caught us kissing in his bedroom."

"What were you doing in his bedroom?" Will asked.

"I was cleaning it when he came home, so that's where I talked to him."

Will shook his head. How could any young lady — even Sarah — be stupid enough to be caught alone with a young man in his bedroom?

Mrs. Blackmore had not been so stupid. When she had come home and heard giggling behind her son's closed door, she had not hesitated to open the door without knocking. She had found her son lying on the bed with the housemaid, their lips locked together. That they were fully clothed only told Mrs. Blackmore she had arrived in the nick of time.

"Mother, I love her. I want to marry her!" Lysander had protested when Mrs. Blackmore ordered Sarah to leave the house.

"Over my dead body will my son marry a common tramp," Mrs. Blackmore had replied.

Lysander was afraid of his mother. She sternly ruled her family with a ladylike thumb of iron. Lysander would have caved to her wishes right then by sending the wronged girl away had Sarah not declared, "We will so get married. We have to."

Then Lysander had turned pale. Mrs. Blackmore had clutched her heart.

"We'll get married," Sarah had added, "unless you want everyone in Marquette to know you have a bastard grandchild."

"What! What!" Mrs. Blackmore had shrieked until her husband came running. When all had been explained, Mr. Blackmore told his son, "I wish you were still small enough for me to take you over my knee."

"He promised to marry me," Sarah said, "so you can't stop us."

"You're a stupid girl if you think I'll let you ruin my son's life," Mrs. Blackmore replied. "I hope your parents have more sense."

Mrs. Blackmore had then stormed from the room, followed by her husband.

Lysander had stood up to buckle the belt Sarah had been unbuckling when they had been interrupted.

"What did she mean by that?" Sarah asked him.

"Come on," he replied, pulling her off the bed and downstairs.

"Mother, if you do this — " Lysander began as they came downstairs.

"You'll thank me for this later," Mrs. Blackmore had replied in the front hall. "Now unless you want to be living on the street, you'll let me take care of this."

Lysander, seeing his mother's eyes flash, knew he was defeated. Lowering his head, he went and locked himself in the library.

"Ly, where are you going? Ly!" Sarah had called helplessly, but he was too weak to return and fight for her.

"Come along, Missy," Mrs. Blackmore had said. "We're going to have a talk with your parents."

Sarah, abandoned by her lover, had found herself pulled down the street to her home. She had cried and tried to run away when they reached her parents' house, but Mrs. Blackmore, afraid to lose her grip on the collar of the girl's dress, had roared out, "Mr. Dalrymple!" When her father had come onto the porch, Sarah had broken free from the horrid woman and run into the house, burying herself in a corner of the parlor sofa. She had heard her father talking in a loud voice, and her mother run to the door, asking, "What's wrong? What is it?"

Then the horrid woman had followed her parents inside to the parlor where Sarah had to confront all three of them. She was so terrified she could scarcely follow what was being said until she saw her father take a bank check from Mrs. Blackmore.

"If I ever hear anyone make mention of this," Mrs. Blackmore had warned, "I'll make sure, Mr. Dalrymple, that you never work another day in this town."

"She's just a girl," Mrs. Dalrymple had protested.

"You heard me. I'll turn everyone in Marquette against you. Send her away!"

Then Mrs. Blackmore had gone out into the black night.

"What did Mother and Father say when she left?" Margaret asked when Sarah had finished her tragic tale. The tea had grown cold during the recital. Not knowing what to say, Will collected tea cups and carried them into the kitchen. He took his time washing them. He would be of no use while Margaret comforted her sister. He wondered why one's siblings always had to bring trouble to a family.

"They said I'll have to go stay with Uncle Alexander and Aunt Maud in Chicago," Sarah replied. "I hardly even know them, but Father says they're family so they'll help. He says I'll have to tell people in Chicago I'm a widow who's come to stay with my aunt and uncle. I'll be treated as a poor relation to them."

"Do Mother and Father know you already told me?" asked Margaret.

"Yes, I told them that's why I was coming here."

"Now they'll be angry with me for not telling them," Margaret worried.

Sarah was not concerned about her sister's distress. She had enough of her own. "What can I do, Margaret? I don't want to go to Chicago."

"I can't believe Father took money from that woman," said Margaret.

"He only did it so I would have money to buy things for the baby."

"I suppose," said Margaret. She did not want her sister to go. Sarah had always gotten into trouble and embarrassed her, and now she was getting her just deserts, but Margaret hated to see her go. Sarah had helped her with Henry, and now that she was expecting another baby, she wanted her sister close by. "It's just not fair. That scoundrel's as much at fault as you."

"Maybe so," said Will, returning to the room, "but he's rich and Sarah isn't."

"I guess I have no choice but to go to Chicago," said Sarah. "Uncle Alexander manages a dry goods store so he can probably get me some nice things for the baby, and I bet there are lots of eligible young men in Chicago, men who will believe I'm a widow and still show an interest in me."

Margaret shook her head. In a few minutes, Sarah had gone from lamenting her lover's betrayal to fantasizing about a Chicago husband. But Margaret doubted Sarah would ever find a husband now; who would want a spoiled girl with a bastard child? And Margaret knew Sarah was not smart enough to pull off playing a widow — the secret would out.

"When are you leaving?" Will asked.

"Next week. Mother says I don't have to go until the baby starts to show, but I want to go as soon as I can. I don't want to see Ly around town."

Margaret promised to go shopping with Sarah the next day to help her buy necessities for her trip to Chicago. Sarah then left, more excited about her trip than regretful for her misdeed.

Clarence came to visit again that autumn when the dead, falling leaves matched Margaret's mood. She had been depressed since Sarah left. Between the loss of her sister, her brother-in-law's arrival, and the baby soon to be born, she thought she might have a nervous breakdown.

But Clarence gave her little trouble this visit; he barely spoke, and when he did, his words were more kind than usual. Will always insisted that Clarence's visits were vacations during which Clarence was not to do any work. Margaret was annoyed that Will did not consider how his brother's presence increased her own labors. But this visit was different. In the past, Clarence had eaten breakfast, then not even thanked her for the food. After breakfast, he would go off for long walks, look up old friends or visit restaurants and bars and not come home until late so that Margaret had to reheat his supper. This visit, however, he stayed home every day. Margaret was surprised when he devoted himself almost completely to Henry, and after supper, rather than sit and smoke on the porch with Will, Clarence helped her with the dishes so she would not have to be on her feet so much when pregnant. Margaret was almost ready to forgive him for his previous grudge toward her for marrying Will.

Clarence had reason to remain close to home. He felt exhausted. He first feared he had the flu, but when he found that just walking from his room to the kitchen table made his legs shake and his head become woozy, he knew he had more than a common virus. Then his vision would became blurry; other times his head ached until he nearly saw double. He did not want the family to know. The one time Margaret suggested he looked pale, he dismissed it with a laugh and said it was just because it was a cold day.

Only one morning when he felt strong did Clarence go out for a long walk; he did not inform Margaret or Will where he was going. He returned home for lunch in a merrier mood than during the entire visit. That afternoon he offered to take Henry to the drugstore for ice cream so Margaret could have a rest; poor Henry never got out of the house now that his mother's pregnancy meant she could not appear in public. Thankful for the respite from her active three year old, Margaret did not even notice when they were gone over two hours, and Henry was too little to explain that Uncle Clarence had sat on a park bench and dozed for an hour, leaving his nephew neglected; Henry had felt so awkward he ate his ice cream, then simply sat silently beside his napping uncle.

The next day, Clarence departed again on his ore boat.

"Did you think Clarence looked tired while he was here?" Will asked after he and Margaret had seen his brother off. "I worry that he works too hard. I wish he would come back here to find a job. Then he'd have a family around him."

"You worry too much," said Margaret, wondering why Will never noticed how tired she was. "I think he's fine. He said he had a good time with Henry yesterday, and they were gone out long enough."

"He adores Henry," said Will, "which is more reason why he should be here to enjoy his nephews."

"Nephews?" Margaret thought he meant Sylvia's sons.

"Yes, nephews," said Will. "I have a second son on the way."

Relieved to be spared intimacy with the Cummings, Margaret teased back, "No, this baby will be a girl."

Clarence found himself too ill to stay aboard ship. When his boat docked in Ohio, two of Clarence's shipmates took him ashore to a boarding house where he was placed in the landlady's capable hands. Clarence suffered from a fever for several days, and the doctor came to attend him frequently. When he recovered, he refused to rest, but insisted he would go home for Christmas. The landlady and doctor argued that he was too weak, but he soon found work on another ship, the *D.M. Clemson*. After loading coal in Lorain, Ohio, the *Clemson* began its journey on November 28th, north to Duluth. From Duluth, Clarence planned to find passage on another ship to Marquette, so he could spend the holidays and the winter with his brother's family.

He could feel his immune system failing him throughout the trip, but he also had a strange sense of fearlessness. He felt he had been wrong to act so courageous and not tell his family how sick he was. He became resolved to see his new nephew or niece. If God would grant him one more month of life, he would spend the holidays with Will's family.

Two days after leaving Lorain, Clarence's ship passed through the Canadian Soo Locks at nine-thirty in the morning. Four hundred miles of Lake Superior would need to be traversed before the ship reached Duluth.

The *Clemson* was a modern state of the art sea vessel. The old schooners that had brought Clarence's grandparents to Marquette nearly sixty years before had long since been replaced by wooden steamers, and even those had become obscure in the last decade. By the start of the twentieth century, it was more economical to build ships from iron and steel than wood. Vessel size had also increased until nineteenth century schooners were viewed as unseaworthy beside the solid steel giants that now coursed the Great Lakes. The *Clemson* could hold five thousand tons of iron, steel, or coal and deliver its cargo in record time.

But Lake Superior mocked the growing strength of these industrial mari-
ners. Many a lesser ship the lake had swallowed, and it was not yet willing to
relinquish dominance over its own waters. Shortly after the *Clemson* passed
through the Soo Locks, a terrible gale rose up. The storm was not the first the
ship had passed through. The previous October a strong current had pushed
the ship into a pier while entering the harbor of Ashtabula, Ohio; although ten
hull plates were smashed and the water tank on the starboard side badly
damaged, repairs were made and the *Clemson* had sailed again. Then a month
later, a sharp Lake Superior gale had covered the ship completely in ice, but it
had sailed on without major damage done. Twice the Great Lakes had tried to
destroy the ship, and twice it had failed.

Now Nature's enigmatic forces surged up to create the most vicious storm
yet. As the tempest began, Clarence struggled to help secure the ship. He well
knew Lake Superior's fury after five years of riding through torrential storms;
he knew better than to mock Superior's power. Today, struggle as the sailors
might, the waters were determined to show themselves masters. The ship's past
repairs became its weak spot as roaring waves and high winds tossed it up and
down upon rough waters. The tumult soon shifted the cargo, then slid it
completely to one end; whipped up and down and around in circles, the ship
could not bear the pressure of sliding cargo as it tilted upward on towering
waves.

Then Clarence heard the deafening tear of metal; he knew the ship was
ripping apart. Within seconds, the hull filled with water; the weight snapped
the ship in two pieces which immediately separated into the waves. Water
engulfed everything. For a second, Clarence watched in horror as his fellow
sailors were hurled beneath the pounding waves; then he felt terror as his body
was pulled down beneath the water. Somehow the current swept him out of the
sinking ship, and after what seemed an eternity, he managed to surface. For a
second, he bobbed above the water until a massive wave lifted him up, then
catapulted him into another wave, which hurled him again below the surface.
Pain surged through his body. Something hit his back, perhaps a wave, perhaps
a piece of the ship, either would hurt equally in that tremendous storm. He
knew his back was broken. As he gasped from the pain, his lungs filled with
surging water. He blacked out. He felt himself sinking.

Then came light. It was impossible. He knew he should be dead now. He
could feel the water inside his lungs. Had he resurfaced? Was it moonlight he
saw? Something brushed against him, but it was not water, not debris from the
ship. He felt a hand on his shoulder. He opened his eyes. A beautiful woman's

face was before him. He did not understand. No woman had been on the ship. She was not one of his drowned comrades. Could she — a mermaid? Could she be such a creature? She was beautiful, like the photograph he had seen of his mother.

Her lips did not move, but her face said, "Be not afraid."

She need not speak. Her presence brought him unspeakable peace.

Then he knew death was not punishment, nor was it an end. His debilitating disease was nothing to fear. His spirit was eternal. He was leaving life when it would most benefit those he loved. The mermaid, or whatever grace she was, took his hand and led him toward the glowing light. He floated beside her, all his pain, fear, anxiety washed away.

On December 2nd, the *Clemson* became overdue in Duluth. Everyone believed the ship had sought shelter from the storm in another port, but no word was received. In a few more days, debris from the ship began to surface. Searches were made. Lifejackets, hatch covers, a barrel bearing the ship's name were washed up on shore. No luck occurred in the search for survivors. Only two bodies were recovered while the other twenty-three sailors rested in a watery grave.

Once the ship was reported overdue, Will and Margaret began to pray all day and lie sleepless all night. When the situation was known to be hopeless, Will was inconsolable. Margaret had thought Clarence a difficult brother-in-law, but she sincerely mourned his loss, and she grieved that she could not relieve the depression her husband fell into.

Then, one sleepless night, Margaret's labor pains began. Her contractions were so painful that Will, devastated by his brother's loss, now feared the loss of his wife and child. He quickly hitched up his horse, ran back inside the house to carry Henry to the buggy, then made yet another trip to help Margaret. By the time the sun broke over Marquette, the expectant mother had been checked into St. Luke's Hospital on West Ridge Street. By noon, another Whitman had entered the world.

Later that afternoon, Molly Montoni was visiting a sick friend at the hospital when she overheard a nurse say, "My old schoolmate, Margaret Dalrymple, just had a baby."

Before leaving the hospital, Molly sought out the new mother, remembering how years before, she had delivered Margaret herself into the world.

"How splendid," said Molly when she saw the proud mother holding her newborn son. "Do you remember me, Margaret? I'm Mrs. Montoni."

Christina Dalrymple was there visiting her daughter. She greeted Molly by saying, "This just shows your good work has rewards beyond what you could have known. I doubt I would have survived Margaret's birth if you had not acted as midwife, and now my little girl has lived to be a mother twice as a result of your kindness."

Margaret smiled politely and let Molly hold the baby. Margaret had never forgotten her boarding house origins, but with her new son safely born, she could forgive Mrs. Montoni for being present at her own inauspicious birth.

Margaret had gradually made peace with being born in a boarding house, but she had not yet relinquished her aspirations. When Will asked what they should name the baby, Margaret replied, "Royal Whitman, to show he comes from good stock. He'll hold his head up because he'll know his father's ancestors were American patriots who helped to found this country, and because his mother's ancestors were Scottish royalty. I don't think our son deserves any lesser name."

Will thought such a name pompous, but before he could object, Margaret added, "And his middle name will be Clarence. Not his first name because that might be too painful a reminder for you, Will, but his middle name to honor your brother. I always did like the name of Clarence. I believe there are Dukes of Clarence."

Will knew Margaret had not cared for his brother, so he gave in to the first name when she kindly suggested the middle one. He told himself that his second son's birth would begin healing the pain of his brother's loss. He also told himself he would call his son "Roy" so the name sounded no more grand than Henry. Had he asked Margaret, however, she would have reminded him just how many kings had been named Henry.

"I am sorry for Clarence's loss," said Margaret, "but now that we have a new son, and a new year is coming, I feel things will be better for us."

Will replied by kissing Royal on the forehead and Margaret on the lips.

Molly walked home from the hospital, watching her step so she would not slip on the ice. The distance from the hospital to her home was a mere eight blocks; in her youth, she could have walked the distance in ten minutes. Today, it took half an hour, and when she reached the bottom of the hill, she had to pause to catch her breath. Then she wrapped her scarf tighter over her mouth to avoid inhaling the crisp December air and plodded on.

Kathy had not wanted her mother to go out on such a cold day, not even to visit a sick friend at the hospital. When Molly returned home, she complained that she felt a little shaky. Kathy quickly removed her mother's coat, insisted on brewing her a cup of tea, then escorted her upstairs, ordering her to lie down until supper.

Molly made little argument. She lay down, but she did not sleep, and when Patrick came home from work, she half-heard murmurings from her daughter downstairs. "Looking pale since this summer . . . shouldn't have let her go out today . . . what if . . . and Karl isn't here."

Molly knew she had lost quite a bit of weight in the last few months. She felt tired lately, but she had not thought herself seriously ill. She could not remember a day in her life when she had been so sick she had remained in bed. She had no time to be sick, not when first her parents and siblings, then Fritz and her children, then Montoni, and now all these grandchildren constantly needed her.

She felt cold. The bedroom door was shut — she told herself it was just blocking out the heat. She could smell potatoes and turnips cooking. If she got up to open the door, she knew the windows would fog up from the steam in the kitchen. She always felt cozy when that happened. If she just got up and opened the door a crack, she would feel warmer. She really should go downstairs to help Kathy. She felt lonely not being down in the kitchen; she missed hearing the boys' banter and Thelma babbling about her doll. She felt disoriented, especially as it grew dark, yet she was too tired to get up and light a lamp.

She turned her head when Patrick carefully opened the door to see if she were awake. When he saw her struggle to sit up, he stepped inside the room.

"How are you, Mother?" he asked, although he was her son-in-law.

"Fine, just a little tired." She would not worry anyone by admitting just how tired.

"Will you come down for supper?"

She debated, but then admitted to herself she did not have the strength.

"No, I'm not hungry," she fibbed.

"Well," he said, hiding his fear, so he could cheer her up, "after supper maybe we'll have a shot of whiskey together."

Molly smiled. "You're a good Irish boy, Patrick, and a comfort to me. Fritz was a beer drinker, but much as I loved him, it's good to have someone in the family who knows what a real drink is. I'm just going to take a little nap while you go eat, and then we'll have that drink."

Patrick closed the curtains for her, then returned to the kitchen. An hour later, Kathy and Patrick came back upstairs. Patrick carried the whiskey, but Molly did not answer when they spoke to her. Kathy felt her mother's forehead. "She's burning up," she said. Patrick ran downstairs and sent Jeremy off to fetch the doctor. Meanwhile, Molly began to mutter, and her eyelids fluttered as she tried to awake from confusing dreams. At one point she opened her eyes long enough to see Kathy and tell her, "I have to get up or your stepfather will be angry that I haven't made supper."

Patrick returned to hold his wife's hand, but Kathy still cried until the doctor came.

Pneumonia was the diagnosis. "It's a severe case," said the doctor. "She's been fighting it several days now. At her age, it could be critical."

He left a bottle of medicine and promised to return tomorrow.

"What if we lose her?" Kathy asked when Patrick finally insisted she go to bed, leaving one of the boys to watch over their grandmother. "She's always been there for me. I hate feeling so helpless."

"She's a tough old lady. She'll pull through. You'll see," he said.

"And Karl isn't home. He'll be heartbroken if anything happens," Kathy moaned.

"When did you last hear from him?"

"Not since that postcard in October. He was in Dresden then I think, but he said he'd be home by winter."

"I would think he'd be home by Christmas, for Thelma's sake if nothing else."

"How could I tell him if he came home and Mother — "

"Shh." Patrick held her to his chest. "Just try to get some sleep. I promise I'll worry enough for both of us."

Many years ago, Will's father had told him that the voices of those who die at sea can be heard in a storm's fury. Will wished it were so — he wished his brother's voice would speak in the wind to tell him he was free from suffering. If Clarence's body had been recovered, Will felt the loss would have been easier. Even the birth of his second son only momentarily lifted his spirits. The blow was all the harder because he had inherited Clarence's savings from the bank.

He and Margaret definitely needed the money, but Will felt guilty reaping what Clarence had worked so hard to sow. He could not bring back his brother, although he would have given every cent away for just one more day with him, especially one of those carefree childhood days spent on the farm when they would run and laugh and climb trees and fish until dark, then bring home a catch to make their father proud.

Will wondered what was wrong with him that he spent so much time remembering the past, longing for his childhood. He loved Margaret and his sons, even more than he had loved his parents and siblings, but his responsibilities as a husband and father gave him constant worry. Margaret believed they had little to worry over now that Clarence's savings would be their nest egg. When Will suggested splitting the inheritance with his sisters, Margaret adamantly refused, especially since their only contact with Will's sister Mary had been two Christmas cards since their marriage, and they had been estranged from Sylvia's family for six years.

Later, Margaret would blame herself for not being more considerate of Will's grief, but she was also mourning Sarah's absence, and her two sons constantly distracted her thoughts. Later, she would blame herself; had she been more attentive to her husband, she would not have been so caught off guard when he announced his ridiculous plan for Clarence's money.

"Maggie, I want to buy a farm."

"What?" Her mouth hung open at such insanity.

"I want to buy a farm. There's a perfect one just past Harvey. Cherry Creek runs alongside it. My father and I used to go fishing near there."

"But Will, you're a carpenter; what do you know about running a farm?"

"I grew up on one. It'll give us an extra income, and I'll do carpentry work on the side."

"We can't take care of a farm by ourselves," she said. What she really meant was that farming was beneath her.

"We can if we start out small. As the boys get older, they can help us. We'll just plant a few crops and have some chickens, maybe a cow to milk. We can see how it goes from there."

"But I'm a city girl. I don't know anything about farming."

Will knew what she was trying to say. He always let her have her way in everything he could. But this time he would stand firm. He knew his notion might be foolish, but he had not wanted anything so badly since he had realized he wanted Margaret.

"I can teach you all you'll need to know," Will replied. "Please, Maggie. You know how I felt about my brother-in-law selling my father's place — it was my Great-Grandpa Brookfield's farm originally. I wish I could buy it back only the man whom Harry sold it to was a lot smarter than him — he divided it up into plots and now it's becoming city blocks on the edge of town. Best I can do now is try to recreate that farm out in Cherry Creek."

"But it's so far from town, Will."

"Only five miles. Think what a great place it'll be to raise the boys. They'll need room to run around in. Marquette's getting too big, and I don't want my boys soft from city living."

"But Will, we can't buy a farm just because you're nostalgic over your childhood."

"Of course not," said Will. He knew he was not being logical, but he still wanted the farm. "I'm not sentimental like that. After all, right now we live in my grandparents' house, but I'm willing to sell it."

Margaret did not believe him. But then he started explaining the potential profit to be made by selling eggs, potatoes, corn, milk, and tomatoes; he reminded her his father had operated a little dairy, concluding, "We'll still have money left over because we'll use Clarence's money to buy the farm, and the money from selling this house will be our nest egg."

"Let's think about it a little while longer," said Margaret.

"Just come to see the place," Will said. "That's all I ask."

"But how can we look at a farm in the middle of winter when the ground's covered in snow?"

"That's another advantage. Winter will give us time to fix up the place before planting season begins."

"Fix it up? What's wrong with it?"

"I didn't mean 'fix it up.' I meant, time to settle in and decide what we'll plant and what livestock we'll raise."

Margaret knew she was losing the battle. She was afraid to say more.

"Just come see the place," Will cajoled. "I know you'll love it. The kitchen is huge. You'll have so much more space. All your friends will be envious."

He knew if she agreed to see the place, he could convince her to buy it. Not that he needed her permission — Clarence's money was his, and despite their efforts, women were not emancipated yet so Margaret had no real say in the matter, but he knew he would not be so inconsiderate, and if he bought the place against her will, she would have plenty of words for him later if the farm did not work out.

"For five years," said Margaret, "we've struggled day by day to live. Clarence's money gives us some security, and I just don't want to lose that security if this farm fails."

"For five years," said Will, "we've survived because we have each other. After all those rough years, we can make this work as well."

Margaret loved Will. He was not a man to put a woman down; she knew plenty of women with husbands who did. Will considered her his partner, even if he did not always say so. She felt if she now said "No," she would be saying she had no faith in their partnership. She knew he needed reassurance that she believed in them as a couple.

"All right. We'll go look at the farm tomorrow."

"You won't regret it," he said, kissing her cheek. "When Roy was born, you said it was the start of better times for us. This is just further confirmation."

The next day, Margaret went to see the farm. The house was much larger than their current home. Each of the boys could have his own room, and there would be an extra room in case they had a little girl. Margaret could not help but love the kitchen. The low winter sun bathed the floor where the breakfast table would be. She had always thought her current kitchen dark and gloomy. The snow was not yet deep enough to hide a large flowerbed along the front porch. She envisioned the rows of daffodils she would plant there. And there was an apple orchard — oh, the apple pies she could bake! Will loved apple pie. They could have pie for breakfast, as she had heard people in New England did. And the farm really was not that far from town. Of course, she would have liked to be something more elegant than a farmer's wife, but Will wanted to be a farmer, and she was still proud to be Mrs. Will Whitman. She would make the best of it for his sake. She did not have all she wanted, but Will had done his best to provide for them — better than Harry Cumming did for Sylvia or that Blackmore scoundrel had done for Sarah.

On Christmas Eve, Margaret and Will went to the bank to sign the mortgage papers.

After a couple days, Molly insisted she felt well enough to come downstairs and eat supper and even sit up in the parlor for a couple hours that evening. But the next morning, she was so weak again that she could not get out of bed.

The relapse terrified Kathy. Again she sent for the doctor. Again Molly had a dangerous fever.

While the doctor diagnosed his patient, Patrick insisted Kathy have a cup of coffee with him in the kitchen. Patrick had just filled the coffee cups when Jeremy brought in the mail.

"Here's a letter from Uncle Karl," he said, handing a hefty envelope to his mother.

"Maybe he writes when he'll be home," said Patrick. Kathy had the envelope ripped open before her husband finished the sentence. Numerous pages were scribbled in her brother's illegible handwriting. She was too anxious to read it all. She skimmed over the paragraphs, noting he had met some relatives in Germany. He launched into some weird philosophical comments. She wished he had not written all this gibberish but just gotten to the point of stating when he was coming home.

"He keeps going on about some distant relatives in Germany," she huffed, "as if they're more important than his family back home."

"He knows his family here is important," said Patrick.

"Then why isn't he here for his little girl, and how could he go so far away when he knows he has an elderly mother?"

"Mother, the doctor wants to speak to you," said Frank, stepping into the kitchen. Kathy shoved Karl's letter in the top drawer of her writing desk, then rushed upstairs.

The doctor explained that he had given Molly a sleeping draught so she would rest peacefully, but he had little hope she would make it to morning. Would they like him to stay and watch with them through the night?

Kathy thanked the doctor, but she told him to go home to his family since tomorrow was Christmas Eve. The doctor insisted they send for him if Molly got worse. Hour after hour then dragged along until night fell. Patrick made Kathy lie down for a few hours while Frank and Jeremy watched over their grandmother. The boys sat together, afraid to be alone when death came. Every slight irregularity in their grandmother's breathing, every soft moan, terrified them. Both were thankful when their father relieved their watch so they could go to bed.

Kathy slept little that night. She took over the watch at midnight. At six the next morning, Patrick found her wide awake beside her mother's bed. Rather than go to sleep then, she made breakfast for the family, did the dishes, and insisted she would go back upstairs to watch over her mother.

By late afternoon, Molly had not yet woken, and her breathing had become labored. When Kathy went to make supper, leaving the boys to watch over their grandmother, she constantly dreaded a shout from upstairs, announcing the end. She was so nervous she dropped and broke a plate, then dropped a knife, then overturned the gravy bowl. Overwhelmed, she shouted, "Damn it!" and terrified Thelma and Michael who had never heard her speak such words before.

Patrick calmly cleaned up the mess. They ate in silence, Michael and Thelma afraid to speak. Patrick brought plates upstairs so Frank and Jeremy could eat, but under the shadow of death, they could only poke at their food, then set their plates on the floor to grow cold until they could escape the sick room. Patrick did the dishes while he insisted Kathy lie down, if only for half an hour. Kathy did go to her room and have a good cry, but she could not rest. Christmas morning was fast approaching. She had to wrap the children's presents and get the turkey ready for dinner tomorrow. And there was Midnight Mass to attend. She would have to miss Mass this year. God would understand. She could not leave her mother. Her mother had been such a good Catholic, and loved her neighbors so well; it was not right she should die at Christmas.

"Poor Karl will be heartbroken," she told Patrick when he came to check on her.

Patrick was less generous now toward his brother-in-law because of the strain his wife was under. "I think if Karl cared, he'd be here."

"He doesn't know Mother's sick," Kathy said, although secretly she agreed with Patrick.

"Well, then he has a little girl he should be home to spend Christmas with."

Kathy was too drained to argue. "You take the children to Mass," she said. "I almost hope she goes while you're gone. I think that'll be easier for me, to be alone with her when it happens."

"I'll go tell the kids to get ready," Patrick replied.

The children were relieved that they would soon leave the house, even if it were midnight and they were all tired. As night progressed, Michael and Thelma became rambunctious for Christmas to come, and Patrick did not want to dampen their spirits although he shushed them several times so they would not disturb their grandmother. Thelma did not understand her grandmother was dying, and Michael had never known anyone who had died.

When Michael went to his room to change his clothes, he paused in the upstairs hall before his grandmother's half-closed door. He peered into the room and saw his mother sitting, trying to tat while every few seconds she stopped to look at the stiff form beside her. A creaking floorboard made her notice her son.

"It's all right, Michael," she smiled.

"Is Grandma going to be all right?" he asked, tiptoeing in.

"I sure hope so. Pray for her when you go to Mass, okay?"

"All right," he said, laying his head on his mother's shoulder; he was frightened, but Kathy had no comfort to give at that moment.

"Go get ready for church so you don't keep your father waiting," she said.

"Yes, Mother," he replied.

"Oh, Michael," she called him back. "Could you go in my room and bring me my shawl? I'm feeling a little chilly."

"All right."

Kathy returned her attention to her mother, who still struggled to breathe. Kathy thought she heard it — the death-rattle in her mother's throat — but she could not be sure. Where was Michael? He should have come back by now.

"Mother, where did you get all this candy?" the boy asked, returning with a box of chocolates in his hand.

His voice was loud. He might wake his grandmother. Thelma might hear him.

"Put that back where you got it!" Kathy yelled.

"Where'd you get it, Mother?"

"Put it back this instant, and if you tell Thelma, I'll spank you. Do you hear me?"

Michael stared in horror. His mother had never shouted at him like this. Not since he had become a big boy. He never got spanked now.

"Put it back right now! You're a very bad boy."

Michael started to tear up, but Kathy took no pity on him. The last thing she needed right now was two children devastated to learn the truth about Santa Claus.

Michael went back to her room. Then she listened to his footsteps as he went to his own room to change his clothes. A couple minutes later, she heard him go down the back staircase. She could hear him crying in the kitchen and Patrick speaking to him gently. The darn kid had forgotten to bring her shawl; she was freezing. She hated to move, but she needed to make sure Michael had put the candy back where Thelma would not find it. Had he understood? He would tomorrow when he found the same candy in his stocking. In her room, she checked to make sure none of the packages under the bed had been moved.

She reassured herself the candy was closed up in the drawer. Then she plucked up her shawl and again wondered why this had to happen at Christmas.

Patrick came upstairs to find her back beside her mother's bed.

"The children and I are leaving. Will you be all right alone?"

"Yes."

"Any change?"

"No. How will I make it without her, Patrick?"

"How will any of us?" he said.

"I'm almost glad my father died before I knew him. I don't think I could bear losing two parents."

Patrick squeezed her shoulder, then left the room.

She heard the front door open and shut. She was alone now with her mother. After a few minutes, the candles burnt out. She told herself to get up and light new ones, but she felt too lazy. The streetlight shined into the room. She could still dimly see. What did it matter whether the candles were lit?

She sat for a long time staring into the dark, waiting for her family to come home. Now she felt frightened to be alone. She listened to her mother's labored breathing. She wished Patrick had stayed with her. Frank and Jeremy were old enough to watch over Michael and Thelma at Mass. She tried to pray — to think about the Christmas mystery — to assure herself that Christ's coming into the world and His death for our sins meant that she would see her mother again. Then she must have drifted asleep. She thought she heard a branch hitting against the window. She did not remember a tree being beside the house there. She tried to open her eyes, to get out of bed. Then she remembered she was in a chair, but why was there a blanket over her?

"Kathy, wake up."

It was her mother's voice. She instantly remembered the crisis.

She opened her eyes. Her mother was sitting up in bed.

"There's someone knocking on the front door," her mother said.

Kathy heard the knocking, but first she asked, "Mother, are you okay?"

"Fine, fine. The fever broke. I've been waiting for you to wake up so we can have Christmas breakfast. It's almost daylight."

"You're sure you're okay?" Kathy said, wondering whether she were merely dreaming.

"Yes, just a little weak and hungry. Go see who's at the door."

She now felt startled awake by the knocking. She started from the room and to the stairs. Was Mother really all right? She heard voices. Patrick had answered the door. She had never even heard him and the children come home from Mass. She heard another male voice. Then she knew —

"Karl!" she cried. She nearly leapt down the stairs and into her brother's arms.

"Is this any way to greet me?" he roared, stumbling back against the wall, "by knocking me plumb upside down?"

"I'm so glad to see you. Mother's been so ill, and I was afraid you wouldn't be back before she — "

"Mother, where is she?"

"She — oh, but she says she's better now. Come see her."

She grasped his hand and led him upstairs. Thelma met them in the upstairs hall. She had heard her father's voice and was running to greet him. Now when she saw him, she stood back, feeling shy. She barely recognized him because he had shaved off his bushy beard to sport a dapper curly mustache.

"Kaiser Wilhelm has one just like it," Karl would later explain.

He picked Thelma up, lifting her over his head.

"How's my best girl?" he asked.

"I'm just fine," Molly called before Thelma could answer. "Are you coming in here to see me or not?"

The entire family was now awake and crowded into the hall. Everyone laughed with nervous relief to hear the familiar lilt in Molly's voice. Then they made the rush into her room.

"How was Germany?" Molly asked. After Karl had left, Kathy had confessed to her mother where he had gone.

"Wonderful," he said. "The most beautiful place in the world, after Upper Michigan of course. It's good to be home."

"Why didn't you write or telegram that you'd be home for Christmas?" asked Patrick.

"I wasn't sure I'd make it. I had some trouble with my automobile."

"Automobile?" shouted Jeremy, Frank, and Michael together.

"Sure, I bought one in Chicago. Drove it all the way up here. It wasn't easy going. I had to buy a new tire in Green Bay, which is hard to do on Christmas Eve."

But the boys did not listen to the explanation. Christmas presents forgotten, they ran downstairs and outside, still in their night shirts, barely taking time to put on their boots. In front of the house, parked beside a snowbank, was Uncle Karl's glorious, sparkling new Model-A.

"Everyone quit fussing over me so I can get dressed," Molly warned Karl, Kathy, Patrick, and Thelma. "I can't cook breakfast in my night clothes. And don't you start opening Christmas presents until I come downstairs."

They all obeyed by evacuating the room. Molly still ruled as matriarch. They were all thankful for it. Having her well and cheerful was the best Christmas present possible. Even when the boys came back inside, their arms loaded with the gifts they had discovered in the seat of Uncle Karl's automobile, they agreed having Grandma and Uncle Karl for Christmas was the best present of all.

If Karl were an eloquent man, he would have told everyone at breakfast, "I won't be going away again. I found what I was searching for." But Karl was not eloquent in speech; that was why he had written about everything he had experienced in the letter his sister had shoved in her desk drawer. Today held too much holiday cheer for anyone to remember that letter.

1917

Michael's parents were stunned when he told them. Kathy did not know what to say. Patrick was opposed to it. He had seen enough of how the Church oppressed people back in Ireland — look at the recent Easter Riots against the British government; what had the church done to help?

But Michael's grandmother said, "I think it's wonderful. I don't think there's ever been a priest in our family, and I say it's about time."

"It's such a big commitment," Kathy worried.

"It's a wonderful vocation," Molly replied.

"I knew you would understand, Grandma," said Michael, and he kissed the devout old woman on the cheek. Molly knew her wrinkled old face repulsed her other grandchildren, but Michael never shirked from kissing her.

"Michael, you're too young to go to the seminary," said Kathy. "You're only sixteen. Wait another year to make sure it's what you want."

"I'll be seventeen this year, and I know it's what I want," said Michael. "More importantly, I know it's what God wants. I've prayed over it until I'm absolutely sure."

"I don't know," said Kathy.

"Then can I be a nun, Mama?" asked seven-year old Beth. She was the youngest of the McCarey children, and a complete surprise to Kathy, who had been forty-three when she was born.

"Hush, Beth," said Kathy. "You're much too young. You haven't made your first communion yet."

"Marquette has had some mighty fine priests," said Molly. "You're all too young to recall Bishop Baraga, but he was a living saint." She remembered Marquette's founding bishop well, remembered that when Kathy had been sick as a baby, Bishop Baraga had placed his hand on her forehead and she had been healed instantly. Molly remembered now how the good bishop had told her

God must have great reason to save her little girl's life if she healed so quickly. Could God have intended Kathy to be the mother of a priest?

"I don't care for priests much," said Patrick, "but I won't oppose you, Michael, if it's what your heart is set on. Just make sure you're a good one." Then he muttered, "You always were different from your brothers."

"You'll make a fine priest, Michael," said Kathy to compensate for her husband's disappointment. "I just want to make sure it's what you want."

"It is," Michael said. "And more importantly, it's what God wants."

"Have you told anyone else?" Molly asked.

"No, I wanted to tell my family first."

"Well, there's no sense in wasting time," said Molly. "I'll go with you to tell the bishop."

"Let's wait a few days," Kathy pled.

"No, I want to go now," said Michael, and both he and Molly rose to leave.

"Right now?" said Kathy. It was too soon for her. "But your Uncle Karl and your brothers are coming today."

"There'll be plenty of time to visit with them when we get back," Molly said.

Kathy felt annoyed with her mother. At eighty-seven, the old woman should stay home to doze in her chair by the fire. Instead, she was ready to clatter down the street with her cane to enroll her grandson in Holy Orders.

"I'm proud of you, Michael," Molly said as she walked with him to St. Peter's rectory.

"Grandma," he replied, "I'm glad I told you, but I'm afraid to tell my brothers."

"They're tough men like your Uncle Karl," she replied. "They won't think religious orders as manly as working in the woods, but still, they're good boys. I don't think they'll tease you much. Being a priest is a tougher life in many ways than being a lumberjack, but there'll be a lot of comfort in it too. You'll be there to baptize newborns, celebrate weddings, and comfort the dying. You'll be a caretaker; there's nothing better a person can be. Your mother knows that because she's a mother, and once she gets used to the idea, she'll be proud of you."

"I know," said Michael. "She just worries because she's a good mother."

"Exactly," said Molly.

When they reached the rectory, Molly knocked on the door.

"Good morning, Mrs. Montoni, Michael," Father Bucholtz greeted them.

"Father, I'd like to introduce you to a future member of the clergy. My grandson here wants to become a priest."

"Why am I not surprised?" he said. "The sisters have given me glowing reports of Michael's performance in school. I've been meaning to talk to him about the priesthood, but it looks as if God sent him to me before I could come to him."

Father Bucholtz invited them inside. Once Michael had helped his grandmother into a chair, he answered the priest's questions about his intentions.

"I want to serve God," said Michael. "There's so much pain and suffering in the world, especially now with the war in Europe. I want to comfort others by letting them know God loves them."

"Many ways exist to help others that do not include devoting yourself to the religious life," said the priest. "Have you heard God's call?"

"Yes, Father. I've read the story of Samuel in the Bible, how God called to him at night. I've often waited for God to call me like that, or for me to see a vision. I can't say I've had one, but my heart burns with love for God when I'm at Mass. I often feel like crying from joy when I receive communion."

Molly's heart exulted at the boy's words. She had known similar spiritual moments, but not until she was far older than her grandson. At sixteen, her thoughts had been on worrying over money and daydreaming of handsome Irish boys.

"Those are eloquent words, Michael," said the priest. "And I commend you for knowing your Bible stories. Most Catholics don't. I think you'll make a fine priest. Anyone who knows you would think so. Come back on Monday. The bishop will be here then. He's noticed as well what a faithful Catholic you are. I know he'll be pleased to talk with you."

Michael was overjoyed. He warmly clasped Father Bucholtz's hand. "Thank you, Father. God bless you."

In a glow of enthusiasm, Michael and Molly found their way back outside.

"What do you think of that?" Molly said as they walked home. "Even the bishop is impressed by you."

"I didn't think he even knew my name," said Michael. "I've only met him once."

"Good names get passed along," Molly grinned, "and don't forget that your grandmother was once president of the Altar Society. That helps."

Michael smiled as she took his arm for support.

"My grandson will be a priest," said Molly. "I think this is the proudest moment of my life."

Michael was deeply touched by his grandmother's faith in him. She was so ancient, so steadfast in her belief. She had lived here before the walls of St.

Peter's Cathedral were raised, before the walls of the cathedral that preceded the present one were even raised. Yet after eighty-seven years, she considered this moment her proudest.

Karl's automobile was parked along the sidewalk when they reached home. Michael's uncle and Thelma must have already gone inside, but his brothers, Frank and Jeremy, were standing on the front porch, smoking cigarettes.

"Hey there, Father Michael!" called Jeremy.

"Father?" said Frank. "Won't be long before he'll be Monsignor."

"Don't you boys laugh at him," Molly scolded as Frank stepped down to help her up the porch steps. "He'll make all this family proud. Now put out those cigarettes and come inside. I haven't seen you boys for two months. I wish you would understand those trees can wait to be cut down, but I don't have many days left."

"You know we love you, Grandma," said Frank, pecking her right cheek. Jeremy dutifully kissed the other wrinkled one.

"Is it true you're going to be a priest?" Thelma asked when Michael went inside.

"Yes," he said.

"I'm glad," she said. "I always knew you were my goodest cousin. Your brothers nag and harass me, but you're my favorite because you're always kind."

Michael knew Thelma was a bit simple minded. His brothers joked that no man would ever marry her, although they never said so before Uncle Karl. Yet what Thelma lacked in intellect, she compensated for in blunt honesty. Her compliment pleased Michael as much as his appointment to meet the bishop.

"Thelma, come see my new doll!" Beth shouted while running downstairs to drag her cousin upstairs. The girls were seven years apart, but Beth scarcely noticed, for at fourteen, Thelma could play dolls as well as any little girl.

"Hello, Michael," said Uncle Karl, entering from the kitchen. "I hear you're going to be a priest."

"Yes, sir," said Michael. "How are you, Uncle Karl?"

"Fine, just fine. Well, Mother, how are you feeling?"

Molly settled into a chair, a bit winded from the walk. She told her son about her last doctor's visit and how her rheumatism had been acting up all winter.

"You boys must be thirsty after the long drive from Calumet," said Patrick. "What do you say we open a bottle of whiskey to celebrate my son becoming a priest."

Kathy, knowing Patrick would use any excuse for a drink, frowned, "I thought you got rid of all that whiskey. And you, a state employee — I'm surprised at you."

"What's there to be surprised about, woman? You know you married an Irishman. Just 'cause Marquette County's crazy enough to pass prohibition doesn't mean I have to agree to it. This country's a democracy so I have individual rights. Haven't you ever heard of civil disobedience?"

"Democracy means the majority rules," said Kathy, "and they say the whole country will be under prohibition soon."

"It would never happen if Roosevelt were still president," said Patrick.

"Yes, but look at the trouble his drinking got him into," said Kathy.

"Yes, and look how he cleared his name," Patrick replied. "He proved that a drink never hurt anyone."

Patrick referred to the famous lawsuit former President Theodore Roosevelt had filed in 1913 against an Upper Peninsula newspaper, the *Iron Ore*. Roosevelt had visited Marquette by train in October 1912 to campaign for the presidency. His speech was well received in Marquette, but his voice was raspy, causing some people to speculate whether he had been intoxicated. Rumor spread until the *Iron Ore* ran an editorial that slandered the former president as a drunk. When Roosevelt heard the accusation, he had the newspaper investigated, then ordered his attorneys to start a libel suit. The trial began May 26th, 1913 at the Marquette County Courthouse. Roosevelt had arrived early that morning on the Chicago and Northwestern Railroad to be greeted by a cheering crowd. He joked with reporters and appeared completely fearless.

When the trial began, Roosevelt painstakingly listed every drink he could recall having in his life, and with forty witnesses on his side, many of them holding high political office in Washington, his opponent scarcely had a chance. After five days of trial, the newspaper editor finally read a prepared statement admitting he was mistaken in his accusations against the former president. Theodore Roosevelt could have been awarded $10,000 under Michigan law, but instead, he requested only six cents for compensation because "That's about the price of a GOOD paper." The *Iron Ore* cost only three cents.

"There's no reason a man can't have a drink in his own home," Karl agreed with his brother-in-law. "It's good for the heart, and I don't see anyone here who'll tattle on us."

"I don't see anything wrong myself with a little sip of whiskey," said Molly. "After all, we Catholics always drink wine at Mass."

"I just don't want my boys to be alcoholics like those Cummings," said Kathy.

"Well, now that Michael's going to be a priest, his brothers can always get him to absolve them from their sins," Patrick laughed.

"Don't be blasphemous," Molly replied. Patrick might joke with his wife, but respect for his mother-in-law sobered him instantly. Karl turned the conversation to his lumber profits over the past winter, and then Patrick told stories of recent difficulties at the Marquette Branch State Prison where he worked. Jeremy, Frank, and Michael respectfully sat and listened while the women did their needlework. Molly's eyes were not as strong as they used to be, so many of her stitches were in the wrong place, but no one dared point out her errors. Occasionally, some cackles floated downstairs from the girls who were imitating their dolls' voices. The family passed Sunday afternoon well pleased to be together again after a long winter. All were content, save Michael, who burned to begin his new life serving God.

Margaret Whitman was a farmer's wife. She had by now accepted that she would never be the Scottish princess she had dreamt of being; few princesses were left in this modern world of anarchists and revolutions; she had also dreamt of being an opera singer — when her grandfather had taken her to the Marquette Opera House, she had felt an exhilaration she had never known before, but her parents had had no money for her to take voice lessons. So she had settled for being the wife of Will Whitman. Even then she had expected her husband to be a talented carpenter and successful contractor. That dream had been distorted when he became a farmer, and she a farmer's wife. She had no jewels to admire, no evening gowns to wear, no arias to practice, no dinner parties to arrange. Margaret spent her days churning butter, canning preserves, and worst of all, plucking chickens. Today, she had just finished peeling potatoes for supper when her brother and his new bride pulled up to the farm in their horse and buggy.

Charles Dalrymple Jr. had married his Harriet Bryon the year before. Bride and groom were both twenty-two years of age, old classmates from school. Margaret had been silently opposed to the marriage. She did not want Charles to marry too young before he knew what he wanted in life, and from the start, she had found Harriet rather tactless. But Margaret also knew war was raging in Europe and it was inevitable the United States would become involved in the conflict, despite President Wilson's isolationist policy. If Charles married and became a father, he might avoid being drafted.

"Father says you got a letter from Sarah," said Charles as he and Harriet settled themselves at the kitchen table.

"Oh, yes," said Margaret, washing her hands at the kitchen pump. "I might as well read it to you before Will comes in from the barn. He's already heard it."

But before Margaret could fetch the letter, baby Ada started to cry; she in turn woke up little Eleanor, who until now had been napping peacefully. After some fussing, Eleanor found a seat on "Aunt Hairy-yet's" lap. Margaret cuddled Ada with one hand while holding Sarah's letter with the other.

"Here's what she writes," said Margaret, in a tone that expressed her annoyance with the letter and its composer.

March 31, 1917
Dear Margaret,
What do you think of your little sister now? It's true. I'm Mrs. US Senator Joseph Rodman of the grate state of California. It was a quite little wedding. Just me and Joseph and Theodore. I am so happy now that my sweat little boy will have a father, and a good one to. Joseph has been so good about everything. He insisted all the girls at the hotel where I work be invited so they could enjoy the fun. And he had special gifts for Uncle Alexander and Aunt Maud. He said he had never seen a lovelier vison than me when I appeared in my white silk dress in the hotel front parler. Of course, I'd rather of been married in a church, but you know, we were in a hurry because he had to get back to Washington so he could continue leeding his country. He is on a special comittee for some sort of defense now in case we go to war. Since that boat, the Lusatanya sank, he thinks war is definate. Of course, I don't want a war, but I think it would be good for his career. Just imagine little old me soon assocating with all those fine ladies in Washington! Joseph says he'll introduce me to Mrs. Wilson at the first chance he gets.
Theo is so excited. Before he had to share a room with me at the hotel, but now he'll have his own bedroom and a seperate playroom all his own says Joseph. Just as soon as he's able, Joseph will adopt my boy so he'll officely be the son of a US Senator. Isn't that something?
Please give my love to everyone. I have to pack for the train trip but I wanted to let you know. I'll right to Mother and Father later.
Love, Mrs. Senator Joseph Rodman

"It's not much of a letter," said Charles.

"I suppose when you're so important that you're married to a senator," said Harriet, "you don't have time to write long letters."

"Or learn to spell," thought Margaret.

"Who knows," muttered Charles.

"I'm surprised," Harriet added, "that she didn't have her husband's personal secretary write the letter for her."

Margaret thought Harriet had a shrewish tongue, but today she felt comforted to have it side with her.

"How'd she meet this senator fellow anyway?" asked Harriet.

"He was at some sort of convention at the hotel where Sarah worked. He probably just wanted a pretty girl to show him around town. You know what politicians are like, especially Democrats," said Margaret.

"I don't know why any self-respecting U.S. Senator would marry a woman with an illegitimate child," said Harriet. "Even if he adopts Theodore, the boy's nine, so no one will believe he's the senator's son."

"I don't know why either," Margaret replied. Inside she seethed with rage at the world's injustice, that her sister should marry so far above her station in life, not deserving such good fortune, after the sin she had fallen into. Initially, Margaret had blamed Lysander Blackmore for her sister's misfortune, but as the years passed, the tone of Sarah's letters had made Margaret suspect her sister was a flirt, maybe even a vixen, fully capable of seducing a man. Neither party had been wholly innocent in Theodore's conception. Margaret did not pretend she was so good as to deserve the wealth Sarah had suddenly achieved, but neither did Sarah. Yet Will was a hardworking man, worth two of any Senator Rodman; if anyone deserved the good life, it was her husband.

Before more comments could be made about Sarah's illustrious marriage, Will came inside with the boys.

"Hey, Uncle Charles, Aunt Harriet," Henry said. "Ma, we finished cleaning the barn."

"Henry found a penny," Roy added.

"What good luck," said Uncle Charles. "I s'pose you'll be buying candy with it?"

"No, it's an Indian head cent, so I'll have to save it."

"Why?" asked Roy. "There's lots of Indian heads."

"Maybe so," said Henry, "but they quit making them. Someday they'll be rare, so I'm going to save all mine. They might be worth money someday. Don't you think so, Ma? You should save all yours too."

Margaret laughed, "I'm afraid pennies are too tight around here, Henry. Your father and I can't be picky about which ones we use."

"Still," said Will, "I'm glad my son is learning to save money. Here's the quarter I promised you boys for cleaning out the barn. You better get going if you're going to walk to town in time for the movie."

"Will, don't give them a whole quarter," said Margaret. "The picture show doesn't cost that much."

"Well, they need to buy treats, don't they?" said Will.

Margaret grimaced. She wished Will would discuss it with her before he gave the children money, and candy would only spoil their supper. "Boys, go wash your hands and faces and comb your hair before you go."

"Yes, Ma," said Henry. "Goodbye Aunt Harriet, Uncle Charles." He turned to follow Roy, who had already raced outside to wash himself at the pump.

Downtown Marquette was five miles from the Whitmans' Cherry Creek farm, but the boys easily ran most of the distance.

Marquette had already had a few short-lived movie theaters, but when the Opera House began showing moving pictures in 1912, it soon put the smaller theaters out of business. Then in 1914, Fred Donckers, best known in Marquette for his long running candy store, opened the Delft Theater. From that day on, it would be the place to go for a late night show or an afternoon matinee. Named for the Dutch china-manufacturing city, the Delft looked as if it had been transplanted to Washington Street from Amsterdam. Its facade was elaborately gabled and painted in blues and whites to attract a movie fan's eye. Its doors were the gateway to a magical silver screen that could electrify the minds of two simple Marquette farmboys. For twenty-five cents, Henry and Roy could see a double feature, eat candy, and become cowboys for a couple hours. Perhaps the greatest advantage was that the films lacked sound, so the boys could roar, laugh, and jeer the villains to their hearts' content. The Delft was vacationland for Marquette's children who otherwise endured short summers, cold winters, and hard lives; they could escape and travel around the world simply by purchasing a theater ticket.

Today the boys arrived at the Delft with fifteen minutes to spare, enough time to buy their tickets, order their candy, and begin munching popcorn while they chattered contentedly about their love of Western movies and the most recent Tarzan book Henry was reading.

"Is Tarzan's son as strong as Tarzan?" Roy asked, while devouring popcorn.

"Stronger I think," said Henry.

"No, no one can be as strong as Tarzan," said Roy.

"I don't know," said Henry. "Korak picked his tutor up over his head when he was just a boy, maybe ten years old or so I bet."

"That's about our age. No boy our age could do that."

"Korak can," said Henry, biting off a piece of licorice.

"I wonder whether they'll ever make a Tarzan movie?"

"I doubt they'd ever find an actor strong enough to play Tarzan," said Henry.

"I wish I were strong like Tarzan," said Roy. "Then when I grow up, I can go to Africa to have adventures."

"You can't go to Africa."

"Why not?"

"It's thousands of miles away."

"That doesn't mean I can't go there."

"You couldn't afford it. The train and boat tickets would cost hundreds of dollars."

"I'd find a way," said Roy. "I'm going to make all my dreams come true. I don't want to live on a farm all my life."

"Neither do I," Henry said. "I'd rather be a carpenter like Pa."

"You can't make money being a carpenter. I'm going to California to find gold, or to Africa to find diamonds. Then I won't have to work."

"Shh, the movie's starting."

The boys loved Westerns; Roy could scarcely separate them from reality. As the hero rode his horse across the prairie, Roy felt himself on that same horse, and although the films were only black and white, his imagination was strong enough to see all the vibrant prairie shades; if asked the color of the film's saloon, Roy would have said yellow; if asked the color of the pretty girl's dress, he would have said pink; if asked the color of the hero's horse, he would have answered black. And of course, the hero's cowboy hat was white. During that hour, Roy felt as if he had lived on those prairies all his life, even though he had never set foot outside Marquette County. He felt he belonged anywhere except this small town and his parents' even smaller farm. And he believed he could accomplish all the same wonderful deeds as his silver screen heroes.

"That was one of the best movies yet," Henry said when they were back outside.

"Yup, it was," said Roy, completely dazzled by cinema magic.

"I thought the Indians were — " Henry began, but he was interrupted by the troubling sight of a mother and father standing at the theater door.

"Have you seen Mags Lawson?" the mother asked every child until her daughter appeared, accompanied by a younger sister.

Mrs. Lawson looked scared. Henry paused to learn what was wrong.

"We have to go home," the woman told her daughters. "War's been declared."

"I'm going to enlist," their father added.

"Shh," Mrs. Lawson told him. "Don't scare the girls like that."

The oldest girl looked troubled but said nothing. The younger girl, who was about Roy's age, began to ask questions about the war.

Roy and Henry looked at each other. Neither could fully conceive what war meant. Both knew they were too young to go away to fight. They did not know anyone the right age to fight, except — the thought of their father or Uncle Charles being drafted to go fight the Germans — it made them both sick to their stomachs with fear.

"I think I ate too much candy," said Roy.

"Me too," said Henry. "We better get home."

"It was a good movie," Roy said as they started down Front Street.

"Yeah, it was, but we better get home."

Roy did not know what else to say. He had no idea what the war was about. Since Henry was older, he figured Henry could explain it to him, but he did not ask for an explanation; he did not want to show his ignorance, and he was afraid to learn more than he wanted to know.

The Mining Journal, August 15, 1917:

MRS. MONTONI PASSES AWAY

Mrs. Molly Montoni, eighty-seven years of age, died at 7:30 Monday evening at her home. Dropsy was the cause of death. The funeral will be held at 11:00 Friday morning at St. Peter's Cathedral with internment in Holy Cross Cemetery. Mrs. Montoni came to Marquette the year of its founding in 1849 and was one of the oldest residents of this city. Among her neighbors and friends, Mrs. Montoni will long be remembered for her many acts of kindness.

The Mining Journal reporter had added that last line, having been one of the many recipients of Molly's charity. The family had been surprised by that last sentence, but they had also been pleased. The words were a greater memorial to Molly than any grand mausoleum. Michael had just read over the obituary clipping in the privacy of his bedroom. He had decided he would bring it with him; after carefully folding it, he placed it in his catechism, then packed the book in his suitcase. His grandmother had wanted him to go to the seminary. He wished she had lived to see him leave, but at least she had died knowing he would be a priest. As he packed his suitcase, he could hear his parents downstairs.

"I'm glad he's going to the seminary," said his mother. "He'll be safe there. He won't end up being drafted."

"Maybe so," said his father, "but I don't see the church making any effort to preserve freedom. In times like these, people can't just pray. They need to act."

"Two of my sons have been drafted," said Kathy. "Isn't that enough? Can't one of my boys be protected? Michael's only seventeen. The war might be over before he's old enough to go anyway."

Michael hoped his parents' agitated voices would not wake Beth. Beth was the one sibling he felt he would miss. He was sorry his brothers were going to the war, but he had never been that close to them. He worried for his mother more than anyone because all three of her sons were seemingly deserting her, especially now, after Grandma had died.

"Mother was so pleased Michael would be a priest," Kathy's voice drifted upstairs. "It was her dying wish. You know that."

The mention of his grandmother made Michael's eyes tear up. She had only been gone four days. He remembered how he had sat beside her that last day as she slept. She had passed away with one hand held by him, the other by his mother. It had seemed so sudden, despite how old she was.

He had not mentioned it to anyone, but later when he had gone alone into the room where his deceased grandmother lay, he had noticed a sweet, comforting perfume. He had read enough lives of the saints to guess what caused the scent. Since war was declared, Michael had been torn between going to the seminary or waiting until his eighteenth birthday to join the army. But that scent — like the sweetest incense used at a High Mass — he interpreted as a sign to carry on his grandmother's work of serving God.

"There's so much suffering, so much unhappiness in the world," he had cried into his pillow that night, overcome by the loss of his grandmother and the weight of his future cross. "All I want is to help ease that misery in whatever small way I can. Killing people is not the answer. I have to learn and then teach others to love one another. Maybe I'm too tender hearted; maybe I'm not thick skinned like my brothers, but I don't see how being a soldier is preferable to being a priest. Someone has to comfort all those who will be widows and orphans as a result of this tragic war; someone has to help people keep faith in God through it all."

He would leave for the seminary tomorrow. He did not care whether anyone understood his reasons. Did not the Bible say no man was worthy who was not willing to leave his family to follow Christ? Michael loved his family, and he did not want to leave them, but he loved God most of all. By serving God, he would show love for the entire human family.

❦   ❦   ❦

"Beth, honey, wake up. You need to hurry, or you'll have to stay home."

Beth McCarey rubbed her eyes, then gazed up at her mother, not fully understanding.

"Beth, honey, come on. Your brothers have to leave today; remember, I told you that you don't have to go to school so you can see them off. But we can't keep them waiting."

"No, you can't keep the war waiting," Frank hollered from the next room.

Frank and Jeremy were going to the war today! Beth had almost forgotten. She knew the war was a lot of fighting with horses and guns and airplanes — but she did not know who her brothers would fight or why. It sounded fun, to go kill the bad guys, but Mama said only boys could go, and only Frank and Jeremy were old enough, and Mama wished they were not going. Michael had already gone away just a couple days before.

"Come on, Beth. Sit up. Let me pull off your nightgown," said Kathy, pushing her only daughter — today she wished she only had daughters — into a sitting position to pull the nightgown over her head.

"Where are Frank and Jeremy going, Mama?"

"Far away, dear."

"And we can't go with them?"

"No, thank God," said her mother. "We just have to walk them down to the train station."

"Will we see a train?"

"Yes, dear. Your brothers are going to ride on one."

"And the train will take them far away?" asked Beth. She felt excited; she had never actually seen someone she knew ride a train before. She did not have any friends who had ever been farther than Negaunee, and she was not even quite sure how far that was.

"Yes, dear, they'll take the train, and then they'll have to take a boat over the ocean to Europe."

"Yer-yup? Where's that?"

"Far away, dear, over the ocean."

"You mean like Canada where the boats come from?" asked Beth.

"Yes, dear, only it's even farther away than Canada. Now no more time for questions. I still have to pack your brothers' lunches." Kathy was too anxious to explain more. She wanted to think as little as possible about her sons going away.

Beth had been struggling to find her dress sleeve, but now that she had found it, and her mother had managed to get her into her underpants without major complaint — Beth was too excited to complain this morning — she only had to get her shoes on.

"I can lace them myself, Mama. You go make the lunches."

Kathy smiled. Beth was trying to be helpful now that she was wide awake. That made things a little easier.

"All right, dear. Hurry down for your breakfast."

Kathy went down to the kitchen, telling herself she would have to bear it. She had no choice.

"Cheer up, Mother," Frank said when he saw the look on her face. "The war will probably be over before we finish training at Fort Custer."

She made no reply but set to making sandwiches for the boys' train ride.

"I don't want the war to end," Jeremy said, "before I get to kill a few Huns."

"Be quiet! You don't know what you're talking about!" Kathy snapped. She swung around in such a frenzy that the butter knife in her hand nearly smacked her son's face.

Jeremy was speechless, especially when his father frowned to remind him how difficult this parting was for his mother.

Kathy went back to making sandwiches. Jeremy had always been obnoxious in his speech, and she knew his fear only made him more obnoxious in his attempt to be brave. But she hated to hear the Germans referred to as Huns. Her father had emigrated from Germany, and although that was seventy years ago, and she did not know whether she had any relatives left in that country, her own family was proof that the Germans were good people. She understood the German government was in the wrong, but it made little sense to her that the United States would side with Great Britain — Ireland's enemy for centuries. Patrick hated the English, and since she was half Irish and half German, Kathy equally found it bitter that the United States was Great Britain's ally.

Beth stepped into the kitchen while buttoning her coat. Her brothers hailed her arrival to divert attention from their mother's irritable temper. Beth was the baby, much loved and much spoiled by all the family. Everyone constantly fussed over her, as now when Frank swept her up into his arms and placed her on his knee.

"Are you going to miss me, Lollipop?"

"Yes," she said, running her hand along his freshly shaved chin. She loved the scratchy feel of his whiskers against her fingertips. "Are you going to be gone long?"

"I don't know, but I'll come back as soon as I can, and I'll bring you a present."

"Promise?"

"I promise," said Frank.

"Don't make her a promise you can't keep," warned his father.

"Patrick!" Kathy barked.

"Well, I don't want her to be hurt anymore than necessary," Patrick replied. "She has to understand what's going on just like the rest of us."

"She's just a child," said Kathy.

Patrick did not know what it meant to be a child like Beth. He had never known the innocence, the ease she knew, not even when he was seven years old. He had been Beth's age the first time he had seen an Irishman beaten by a British soldier. He had lived in fear from that day; he had lived in anger and in hunger, and he believed those soldiers were the reason. But Kathy was right. He did not want his daughter to know such horror, even if his sons would know it. He had come to America to avoid the horrors that existed in the old country, but now his sons would have to go and straighten out the mess being made over there. They would never succeed. The Europeans had fought among themselves for so many centuries that he doubted peace would ever exist among them. He just hoped his boys would come home.

"Don't worry, Mama," said Frank. "Jeremy and I'll be in the same unit, so I'll keep an eye on him. No Hun will get my brother."

Again Kathy cringed at the derogatory word. She could barely stop herself from snapping, "Your grandfather was a Hun." Today, she was thankful her father was dead so he need not see his grandsons forced to fight against his fatherland.

"Here are your lunches," she said, handing them to Frank and Jeremy.

"Are we all set to go then?" asked Patrick.

"I am," said Frank.

"Me too," said Jeremy.

"At least it's a nice morning for a walk," said Patrick, giving his wife an encouraging smile as they went out the door.

Kathy did not have the energy to smile back; she grasped Beth's hand and stepped onto the porch, then locked the door behind her. Marquette scarcely had any crime, but today, her life seemed filled with insecurity.

The train station was a good six blocks away, but the McCareys walked most of the distance in silence. Beth felt sleepy, despite the cool morning air. She had slept in later than usual since she did not have to go to school today, but the extra sleep had only made her groggy. Halfway to the train station, her father lifted her into his big strong arms. She nuzzled her face into the comforting fabric of his cigar-scented coat. She had nearly drifted back to sleep when they reached the train station. When she was set down on the ground, she let out a little whine, until she opened her eyes to the sight of a train and remembered why they had come.

"Frank, are you really going to ride on that train?" she asked, proud that her brothers were so privileged.

"Yes," Frank said, but she noticed he did not smile or look excited as he had in the house.

"Are all these fellows riding on it?" Jeremy asked. Several young men stood about, most scarcely more than boys in the eyes of parents who had come to wish them goodbye.

"You boys make sure you're careful," Kathy said. "Keep your clothes in good shape. Wash them and keep them as clean as you can because you never know what the army will give you to wear."

"Yes, Mom, we will," Frank replied.

"Your father and I will send you a little money when we can. I'm sure army food isn't very good, so you use the money to buy yourselves some decent meals; don't waste it on cheap magazines or cigars, and especially not on those foreign girls."

"Yes, Mother," said Jeremy, rolling his eyes.

"And don't forget to write everyday you can. I know you'll both be busy, but your letters will be the only way I'll know you're both — "

"Yes, Mom, we know," Jeremy softened.

"Take turns writing if you want, just so long as you do write. Promise me."

"We'll write, Mother," said Frank.

"ALL ABOARD!" shouted the conductor.

"So soon?" gasped Kathy. "Oh!" She clutched Jeremy around the neck. "I love you boys." She released Jeremy so she could squeeze Frank just as hard.

"Take care of yourselves," said Patrick, shaking his sons' hands. "Make us proud. Look out for one another."

"Bye, Lollipop!" said Frank, kissing Beth on the forehead.

"Don't forget you promised to bring me back a present," she said.

Frank tried to smile. He was glad she did not really understand what it meant that her brothers were leaving.

"Hurry, or you'll miss the train," said Patrick.

"Goodbye," everyone repeated quickly. Then the brothers climbed aboard the train. The whistle blew. The locomotive pulled out of the station. Two new soldiers found window seats, then waved to their parents.

"Be brave, Kathy," said Patrick, squeezing his wife's hand as she waved with the other.

The train whistle blew again. Beth jumped up and down with glee. Then she noticed that while everyone else was waving, they all had long faces.

"What's wrong, Papa? They'll come back right?"

Patrick knelt down and put his hands around her waist. "We hope so, honey. But you have to pray very hard that they will. Pray every night that God keeps them safe. Do you understand?"

"Yes," said Beth, disconcerted by his serious tone.

Kathy smiled now. Patrick seldom spoke of God, but at difficult times, he revealed he still believed, even if he only rarely went to Mass with her and the children — her and Beth, she meant. Now only Beth was left at home with them.

"Let's go," she said as the train disappeared.

But when they turned around, their attention was distracted by loud weeping.

"Quit crying! You're making a scene!" grumbled a man, turning from his wife in embarrassment.

"It'll be all right," said Kathy, stepping up to the grieving woman. Any other day, she never would have approached Mrs. Cumming. She did not know the woman, only knew of her, knew her husband was a drunk, and that her children were trouble. Until now, she had always thought Mrs. Cumming had a harsh way about her.

Mrs. Cumming looked at her oddly, trying to place her face.

"I'm Kathy McCarey."

"Kathy McCarey?" Mrs. Cumming replied. "I know you. I was at your wedding."

Kathy felt confused by the remark.

"I used to be Sylvia Whitman," said Mrs. Cumming. "I was just a girl when you got married, but my grandparents knew your mother. I think so anyway. It was many years ago."

"Sure, I remember you," said Kathy, although it would be hours before she connected this middle-aged face to that of the twelve-year old at her wedding. This must be one of Jacob and Agnes Whitman's daughters, one of those obnoxious little girls she remembered from picnics when she was a child. One of the girls who had been so mean that time Agnes had invited her to go sledding. Kathy almost felt pleased to know the obnoxious girl had grown up to marry a drunk, but she also realized the obnoxious girl was now a worried mother.

"Your son was drafted?" asked Kathy.

"Yes," Sylvia replied. "Two sons."

"Two of my sons have gone also," said Kathy. "Only my daughter's at home now." She did not mention she had another son studying for the priesthood; the Cummings were not the type of people to understand that.

"I worry so much about them," Sylvia said.

Kathy looked about for Mr. Cumming, but he was walking up the street, smoking a cigar.

"All we can do is say lots of prayers," Kathy consoled.

"Ye-es," Sylvia replied, thinking that God did not answer her prayers.

"It was good seeing you again," said Kathy, afraid if she said more this woman would claim her friendship because of their families' past acquaintance. "Be strong for your sons' sake."

"Goodbye," Sylvia replied, her heart too anxious to say more.

"Poor thing," said Kathy, rejoining her husband and daughter.

The McCareys walked the first block home in silence. Then Beth began to ask her father about trains; he tried to pacify her, making up fanciful answers when he did not know the real ones to her questions. He saw Kathy did not want to talk, but he was proud she had tried to comfort someone else.

He did his best to keep Beth occupied the rest of the morning. He would have preferred to be at work today if he had not had to see his sons off and try to keep his wife company. By afternoon, he had spent all the time he could bear with his rambunctious daughter. When he saw the neighborhood children coming home from school, he sent Beth outside to play until supper.

But Beth could find no one to play except Joe, who was nine and lived next door. She did not particularly like Joe, but he was better than no playmate, and she felt lonely now that her grandmother and three brothers were all gone. She marched across the yard to where he sat on his front porch. She told him proudly, "My brothers went off to the war today. They're going to kill all the bad Germans."

"One of my cousins went too," Joe said.

"What are you doing?"

"I got a new slingshot," he said. "I'm pretending to shoot Germans with it."

"Let me see."

"Here," said Joe, pointing to a tree branch in his front yard. "See that squirrel. We'll pretend it's one of the Germans, okay?"

"Okay," said Beth. She thought it silly to pretend a cute squirrel could be a mean German, but she went along with the game to see what Joe would do.

"Okay, now I'm going to shoot it," he said.

Beth watched as Joe pulled back the slingshot, carefully positioning the stone. Then, with a swift yank, he released the sling, and the rock soared toward the tree.

Beth did not turn her head fast enough to see the stone collide with the little animal's skull, but she saw the squirrel fall into the bush below.

"Bang! He's dead. The filthy German!" shouted Joe, jumping up in triumph.

"Did you really get him?"

"Sure. Didn't you see him fall?"

"Yeah."

"Come on, let's go find him," said Joe, racing to the bush with Beth trotting behind. "He fell in here somewhere." Joe searched in the shrubbery. "Here he is."

"Is he dead?" asked Beth.

"See for yourself," Joe replied. He lifted up the dead squirrel by its tail. Then the stone dropped from where it had embedded itself in the skull. The creature's face was deformed, one eye smashed shut, the other gruesomely glaring. Blood and guts oozed from an ear.

"Ooh," said Beth, unsure how to react. "He's really dead?"

"Yup, dead as a door nail. One less German for the Yanks to kill."

"We can't fix him?" she asked.

"Fix 'im?" said Joe with scorn. "No, you can't fix 'im. He's dead!"

"Do — do Yanks get killed like that too?" She felt she would be sick.

"Oh sure, I s'pose, but not as often as Germans. Huns are nothing like Yanks. Why, one Yank can lick ten Huns."

"But a Yank can still die?" asked Beth.

"I s'pose. You wanna see what other animals we can pretend are Germans?"

"N-no, I think I'll go home now." Beth took a couple cautious steps backward. Her eyes stayed fixed for a minute on the dead squirrel still hanging by its tail from Joe's hand. Then she turned and ran. She ran past the bush, past Joe's house, and into her backyard. She ran around the corner, past the flowerbed and her swing, and then down the steps to the outside entrance of the basement. There she crumpled down against the closed door. It was the darkest hiding place she could find.

"I don't want them to die!" she shrieked. "I don't want Jeremy and Frank to die! I hate war! I hate the war!"

Patrick heard her cries. He opened the basement door, scooped up his little girl, and listened to her tell about the dead squirrel as he carried her inside to bed. After she slept, he knew she would forget. He wished an adult could forget so easily.

*   *   *

"Will," said Margaret, passing *The Mining Journal* to her husband, who was resting in his chair. "Look. Your nephews are in the army."

Will read the names of those enlisted, including Harold Cumming Jr. and Douglas Cumming. It surprised and disturbed him to think they were so grown up they could be soldiers. It seemed just yesterday they had sat on his lap as he taught them their ABC's. But he only said, "Humph!"

"What do you mean by that?" asked Margaret.

"What am I supposed to say?" he asked.

"I don't know. I just thought you'd want to know."

Will turned over the newspaper. He pretended to be deeply engrossed in the stock market report. Margaret picked up her sewing bag to darn her sons' socks.

"We're going to knit socks and scarves in school for the soldiers," said Henry when he saw his mother at work.

"That's good," she replied. "We need to do all we can for our brave boys."

"I wish I was old enough to be a soldier," said Roy.

"The war'll be over long before then," Henry told his brother.

"Girls, it's time for bed," said Margaret, glancing at the clock.

"Just five more minutes, Ma?" begged five-year-old Eleanor. Two-year-old Ada just stared with displeasure.

"Clean up your toys. It's bedtime," Margaret repeated.

"I don't know why we get the darn newspaper anyway," Will muttered, tossing it down beside his chair. "There's nothing in it worth reading; just a waste of money."

"Yes, dear," said Margaret, ushering the girls off to bed.

She helped Ada pick up her blocks, and she kissed Eleanor's dolly's booboo. Then she took the girls' hands and walked them upstairs. Margaret knew her brother-in-law was totally useless, but she had expected more of a reaction from Will; those boys were his nephews. Maybe she should go see whether Sylvia needed anything. At least she could let Sylvia know the family still cared about her. Granted, the Cummings were horrid people, but no woman should have to send her sons off to war.

An hour later, when Will turned off the kerosene lamp in their bedroom, Margaret took a deep breath and said, "Poor Sylvia, having her boys go off to war."

"Yeah," grumbled Will, pulling back the covers to crawl under them.

"Maybe you should go see whether she needs anything," said Margaret.

"If she does, she knows where I am."

Margaret wished she had spoken before he turned off the light; she wondered whether his face were softer than his words.

"It's harder for her to come to you," she said.

"It was her choice to marry that man. Until she does something about that, there's nothing I can do."

"She can't just leave her husband, Will. It's different for a woman. We can't support ourselves like men."

"Now that her children are grown, maybe she could — "

"But she still has a little girl, doesn't she?"

"That girl must be almost grown by now."

"She is your sister — "

"Goodnight, Maggie."

Margaret laid her head against the pillow. It was no good talking to Will when he was in this mood, and he only got into this mood when his sister's family was mentioned. She did not know why she bothered.

But after Margaret fell asleep, Will lay awake, remembering the nephews he had loved so well he had not thought he could love his own children more. He wished Sylvia would come speak to him. He wished he could have seen the boys before they left. Sometimes he wished God would strike Harry Cumming dead so they could be a family again. Before he fell asleep, he decided to go see his sister in the morning.

But when morning came, he put off going until he had milked the cow and fed the chickens, and then a man came over to give him a quote on building a stable. He decided he would go see his sister tomorrow, or next week, or whenever he got the chance.

1918

For the next year, common conversation on the streets, in the stores, in the parlors and kitchens of Marquette followed the same patterns.

"Hurry, the parade is about to start."
"What do those banners say?"
The first one says "We Lead the Draft" and the other says "Draft for Defense."

"I hear those Cumming boys were both drafted."
"Good riddance; their mother will be better off without them."
"I don't know. I heard from Kathy McCarey that their mother was very upset when they left on the train."
"Mrs. McCarey has a couple boys who went as well, doesn't she?"
"Yes, the two oldest. But the youngest is becoming a priest. He's only seventeen, but I imagine he only did that so he wouldn't be drafted."

"The Molbys have a son going to the war."
"Really? Well they have enough sons, so I suppose they can spare one. Eight boys aren't there?"
"Yes, and a couple girls."
"Do you know which boy is going?"

"Yes, William. He'll be going to Fort Custer to train."

"I guess they can be thankful all the boys aren't going. Still, I imagine it's no less hard for them to worry about one son."

"I'm just glad my boys are too young to go."

❦   ❦   ❦

"I hear Kathy O'Neill has gone down to South Carolina," said Florence Mitchell to her equally spinster sister Mary.

"To visit relatives?"

"No, since her daughter, Cynthia, just died and her son-in-law is away at the war, she's gone to pick up her grandson, Robert. He's going to stay with her until his father returns, if he returns."

"The poor little boy."

"I imagine we'll see him when we go over there for Thanksgiving," said Florence. She waited to withhold judgment on whether he were a poor little boy until she had seen him for herself.

"That's funny," said Mary, "because I just heard Mrs. Lawson has a niece coming to stay with her. The poor woman, she's already got three girls to take care of and a husband who was foolish enough to enlist and leave his family."

"Why's the niece coming?"

"Seems her mother's dead and her father's in the war. She's been living with her grandmother until now, but the old woman can't take care of her anymore."

"That's what happens when you're married," said Florence Mitchell, promoting spinsterhood under the pretense she had chosen it. "We're better off single; all those husbands, children and in-laws just complicate your life."

"I wonder," said Mary, "if President Wilson even thought of all the poor mothers and children who would be left behind to worry when the men went off to war. We're lucky our brother is too old to go; what would we do without him to take care of us?"

"Seems to me," said Florence, "that we're the ones who take care of him."

❦   ❦   ❦

"I think we should buy Liberty Bonds," said Kathy McCarey to her husband.

"Why?" Patrick asked. He remained opposed to the war despite his sons having been drafted.

"It will help the war effort. It might help the U.S. win a little sooner, and we still have some of that money my mother left us that we could invest."

"I don't know," Patrick grumbled.

"It's our patriotic duty," said Kathy. "And it'll be a way to support our sons. If we don't help the country, who's to say the war won't reach American soil?"

"That's true," said Patrick, remembering the English occupation of Ireland. "I'll go buy some bonds at the bank tomorrow."

"Margaret," said Will Whitman to his wife. "I want to plant a Victory garden."

"We barely get by on what we grow now," said Margaret, but by her tone, Will knew she was not arguing with him.

"Seems as if everyone is doing something for the war effort. Most people have someone in their family in the army, but our sons are too young to go, so I thought a Victory garden would be our way to help."

"All right, Will. Though it seems to me, that in times like these, it's us poor people who give the most."

"That's true, but that's because we understand suffering better than the rich. We should just be thankful our children are too young to go."

"I want to go," said Roy.

"You're too young," Margaret told her son, "but I'm proud you're willing to serve your country."

Then came the sad conversations:

"Did you hear about old Mrs. Smith's grandson?"

"Mrs. Smith, the judge's widow on Ridge Street?"

"Yes."

"No, what?"

"He died in the army. Wasn't shot either. Died of sickness in France."

"What was his name again?"

"Hampton. Mark Hampton."

"Didn't he just get married to Eliza Graham last year?"

"Yes, poor girl. She married him just before he left. He was only eighteen and she seventeen. Imagine being a widow so young."

"Wasn't he the old lady's favorite?"

"Yes. His grandmother left him everything when she died last year. Now Eliza will get it all."

"What a shame to die so young. He was so good-looking too. The war is ruining so many lives."

"Did you hear about poor Bartlett King?"

"No, what?"

"Died in the Argonne in France."

"Oh, his poor family. How awful. Was he shot?"

"No, pneumonia from spending days in those mud filled trenches."

"What a shame. My boy was in the same boyscout troop as him. I wonder how his family's holding up?"

"My sister just went over to see them yesterday. There'll be a memorial service tomorrow."

"And they say the war is almost over. Why did he have to die so near the end?"

"Poor Mrs. Lawson. Ever since her niece, Helen, heard of her father's death, the girl's been so depressed and crying constantly. Mrs. Lawson doesn't know what to do to comfort her."

"How awful! Oh, the poor little girl."

"Yes, and Mrs. Lawson has enough worries. Her own husband is enlisted, so I imagine she worries all the more now that her brother-in-law has been killed. And her with three girls and now a niece to care for. I don't know how she'll support all of them if anything happens to her husband."

"All any of us can do these days is pray the war will end before many more are killed."

"Did you hear about the McCareys?"

"No, what?"

"Last night they learned their son, Frank, was killed."

❦   ❦   ❦

When the telegram arrived announcing Frank's death . . . . But the family's grief was too painful for the reader to invade the family's privacy. It is sufficient to say that Kathy, who previously had been unable to imagine anything worse than the death of her mother, now felt her entire world had fallen apart. Patrick wanted to crawl into the grave and join his son, but he had a little girl to care for, and a wife he loved too dearly to leave alone in her grief. Yet he could not find words to comfort her. Desperate for help, he sent a telegram to his brother-in-law.

"To Karl Bergmann Stop Frank Killed Stop Come Immediately Stop Patrick"

The same hour Karl received the telegram, he jumped into his automobile and drove to Marquette. He brought Thelma along, hoping the girl would be a comfort to her grieving aunt.

Heavy autumn rains accompanied the Bergmanns. The roads between Marquette and Calumet were a muddy mess. Karl's automobile had a flat tire on the way, so they were forced to stay overnight at a hotel in the village of Baraga. By the time Karl and Thelma reached Marquette the next afternoon, the McCareys had known their son was dead for three days. That morning, Kathy felt so overwhelmed, she had retreated to her bed. She had herself been caught in a rainstorm the day before while out walking to try coping with her restlessness; grief and wet clothes had broken down her immune system.

"Kathy's sick in bed," Patrick told Karl after receiving his sympathies. "She has a bad fever. I was just about to send for the doctor."

"Is it influenza?" asked Karl.

An influenza epidemic was currently sweeping the nation. In March, forty-eight men had died at Fort Riley, Kansas. From there the epidemic spread across the Midwest, until the entire nation trembled. Dozens of cases had already been diagnosed in Upper Michigan.

"I hope not." Patrick was alarmed by the possibility. "She looks awful. I thought losing my son was horrible, but I can't imagine losing my wife."

Karl went upstairs. Patrick was too nervous to accompany him. Twenty minutes later, Karl returned to announce, "She has liberty measles."

"You mean German measles?" asked Patrick.

"That's what they were called before the war," Karl said. "Seems as if the name should have been kept considering how unfairly they attack a person."

"Oh God," said Patrick, collapsing into a chair. "I was hoping it was just a bad cold. I never expected the measles."

"Have you ever had them?" Karl asked, his face going pale.

"Yes, back in Ireland when I was a boy."

"I had them once too," said Karl, "but that was before Kathy was born."

Patrick did not answer. He feared something horrible.

"You better send for the doctor," said Karl.

"What about Beth?"

"Is there someone she could stay with?"

"I don't know who," said Patrick, trying to think of a neighbor who would be willing to take her in until the danger was past, but most would fear his daughter was already a carrier of the disease.

"Then I'll take her back to Calumet with me," said Karl. "Thelma would love to have her visit; they get along so well."

"What about school?"

"Beth's a bright girl, and at her age, it won't be hard for her to catch up. It'll only be for a few weeks."

When told, Beth was not at all happy about staying with Uncle Karl and Cousin Thelma. She loved them dearly, but she wanted to stay home and help care for her mother. She was not quite eight, yet she thought herself a good caretaker. She already helped her mom around the house with the dishes and setting the table.

"It's just a visit, Beth, honey," her father said. "You'll be back home before you know it."

But Beth cried all the way to Calumet. Patrick hated to see her leave, but he knew it was for the best. The doctor told him he had done the right thing to send the girl away. Kathy was too ill to object.

If Kathy McCarey were spared from the influenza only to receive the measles, hers was a rare case. During that winter, nearly eighteen hundred people in Marquette County were diagnosed with influenza. Soon a ban was placed upon public assemblies to hinder the virus from spreading. Even in the dead of winter with subzero temperatures, people avoided enclosed spaces, and Marquette's streetcars whizzed along with open windows, the passengers preferring to breathe in the cold than inhale fatal germs. War worries continued, but the locals fought their own epidemic battle at home.

Three-year old Ada Whitman was the first in her family to contract the influenza. Margaret immediately panicked. The family already scrimped to get by; they could scarcely afford doctor bills, or worse, a funeral. Margaret did not know what they would do if the other children contracted the disease.

"We need to keep the other children safe," she told Will. "They can't stay with your sister, and with Harriet expecting a baby, we can't bother her and Charles."

"What about your parents?" said Will.

"They're too old to chase the children around."

But Will rode into town to ask his in-laws anyway.

"Of course," said Christina. "We'd love to have the children here, and you and Margaret already have enough to worry about with Ada being sick. The house has been lonely ever since my children all married, so I'm sure having the grandchildren will cheer up Charles and me."

A few hours later, the Whitman children were dropped on their grandparents' front door step. None of them were pleased. They loved their grandparents, but they felt awkward about staying with them. Their mother had lectured them on not being too rambunctious so they didn't give Grandma a stroke.

But the next morning at breakfast, Christina Dalrymple told her grandchildren:

"Your grandpa and I think it best you all stay home from school for a few days. If you've gotten the influenza from your sister, you don't want to infect the other children, and of course, we don't want you to catch anything from your schoolmates."

"What will Pa and Ma say?" asked Henry. As the oldest, he felt the burden of responsibility, although he did not want to go to school any more than his brother or sister.

"Your grandpa and I can handle your parents, and it can't hurt for you children to have a little vacation."

Eleanor smiled. She would have jumped with pleasure except that she feared her grandparents would disapprove.

"What will we do all day?" asked Henry, wanting to know the price of freedom.

"Anything you want," Grandma replied. "I'm going to make us all some sugar cookies this morning if anyone wants to help."

"I'll help," Eleanor said. "Mama never lets me help because I make too much mess."

"Well, I'll just have to teach you how not to make a mess, although messes are much more fun, I admit."

Eleanor beamed. At last an adult who understood her.

Roy said, "I'm going to read upstairs." He set his empty plate on the kitchen cupboard and disappeared.

His grandparents exchanged glances, their fun somewhat spoiled by Roy's departure; they rarely had an opportunity to be doting grandparents because the children lived out on the farm and only came to town for school or church.

"What do you plan to do, Henry?" asked Grandpa Dalrymple.

"I don't know," he said. He liked to keep himself occupied, but he could not imagine what he could do at his grandparents' house. He almost thought school would be more interesting. He would miss the math competition today.

"I have some work to do in my woodshop," said his grandfather. "If you want to help me, Henry, maybe we could make something for you kids."

"Okay," Henry said. "I help Pa at home a lot. I'm good at pounding nails and measuring."

"I bet you'll make a fine carpenter someday," smiled Grandma.

Charles and Henry left the females to their baking and went outside.

Charles Dalrymple's woodshop behind the house stretched for twenty feet and every foot of it was packed with wood, sawdust, nails, shingles, shavings, saws, sandpaper, and rulers. Henry thought it the dirtiest, finest smelling place imaginable.

"I just have to finish sanding the cabinet I'm making for Mrs. Haslett," said Charles. "It shouldn't take me long, and then we can make some things for you kids."

"It's so fine looking, Grandpa," said Henry, running his hand along the already finished side of the cabinet. "It must be wonderful to make such beautiful things."

"Yes," said Charles. "Only bad part is I end up giving away what I make. After working on them so long, they're sometimes hard to part with."

"I would think it's worth it to give them up when you see how pleased people are with what you've made."

"Well, I guess that's true," frowned Charles; it was true in most cases, but he knew Mrs. Haslett found little to be pleased about.

"What can I do, Grandpa?"

"I have several scrap pieces over there in the corner. Why don't you look through them and pick out some good pieces to make things with, toys for your brother and sister, like a wagon or some doll furniture or a little play-house."

"I can't yet make a big cabinet like you, Grandpa, but maybe I can start by making a small one for Eleanor to put her play dishes on."

Henry walked over to the woodpile, stepping over the little mound of sawdust on the floor. Rather than step over the pile of curlicued wood shavings, however, he picked up several, thinking perhaps Eleanor would like to use them as decorations for something. He set them on a workbench, then turned to the cluttered wood stack in the corner. While he examined the wood, he soaked in the sawdust smell and the musty dampness of the shop that remained noticeable despite a fire in the barrel stove. Years later, when he would have his own woodshop, when his grandfather was long gone, Henry would remember that sawdust smell from his grandfather's haven, and when he touched sandpaper, he would recall the feeling of his grandfather's whiskered cheek when he kissed it. But today, he was too young for such sentimentality. He had woodworking to do.

Henry dug through the woodpile, trying to match up similarly shaped pieces to create walls for a dollhouse. The oddly shaped pieces — rejected as trim for porches, lattices, and decorative furniture — Henry saved so Eleanor might paint or color them. In these awkward shapes, he imaginatively saw Cinderella's slipper, a parrot, a mushroom, and numerous other strange shapes to please his sister. The pieces could remain separate, or be nailed together to form fantastic sailboats, wagons, chariots, trees, and uniquely shaped boxes to hold childhood's secret treasures.

Once Henry decided what to make, his grandpa showed just what an expert carpenter he was. Henry had never realized the multitude of sizes and types of nails and screws, each appropriate for a different size of wood. His grandpa explained how the grain of the wood revealed which type of tree it was from. Henry had never paid attention to the grain before, but now he saw faces in it, and he appreciated the natural beauty of its patterns. Grandpa taught him how to pound nails straight, or to bend and twist them so pieces would hold together as if they were one original board.

In the kitchen, Eleanor created her own fascinating shapes. Grandma had plenty of cookie cutters, but she also creatively took a knife to carve out new shapes. Eleanor wanted to make a bunny, so Grandma shaped a rabbit's head. Then came a pumpkin, and a dolly, an automobile for Roy and a baseball bat for Henry. Best of all, Grandma said half the cookies would be frosted and the rest would be sugared. "So what if there's a war on," said Grandma. "The government can't expect us to go without cookies. There's not too many things more worth fighting for."

Eleanor had never imagined making cookies was fun the way her mother always frowned as she rolled out the dough and then snapped at the children when they came near her because they might get flour on the floor. Grandma only laughed about spilled flour, saying, "I can always mop it up" and then she would pop a piece of dough in her mouth because, "Frankly, I like them best before they're baked."

The morning passed too quickly for grandparents and grandchildren alike. When Charles and Henry came inside for lunch, Henry immediately told Eleanor about the dollhouse he and Grandpa were making for her, but when she wanted to see it, he insisted she had to wait until it was done.

"Is Roy coming down for lunch?" Charles asked.

"I was just about to call him," Christina replied. "I worry about that boy. I haven't heard a peep from him since he went upstairs. He said he'd be reading, but I can't imagine a ten-year old boy burying himself in a book like that. I'm not sure it's healthy."

But Roy was enjoying himself perhaps more than anyone. For the first time he could remember, he was free to lounge around rather than have to collect eggs, rub down a horse, or be at school. He never could understand why Henry worked so diligently on the farm and at school, and then on a vacation day like today, Henry still wanted to be in a woodshop, helping Grandpa do more work. Not that Roy was a lazy boy; he was all too willing to work at what interested him, but in Marquette, he found little of interest. Life here seemed drab and dull, so at an early age, he started to escape by reading about the greater outside world. Most days, he only snatched a few minutes to read, and few books beyond the *Farmer's Almanac* were at home. But today, in what had been his Great-Grandpa Dalrymple's room, he discovered nine tall, green cloth volumes with gold engravings of Scottish symbols upon them. Each volume was distinguished with a picture of Sir Walter Scott and contained three or four stories to comprise the complete Waverley novels. Roy had never heard of these books, but the gaudy covers attracted him with their promise of inner splendor, especially because the stories took place in Scotland — had not his mother named him Royal because he was descended from the great houses of Scotland? He spent a half hour paging through the books to look at the fantastic pictures of men in kilts with bagpipes, crumbling castles, splendid palaces with gardens and fountains, beautiful maidens persecuted by highwaymen, and gypsy robbers who hid in caves while their exotic daughters were courted by handsome soldiers. When Roy could bear the excitement of the pictures no longer, he turned to one of the stories and soon found himself engrossed in *Guy Mannering*. Roy had heard of Scotland, but now for the first time he visited it; he could not have been more stunned and pleased if he had leapt off Ben Lomond to find himself flying over a field of blooming heather.

Charles Dalrymple went upstairs to find Roy lying on the bed, wrapped in a quilt and reading a book long forgotten to be in the house.

Roy was almost embarrassed when woken from his daydream; he quickly stumbled downstairs, feeling how cold was the ordinary world compared to Sir Walter Scott's imaginative one. But when he complained of being cold, Grandpa said, "That's because you were lying under that quilt," and Grandma said, "Drink some coffee. That'll warm you up."

Roy made no reply when Grandma filled his coffee cup, but Henry said, "Ma and Pa don't let us drink coffee."

"Well, what they don't know won't hurt them," Grandma said. "Do you like coffee, Henry?"

"I think so, but I've never had any."

"At thirteen? How silly!" said Grandpa. "It's best with cream and sugar."

Grandma filled a second cup an inch from the rim for Henry.

At first, Henry wondered why she left it so far from full. But then he watched Grandpa generously measure three teaspoonfuls of sugar and nearly an ounce of cream for his own coffee. The Dalrymples had never been rich, but cream and sugar were not to be skimped on, war or no war.

Henry followed his Grandpa's example, stirring his coffee until it was a light cream color.

Grandma asked Eleanor whether she would like a sip of coffee. She eagerly picked up her grandmother's cup, but instantly regretted it.

"From the face she's making, I guess she'll stick to milk," laughed Charles.

Henry now told Roy about the dollhouse he was making for their sister; Eleanor constantly chimed in with questions or ideas to improve what she had not yet seen. Henry promised that tomorrow he would make Roy a little wagon. Roy seemed uninterested, but Henry was too enthusiastic to notice.

"What will you women do after lunch?" Grandpa asked.

"At the rate you're eating the cookies, we may have to bake another batch," Grandma teased. "Actually, I was thinking Eleanor and I could make her some paper dolls for that dollhouse."

Eleanor grinned so widely that the loss of her first tooth was visible.

"I'll have to do the dishes first," said Grandma. "But if Eleanor will wipe, we'll be done soon."

"I'm going to finish reading my book," said Roy, pushing back his chair to escape after a hurried meal.

The afternoon passed as pleasantly as the morning. At night, after the children were gone to bed, Christina confessed to her husband, "It's hard work keeping a six-year-old girl occupied. Eleanor has me totally worn out, but it was a wonderful day."

"Henry will be a fine carpenter someday," Charles said.

"I worry about Roy," said Christina. "I don't think he likes being separated from his parents."

"Maggie always says he's quiet so I wouldn't worry about it," said Charles. "Maybe tomorrow, he'll come out to the woodshop when we start to make his wagon."

"Somehow, I don't think he'll care whether he has a wagon."

Indeed, Roy had found something better than wagons. He had discovered the world beyond Marquette, the world of historical fiction, the glories of other lands and times. He had discovered his imagination could transcend the dullness of everyday life. He felt he was moving toward an answer to all that troubled him, to what he had sought all his life without knowing it. Ambitious thoughts and desires were now planted in his young, impressionable mind.

For three weeks, Beth McCarey longed to go home. She loved her uncle and cousin, but a heavily bearded lumberjack was not the same as a mother, and while Thelma was fun to play with, sometimes Beth could not understand her cousin, who seemed more like a little girl than she was, despite being seven years older.

When the day finally came to go home, Karl sat Beth down to talk with her.

"Honey," he said, "maybe I should have told you sooner, but I just couldn't bring myself to do it. Your mother's gotten over the measles, but they left her deaf in one ear and hearing impaired in the other. From now on, she'll have difficulty understanding when you talk to her."

Beth stared at her uncle.

"You mean she can't hear anymore?"

"She can a little, but you may have to shout or use your hands to help her understand."

"Let's go," Thelma told her father. "Beth'll understand when we get there."

It was a long drive from Calumet to Marquette, and Beth worried all the way home. She wondered whether her mother would look any different because of the measles. Thelma had, in an indiscreet moment, told her they might scar her mother's face. Beth was a little afraid to see her mother again.

November had arrived, and the cold winds blew through the cracks in Uncle Karl's car, making Beth sleepy. She drifted into a dream of her mother; the bumps in the road made her dreams confused, and her mentally exhausted body fought hard to keep her asleep. She felt miserably uncomfortable; once she woke up, wanting to cry, wanting to be home, tucked into bed, and kissed goodnight by her mother. Upon arriving at the McCarey house, Karl had difficulty waking her. She nearly rolled out of the car, then stumbled up the steps to the front door.

"Beth," whispered her father, kneeling down to kiss her. She flung her arms around him, relieved to be home.

"Kathy's upstairs," Patrick told Karl. "She's resting, but she wanted me to wake her when you came. I'll bring her right down."

Karl followed Patrick upstairs, while the girls sat on a bench in the hall, afraid to venture anywhere until they saw how badly the illness had afflicted Beth's mother.

After a few minutes, the girls heard footsteps upstairs. Both became nervous. Thelma clutched Beth's hand. Karl came downstairs, but they scarcely looked at him. Then they saw Patrick's feet, his legs, and they heard the swish of Kathy's skirt. Just as she came into view, the front door flew open.

"It's over! The war's over!"

Joe, the neighbor boy, was standing in the hall, shouting at the top of his lungs.

"What?" asked Karl. He had heard but not yet taken in the words.

Beth ignored Joe. She longed for her mother, but Kathy did not look at her daughter. She stared at Karl and then Joe and tried to understand why they had such a strange reaction to words she had not heard well enough to understand.

"Is it true?" Patrick asked. His heart leapt and shivers ran through him from fear he had misunderstood.

"The war's over," Joe repeated. "My father heard it downtown. It came through the telegraph office, and it'll be in the next newspaper."

"Then Jeremy will be coming home," said Patrick. He longed too deeply for his absent son to find more words.

Beth watched her mother. She wanted to run to her, but she was frightened when her mother did not rejoice like everyone else.

"What is it?" asked Kathy, her voice faltering, as she touched Patrick's shoulder.

Patrick squeezed her hand, both of them still standing on the stairs. "The war is over," he said, placing his mouth to her ear.

"Oh."

The word meant quiet acceptance, and awe that such horror was over, and regret that so much blood had been shed, so much misery suffered in trenches and on battlefields, on air machines and ships. So many people slaughtered pointlessly. Patrick thought of the son who would come home. Kathy remembered the son who would never return.

"Mama," said Beth, longing to hug her mother, but bewildered by her mother's unchanged expression. Kathy still did not hear her daughter.

"Everyone's celebrating!" Joe yelled. "I have to go tell the other neighbors."

"Thank you for letting us know," Karl said, but Joe had already torn down the street, shouting the news. People heard and came outside, to stand and stare, to take in the news. Women broke into tears; men felt a yoke lifted from them. People looked out their windows. Seeing their neighbors in the streets, they stepped outside to hear the news. Because of the influenza epidemic, public assemblies had been banned, but now people were running up and down, whooping for joy, marching, singing the "Star Spangled Banner," "When Johnny Comes Marching Home Again," and "Over There." Even with liquor prohibition in Marquette County, not a few bottles were broken open right on the streets.

The McCareys and Bergmanns stepped outside to join in the celebration. Then, awkwardly, Beth took her mother's hand. The changed woman bent down to hug her little girl; she had feared she might never see Beth again.

The war was over; her mother's illness was over; in the past year, Beth had known more unhappiness than a little girl should. She hoped everything would be back to normal now. But a new war had begun in the McCarey household, a battle against silence that Kathy McCarey would have to fight each day.

1919

The men were home. A parade was held to welcome them back. Jeremy McCarey marched with his fellow soldiers, amid much fanfare, through a giant welcome arch, to the beat of a band whose music sang the joy in everyone's heart. Thousands of well-wishers turned out to cheer the men who had fought so bravely.

Patrick and Kathy McCarey stood on the sidewalk with their neighbors and friends, their fellow Americans, celebrating the war's end and the return of boys they had watched grow to manhood, then sent overseas to make their hometown proud. Nor were anyone's thoughts far today from those many fine young men who had given their lives in their country's service.

Kathy spotted Sylvia Cumming in the crowd. She recalled how upset Mrs. Cumming had been the day the boys had gone off to the war. She imagined Mrs. Cumming was now as relieved as she was to have her sons back home.

Knowing Jeremy was safely home made this one of Kathy's happiest days. The music was so loud she could actually hear it, and the crowd was especially uproarious after being isolated all winter because of the influenza epidemic.

But when the soldiers passed, Kathy saw Jeremy marching beside the two Cumming boys. Then she looked across the street at Sylvia Cumming and asked herself, "Why should that woman have both her sons return home while one of mine is dead? Her boys have always been in trouble. It isn't fair; Frank deserved to live more than either of her sons."

Kathy grew angry; she nearly broke into tears, not from patriotic fervor or relief, but at the injustice of life. Everyone in Marquette knew those Cummings were nothing but white trash, while the McCareys were a respectable God-fearing family.

Farther down the street, the Whitmans watched the parade with Margaret's parents. Straining her eyes to watch the approaching soldiers, Margaret was the first to spot Sylvia in the crowd; she nudged Will, who then noticed his sister but made no comment; he and Margaret had long ago agreed not to mention the family feud before the children. But Will kept sneaking glances toward his sister, her husband, and her daughter — Will's own niece, whom he had never met. He remembered Sylvia had been expecting this last child when he had moved out of his brother-in-law's house, and now the girl was — why, she must be seventeen now. Seventeen years he had not spoken to his sister.

"How about we all go into Donckers; I'll buy cokes and candy for everyone," said Grandpa Dalrymple when the parade had ended.

"Yeah!" cried Eleanor.

"Let's hurry," said Margaret. "Ada's better, but this cold air isn't good for her."

"Margaret," Will held her back as the rest of the family walked to the candy store. "I'm going to speak to Sylvia. I saw Harry walk down the street, probably in search of the boys, so I might have a minute."

"Are you sure, Will?"

"Yes. It's been too long."

Margaret nodded in consent, then scurried after her parents and children. Will quickly strode across the street to where Sylvia and her daughter were already turning to walk home.

"Sylvia!" he called to keep her from escaping. She stopped and waited, although she looked as if she would rather run than speak to him.

"Who's that, Mother?" asked the girl.

"Serena, this is your Uncle Will," said Sylvia.

"Hello," said Serena, startled but polite. She had never thought to ask about her mother's family since her parents did not speak of them. A couple times, Serena's brothers had recalled memories of their uncles, but their father had always put an immediate stop to such talk, and Serena had never been curious.

"Hello," Will said. "Hello, Sylvia. How are you?"

"Okay," she said. She looked afraid.

"You look well."

"So do you," she replied. "What do you want, Will?"

"Just to see you."

"Please, Will. You'll only make it harder for me."

"Why?" he asked.

Sylvia turned to her daughter. "Serena, go find your father. Tell him I'll meet him at home. Tell him I have an errand to run. Don't tell him I'm speaking to your uncle."

Serena hesitated, but said, "All right." Will saw she was intelligent enough to understand without questioning. He imagined her father had made her life difficult enough that like her mother, she feared his anger.

"She's beautiful," said Will as Serena disappeared into the disbanding crowd. "She looks like you did at her age."

"I can't remember ever being her age."

"Is it awful for you, Syl? Will he hurt you if he learns you spoke to me?"

"No."

"Then why did you say that talking to me will make it harder for you?"

"He'll yell at me, but he won't hurt me. It'll be harder because when I don't see you, I can go days without thinking about you. But now that I'm talking to you, I'll think about you for days to come, and that'll be hard because I won't know when I'll get to speak to you again."

"I'm sorry."

She stared at the ground. He stared at the dispersing crowd.

"I'm glad," he said, after a minute, "that my nephews came home safely."

"Thank you." She tried to smile.

"Do you ever hear from Mary?"

"No. I'm sure Mary's far too busy, living in Chicago, to bother with a brother and sister in a little town like this."

"I have bad news for you," said Will. "Aunt Edna wrote that Grandma Whitman died in October."

"Did she?" said Sylvia. "I thought she must have died years ago and no one ever bothered to tell me."

"No, just recently. She was ninety-seven."

"She was a good woman. I hope she rests in peace. How's Aunt Edna?"

"Okay, I guess. She didn't say much. I never really knew her."

"No, she moved away when I was little, so I barely even remember her."

"We're really the only family we have left," said Will. "Of course, there's our children, but we're the only ones who remember the old days."

"I think about those days often. I was happy then without knowing it."

"The war's over now," said Will. "Good times will come again."

But he knew the war had nothing to do with good and bad times for them.

"I better go. Harry will wonder where I am."

"All right," he said. He did not want her to go, but he did not know how to stop her. Unconsciously, he leaned over to kiss her cheek, just as he had in their youth.

She broke away and walked quickly up the street. For a second, Will felt like crying; then he turned to look after her. She was already a block away, far enough that she must have felt safe when she turned back to wave before climbing the hill.

Will pretended to be jovial when he joined his family inside Donckers.

Kathy had recovered from the sadness she felt during the parade. She found comfort in having her family together again. Jeremy was home from the war, and even Michael had left the seminary for a couple days to welcome his brother. Kathy knew nothing would ever fill Frank's place, but at least tonight the rest of her loved ones were under the same roof. Even Karl and Thelma had come for the day. Karl immediately engaged Jeremy in a long conversation about what they had each seen on their respective visits to Germany. Patrick occasionally chimed in that he would never visit Europe again; he wanted to know what good the war had done for Ireland; why would the United States not intervene to help his oppressed country when it went to the aid of every other nation in Europe?

For Beth, the end of the war left only one mark on her memory. After supper, Jeremy said, "I almost forgot." Then he went upstairs and returned a couple minutes later with a small square box he presented to his sister.

"I know Frank promised you a present," he told Beth. "I couldn't bring much home with me, but since Frank couldn't get you a gift, I brought you this." Beth carefully opened the little box. Inside was a small piece of cloth. She set down the box, took out the cloth, and unfolded it. The fine piece of silk was light pink, with intricate lace along its edges. Beth McCarey now possessed a dainty handkerchief, fit for a fine French lady. Embroidered across it were the words "Paris 1918."

Jeremy had brought it to her, but Beth would always think of Frank when she saw it. It should have come from Frank, her brother who lay buried in a field in France.

"You should take it to school to show all your friends," said Thelma.

But Beth did not want to share it. Even as a little girl, she felt it too personal an item; she feared losing it if she brought it to school. To lose it would be like losing her brother all over again.

1920

On this beautiful August morning, Kathy McCarey felt all was finally right again with the world. This time two years ago, the war had still been raging, but now some good might be detected as having resulted from it. She would never cease missing Frank, but the worst pain of his loss had been dealt with, and while a day never passed without her thinking of him, she found life remained abundant about her. Jeremy had come home from the war, and a year ago, he had married. Now Kathy and Patrick were expecting their first grandchild. Jeremy had met his bride, Caroline, while training downstate at Fort Custer; after the war, he had gone back to Battle Creek to visit her family and bring her home to be his wife. Caroline missed her family downstate, but Kathy felt once the baby was born, her daughter-in-law would adjust to the change of location and feel her life was complete, just as Kathy had felt when her first child, Frank, had been born. She had become a mother so many years ago, yet Kathy found it hard to believe that only her baby, Beth, was still at home. And now Beth was a big girl of ten and would be running off to get married before she knew it, but by that time, Kathy imagined she would have Jeremy's children to spoil.

"Mama, hurry, or we'll be late!" Beth shouted.

The girl had learned to yell for her mother's attention, and usually Kathy heard her. At first, the deafness had been difficult for Kathy, but she soon found she knew her family so well, she could guess what each one wanted even if she only caught a couple words. She had become very good at reading lips, especially when speaking to people outside of her family. At other times, her family might speak loudly to her, but because she was not facing them, she pretended she did not hear them; she had found that a little exaggeration of her deafness helped to prevent many unnecessary family conflicts.

"Thelma's already waiting outside," Beth continued to holler.

Thelma was making her annual summer visit. Kathy felt the girl was a good companion for Beth, old enough to watch over her, yet young enough to play with her. That Thelma was a bit slow for her years made the two girls all the more compatible. Kathy had often feared Beth would become a tomboy because she only had older brothers to model herself after, but Thelma was decidedly feminine with her fancy white gloves, expensive dresses, and refined taste in music. And Thelma had not yet acquired any of those silly notions about boys that so many young women had these days. Kathy had been married at Thelma's age, but Thelma was a late bloomer, and Kathy was thankful because then Beth was less likely to get any ideas while so young. Thelma's eccentricities actually dissuaded several young men who might otherwise seek her hand solely from interest in her father's wealth.

"Mama!" Beth hollered again.

"I'm coming," Kathy called. She had promised to take the girls blueberry picking. Last year a huge forest fire near Birch and Big Bay had resulted in this summer's mammoth blueberry crop. A "blueberry train" had been organized to take people to the berry fields north of Marquette so they could spend the day filling their pails. When Kathy heard reports that people were returning with tubs full of berries, she was determined to go; she just hoped the fields were not completely picked over; she longed for blueberry pie and did not want to disappoint the girls.

Kathy, Beth, and Thelma soon walked to the train at the depot with a few dozen Marquette residents, all fiercely intent upon blueberry picking, and even more intent on having a good time. Smiles and general gaiety marked the group, for it was a pleasant summer day, with a slight breeze to cool them from the sun's rays, and the low humidity meant the woods would not be stiflingly hot. True Marquettians are always ready for an excuse to get out of town, no matter how much they love their distinguished city of sandstone and scenic views; they have an innate desire to get lost among trees, to forget civilization's existence, to renew their spirits amid Nature's serenity.

The train trip was uneventful, but all the more pleasant for it. Quiet yet eager conversations filled the railway car, and Kathy found herself surrounded by several of her acquaintances. Marquette's population now surpassed ten thousand, but it remained small enough that if everyone did not know everyone else, people were sure to have mutual friends and acquaintances. Because she could read lips, Kathy could better converse on a noisy train than most of her neighbors with perfect hearing. She felt she hadn't known such fun since long before the war. Thelma and Beth occupied themselves by looking out the windows. Beth tried to count the birch trees, but she soon gave up — they flew past so rapidly. Thelma willingly entertained her younger cousin, pointing out pretty little meadows or oddly shaped trees. They spotted a few deer, including a princely young fawn. The morning sun glistened through the trees, casting a medley of sunshine rays through the train windows. The ride felt all too short on such a glorious morning, but after a long day of berry picking, they knew they would all appreciate the shortest return trip possible.

When the train stopped at the berry fields, the passengers scurried across the meadows and copses, laying claim to large shady trees under which they could leave their excess belongings until lunchtime. Several people had brought multiple buckets, one even brought a small washtub. People went off with one pail, returned to place it under their claimed spot, set off into the fields to fill a second, and then started on a third. Little fear existed of anyone stealing berries amid such a multitude of overflowing bushes.

Kathy selected a spot for lunch while Thelma led Beth across the berry patches; Beth anxiously followed her cousin, but her enthusiasm was not bound to last.

After fifteen minutes of berry picking, Beth was tired enough to want a break. Thelma, too focused on picking berries to bake a pie for her father's visit next weekend, ignored her cousin's complaints.

Seeing that Thelma wasn't paying attention, and that her mother was across the field, Beth decided to quit picking and go for a walk by herself. As she crossed the fields, she spotted another girl close to her age. She did not recognize the girl from Bishop Baraga School, but that did not matter. Beth went over to introduce herself; in a few minutes, the two girls were best friends, chasing each other and playing hide-and-go-seek among the trees; they completely neglected the blueberries, save for trampling over some of the bushes.

When Kathy looked up, she was concerned not to see her daughter near Thelma, but after a minute, she saw Beth and the other little girl. Having known Beth's work ethic would not last long, she smiled to see her daughter had found a friend. Kathy returned to berry picking until Thelma had picked her way in the same direction. When the two were close enough, they started to chat and momentarily forgot about Beth until Thelma heard her scream from across the meadow.

Thelma told her aunt what she had heard, and then Kathy, who had not heard anything, quickly looked about for the source of her daughter's cries. Then Beth came running toward her mother, her dress ripped, her eyes filled with tears, clutching the handle of her berry pail, only half connected to its handle so that the berries were haphazardly plunking from the bucket to the ground as she ran.

"Beth, what's wrong?" asked Kathy, rushing to take her girl in her arms.

"I saw a snake! I nearly stepped on it before I saw it," she said between sobs. "And that girl, Amy — I hate her — she just laughed, and she picked up the snake and shoved it at me; it hissed and tried to bite me!"

"There, there, dear. There aren't any poisonous snakes around here. What color was it?"

"Green, and it was really big, like this." Beth held up her hands to indicate a foot and a half.

"Ha," laughed Thelma. "It was just a little garter snake. It won't hurt you. I know a boy back in Calumet who keeps a half dozen of them as pets."

Rather than be consoled, this news ran shivers up Beth's spine.

"There, dear, it's okay," said Kathy. "It wasn't nice of Amy to do that, but it didn't hurt you any. Now tell me, how did you rip your dress?"

"Oh," said Beth, forgetting she had intended to carry her pail in front of the rip so her mother would not see it. The snake ordeal had broken her cunning, so she had to confess. "I tore it on a branch while Amy and I were climbing a tree."

"Well," said Kathy, "it's one of your older dresses, and I imagined you'd end up with berry stains on it, but I wish you wouldn't climb trees."

The mention of berries made Beth look to see how many she had picked. Then she discovered her bucket handle had broken. The bucket hung down at a forty-five degree angle. Inside, only six berries and some blueberry leaves were to be found.

"I lost all my berries!" she cried.

Twenty feet away, a young boy heard the lament. He had witnessed the snake incident and been unable to restrain from silent laughter, but now he felt sorry when Beth looked devastated by the lost blueberries.

"Come, dear," said Kathy. "Let's have lunch, and then we'll fix your pail so you can still fill it this afternoon."

"But I had it almost full," sobbed Beth. "I wanted to pick two pails worth."

In truth, the pail had barely been a quarter full, but Beth exaggerated her loss so her mother would not chide her for slacking in her berry picking.

Kathy and Thelma continued to console Beth as they found their shady tree and set up lunch. While they unfolded the picnic cloth, the young man who had witnessed Beth's tragic scene approached. He waited to be noticed, then said hello.

"I saw you spill your berries," he told Beth. "You can have my pail full if you want. I don't really need so many."

"Oh no, we couldn't," said Kathy.

"I insist," he said, turning to Kathy. "It didn't take me long to pick them, and I already filled two other pails this morning. I have all afternoon to pick, and I know little kids get tired quicker, so now she won't have to pick all afternoon to make up her loss."

Kathy was going to object again, but the young man said, "Please. I really do insist."

"What do you say, Beth?"

"Okay," Beth agreed, too surprised by such kindness to remember her manners.

"We thank you, Mr. — "

"I'm Henry," he replied, although pleased to be called "Mister" when he was only fifteen.

"It's a pleasure to meet you, Henry," said Thelma, holding out her hand. "Would you like to have lunch with us?"

Henry did not wish to impose. He waited for permission from the adult.

"There's plenty of food," Thelma said. "Isn't there, Aunt Kathy?"

Kathy smiled. "We have more than enough. Please join us."

Henry accepted by sitting down. Thelma introduced everyone, explained that she was visiting her relatives in Marquette, then launched into her life story, which despite her short lifespan she described in enough detail that it could have rivaled *War and Peace* if written down. Beth sat quietly, too shy to say anything, but she adored the kind young man. Kathy emptied the picnic basket and spread out everything while Thelma continued to chatter.

"Henry, are you here by yourself?" asked Kathy, breaking in as Thelma paused before beginning to describe her life at age nine. Kathy was surprised the boy did not eat with his own family or friends.

"Yes, my pa is working for the Kaufmans over at Granot Loma. I usually work with him, but today there wasn't much I could do, so he suggested I pick berries, and I'll meet him when he's ready to head home."

"Oh, you've seen Granot Loma!" squealed Thelma, although less interested in Granot Loma than in gaining the boy's attention. He was younger than her, but boys rarely spoke to her, so she was not choosy.

"Yes, it's incredible. It's so big, and it's progressing beautifully."

"What is your father doing there?" asked Kathy.

"He's a carpenter, just like me," Henry replied.

"You're not old enough to work," said Beth. "Don't you go to school?"

"I did until this year, but from now on, I'm going to work with my Pa to help out the family. I have four younger brothers and sisters; the youngest one, Bill, is just two months old, so we need all the money we can get."

Kathy smiled. She believed in the importance of education, but Henry seemed intelligent from his manner and speech, and a boy who helped his family was often of better character than one who received honors at school. It was unfortunate he knew tough times at his young age, but she suspected he might persevere all the more because of it.

"You look familiar," she said. "Who are your parents?"

"My pa is Will Whitman, and my ma is Margaret. She was a Dalrymple."

"I used to know Jacob Whitman and his wife Agnes. Are you related to them?"

"They were my grandparents."

Then the names clicked in Kathy's head. So this was Will's son — Jacob and Agnes's grandson. She had not seen Will in years — would not recognize him if she did see him. He must be middle-aged now, although she could only picture him as the little boy she had once gone sledding with. That meant, if Will were Henry's father, then Sylvia Cumming was Henry's aunt. Well, she mustn't hold that against him.

"I remember your father when he was just a baby," said Kathy. "When I was a girl, my mother was good friends with your family, especially with your grandma, and I think your great-grandparents. When your Grandpa Whitman moved the family out to his farm, though, we didn't see much of them after that."

"My pa did grow up on a farm," Henry said. "But I never knew my grand-parents; they died before I was born."

"Mine and Beth's grandparents are dead too," said Thelma. "Grandpa and Grandma Bergmann I mean. We never knew our grandpa, but our grandma only died a few years ago."

"Tell us more about Granot Loma," said Kathy. She did not want to talk more about Henry's family; his connection to the Cummings reminded her that Sylvia's sons had come home from the war while Frank had been killed in France.

"Is Granot Loma as grand as everyone says?" asked Thelma. "It sounds like a castle in the wilderness."

"Sort of is, like a castle masquerading as a log cabin," laughed Henry.

He launched into a description of the Kaufman family's magnificent mansion on the shore of Lake Superior. Intended as a summer home, it far outrivaled any cabin in the great North Woods, even those at the exclusive Huron Mountain Club. The Kaufmans had named the cabin for their children by using the first two letters of each of their children's names to spell out Granot Loma. The famous architect, Marshall Fox, had been hired with several assisting architects to design the monstrous getaway. The main sitting room alone was to be a tremendous eighty feet long, forty feet wide, and thirty-six feet high. Henry did not know all the details, but he remembered those dimensions because they were so unfathomable. His parents' entire house could fit into that one room. Stonemasons, plumbers, electricians, all were working constantly, yet completion of the building, already begun a year earlier, was estimated to take another five years. Rumor said the Kaufmans would build several smaller yet ornate cabins in the surrounding woods, one for each of their children, locally known as the "million dollar babies."

"I just can't imagine anything so grand in Upper Michigan," said Thelma, jealous that despite her father's own lumberjack prosperity, he would never be able to afford anything a quarter so splendid.

"Oh, great homes have been built here before," said Kathy. "You're all too young to remember the Longyear mansion, but it was a marvel in its day."

"My pa told me about that," said Henry. "He and my Grandpa Dalrymple were among those hired to take it apart."

"It must have been quite a job," said Kathy. "It was so enormous it filled an entire city block, and when the Longyears decided to move, the whole house was taken apart and shipped out East on railway cars."

"My ma," said Henry, "went inside it one day when my grandpa was working there. She got lost in it, it was that big."

"It must be grand to be so rich," said Thelma, although she had far more than most young ladies.

"Well," said Kathy, "let's have our cake and then get back to berry picking. I spied a good patch just before lunch, and I don't want anyone to snatch it up."

When the cake was gone, Henry thanked Kathy and the girls for their hospitality, then said, "I better get back to work. I promised to bring my ma back enough berries for two pies, and I want to bring some home for my grandparents too."

"We're glad you could join us," Thelma said. She was sorry he was leaving; he was a cute boy; she wondered what chance she had to see him again.

Beth was more forward than her cousin. "Henry," she asked, "can I go pick berries with you?"

"No, Beth, you stay with me," said Kathy, not wanting to impose on the young man's kindness.

"But Henry might know where the best berries are," Beth said.

"She can come with me if she wants to," said Henry. "I won't mind."

"I'm afraid she'll be a trouble to you," said Kathy.

"Oh, no," he replied.

Kathy suspected he was only being kind, but she gave in. "All right, if you're sure. Beth, you mind your manners, and be back in a couple hours so I don't have to go looking for you and then miss the train."

"Yes, Mama," said Beth, clutching her berry pail, then disappearing with Henry.

Thelma looked after them, wishing she could go along, but she dared not ask — she knew she was no longer a cute little girl who could get away with joining a handsome boy. She stayed behind to help her aunt clean up the picnic.

"Don't you want to go with them, Thelma?" asked her aunt.

"No, it wouldn't be fair to leave you alone, aunt," she said. She was embarrassed that her aunt should ask. She wanted to pick berries with Henry, but having Beth along would just spoil it anyway.

Kathy was pleased such polite young people existed as Henry and her niece, who was always attentive to her. It made her hopeful for the future. The war had not destroyed everything, not when such a beautiful day existed for berry picking, and when grand homes like Granot Loma were being built right here in Upper Michigan. She could not imagine having enough wealth to build such a home. But she was here to collect berries, not dollars, and if she wanted to make those pies, she had better get back to work.

Two berry picking hours later, Henry returned Beth to her mother. Then after saying goodbye, he started for the main road to meet his father and get a ride home.

"He's so nice," said Thelma, already starving for another look at the cute boy.

"Yes, the Whitmans were always good people," said Kathy, thinking the Cummings did not count since they did not share the same name. Kathy thought Agnes would be pleased to know she had such a fine grandson. She wished Agnes could hear how beautifully Thelma played the piano. Agnes had taught Kathy to play and Kathy had first interested Thelma in the piano, and now Thelma was quite an accomplished pianist. Kathy wished Agnes knew how her influence lived on, although more than thirty years had passed since her death.

As they were stepping onto the train, Kathy's thoughts were interrupted by Mrs. Quigley, whom Kathy knew from church.

"It's a wonderful blueberry crop this year, isn't it?" Mrs. Quigley said.

"Yes, I can't get over how big the berries are," Kathy replied.

"Listen to this," said Mrs. Quigley. "I got me a cousin in Chicago, born there, lived there all her life. She called me up on the phone this mornin' and when I told her I was goin' to go pick blueberries, she asked whether I was bringin' a ladder with me. 'For what?' I asked. 'So you can reach them on the trees,' she said. I said, 'Blueberries don't grow on trees, they grow on bushes.' 'Oh, I thought they was fruit,' she says, 'like oranges and apples.' 'They are,' I says, 'but lots of fruit grows on bushes.' And then she got kinda mad at me and said 'Well how was I to know?' She ain't never seen a blueberry bush in her life — only seen blueberries at the grocer's. Can you imagine that?"

"How stupid she must be?" laughed Beth.

"Beth, we don't use that word," said Kathy.

"I'm not sure that she's stupid," said Mrs. Quigley, "but it goes to show you that livin' in the city distorts a person. I wouldn't want to live anywhere there wasn't all these woods and open country as we have around here."

"Chicago must be horrible!" said Thelma.

"Well, some must like it," Mrs. Quigley replied, "else they wouldn't live there."

"People only live there to make money," said Kathy. "But they don't realize how little money is worth it. I wouldn't live there for a million dollars."

"Me neither," said Beth.

"Well, I've been to Chicago a couple times," said Mrs. Quigley, "and it's a dirty, noisy place. It's nothing compared to the fresh air and clean water we have here. And it's too crowded, not quiet like here where you can at least hear yourself think."

"That's true," Kathy nodded as the train started to chug down the track, leaving the blueberry meadows far behind.

"Looks like you all made out well," said Mrs. Quigley. "Must be nice to have helpers. Couldn't get any of my family to come out. My husband just wants to lay around the house. I've three big boys, but do you think I could get one of them to come? Not that they'll argue when it comes time to eat the blueberry pie and muffins. But I shouldn't complain. It was a nice quiet day for me. A woman needs a break now and then, especially when she lives with all men. Nice to be out in the woods like this."

Kathy smiled in agreement. She felt her spirit refreshed by these beautiful dark woods.

Everyone on the train felt content. Bending down all day to pick berries was hard work, but everyone had a full bucket to make blueberry muffins, blueberry pie, blueberry pancakes, blueberry cookies, blueberry jam, blueberries on cereal and blueberries on ice cream. For the especially brave, there would be blueberry soup, that looked like paint and tasted worse, but even these people had to be admired for their blueberry passion. Yes, it had been a fine blueberry-picking day.

Will was pleased to see how many berries Henry had picked and to hear he had found some friendly people to lunch with. He could not place who the McCareys were, but since his parents had passed away so many years ago, he could remember few of their old friends' names, and caring for a family gave him little time to reminisce about happier, bygone days.

He hoped Henry would never know the worries he knew, yet he already felt he had failed his oldest son. He had long ago lost count of how many times Henry had come home from school with some award for winning a spelling bee or a math competition. Will and Margaret loved all their children, but they had had the greatest hopes for Henry. One night last winter, Henry had overheard his parents' fretting over money; he had then volunteered to leave school and go to work. His parents had insisted he finish school, but he had argued that he wanted to be a carpenter like his father; why delay his working when he could earn money for the family? For two days, Margaret had cried with frustration, but then she had begrudgingly agreed that Henry was right. Will remembered how he had argued and lost when Clarence wanted to go on the ore boats; now he wished he had told his brother how proud he was that he had followed his heart's desire. Henry viewed carpentry as a noble vocation, even a family tradition since his father and Grandpa Dalrymple were carpenters, and the family needed the money, so Will did not dissuade him.

"There are always the other children," Will consoled Margaret. "Perhaps with Henry's income, we can put something away to send Roy to college."

Margaret accepted the situation, not as the destruction, but only the deferral of her dreams for her children.

But Margaret had other worries than her children today. Will and Henry arrived home to find her in the kitchen with red eyes.

Will, expecting the worst, asked what was wrong.

"My parents are crazy, that's what," said Margaret.

"Why? What's happened?" he asked, sitting down and taking her hand, while Henry stood in suspense; the boy's role as a breadwinner had made him sensitive to family crises. His parents worried he would become hardened by their troubles, while he worried his younger siblings would lose their innocence as he had. He had taken up a heavy burden to lighten his parents' own, but now his mother's tone made him fear something worse than financial troubles.

"My brother was just here," said Margaret. "He says Mother and Father are coming out to see us this evening."

"So?" said Will.

"They're coming to tell us they're moving to California."

"California!"

Will and Henry gasped together.

"Yes, they're going to live near Sarah. I don't know why I'm surprised; Sarah always did get everything, even though she was the laziest of us, but I never thought she'd get our parents."

Before more could be said, Eleanor ran in to announce that Grandpa and Grandma's wagon was coming down the road.

Will went to wash up before his in-laws arrived. Henry followed his mother outside. When her parents climbed down from the wagon, Margaret said, "I already know. Charles was just here to tell me."

"Oh, honey," said Christina, climbing up the porch steps. "I wanted to tell you myself. I was afraid you'd be upset. Let's go inside. I'll make you some tea. You look tired."

Margaret followed her mother, willing to be spoiled considering the current state of her nerves.

"It's my fault," Charles Dalrymple said, while giving his grandchildren candy despite their mother's protests. "You know the bronchitis I had last spring is still hanging on. At my age, the doctor says it could be fatal if I get seriously ill again. He suggested we move to a warmer climate."

"We thought California would be best since Sarah is there," Christina said. "You know we hate to leave all of you, but we would like to see Sarah, and poor Theo is already twelve and has never met his grandparents."

Margaret could care less about Theodore. The kid had a senator for a stepfather so what did he need with grandparents? Was it not enough that Sarah had a rich husband? Did she have to have their parents as well?

"And Sarah gets lonely out in California," Christina added. "She can't always be in Washington with her husband. She's looking forward to our coming."

"I'll miss you," Margaret started to sob.

"We can always come back to visit," said Charles, "and we can write letters and talk on the telephone."

Margaret had never made a long distance telephone call in her life. She and Will could never afford such a thing.

"Hello, Charles, Christina," said Will, trying to be cheerful as he joined the family in the kitchen. "I hear you're moving away."

"Yes, in a couple months," said Charles. "Before the snow comes anyway."

"We have to sell the house first," said Christina. "We've started cleaning it out, so we brought you a few things we thought you might like."

The "few things" were a mammoth load of household products from dishtowels and throw rugs to toys the grandchildren played with when visiting. From one sack, Charles drew out an old but sturdy hammer.

"This is for Henry," he said. "It's the hammer my father bought for me when I started out as a carpenter. I won't be pounding too many more nails at my age, so I thought Henry could use it."

Henry accepted the hammer with reverence.

"The rest of what's in that sack is for Roy," said Charles. "I can't imagine those old books are very interesting, but he seems to like them."

Roy looked inside the sack to discover Sir Walter Scott's Waverley novels piled one volume on top of another.

"Oh, Father, those were Grandpa's," said Margaret.

"Thank you," said Roy, instantly claiming them when he sensed his mother's disapproval. "I'll take good care of them. I promise."

"Those silly books," Margaret said. "All they do is put foolish ideas into people's heads, making them wish for things that will never happen."

"I remember you enjoyed them when you were Roy's age," Christina said.

"I hope they'll make him dream big," said Will. He thought tales of valor might inspire Roy to strive for more beyond what his parents would ever have.

"I just don't want the boy to grow up disappointed in his dreams," said Margaret.

"You aimed high when you went after me," joked Will, "and you won the prize."

"I wouldn't call you much of a prize when I have to clean out your spittoon," Margaret snapped. Then, instantly ashamed by her rudeness to her husband before her children and parents, she fled upstairs in tears.

"I'm sorry," said Charles. "We didn't mean to upset her."

"She just needs time to get used to the idea of our going," said Christina. "Let's go home, Charles. We'll come back tomorrow to talk with her."

Will saw his in-laws out, after reminding the children to thank their grandparents for the gifts.

"It's silly," Margaret said when she and Will went to bed. "Lots of people get bronchitis in winter, but they don't move to California."

"Maggie, don't be selfish," Will warned, his own patience wearing thin after she had snapped at him. "You know you want what's best for your father; you should be thankful for all the years you've had them here. It won't hurt to share them with Sarah."

"Why should I share them? Sarah has everything, and she didn't even work for it. We work our fingers to the bone, and we still have nothing. Not everyone can marry a rich husband."

"Since I'm such a poor provider," Will snarled, "maybe I should sleep on the sofa."

"Will!" Margaret shouted, but he was already stomping downstairs with his pillow and an afghan. She did not go after him. She was relieved to be alone to mope, and she felt too guilty to apologize yet. Will settled himself down on the sofa, feeling what a failure he was at supporting his family. He loved Maggie, but a man did not need his weaknesses thrown in his face.

1921

Nearly three years after the cease-fire of World War I, Marquette honored one of its favorite sons who had died for his country. Perry Hatch, local scoutmaster, organized boys throughout Upper Michigan to build a monument to Bart King, former leader of Methodist Troop I, who had fallen at the Battle of the Argonne. Throughout that summer and into the autumn, the scouts hauled four thousand pounds of sand, sixteen hundred pounds of cement, ten tons of trap rock, and fifteen hundred white boulders four hundred feet above Lake Superior to the top of Sugarloaf Mountain. Bartlett King was well remembered by the older scouts, and those too young to remember him had heard many stories about what a good scoutmaster he had been. Others were willing to honor him as a means to heal their own proud but grieving hearts for brothers and friends lost during the war. The end result of the scouts' repeated exodus up Sugarloaf Mountain was an obelisk that rose twelve feet into the sky on top of a four hundred foot cliff. Attached to the monument was a plaque to honor the beloved scout leader.

Years later, when these scouts, and even their children and grandchildren, had passed away, the obelisk would remain, overlooking Lake Superior and the City of Marquette, almost as permanent a landmark as the granite cliffs and great lake itself. Sugarloaf Mountain would become a popular tourist attraction, with each year thousands hiking its rugged trails to its rocky summit from where they could look down as if perched atop clouds at the rising, cold fog from frigid blue waters below. Here Father Marquette had once stood, admiring the rugged wilderness home of the Chippewa he served. Today he would have found a different people in this land, but the air was still as pure, the lake the same unchanging multitude of blues, the breeze as crisp, and the people just as devoted caretakers of this land as those who came before them.

But Upper Michigan is not always a paradise. Had the scouts looked down to the winding road below them, they would have seen a small vehicle racing along at an alarming speed.

The Big Bay Road points north from Marquette, curves along Sugarloaf Mountain, skirts the shore of Lake Superior, then blazes through the forest to the little village of Big Bay and on to the Huron Mountain Club. Originally built to provide easy access to the Club for its wealthy members, the road also served as access to little mining communities like Birch, which had operated for only a few years. The rugged terrain and rocky hills had resulted in one of the most treacherous, sharp twisting roads in the country.

Harry Cumming Jr., formerly a soldier in the United States Army, was racing down the Big Bay Road in his automobile; in hot pursuit were the Michigan State Police. Harry Jr. had returned home from war, traded his uniform for civilian clothes, and gone into business as a bootlegger.

Many upstanding citizens viewed prohibition as the most unreasonable law ever passed in Marquette County or the United States, and plenty of people were willing to break the law for a good drink. Harry Cumming Jr. was willing to aid all these willing lawbreakers. Harry had a friend with a cabin hidden in the woods off the Big Bay Road. This friend had his own still where he made liquor, and Harry had quite a profitable little business selling his friend's liquor to dozens of discreet clients across Marquette County. He had pursued this illustrious career for the past year, but in the last few weeks, the law had caught on to Harry Jr.'s activities. The police did not know whether he were carrying alcohol today, but when they caught him speeding, they found a reason to pull him over. And Harry, who was carrying liquor, decided he had better try to outrun the law.

A mad chase ensued through Big Bay and Birch, down the Big Bay Road and into Marquette. Harry Jr. raced through the Normal School's campus, past churches, past residences, down Washington Street, down Front Street and then out of town, past the Rock Cut and the prison, through Harvey and Chocolay Township, then down a dirt road, always trying to shake the patrol cars. But before he could reach Skandia, he ran out of gas, and five minutes later, he was surrounded, then handcuffed, and his vehicle searched. To the Marquette County Jail he went to await his trial and sentencing.

🍁   🍁   🍁

Will had often thought that to buy *The Mining Journal* was a waste of money when the family could barely afford food for the table. Margaret, however, insisted the newspaper be purchased whenever she went into town. She would have bought *Harper's Bazaar*, the fashion magazines, or those rags about the movie stars if she could afford them. Deprived of such simple entertainments, *The Mining Journal* had to fulfill Margaret's longings for gossip. In the "City Brevities" column, she discovered who was visiting Marquette, who had gone on vacation, who was recently engaged, and who had married. She perused it with avid interest.

Today Henry had brought *The Mining Journal* home from town, but scarcely glancing at it, he had completely missed the headline about the wild car chase that resulted in the arrest of a moonshine dealer. Margaret believed alcohol consumption one of mankind's greatest sins; she would have passed over the article without interest if her eye had not caught Harry Cumming Jr.'s name. Then she read with fascinated alarm. Those Cummings had shamed the family again. Thank goodness they did not have the Whitman name. She knew Will wished to be on better terms with his sister's family, but again Margaret felt they were better off without such undesirable relatives. She would have to tell Will about his nephew's crimes, but she hoped he would not contact the Cummings as a result.

"It's too bad, but I can't do anything about it," said Will, after reading the article. "I'm sorry my nephew's in trouble; he's going to need a good lawyer, but we don't have the money to help him out, and I sure can't be a character witness for the boy."

Margaret was surprised by her husband's indifferent response. But Will could not express his sorrow even to his wife. He had long wanted to march into that house and take away Sylvia and her children to live with him, but now the children were grown, and today's news verified that they resembled their father more than their mother. Will grieved that the sweet little boy who had sat on his lap, whom he had taught to play pattycake, whom he had helped to build castles out of blocks, was now a criminal. If only — but why think about it? He could do nothing to help.

"I won't be in here long. My lawyer will appeal; he'll get me out."

Two Marquette prison guards smiled knowingly at Harry Cumming Jr.'s boasts.

"If your lawyer was any good, you wouldn't be here now," said one. He was a young guard, cocky but not as foolhardy as the prisoner. The other guard was a tall, solidly built man whose piercing blue eyes stared out of a deeply jowled face. Sixty years of hard living had written sympathetic tolerance on his face.

"Just behave yourself and you'll get out early for good behavior," he counseled the inmate.

"I'll be out in a few days," Harry retorted. "I don't need advice from you goons."

"I'd watch my tongue if I were you," said the older guard. "I'm sure you've already broken your mother's heart. You don't want to give her any more grief."

Harry had intended to make another smart-aleck remark, but as prison guard Patrick McCarey had long ago discovered, the mention of a boy's mother could set guilt into his conscience, and a boy who did not wish to hurt his mother was not lost yet.

Harry Jr. was only one of many young men, scarcely more than boys, who found themselves in the Marquette Branch Prison. Almost since the prison had opened in 1889, Patrick McCarey had served there as a guard. During those years, Patrick had seen hundreds of young men come into the prison; some were deeply hardened criminals, but most had just made bad decisions. After all these years, Patrick remained amazed that his occupation was as a prison guard. He knew that but for his own good luck, he could have been one of the confused young men behind bars. Only, he would have been in a British prison, unless he had instead been shot for treason, including slaying an officer of the British crown. Patrick had committed murder in self-defense, but he had chosen to place himself in a position where he had been forced to defend himself. He had fled to America to escape arrest, and to change his life after that.

Many of the prisoners reminded Patrick of the rash young man he had been. These young men saw themselves as rebelling against an oppressive government, but while Patrick had fought for his nation's freedom, these boys broke the law to drink liquor; Patrick knew the situations were not comparable; still, he liked a drink himself; he had his own stash of whiskey hidden away in his basement. He never would have said so in public, but if drinking liquor were against the law, then the law was against the American right to pursue happiness.

When he went home that evening, Patrick told Kathy that a young man named Cumming was in the prison.

"It doesn't surprise me," Kathy said. "Those Cummings are nothing but white trash."

"Why do you say that?" asked Patrick, shocked by her vehemence.

Kathy paused a moment. She could not tell Patrick how upset she was that those Cummings boys had returned from the war when her own Frank, her good sweet boy, had not.

"Don't we know some Cummings?" Patrick asked. "The boy looks familiar."

"You probably saw his picture in the papers," said Kathy. "He was in the war. Even got decorated for something or other."

"Really? Then how does a good soldier end up in prison?"

"He comes from a bad family," Kathy replied.

"What do you know about the Cummings?" asked Patrick. "I can't seem to place them."

"We knew his grandparents. His mother is Sylvia Whitman, Jacob Whitman's daughter. Sylvia married a Cumming, a horrible man from everything I've heard; apparently the boys take after their father."

"Maybe so," said Patrick, "but if the boy has Whitman blood in him, he can't be all bad; he just didn't get a proper upbringing. His great-grandfather, Nathaniel Whitman, was very kind to me when I first moved to Marquette. His great-grandmother, Cordelia Whitman, took a while to come around to liking me, but she was the one who sent me to shovel snow for your mother, remember? We probably wouldn't have met if it hadn't been for the Whitmans."

"Oh, we would have met," Kathy smiled. "I would have seen you around town and laid my snare for you. I wouldn't have let a goodlooking fellow like you get away."

Patrick forgot about Harry Jr. until the next day when he made his prison rounds. Harry was sitting alone on his bunk, staring at the wall, his back to the cell bars. Patrick stopped and debated whether he should speak to him. Harry heard Patrick's footsteps, and after a few seconds, when he did not hear them move on, he turned around to see the husky old man spying on him.

"What the hell do you want?" he spat out.

"Just came to see how you are," said Patrick. "Are you comfortable?"

"I'm in prison," said Harry. "Am I supposed to be comfortable? What do you care?"

Patrick hesitated. He had known worse criminals who had left prison to live straight, decent lives. He thought he could win this young man over. He felt he owed it to old Nathaniel and Cordelia Whitman.

"I hear you were in the war," he said.

"Yeah, so."

"My sons were in the war."

"Yeah, so were about a million people."

"One of my sons was killed in France."

"Yeah," said Harry. He wondered what the damn mick wanted.

"I've heard you were quite a soldier, a staff sergeant they tell me," said Patrick.

"It wasn't anything," Harry replied. His war record had been filled with merit, but he did not want to talk about it when he had fallen so much since he returned home.

"If you did well in the army, how'd you end up here?"

"How else was I supposed to end up? The war ended so I came home."

Patrick persisted, wanting an honest answer.

"Why did you go from serving your country to breaking the law?"

"You don't know anything about me," said Harry. "You can't understand. You've got a decent job as a prison guard so you're respected in this little town. Me, I got a drunk for a father; no matter what I do, I won't never live that down around here. I have to do something to make money to support the family since my old man is too drunk to work. I got my parents and a sister to look after, and my younger brother's about as useless as my old man. Selling liquor makes me a nice little profit, plus I can get booze for the old man real cheap — if he goes long without a drink, he starts smacking around my ma."

"Your family might need the money," said Patrick, "but I bet your mother needs her son more. Now that you're in here, who's going to help her?"

"Leave my mother out of this; my family's none of your damn business."

Patrick walked away without another word. He would try again when Harry was not so angry. Then he would tell the boy that his mother came from good people, that he had known the Whitmans, and he believed the same good was in Harry. If the boy had been such a good soldier, he could still be a good citizen.

When Patrick arrived home that evening, Kathy handed him the newspaper with the comment, "I told you those Cummings are nothing but white trash. They're all alike. It's a shame, but it's the truth."

Patrick skimmed the front page of the paper, searching for his wife's meaning until he saw the headline "YOUNG WOMAN DIES IN CAR ACCIDENT." Serena Cumming, age eighteen, had been killed on the Big Bay Road when her car hit a patch of ice and was spun off the road into a tree. She had been accompanied by a young man, who had suffered only minor injuries.

"Probably her lover," said Kathy, referring to the boy. "I'll bet she was drunk too. Probably making her brother's liquor deliveries since he's in prison."

Patrick said nothing. He would not judge a girl he had never known. What troubled him was how Harry Jr. would react to his sister's loss.

"What are you doing here?" Harry Cumming Sr. laughed when his oldest son stepped into the funeral home. "Did you break out?"

"No," Harry Jr. replied. "They let me out just for the funeral. They weren't going to, but this guard named McCarey talked the warden into letting me come. Of course, there's a couple cops outside the door so I don't make a run for it."

"Come on in. It's a closed casket so you can't see your sister. She was too bruised and broken up for anyone to look at her."

Harry followed his father into the funeral parlor. They slowly approached the casket, but neither knelt down to pray. When his father stepped away to greet another guest, Harry stood awkwardly, afraid to look around for his mother; he did not know whether he could bear her tears. He wondered whether his brother had come home for the funeral.

When he turned around, he saw the room was mostly empty. His parents and a few neighbors were the only ones present. There was no one he dared talk with.

"Please be seated. The service will now begin," said the funeral home director as the minister stepped up to the pulpit.

Harry waited for everyone else to find seats. The chair beside his mother was left open; he felt he should sit with his family, so he slid into the empty chair and whispered, "Hello, Ma." She only stared forward as the minister began to speak.

He bowed his head to mourn his sister and the poor example he had set for her. He had been gone to the war when Serena had most needed his guidance; had he been home then, maybe he could have stopped her from becoming an alcoholic like his father. A couple times, he glanced at his mother, wanting to express sympathy to her, but her face remained set like stone; her eyes were dry, too exhausted from grief to cry more.

When the service ended, Harry turned to his mother, but Sylvia immediately stood up and stepped away to thank a neighbor for coming. Harry realized she would not speak to him. His brother had not come. He only had his father to speak to.

"How are you holding up, Pa?" he asked of the family member who least deserved sympathy.

"Okay," Harry Sr. replied. "Can't wait to get out of this monkey suit. I could really use a drink. Ain't had one all day."

Harry Jr. observed it was only two in the afternoon. He was silent a few seconds, then said, "I better go. The cops are waiting for me. Take care of yourself."

"Bye."

His old man could not find a kind word for his son, not even when he was returning to prison. Harry Jr. walked quickly out the door, where the cops grabbed his arms and escorted him to the car. Soon he was back behind prison bars where he could no longer endanger society, where he would not see the stares or hear the whispers of the townspeople who believed he and his family were less than them.

After the funeral luncheon, Sylvia and her husband returned home. Harry was restless after the sober ritual of politeness he had barely endured. He poured himself a drink, then left it half full beside the sofa while he drifted into his daily nap.

Sylvia went into the kitchen to tackle the pile of dishes from the few neighbors who were Christian enough to have stopped by, and to whom she had offered refreshments, less to be a good hostess than to divert conversation from her daughter's tragic death.

As she finished rinsing the last plate, she saw the mailman pass by. After drying her hands, she peeked into the parlor where her husband remained crumpled up on the sofa. Then she went out to the mailbox.

Her brother had sent a sympathy card; she had not expected one, much less the ten dollar bill inside the card. No note was attached, just her brother and his wife's names — the wife she had never met; whenever she had seen Will's wife downtown, Sylvia had crossed the street or ducked into a store to avoid their meeting, as much for Margaret's sake as her own. Sylvia knew Will could not afford such a generous gift as ten dollars. She also knew if Harry found the money, he would use it to buy liquor. She did not know where he would find alcohol with Serena dead and Harry in prison, but he would find a way.

Sylvia found an envelope and placed the ten-dollar bill inside. Then she found a scrap of paper; before inserting it in the envelope, she scribbled:

> Thank you, Will, but I'm sure you need this more than me. Put it away for one of your children. I pray they end up happier than my children have.
> Love, Sylvia

Many times Sylvia had successfully blocked her estranged brother from her thoughts. Other days her heart ached for him. Whenever she glimpsed his sons around town, she was struck by how much they resembled their father. Then she longed for happier times. The sympathy card confirmed that no matter the distance between her and Will, they still loved each other.

"It's Sunday," said Kathy. "After all your years of service at that prison, they ought to let you have the Lord's Day off from work."

"I'll have three days off for Christmas," Patrick replied. "Besides, it'll be an easy day; we're showing a movie this afternoon; that always cheers up the prisoners so they'll behave. I'll see you tonight." He kissed her on the cheek.

"All right," she sighed. "I haven't figured out what we'll have for supper yet."

"I'm not fussy," said Patrick. "Say, did I tell you there's talk of building a sunken garden at the prison this spring? That'll keep the inmates busy."

"That'll be nice; the prison is such an imposing building that a garden might soften it up a little. Have a good day. I hope everyone treats you well."

Patrick frequently walked to the prison, even in winter. He made his way to South Front Street, then started up the hill toward Harvey. Hardly any snow was on the ground yet compared to what there would be in February and March when the banks might be as tall as Patrick's own six feet. At age sixty-one, Patrick felt his lengthy walks to the prison were beneficial to him.

Kathy wanted him to retire, but he would not quit working until necessary. He was as large and strong as when he was young, even if a bit more stout now. His walks kept him fit, despite his cheeks sagging into jowls.

He spent a quiet morning making his rounds. Church services usually kept the prisoners well behaved on Sundays. When time came for the movie, Patrick found a seat in the back of the room where he could keep his eye on the men. Sitting up front was Warden Catlin and a couple other guards. A movie in a dark room allowed the prisoners temporarily to escape their feelings of guilt or anger, and it gave them relief from worrying over their loved ones at home, whom they hoped still loved them.

For thirty years, Patrick had been an alert, conscientious guard. Last night, however, he had not slept well, and despite his protestations that he felt as young as ever, he was a bit sleepy after his brisk walk to work, so he fell into a little doze.

Then three convicts, Harper, Perry, and Roberts, made their move. The sudden ruckus and shouting immediately woke Patrick. He opened his eyes just as one of the guards turned on the lights. Chaos was everywhere. Four hundred shouting prisoners, guards whacking convicts with canes. Desperate men seizing this moment as their chance to escape. The warden found himself surrounded and fighting to break free from the mob.

Patrick pushed his way across the room, trying to reach the center of the melee. Before he had moved three feet, a burly prisoner threw him to the ground, took his cane, and started to strike him with it.

"The warden's been stabbed!" someone shouted. Patrick's stomach cringed in fear.

He only let himself be struck once. Then he grabbed the end of his cane and pulled his assailant to the ground while jumping to his own feet. He had to reach the warden; the man's life depended on fast action. The other guards were also trying to reach their leader and pull him from his attackers. Across the crowded room, Patrick saw his boss surrounded by guards; the warden was struggling to walk, but excruciating pain was already soaring through him from the stabbing. His men pulled him from the room while the other guards fought to restrain the prisoners.

Suddenly, a convict jumped in front of Patrick.

"No chance, old man!" he shouted. He had a knife. Patrick realized he had lost his cane somewhere. He was helpless, unarmed. He put up his arm to ward off the lunging knife, but the prisoner was faster and stronger than him.

"Stop!"

Another prisoner jumped between Patrick and his assailant. Patrick watched as a powerful hand gripped his attacker's wrist and squeezed it until the knife fell from a hand of white knuckles. Patrick's savior twisted the man's arm behind his back and forced him to his knees.

"Boys, over here," shouted the hero. In a minute, two guards had come to restrain the convict.

Patrick felt shaken by how helpless he had been during the attack; he was also stunned by who had rescued him.

"You okay, Patrick?" one of his fellow guards shouted.

"Fine, fine," Patrick called. Then slowly, he said, "Thank you, Harry."

"Don't worry about it. You stood up for me when I needed help," Harry Jr. replied, referring to how Patrick had gotten him permission to attend his sister's funeral.

Patrick smiled. He had been right about Harry's character all along.

"Cumming, get back to your cell!" shouted a guard.

"I'll see ya," Harry said, then obeyed the order. Patrick went back to his rounds, making sure none of the prisoners had escaped during the conflict.

The warden and deputy warden had both been fatally wounded. For Patrick, the greatest horror had been how easily he was overcome and nearly victimized by the prisoners. He realized he was getting too old to remain at the prison. Within a couple months, he would quit working there.

Kathy was upset when he told her about the attack. Patrick would have kept it from her, but he knew she would read about it in the newspaper. After her initial concern, Kathy grew silent as Patrick described how the Cumming boy had saved him.

"It's okay. I'm fine," he said, when she made no reply.

"I'm glad," she said, taking his hand. "I wouldn't want to lose you."

That night, Kathy silently prayed, "Dear God, forgive me for hateful, selfish thoughts. It was wrong for me to question why the Cumming boys should come home from the war when Frank did not. You understand the reasons for these things better than I do. I don't know why You took my son from me, but it was wrong for me to be angry with Sylvia because misfortune was not brought upon her. I think the lesson I was supposed to learn is to trust You; I think You brought Harry Jr. home from the war to save Patrick's life. Thank You, God, for saving my husband and for bringing Harry home from the war. I hope he does much more good in his life. I still miss my son, but I will not be jealous of others because of my own misfortune."

The cease-fire had been three years earlier, but only tonight did the Great War end for Kathy McCarey. Now she finally released the pain. Always there would be wars, always injustice and misery in the world, but good existed as well, and she would concentrate upon finding it.

For Christmas, she sent Sylvia Cumming a giant fruit basket with a kind note. She hoped her double expression of gratitude for Harry Jr's actions and sympathy for Serena's loss would lighten the grieving mother's heart.

1926

"The poor boy wants to go to college, and he's worked so hard, earning all those perfect marks in school."

"I know," said Will.

"It's just hard, especially since we couldn't send Henry."

"I know," Will repeated. He wished Margaret would drop the subject.

"Roy deserves to go. Not that I don't love all my children, but I think he's the smartest and most likely to succeed."

"He'll just have to work like Henry," said Will. "He can always save his money to go to college later."

"Henry didn't even finish school because he felt he needed to help us out. I don't want Roy to feel that way."

Will was tired of discussing it. Margaret was convinced he had talked Henry out of college, but Henry had felt no desire to go, preferring to work with his hands. But Margaret was right — Roy was different. Roy would make a fine professor, or lawyer, or doctor. The boy was interested in everything. Will was constantly amazed by Roy's observations about the smallest things Will had never thought to consider — everything from tadpoles and the migration of birds, to chemistry and theology. Will would gladly have sent Roy to college, but he saw no way to do it. There simply was no money. Roy would have to earn and save his own money if he wished to go to college.

"There's no point in waiting any longer to tell him," said Will.

"But how do we break it to him?" asked Margaret.

"He knows we're poor. We never promised to send him to college. We told him we would try is all. I'll talk to him when he gets home from school."

Will did not want his son to witness his mother's tears, which would only make the situation worse. He waited until Roy came home from school and went out to the barn to do his chores. Then Will followed him.

"Roy, you'll graduate from high school next week," he began.

"Yes," said Roy, stopping his raking when he heard his father's serious tone.

"You've done well in school. Your ma and I are both proud of you."

"I know, Pa. I want you to be proud of me."

"Your ma and I," said Will, taking a deep breath, "have been hoping for a long time to send our boys to college. We wanted Henry to go, but we couldn't afford it, and he didn't want to go anyway."

"I know," said Roy, his heart surging with hope his future would be different from Henry's.

"Your Ma and I wanted to send you to college too."

Roy waited. He grew afraid.

Will took the rake from his son's hand and leaned it against the wall.

"Roy, you know we'd do anything for you, but we just can't afford to send you to college. We're in debt actually, although we've never said so because we didn't want you children to worry. We're sorry."

Roy was disappointed, but when he saw how his father struggled, he interrupted him. "It's okay, Pa. I understand. I didn't expect — "

Both grew silent as they heard Henry open the barn door and saw his shadow cast across the floor by the late afternoon sun.

Henry knew Roy longed to attend college. Roy had confessed to him, in their cramped little bedroom, how he thirsted to learn, to spend hours in a giant library where people actually read important books and took time to study rather than just work all summer and shovel snow all winter. Roy wanted to be respected for his talents, for his intelligence, and not always to be looked down on because he was poor. Now Henry knew from the suffocating look on Roy's face that his brother would never see those grand libraries.

Henry was embarrassed to have interrupted, but he knew Roy would have to accept the situation rather than dwell on it.

"Roy, what will you do now?" he asked.

"I don't know. Work on the farm I guess."

"We thought," said Will, "that if you found a job and made your own money, you could save up for college; don't give up on going; you just have to postpone it a while longer."

"Maybe," Roy frowned. He was not afraid of hard work, but it would take years of saving before he could go to college. He felt hopeless.

"Your ma and I," said Will, "want you to keep any money you earn. You can live with us rent-free and find a job in town. That'll help you save faster."

"What kind of job could I get?" asked Roy. "What can I do?"

"I know a guy who works up at the Huron Mountain Club every summer," said Henry. "Maybe you could start by working up there. I know he makes good money."

"That's an idea," said Will. "There's millionaires who spend their summers there in cottages bigger than our house. You might meet someone who'll take a liking to you and help you get ahead in the world."

Henry and Will both sounded optimistic, but Roy remained doubtful.

"What would I do at the Huron Mountain Club?"

"All kinds of things," said Henry. "They need carpenters and maintenance people, tour guides for hikes and fishing expeditions. You're a great fisherman, and nearly as good a carpenter as me and Pa. Even if you started out waiting tables, they would soon realize what an asset you are to them."

"I don't want to wait tables. I'd rather be outside."

"Well, you probably could be," said Henry. "I'll talk to this guy I know tomorrow when I go into town. I just saw him a couple days ago, and he said he'd be going up to the Club next week. I'll tell him to mention your name there. It can't hurt."

"I don't know," said Roy. He had never worked anywhere except on the farm. He had always worked hard at school, but to enter the work force was unnerving.

"Henry, you mention Roy's name to this fellow you know," Will decided for his son. "Think what an opportunity it'll be to meet all those rich folks up there. Besides, when you go to college, Roy, you'll have to be far away, so this'll give you a chance to adjust to being away from home."

"I guess," Roy said. He thanked his brother for his help, but all he really wanted was to be left alone so he could hide up in the hayloft and mope.

Margaret remained determined that Roy would go to college. She did not tell the family her plan, but everyday when she went to get the mail, she hoped to find there what would make their lives easier.

She had put her plan into effect weeks before after attending a funeral at the Baptist Church. Mr. Bissell, one of the church's oldest members, had passed away. Margaret had agreed to help with the funeral luncheon. After everyone had eaten and the dishes were washed, Margaret had gone over to give the widow her sympathies. She had found Mrs. Bissell and her daughter looking at old photographs.

"They're pictures of my Zeb," Mrs. Bissell had explained. "Here's one of him in his Civil War uniform."

Margaret had looked at the faded old picture. She had never known Mr. Bissell as anything but a withered, old prune of a man. From the picture, she did not think he had looked much different when twenty.

"You'll still receive father's pension now, won't you, Mother?" Mrs. Bissell's daughter had asked.

"Your husband got a pension for being in the war?" Margaret had asked in surprise. Suddenly, her thoughts were racing. Will's father had fought in that war — had he received a pension?

"Yes," Mrs. Bissell had explained. "Soldiers can apply for pensions. So can their widows or children who were minors when their father died."

That night, Margaret had asked Will whether his father had gotten a Civil War pension. Will was uncertain, but he did not think his father had ever applied for one. Margaret had said nothing more, but she was convinced her father-in-law had been denied one of his rights. Furthermore, both Will and Clarence had been under eighteen when their father died. Perhaps pension money was due to them. The next day, she had walked into town, and at the Marquette County Courthouse, she asked for the address to write to. The result was the following letter.

April 5, 1926
Dear Sir,

I am writing regarding the pension of Jacob Whitman, a corporal in the 27th Michigan regiment during the Civil War. I am writing for my husband, William Whitman, the only living son of Jacob Whitman. He is unable to write because of bad arthritis in his hand. I believe my husband should have received money from his father's pension when his father died as both he and his younger brother, now deceased, were under age at the time of their father's death. Their mother had died before their father so she never received pension money either as his widow.

I am writing because I believe this money was due to my husband at the time of his father's death in 1897, although it was unknown to him at the time that he could receive pension money.

Times are very hard for my husband and me. We live on a farm, but it barely produces enough to support us and our five children. My oldest son is twenty-one and he works hard to help us, but he needs to have an operation for appendicitis. I have another son, eighteen, who is very smart and wants to go to college, but we cannot afford this for him. He is a good boy and if he could get an education, he would be able to help us out better with money. My other three children are all under fourteen and too young to work. If we could have just a few hundred dollars, it would make our days less dark and life easier.

I know you will be reasonable, and may Jesus bless you. Times are hard but our Heavenly Father is always ready to lighten our burdens when we trust in Him.

Yours respectfully,

Mrs. William Whitman
Rural Route 1
Marquette, Michigan

Margaret had written and rewritten this letter, obsessing over whether it would bring sympathy. She believed the money was owing to them, but she did not know whether the government would give it to her. She had tried to explain the situation truthfully, although perhaps she had exaggerated about Will's sore hand, and while Henry's stomach was always upset, he had never been diagnosed with appendicitis, but she worried he might, and how could she know for sure what was wrong with him if there were no money for him to go to the doctor? And certainly the government should invest in a smart young man like Roy. If the government truly cared about the American people, it would aid her family out of gratitude for her father-in-law's service in saving the Union sixty years ago.

But today when a letter arrived from the government, Margaret's heart sank.

Re: Widow Division
Jacob Whitman
27th Mich. Inf.
April 29, 1926
Dear Madam:

We have reviewed the request you have made and apologize that we are not able to concede with your request for payment regarding the pension of your deceased grandfather. Our records show that his widow received his pension up until the time of her death in 1908. As pensions are only payable to widows or underage children, you are not entitled to further claims.

Sincerely,

A.Q. Edmundson
Acting Commissioner

Margaret was baffled by this letter. She had first only glanced through it to find out whether they would receive any money. Then she reread it. The government must have made some mistake. They thought she was writing for her grandfather, and they said his widow died in 1908. Margaret knew Will's mother had died right after Clarence was born in 1884. She was extremely irritated by the mistake. Was this not what one always expected of the U.S. Government — to make a mess of things? But there was still hope. She waited until the children had gone to bed and Will went to take his Saturday night bath. Then she wrote again.

Mr. A.Q. Edmundson
Acting Commissioner
Pension Claims Office
Washington D.C.
May 17, 1926
Dear Sir:

I am writing once more in regards to the pension of Corporal Jacob Whitman. In your last letter you spoke of him as my grandfather. He was not. He was my husband's father. I am writing for my husband because he has arthritis and his eyesight is not so good for writing letters. You also stated that Jacob Whitman's widow received his pension until her death in 1908. All Wrong! His wife died before him in 1884. He died in 1897, leaving behind two underage children: my husband, William, and his younger brother, Clarence.

I do not know where you got your information but the Marquette, Michigan County Courthouse records will verify these facts. I do hope you will not take this as a joke. I have never been so serious in my life. We are very poor. We have a small farm but cannot make a full living off it so my husband has to do carpentry work as well, leaving me and my little ones to run the farm. My two oldest boys also work to help us, but they cannot afford anything for themselves. My oldest son needs to have an operation for his appendix. My second oldest son is an honor student at school and should go to college, but we cannot afford it. If we had some money, he could go and then he would be better able to help us. Both my older children are good boys who do all they can for their parents. Even if you could see to send us just a few hundred dollars, I would ask God to bless you as it would be of great assistance to us.

Sincerely,

Mrs. William Whitman
Rural Route 1
Marquette, Michigan

Margaret laid down the pen and sealed the envelope. She hid the letter where Will would not see it before she could mail it in town on Monday. She hoped this time the commissioner would be kind enough to help her.

🍁   🍁   🍁

When the time came to leave, Roy borrowed an old suitcase from a neighbor and packed up his few clothes and a couple of his favorite books. No one in the family ever traveled, so a suitcase was a luxury the family did not possess. Roy felt frightened today. He would be nearly fifty miles from his family and only able to see them on the rare weekend when he could get a ride to Marquette. Henry had bought a used automobile last year — the first one owned in the family — so he promised to come visit his brother. But Roy knew his parents would never visit him; both refused to ride in Henry's "contraption," insisting they did not trust automobiles. Will had kept his horse and wagon, but the drive to the Club was too far for a wagon.

Margaret tried to smile and warmly hugged Roy, then gave him a sack lunch and some extra cookies. Roy had been annoyed with her that morning — she insisted he wear a freshly pressed shirt and a necktie because he would be "meeting all those millionaires at the Club" and he would "want to make a good first impression." Roy hated wearing ties, but he put up with it when he sensed how hard it was for his mother to see the first of her children leave home, even if only for the summer. His father and Henry had already left for work — they were helping to build a new house in town. Roy had said goodbye to them earlier, and since it was only seven in the morning, Eleanor, Ada, and Bill were still in bed. Roy had asked his mother not to wake them so his leaving would be easier. He stood now on the front porch with his mother, waiting for Lex, Henry's old schoolmate, who had gotten him the job and was coming to drive him up to the Club. His mother had promised not to hug him again before a stranger, so when Lex arrived, Roy quickly muttered goodbye and crawled into the passenger seat of the car.

"Aren't you going to kiss your mother goodbye?" asked Lex, tossing Roy's suitcase into the back seat.

"I did in the house," Roy blushed.

"All right, you ready?"

Roy nodded. Lex revved up the engine and turned the car down the dusty driveway onto the road.

They had to drive through Marquette, then north to the Big Bay Road, a series of sharp curves and potholes, the favorite drive of the well-to-do Huron Mountain Club members. Roy had never even seen the Club before. He wanted to ask Lex all about it, but Lex just stared ahead, looking confident and sure of himself. He was twenty-one, the same age as Henry, but taller, more solidly built, blond, and self-assured in a cocky way. At least, Roy assessed him as such while the car rolled down the road, the engine roaring so loudly it defeated any chance for conversation. Roy had plenty of questions, but he was too shy to ask them even if they could have been heard.

As the car passed among the hills, speeding by tall pine trees through which they could catch glimpses of Lake Superior, Roy felt increasingly alarmed. He had never been farther from home than Ishpeming. What if he did not like it at the Club? Would he be able to come home before the summer was over? Henry had promised he would visit him, but when would that be? It would be three months before summer was over, and maybe two months before Henry made good on his promise. Roy felt as if he would panic. If he could get Lex's attention, he thought he would ask to turn around. Instead, Roy closed his eyes so he would not see the miles pass, so he would not feel so far from home. He woke with a jolt when Lex hit a pothole. They were passing through the little town of Big Bay, the last outpost before the Huron Mountain Club.

"I hope you had a good nap," said Lex. "There's no time for napping at the Club."

Roy dared not ask what Lex meant. He hoped the cocky fellow was only trying to make him nervous. Henry had said Lex was an "okay guy" but Roy did not trust someone who had not tried once to make him feel comfortable on the trip up.

"There's the entrance," said Lex. A wooden gate stretched across the road with a little building beside it where sat the gatekeeper, endowed with power to determine who was worthy to enter this privileged realm.

The gatekeeper took one look at Lex and waved him through, saying, "This must be Roy. Welcome, son."

Roy could only nod before the gate opened and Lex whizzed the car through. Roy found himself on a thin winding road among the trees. For a moment, he wondered whether they would ever reach anything; then into view came a little village of cabins, each larger than his parents' farmhouse.

"Lake Superior's over there," Lex pointed, "and there's the dining hall, and there's the Fords' cabin, and over here are the rooms for the hired help."

Roy was dazzled. He had expected to see men in business suits, the Club's millionaire members; instead he saw a portly middle-aged man with a fishing pole over his shoulder, walking down to the lake. Lex parked the car. Roy got out, then reached in for his suitcase.

Lex came around to where Roy stood beside the car. He was taller than Roy. He stood and sized Roy up, from head to toe, making Roy feel inadequate. Lex sort of frowned — at least Roy thought so — then said, "Come on, I'll show you to your room, then give you the tour."

"Hello there, Lex," said a gentleman, coming around the corner of a building. "I see you brought an addition to our family here."

"Hi, Mr. Hebard. This is Roy Whitman," Lex replied. "Roy, Mr. Hebard's the Club President."

"Pleased to meet you, sir," said Roy, shaking hands.

"What was the name again?" asked Mr. Hebard.

"Roy — actually, it's Royal, but everyone calls me Roy."

"Royal, hey? Where'd you get a name like that?"

"Um — " Roy wondered why he had been dumb enough to mention his full name. He did not want to brag, but his mother's proud Scottish blood surged up in him, and his intimidation from being around this rich man made him unable to stop himself from explaining, "On my mother's side, I'm descended from the Stewarts, the royal family of Scotland, so that's why she named me Royal."

"Well, we're glad to have you, Royal. Only, I hope your royal blood doesn't mean you're unwilling to sweep floors and pound nails. Well, I'm off to go fishing. I'll see you boys later."

"Goodbye, Mr. Hebard," said Lex.

"Goodbye," said Roy, wishing he had never left home.

"Come on, Royal. I'll show your majesty to your regal bedchamber," Lex grinned.

Roy said nothing, just followed Lex across the yard, then up a flight of stairs. Roy wished Lex would help him with the suitcase. It was not heavy so much as awkward to carry up the narrow stairs. But Lex just stood and waited until he reached the top. Then he led him into a small room with two twin cots.

"Look, I told your brother you could bunk with me," said Lex. "That way you'll have someone to look out for you. Just remember this is summer camp for everyone except us. We're here to work. Don't mix too much with the members unless they ask you, and even then, remember your place. Since they're on vacation, for the most part they're in good moods, but you can never forget they're your bosses."

"I understand," said Roy, staring at the two twin beds squeezed into a little room. The room was smaller than what he and Henry shared at home, but he was thankful for a roommate, even if it were Lex.

"Do you want to change before we go to work?" Lex asked. His tone suggested the inappropriateness of Roy's clothes. Roy wanted to protest he had only worn the dress shirt and tie because his mother had insisted, but he feared he would only appear more foolish then, so he simply said, "Sure."

Lex sat down on the bed. Roy thought about asking him to leave the room. Even he and Henry never dressed in front of each other, but he did not want to seem prissy. He turned around and quickly changed his clothes, wishing he could be alone for just one minute.

"Looks like you've got some baby fat on you," laughed Lex as Roy changed his shirt. "We'll work that off you soon enough."

"I work hard on the farm," Roy defended himself.

"Yeah, your body just hasn't finished growing yet, but don't worry; we'll make a man of you. You ready?"

"I guess," said Roy, buckling his belt.

They went downstairs and back outside.

"How many other fellows live in this building?" asked Roy.

"Oh, about eight I'd say. I never took time to count. You won't see them until suppertime I imagine. Let's go down to the office to see what work you'll be doing."

"Hello, Lex," said a woman they met as they stepped outside. "How are you?"

"Just fine, Mrs. Paul," he said. "This here's Roy. He's starting work today."

"How nice," she said. "I'm going to need a little work done at our place. I'll let Mr. Hebard know to send you boys over to help."

"Sure, Mrs. Paul," said Lex. "Have a nice morning."

"Thank you. I will," she smiled and passed them by.

"Who's she?" asked Roy.

"Mrs. Paul."

"I know, but is she a club member?"

"Oh sure. She's one of the Longyear daughters. They live out in the Stone House on Ives Lake."

"Oh," said Roy. He remembered his mother telling him about the fantastic Longyear Mansion that had been moved from Marquette to Massachusetts. He wished he had met Mrs. Paul when he still had his necktie on, not this horrid old work shirt and his denims. His mother would be so excited to hear he had met a Longyear.

They went to the office; on the front steps, Lex met a couple of his pals who bunked in their building. He introduced Roy, who tried to join the conversation, but was quickly forgotten by the other boys. Instead, Roy stared about him. Part of him felt as if he had arrived in a ghost town, save for the few people leisurely walking about. The buildings were all old and rustic looking, like something out of a Western, except that they were surrounded by trees, and in Westerns, the towns were usually out on the plains or prairies. There were several simple, but large buildings, built like log cabins. None were painted, but a few were stained or treated so they would look weathered and blend in naturally with the trees, the lake, and the Huron Mountains. Roy liked how simple everything appeared; he wondered why the rest of life was not this way — here were all the necessities of life; what more could one want? To be surrounded by all this beauty would be worth going without running water or electricity — people had gone without them until just a few decades ago anyway. What mattered was that everyone seemed happy here where time appeared to have stopped or never existed; there was no urgency as in the modern, industrial, chaotic world. More peace was here than on the farm back home. Roy was too naive yet to learn the expense of such peace.

"Well, I better take Royal in to see what he has to do," said Lex, smacking his charge on the back to usher him away from his friends. Roy entered the office, hoping the other fellows had not heard how Lex had said his name.

Inside, he was soon given his orders. He would work side by side with Lex repairing the roof of a cabin. He was well suited for such a task after years of helping his father and brother with carpentry work.

"Next month," the office manager said, "we'll be at the height of the season. Then we'll need you and Lex to lead some nature hikes, but the next couple weeks will give you some time to learn the trails so you don't get lost. We have miles and miles of trails and woods to get lost in. Lex can lead the hikes this summer and you can go along as his assistant until you learn them yourself. By next summer, you should be an expert trailsman. That is, if you decide to come back next summer."

Roy thought it too early to decide, but he liked the looks of the place, and he wished to be polite. "It's a beautiful place," he said. "I can't imagine not wanting to come back next summer."

"That's a fine answer," said the manager. "Lex tells me you're some kind of genius in school, but you'll find all that booklearning is nothing compared to what you can learn about Mother Nature in the great Northern Woods."

"I'm always willing to learn," said Roy.

"Come on," said Lex, "we'll go see what repairs need to be done at that cabin."

The boys had barely stepped outside when a car cruised into the yard. They jumped back to keep from being hit as the vehicle screeched to a stop.

"Hello, Mr. Ford," said Lex.

"Hello," said the gentleman in the back seat.

Roy goggled. Was this *the* Mr. Ford? He had a chauffeur too. It must be.

"Mr. Ford, this is Roy," Lex said. "Roy is starting here this summer."

"Good," said Henry Ford. "I'm sure I'll see you boys around. It's a great place to be, Roy. Just watch out for the wild bears."

Roy laughed politely.

"It's no joke, boy," snapped Mr. Ford. "Those bears'll eat you alive if they get a chance."

Then seeing how quickly Roy sobered, Mr. Ford laughed. "Don't worry. The bears don't come into our little village too often. You mostly have to watch them out on the trails. Well, I'll see you boys around."

Mr. Ford gave the order for his chauffeur to drive on to his cabin.

"I bet you and Henry Ford'll get along great," said Lex. "You have so much in common."

"What do you mean?" asked Roy.

Lex laughed. "Why, Henry Ford is king of the automobile industry, and you're bona fide royalty."

Roy wished Lex would lay off him, but he was glad to be here. He wished his mother could know all the important people he had already met. He told himself this summer would be an adventure. Even if Lex were rather annoying, and even if he only pounded nails everyday, Roy decided he would make the best of things.

"Finally," said Margaret, ripping open another government letter.

June 14, 1926
Mrs. William Whitman
Rural Route 1
Marquette, Michigan
Dear Madam:

In regard to your letter of the 17th ultimo relative to the above entitled case of your deceased grandfather, it would appear that your letter was inadvertently filed regarding the case of another veteran of the Civil War. We thank you for clarifying the situation.

With reference to your grandfather, Jake Whitman, I have to advise you that he died in 1897 leaving no widow behind to receive his pension. Since she predeceased him, we are unable to appease your request of pension money for your family. We apologize for the confusion.

Sincerely,

A.Q. Edmundson
Acting Commissioner

"My grandfather again!" gasped Margaret, almost seeing red in her frustration with the government's mistakes. "What a fool this commissioner must be." Then she dug in her desk for paper to compose yet another letter.

June 21, 1926
Dear Mr. Edmundson:

For the third time, I am writing in regard to my deceased father-in-law, Jacob Whitman, who served in the 27th Michigan Infantry during the Civil War. You referred to him in both of your last letters as my grandfather. He was not. He was my husband's father. You have clarified your own error when you stated that his wife received no pension money because she died before him. However, you neglected to note that his sons were underage at the time and therefore should have received said pension. Jacob Whitman died in 1897. My husband William was born in 1880 and his brother Clarence was born in 1884 so they both would have been under eighteen years of age at the time of their father's death. Therefore, I believe pension money is due to us for both of them.

It is very good of you, kind sir, to take interest in this case. I am sorry to have continued to trouble you, but as I said before, we are very poor, and we need to know whether anything is due to us that might help our situation. May God aid you in doing what is right.

Sincerely,

Mrs. William Whitman
Rural Route 1
Marquette, Michigan

Margaret mailed the letter, hoping she had restrained the annoyance she felt while writing it. She also hoped she had made that dimwitted commissioner feel some sympathy for her family. Maybe when he realized all his mistakes, he would be all the more generous.

Then Margaret waited. She wished she could tell Will about the letters; she wanted to explain she was only writing them in hopes to get Royal money so he could go to college. She was proud of her son for working so hard. He had even sent her home ten dollars last week; she had only used five and then hidden the other five in her bureau drawer to save for his education. Everyday she calculated how many days it would take for a letter to reach Washington D.C. and then an answer to be returned. Whenever the mail came, she flipped through it quickly, seeking an envelope from the government. Finally, the expected letter came.

July 2, 1926
Mrs. William Whitman
Rural Route 1
Marquette, Michigan
Dear Madam:

Thank you for your letter of the 21st ultimo clarifying our error. We regret to inform you that pension money is only payable to heirs if the children are under sixteen years of age at the time of the father's death. Your husband would have been seventeen at the time of his father's death in 1897, and therefore, he is ineligible to receive any money. His brother, Clarence Whitman, however, may be eligible, having been thirteen years of age at the time of his father's decease. If you will inform Mr. Clarence Whitman of this, he may write to us to make his own claim and then we will determine its eligibility.

Sincerely,

A.Q. Edmundson
Acting Commissioner

Margaret lay her head down on the table. Why did they not tell her in the first place that only children under sixteen were eligible? The government was never coherent or organized about anything. Look at how they had made the mistake of thinking she was writing about her grandfather. Did they have any idea how much postage she had wasted in mailing all these letters, not to mention time spent writing them and delivering them to the post office; why could they not realize she had work to do, a house, a farm, a husband and children to look after? But if she could just get the government to send her a few hundred dollars, it would be worth it. "The Lord says 'Knock and the door shall be opened,'" she told herself. "I guess that means I have to keep knocking until they hear me." She got up and brewed herself a cup of tea, even though she had no sugar to put in it — sugar cost money. Still, she needed something to steel her nerves before she wrote again.

July 7, 1926
Dear Mr. Edmundson:

Thank you for your letter regarding the pension claim for my father-in-law, Corporal Jacob Whitman of the Michigan 27th Infantry in the Civil War. I did not realize that the pension money for children was only possible if the child were under sixteen. I understand, therefore, why my husband William, son of Jacob Whitman, was not eligible for such money. As you state, his brother Clarence Whitman would have been eligible for pension money, being only thirteen at the time of his father's death.

Unfortunately, Clarence Whitman has been deceased for eighteen years so he cannot make a claim for his father's pension. However, my husband is his only brother and heir. Therefore, my husband and I would like to claim the money in Clarence's name as his legal heirs. I trust this clarification will settle the matter. It is certainly fine of you to trouble yourself so much for us. I know you must have a wife and children of your own to support, or perhaps an aging mother like myself, so I know you will do what is right. I look forward to your gracious response. Times are hard now, but I trust our Heavenly Father will lighten your burdens and help you in your good work. Please answer soon.

Yours respectfully,

Mrs. William Whitman
Rural Route 1
Marquette, Michigan

Margaret read over the letter. She hoped this commissioner was a God fearing man. She had already told him how poor they were, how Henry needed an operation, how Roy needed money for college, how she had three smaller children to feed. How could he turn down the pension money to them? If he were at all a Christian, he would take pity on them. She looked at the clock; Will and Henry would be home soon. She stuck the letter in an envelope, addressed it, then hid it where no one would see it until she mailed it in the morning.

After a minute, she remembered to flip through the rest of the mail. At the bottom of the stack was a letter from Sarah. After not yet receiving any pension money, the last thing Margaret desired was to read about her sister living the high life in Washington D.C. where her husband was serving yet another term in the United States Senate. She especially did not want to read her sister's complaints about lazy servants and how hard it was to find a good cook; Margaret would have willingly eaten burnt food in exchange for not having to cook. But perhaps Sarah's letter would mention their parents. Margaret had not heard from them in over a month. They had originally planned to come visit this summer, but then her mother had written in the spring that her father did not feel well enough to travel. Now that her father was seventy, Margaret feared they would never come. Hoping Sarah's letter might say her parents had changed their minds about not visiting, Margaret tore open the envelope.

July 2, 1926
Dear Margaret,

I'm sorry I haven't written for so long. You would not believe how busy a social life one has in Washington. Constantly there is some party to attend, and one always has to go if one wants to help out one's husband's career. Poor Joseph, I really think he would be lost without me to help him make the rounds of the social circles. And then, one is always trying to keep one's own household in order and seeing to arangements for one's parties so none of one's acquaintances feel snubbed. Political life is a never ending cycle of such social duties.

But I had spoken to you last year about paying you a visit. I have decided that I will stop in Marquette for a couple days on the way out to California for the remainder of the summer. I know you would like Mother and Father to come visit as well, but I think they are now too old to be traveling so much so I have talked them out of the trip. I would hate for them to travel alone, furthermore, and it just simply would be too dificult to go all the way to California and then backtrack by bringing them to Michigan. I have tried to get them to come to Washington several times, but they never will and prefer to be near father's relatives out there in California.

There is much to do since Independence Day is coming and there will be more gallas to attend. I must go out this afternoon to find a new gown for the occasion, so I'll get to the point. Poor Joseph cannot get away from Washington right now, so Theodore is going to acompany me to Marquette. He has always expresed an interest in seeing the place where his mother was raised, although I'm afraid he'll be teribly bored in my little hometown after years in Washington D.C. and San Francisco. In any case, we'll be arriving on the train in Marquette on July 8th. I forget what time, but we'll be coming up from Detroit and then on the ferry over the Mackinaw Straits, so I trust you can check the time table with the railroad there and meet us at the station.

I'll look forward to seeing you.

> Much love,
> Mrs. Senator Joseph Rodman

"She can't even just sign her name as Sarah," thought Margaret. "And tomorrow's the eighth. I'm lucky I got the letter before she showed up. If she's going to give me such short notice, the least she could do is send a telegram; she's probably the only one I know who can afford to send one, but I guess when you're important enough to go to dinners at the White House, you don't worry about inconveniencing a poor farmer's wife."

"What's wrong?" asked Will. The moment he stepped into the room, he saw his wife's vexed look.

"O-oh," huffed Margaret, "that darn sister of mine."

"Sarah? Why? What's wrong?"

"She's coming to visit."

"Oh, that'll be nice," said Will, wondering why Margaret did not think so.

"I just got a letter saying she'll be here tomorrow! What am I supposed to do? The house is a mess, and how will we feed her? She's so used to fine things. How can I even bear to let her see the inside of my house?"

"She knows we live a simple life and are the happier for it," said Will, rubbing his wife's shoulders.

Margaret grimaced. Why did he have to pretend they were happy? Yes, they loved each other, but what was simple about constantly worrying where the next meal would come from? Sarah had no such worries with all that money and two beautiful homes filled with servants.

"She won't understand how we live," said Margaret. "She's such a snob — just look at how she signs her name, always acting as if she's better than us because of her husband."

"Well," Will laughed when he saw the pretentious signature, "some people just have to promote themselves. Luckily we're more confident from being self-reliant."

"But Will, it'll be so hard to have her here, always looking down her nose at us."

"People can't make you feel inferior unless you let them," said Will. "Now cheer up. You don't want the children to see you angry with your sister."

He kissed her cheek. She was unresponsive. He turned his head and gave her a long kiss on the lips.

"I bet no senator can kiss his wife like that," he boasted.

"No, I guess not," Margaret smiled, but inside she still fumed. If she continued to complain to Will, he would only accuse her of being jealous of Sarah, and if that happened, he would think she regretted her marriage because he had not given her as much as the senator had given Sarah. She knew Will well; he tried to be courageous, but internally, he beat himself up when his wife was unhappy. She did not want that. She loved him; he worked harder than any man she knew; it was no one's fault if they could not get ahead. And it was not even that she wanted her sister's riches; she just wanted her children to have decent clothes, and she wanted to have a little money put aside for emergencies, and for Will to be able to relax a little.

She could not remember a day since her marriage when she had not had something to worry about. And with Sarah coming — well, it was more than her nerves could take.

The following appeared in *The Mining Journal* on July 9, 1926.

City Brevities:

Mrs. Joseph Rodman, wife of the U.S. Senator from California, and her son, Mr. Theodore Rodman, arrived yesterday to visit with family in Marquette. Mrs. Rodman is the daughter of Mr. and Mrs. Charles Dalrymple, formerly of Marquette. She will be staying with her sister, Mrs. William Whitman.

When Margaret saw her name in the newspaper as sister-in-law to a U.S. Senator, she felt some small reward for her pains. Even if Sarah looked down on her for being poor, perhaps now the neighbors would respect her more. Will might even make better business contacts when his illustrious connections were known.

But her sister's visit soon strained Margaret's patience.

Sarah was disdainful from the moment Will, Margaret and Henry went in the wagon to pick up her and Theo at the train depot. Even though Margaret had not seen her sister in several years, and she found some satisfaction in seeing Sarah was growing stout, she still found her sister's attitude difficult to tolerate.

"I didn't know anyone still drove wagons," said Sarah. "Everyone in Washington and San Francisco owns an automobile."

"I don't trust those contraptions," said Will.

Theodore laughed and said, "What a lark!" as though traveling in a wagon were equivalent to a carnival ride. Henry shook his cousin's hand, then the two young men piled into the back of the wagon with the luggage. The children had stayed home with instructions to straighten up the place before the guests arrived; Margaret might be vexed with her sister, but she wanted her children's self-esteem to feel the honor of having a great political leader's wife in their home.

"How Marquette has changed," said Sarah as they drove out of town toward Harvey and then on to the Whitmans' Cherry Creek farm. "Look Theo, there's the Hotel Superior — remember me telling you about it?"

Theodore looked up at the rising cliff where the castle-like hotel perched.

"It's abandoned now," said Margaret.

"That doesn't surprise me," said Sarah. "You can't expect a big hotel like that to prosper in the middle of nowhere. Still it was a pretty hotel in its day."

Sarah then went on to make several more choice comments about Marquette and its lack of attributes — comments that made Margaret feel she, her family, and neighbors were nothing but hicks for remaining in their hometown when they could be living in glorious Washington D.C. or splendid San Francisco, where "the climate is warmer, the landscape prettier, and there's far more to do."

As they pulled up to the farm, Margaret keenly felt how badly the house needed painting, and the squawking hens in the chicken coop made Margaret feel downright seedy.

Then the children came out of the house to meet their aunt. They had changed into their second best clothes — their best were only worn to church.

"Margaret, the girls look just like you, and they all look so healthy!"

Margaret heard the implication that poor children are not supposed to be well.

"They have rosy cheeks from all the fresh air," Will smiled.

Before going inside, Sarah stopped to admire Margaret's little flowerbed along the front porch.

"Your pansies are quite pretty," she said. "Oh Margaret, you should see the fine gardens in Washington. My garden is quite a bit larger than yours, but nothing by comparison to most there, but then our yard boy only comes once a week to care for it. I really need to find a full-time gardener."

All afternoon, Margaret cringed as her sister made little jabs at her life. When she went to make coffee in the kitchen, she started to mutter under her breath, and then Will whispered to her, "Maggie, don't let her get to you. She doesn't mean it; she just has no tact. If you get upset, you'll just make a mountain out of a mole hill."

Margaret knew he was right, but her blood pressure still rose when she brought the coffee into the parlor, only to hear Sarah complain about how uncomfortable the train had been even though she had traveled first class. She grew further irritated when she saw Ada and Eleanor's eyes grow larger with each word Theo and Sarah used to describe their high society life. Fortunately, the girls asked so many questions about Washington that Margaret need not speak; she may have lost her temper if she had.

When supper was over, Eleanor dutifully began to clear the table.

"Eleanor, dear, go play," Sarah told her. "I'll help your mother clean up."

Margaret nearly dropped her glass at this offer. Senators' wives do not wash dishes. What if Washington's ladies heard of it? Joseph Rodman's career might be ruined by his wife's folly.

Sarah then turned to Margaret and added, "I thought that way we could have a little talk."

Margaret did not reply but carried the dishes to the counter. Everyone else filed out of the house to sit on the porch where there was a breeze. Margaret began to prime the pump to run the dishwater.

"You don't have electricity?" Sarah gasped, when she saw the pump.

"Not way out here on a farm," Margaret replied, trying to stay calm.

Sarah stood in dismay.

"We had a hand pump at home when we were girls," Margaret reminded.

"I guess I'll wipe," said Sarah.

Margaret became deeply engrossed in scrubbing gravy off the plates. She did not feel like talking.

"Margaret, I'll come straight to the point," Sarah said. "I want to help you and Will. I'm afraid it's very obvious you're having financial difficulties."

Margaret paled. She knew Sarah would notice their poverty, but she had hoped her sister would be more respectful than to mention it. And Sarah should know she and Will were too proud to take charity.

"I know you'll never take money from me," said Sarah, "so I have a proposition for you."

Margaret guessed where the conversation was leading. Sarah wanted her to move to California, but Will would never go; he was too attached to Marquette, no matter how much money he might make elsewhere.

Sarah was a bit taken aback by her sister's silence, but she forged ahead anyway.

"No farm family can expect to get along well with five children to feed," she said. "By comparison, I only have Theo, and he's going to college this fall."

Margaret's heart dropped. College. The future she had dreamed of for Roy.

"And with Joseph always traveling on business," said Sarah, "I have lots of lonely hours. I've always wished I'd had more children."

"You're still young enough to have another child," said Margaret, puzzled over what her sister was getting at. But for a moment, Margaret felt pleased to think she had surpassed her sister in the wealth of children — and each child was legitimate.

"We've tried," said Sarah, "but Joseph isn't able to have children."

"Oh." Margaret turned from the dishwater to look at her sister. "I'm sorry," she said, but she exulted that her husband was greater than the senator in at least one way.

"It's all right. I've made my peace with it," said Sarah, "and it might be a blessing for all of us. You see, I always wanted a girl, and since you and Will have so many worries, I thought you might let me adopt one of the girls — maybe Eleanor. She'll be fourteen this year. She's at an age where she deserves a better chance at life."

"Adopt!"

Margaret wiped her hands on the dishtowel, then sat down at the kitchen table. She had never expected such a proposition.

"Yes," said Sarah. "I know you'll miss her, but think of the advantages for her."

"But she's my daughter," said Margaret. "It would be like selling her to you!"

"Oh, Margaret, it's not like that," said Sarah, sitting down and taking her hand.

"She's my oldest girl. I couldn't part with her," said Margaret. "She's so much help to me, probably even more so than the boys, and she — "

"I'm sure she helps you, Margaret, but the question is whether you're helping her. Of course, it may seem selfish for me to want a girl of my own, but wouldn't you be selfish to keep her here when she could have all the finest advantages in life? She'll be a woman soon. I can send her to a finishing school, buy her decent clothes, and teach her how to behave in society. In time, I'll introduce her to the right kind of men so she'll make a prosperous marriage. Once she has those advantages, she might be able to help your other children get ahead."

Margaret weighed her sister's words; she could hardly believe Sarah dared ask her such a thing. She wanted to shout "No!" but she feared she would be selfish to hold Eleanor back from such a fine life.

"But would such advantages outweigh her being separated from her family?" Margaret asked.

"I'll love her," Sarah said, "and Joseph will treat her as his own daughter."

"But she barely knows you. She loves me and her father, and she would be so lonely without her siblings."

"But if you love her, do you really want her to share a cramped little room, and wear hand-me-downs from the neighbors, and coarsen her hands from farm work? She deserves to have fun with girls her own age, proper, educated girls."

Margaret did not wish to deny her daughter all these things, but she could not overpower her heart, even if it were selfish. "No, I can't let her go. It's impossible."

"Don't decide now," said Sarah. "I know this is a surprise for you. Talk it over with Will, or better yet, let Eleanor make her own decision; she's old enough."

Margaret had not thought to ask Eleanor. If she did not ask her, and Eleanor later found out, would she blame her mother for denying her a fair chance in life?

"I'll ask Eleanor," she said, "but whatever her answer, it doesn't mean I'll agree."

"Just try not to be selfish," Sarah said.

Mixed guilt and love exploded inside Margaret.

"Selfish! When have I ever been selfish?" Tears sprang into her eyes. "If anyone's selfish, it's you, Mrs. Senator Joseph Rodman. Just because you have all that money doesn't mean you can buy one of my children."

She got up from the table, went back to the sink and wiped her best bowl, then set it on the hutch cabinet. By then, Sarah had recovered from shock over the outburst.

"Margaret," Sarah pled, "I just want to help you as a sister should."

Margaret tried to maintain her self-control. "I'll talk to Will, but I can tell you the answer won't change. Now I don't want to talk about it anymore."

She drained the dishwater, then without a word, went up the backstairs, leaving Sarah to finish drying the dishes. In her bedroom, Margaret asked herself for the thousandth time why Sarah should be so fortunate after the terrible sin she had committed.

On Saturday morning, Henry took pity on his cousin. The city-bred Theodore had appeared terribly bored since his arrival, having spent the past two days with his mother, aunts, and young cousins, while Henry and Will were at work. Henry felt responsible for entertaining Theo, and since he had not seen Roy in weeks, he suggested the two of them go up to the Huron Mountain Club for the day. "You and Roy are the same age," Henry explained to Theo. "Roy's interested in books and science and all that, just like you, so I bet you'll both get along well."

"Is Roy going to college?" asked Theo, who had still not fully grasped the economic disparity between himself and his Upper Michigan relatives. In one of his frequent philistine moments, he had bragged he would attend Harvard that autumn.

"No," said Henry. "Roy probably won't go to college until next year. He has to work first to save some money."

"Oh," said Theo, wondering why his aunt and uncle did not pay Roy's tuition.

Henry changed the subject. "Maybe we can climb Sugarloaf Mountain on the way to the Club. I think you'll be impressed by the view from up there. I doubt there's anything like it in Washington."

"Is the mountain as tall as the Washington Monument?" asked Theo.

"I don't know," said Henry, "but the view is spectacular."

After an early breakfast, the cousins set off down the Big Bay Road in Henry's car.

"Where's this mountain?" asked Theo when Henry parked the car in a dirt parking lot just off the road.

"You can't really see it here because there are so many trees," said Henry, "but it's very steep toward the top. It's really a giant cliff overlooking the lake."

"It can't be much of a mountain," said Theo.

But then he began to climb it. At first, a long path stretched amid the birch, pine, oak, and maple trees, a path that inclined so gradually it seemed never to ascend. Then came a steeper hill, followed by several little slopes; rocks jutted out among the leaf covered ground, and ahead, trees, ferns, and berry bushes buried the side of the mountain. Next came steep glacier rocks carved from Lake Superior several millennia before. Beneath the vegetation was thick granite, composing one of the highest cliffs along Lake Superior, rising a thousand feet above sea level, five hundred feet above the lake, every foot of its climb rigorous. Henry strode up the rocky summit like a mountain goat, nimbly jumping from one rock to the next, ignoring the branches that threatened to snap in his face. Theo panted after him, his legs beginning to ache. Several times, Henry paused to wait, pretending he was in no hurry so Theo would not be embarrassed by his lack of physical vigor. When they finally reached the top, the perspiration was profuse on Theo's brow; Henry thought his cousin would have sweated less had he worn more practical hiking clothes. There was no understanding big city people.

"It's quite a climb," Theo huffed, but he dared not complain for fear Henry would think him soft.

"It is a little rough going," said Henry, "but I guess I don't notice anymore; I've come up here so many times. Come on, I want to show you the memorial I helped build."

Theo followed, surprised to see Henry was not sweating; actually, Henry was wearing shortsleeves, which had made Theo think his cousin would shiver in this abominably cold climate. Now he wished he had left his spring blazer in the car, even if it were only sixty degrees this morning.

Theo forgot about the temperature when he reached the rocky summit and saw the memorial obelisk jutting upward. Below him were miles of trees; to his right was the miniature city of Marquette, and directly in front, as background to the obelisk, was the dazzling deep blue of Lake Superior, the morning mist still rising up from it as though it were clouds, and Theo were standing on a mountain summit above them.

"I helped build this a few years back," said Henry, referring to the stone monument. "It's a memorial to our Boys' Club leader when I was a kid. He died in France during the war, so our troop hauled these rocks up here to honor him."

Theo looked at the pillar of large, mortared stones, then shook his head.

"I don't know how you could have carried all those rocks up here. It must have taken about a hundred men to do it."

"No, not nearly that many. Most of us just made several trips up."

Theo knew he never could have carried all those rocks up — how could anyone when your hands were needed to brush away all the scratching tree branches along the path?

"Look at how beautiful the lake is," said Henry.

Theo agreed Lake Superior was beautiful, but it looked so cold. He longed to reach California where the sun danced on the warm water of the Pacific. He missed the city's bustle — here you could see nothing because trees blocked the view. On the horizon, an ore boat from Canada headed into Marquette's harbor. Theo thought even the harbor looked desolate compared to San Francisco's thousand ships.

Henry breathed in the cool air blowing off the lake. Theo said, "You people sure are mountain men living in such a remote area."

"Yup," Henry smiled. "I doubt any of your Washington politicians could survive in our Northern woods, especially not camping in winter with four foot snowbanks."

"Why would anyone want to camp out in winter?" asked Theo. "It's so cold here, and Marquette's so small there isn't anything to do."

"There's plenty to do," said Henry. "Swimming, fishing, hiking, boating."

"But everyone here is so poor," said Theo, collapsing onto a rock. He had wanted to sit down since he had arrived on the summit, but only now did his fatigue overcome his concern for soiling his pants. "If you moved to San Francisco or Washington, you'd find better jobs and have a better life."

Henry wanted to lecture Theo that "A better life is a state of mind," but he could hear the superiority of such words, so he softened. Despite Theo's prissiness, he did like his cousin. "Lots of people up here are poor," he said. "The iron mines were supposed to make Upper Michigan one of the richest areas in the country, but it never quite happened. Still, most of us would rather live here than anywhere else, and those who move away usually end up coming back, deciding that peace, and beauty, and friendly people outweigh making big money in a noisy, polluted metropolis."

"I don't like noise or pollution either," said Theo, "but they beat blizzards. My mother's told me stories about winters here where the snowbanks are over your head and you're stuck in the house for three days during a snowstorm."

"Winter can be rough," said Henry, "but it's worth it on a sunny winter day when you step outside to be blinded by the sun reflecting off the snow. And the summers here are rarely too hot, and the autumn leaves are more spectacular than even in New England."

"You act as if Marquette is the best place on earth," said Theo, "but that's because you've never been anywhere else. If you visited San Francisco, or Boston where I'll be going to school, you'd see a whole new world and change your mind."

Henry felt annoyed. He admitted to himself he knew little about the world beyond Upper Michigan, but he had brought Theo to the top of Sugarloaf to see the land he loved, and Theo was blind to its beauty.

"We better get going," he said. "Roy'll be waiting for us."

He started back down the hill. Theo had barely caught his breath, but he quickly followed, afraid to be left alone on this wild mountain top.

It was late morning when Henry and Theo arrived at the Huron Mountain Club. Henry had only visited Roy once that summer to bring his brother a care package from home, and Roy had given Henry a brief tour of the Club; since then Henry had long anticipated a return to this forbidden land, preserved like a giant garden within the Club's gate, protecting the Upper Peninsula's natural beauty from the encroachments of logging and civilization. Henry imagined the Club looked a lot like Marquette must have in its pioneer days. As for Theo, the winding road to the Club was so long he thought they were driving clear to Canada — Theo's geographical understanding did not include Lake Superior separating Upper Michigan from the neighboring country.

Roy always had Saturdays off, and each weekend he hoped his brother would visit. He knew if Henry came today, it would be before noon, so he hung around his cabin, paying little attention to the book he was reading and constantly glancing out the window to see whether a familiar vehicle appeared. The day was breathtakingly sunny, without being too humid; Roy felt an urge to stroll through the forest of giant pines whose needles carpeted the earth of the Huron Mountains. He knew if Henry did not come, he would be so depressed, he would have to go off into the woods to hide his loneliness, to be alone where no one could see he was alone. The forest would keep him from moping — once surrounded by trees, he could forget himself and find pleasure in walking the miles of trails, climbing a hill to look out at beautiful Lake Superior, or just lying down in his favorite valley to listen to the forest sounds.

Finally, Roy closed his book, unable to read on such a gorgeous day. One final time he looked out his window. No Henry in sight; he trembled a moment as his anxiety faded away. Then he resolved himself to a lonely day. He went outside and started toward the kitchen building to get a sack lunch for his afternoon excursion. Then he heard a motor. He turned just as Henry and another fellow pulled up beside him in a car.

"Hi, Roy? Did you guess I would come?" asked Henry as his brother's face lit up.

"I hoped so, but I didn't know," said Roy, trying not to shake, he was so excited to see his brother.

"Well, I'm here now. This is our cousin, Theo, Aunt Sarah's son. They've come to visit for a couple days, so I brought him up with me. You're free aren't you?"

"Sure am," said Roy, stepping around the car to shake Theo's hand. "It's nice to meet you. I was just going to get some lunch. You hungry?"

"We're starved," said Henry. "We hiked up Sugarloaf this morning, and Theo here, being from the big city and not used to such strenuous activities, has worked up an appetite."

Theo smiled good-naturedly, although he felt Henry was mocking him. "Is there a restaurant in this little village?" he asked.

"Not in this rustic place," said Henry. "There's a dining room for the millionaire members where you'd fit right in, but you're the guest of one of the workers now."

"I was going to get a sack lunch," said Roy. "I can get one for each of us, and we'll have a picnic."

"Sounds good," said Henry. "We'll wait for you."

Henry parked the car while Roy practically skipped to the kitchen building to place his order. He would not have to spend today alone.

"Watch out for the bears," Henry warned as Theo got out of the car. "They're all over this place."

Theo looked about, although he suspected Henry only wanted to give him a hard time; he felt Henry was annoyed with him, but he was not sure why. He thought Henry a little rough around the edges, but he liked him anyway, and both Henry and Roy seemed like real people to him, not like the hundred fellows he had known at prep school or imagined he would meet at Harvard who tried to impress you and only bored you instead. Sometimes, Theo dreamt of joining the army, to make a man of himself — all his life he had been conscious he was a bit soft compared to other boys — but his mother had once told him, "I never dreamed when I got into trouble and you were born that someday I would send my son to Harvard. With such an opportunity, there's no way you'll turn it down. I want you to have a better life than I had at your age." Theo understood he was expected to erase the stain of his mother's youth by living that better life.

In a few minutes, Roy joined his brother and cousin. He gave each a sack lunch.

"Where will we eat?" asked Henry.

"We can take a boat across Pine Lake and eat on the other side," said Roy.

"All right," Henry agreed. Theo said nothing, but followed.

They walked to the boathouse, noticing the day was getting warmer. The sunshine of midday was now breaking through the branches and cast wavering tree shadows over the grass. After a minute, Henry started to tell Roy about what the family had been doing since Theo and Aunt Sarah had come to visit. Roy became interested when he heard Theo was going to Harvard.

"Mother wants me to go into investment banking," Theo said, "but my father supports my interest in science, so I might go into astronomy or biology. I haven't really decided yet. What school are you going to, Roy?"

"I don't know," said Roy.

"Probably the Northern State Normal School," said Henry.

"Where's that?" asked Theo.

"In Marquette," Roy replied, "but it's a teaching school, and I don't want to teach."

"Then what do you want to do?"

"I don't know. That's the problem. I can't decide. I'd like to be lots of things, maybe a professor, or an archeologist, or a philosopher."

"A professor might be okay," said Henry. "I don't know that archeologists or philosophers are much use. You need a job that'll make money to help the family."

Roy did not reply. He knew his parents were poor. They worked hard, but he suspected if they had made better choices, they would have succeeded like Aunt Sarah. He did not see why he should be obligated to provide for them. Henry was already doing that, and where was it getting him?

"Here's the boathouse," he said to change the subject.

The boys quickly chose a boat, laid their lunch sacks inside, then pushed off from shore. Henry asked Theo whether he wanted to row. Theo had never rowed before, but he agreed he would. He sat in the front of the boat, with Henry in the back, and Roy in the middle.

They started across what suddenly appeared to Theo as a gigantic lake when he realized his oars would not cooperate with his rowing strokes. He could not coordinate his movements with Henry's, but kept whacking against Henry's oars. Finally, Roy placed his hands over Theo's to show him how to row in unison with Henry, but then Theo felt embarrassed, and with curling lip, told Roy, "Why don't you just row yourself then?"

"Are you sure?" asked Roy, trying not to upset his cousin.

"Yes," Theo snarled. So they could trade places, he stood up and nearly toppled over the boat, but Roy grabbed him in time to pull him down and prevent a spill. Frightened, Theo quietly slid into the middle seat.

A few moments of uncomfortable silence followed before Henry said, "Sure is a gorgeous day."

"Sure is," said Roy, enjoying the pressure against his muscles as he rowed in time with Henry's own strokes to send the boat placidly jetting across Pine Lake.

The water was a deep, dark blue. The pine trees around the lakeshore stood tall and lush in every shade of green, and a cloudless sky covered the lake. A light pine scent wafted on the breeze. A ticklish splash of water hit their bare forearms. A lazy warmth filled the air, and a dragonfly buzzed over the lake. Despite his recent irritation, Theo felt content to be alone on this lake with his two mountain men cousins; he thought he would feel just fine if they were the only three left on earth. No more nagging mothers, political stepfathers, or attempts to one-up your phony friends at school.

Too quickly the rowboat reached the shore for too strong were Henry and Roy's rowing arms. The boat docked. The trio stepped onto dry land. They walked up a slight hill, then stopped for lunch. Theo looked about for a stump or log to sit on, but when his cousins plopped down on the ground, Indian style, he joined them, trying to be nonchalant about knowing he would stain his pants.

"So, you're going on to California," said Roy, before biting into his sandwich.

"Yes," said Theo. "I'm glad to. I like California better than Washington."

"How are Grandpa and Grandma? Have you heard from them lately?"

"Mother has, but I don't write to them much. I hardly ever see them."

"We used to see them every week when they lived here," said Henry. "It was Grandpa who made me want to be a carpenter."

"Hmm," said Theo. He did not know what to say. He always felt awkward around his grandparents. They were rather dull — Grandpa always pounding nails into blocks of wood, and Grandma always fussing with her flower garden. Neither was interested in things that really mattered like politics or science.

"I think I'd like Washington," said Roy. "All of American history is there."

"I guess," said Theo. "But you get so used to living there you forget about the history."

"How could you forget it?" asked Roy. "Everywhere you go must remind you of Thomas Jefferson or Abraham Lincoln."

"Well," said Theo, "it's hard to think of past presidents considering the ones we've had lately. I didn't think much of either President Harding or President Coolidge when I met them."

"Don't say that to my mother," laughed Henry. "She's a die hard Republican."

Roy smiled at his brother, as if they were remembering a shared memory of their mother. Theo saw by the way his cousins' faces lit up around each other just how much they enjoyed each other's company. He had never had anyone feel that way about him. His cousins were rather hicks, but he still wished he had a brother like they did. Spontaneously, he said, "You should both come to San Francisco with me, or better yet, come with me to Harvard in the fall."

"We can't afford to go to Harvard," said Henry.

"I could help you out, or maybe my mother would. It would be nice to have some family around. I don't know too many people going to Harvard so I could use some friendly faces."

Henry did not know what to say. He and Roy scarcely knew Theo. He dug in his lunch sack for his apple. Theo was soft and a bit spoiled, but Henry pitied him; he was obviously lonely. Henry could not imagine what it must be like not to be surrounded by family.

Roy stared across the lake, upset by Theo's suggestion. He wished he could go to Harvard, but he knew discussing it was pointless.

When neither cousin replied to his plea, Theo felt embarrassed. He wanted to tell them how scared he was, that he needed some friends — for a foolish second, he had thought they would understand, but how could they? They were just farmboys.

"Tell us about San Francisco," Roy broke the silence. "Grandpa and Grandma's letters make it sound so wonderful."

"It is," said Theo. He began to describe San Francisco Bay, Chinatown, the beautiful homes, the steep hills, and the palm trees.

"You really should come visit," he repeated. "It's so beautiful you can't even imagine. You've nothing like it around here."

"I don't think I'd like it," said Henry, feeling it an insult to Upper Michigan to compare it to San Francisco. "It's probably too hot there."

"Oh, no, it gets cold. Winter days are often forty degrees."

"Winter days are often forty degrees here too," Roy grinned. "Forty degrees below zero."

"All the more reason for you to come out there. Roy, you want to go to college. Maybe if you came to California, we could both go to Berkeley instead of my going to Harvard. I bet my parents would help you pay your tuition. You're family after all."

"Roy doesn't need to go out there," said Henry. "There's nothing in California he needs that he can't get here."

"How can you say that when you've never been there?" asked Theo. "Everyone talks about San Francisco. No one ever talks about Marquette."

"Why do people talk about San Francisco?" Henry asked. "Maybe because of the California Gold Rush of 1849. Well, let me tell you, Marquette was founded that same year because iron ore was discovered, and our iron ore has produced more wealth than all the gold from California. And what else is San Francisco famous for except that big earthquake twenty years ago? No Michigan blizzard ever did as much damage. I wouldn't live where there are earthquakes like that. I can't see one single advantage San Francisco has over Marquette."

Roy longed to see California, but he felt proud of how quick Henry was to defend their hometown. Still, he did not wish to hurt Theo's feelings, so rather than let his brother and cousin debate further, he suggested they go for a walk.

"I'll show you the beauty of the Huron Mountains, Theo," Roy said. "Then when you take the train over the Rockies to California, you can make a better comparison."

For two hours the cousins wandered about the woods. Henry and Roy kept admiring the trees, tall enough to form a cathedral ceiling. Once when they came around the edge of a hill, before them stood a doe and her fawn. Theo, first to see them, stopped in shock and awe, not a dozen feet from the graceful creatures. All three boys let out a little gasp, then laughed at their own surprise. The doe, sensing no danger to her fawn, turned her head in disdain at the sight of the inferior two legged beasts; with great dignity, she stepped into the deeper forest, followed by her babe. In a few seconds, the white tails and golden coats were only a memory to the boys. Henry and Roy exchanged looks of shared pleasure. Theo was dumbfounded.

"I never saw any wild animal before, except birds and squirrels," he said.

"See why we love it here," said Henry. "You can't see that in San Francisco."

After the long walk, Theo had been feeling fatigued, his leg muscles tightening up, but this pastoral moment invigorated him. Until the vision of the deer, he had wanted to turn back; now he only wanted to continue through this magnificent forest in search of more illuminating moments.

But the trail eventually did curve back around to the edge of Pine Lake, and the trio traipsed along its shore toward where they had left the rowboat.

Up ahead, they heard laughter and tumultuous water splashing.

"Someone must be swimming," said Roy. He heard several male voices but did not recognize them. Then a break in the foliage gave a glimpse of three bare male torsos, half submerged in the lake.

"Hello!" called Henry as they approached the bathers, each in his late teens or early twenties.

Roy strained his eyes to discern their faces.

"Hey, Roy!" Lex called out.

"Hello," said Roy, distinguishing his roommate from the other two boys.

"Theo Rodman?" called another voice.

"Yes," said Theo, not expecting to meet anyone he knew.

"It's Marcus Van Kamp."

"Marcus?" said Theo with surprise.

"Hi, Theo," called another boy.

"Hi, Aaron," Theo replied, recognizing yet another of his Washington schoolmates. "I never expected to find you boys here."

"My uncle's a member," said Marcus, "so Aaron and I came up to visit. Don't tell me your parents are members too?"

"No," said Theo. "These are my cousins, Henry and Roy. Roy works here."

"Oh," Marcus said.

"Come and join us for a swim," Aaron invited.

Theo looked askance at his cousins.

"Come on in, Roy," Lex called. Roy was surprised by the invitation. Lex had been the one who told him workers should not mix with Club members or their guests. Just Thursday night when he was serving in the dining hall, this same Marcus and Aaron had been rude to him, torturing him with complaints about their food, then laughing when he tripped and dropped a plate. He had despised and avoided them ever since. He was not surprised, however, that Lex was swimming with them — Lex would go to any length to curry a member's favor.

"Come on, Roy; we don't bite," said Lex. "We're all the same when swimming in the lake."

"Do you want to swim?" Theo asked his cousins.

"Sure, but we don't have any trunks with us," Henry replied.

"That doesn't matter," Marcus said, stepping into shallow water to illustrate. "We're all skinny dipping."

Roy was repulsed by this ungentlemanly display of nudity, but Theo replied, "All right, here I come," and pulled down his trousers.

Roy turned to Henry, only to find his brother also stripping.

"Shouldn't we leave our underwear on?" he asked.

"No," said Henry, "then it'll be wet, and we won't be able to wear it later."

"I think I'll just sit here instead and enjoy the sun," said Roy.

"Suit yourself," Henry replied, already wading into the water.

"Glad to meet you," said all the boys, shaking hands and nodding as the newcomers entered the lake.

"Roy, don't get sunburnt anywhere," Lex laughed.

"No, I'm staying dressed," replied Roy, smiling with false amusement; he would have felt ashamed to be naked. He was surprised his brother and cousin, especially his cousin, did not have a sense of decorum. And these were his cousin's friends from school — he did not think them nice boys, not the gentlemen he had expected would attend Harvard. Why should such young men go to college when he could not?

"So tell me about that Evelyn girl," Marcus said to Lex. "Every night in the dining hall I eat her up with my eyes, but it seems you're the one she's got it bad for."

"No, it only happened once between us. She's too cold for me."

"That Indian girl looks pretty fine," said Aaron. "She could keep me warm all night."

"Yeah, she could," said Lex. "Ask any of the guys, and they'll tell you so."

"You don't say? I didn't know she was such a total whore. You've had her too?"

"You kidding? Who do you think broke her in?" Lex laughed.

Marcus gave Lex a splash of approval.

"I hear there are lots of pretty women like her around here," Theo said. Roy could not imagine who would have told him that — certainly not Henry.

"Not as fine as the girls back in Washington," said Marcus.

"That's true," Theo said. "Especially not like those Southern girls; they always know how to satisfy a man."

Roy looked at Henry, who abstained from the lurid conversation, but nevertheless had a mischievous grin.

The boys continued their suggestive talk, while splashing each other when they boasted. A couple times they caught each other in wrestling moves until one mastered the other and dunked him beneath the water. Roy watched the horseplay, observing that they behaved like little boys despite their powerful glistening torsos. They were all larger than Roy. Even Theo was slightly taller, though less wiry and with a bit of a stomach roll. Only Henry was weak chested, and consequently, thin and prone to illness despite the incredible stamina that let him be a workaholic. Roy was surprised his brother, hardly more than skin and bones, was so little self-conscious as to take off his clothes and jump in the lake. Roy would not be naked, although he knew his physique was better than his brother's.

Even more, Roy was unnerved by the conversation. He dreaded lest one of the boys ask him about his own relationships with women — dreaded that because he had had no relationships, he would save face by lying. He had honestly never thought that way about a woman. Of course he noticed girls were beautiful, soft and tender, and he knew the mysterious yearnings, but his thoughts had never been as vulgar as his companions' suggestions. He did not like Evelyn, but he found no satisfaction in hearing her derided for her escapades with men. As for Ann, who was half-Indian, he had thought her a sweet girl, even his friend. He could not believe she had really slept with all the other young men at the Club. He pitied her for not knowing she was the laughingstock of these scoundrels. Had she really done those acts, and if so, why? How could she fall so low to please such immature bastards as these?

He was proud he had not stooped to the level of these sordid boys, yet he felt lonely, felt an urge to run into the woods, to escape, to hide from all his kind, who spent their lives controlled by their lusts. But even this greenwood could not hide him. He knew the world was becoming too small. He could just as easily hide in a big city like San Francisco, become nameless in a crowd, yet he would still be afflicted by the philistine human herd. He doubted he would ever find anyone just to have an intelligent conversation with, not when even Harvard students were so vulgar.

"We better head back or we'll miss supper," said Lex, wading toward shore.

Roy was startled from his thoughts when he observed how Lex's authoritative stride made arrogant Marcus and Aaron follow behind a man socially so far beneath them. As Lex emerged from the lake, he flexed his muscular arms; they were stunning as the sunlight glistened on their immense hardness. Then Roy understood why these rich boys admired Lex. And Roy hated the world all the more for its adoration of men, who succeed because of unearned physical beauty. Behind Lex and his disciples emerged Theo, and then finally, Henry, looking shriveled and malnourished in comparison to the others. Yet Roy felt Henry was more deserving of good looks and wealth than these other ignorant young men.

"Are you staying for supper?" Aaron asked Theo, as the boys shook the water from themselves and stooped to pick up their clothes.

"No, we have to get back to Marquette," said Theo. "My mother and I are leaving for San Francisco tomorrow."

"Plus Aunt Harriet and Uncle Charles are coming over for a family get-together this evening," Henry reminded Theo.

Roy felt anxious to get away from the horrid lake, to forget he had ever been here with the others. Once dressed, everyone walked back to where Henry and Roy had tied up the rowboat. Lex's rowboat was beside it, so the two groups rowed back across Pine Lake, good-natured jeers impelling their race to the other side.

Once on shore, Lex told Roy, "You're lucky to have the evening off. I better hurry or I'll be late to serve in the dining hall." He then rushed off to change his clothes.

"We'll see you around, Roy," said Marcus, cordially shaking hands with him, then with Theo and Henry. Roy knew Marcus was only polite now because he knew Theo. In a day or two, he would be just as ignorant to him as before.

"Theo, are you ready to go?" Henry asked as they stood tilting their heads to drain water from their ears.

"Just let me use the restroom," said Theo.

Roy pointed out a bathroom, then leaned against the car with Henry to wait.

"Why didn't you swim with us?" Henry asked his brother.

"I just didn't feel like it," said Roy, unwilling to admit shame over his physique.

"I'm guessing you don't like those fellows," said Henry.

"Not really."

"Has Lex treated you all right?"

"Yeah," said Roy. "We just don't have anything in common."

"I can see that. I didn't know he was so coarse until today. I'm sorry. It's best you stay away from fellows like that."

"I imagine they're like most our age. I'm probably the odd one."

"They're just a bunch of braggarts," Henry replied. "Half of what they say isn't true, especially about girls. They make up stories to look like big men in front of each other. They have no respect for themselves, or anyone really; that's apparent."

"I know," said Roy, thankful his brother shared his opinion. "Funny thing is, no matter how they behave, they seem happier than me."

"I doubt they are."

"They should be," said Roy. "They're going to college. They've got money so they can do anything they want. By comparison, what reason do I have to be happy?"

"Lots. You don't have half what they do, but what difference does it really make? Look at Theo; he has plenty but you can tell he's not happy."

"How do you know?"

"For one, he complains a lot. If he were happy, he'd be more carefree, more willing to go along with things. You should have seen him this morning, so afraid to get his pants a little dirty. I'd never want to be like that."

"Well, he's used to fine things; you can't expect him to fit in with people like us. And what's so great about being like us? I'd rather go to Harvard or Berkeley as he suggested and do something I want with my life."

"You'd never fit in with his type of people. Sure, he thinks it would be fun to have us around, but that's just because we're a novelty to him. He'd soon be embarrassed by us. Out West, he'd treat you as his poor cousin, with pity, or worse, disdain. You don't need that. You belong here with your family."

"You're too judgmental, Henry. You barely know Theo."

Roy knew his brother was right, yet he could not help feeling Theo might be his ticket out of Upper Michigan. Theo's family might help get him into a school where serious people cared about what mattered: art, literature, religion, philosophy, the purpose of it all, the knowledge for which he yearned.

Theo returned before Henry could reply to his brother.

"It was nice meeting you, Roy," said the Californian. "I didn't know until today how much fun it was to have cousins. I sure hope you'll come out to San Francisco."

"Maybe next year," said Roy. "I'll need to save up money for college, but maybe then I could go to school out there like you said."

"You could stay with us. I'm sure Mother and Father wouldn't mind; they'd probably be willing to help with your living expenses."

"We don't take charity," said Henry.

Roy glared at his brother.

"Goodbye, Roy," Henry said. Roy might be angry with him, but he knew Roy had enough common sense to admit he was right. The brothers had always been good friends, and any misunderstanding between them was always forgotten in a few minutes. But as Henry drove home, he regretted he had introduced Theo to Roy. He feared the meeting had stirred up longings in Roy that would never be fulfilled. Henry had always known he belonged in Marquette; he believed Roy would be happier with his lot if he would learn the same.

Margaret had promised Sarah she would at least mention the possibility of adoption to Eleanor, but whenever she tried to broach the subject, she felt a sudden need to hide in the outhouse before anyone saw her break into tears. After two days, she confessed her dilemma to Will. He was not one to lose his temper, but tonight he was restrained only by the presence of guests under his roof.

"That woman has some nerve," he seethed as he turned off the lights and crawled into bed. "Most years we're lucky even to get a Christmas card from her, yet now she thinks we'll give her our child."

"Well," said Margaret, "I do think she means well."

"If she meant well, she wouldn't interfere with our family."

"I told her the answer was 'No' but I felt I should tell you," said Margaret.

"I don't see how she could ask. It's selfish of her and completely unthinkable on our end."

"Of course," said Margaret. She would never want to lose one of her children. But she could not help fearing she and Will were being equally selfish. Were they taking away Eleanor's chances? They had to do what was best for their daughter, but was being with her family really best for Eleanor? Times were hard, but Margaret had to believe that if they loved each other and stayed together, everything would eventually be all right. They had had plenty of difficult times, but they had always scraped by, and they would continue to do so. She cuddled into the nook of Will's arm, then fell asleep believing she and Will had made the right decision.

But Will remained awake, first angry at his sister-in-law, then angry at himself. Sarah was ignorant to suggest they give up their daughter, but she would not have made such a suggestion if he could better provide for his family. He had worked hard all these years to support them, yet they rarely had a penny in the bank. He often felt Margaret never should have married him; she was ambitious and capable, and he felt perhaps he had just held her back. She had a beautiful voice; she might have been an opera singer instead of a farmer's wife. Now he rarely heard a song pass her lips, and he blamed himself for that change. He had made life a disappointment for his wife and children.

In the morning, Margaret got up early and went out to the chicken coop to collect eggs for breakfast. She dreaded speaking to her sister today; she knew Sarah would bring up the subject of adoption before leaving on the train at noon. She found her sister sitting in the kitchen when she reentered the house.

"Do you need help?" Sarah asked.

Again Margaret thought it odd that a senator's wife help in the kitchen.

"You can crack those eggs if you want," she replied. "There's only a dozen. I hope that's enough. There'll be eight of us for breakfast, but I'll only eat one, and Bill doesn't like eggs so he won't eat any."

Sarah dutifully cracked the eggs.

Margaret tried to control the conversation by commenting on what a nice sunny day it would be for a train ride. Sarah skipped the small talk.

"Did you ask Eleanor whether she would come to California?"

Margaret paused. "No, but I discussed it with Will. She's our daughter. We can't let you adopt her."

"Who's going to be adopted?"

Ada had asked the question. She had just stepped into the kitchen, unseen by the women, catching only her mother's last words.

"No one," Margaret replied.

"But you said one of your daughters would be adopted."

"No, I didn't," Margaret replied. "Just be quiet, Ada."

"Aunt Sarah, I'll go with you to California," Ada said.

"You will not," said Margaret. "And if I hear one more peep from you, I'll slap you across the face; do you understand?"

Ada was so stunned by the reprimand that she ran to her room. She had never seen her mother so angry, not even the time Eleanor had broken Great-Grandma Zurbrugg's teapot that had come from Geneva.

"Margaret, you shouldn't have yelled at her," said Sarah.

"You shouldn't tell me how to raise my children," said Margaret, nearing her boiling point.

"I'm sorry," said Sarah. "Do you have a whip so I can beat the eggs?"

"Just use a spoon," Margaret replied. Did it look as if she could afford a special whip just for the eggs? This was a farm wife's kitchen, not some fancy San Francisco restaurant.

Sarah knew the adoption subject was closed, never to be opened again. An emptiness settled over her; she thought she would cry; but then Will and the children poured into the kitchen, flooding the house with their rambunctious voices.

The two sisters did not speak again until it was time to leave for the train station. Sarah gave Margaret a hug, which was cordially returned. Theo shook hands all around with his cousins. Then mother and son climbed into the back seat of Henry's car, and Henry and Will took them down to the train station. Margaret went upstairs to lie down. The children imagined she was tired from all the extra work of having had visitors. They could not understand the strain she had been under of having her sister constantly looking down her nose at her.

A week later, Margaret and Eleanor were leaving to attend a luncheon at the Baptist Church. Eleanor was fourteen this year, so Margaret thought a church luncheon would be good training to teach Eleanor how to be a young lady. Just before they were about to leave, Henry brought the mail into the kitchen, then went out to the barn. There were only two letters, one from the pension bureau in Washington D.C., the other from the bank. Margaret had to leave in five minutes, and she still had to pin on her hat, but she ripped open the mail.

July 20, 1926
Mrs. William Whitman
R.R. 1
Marquette, Michigan
Dear Madam:

In reply to your letter of recent date, I must inform you that pension money can only be disbursed to children under the age of sixteen at the time of pensioner's decease. Although Clarence Whitman was a minor child at the time of his father's death, the fact that he did not file for pension collection prior to his own decease is an irreconcilable misfortune because a pension is not an asset of the pensioner's estate and is not payable to his heirs. In such cases, pensions are only available as reimbursement of funeral expenses and fatal illnesses if sufficient assets were not left to cover costs.

I regret I am unable to assist you further in this matter.

Respectfully,

J.E. Edwards
Commissioner

Margaret did not understand; Clarence had been under sixteen when his father died. She read the letter again, angry to see the phrase "a pension is not an asset of the pensioner's estate and is not payable to his heirs." All right, fine. She understood. But why couldn't they explain it in plain English?

She looked at the letter's signature. J.E. Edwards, Commissioner. He was not the same man who had written the earlier letters. That other man had only been Acting Commissioner. Why hadn't the commissioner written to her in the first place? Then everything would have been settled sooner, and she would not have kept her hopes up, or wasted money on postage for all those letters. The Acting Commissioner had obviously been incompetent. Margaret was not surprised, considering it was the U.S. Government she was dealing with. Jacob Whitman had been wounded while fighting to save his country. How ashamed he would now be to see the U.S. Government run by such ingrates and fools as these commissioners.

Angry and feeling rushed because she would be late for the luncheon, she ripped open the letter from the bank. A few words blurred her eyes with tears.

"foreclosure of your farm from lack of payments"

Those words were all she needed to see. Lose the farm! Yes, they were behind in their payments, but they were doing the best they could. What did the bank expect? Upper Michigan with its short growing season was not exactly ideal farming territory. She and Will paid whenever they could. How could they keep up on their payments when the children needed clothing and visits to the doctor? What was wrong with this country that it constantly ground the poor into the dirt?

"I'm ready to go, Ma," said Eleanor, coming downstairs.

"Wait for me on the porch. I'll be there in a minute."

Margaret went upstairs and stuffed the letters into her dresser, beneath her underwear where Will would not find them. She would have to tell him about the foreclosure, but first she had to resign herself to the task so she would be strong enough to console him. She would need composure, but right now she only felt panic that they would all end up at the poor farm.

"Mother!" Eleanor called from the porch.

"I'm coming!" Margaret shouted out the window.

She shook her head, wishing she could be like Eleanor again, innocent, excited over something as silly as a little church luncheon. Poor Eleanor; her mother had ruined her life; she could have been in California now, with her rich aunt and uncle, but instead she had to live with her selfish mother. Margaret considered writing to Sarah, apologizing profusely, begging her to take the girl, maybe Ada and Bill also, so they would not have to join their parents at the poor farm.

She reached for her handkerchief, then resolved, "No, I won't cry. Not until after the luncheon. I'll think more clearly after I'm back home and used to the idea. Then I'll be able to think of something to do other than going to the poor farm."

She breathed deeply, then went downstairs. As she stepped onto the front porch, she forced a smile and said to Eleanor, "It looks as if it'll be a beautiful day."

"Henry went to bring the car around," Eleanor said.

"That's thoughtful of him."

Henry pulled the car up to the front steps, then got out to open the door for his mother and sister. The automobile was loud and rumbling, but Margaret was glad because its sputtering motor prohibited conversation. She would find it difficult enough to make small talk at the luncheon. If she spoke to her children, she feared she would break down.

Henry dropped Margaret and Eleanor at the church and promised to return in a couple hours. Margaret's sister-in-law Harriet met them on the doorstep.

"Margaret, where are the buns you said you would make?"

"Buns! Oh dear, I forgot them at home. I don't know where my head is today," said Margaret.

Harriet restrained herself from rolling her eyes. Margaret was so cheap she would use any excuse to avoid bringing something to a luncheon.

"Well, here," said Harriet, "take my tray of brownies. We can say you brought them. I made potato salad too, so no one will know the difference."

"Thank you, Harriet," said Margaret. She did not like being credited with Harriet's dry brownies, but that was trivial beside her other problems.

Soon she was surrounded by gossiping church ladies. Margaret smiled, praised everyone's dishes and diplomatically sampled each one even though she had no appetite. A couple times she felt she could not even breathe.

She saw Mrs. Bissell across the room. Mrs. Bissell had given her the idea to write to the pension board. Now she wished she had never heard of the darn pension board. Why had she gotten her hopes up? But what mother would not want to pay her farm mortgage, put one son through college, send her oldest son to the doctor for stomach aches she knew were caused by the stress of helping support his family? She had such good children — they deserved better than what they had received, deserved better parents, or at least a better mother. She and Will had done their best — she had gotten no easy breaks like Sarah, who for being a hussy in her youth, had been rewarded with a rich husband.

"I hear your sister came to visit," Mrs. Boardman interrupted Margaret's thoughts.

"Yes, she and her son," said Margaret.

"Did your brother-in-law come too?"

"No, he's far too busy."

"Oh, what does he do?"

"He," Mrs. Vincent intruded, "is a U.S. Senator. You didn't know we had such a celebrity in our church as the sister-in-law of a senator, did you, Mrs. Boardman?"

"No, I had no idea. He lives in Washington then?" asked Mrs. Boardman.

"Oh yes," said Margaret, pleased to be termed a celebrity. "He and my sister have a beautiful home in Washington where they stay when Congress is in session, and they have another home in San Francisco, near my parents."

"That's right. Your parents moved out West," said Mrs. Vincent. "How are they?"

"Just fine," said Margaret. "They enjoy being near my sister when she's in California."

"How long did your sister stay?" asked Mrs. Boardman.

"Just a few days before going on to San Francisco. My nephew has been studying so hard so he wanted to get home and rest a few weeks before he starts at Harvard this fall."

"Harvard, oh my," said Mrs. Boardman.

"How did your sister ever meet a senator?" asked Mrs. Vincent.

"They met in Chicago, at a ball."

That was almost true. Sarah had been a waitress at the hotel holding the ball.

"Has your sister ever met the president?" asked Mrs. Boardman.

"Oh yes, she's met Wilson, Harding, and Coolidge," said Margaret, "and she's been to teas and luncheons with all the first ladies and several governors' wives. She's even met the President of Mexico and the President of France."

"How grand," said Mrs. Boardman.

"Some people have all the luck," Mrs. Vincent agreed.

"Margaret," Harriet Dalrymple frowned, "you don't want everyone thinking Sarah's so special. You'll make poor Eleanor feel inferior."

"Well, it's not everyday someone from Marquette marries a senator," Mrs. Boardman said.

"That was just luck on her part," Harriet blabbed. "She never would have met him in Chicago if she hadn't had to leave Marquette in disgrace."

"Harriet!" Margaret yelped.

"Well, it's true. I get so sick of hearing about grand old Sarah. The woman has to leave town because she gets herself into trouble, and next thing you know, she thinks she's Queen of Sheba. I'd like to know what kind of a senator marries a loose woman like that."

"Excuse me," gasped Margaret, holding back her tears as she rushed to the bathroom. She had never been so embarrassed. Why, when everything else was so awful, did she need this added irritation? How could her brother have married someone so coarse and tactless as big-mouthed Harriet?

"Harriet, why did you have to say that?" Mrs. Vincent chided.

"Well, it's the truth," said Harriet. "We're all God fearing women, and someone like Sarah doesn't deserve to be admired just because she married a rich man."

Eleanor remained at the table, stunned by the entire conversation. She was fourteen, and had vague ideas about how things worked between men and women. She thought she understood, but she wanted to make sure.

"Does that mean Uncle Joseph isn't Theo's father?" she asked.

"Yes," Harriet replied.

"Eleanor," Mrs. Boardman said, "you should go check on your mother."

Eleanor dutifully went to the bathroom, but her mind burned with the scandal. Now she understood — now she knew why her mother reacted so strangely whenever Aunt Sarah was mentioned. Aunt Sarah had a secret her mother had been hiding.

"Ma, are you all right?" she asked.

"Yes," said Margaret, pretending to adjust her hat in front of the mirror. Eleanor saw she had been crying. "Are you ready to go? Did you finish your dessert?"

"Yes."

"Good. Your brother should be here in a few minutes. Let's wait outside. I can't talk to your Aunt Harriet right now."

Eleanor said nothing. She obediently followed her mother.

While they stood out on the sidewalk, both prayed no one would come out of the church to speak to them.

"Your Aunt Harriet," said Margaret, "is the last one who should talk considering she named her son after your Uncle Joseph."

Eleanor did not reply. She was glad when Henry's car pulled up. For the first time, she realized her mother was a hypocrite, pretending to be something more than she was, willing to brag about the family's connection to a senator, yet always hiding the truth behind her delusions of grandeur. Eleanor wondered why her mother had to be so full of pretense; why she cared so much what others thought. But Eleanor was also a good daughter; she decided she would try to make money or to marry well so her mother could hold up her head. Whatever she did, she would not disgrace the family like Aunt Sarah had.

Margaret did not tell Will anything. She burnt the letters from the pension board. The bank's foreclosure letter she left in her underwear drawer until Monday morning. Then, once Will and Henry went to work, and Eleanor was safely watching Ada and Bill, she put on her best Sunday dress, her finest hat, and her gloves, which despite a small tear in the wrist of one, made her feel bastioned with formal authority. She placed the threatening letter in her handbag, then walked slowly down the road, so she would not sweat too much on the long walk into Marquette.

When she reached the downtown bank, she entered the lobby and looked about. She did not see him anywhere. She trembled; would she be able to pull it off?

"Can I help you, ma'am?" asked the lady teller.

"Ye-es," she said, stepping up to the counter.

The teller looked at her blankly, while Margaret struggled to find words.

"What can I help you with?" she asked, becoming impatient.

"I'm here to see Mr. Blackmore," said Margaret.

"Do you have an appointment?"

"No."

The teller looked annoyed. Margaret realized she had placed her hands on the counter. The rip in the seam of her glove was visible. Self-consciously she pulled away her hand.

"Mr. Blackmore does not see people who do not have an appointment."

"Would you tell him I'm here," said Margaret. "It's very important."

"Your name?"

"Mrs. William Whitman."

"What is it in regards to?"

"The mortgage for my and my husband's farm."

"I'll see whether he's available." The woman disappeared before Margaret could even say, "Thank you." She watched the woman go through a door leading to a staircase. Nervously, Margaret retreated to the nearest chair in the lobby.

She looked about, hoping not to be noticed by anyone she knew. No one ever sat in a bank lobby without an important reason. Everyone knew the Whitmans had nothing to invest, so if she were seeing a bank officer, they would suspect she had financial troubles. Such moments made her hate living in a small town. She wondered whether she had time to sneak out the door before anyone except the teller knew she had come. But she could not go; she had to stay for the sake of the farm, for the children and Will. She had to be steadfast. She could not fail. The man she must face was just one more example of the world's injustice, of how the poor and virtuous are downtrodden to satisfy the dictates of millionaires and tyrants.

"Mrs. Whitman?" The teller shouted her name across the lobby.

"Yes," said Margaret, scurrying back to the counter before her name was repeated and everyone stared at her.

"Mr. Blackmore cannot see you now. If you would like to make an appointment for later this week, I could — "

"No, I must speak to him immediately. It's urgent."

"It's not possible," said the teller. "He's in a meeting right now."

"Then I'll wait until he's out, but I must talk to him today."

"He'll be in meetings all day."

"Then I'll wait all day," Margaret insisted.

"Really, Mrs. Whitman, if you will — "

"I'll wait," Margaret repeated. She returned to the lobby chair. She did not care whether they tried to throw her out. She would not go until she had seen Mr. Blackmore.

The teller sighed as if Margaret were being completely unreasonable, then walked over to a man at a desk in the corner. When the two of them glanced at her, Margaret felt she was making a scene, but she would not give up now. She had impressed herself with how forcefully she had spoken to the teller; it only made her more determined. She had not intended to be rude or troublesome, but she must see Mr. Blackmore.

The teller and the man behind the desk came across the lobby to her. He introduced himself, but Margaret did not listen to his name.

"Is there a problem, ma'am?"

"No problem. I'm just waiting to speak to Mr. Blackmore."

"Mr. Blackmore is unavailable."

"I will wait until he is available."

She would not stand up so it would be more difficult for them to move her.

"He will be unavailable all day."

"It is imperative that I see him," Margaret stated. The bank patrons turned around at her loud voice. She did not care; the bank employees would pacify her before they would allow a scene in the lobby.

"Mrs. Whitman, it's not possible today. If you want to make an appointment — "

"No, I don't want to make an appointment. I want to see him now."

"Ma'am, Mr. Blackmore is a very busy man."

"And I'm a very busy woman. Just because he's vice president of a bank makes him no more important than me in the eyes of God."

Margaret thought if this man were a Christian, those words would get him.

"Ma'am, you're being unreasonable. I'm afraid I have to ask you to leave."

Obviously, he was not a Christian. Before she could think what next to say, from the corner of her eye, she saw Lysander Blackmore enter from a side door.

Ignoring the other bank employees, Margaret jumped up and marched across the lobby.

"Mr. Blackmore, I need to speak to you," she said, blocking his way.

"What is it?" he barked. He had on his hat and coat. He had an important lunch meeting to attend.

"I need to speak to you about the mortgage on my farm."

"You can speak to someone in the mortgage department. Robert," he called the gentleman who had tried to oust her, "show this woman to the mortgage department."

"I need to speak to you directly," Margaret said.

"I don't handle mortgages. Excuse me, I have an important meeting." He tried to pass her, but she would not let him.

"It's a personal matter. Only you can help me," she said.

"Madame, please, I'm pressed for time. Robert will assist you."

"Perhaps you don't recognize me," said Margaret, ready to play her trump card. "I'm Mrs. Will Whitman. My maiden name was Dalrymple. My sister is Sarah Dalrymple."

Lysander Blackmore stared blankly until the name registered in his brain. Margaret's trepidation disappeared as his face registered guilt. How she loathed him.

"What can I do for you?" She heard his voice quiver.

"Let's speak privately in your office," she replied.

Without a word, he turned on his heel and walked back to the side door. He stood and held it open for her. She passed through, then waited to follow him upstairs so he could not turn around and escape. She would not put an escape attempt beyond such a rogue. She followed him upstairs, then into his office.

"What can I do for you, Mrs. Whitman?" he asked, gesturing for her to take a seat while he sat down behind his desk, too nervous to take off his hat. His question reflected his pretense that he still did not know why she wished to speak to him, and his hope that he had misunderstood her overtones.

"You can help me with this," said Margaret, slapping the foreclosure notice on his desk. "My husband and I work our fingers to the bone to feed our five children. Our two oldest boys work to earn extra money and all the children help on the farm. We barely scrape by, but we pay every penny we can when we're able."

"I see," said Mr. Blackmore, hesitantly pulling the letter toward him to study it. He feared to meet her eye. From his pocket, he extracted his glasses — a ridiculous little pince nez that made him look effeminate despite his being quite a large man.

"This is a final notice," he said. "We've sent you warnings before. The bank has no choice but to foreclose. You're too far behind in your payments."

"Can't you do anything?" Margaret asked.

"No, if we made an exception for you, we would have to for everyone."

Margaret knew what she must do. She felt almost as low as the weasel before her, but she would do whatever was necessary for her family's survival.

"Perhaps you can't keep the bank from foreclosing," she said, leaning over his desk to intimidate him with the entirety of her hundred twenty pounds, "and perhaps I can't keep myself from telling everyone in Marquette about the skeleton in your closet."

"Ma'am, don't threaten me. As I've told you, there's nothing I can do."

He believed she was bluffing, but she would not be put off.

"I suppose 'There's nothing I can do' is what you told my sister when she became pregnant with your child!"

He tried to interrupt her, but rather than be silenced, she only raised her voice.

"I suppose you'll explain to your wife and children that there's nothing you can do about having a bastard child. I sure know there's nothing you can do to keep me from telling everyone the truth about you."

"You can't prove it."

"And you can't prove it's not true. Your parents are dead so they can't back you up, and my husband knows the truth, and my parents, and God knows my sister knows the truth, and so does her husband, who happens to be a U.S. Senator. He could find a fine lawyer for me if you try to take me to court for slander. And unlike you, I'll have nothing to lose if you take my farm away."

"Madame, would you really stoop to blackmail?" He had seen in *The Mining Journal* that Sarah Dalrymple had recently been in town, that she had married a senator. Even with all his money, Lysander Blackmore had no friends powerful enough to fight such a man. He was not ashamed of his past deeds, only disgusted that a farmwife could get the better of him.

"Stoop to blackmail?" Margaret mocked. "Blackmail is not as low as being a fornicator, or someone who throws people out of their homes so their children are left to starve!"

Lysander Blackmore pulled nervously at his shirt collar. She stared at him without blinking. Internally, she marveled at her own fierceness.

"I can't erase your debt," he said.

"I'm not asking that. My husband and I will pay when we can. We just need more time. We want an indefinite extension to pay the debt, and we will pay every penny of it. We're respectable, hardworking people, unlike some who get ahead by deceit and family connections."

Lysander would not defend himself further. He only wanted this woman out of his office. Any other time, he might have withstood the blow Margaret threatened, but another scandal was about to erupt against him; he could not risk his wife knowing he had made multiple indiscretions; he feared Mrs. Blackmore above everything.

Without a word, he took the foreclosure notice and stepped out of the office.

Margaret was surprised by his sudden departure. Her head throbbed. She collapsed into a chair and struggled to catch her breath. Where had he gone? Had she won? If he were not going to comply with her demands, he would have told her to leave — unless he were going to call the police and have her thrown out. She felt like crying, but she would wait until she got home. She would not give him the satisfaction. Whatever happened, she respected herself for standing up to a bully. She closed her eyes. She had begun to recite the Lord's Prayer to calm herself when the door reopened.

"Mrs. Whitman?"

It was the bank teller she had initially confronted.

"Where's Mr. Blackmore?" Margaret asked, nervously standing up.

"He apologizes that he had to go to his lunch meeting. He asked me to give you this."

The coward. He had retreated from his own office. She took an envelope from the teller.

"What is it?" Margaret asked.

"We've refinanced your mortgage — reduced the payments so it will be easier for you. There's a letter inside explaining it all. Everything should be fine now."

Margaret's tense shoulders drooped with relief. She wondered whether the teller knew the full situation. No, that Blackmore was too cowardly to explain his reasons for making such an exception.

"Thank you," she said, turning toward the door.

"You're welcome," said the teller. "Mr. Blackmore said he was happy to help out an old friend."

Margaret could not help grinning.

"I daresay," she replied. She went out the door, down the stairs, through the lobby, and onto the street. She stayed calm until she had walked several blocks south down Front Street. Then she gasped in disbelief at her triumph. Now she would not have to tell Will they had almost lost the farm. God was merciful to the poor.

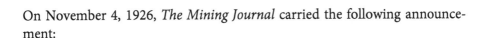

On November 4, 1926, *The Mining Journal* carried the following announcement:

Births - Marquette, St. Luke's Hospital

Blackmore, Scofield - born November 1, 1926, son of Hattie Scofield of Marquette.

Had the announcement been noticed, it would have caused a flurry of gossip among Marquette's residents. That no father was listed for a bastard child was not surprising, but that the child bore its father's surname and its first name was its mother's maiden name was evidence of what had been rumored for years about one of Marquette's most prominent citizens. That a greater scandal did not erupt from the announcement was Lysander Blackmore's timely luck. Marquette County was too overwhelmed with grief to gossip. That same day, *The Mining Journal*'s headline announced:

52 MINERS LOSE LIVES

Jeremy McCarey had lived through the tragedies of World War I. He had then returned to marry a girl he had met while training in Fort Custer. Once married, he and his wife had moved to Marquette. Jeremy then found a job at the Barnes-Hecker Mine just west of Marquette, near Ishpeming. Kathy and Patrick McCarey were delighted by their son's marriage, and even more delighted when their first granddaughter, Emily, was born. For the young couple, life seemed perfect. Even the sadness of war was vanishing away; when his wife became pregnant with a second child, Jeremy stated if it were a boy, he would name it Frank, after the brother he had lost in the war.

Every morning, Jeremy took the bus to the Barnes-Hecker Mine with his coworkers. Today, his thoughts were filled with his expected son. Too bad the baby would not be born before Christmas, but his wife still had a few months left to her pregnancy. Little three-year old Emily would bring plenty of enjoyment for the holiday. Jeremy and Caroline had already bought her some dresses and toys for Christmas, and he knew his parents would spoil her.

The miners disembarked from the bus. Jokes were made. "What did you do last night?" was asked. They bragged about their children, their beautiful wives, or the girls they were going out with on Saturday night. The miners made their way to the elevator, then descended down the shaft to various levels. The first group of men stepped off the elevator six hundred feet underground; then the elevator descended again and more men stepped off eight hundred feet down. Finally, Jeremy joined the last group of men one thousand feet below the earth's surface. Jeremy was already thinking about when he would get home that night. Caroline had promised to make pork chops for supper, and she could make them like no other woman, not even his mother or grandmother. If there were leftovers, he would have one for lunch tomorrow, which would sure beat his usual bologna sandwich Caroline always brought him.

What happened next was something never fully understood. A blasting job apparently ruptured an underground spring-fed lake. In fifteen minutes, the mine shafts were filling with water. Jeremy suddenly found himself caught up in turmoil.

First he hears the cries of his coworkers. When he understands what is happening, he runs toward the elevator. Already the water and sand surround his feet, rush up to his waist, pull him back, suck him down. His nose, eyes, mouth fill with mud. Jeremy McCarey loses consciousness, then his life.

On the mine's upper level, men hear the explosion and struggle to climb ladders that rise hundreds of feet up the shaft and to the open air. Twenty-three year old Wilfred Wills leads the men in climbing up the ladder. For ten minutes he struggles upward. He warns himself not to listen to the cries of the men below. Up, up, one rung after another. What's that on his feet? It must be the water. It's rising up above his heels. At one point, it rises to his waist and his feet slip from the ladder, but his grip is strong and he hangs on until he can regain his foothold. His legs rush quickly up the ladder, his shoes are wet, his feet slip, but he remains determined. He climbs hundreds of feet. Wilfred Wills sees the light. He comes into the air, collapses on the frozen ground. His body convulses with muscle spasms from his strenuous exertion.

As Wills emerges from the shaft, he is met by miners who struggle to help him up. Other men stand, heads bent down, as they worry about the men trapped below. Fearful anxiety soon gives way to despair and grief. Then a few women arrive with lunches for their husbands, Caroline McCarey among them. They stand and wait. Soon, word spreads to the neighboring mines, then to Ishpeming, Negaunee, and Marquette. A crowd gathers at the Barnes-Hecker Mine, waiting for news, praying that others will be saved, but soon everyone knows it is hopeless. Caroline goes home with little Emily; she knows she will never see Jeremy again. Her little girl and soon to be born child are fatherless. Other family members remain gathered together at the mine to comfort each other.

Fifty-one men — *The Mining Journal* would miscount — perish in the disaster. Only six bodies are recovered from the Barnes-Hecker Mine. In a couple months, all attempts to reopen the mine or recover the bodies are abandoned. The dead miners are left in their underground tomb. Their names are memorialized on a six foot tall, one ton marker. The dead men's horror and pain only lasted for seconds. Years pass before the pain ends for the forty-two newly made widows, one hundred-thirty-two fatherless children, the brothers, sisters, parents, grandparents, friends, and neighbors.

🍁　　　🍁　　　🍁

"What will you do now?" Patrick asked his daughter-in-law after Jeremy's funeral. They had bought a stone for the Holy Cross Cemetery, although no body had been recovered to place beneath it. Kathy also wanted to know Caroline's plans, but she was too heartbroken to ask.

"My parents want me to move back home to Battle Creek," said Caroline.

"But the children — we won't be able to see them then," said Patrick.

"My mother wants me home when the baby is born. I feel I need her now."

Kathy wrapped her arms around Caroline and began to sob. "Please don't go," she said.

Caroline returned the hug but said nothing. She was sorry to add to her in-laws' pain, but she could not stay in this place that had taken her husband.

"I won't leave for a couple weeks yet," she said. "I'll see you again before then."

Another newly widowed miner's wife drove Caroline and Emily home from the funeral service. The McCareys were left to walk home alone.

"Michael gave a beautiful eulogy," said Patrick. His only remaining son was pastor of a western Upper Peninsula parish, but he had come home for his brother's funeral.

"I wish Michael could stay overnight," said Beth.

"He has to say Mass at his own parish tomorrow," Patrick replied.

Beth fell behind her parents as they walked home. She watched her father take her mother's hand, but doing so scarcely eased their breaking hearts.

"It's too bad Uncle Karl and Thelma couldn't come," Beth said.

"It's better Karl doesn't travel when he's recovering from the flu," said Patrick, "and we'll see them at Thanksgiving."

Beth thought it would be a grim holiday. What was there to be thankful for? And Christmas! Christmas would be awful. She had a doll hidden away for her niece. Now she would have to wrap it up so Caroline could give it to Emily on Christmas morning in Battle Creek. She had so been looking forward to seeing Emily's face light up when she saw the doll. Now Beth would only get a thank you note for the gift.

"I think I'll take a nap," said Patrick when they reached home.

"Mother, why don't you go lie down too?" Beth said. She put her hands together and laid them against her bent head in case her mother had not heard her.

Kathy shook her head.

"No, I can't sleep. I'll sit down and work on my embroidery."

Beth watched her mother hang up her coat, then sit down in the front room and pick up her needlework. Beth went upstairs to take off her own coat, then came back downstairs to find her mother staring into space. Kathy did not hear Beth enter, but when she saw her daughter sit down on the sofa, she picked up her work, embarrassed to appear lazy.

Beth opened the newspaper lying on the sofa. It contained her brother's obituary. Her mother wanted it cut out, so Beth got up to find the scissors in the kitchen.

"Don't go, Beth. Sit with me for a while," said Kathy.

"I'll just cut out the obituary and come back," said Beth, gesturing with her fingers as if they were scissors.

Kathy nodded. "Would you make me some tea, please?"

Beth went into the kitchen. She put the water on to boil, then found the scissors and cut the article from the paper. While she waited for the tea to brew, she reread the obituary. Then she stuffed it in a drawer of the hutch cabinet. She would later tell her mother where it was, but she did not want to leave it in the open as further reminder of their pain.

She brought the tea to her mother and sat on the sofa with her own cup. She did not like tea, but she sipped it politely for her mother's sake. When her mother set down her tea cup, she did not pick up her needle. She stared out the window. She made Beth nervous.

It was November. A gloomy, gray day. Fog came in from the lake, slowly permeating its way westward through the city, between the houses, the trees, the telephone poles, the streetlamps until it surrounded and seemed to smother the McCarey house. Beth felt the fog was like a grief that could not be lifted. There was nothing to do now. The funeral was over, the lunch eaten, the stone placed over an empty grave. Only emptiness remained.

Beth was sorry to have lost Jeremy — he had often teased her, but he had also bought her treats and even trusted her to babysit Emily. Yet Beth grieved more for her parents than for her brother. She was so much younger than Jeremy that she could scarcely remember when he had lived at home; for years now, she had been the only child in the house. Now she was sixteen, and with Emily moving away, no more children's voices would be heard in the McCarey home.

Beth sipped her tea again, but it had turned cold and disgusting. She and her mother had spent half an hour staring into space, not even noticing one another. Beth got up to carry the teacups into the kitchen.

"Don't go, Beth."

Beth gestured that she was only bringing the cups into the kitchen.

"Come back. I — I don't want to be alone today."

Beth smiled in assurance she would return. She felt unnerved by her mother's request. She rinsed out the tea cups, turned them upside down to dry, then went back to sit with her mother. Neither said anything. Kathy slowly worked at her embroidery. Beth sighed and got up to find something to read. When she stepped toward the bookshelf, she sensed her mother again staring at her, anxious that she not leave.

"Do you want me to read to you?" Beth asked, motioning to the book she had taken from the shelf.

Kathy could read lips well enough that if she watched Beth read aloud, she would understand, but she shook her head.

"I don't think I can concentrate today."

Beth was relieved. To read aloud on such an emotional day would have been trying.

She opened up a volume of poetry. It was boring — she could make no sense of its elaborate conceits. She longed for a good storybook to forget herself in, but all her books were upstairs, and her mother would be distressed if she left the room again. The house was so silent she could hear the kitchen clock ticking. She wondered whether her mother's world were always this terribly silent.

She had nearly dozed off when footsteps upstairs jolted her awake. Her mother was startled by her movement and looked askance at her. Beth just stared toward the doorway until her father entered. He looked more exhausted now than before his nap. He sat down in his chair next to his wife.

"How was your nap?" Kathy asked.

"All right," he said. She read his lips, then looked in his eyes, searching for how deeply the blow had hit him.

"Are you hungry?" she asked. "I should make supper."

"No, I don't feel like eating."

"Maybe just something light?"

"Maybe. I feel warm. My stomach gets upset when I sleep in the day."

"We're all exhausted. Maybe we could just have some scrambled eggs and toast."

"Okay," Patrick said. He took her hand. Neither got up.

Beth could not bear to watch a tender moment between her parents. She wanted to cry when she saw they were trying to be brave for each other. She went into the kitchen, free now to leave the room because her father was sitting with her mother. She wanted to go upstairs, to slip into unconscious sleep. Instead, she set the table, found the frying pan and cracked the eggs.

Then she heard sobbing. She tiptoed to the doorway.

"All my children gone," she heard her mother sob. "First the girls I never knew, then the boys. Now only Beth is left."

"Michael is still — " began Patrick.

"No, God took him too. I willingly gave one child to God, but He took four more."

"Let's be thankful we still have Beth," Patrick soothed.

"She's almost grown. Soon she'll marry and leave us. I don't think I can bear that."

Beth felt paralyzed. Could she marry and leave her parents? Would she have to wait until they were gone? They were both becoming elderly, but they might still live for years, and then, would she be too old to find a husband? Would she become an old maid like Thelma? She told herself she was being foolish, but she suddenly felt terrible fear. Did Jeremy's death mean the end of her life before it had barely begun? She felt the walls of her parents' house enclosing her into a tomb.

1928

September 17, 1928

Dear Brother Patrick,

Here the whole summer has gone and I have been meaning to write to you everyday. We are all prospering here and business in our shop is so good I have little free time to write. When I do have a free day, I spend it with my grandchildren. I think St. Patrick himself would be pleased to see our Ireland today. I wish you could see it — our people have now been free these seven years, and we have men like you, not rebels any longer, but Irish patriots, to thank for keeping our hopes and spirits alive during all our years of struggle. My son is now part of the Irish Parliament — I told him he reminds me of his fiery uncle — he is after all named for you, born as he was the year you left us. But unlike you, he is allowed to fight for laws to benefit his people, not against laws that oppress. He tells me to send you his love, and that he wishes you could come to visit, for you would be a hero here now, whatever accusations may have been made against you in the past. Of course I know you and I are too old to travel over the ocean, but we are always together in thought and heart.

Uncle Seamus had his birthday a couple days ago. He is ninety now. You should have been here to celebrate. He mentions you often; he is always remembering the past, and he tells us now, what he never mentioned when he was younger, stories of his childhood, of what he and Father were like as boys, about the great potato famine, about the time he went to the Abbey Theatre and saw William Butler Yeats, and a thousand other stories, half of them stretches of his imagination. When I laughed at him for telling us how he thumbed his nose at Queen Victoria the time she came to visit Ireland, he said, "She was never our Queen, and now we have our own government." And then he reminded me of what Father used to tell us, "That we Irish are all of us the sons and daughters of kings" and that we O'Connors are descended from that King of Ulster, who was foster father to Cuchulainn and husband to the star-eyed Deirdre. Uncle's claims are all a bit too grand for you and me, Patrick, but my son enjoys all these stories; he feels a great pride in his heritage, a pride he need not fear to display as we did in our youth. Ireland has truly been reborn.

Write when you get a chance. Let me know how your wife Kathy is. I hope her hearing does not deteriorate any more. It must be very difficult for both of you. Tell me again about your fierce Lake Superior and the multicolored autumn leaves, but do not expect me to believe them any finer than the beautiful Ring of Kerry. Let me know how my nephew Fr. Michael prospers in bringing souls to Christ, and finally, tell me if Beth has found herself a good Irishman for a husband. Write soon, Brother. Uncle Seamus, for all his high spirits, is not likely to live much longer, and then you and I will be the only ones who remember the old days. Even if they were not good old days, at least we were together then.

Much Love, Bridget

Patrick had been so engrossed in reading his sister's letter that he did not hear Kathy enter the dining room until she asked, "Who's the letter from?"

"My sister," he replied, turning to face her so she could read his lips.

"Why is it addressed to Patrick O'Connor?"

His sister had forgotten to write "McCarey" on the envelope. For a moment, Patrick sought to avoid explanation. Then he remembered what his sister had said — Ireland had changed — and for years now he had been a citizen of the United States. He no longer had to hide.

"Because that's my real name," he said.

Kathy stared at him. He was not worried. After all the years of love between them, she would understand when he explained. Then the demons would finally be behind him.

"Bridget must have forgotten to write my fake last name on the envelope," he said. "She's getting forgetful now that she's older."

Kathy had always suspected something wrong about her husband's past, but she had never questioned him. She remembered the night they were engaged, when her mother and Patrick had talked together for a long time, without her being allowed in the room. Her mother had found out everything, and trusting her mother's judgment, Kathy had never asked but simply let Patrick keep his secret. She did not ask now, would not even have asked about the name on the envelope if she had thought a moment before blurting out her question. But now Patrick was ready to tell her.

"I had to change my name because I was in trouble when I left Ireland. I couldn't risk being tracked down here. If I hadn't left, I might have ended up in prison."

"Did you do something awful?" she asked.

"Yes. I was young and foolish then, but I acted from what I thought were the right motives, although I later realized I was wrong."

"You don't need to tell me," said Kathy, seeing how nervous he looked. "It doesn't matter since it happened before we knew each other."

"I told your mother," said Patrick. "We agreed not to tell you because we didn't want to upset you. Are you mad?"

"No," Kathy smiled and took his hand. "I forgive you, if you need forgiveness."

"I confessed to the priest years ago," said Patrick. "God has forgiven me."

Kathy remembered he had gone to confession only once, back during the war, saying he did not want any of his sins to hurt his sons. Frank had died anyway, but Patrick had been different, calmer after that day.

"I can't imagine even God could stay mad at you for long," said Kathy. "Now take off that long face before Karl gets here."

Patrick pushed the letter back into its envelope. He heard the door open. Karl bellowed "Hello!" and Thelma shouted, "We're here, Aunt Kathy and Uncle Patrick!"

"Hello, everyone. Who'd you get a letter from, Patrick?" asked Karl, stepping into the dining room and seeing the envelope in his brother-in-law's hand.

"My sister."

"Sister? You never mentioned having a sister," said Thelma.

"She lives back in Ireland."

"You must miss her," said Karl, sitting down at the table after his daughter took his coat and went to hang it in the hall closet.

"Not so much anymore," said Patrick. "I used to miss Ireland, but I doubt I would recognize it now. My sister says it's changed so much — especially since its independence. Changed for the better, I'm thankful to say, but Marquette is my home now."

Kathy smiled.

"That's how I feel about Germany," said Karl. "I wanted to see my father's homeland, but I came home realizing here is where I belong. I guess I never had any desire to see Ireland because Mother never talked about it."

Patrick knew why his mother-in-law had been silent about Ireland, but he kept her secret from her children as she had kept his.

"Germany's changed too," said Karl. "The war left the people impoverished and oppressed. It's sad because they were fine people when I met them. I couldn't bear to visit there again and see their broken spirits. They're a proud people so I hope someday they'll rise again."

"Where's Beth?" asked Thelma, returning into the dining room.

"She's at work," said Patrick.

"At work?" said Karl. "I didn't know she was working."

"She just started this week," said Patrick. "When she graduated from Bishop Baraga, she didn't know what to do with herself so she found a job at St. Luke's Hospital in the diet kitchen."

"I don't know why she wants to work," said Kathy. "She could stay home and help me keep house. There's plenty to do around here. I was looking forward to having her at home more."

"I imagine it's a good thing," said Karl. "Maybe she'll learn to cook so she can find herself a husband."

"She's too young to marry," Kathy replied. "I won't let her yet."

"She will eventually," said Karl.

"I'm not married yet," said Thelma, "and I'm a lot older than her."

"Your father's the only man you need in your life," Karl replied.

Thelma was twenty-five, and none of her family was surprised she was not married. No one would say so, but they all knew she would not find a husband. Even if her plainness could be overlooked, her running tongue, and her simple mind would deter the most desperate men. Yet God had compensated her by making her a gifted pianist and giving her a rich father who doted upon her.

"When will Beth be home?" Thelma asked.

"In time for supper," said Kathy.

Thelma looked at the clock. Supper was two hours away. Sulking, she went into the front room and stretched out on the sofa, then opened a movie magazine so she could ogle the gorgeous young men of the cinema.

"How did you luck out, getting a date with a beautiful girl like her?" Roy asked.

Henry grinned as he combed his hair before the bathroom mirror. "What do you mean, 'How did I luck out?' Don't you know all the dames swoon over your older brother?"

"I doubt it, but you did luck out with this one — she's gorgeous," said Roy, although he was not interested in love — he did not trust it. It held a person back. Look at his parents — his father could have been a great architect, his mother an opera singer if they had applied themselves, but instead they had married and raised a family. Still, Roy admitted he would not mind one night out with a pretty girl like the one Henry would see tonight. "Didn't she just break up with that Lundgren fellow?"

"Yeah, so? She found a fellow she liked better," Henry bragged.

"Henry, you dog!" said Bill. At eight years old, he enjoyed American slang. He had come into his older brothers' room and plopped himself on a bed. He found their conversation highly educational.

Roy grimaced at his little brother's coarseness.

Henry saw Roy's expression in the mirror and said, "Cheer up, Roy. Maybe she has a friend I can fix you up with."

"Not interested," Roy replied.

Henry did not waste time asking why. He knew his brother's only interest was in moving away. Roy had begun college last year, but after a few weeks, he had left school, saying it was not for him. He had taken an astronomy course, only to decide the teacher knew nothing of importance. "There's all this emphasis on light and gas and I don't know all what, but there isn't any appreciation for the Creator, for the sheer beauty and miracle of the stars. These professors know the individual facts, but miss the big picture, the real point of it all."

Henry had heard these complaints many times. Roy had also said he would not settle down with any woman. These comments had begun shortly after Theo's visit two years ago. Since then, Roy had gotten it into his head that he wanted to go out to California, to see the country, to see the world. Since he had dropped out of college, Roy had worked to save money so he could move away. He intended to travel. He would work only as needed to earn enough money to journey on to the next place.

"Roy, if you had yourself a beautiful woman," Henry told him, "all those wild thoughts would disappear from your mind."

"Women only weigh a man down," said Roy. Henry did not answer. He had to go pick up his date so he ran downstairs.

"Goodbye, Ma," Henry said, kissing his mother on the cheek as she set a platter of food on the dining room table.

"Don't you want something to eat before you go?" Margaret asked.

"Nope, we're going out to a restaurant."

"I don't know why you waste your money on girls," she said.

"Let him go, Maggie," said Will. "He's only young once."

"What's this girl's name again?" Margaret asked.

"Millicent Maki."

"A Finn," Margaret frowned. "They're so clannish. Can't you find a nice American girl? Does this Millie even speak English?"

"Of course, Mother. She was born in the United States."

"Well, it's a ridiculous name," said Margaret.

"I better go," said Henry to avoid further questions. He climbed into his car and roared toward town while trying to smell his own aftershave to make sure he had put on enough. Fifteen minutes later, he arrived at the kitchen entrance to St. Luke's Hospital. He trembled as he went to the door. He hoped Millie would still be wearing her hairnet so he could watch her take it off. He loved when she shook out her hair, displaying golden tresses, as shiny as those of the goddess Freyja. They gave him a chill everytime he saw them.

He had dreamed of going out with Millicent for months. Since he had first seen her in Donckers, he had asked every guy in town about her. Then he had arranged to bump into her one day when she came out of work. Only, he had not expected she would be crying when they passed on the sidewalk. He had seized the opportunity to offer her his handkerchief and give her a ride home. In exchange, she had given him a beautiful smile of gratitude. The next day, even though he had finished work an hour earlier, he happened to be driving "home from work" when she stepped out of the hospital. He had again offered her a ride. This time, she had told him why she had been crying — her boyfriend had been mean to her, so she had broken up with him. Then Henry had boldly asked whether she would go out with him that Friday night. She had agreed. He had come home to brag to Roy, who could scarcely believe it. Millicent was renowned as one of Marquette's great beauties. Roy could not imagine what his overalls-clad, skinny brother could have done to attract her attention.

"Her broken heart must have affected her brain," he said. "She's far too pretty for someone like you."

But Henry remained in high spirits. He intended to kiss Millie tonight and make her promise him a second date. That would show Roy.

"Good evening," he said to the woman closest to the kitchen door when he arrived at the hospital. "Is Millie here?"

"I don't know. Let me go check," she replied.

Another, slightly plump girl approached him.

"Millicent left with her boyfriend five minutes ago."

Henry did not understand. "Her boyfriend? No, she couldn't have. I'm here to pick her up for the evening."

"All I know is she left with her boyfriend, the same guy who's always come to pick her up in the past."

"You're sure it was Millie?"

"Sure. I've been working here for a month now. I know all the girls," she replied. She was hot and tired from the steamy kitchen, and she did not like Millicent, who always talked in that odd Finnish language to the other Finnish girls, and made her feel as if they were laughing at her. She did not know what the boys saw in her.

"Oh," said Henry.

The girl saw his shoulders droop.

"I thought she had broken up with him," Henry said.

"She does every week; they fight constantly, but they always get back together."

"Oh," said Henry.

"I'm sorry," said the girl.

Henry did not know what to do. He was too embarrassed to go home. The girl looked as if she rather pitied him. He had scarcely looked at her until now. She was no beauty, but she did have pretty brown hair and a cute nose, even if she were on the plump side. She did not look too many years younger than him.

"Say," he said. "Are you doing anything tonight? You wouldn't want to — what time do you get off work?"

"Not until seven," she said.

"Oh, well, I could wait around if you'd like to go get a bite to eat."

"My parents'll worry if I'm not home."

"Oh, well, maybe some other time then."

"I guess I could call them," she said. She wondered why she said it. They would not want her going out with any young man, least of all a stranger. She would tell them she was working late so they would not worry.

"Great, I'll see you in an hour then," said Henry. At least he would not have to lie to his family that he had been on a date. He would just avoid specific questions about whom he had been with.

"Okay," she said, turning to go.

"Wait! What's your name?" he asked.

"Beth."

♣   ♣   ♣

Morning sunlight broke through the upstairs window and woke Karl Berg-mann. He groaned and rolled over, realizing he had forgotten to shut the bedroom curtains the night before. Once he knew he would not be able to fall back asleep, he glanced at the clock. It was still early. Thelma would not be up for an hour. He did not want to disturb her. His valet would not even have the fire going yet in the dining room. He could get up, but he had nothing urgent to do. He usually went to his office a few hours every day, but mostly he let other men take care of his business now. Maybe he and Thelma could go for a drive this afternoon, just to get out of the house — maybe drive up to Copper Harbor, to stand on top of Brockway Mountain and look out on the lake. It was autumn, the most beautiful time of year, and a perfect day for such a trip.

He debated whether the view from Brockway Mountain could be much better than that from his window. He and Ben had picked the perfect location when they had built their lumberjack mansion on top of this hill, just outside Calumet. Here they could look down on the forest, with Calumet in the distance, and on a clear day, they could even see Hancock and Houghton. They had built their house from trees they had personally cut down, then hired carpenters and an artisan to carve intricate doorframes and lay hardwood floors to create one of Calumet's finest homes when Calumet had outrivaled Marquette in population and wealth. Now as prosperous mining days were fading into memory, Karl's mansion spoke of another time when mining and lumbering were the lifeblood of Upper Michigan. Those years had climaxed at the same time Aino had decorated Karl's home with a woman's touch. Now Aino and Ben were gone, and Thelma had grown restless to escape the old house, whose glory had vanished with Karl's youth.

Karl looked out his window; autumn's early morning mists rose up from the forest's little pools and rivers. Despite the cool air, sunbeams highlighted the tree tops so bright reds, oranges, and yellows blended with the pine trees to create a speckled collection of color. "It's Nature's own Oktoberfest," Karl thought. Only once before had the autumn colors appeared so brilliant to him, the year he had gone to Germany, to see the fairyland of his father's stories. He remembered how in the Black Forest he had realized what he should have known all along, what had made him come home, although he had never been able to tell anyone. Never again had he desired to leave Northern Michigan's forests or his family.

He was getting old. He had not chopped down a tree in a year. He could feel himself getting soft. His stomach was no longer hard. His pants had grown tighter these last couple years, and when he lifted an axe, it had felt heavier. While his shirts were more full in the waist, they were looser in the shoulders.

He should get up and read to block out these melancholy thoughts. He would ask Thelma at breakfast whether she wanted to drive up to Copper Harbor. Riding down roads surrounded by trees always cheered him up. He pushed back the blankets and started to lift his leg out of bed when he found he could not move it. A sharp pain passed up his left side. A great jolt slammed him backward. He felt as if he had fallen onto a soft pillow of crunchy autumn leaves.

"I got you," laughed Ben, pinning Karl to the forest floor.

"I'll beat you one of these days," said Karl, trying to sound furious, but he could not keep from laughing.

"Only if you chop off both my arms with your axe," smiled Ben, his hands holding down Karl's wrists, while Karl lay helpless, his giant muscles unable to aid him against the viselike grip of Ben, the forest god.

"I could never hurt you," said Karl. "I doubt anyone could."

Ben tapped him on the head, then jumped back to his feet.

"Come on," he said, "let's go. Paul's waiting for us. We've a mile worth of trees to chop down today."

Karl bounced onto his feet, then brushed the dead oak leaves off his flannel shirt. He looked about for his axe, which he found leaning against a tree. Ben stood up ahead on the forest trail, motioning for him to follow. Robins chirped overhead. The sun glistened through the tree branches, illuminating Ben's blond hair into a halo. Karl grabbed his axe and started down the trail into the eternal forest.

"Thelma!" said Patrick. "We had no idea you were coming today!"

He had just opened the door to his niece; he peered behind her to look for Karl. "Where's your father?" he asked, not yet noticing she had been crying.

Beth came to the door, having heard the bell. "Hi, Thelma. What are you doing here? Where's Uncle Karl?"

Thelma had cried all the way to Marquette. Now her throat was so dry she could scarcely speak.

"He's not coming," she said. "Never again. He — I found him in his bed this morning. He's gone."

Beth did not understand at first, but Patrick did.

"You poor girl. Did you find him all by yourself? How awful for you."

"He usually comes to my room after I'm dressed," said Thelma, "and we walk downstairs to breakfast. This morning when he didn't come, I went to his room. He didn't answer when I knocked, so I opened the door to see whether he had already gone down to breakfast without me. When I saw him, I thought he was sleeping, but — "

She started to choke, her throat too dry for her to sob more.

Patrick took her arm and drew her into the house.

"And you drove here?" asked Beth.

"I didn't know what else to do?"

"What did Roger say?" asked Patrick, referring to Karl's valet.

"I didn't tell him. I was so upset I just ran out of the house. I guess I panicked. I just wanted to be with my family, so I got into Papa's car and drove here."

"By yourself?" asked Beth. She did not know that Thelma could drive.

"Beth, go get your mother," said Patrick, walking Thelma to the sofa.

Beth did as she was told, leaving her father to comfort her cousin. She found her mother bent over the washing machine. How would she tell her mother that Uncle Karl had died? But since her father was comforting Thelma, Beth would have to comfort her mother. Awkwardly, she put her hand on her mother's shoulder. Kathy turned, startled, then felt alarmed by her daughter's face. She let Beth pull her toward a chair. When she read the sad words on Beth's lips, she lowered her head. Beth reached over to lift her mother's face, so she could also explain that Thelma had just shown up on the doorstep.

"The poor girl," said Kathy, wiping her wet hands on her apron. "I better go see to her. Beth, will you wring out those last two sheets and hang them to dry?"

Beth obeyed, glad her mother's first thought was for Thelma. She was relieved to finish the laundry, to have something to do other than comfort her mother.

She finished wringing out the sheets, then brewed some tea, hoping it would soothe Thelma's nerves. Her poor cousin must be exhausted after finding her father dead, and then driving for hours from Calumet.

Thelma drank the tea quickly, being terribly thirsty after constantly sobbing on the way to Marquette. Beth perched on a chair arm while her parents sat on the sofa, one on each side of Thelma.

Beth did not know what to say. She hated death — it always made a person uncomfortable. She wanted to cry herself — she could not imagine life without Uncle Karl's hearty laugh; she recalled his past visits, all the times he had told his tall tales, making her brothers' faces light up; in those days, when all their lives seemed so hopeful, he had been the boys' hero. Since the war, life had only gotten harder. She hoped all of adulthood was not this way.

"Thelma, dear, why don't you take a little nap upstairs," said Kathy.

"I'll call Roger to tell him you're here," said Patrick, thinking poor Roger was probably at a loss what to do with no one to instruct him.

Kathy led Thelma upstairs while Patrick and Beth went into the kitchen. Beth took her time washing Thelma's teacup and saucer, then wiping the cupboard while she listened to her father telephone Uncle Karl's house. Only it was Thelma's house now, that entire enormous house. How funny to think of Thelma living there alone.

"The poor girl," said Kathy, when she rejoined her family in the kitchen.

"Roger seems all right," said Patrick. "He's going to call the funeral home to take the body. He said he'd pick out Karl's best clothes for him. I told him we'd bring Thelma back tomorrow. I don't think she's in any state to travel more today."

"All right," said Kathy, collapsing into a chair. "Beth, I don't suppose you'd make me a cup of tea?"

Beth set more water on the stove to boil, then dried out Thelma's cup.

"Mother, what will Thelma do now? I don't think she can take care of herself alone in that giant house."

"I don't know," said Kathy. "I'm sure Roger would stay to take care of her, but he's not all that young, and she has no real friends. We're the only people she has now that her father is gone."

"Maybe," said Beth, "she could stay with us until she decides what to do."

Kathy said nothing, waiting for her husband to answer.

"It would be a good idea," Beth added. "Now that I'm working, I'm not home to help as much, and Thelma would be company for you, Mother. She probably doesn't want to be alone, at least not for a while. I think we should at least make the offer."

"She'll have a house to herself now," said Kathy, "and with all her father's money, I imagine she can do whatever she likes."

"Yes, but we all know she's not very levelheaded," said Patrick. "Look at how she bolted from the house when she found her father this morning."

"You can't blame her for that," said Kathy.

"No, but a sensible girl would have told someone rather than just running out of the house and driving for four hours. Roger was worried sick about where she had gone to."

"I agree with Father," said Beth. "Thelma's not very logical, and she's going to need someone she can trust to help her manage all that money. I think we should try to help her."

"It can't hurt," said Kathy. She thought it would be nice to have her niece around. The house was so lonely without the boys, and upstairs were two empty bedrooms. Thelma could have her grandmother's old room if she wanted to stay.

Beth smiled. She knew Thelma would cheer her mother. And with Thelma here, Beth would not have to keep her mother company every evening. Beth had barely been allowed out of the house these past two years, and she had nearly fought with her parents to be allowed to get the job at the hospital because her mother worried about her riding the streetcar across town by herself. With Thelma around, her mother might not depend on her so much. She might have a more normal life now.

Not that she was ready to tell her mother about Henry. After all, they had only gone out once, just last night. She could still not believe he had asked her out, especially after she had been sharp with him when he had come to pick up Millicent. She had almost expected he would not come back to get her, but he had. She did not know what had possessed her to go out with him, except that she could not bear the thought of another dull evening with her parents. Thinking she must be a disappointment to him compared to Millicent, who was such a beauty, she had been unable to refrain from asking him why he had asked her out.

"You seemed nice," he had said, "and I didn't want to go home and be alone."

Funny, but she had liked him after that. She had not known what to say, but she had understood how he felt. She had never been anywhere with any boy other than her brothers. Once she was in his car, she had been so nervous she had nearly asked him to drive her home. When he had asked where she wanted to go, she had said, "I don't know."

"Are you hungry?" he had asked.

"Um, not right now," she had replied, instantly thinking how silly it sounded.

"Why don't we go for a drive then, so we can talk and get to know each other?"

"Okay." He had seemed nice. Real friendly. He reminded her of Frank. She still missed Frank.

Henry had driven away from the hospital. He drove awfully fast, faster than Uncle Karl —

How could she be thinking about last night when Uncle Karl was now gone?

"I think I better lie down for a little while," said Kathy, sighing and then going up the back stairs. Patrick followed to comfort his wife.

Beth went into the front room and stared out of the window. She tried to think about poor Uncle Karl, and how they might help Thelma. But every automobile that passed the house made her crane her neck to see whether Henry were in it. She almost wished he would show up to take her for a ride. She hoped she would see him again. Maybe he would pick her up at the hospital the next time she worked? That would be better; how would she explain to her parents if he showed up at their house?

He had been kind to her, asking her questions about her family. Had she liked school? Had she thought about college? Did she want to be married someday?

"My parents need me at home," she had replied. "I'm their only child left."

"There's five of us in my family," he had said.

"I had three brothers and two sisters," she had replied. "My sisters died at birth, and two of my brothers died just after they became adults. My only living brother is a priest so I don't see him much."

Then she had realized she had just told him she was Catholic. She had wondered what religion he was.

"I'm a Baptist," he said, as if reading her mind.

Her mother would not want her going out with a boy who was not Catholic. She had thought she had better tell him to bring her home before trouble started, but he said, "I know you said you weren't hungry, but I was going to take Millicent out for supper. Could I at least buy you some ice cream?"

"Ice cream sounds good," she said, "but I have my own money."

"No, it's my treat."

"No, that's not fair. This isn't really a — "

"What?"

"I mean, it's not as if we're really going out, is it? So you don't need to treat me."

"I want to."

Beth had felt immature then, afraid he would think she were worried about his intentions, but he had taken it all in stride, never being scornful or less than a gentleman. They were then north of Marquette, heading up the Big Bay Road.

"Maybe we can stop in Birch to get ice cream," he suggested.

She said that would be fine. But they had been disappointed when they reached the little town. Birch had once been a prosperous village, home to a sawmill and close to Frank Krieg's gold mine, but the sawmill had closed and the mine had long since failed to yield enough gold to make a profit. Only a few families and a street full of empty buildings remained of what was fast becoming a ghost town.

"I haven't been here in years," Henry said, "but I remember getting ice cream with my father one summer when he was working around here."

Birch's present state was a sign that the great days of logging and homesteading had passed. Beth had not thought of Uncle Karl last night, but now she realized he was like Birch, part of the old world of great lumberjacks and mining. She and Henry had driven down Birch's deserted main street. The car's headlights had lit up ghostly houses and former stores. The rumbling car engine had been the only sound. An eerie silence had settled over Beth's soul.

Then in the gathering dusk had burst out the song of a whippoorwill. The sun had disappeared; it was mid-October; most of the birds had migrated south, but this whippoorwill sang anyway.

"It's beautiful," Beth said. Henry said nothing. Instead, he had stopped and turned off the car, and a look of great pleasure had come over his face as he listened to the song. Beth had decided that when he smiled he was good-looking, but not quite handsome.

When the bird had stopped warbling, Henry said, "Let's go on to Big Bay. We can probably find ice cream there."

Beth had known her parents would worry if she were not home by nine o'clock. But she had not wanted to go home yet.

"Okay," she said.

They had pulled out of Birch and started down the road to Big Bay.

They had been quiet, but the silence had not been awkward. It was an appreciative quiet. Henry had his window cracked open so the cool autumn air filled the car, bringing in the comforting smell of decaying leaves. When they had reached Big Bay, Henry pulled the car into a small restaurant. They had gone inside and found a table. A waitress had quickly come over to take their order.

"We're closing in fifteen minutes," she stated.

"We just wanted some ice cream," said Henry.

"We're out of ice cream."

"Oh," said Beth. For a minute, she wished she had not come — even felt a little afraid. What would this woman think of her being out with a man after dark?

"What do you have that won't be any trouble to fix?" Henry asked.

"We got some pie."

"What kind?"

"Apple and blueberry."

"Blueberry for me," Henry said. "What will you have, Beth?"

Beth wished he had not used her name. Of course, she did not know the waitress. Her parents need never know she had been here. But she still wished he had not said her name. "Um, blueberry I guess," she replied.

The waitress looked scornfully at her, then went to slice the pie.

"I don't imagine we'll have blueberry pie again until next summer," Henry said.

"No." She felt so nervous she could think of nothing interesting to say, but somehow she came up with, "We used to have blueberry pie all the time when I was younger, but now my parents are too old to go picking berries."

"Did you ever take the berry train from Marquette?" Henry asked.

"Oh yes, every summer when I was a girl."

The ornery waitress returned to hand out the pie without a word. Henry smiled kindly and said, "Thank you," to the waitress, as appreciative as if she had cooked him a seven-course meal.

Then a memory had triggered in Beth. She had seen that smile before. Was he the same boy? The boy from the blueberry fields? She remembered she had looked for him the next year but had not seen him, and when she had mentioned him to her mother, her mother had not even remembered him. But Beth had liked him so much. Hadn't that been the summer after Frank died in the war, and she had been missing Frank so much, and this boy had let her follow him around all afternoon and even helped her fill her berry bucket?

"What do you do?" she asked.

"I'm a carpenter," he replied. "I help my Pa mostly. We build houses, or do little things like build bookshelves or fix porches, or whatever people need."

"That's interesting," she said. "More interesting than my washing dishes."

The waitress then returned, demanding payment. Henry reached into his wallet and gave her some money, tipping her generously.

"Did you make the pie?" he asked.

"Yeah," she grunted.

"It's as good as my mother's," he smiled.

The waitress returned to the register without a word.

Henry rolled his eyes and Beth giggled. She had thought him charming, the way he could joke, yet be polite. He was a gentleman, even when people mistreated him.

"I guess I better be going home now," she said when they were outside and he opened the car door for her.

"All right. I imagine my parents will be worried too."

"Do you still live with your parents?"

"Yes. I'm saving up money to build my own house someday, but my parents need me right now. My brothers and sisters are still young and need looking after, so I try to help out where I can. I don't really need the money for myself. It's not as if I have my own family to support yet."

"Same here," she said. "My parents don't need my money, but I stay with them because I'm the last of their children and they'd be lonely without me. They're in their sixties now so I worry about leaving them alone."

"My folks are only in their forties," Henry said, "but I know what you mean. I worry about them as much as they worry about me."

They talked about school then. He explained that he had dropped out after eighth grade to help his parents, but he had a brother who had finished and even gone to college for a semester. "I don't know about Roy though," he said. "We all agree he's the smart one in the family, but I don't understand him when he talks about how knowledge isn't found in colleges but in life. I don't know much myself, except that I'm content just pounding nails with my hammer."

Beth had thought Henry a simple, unassuming boy. She had known many boys in school who bragged they would become doctors or lawyers. She doubted any of them would do better than Henry at finding contentment in life.

"Where do you live?" he asked. "Tell me how to get there."

Not until this moment had Beth realized he would have to bring her home. Could she have him drop her off at a corner where she could take the streetcar home? But it was too late now for the streetcars to be running. What would she tell her parents if they saw a man bring her home?

"Just drop me off on Fourth Street by the courthouse," she said. "I can walk from there."

"No, I'll drive you to your door. You shouldn't walk alone in the dark."

For the first time, she had wished he were not so polite. Still, she had not wanted him to think her a silly girl, afraid of her parents. She had given him the directions. As they had approached her house, she had strained her eyes, hoping the front curtains were drawn, the lights out so her parents would not look out to see her.

He had pulled into her yard. She had cringed at the sound of the engine. She had quickly opened the car door. "Thanks. I had a good time."

"Maybe I'll see you again sometime."

"Okay, bye," she had said, quickly shutting the car door. Then she had run to the house, opened and closed the house door behind her, all the while listening for the car to pull out of the yard, hoping it would be gone before her parents looked out the window.

"How was work?" her father had asked when she went into the kitchen.

"Fine."

"Who drove you home?"

"One of the girls." Even now, she still felt horrible that she had lied. She had not lied since she was a child, but life had given her little to lie about until now.

"I'm going to bed. I'm really tired," she had said to avoid further questions.

She had kissed her mother and father goodnight, then gone upstairs. When she was alone in her room and had changed into her nightgown, she began to remember every detail of the evening.

Now she stared out the window, trying to remember the color of Henry's car so she would know it if he drove by.

"Maybe I'll see you again sometime," he had said. Maybe they were just polite words he would have said to any girl. He had not kissed her. If he had really liked her, he would have kissed her. Or maybe he had wanted to, but had felt it would be too forward — it had been only their first date — had it even been a date? Besides, she had gotten out of the car so quickly she had not given him time to kiss her if he had wanted to. What if he showed up at the hospital tonight and she were not there? She had forgotten to tell him which days she worked. And now she would be going to Calumet for a couple days for Uncle Karl's funeral. If Henry came here or to the hospital and did not see her, would he think she was avoiding him? Would she ever see him again? Did he even want to see her again? He was the only boy she had ever been with. She felt foolish when other girls had plenty of young men pursuing them. But now she had been out with one boy. She felt braver, better about herself for it. She hoped she would see him again.

❦   ❦   ❦

The day after his date with Beth, Henry was nervous that his family would ask how it had gone with Millicent. He dreaded to admit she had gone back to her old boyfriend, and worse that he had been too embarrassed to come home so he had asked out another girl.

But when at breakfast, Roy asked, "Are you going to see Millicent again?" Henry just said, "I don't know. We'll see."

Then Bill started yelling because he still did not have any pancakes when everyone else did, and Roy told Bill to behave himself while Margaret scurried to finish putting breakfast on the table. Henry was relieved the subject had been changed; he hoped his date would not be brought up again.

"Will, did you read *The Mining Journal* yesterday?" asked Margaret when she sat down at the table.

"No," he replied, pouring syrup onto his pancakes.

"Don't use all of that. It's all we have left. Leave some for Bill and the girls," Margaret said.

"What was I supposed to see in the paper?"

"Your nephew's name."

"Harry?"

"No, the other one. I can't remember his name."

"Douglas," said Will.

"I didn't know we had a cousin named Douglas," said Ada.

"We don't talk about him," Eleanor said. "He's one of Aunt Sylvia's children."

"Oh," Ada nodded. She understood from her mother they were not to be involved with those Cummings.

"What about him?" Will asked.

"He got married," said Margaret. She got up and dug out yesterday's newspaper, then turned to the wedding announcements. "Here it is," she said, shoving the page in front of her husband. "He married some girl in Escanaba. Oh, and look at this. They were married in a Catholic church. As if those boys haven't already given their mother enough grief without one of them marrying a Catholic."

"At least he was married in a church," Eleanor said. "You never know with those Cummings."

"That's enough Eleanor," said Will. "They are your cousins. You're no better than they are."

Eleanor scowled. She knew she was better than them. Her mother had told her how the Cumming girl had been killed while intoxicated and speeding with her lover. And one of the boys had been in prison. And everyone knew Aunt Sylvia's husband was a useless drunk.

"Poor Sylvia," said Margaret. "At least Douglas and his wife live in Escanaba so we don't have to see them. The last thing we need is a Catholic in the family."

Henry had not been listening until he heard this comment. All his thoughts were of Beth, the wonderful girl he had met last night. She had been so nice, even when that waitress had given them stale blueberry pie; she had pretended to appreciate it and to be grateful for his treating her to dessert. Millicent would have complained if he had bought her anything less than prime rib. Why had he not met a girl like Beth before?

"What's wrong with Catholics?" Ada asked her mother.

Margaret nearly snorted. "They worship idols for one. They pray to the Virgin Mary so there's no way they'll ever get into Heaven. They have ties to the mafia. They — "

"Maggie, don't put ideas into the children's heads," said Will.

"Well, it's true."

"I doubt Doug will get involved with the mafia," Will said.

"You never know. His brother went to prison for selling liquor, and that Al Capone, isn't he a bootlegger and in the mafia. He's Italian so he must be Catholic."

"So Henry, what did you do last night with your girl?" Will changed the subject. He loved Margaret, but sometimes she was not quite reasonable.

"Not much. We went for a drive and then we stopped at a restaurant and had some pie. We just talked mostly."

"Sounds boring," said Roy.

"Some of us are content with simple things," Henry replied.

"Some of us will rot in this little town," Roy retorted.

"Then why don't you leave?" Henry asked.

"I will next spring. As soon as I have enough money, I'll be gone."

"Boys, don't argue at the breakfast table," said Will. "Really, Roy, I don't know what has gotten into you lately."

Henry was tired of hearing Roy talk about leaving. He suspected his brother used money and winter as excuses for why he did not leave. He was starting to doubt Roy would ever go anywhere. He did not know how to take Roy anymore. His brother needed to find a nice girl, like Beth, to settle down with. Henry wanted to see Beth again, real soon. But he understood that if he kept seeing her, problems would arise. His mother obviously did not like Catholics.

1929

Karl Bergmann was laid to rest in the Calumet cemetery between his wife, Aino, and his best friend, Ben. A tremendous oak tree rose above them, providing shelter to the graves of these pioneers. Acorns would fall there. Squirrels would bury them in the ground. New trees would rise. Nature would continue its cycles.

But for the present, grief remained. Thelma was so devastated by her father's loss that her aunt and uncle let her stay with them indefinitely. With Beth's encouragement, the stay became long-term. By the following spring, Thelma had sold the house in Calumet and stated she had no intention of living anywhere other than with her aunt and uncle. Her companionship was a great comfort to her aunt, and her inheritance meant she need not work.

"Perhaps someday I'll marry," she confided to Beth, "so Aunt Kathy can teach me to keep house. I never had to for Papa because we always had servants."

Beth could not imagine any man wanting to marry Thelma, and she pitied her cousin for thinking otherwise. Yet Thelma amused Beth; although she rarely meant to — seldom realizing how outlandish were many of her simple remarks — she had brought laughter back into a house that had been grim for two years after Jeremy's death. Best of all, Thelma's presence made Kathy less dependent on her daughter; not that Beth was officially allowed to date boys, but she secretly managed to see Henry, and they liked each other enough that neither saw anyone else.

Then one spring day, Thelma complained of being cooped up in the house. The snow was melting, the daffodils blooming, the great outdoors calling. Since Beth had the day off, she agreed to go shopping with her cousin. Patrick stayed home to keep Kathy company since her deafness made her nervous about being left alone. The young ladies enjoyed browsing through downtown Marquette's various shops. Thelma freely spent money, having a substantial yearly income. Eventually, Beth grew tired of watching her cousin's frivolous spending when she only had a few dollars and worked too hard to part with them so easily.

"Aren't you going to buy anything?" Thelma asked as she paid for a new scarf.

"I was going to offer to buy us cokes at Donckers," Beth replied.

"All right," said Thelma. "All this shopping has made me thirsty."

The girls were soon seated in Donckers. Thelma had her back to the door. Beth was the only one to see the two young men in their work clothes come inside.

"I can at least buy you something for your trip," Henry Whitman told his younger brother. "If you're going to travel across country, you'll need some chocolate."

Roy did not want any candy, but he let Henry buy it so his brother would feel better. He would miss Henry just as much as Henry would miss him.

As the soda jerk filled a bag with chocolates, Henry spotted Beth. An awkward moment followed. Neither had told their families about the other. Should they, in a public place, with family members present, acknowledge each other? Henry recognized Thelma from Beth's descriptions. He did not know whether they could trust Thelma to be silent, but he figured Roy could keep the secret for one day until he left town.

"Where are you going?" asked Roy as Henry stepped over to the girls.

"Hi, Beth," said Henry, as if there were nothing unusual about their meeting.

"Hello," she said.

"Who are you?" Thelma demanded.

"Thelma, this is Henry. Henry, this is my cousin, Thelma."

"Pleased ta meetcha," said Thelma.

By now Roy had stepped over. Henry introduced his brother.

"Are you having cokes?" Henry asked. It was a stupid question. Full coke glasses were in front of the girls. But he did not know what else to say.

"Yes," said Beth. "What are you doing here?"

"Buying candy for Roy. He's going on a trip tomorrow."

"Where are you going?" asked Thelma.

"Out West."

Beth had heard all about Roy's intended trip. She smiled. "I hope you have a good time."

"Are you going to be a cowboy?" asked Thelma. "You look too scrawny to me."

Roy felt insulted but said nothing. Henry stood awkwardly. Beth sipped her coke.

"Beth, how do you know Henry?" Thelma asked.

"I don't remember," said Beth. "We've just seen each other around town."

"He's good looking," said Thelma, as if Henry were not present.

Roy poked his brother. "At least she approves of one of us."

Henry blushed.

"He is good looking," Beth smiled.

"You two would make a nice couple," said Thelma.

"Well, I'll see you around," said Henry, thinking it best now to retreat.

"Goodbye," said Beth.

The brothers returned to the counter to pay for the candy.

Henry could not resist one last glance back at the booth.

"Goodbye, Henry!" Thelma shouted. "Goodbye, Henry's skinny brother."

"She's a pain," Roy said when they were outside.

"I don't think Thelma's right in the head," Henry replied.

"How do you know?"

"Beth told me."

"How do you know Beth anyway?"

Henry had figured if he told his parents about Beth an explosion would follow because she was Catholic. But he felt he could trust Roy with his secret.

"You remember last fall I was supposed to go out with Millicent Maki?"

"Yeah," said Roy.

"Well, she stood me up so I took Beth out instead."

"Oh," said Roy. He had been meaning to ask what had happened to Millicent.

"I mean," said Henry, "that Beth and I are going out. We have been for several months. It's just once every couple weeks, but we really like each other."

"As long as she's not like that cousin of hers," said Roy, as they climbed into Henry's car. "She's not that pretty though. You can probably do better."

"I think she's pretty," said Henry. "It doesn't matter what you think."

"Cripe, you don't need to get so defensive about it," said Roy. "If you like her so much, why didn't you tell me before?"

"Because Ma and Pa won't approve."

"Why not?" asked Roy, shoveling down the chocolates meant for his trip.

"She's Catholic," said Henry.

"Oh," said Roy. His face drooped as he watched his brother's face do the same. Then he thought aloud, "Maybe she'll convert for you."

"I don't think so," said Henry. "Her family is really Catholic. I mean, her brother's a priest."

"Then you better stay away from her, Henry. Ma'll be furious if she finds out. There's plenty of other girls."

"Not like Beth. She's so sweet. She doesn't care that I don't have money. She's polite, and she doesn't fuss over her clothes or her hair. I think she's the one."

Roy had been unprepared for such a speech from his brother. He looked out at Lake Superior as they drove toward Harvey. Tomorrow he would be on a train headed West. He planned to go to San Francisco, maybe stay with Theo, see Aunt Sarah and her infamous husband, and his grandparents. But first he wanted to see America. He wanted to ride the rails, to stow away on trains and go wherever they might take him — the Dakotas, Montana, Louisiana, Texas, wherever. Marquette was too small, too remote a place when all the world was out there to be explored. Small towns were too repressive — that was apparent just from Henry and Beth's situation — if they went together, everyone in Marquette would talk, and the Catholics and Protestants would split lines. Roy wondered whether Beth's parents approved. He knew his mother would not — she seldom approved of anything — he loved her, but she was one reason he was glad to be leaving.

"If you love her, Henry, then don't worry what anyone else thinks," Roy nearly shouted. "If she makes you happy, marry her. It's your life, no one else's."

Henry was surprised but pleased by his brother's vehemence.

"Thanks, but it's not that easy. Ma's anger alone will be hard to deal with."

"She's your mother; she loves you; she'll get over it."

"I don't know."

"Don't live scared all the time, Henry. You've always worked hard and done everything you could for the family. You deserve some happiness."

Roy seemed fearless these days. Henry admired his brother for finally finding the courage to leave, but he knew he could not do the same. It was less, he told himself, from fear than because he had responsibilities to his family — Roy did not or could not understand that because he was not the oldest sibling. Roy did not realize how their parents had struggled for them, and because of that struggle, Henry could not hurt them. He just wished he could take care of his family and Beth as well. Beth understood; she felt the same loyalty to her parents. He knew he and Beth could be happy together and he was certain everything could work out if it were not for their religious differences. He wanted it to work out. He would find a way. Roy was leaving on a train, looking for something Henry had found right here; he just needed to figure out how to hold onto it.

"Is Beth there?"

Henry had waited an hour until his mother had gone to the outhouse, his father was in the barn, and Bill and his sisters were playing outside. Finally, he could talk on the telephone in private, but he knew he only had a minute before someone would intrude.

"Just a minute," said Patrick, assuming the man on the other end of the line must be his daughter's boss. He wished they had never bought a telephone. The only calls they ever seemed to get were from the hospital when some lazy girl called in sick and Beth had to take her place.

"Beth, it's for you," Patrick called. She took the phone, silently asking her father who it was.

"Someone from work, I guess," he muttered.

"Hello," she said.

"Hi, Beth. It's Henry."

"Oh, hello," she said. She had wondered whether he would ever dare call her at home. How would she explain it if her parents asked?

"I'm sorry about the other day at Donckers. Is it all right?"

"Yeah, Thelma didn't say much about it."

"I told my brother about us," said Henry.

"Oh." Was it significant that he had told his brother?

He cleared his throat.

"What are you doing?" he asked.

"Just reading a book."

"A love story?" he laughed, then felt he sounded stupid.

"No. *The Girls of Gardenville* by Carroll Watson Rankin. It's just a children's book really, but since it's by a local author I thought I'd try it out."

"Mrs. Rankin's a nice lady," said Henry, "but I don't read girls' books."

"You don't read anything, Henry."

"I've read *The Autobiography of Buffalo Bill*."

"Yes, I know, about half a dozen times."

"I've read most of the Tarzan books."

"Oh, those." Beth rolled her eyes.

Henry heard his mother open the back door. Quickly he said, "I wondered whether you'd want to go for a ride."

"Okay," she said, trying to think of an excuse to give her parents.

"Now?"

"Sure."

"I'll meet you at the corner of your block in half an hour."

"Okay."

"Bye."

"Bye."

Beth hung up the phone. She turned around. Her father stood behind her. She thought he had gone into the front room after handing her the telephone.

"Who was it?" he asked.

"On the phone?"

"Of course. Was it your boss from work? It didn't sound like him."

"Actually," she began. She wanted to tell the truth. It would be hard to tell her mother, but she thought her father might understand. "He's a young man I met. I like him a lot, and he likes me. He asked whether I could go with him for a ride."

"Where?" asked Patrick. He thought it time his daughter had a young man. She was nineteen now.

"Just for a ride in his car."

"Where did you meet this young man?"

"At the hospital."

"What's his name?"

"Henry Whitman."

"Whitman? I used to know some Whitmans. They were good people. You sure he'll behave himself?"

"Yes, Father."

"Be home in time for supper, then," he said, taking out his wallet. "Do you need some money?"

"No, thanks, but do you think Mother will be angry?"

"She shouldn't be; she was married at your age. I'll talk to her."

"Thank you, Father," said Beth, kissing him on the cheek. He was such a wonderful father! Then she grabbed her coat and went out the back door before Thelma could ask nosy questions. She walked to the street corner to wait for Henry so he would not have to stop at her house.

"I told my father," she said when she got in the car.

"I thought you said your parents wouldn't approve."

"My father said he knows your family and that they're good people."

"Hmm," said Henry. He doubted his mother would approve so easily.

"Why are we so sure our parents won't like us together?" asked Beth. "My father seemed okay with it."

"Because you're Catholic," said Henry. "My mother won't like that."

"Well, she'll have to learn to."

Henry liked Beth's spunk, but he was not ready to broach the subject with his parents.

"So your father didn't mind?"

"No. He didn't even warn me about the dangers of automobiles."

"Don't you own one?" asked Henry.

"No, never. My Uncle Karl had a few; my cousin Thelma has his now; my parents will ride in it, but both refuse to drive one. They both say they're too old to learn."

"Do you drive?"

"No. I'm afraid too."

"It's a great feeling," said Henry. "It gives you such a sense of freedom. Whenever I'm in a bad mood, there's nothing better than going for a drive."

Beth thought nothing was better than going for a drive with Henry.

"Want to try driving?" he asked. "I'll teach you how."

"No."

"Come on, you'll do fine. We'll go out on a back road where there isn't any traffic. You should learn. Girls need to be independent these days."

They were already out of town and driving through Harvey. Beth did not object as Henry turned toward Munising, then onto a back dirt road. Once out of sight of civilization, he stopped the car, then got out and walked around to Beth's door.

"Henry, I — "

"It'll be fine," he said.

She slid across to the driver's seat. She was trembling, but she did not want him to be disappointed in her.

"Now this is your brake," he said, "and this is the gas pedal. And this is the gear shift, and — "

She would never remember all this! He kept naming parts and she was supposed to touch or grab the different pedals and gears. But he seemed patient with her. She thought he was a good teacher. He seemed very knowledgeable about automobiles. She imagined he was knowledgeable about a lot of things. He had not finished high school, but she felt he could do just about anything. She felt safe with him.

When she started the engine, he scooted right up beside her. His leg was brushing against hers. He put his hands on the wheel above hers to guide them. He was so close he made her nervous, but it was a good kind of nervous. Still, they were alone on a back road; her father had worried whether Henry would behave himself, but Henry could have taken advantage of her many times before if he had wanted, especially on that first night when they had driven up to Big Bay.

"Put your foot on the gas a little," he said.

She tapped it and nothing happened.

"Harder."

She gave it another tap and the car jolted forward a foot.

"No, put your foot down and leave it there."

She pushed down her foot. The car jolted again, then ran down the dirt road at twenty miles an hour. She was terrified to go so fast.

"Let your foot up halfway," said Henry.

She did, and the car slowed up. They were on a straight stretch. They were going along nicely.

"Good," Henry praised her.

Then came a curve. Beth turned the wheel. Henry's strong grip made sure she did not turn it too far so they made the curve smoothly.

"See, it's not so hard," he said.

"Not with you teaching me, it isn't," she said.

They drove a few more minutes. Henry said, "I think you can manage without my hand on the wheel now."

He let go before she consented. She began to panic. She struggled to keep the wheel under control. She felt as if it wanted to jerk out of her grasp.

"You're doing fine. Slow down a little if you don't feel comfortable going this fast."

They came to another curve. Beth tried to slow down, but she confused the brake and gas pedals. Suddenly, the car roared around the bend at a ninety degree angle, kicking up a cloud of smoke.

"Hit the brake!" Henry yelled.

Beth's foot found the brake, but already the wheel had started to straighten out of the curve; slamming her foot on the brake made the car jerk off the road and spin into a pine tree.

"Ah!!!" she screeched.

Henry's shoulder slammed against the dashboard. Then the car came to a standstill.

They were both out of breath.

"Ow," Henry moaned, sitting up straight to rub his shoulder. "Are you all right?"

Beth lay slumped in the driver's seat, the blood gone from her face.

Henry moved his arm about to make sure it worked.

"Are you all right?" he repeated.

"I ruined your car." She began to cry.

Henry got out and looked at the car's hood. It was a little dented, but she had hit the brake before the car had done much more than scrape the tree.

"It's not that bad," he said.

She continued to cry.

"It's okay," he insisted.

"I told you I didn't want to drive. You shouldn't have made me!"

He felt guilty for having terrified her.

"It's all right," he said, climbing back into the car. He wrapped his arm around her shoulder to calm her.

"I wrecked your car. I'm so sorry."

"Please quit crying," he begged. He hated when girls cried. His sisters annoyed him when they cried, but Beth's tears hurt him.

He did not know what to do. He wanted to comfort her. He took her face in his hands. Then her sobs suddenly stopped. She looked surprised. She was beautiful. He dared. He kissed her on the lips.

Beth wondered whether he now intended to take advantage of her. She wondered whether she would want —

Then he pulled away.

They sat silently.

"Henry, I — "

"I'm sorry," he apologized for the kiss.

"Don't be," she said. She felt sinful. She had encouraged him. What would the nuns at Bishop Baraga School have said? Now she would have to go to confession. But maybe he would kiss her one more time before she went.

"I'll start up the car. Hopefully it'll still run," he said.

They switched places. The car started down the road without a problem. She said nothing. He thought he had ruined everything. They drove in silence until they reached her house.

"I'm sorry, Beth. Please forgive me. I should have asked you first. It's just, you were hysterical, and I didn't know what else to do."

She wanted to say it was okay, even that she wanted him to kiss her again. Instead, she got out of the car.

"Are you mad at me?" he asked.

"No," she said. "But I better go now. It's almost suppertime. You can call me again sometime."

"Goodbye," he called after her.

He had thought she was mad, but her tone had not sounded mad at all. As he watched her walk listlessly down the street, he realized something had changed between them. He could not describe what had changed, but he knew it was for their good.

Rather than going home, he drove to a friend's house. Together they pounded out the dent in his car hood so his parents would not ask questions. He knew the time for questions would come soon enough.

"Henry, I got a new job for us," said Will the next morning.

"Oh yeah, what?" asked Henry, generously spooning sugar into his coffee.

"There's a Green Bay company tearing down the Hotel Superior. They want to salvage as much of the lumber as possible. They figure there's about a million boards they could reuse. It'll pay — "

"The Hotel Superior!" said Margaret. "Oh, no!"

"Well, it's been closed for years," said Will. "I guess it has to be torn down since no one can make a go at running the place."

"But it's such a shame. It was always such a majestic part of Marquette's landscape. I don't think I can remember back to before it was there. What a sad day in this city's history."

"Yes, it was grand in its day," said Will, although he felt less nostalgic than glad to make the extra money. In his youth, he had often felt angry toward progress; then he would have despised tearing down an elegant building for material gain, but having a family to support left little room for sentiment.

"Ma, were you ever inside it?" asked Ada.

"Yes, a couple times," Margaret replied.

"I was in there twice," said Will. "The first time I had dinner with Peter White."

"Sure you did," laughed Margaret.

"I did too," said Will. "Clarence and I went there once when my Grandpa Henning visited. My grandfather and Peter White were old friends so when we bumped into him there, he sat down to dinner with us."

"How did your grandpa know Peter White?" asked Eleanor.

"Everyone in Marquette knew each other in those days. I believe my grandparents came to Marquette the same time he did. Marquette only had maybe a hundred people the first few years."

"Your father's grandparents," Margaret reminded her children, "were very prominent citizens in this town."

"The Whitmans?" asked Henry.

"No, the Hennings, my mother's parents," said Will. "They owned a big house on Ridge Street, but they moved away before I was born. I never met my grandmother, and I only saw my grandfather that one time he came to visit while I was a boy. He died soon after that."

"Lunch with Peter White," said Margaret. "Isn't that something? You never told me that before."

"I'd nearly forgotten about it; it was so many years ago," said Will.

"When else were you in the Hotel Superior?" Eleanor asked.

"Oh, some dance there when I was about seventeen," said Will.

"That's the time I was there," said Margaret, "though your father probably doesn't remember me."

"Yes, actually I do," said Will, "because that's the night my father died."

"Oh, I'd almost forgotten that," said Margaret, wishing she had not mentioned it.

"Did you two dance together?" Ada asked.

"We didn't know each other then," said Margaret. "I knew your Uncle Clarence because we went to school together; actually, I rather had my heart set on him — I was only thirteen then. He didn't come to the party, so I figured I would dance with Clarence's brother, only your father ended up dancing with a hussy instead."

"Lorna Sheldon." Will laughed to see Margaret still jealous after thirty years. "She wasn't a hussy though."

"She acted like one that night," said Margaret. "I'll never know what men see in her."

"She was ravishingly beautiful," said Will. "I understand she was heartbroken when I married you."

"Seems to me," said Margaret, "that she married Richard Graham long before we ever married."

Unable to think of a good comeback, Will changed the subject. "Yes, it is a shame the Hotel Superior will be torn down. They used to call it Marquette's glory. It's one of the main reasons we were known as the Queen City of the North."

"We still are the Queen City," Henry replied. "It's the people, not the buildings, that make Marquette great."

Henry loved to hear his parents' tender bickering. He did not know many old married couples who were still playful with each other; everyday, his mother still insisted on kissing his father before he left for work. Henry hoped he and Beth would be that way. He wondered whether his parents would have stayed together if their parents had objected to the marriage. He thought his parents would want him to know the same happiness they had even if it meant his marrying a Catholic girl.

"We better get going, Henry," said Will. "I said I'd be at the job by eight."

"All right." Henry gulped down the last of his coffee. "I'm ready."

He was glad to go to work. While he pounded nails, he could think of Beth without being disturbed by people's chatter. She was always in his thoughts, in his memories of their single kiss, in his longing to hold her in his arms for the rest of their lives, in his wanting to share every little event of every day with her. He wanted her until he could no longer stand the thought of not having her.

On a Saturday afternoon in April, Henry sat alone in his bedroom after having called Beth and asked her to go with him that evening to the Marquette Opera House. She had confessed she would have to tell her parents where she was going or else they would ask why she was so dressed up, but she had promised him she would manage it. Henry also thought he should tell his parents, but instead he had gone upstairs and said nothing. He spent the afternoon in his room, doing nothing but counting the minutes until he would see Beth.

The day was beautiful; spring was bursting through his window, begging him to come out into the sunshine. But rather than go out, Henry sat stretched out on his bed, his back pressed against the wall. He could smell the wetness of the last little patches of snow sure to melt in the next couple days. The cool air made him want to snuggle with Beth. He could not wait for tonight, although he dared not touch her. When he felt the breeze on his skin, he imagined it was Beth's comforting arms, wrapping around his waist, holding him, pressing him to her, loving him, and he loving her even more. His chest was overwhelmed with longing.

He was in love with Beth McCarey. He would never again sneer at all that mushy talk about love. He had never dreamt it was such an all-consuming, life-affirming feeling. This love for Beth — it had grown almost unnoticeably, then had unexpectedly overflowed within him until he knew he must speak or burst. He must ask her to marry him. He could not live otherwise.

Marriage. Men lived in fear of it. But it was what he wanted. He liked himself best when he was the man Beth loved. He felt stronger, smarter, more capable of accomplishment because he wanted her to be proud of him. All his successes would be hers; all her good qualities would rub off on him. They would become one in the sweet mystery of life.

"Henry!" his mother shouted from downstairs. "Supper'll be ready in ten minutes. Can you go find Bill and the girls and tell them to come in and wash up?"

Why did she have to interrupt his thoughts? Yet he did not mind. Such trivial annoyances as his mother's harping voice would no longer trouble him when he had Beth's love to compensate for life's nuisances.

"Sure, Ma," he shouted. He ran downstairs, then slipped on his shoes by the door. As he passed the kitchen, he wondered whether he should tell his mother he loved Beth McCarey, and he was going to marry her.

Would he really do it? Yes, yes, of course. But he would ask Beth before he told his mother. She deserved to be the first to know.

He went onto the porch, then down the steps, and looked about for his siblings. He walked around the house, then toward the apple orchard. He could hear his brother and sisters in the trees, laughing and shouting each other's names. They were making so much noise Henry knew they would not hear him until he was in the orchard. He kept walking toward them, noticing the apple blossoms were more beautiful this year than ever before.

"What a wonderful day!" he could not help but say out loud. He had always loved the green hills, the flowers, the forest surrounding the farm. But never had spring been so gorgeous!

"Henry! Whatcha doing?" cried out Ada.

"It's time for supper," he shouted, bending half-backward to look up at his sister, perched in the bough of an apple tree.

"Already? We just got up here."

"Yeah," said Eleanor. "This is the first day it's been warm enough to climb the trees."

"Aren't you all getting too old for tree climbing?" Henry grinned.

"No," said Bill; at nine, such behavior was still excusable for him. "It's great fun. You can see the Chocolay River from up here."

"I know," said Henry. "I climbed those trees before you were even born."

"Then you know how beautiful it is up here," said Eleanor. "Come on up, Henry."

"No, it's time for supper."

"Oh, Henry," said Ada. "Ma always says it's time to eat, but when we get to the table, the food still isn't ready for ten more minutes. Come on up."

Henry looked up at the branches, each overflowing with white blossoms, the promise of future apples, fruit to nourish them for months to come.

"All right, just for a minute," he laughed. He grabbed a branch above him, then swung up his feet until they were wrapped around the bough. His dexterous arms pulled him up until he was sitting on the branch. He balanced himself until he could stand, and by step and reach, within a minute, he was thirty feet above ground.

"Yeah, Henry!" applauded Ada.

"That's my big brother," said Bill. "He can out-tree-climb anyone in Marquette County."

Henry laughed. He looked out over the magnificent fields to the Chocolay River winding along in the distance.

"See, Henry, wasn't it worth it?" said Eleanor. "Have you ever seen anything so beautiful?"

"Yes, Beth McCarey," he mumbled to himself, remembering a white dress she had worn that made her as beautiful as these apple blossoms.

"Henry, you didn't answer me," said Eleanor.

"Yes, it's beautiful," he replied.

"Look at the river," said Bill. "I wish it were warm enough to go swimming."

"It will be soon," Henry replied. He wondered whether he and Beth might go swimming together this summer.

"I don't think the sky has ever been so blue," said Ada.

"Or the trees so beautiful when the sunlight hits them," Eleanor said.

"This is the most beautiful day of my life," Henry professed.

"That's a funny way to say something," said Eleanor.

"What do you mean?"

"Well, you might say, 'this is the prettiest day I've ever seen' but not 'this is the most beautiful day of my life.'"

"Henry doesn't know how to talk proper," Bill jabbed. "That's what happens when you drop out of school in eighth grade."

Ada thought Bill would be lucky to reach eighth grade considering his marks in school. But Henry did not defend himself. He knew Bill really thought him smart to have dropped out of school because he had learned to do important things like plowing a field, fixing a car, building a house, things far better than sitting indoors all day with a book.

"We better go into supper now before Ma gets angry," said Eleanor, searching for a branch to climb down.

A minute later, the brothers and sisters were back on earth, save for Henry, who spent another minute staring out at the Chocolay River. Today was the most beautiful day of his life. He would never forget this feeling; he did not want it to end. He and Beth were so young they might be married fifty years — this feeling could go on for all those years. His parents must have survived all their troubles because they knew love like this.

"Are you coming, Henry?" asked Bill.

"Yes," he shouted, feeling so carefree he jumped out of the tree. Any other day, he would have been cautious, but today he felt indestructible.

"Wow, Henry! You're the bravest guy I know," said Bill, reverting back to hero-worship of his older brother.

"No, just the luckiest," said Henry, grabbing his brother around the shoulder and giving him a good squeeze as they walked toward the house.

An hour later, Henry could not say what he had eaten for supper, nor recall one word exchanged at the dinner table. He sat through the meal in utter contentment until the time came to excuse himself for his evening date. Then he went to meet the greatest moment of his life.

Beth had not experienced any great revelations that day. But somehow she felt this was the night. She had felt so the last four or five times she had gone out with Henry. Frankly, she wondered whether he would ever ask her. They had only gone out for six months, and she and Henry were both still young, and Henry still had to make his way in the world, but she felt certain he would ask her tonight. Why else would he take her to the opera when they usually just went for a drive or to eat at a diner?

She had had to explain to her parents why she would be so dressed up tonight. She wanted to tell her father and let him break the news to her mother, but that did not seem quite honest. After she had agreed to go out with Henry tonight, she took a deep breath and went into the front room to tell her parents she had a date with a young man. When Kathy read her daughter's lips, her face sunk, and she stared out the window. Beth exchanged a disconcerted glance with her father. He nodded, encouraging Beth, who then sat down beside her mother and took her hand. She explained that Henry was very nice and she liked him a great deal, but she let her mother think tonight was the first time she would be with him. Kathy listened, then was silent a minute before stating, "Thelma will go with you."

Before Beth could object, Kathy purposely turned her head so she could not read her daughter's lips. When Beth raised her voice to protest that Thelma would ruin everything, Kathy pretended not to hear by repeatedly saying, "What?" Beth was furious. Her mother never wanted her to leave home; Thelma would prevent any intimate moments between her and Henry. How could she explain to Thelma that she and Henry wanted to be alone? Thelma would think that leaving them alone would be to stray from her duty as chaperone. And Beth knew if she confided to Thelma that Henry was going to propose tonight, then she would look like a fool if he did not ask her. And Thelma would be sure to tell her parents if the proposal didn't happen. Then her mother would want to lock her in her room forever.

It was pointless even to go now, but Beth still went upstairs to dress. She felt so frustrated she could barely button the back of her dress. She was too irritated to ask for Thelma's help. Her fingers fumbled at everything so that she was not even ready when Henry arrived. When she heard his voice downstairs, she was so nervous she made a mess of her hair. She knew he was being interrogated by her parents and Thelma. She could hear his faint, nervous replies to a dozen personal questions from her father, and she imagined how her mother was glaring at the young man who had come to steal away her daughter.

Her hair was a disaster, but she could not make Henry face her family another minute. No one would see her anyway once the opera began and the building was dark. But if he were to ask her — oh, it would never happen tonight, not with Thelma tagging along, so who cared what her hair looked like?

"Beth! We're waiting!" Thelma shouted.

"We're waiting," Beth mimicked. As if she even wanted Thelma to be waiting.

She took one last look in the mirror, grimaced over how fat her dress made her look, wished she had time to change, then went downstairs to meet her fate.

Henry was at the bottom of the stairs, helping Thelma put on her coat. Beth knew he was a gentleman — he would have helped Thelma with her coat even if her parents were not present to analyze his every move. Poor Henry! What a shock it must have been when he arrived to learn they had to lug Thelma along. He turned when he heard Beth's footsteps, and from cheek to cheek a smile broke across his face.

"You look lovely," he said.

"Thank you. I'm ready," she replied to hasten escape from her parents.

Henry gave her his arm while Thelma trailed behind, yacking about what a nice day it had been. Beth wished she would shut up. It was not such a nice day — it had rained that morning; she had scarcely noticed the sun that afternoon because she had been so busy anticipating tonight, and now it was all ruined. Thelma started jabbering about the review of the opera she had read in *The Mining Journal*. Henry politely tried to answer her, while Beth was unable to get a word in. Forced into silence, Beth felt more nervous because Henry's chatting made her think he was not nervous, and if he were not nervous, then he must not intend what she hoped. How could she be so stupid? He would never propose to a fat girl like her, not when she had such a rummy family, and she had smashed up his car. He could find lots of prettier girls.

By the time they reached the opera house, Beth would have cried if not for the crowd of people. The building was packed. Henry went to the ticket window while Thelma made comments about all the ladies' gowns. Beth strove for stoical composure.

"We have to go upstairs," Henry said when he rejoined them.

"Why up there? Can you afford those seats?" asked Beth.

"They're the only ones I could get," Henry lied. He had purchased the best seats, in a semiprivate balcony, to give him the best opportunity for his plan.

"I do love the Marquette Opera House," Thelma gabbed as they took their seats. "My father used to take me to the Calumet Theatre sometimes. People say it's the most beautiful theatre in the Upper Peninsula, but I think the Marquette Opera House much nicer. But the people who say that about the Calumet Theatre have probably never been here."

The Marquette Opera House was a stately edifice, the grandest in the Queen City's downtown. The building had been constructed in 1892 at the instigation of the city's greatest benefactors, Peter White and John Longyear. The foundation was built of Anna River brick and native Marquette brownstone. The front entrance had a Romanesque arch through which the city's residents passed in their most elegant habiliments. While the building also housed a storefront and a Masonic Hall, the theatre was the building's gem. The interior reflected the height of the Italian Renaissance, while the proscenium arch served as gateway to the grandest scenes ever played on a Marquette stage. Ornate boxes filled the walls, and in one such princely seat, Beth found herself seated between her lover and her annoying cousin.

First Thelma commented about the comfortable seat. Then she fretted over how well she could see the stage. Next she listed the names of everyone in the theatre whom she knew, and since the theatre could hold up to one thousand people, and almost everyone in Marquette knew everyone else, this recital lasted until the lights dimmed and the orchestra began to play.

Beth hoped Thelma would keep her mouth shut during the performance. She vowed she would never forgive her mother for sending Thelma as her chaperone. But what did it matter? Henry clearly had no intentions tonight of asking her to —

He reached over to take her hand. Beth hoped Thelma would not notice. With her hand in Henry's, Beth felt paralyzed — she scarcely heard a note of the opera — she did not understand Italian anyway. She wished she had not worn gloves — they always made her hands sweat; Henry must notice how damp they were. She wished she could just go home. The entire evening was horrible. How could she endure another minute of it?

Finally. Finally. Intermission.

She had endured. Henry had held her hand during all of Act I. Over an hour. Did that mean — but not with Thelma sitting there. As the lights came on, Beth decided her only chance was to speak before Thelma's jaw started yapping again.

"Thelma, do you feel all right?" she feigned concern. "You look pale."

"No, I'm fine," said Thelma, taking out her compact mirror to admire herself.

"No, really Thelma," Beth said. "You don't look good. Almost as if you're going to faint."

"It is warm in here," Thelma replied.

"Maybe you should step out for some fresh air?"

"Well," said Thelma, "maybe it wouldn't hurt. We can be back in a minute so we don't miss the beginning of the next act. Will you save our seats, Henry?"

"Oh, I think I'll stay," said Beth.

"Well," said Thelma — she knew as chaperone she should not leave Henry and Beth alone together. But then Beth gave her the nastiest glare she had ever seen.

"Really, Thelma, you better get some fresh air," said Beth.

"All right. Maybe I'll just go to the ladies' room. I'll be back in a minute."

Thelma stood up, found her purse, and departed. She now understood what Beth wanted; she was surprised Beth had not confided in her before. Sometimes she felt all her family thought her dumb, but she was not. Still, she would not leave them alone more than a few minutes — then they could do no more than kiss. Not that she knew what more they could do, but it was thrilling to leave them alone to see what she might catch them at when she returned.

"Do you like the performance?" Henry asked Beth.

"Yes," she said. Was this his opening line? Should she comment on the opera to show she was interested in his conversation. But she could think of nothing to say — she had no clue what the opera was even about — all that Italian babbling. Thelma might as well have been the soprano.

"I like it too," Henry said.

A long awkward pause.

"If he doesn't ask soon," thought Beth, "Thelma will be back to ruin everything."

More silence.

Finally, Beth asked, "So, how are things going for you, Henry?"

She thought this sentence would let him make a transition into a proposal.

"Fine."

Terrible silence.

"Beth?"

"Yes, Henry?"

"I've been meaning to ask you — "

"What?" she said to rush him. Thelma — back — any second.

"Well, um."

He placed his other hand over hers. She had imagined this moment so many times, but she had not imagined Henry's hand would be shaking. So was hers. She hoped he did not notice.

"Well, um," he repeated.

"Yes, Henry?" she repeated.

"I want to know if — "

The curtain rustled. Thelma plopped down beside Beth.

Henry started to withdraw his hand, but Beth held onto it for dear life.

"It's awful warm tonight, ain't it?" said Thelma, not wanting her companions to suspect she knew they had been smooching while she was gone.

"Excuse me, Thelma," Beth snapped, "but Henry was speaking."

"Oh, I'm sorry," said Thelma, turning to look at the crowd.

"Beth, I — "

Suddenly, even with Thelma there, Henry grew brave. He felt it was now or never, and never was too painful a thought. He could not bear never to be with Beth.

"Please, Miss McCarey, will you marry me?"

There. He had done it. But why had he said her last name? But somehow that had made it easier. Anyway, he had said it. Even though it had sounded stupid. It was the best he could do.

Beth said nothing for a moment. Why had he used her last name? But she was relieved, so relieved she almost forgot to answer.

Then Thelma let out a little screech — she had imagined smooching but not this!

"Ye-es, I will," said Beth.

"Thank you," said Henry. He kissed her trembling cheek.

The violins began to play. The lights dimmed. The curtain opened.

"Oh, there's so much to say now!" thought Beth, disappointed by the orchestra's timing. But perhaps that her hand was still in Henry's said everything. They could bask for the next hour knowing they were to be married. His hand squeezed hers. She looked into his eyes, glazed over with joy. She felt she would love him forever.

As for Thelma, she had never witnessed such a surprising, or for that matter, beautiful moment. She did not know Henry, but she thought he had a kind face. She could tell he was a good man, and handsome too, a real gentleman, money or not; after all, hadn't he helped her with her coat? Still, he could have done more than just kiss Beth on the cheek. Didn't he know enough to kiss a girl on the lips when he proposed? If he were madly in love, that's what he should do, even in public. Rudolph Valentino would have kissed her on the lips after he proposed to her. She had often imagined Rudy kissing her. Too bad he had been dead three years now — she would never forget how she had cried when she heard the news — but even dead, he had been so handsome she could not help still daydreaming about him. Would a man ever kiss her as she imagined Rudy could have? No one had ever kissed her, and here she was twenty-six, seven years older than Beth who was now engaged. Was she destined to be an old maid? Throughout the second act, tears streamed down her eyes.

Beth looked over and thought Thelma was crying over the tragic opera. Beth could not imagine herself ever crying again.

❦   ❦   ❦

"Ma, Pa, sit down. I have something important to tell you."

Henry had just entered the kitchen for breakfast. He was relieved to find his parents alone and his brother and sisters still upstairs.

"Oh, Henry, we got a letter from Roy. Let me read it to you," said Margaret.

"No, Ma, I need to talk to you."

Will looked questioningly at his son. Margaret wiped her hands on her apron, then sat down at the table.

"Is it something bad?" Margaret asked.

"No, it's good. Very good." Henry tried to smile.

"What is it, son?" Will asked.

"I'm getting married."

"Married? To whom?" Margaret asked.

"Beth McCarey."

"How did this happen?" asked Will, completely confused.

"I've gone out with her a few times, and last night, I proposed to her at the opera house, and she said yes."

"Oh," said Will, recognizing the happiness in his son's eyes. "Well, congratulations." He reached over to shake Henry's hand.

Henry shook hands, then looked over at his mother.

"Ma, aren't you going to say anything?"

"Are you sure, Henry? We've never even met this girl. Shouldn't you have discussed it with us first?"

"Ma, I — "

"Maggie, he's old enough to make his own decisions," said Will.

"I love her, Ma. She's fun to be with, and she makes me laugh. We get along really well."

"Having fun is not enough to base a relationship on. What's her family background? What kind of a name is McCarey? Is she Scottish? It sounds like a Scottish name? Is she a Presbyterian? There aren't any McCareys at our church."

"No, Ma, her last name is Irish. Her father is from Ireland, but her mother's family is German I think."

"McCarey, you say?" said Will. "Margaret, isn't that Mrs. Montoni's daughter's married name? Beth must be old Mrs. Montoni's granddaughter."

"Oh," said Margaret. Mrs. Montoni had delivered her in the boarding house, but the old woman had also been well-off. "Does her family have money?"

"She had a rich uncle, Karl Bergmann, but he's dead. He left all his money to her cousin, Thelma."

"Oh, I remember going to Karl Bergmann's wedding when I was a girl," said Margaret. "He was a big logger. My father did some business with him."

"Beth's parents aren't much richer than us," said Henry.

"I can't remember what church Mrs. Montoni went to," said Margaret. "I want to say they're Episcopalians."

"Beth goes to St. Peter's Cathedral," said Henry.

Margaret gasped. "She's Catholic!"

"Yes."

Even Will was speechless. He did not care if the girl were Catholic, but he foresaw the fury to ensue.

"No. You can't marry a Catholic!" said Margaret.

"Who's Catholic?" asked Eleanor, coming into the kitchen.

"Your brother thinks he's going to marry a Catholic," said Margaret.

"Why not?" asked Henry. "She's a good girl, Ma. If you met her, you'd — "

"I don't care if she's the Pope's daughter! No son of mine will marry a heretic!"

"Ma, what's the difference? They believe in God the same as we do."

"Those Catholics have distorted the Bible and they worship statues. They don't go to Heaven. What if you have children with her? Have you thought of that? Do you want your children to burn for all eternity?"

"Maybe she'll convert," said Will to calm Margaret down.

"I don't know," Henry said. "We haven't discussed it."

"No, Henry. Don't talk such foolishness," said Margaret. "You can find a nice Protestant girl."

"Ma, you're being unreasonable."

"I don't think it's unreasonable to be concerned over my future grandchildren's souls," said Margaret, overwhelmed with shock.

"Just meet her, Ma. She's a really nice girl. She's sweet and kind and — "

"None of my children will marry Catholics. You break it off with her right away."

"I won't!" Henry exploded. "I love her! I wanted to tell you about the best thing that's ever happened to me, but instead you have to be horrid!"

That was all he could say. He stamped out of the house, slamming the back door behind him.

"Don't you leave this house while I'm speaking to you!" said Margaret.

Whether or not Henry heard her, he kept walking.

"Will!" Margaret said. "Go after him."

"He's a grown man, Maggie. I can't tell him what to do."

"He can't marry that girl. He just can't!"

"Maybe you could have explained that to him without screaming," said Will.

"If he marries that girl," said Margaret, "I'll never speak to him again."

Eleanor stared at her parents. She had never heard her family members get so angry at each other.

Henry stormed out to his automobile, then hopped in and drove off. He did not know where he was going; he only knew he was angry, extremely angry. He wished he had never told his family. He had known his mother would be upset, but not that she would be so horrible. How could he have ever thought they would accept him marrying a Catholic? Now what was he to do? Be a heel and take back his proposal? Tell Beth he would only marry her if she became a Baptist? Maybe he should convert to Catholicism? That would make his mother mad; it would serve his mother right if he did.

All these thoughts flooded his mind while he drove into Marquette. He would go talk to Beth. He would explain it all to her. Maybe she would despise him for worrying what his parents thought, but he did love them. And he had a good mother, even if she could be unreasonable at times. In his heart, he knew his mother only wanted what was best for him. And Beth was only nineteen — still young. In time, his parents might — but with time, Beth might find another man, a Catholic boy to marry her. The thought of — he felt nauseous thinking about it.

He parked on the street and marched up the steps of the McCareys' front porch.

"Henry!" cried Beth, seeing him through the window and running to the door.

"Beth, don't you dare — " a woman's voice called from inside.

Henry understood instantly.

"Henry, they say I can't," said Beth.

"Why?"

"My mother says I can't marry you because you're not Catholic."

"My mother feels the same because you are Catholic. She's afraid I'll convert."

"Would you?" Beth whispered, fearing yet hoping.

"I — I can't." His chest collapsed. His pride vanished. He detested himself.

"Then it's hopeless," she said.

"No, no, it can't be."

"Then what can we do?"

"I don't know."

"I love you, Henry."

"I know. I love you too."

Beth turned her head. In the house's inner shadows, Henry could make out the figure of Beth's mother.

"Goodbye, Henry," Beth sobbed. She shut the screen door, then ran upstairs.

Kathy McCarey stared at Henry through the screen door.

He stared back. Then ashamed of his cowardice, he turned and walked to his car. He did not know what to do. He cursed himself and all the world. He drove toward Lake Superior, then turned up the Big Bay Road, and on the spur of the moment, decided to climb Sugarloaf Mountain to exhaust himself. He spurted up the mountain with restless energy, trying to defeat mixed anger, despair, and heartbreak. At the mountain top, he thought of jumping into the lake to make his life oblivious. But he knew his family depended on him. He could not be so selfish. And it would take greater courage to end his life than to marry Beth.

Terrified of his own madness, he started down the mountain, his whole body heaving in agony. Halfway down, he collapsed along the path and his cries rang out through the forest and over the lake.

When he was nearly choking, his throat dry from the sobs, he stood up and dusted the leaves and dirt from his pants. Then he drove home and began his chores about the farm. Once his father tried to speak to him, but he shrugged away from him. He did not go inside for supper but walked along the river, again thinking he might drown himself, but the creek was too shallow there. He went to bed without speaking to anyone.

When he woke in the morning, he felt numb, but he went through the motions of his daily work. It was all he could do to survive each lonely moment now.

🍁   🍁   🍁

The Whitmans believed in their ancestors' Puritan work ethic. They worked constantly; they tried to save all they could, hoping someday they would not need to watch every penny. They would not have gambled away a single cent, and they thought those who invested thousands in the stock market with hopes of gaining millions were the most foolish people alive. When the stock market crashed on October 24th, investors nationwide fell into panic, and many Marquette businessmen despaired, but the Whitmans hardly gave the event a passing notice.

"It just proves that riches bring no real security," said Will.

"And that the love of money is the root of all evil," Margaret added, more from envy of the rich than from humility. The Whitmans were too ignorant about economics to foresee how the wealthy's financial woes would trickle down to the poor.

The day after the stock market crash, Margaret joined the ladies of the Baptist Church to plan their Christmas bazaar. The ladies worried few people in town would be willing to participate in charitable events that year.

"People will be too worried about the economy," said Mrs. Vincent.

"Yes, it looks as if we'll have another depression as bad as the one back in '93," said Mrs. Boardman.

"Oh, the government will never allow things to get that bad," said Mrs. Bissell; in her eighty-year lifespan, she believed she had only seen the nation move closer to its manifest destiny of greatness. Fortunately for Mrs. Bissell, she would pass away that winter before the most desperate years came.

"Ladies, have you heard the news?" Harriet Dalrymple burst into the meeting; her bombastic voice drew everyone's attention.

Margaret shivered. Harriet was always so overly dramatic and tactless. She prepared herself to be embarrassed yet again by her sister-in-law, but Eleanor smiled at her aunt's amusing if annoying ways.

Without waiting for a reply, Harriet announced, "Lysander Blackmore has committed suicide!"

First came little shrieks and gasps, then whispered explanations to those who did not know the well-to-do banker.

Afterwards, Margaret thought she had quit breathing for a moment. She tried to conceal the wicked smile of triumph spreading across her face.

"Oh, his poor family," said Mrs. Vincent.

"Are you sure, Harriet?" asked Mrs. Boardman.

"Why did he do it?" others asked. All the women began clucking about possible reasons.

Harriet explained that Mr. Blackmore had been found that morning, lying on the floor of his bank office, having shot himself through the skull.

"His poor wife," said Mrs. Bissell. She had seen many a sad death, but suicide was always the worst.

"But why?" Mrs. Vincent asked.

"Aunt Harriet, how did you find out?" asked Eleanor.

"On the way here, I saw the ambulance in front of the bank. I asked someone in the crowd, who told me he was dead. I bet he did it because he lost a fortune when the stock market crashed, and he was afraid he'd have to live on the streets now."

"I wonder how much he lost," said Margaret.

"Oh, probably thousands," said Mrs. Boardman.

"Ha!" Mrs. Vincent said. "I'll bet he was worth a million."

"Imagine, all that money suddenly gone," sighed Mrs. Bissell.

"Did he leave a suicide note?" asked Mrs. Vincent.

"I don't know," Harriet said.

"Then," said Eleanor, "we don't really know why he did it."

"He had everything — a beautiful wife, children, a fine home," said Mrs. Vincent. "It just shows you that you never know what another person's life is like, no matter how grand it may seem outwardly."

"That's true," Mrs. Bissell said.

Margaret thought it a true statement; she knew things none of the other ladies knew about Lysander Blackmore — not even Harriet, who knew of Sarah's indiscretion, but did not know Lysander had been the other party involved.

"Maybe we should send the family some flowers?" said Mrs. Vincent.

"Why?" asked Harriet. "He wasn't a Baptist. He's Episcopalian."

"But he was one of the town's most prominent citizens," said Mrs. Boardman, "and many in our congregation are members of his bank."

"I think sending flowers would be the Christian thing to do," said Mrs. Bissell.

The church ladies decided flowers would be sent. Margaret halfheartedly donated fifty cents toward their purchase; she pitied the grieving widow, hoping Mrs. Blackmore never knew what a sinful fornicator she had married.

On the walk home, Margaret could barely keep from telling Eleanor her thoughts. Eleanor knew of her Aunt Sarah's disgrace — thanks to Harriet's indiscreet tongue — but Margaret thought Eleanor too young to know the full story. Now that the scoundrel was dead, he should be allowed to rest in peace. Margaret even felt sorry for him — after all, if he had not softened regarding the farm's mortgage, she doubted she would have had courage to expose him. He had helped her, even if she had forced his hand.

When she reached home, Margaret wrote to tell Sarah the news. She did not know whether her sister ever gave thought to the man who had nearly destroyed her life, yet she felt Sarah had a right to know.

1930

Mrs. Joseph Rodman to Mrs. William Whitman
January 4, 1930
Washington D.C.
Dear Margaret,

Forgive me for not writing sooner. I got your letter just before Thanksgiving, but was too ocuppied then to write back because I was planning a large meal to honor some foreign ambasadors who were visiting Washington. Then we had to make preperations to spend Christmas in California with Mother and Father, and we only just returned to Washington yesterday. You know that while I am always busy, eventually, I always respond to your letters.

I apreciate your writing to tell me of Lysander's death. Truthfully, part of why I have not written is that it has taken me so long to adjust to the news. For years after I left Marquette I thought about him. At first, I was angry with Lysander, but now it's been years since I forgave him. I know Mother and Father were set to lay the blame on him for taking advantage of a young girl, but I was probably just as much at fault. I was young and foolish, and he was rich and handsome so I allowed myself to be easily swayed. I'm sorry his life did not turn out better. It's ironic that my life has been so wonderfully happy.

I waited until after Christmas to tell Theo about his father's death so it would not spoil his holidays. I don't think he was very upset about it — I had never before told him anything about his father because I did not want him to go searching for him, but now that Ly is dead, there can be no harm in our son knowing his father's name. Perhaps my fears were unfounded because after I told him, Theo had no qualms about going to a party with his friends. What is an unknown father to him anyway? He has enough already to think about since he will graduate from Harvard this spring and begin his career.

I hope all is well with you, Will, and the children. Your Roy was here for Christmas. He seems a fine boy, if a bit radicall in his ideas. I'm afraid he riled up Joseph somewhat. But Theo enjoyed his visit — they are so diferent, yet they get along well. When Roy left, he said he was going to Texas to find work on a ranch and that he would write you once he was settled.

How is Henry? I hope by now he has forgotten that girl you wrote about. I think you were right in making him break it off with her. He'd only be looking for trouble if he married a Catholic. Now that several months have passed, I imagine he's forgotten all about her — the young are so resilyent.

I will close now as I still have not finished overseeing the unpacking. Write soon, and Happy New Year.

Love, Sarah

Sarah had not realized the irony of her words. For years she had thought of Lysander Blackmore, yet she believed her nephew could quickly forget a girl because the young are resilient. Henry did not have his aunt's luxury of moving to Chicago to escape memories of Beth. In Marquette, two former lovers are bound constantly to meet, especially when those of their own generation rally together against the elders.

Eleanor Whitman was shopping at Getz's Department Store. She had just found a blouse she could barely afford but which was too pretty to pass up. Feeling both guilty and elated, she carried it to the counter.

"One dollar, forty-eight cents," said the cashier girl.

Eleanor dug in her purse for change.

"Aren't you Henry's sister?"

Eleanor looked behind her to see the inquisitor.

"Yes," she said.

"How is he?"

Eleanor did not recognize the woman, but she did notice all the expensive items the woman was buying. Embarrassed by her one meager item, she placed her change on the counter and waited for the cashier to place her blouse in a bag.

"Henry's fine," she told the woman behind her.

"Is he really?" asked the woman.

"I'm sorry. Do I know you?" asked Eleanor.

"I'm Thelma Bergmann." The name meant nothing to Eleanor until the woman added, "I'm Beth McCarey's cousin."

"Oh," said Eleanor. "Yes, he's fine. It — it's nice to meet you."

She did not know what more to say. She clutched her package and walked toward the door.

"I'll be right back," Thelma told the cashier. She dropped her articles on the counter and ran after Eleanor to the annoyance of those in line behind her who did not wish to wait.

Thelma caught Eleanor outside the door.

"Wait, what's your name?" she asked. Eleanor turned around, surprised to be followed. Thelma had shouted, gaining the attention of passersby.

"I'm Eleanor," she said, feeling the stares of everyone on the block.

"Eleanor, is Henry really fine? Because Beth is miserable without him."

Eleanor understood now, but she did not know what to say.

"Beth and Henry love each other," said Thelma. "Just 'cause my aunt and your mother don't approve is no reason to keep them apart. And don't you think the religion thing kind of silly. I mean, as long as we all believe in God, what's the big deal?"

Eleanor smiled. She thought the same thing.

"Well," she replied, "Henry says he's fine, but I can tell he's hurting."

"Is he seeing anyone else?"

"He's gone out with a couple girls, but he said they weren't interesting. He doesn't seem to care for much of anything now, except building his house. He bought a piece of property in North Marquette last summer, and he started building on it last fall. He's got the walls up, so now that it's winter, he's working inside it. I don't know where he gets the energy."

"Maybe he's trying to forget," Thelma said, "or else he wants to be free from your disapproving mother."

Eleanor felt she should defend her mother, but she suspected Thelma was right.

"Eleanor, tell him Beth still loves him. Do you think he still loves her?"

"I think so, but he doesn't talk much — he's been pretty moody ever since."

"Will he be at his house this evening?"

"I imagine so since it'll be a warm night."

"What's the address?" Thelma asked.

Eleanor did not know whether she should give it out. She did not want to anger her mother by getting involved, but neither did she like to see her brother hurting. She gave Thelma the North Marquette address.

"Sometimes we have to help people out a little," said Thelma. "Thanks, Eleanor. I'm sure I'll see you around."

Eleanor walked home, hoping she had done the right thing. Thelma returned inside the store. She found she had to wait at the back of the line because the disgruntled customers had refused to wait for her return.

Henry had bought two vacant lots in North Marquette between the college and Lake Superior. He told his family the property would be a good investment. He told himself the land would give him needed distance from his parents' restrictions. He had helped his parents for years, and he would continue to do so, but he could not live with them any longer. Margaret and Will told their eldest son they understood he was an adult and wanted to be on his own; they did not admit they knew he was moving out because he was angry with them. They decided with time he would get over it and realize what was in his best interest.

By last fall, Henry had bought lumber, dug out a basement, and erected the walls and roof of the house. When the snow came, rather than work outside, he devoted himself to the indoor wiring and plastering. He was enmeshed in dry walling the night Thelma drove Beth across town without telling her where they were headed. Even when she stopped the car before the half-finished house, Thelma refused to explain her reasons.

"Beth, come inside or you'll freeze," Thelma said. "I'll just be a minute. There's someone here I need to talk to." Beth was annoyed, wondering what her cousin was getting into, but she followed Thelma, who was already knocking on the front door.

When Henry opened the door, Thelma said, "I brought Beth over to see you. She's been missing you real bad."

Beth was mortified. Henry was pleasantly surprised. He politely invited them in out of the cold. Thelma quickly entered while Beth unwillingly followed.

"Show us the place, Henry," said Thelma. She thought a little tour of the house would break the tension. Once the lovers had adjusted to each other's presence, they could discuss what mattered between them.

Henry showed them around while Thelma asked prying questions.

"If there's only you, Henry, why do you need three bedrooms?"

"I don't know," he said. "Maybe I won't live here. Maybe I'll just sell the place when it's done."

"I need to use the ladies' room," said Thelma, stepping down the hall. "But I think, Henry, that this would be a good house for raising a family."

Beth blushed. Henry stayed composed enough to explain he had no bathroom yet, but the neighbors would let her use theirs. Thelma was delighted to go next door; it gave the lovers more time to work things out alone. She left Henry and Beth staring at one another.

"How are your parents?" Henry ventured.

"Stubborn," Beth said.

"Oh."

"Henry, I had no idea Thelma was bringing me here. I didn't even know you were building a house." She felt like crying.

"I'm glad you came," he said. He stepped closer but was afraid to touch her. She wanted to feel his arm around her.

"I tried to forget you. To go out with other girls," said Henry, "but none of them were like you. I miss you, Beth."

Now she did tear up.

"I miss you too."

"Couldn't we see each other, even if only as friends? I think perhaps we just surprised our parents, but maybe in time — "

"I don't think our families will ever accept us," said Beth, "but I would like to be friends."

Henry wanted more than friendship. He dropped his eyes to the floor and took a deep breath. "This sounds silly, but even though I started building this house after we broke up, I kind of thought it — that someday it might be ours."

Then she nearly fell into his arms. He held her, buried his face in her hair. Neither knew what to say. They didn't need to. They perfectly understood one another.

"Did you two make up yet?" Thelma asked, coming back inside.

She saw the answer before they could reply.

Careless of Thelma's presence, Henry kissed Beth's lips.

"We'll probably have to wait a long time," said Beth.

"I'll wait as long as I have to," he said. "Someday we'll be married and raise a family in this house."

The next day, Henry whistled while doing his farm chores.

"I'm glad to see you're in a more cheerful mood," his father told him.

Henry decided to be blunt. He would not back down. He also knew his father would be more understanding than his mother.

"Beth and I are seeing each other again."

Will sighed. "You know your mother will be upset."

"I know, but I love Beth, and someday I'm going to marry her. We'll wait a little while for everyone to get used to it, but we won't wait forever."

Will smiled. He was proud of his son. "I'll try to talk to your mother. Maybe she'll come around eventually." Will understood Margaret better than her son did. Her reasons were not always rational, but she behaved as she did out of love for her children. Will knew he would have to be the peacemaker from now on, but that was fine if his children were happy. They were a family — they all wanted the same result, even if they did not agree on the means to it.

That spring, the Whitmans received another foreclosure letter from the bank. Again Margaret did not show the letter to Will. Again she made the walk into town.

At the bank, she asked for the man who had signed the letter. She was shown upstairs to the same room where she had confronted Lysander Blackmore. No visible bloodstains on the carpet testified to the tragedy that had occurred there. A new vice-president of the bank sat behind the desk. He was middle-aged, short, thick-necked, with a bald egg-shaped head. His large-lensed bifocals emphasized his beady little eyes.

"What do you want, Mrs. Whidden?" he barked.

"Mrs. Whitman," she corrected. She felt unsettled when he did not apologize for getting her name wrong. She sat down and tried to formulate a sentence.

"I don't understand this notice you sent us."

"What's there to understand?" he said. "You're behind in your mortgage payments. You've been behind for years. The bank has no choice but to foreclose."

He picked up a pen and began to scribble his name at the bottom of a half-dozen letters. Margaret thought they looked like more foreclosure notices.

"My husband and I work very hard," she said. "We pay as much of our mortgage each month as we can afford. We had an agreement with Mr. Blackmore — "

"Mr. Blackmore was much too softhearted," said the beady-eyed eggheaded man. "If the bank gave such extensions to everyone, the bank would be bankrupt."

He grinned at his own wit, then frowned when he saw she did not laugh; he looked down and scribbled his name some more.

"But," Margaret scrambled, "there must be exceptions. We always pay — maybe not as much as we'd like, but — "

"Madam," he said, laying down his pen and removing his bifocals. "Don't waste my time. This country is slipping into an economic crisis. To protect this bank and the interests of its investors, we cannot afford to bend any rules. For years, Mr. Blackmore was more than generous to you. Frankly, it was poor business on his part to let you get away with what he did. Since you have not caught up but only fallen farther behind, the bank has no choice but to foreclose."

Margaret considered begging for her children's sake, but she observed that this egg-headed pillar of finance wore no wedding ring so he would have no children. She could not imagine what woman would want him anyway.

"In tough times," she said, "good people help their neighbors."

"The discussion is closed, Mrs. Whidden. Unless you catch up on your payments within thirty days, the bank will take your farm. Good day."

Margaret stood up. She turned. She took two steps. Her heart ached. She knew he would not help her, even if she begged. But indignation rose in her. Turning around again, she shouted, hoping everyone on Washington and Front Streets would hear her.

"You, sir, are no Christian!"

She did not remain to see her egg-headed enemy's reaction. She stomped down the stairs and through the lobby. She had to accept she had lost. For four years, she had postponed the inevitable by her showdown with Lysander Blackmore. She had hated that man for bringing disgrace on her family. She had been shocked when Sarah had written that she had long ago forgiven him. And now to be told by the villain's horrid successor that Lysander Blackmore had been "much too softhearted"! To think she really owed a debt to that Blackmore villain; if he had not seduced her sister, she and Will would have been in the poorhouse years before. She had felt a bit triumphant when he had committed suicide, but now she saw his death was her own personal tragedy.

Thunderclouds appeared over Lake Superior as she walked home along its shore. The heavens rumbled. Could God not even be kind enough to keep her dry until she reached home? The rain poured down during the last mile of her walk. She felt her entire life was a disappointment to her. Others might say she should be thankful for a good husband who loved her — but Will could not provide for her. She should be thankful for healthy children — but each child had made the family more poor, made her worry more, caused her stomach to be more upset. Now, straining against the driving rain, shivering under soaked cotton cloth, she felt scarcely able to breathe.

It was lunchtime when she reached home, but she was not hungry. She better get out of these wet clothes. A warm bath might soothe her, calm her so that when Will came home, she could break the news to him. She took off her clothes and ran the bathwater — they had only put in electricity and running water last summer — she had been foolish to think they could afford such luxuries. She shivered even after she was sitting in a tubful of hot water. The pain rose up from her stomach, through her chest, and dissolved into sobs. She wept, her throat choking up, her hands reaching for the handkerchief in her dress pocket, folded up on the cupboard. She wiped her eyes, and blew her nose, then lay listlessly in the tub until the water grew cold.

Finally, she got up and dried herself, then stumbled to the bedroom to find her robe. She intended to go back into the bathroom to comb her hair, but instead, she lay down on the bed, then crawled under the covers. She wanted to cry more, to make the pain go away, but she could only force up dry, empty sobs. She buried her face in the pillow, then fell into fitful dreams of wicked bank vice-presidents who put guns to her head to make her leave the farm.

She dreamt her grandfather was alive again. She went to hug him but woke with a start, realizing he was dead and she had only dreamed. She always remembered his tales of Scotland's glories, but now she also recalled the sad tales he had told her of Highland families driven from their homes and forced to migrate to the New World. She missed him, but his stories had done her no good. At least those poor Highlanders could go to the New World. Where would she go except to the poorhouse? She felt numb. The rain continued to pour down. She saw water streaming down the outside of her bedroom window. She fell back asleep despite the thunder's rumble.

She felt better when she woke. She had always hated the farm anyway. She cared about losing it only for Will's sake. But she wanted to know why life was always so hard. She felt she should be angry with God, but her mother had told her God gave His people trials to make them stronger. Her mother had also told her that in times of trouble, if you randomly open the Bible, you will find there the answer you need.

Margaret pulled herself out of bed, tied up her robe, then took the Bible from the small bookcase Will had built. She blew the dust off the good book, then opened it. She found a parable from the Gospel of Luke:

> Two men went up to the temple to pray; one was a Pharisee, the other a tax collector. The Pharisee with head unbowed prayed in this fashion: 'I give you thanks, O God, that I am not like the rest of men — grasping, crooked, adulterous — or even like this tax collector. I fast twice a week. I pay tithes on all I possess.' The other man, however, kept his distance, not even daring to raise his eyes to heaven. All he did was beat his breast and say, 'O God, be merciful to me, a sinner.' Believe me, this man went home from the temple justified but the other did not. For everyone who exalts himself shall be humbled while he who humbles himself shall be exalted.

Margaret did not understand. Like the Pharisee, she was thankful not to be a horrible sinner. She had committed no wrongs so why did God allow her to suffer? Did the story mean because she was humble, she would be exalted just as the exalted Lysander Blackmore had been humbled? But she was not a sinner like the tax collector, and she could not possibly be the Pharisee if he were to be humbled. This parable was not relative to her situation at all.

She would try again. She just wanted one verse to guide her. She closed and reopened the Bible. Her eye settled on Mark 3:29:

> I give you my word, every sin will be forgiven mankind and all the blasphemies men utter.

Another verse about sins being forgiven. This was pointless. She closed the Bible. The children would be home from school soon. She better get dressed. She would not think about Lysander Blackmore anymore. Only God could judge him and that other horrid man at the bank. She had to figure out how to tell Will.

Margaret waited until after supper, when the children had gone upstairs to do their homework, and Henry had gone to work on his new house. Will sat in his chair, his feet propped up, reading *The Mining Journal*. Margaret perched herself on his footstool. She lay the foreclosure letter on Will's lap, then began to rub his feet. He lowered the newspaper to look at her questioningly.

"Maggie," he said, "you know the children are still awake."

"I know," she said. "That's not what I want, but I do love you. You've been the best of husbands to me."

"You're a fine woman yourself, Maggie," he said, folding up the paper.

She did not want to excite, then disappoint him, so she went to the point.

"Will, I have bad news. A letter came from the bank."

He now saw the envelope on his lap. "What's the matter?"

She let him read the letter. She did not tell him about her meeting with Lysander Blackmore. But she did tell him she had gone to the bank that day, and that nothing could be done. Since she had handled the money for years, she begged him to forgive her for not letting him know earlier how destitute they were.

"You shouldn't have taken this burden solely upon yourself," he said, gesturing for her to come sit on his lap. They held each other. She sobbed a little. He told her he was proud of how brave she had been.

"I'm sorry I haven't been a better provider," he said.

"You've done your best," she said.

"I never should have bought this farm. We could have kept Clarence's money in the bank as a nest egg."

"The farm brought us extra income," Margaret defended his decision.

"It's never been much of a farm — a cow, a dozen chickens, forty acres plus a ten acre orchard. Even with the river running along the edge of the property, it's not worth much I fear."

"It's a fine farm, Will. We could still make it work if this Depression weren't gripping the country. I imagine lots of folks are worse off than us."

Will sighed. "I only wanted the farm so I could recapture my youth, and those happy days on my father's farm. But I can't do that. One should never make a financial decision based on sentiment."

"It doesn't matter now," said Margaret. "It can't be changed."

"So what do we do now, Maggie? I guess we'll be going to the poorhouse."

He was only joking, but the fear rose in Margaret.

"If we sold the livestock and farm equipment, maybe we could put money down on a little house in town."

"I don't know, considering all we owe," he said, "and once I'm done at this job I'm working on, there probably won't be much work to be found. People are afraid to build now when they don't know whether they'll have jobs for very long."

"Could we borrow money from someone?"

"Who?"

Margaret had already thought about this.

"How about your Aunt Edna? Didn't she get a lot of money from your grandmother or someone?"

"Aunt Edna. I haven't heard from her since Grandma Whitman died. I don't even know whether she's still alive. I can't ask her for money."

"What about from Sylvia? Things haven't been good between the two of you, but that's her husband's fault, and after all, he didn't help our situation by spending your inheritance."

"No, Sylvia has nothing," said Will. He had not told Margaret that last week he had bumped into his sister at the butcher shop. She had been counting out her pennies at the counter to buy a pork roast. She had been six cents short. She had insisted she just needed to recount, that she had counted the pennies at home and was sure she had had enough.

Will had stepped up behind her and placed a five-dollar bill on the counter. He had just gotten paid that day. She had turned around, startled by her benefactor.

"Just take it," he had told her. "Don't tell Harry."

"Thank you, Will," she had replied. The butcher wrapped her meat, and then she turned to leave, but first she had given Will a tremendous hug, not caring who saw.

"Why'd you do that?" the butcher had asked Will. "She'll never give it back to you. We all know what those Cummings are like."

"She's my sister," he had replied.

He had not told Margaret of the meeting from fear she would match the butcher's comment, or worse, lecture him for taking food from his children's mouths.

"Could we borrow from your sister Mary?" Margaret asked. "Aren't she and her husband prosperous?"

"We never hear from Mary, except for the infrequent Christmas card."

"Maybe it's time you get back in touch with her."

"Asking for money isn't a way to rekindle a relationship."

Margaret waited for Will to suggest they borrow money from her family, but when he said nothing, she realized he was too proud to suggest it.

"Charles and Harriet can't afford to loan us anything," she said. "I suppose I could write to my parents."

"Your parents need their money. I won't take anything from them."

Margaret knew there was always Sarah. Sarah was the one person rich enough to help them, but Margaret could not ask her for help when she had refused to let Sarah adopt Eleanor as a way to aid them. Margaret knew she would never ask her sister for anything.

"Maybe we can rent a couple rooms in town," said Will. "Henry will have his own house soon. Maybe he could take the girls in since they're almost grown. Bill could stay with us until we — "

"I don't want to break up the family like that," said Margaret.

"There's nothing else to do," said Will. "Even if we sell the cow, the chickens and most of the furniture, we'll only have enough to live on for a few months. I can't depend on any work coming along."

"I guess," said Margaret, "that renting a couple rooms in a boarding house is better than going to the poor farm. I don't care about myself, but what will people think of the children, knowing we've lost everything? I feel so — "

"Hush, Maggie. Everything will work out." He stroked her hair, and she buried her face in his shoulder. "All we can do is trust in the Lord."

Since Henry's house was in North Marquette, and his parents lived in Cherry Creek, he had taken to stopping in South Marquette to pick up Beth when he went to work at the house. They often spent a couple hours together in the evening while Henry worked. Most girls would want a real date, complete with dinner, maybe a movie, but Beth knew Henry was building this house for her. That was enough — it was more than a girl could ask, except to marry the man she loved.

Henry's short visits to Beth's house had made Kathy fond of him, even if he were not Catholic. Henry and Beth continued to wear her down. Margaret, however, had no intention of encouraging her son, and she refused to meet Beth. Then one night Will and Eleanor went with Henry to see his house, and they stopped to pick up Beth. Eleanor came home and told her mother that Beth was a sweet girl, just like the big sister she had always wanted. Will told Margaret that Beth would make a good wife and mother. Margaret remained unmoved.

"The house should be ready to move into by July," Henry told Beth a few nights later when he dropped her off at her parents' house. Beth caught a glimpse of Thelma peeping out the window, hoping to catch them kissing.

"You move in and make the house comfortable until I can join you," Beth said.

"Just make sure you join me soon," said Henry. "Otherwise, I might turn it into my bachelor pad."

"You're awful, but I love you anyway," said Beth, and she kissed him, peeping Thelma or no peeping Thelma.

Beth little expected that by the next night, their plans would change. But she respected Henry's decision; after all, his money had built the house.

How could a dutiful son do otherwise? Henry let his parents move into the new house. Will and Henry quickly finished it before the farm was relinquished. Henry's savings had been spent in building the house, but he had some lumber left over, and he had bought two lots. In time, he intended to build another house beside the first.

Beth was disappointed to lose her house, and she did not relish the idea of someday living next door to her in-laws. She was especially annoyed that Margaret, who would not even speak to her, would be using her intended kitchen. But Beth was somewhat consoled when Eleanor thanked her for being so generous, and added, "Henry is the best of men. He'd do anything for the people he loves." Beth decided a man who loved his family enough to place them first was a man worth waiting to wed. She knew once they were married, he would treat her and their children just as well.

To show there were no hard feelings, Beth bought Eleanor a new dress to wear for her graduation. At the ceremony, Margaret would barely glance at Beth, but to Ada, she said it was a shame Eleanor's dress wrinkled so easily. Beth overheard and ignored the remark, but she steeled herself for a long, difficult engagement. Love is patient.

1933

And now, despite the terrible depression that gripped the nation, despite soup lines stretching for blocks in large cities and farmers surviving in rural areas only because they could grow their own food, despite climbing unemployment, and people leaving the United States to live in communist countries because they felt democracy and capitalism no longer worked, despite all this misery, all the shattered dreams, and the growing fear that America's best days had passed, the Whitmans found themselves enjoying some of their happiest years.

Not that the family prospered — money would never be a source of the Whitmans' happiness, but they now owned a home they need not fear losing. Henry and Will continued to work and the girls sewed or went to keep house for ladies in town to make extra money, and even Bill took on odd jobs to help out. They got by, day to day, and gradually they got out of debt. Henry taught himself to be so frugal that in later years, his daughter would tell him he pinched his pennies so hard he made Lincoln cry, but she would never understand how hard the Great Depression had been, and he would never be able to describe it to her.

For now, Henry was the acknowledged family savior. And on his remaining empty lot, he slowly began to build a house for Beth. It would be no dream home; there would be no hardwood floors, no intricate gingerbread, no bay windows, no concrete swimming pool like the one Aunt Sarah wrote to say she had put into the twenty-acre backyard of her California mansion. But when Henry lovingly pounded each nail, Beth knew nothing could make their home more strong and sturdy.

And during these years, Beth slowly became accepted as a family member, and if she were not liked by the family matriarch, at least, she was tolerated. Henry did better — he found himself invited to Sunday dinners at the McCarey house, even when Father Michael was visiting. Only one crisis occurred during this period for the lovers — Henry went one day to visit Uncle Charles and Aunt Harriet, and sticking out of his coat pocket, Aunt Harriet discovered a Catholic catechism. Suspecting her nephew intended to convert to 'the Church of the Whore of Babylon,' she tattled to his mother. Margaret ranted that she would die before she would see her son burn in Hell, and finally, her manipulative three-day temper tantrum resulted in his promise that he would not become a Catholic. Consoled, Margaret said no more, and Beth continued to be allowed in the house.

Everyone began to think Henry and Beth would court forever and never set a wedding date. When one lover pressed the other, the other would make up an excuse to wait longer, neither wanting to accuse the other's family of creating a problem. Henry's most frequent excuse was partially true; he wanted to wait until Roy came home to be his best man. No one knew where Roy was. He never replied to their letters.

One summer evening in late August, just as supper was finished, Henry went out on the porch to smoke. A slim figure of a man in dusty overalls was walking up the street. By the time Henry put out his cigarette, he knew who it was. A minute later, the fellow was on the porch, grabbing him around the waist and lifting him in the air.

"There's my big brother! How are ya?"

After four years, Roy had come home.

The brothers clapped each other on the back, too happy at first to speak. Then Roy observed, "This is some house you've built, Brother. Ma wrote me about how you've been taking care of everyone. I'm proud of ya."

Rather than reply, Henry opened the front door to holler, "Ma! Come here! Ma!"

"What do you want now?" she yelled from the kitchen where she was sweating over a steaming sink of dishes. "I swear I never get a minute's peace in this house."

"Just come here!" Henry bellowed.

"Don't you yell at me, Henry Whitman. You're not so big I can't still put you over my knee."

But by then she was at the door. As her smile broke, Roy grabbed and lifted her up around the waist same as he had done to Henry.

"How are ya, Ma?" he asked, after kissing her on the cheek.

"Better than you," she said, trying not to cry. "You look so skinny. Have you eaten at all these last four years? Why did you stay away so long?"

First Ada, then Will, then Eleanor and Bill heard the ruckus on the porch. They soon dragged the prodigal son into the house from fear he would get away again. Everyone starting asking Roy about his adventures, except Margaret, who kept asking if he were hungry, then loaded the table with food.

"Well, when I left California, I was in Texas, and then in New Orleans for a spell," Roy said. "I was going to go on to Florida, but I couldn't find work anywhere. At that point, I decided I might as well come home to starve rather than be down there with strangers. I'm afraid I don't have a dime to my name."

"How did you get home without any money?" Ada asked.

"Stowed away on a train from New Orleans to St. Louis, then another going to Chicago, and finally one going to Green Bay and Marquette. I've ridden the rails all over the West and South. Ain't paid once for passage," Roy laughed. "I just jump in an empty boxcar and ride for free."

Bill laughed at his brother's reckless behavior. He had such brave brothers; he admired both of them tremendously.

"Well, I guess in times like these, you couldn't have done much else," Will said to forestall Margaret's objections about cheating the railroads out of their money.

"No, I don't think there's work to be found anywhere," said Roy. "This country sure is a mess, but I've learned more from traveling than I ever did from all the history books in school, and one thing I'm sure of, the American people are strong-willed and will get by. I've worked alongside Mexicans in Texas and California, and Negroes in Louisiana, and Indians out in Wyoming, as well as plenty of white men, and I tell you, there's a lot to this country you'd never know if you didn't travel about. As soon as I get some fat on my bones from my mother's good cooking, I'm heading out East to see the rest of America."

Ignoring the compliment to her cooking, Margaret said, "We hope you won't leave anytime soon."

"We need you here," said Eleanor. "It hasn't been the same since you left."

"I'm glad to be home," Roy replied. "I can't wait to start pounding nails with Pa and Henry. Are there any projects I can help you two with?"

"Actually," said Will, "I just got a contract to build a house for a fellow, name of Vincent Smiley. Do you know him, Henry?"

"No, I don't think so," said Henry. "Why?"

"Well, I thought it kind of strange 'cause he said the house is for him and his future wife. I don't know many fellows his age — he can't be any older than

Roy — who can afford to build houses these days. But what's really odd is his fiancee's name is Thelma Bergmann. Isn't that Beth's cousin?"

"What?" Henry exclaimed. "You must have got the name wrong. Thelma isn't marrying anyone."

"I thought Thelma was Beth's cousin's name, but I couldn't quite remember," said Will.

"What was this fellow's name again?" asked Roy.

"Smiley. Vincent Smiley."

"I know him," said Roy. "Met him up at the Club my first year there. I remember he left that summer to marry some girl in the Sault. He invited us all to the wedding."

"It might not be the same fellow," said Henry, but he dreaded it was.

"Tall fellow. Curly mustache?" asked Roy.

"Yes, beard and mustache. Red hair," Will replied.

"Sounds like the same."

"Has Beth ever said anything about Thelma getting married?" asked Eleanor.

"No," said Henry, "that's what's so strange."

Henry saw Thelma nearly everytime he visited the McCareys; she was not known for keeping secrets. She would have told everyone the second she met a fellow; he was sure of it.

Seeing Henry's confounded expression, Margaret said, "Perhaps you should tell Beth about this." Margaret did not like that Beth wanted to steal her son, but neither did she want a young woman to be taken advantage of — especially one as slow-witted as Thelma. Not all men were gentlemen like Henry; she remembered what had happened to Sarah.

"I'll ask Beth tomorrow night," said Henry. "Pa, did this guy say anything else?"

"Actually, he said they were leaving for Mackinac Island tomorrow on their honeymoon."

"Tomorrow!" Henry jumped up and grabbed his car keys. "Then that means — "

"Henry, you don't think — " said Eleanor.

"I have to stop this. Thelma can be foolish at times, but I hope she's not stupid enough to try something like this."

"She probably doesn't know Vince is already married," said Roy.

"Maybe he's divorced," said Eleanor.

"That doesn't make it much better," said Margaret.

Roy jumped up to join his brother. "I'll go with you. You might need help. At least, I can make certain it's the same man."

In a minute, the brothers were racing across town in Henry's car.

Afterward, Thelma was not quite sure how it happened. She had almost given up on finding love. She did not even know how to look for it. She never knew what to say to a man — even her male cousins had made her feel awkward. The only man she had ever really liked — other than Rudolph Valentino, and Gary Cooper, and of course, Ronald Coleman — was Henry, and he belonged to Beth. She thought she would have liked more men if they would talk to her, but when she tried to talk to them, they always shied away. She liked going to the movies so she could imagine herself as the heroine talking to all those handsome men, each one vying for her hand in marriage.

Then one Sunday, she went to a church picnic for the Lady Maccabees. She had joined the organization because her aunt was a member. Kathy was glad to have her niece attend church functions with her since Beth refused to go where Henry could not. Thelma did not mind going — a picnic got her out of the house, and the church ladies soon became her whole social world. Since Uncle Patrick also went to the picnic, Aunt Kathy had to cater to him, leaving Thelma to fend for herself. Thelma avoided the young married ladies, whom she felt despised her for not having a husband. The old spinster ladies adored her as one of their own, but she felt awkward among women who had given up on finding husbands before the twentieth century had even begun. Two old German ladies, Hilda and Ernestine, were especially revolting to her after they confessed they'd had eyes for Thelma's father when they had been young. Now they were old and fat, and Thelma suspected they flattered themselves in thinking that her father had ever even looked at them. When they beckoned for her to come sit, Thelma pretended not to see them and went up to the refreshment table to find someone with whom she could make conversation.

Then she met Vince. He appeared to be the only single man there, or at least, the only one who did not carry off two cups of lemonade, one for a young lady. Thelma noticed he was also the best-dressed man, and like her father, he had a bushy beard, plus the added elegance of curled whiskers. His dark red hair crowned his stature of six feet. Since she had never seen him in church, he instantly sparked her curiosity.

"It's a warm day, isn't it?" she said, looking him directly in the eye.

He did not blink or shy away, although she feared she was being too forward — Beth always told her she was.

"Yes, dreadfully warm," he smiled. "It makes me thirsty. Might I get you a cup of lemonade?"

"Yes, please," she said, pleased by his attention.

"Did you eat?" he asked.

"Just a small bite," she lied. She had heard men liked women with bird-size appetites.

"I've been so busy visiting with all the kind people here that I've not eaten a thing. Would you care to join me?"

"Are you all by yourself then?" she asked.

"Yes, I just moved to Marquette from Sault Sainte Marie so I don't know anyone here. Perhaps you could tell me about the town if it's no trouble, Miss — "

He glanced at her naked ring finger. She thought such glances only happened in movies.

"Miss Bergmann," she replied. "Thelma Bergmann."

"Let me get you a plate of food." He asked whether she would like ham or potato salad. His kindness made her heart go pitter-patter. Two minutes later, they were seated together beneath a shady tree.

"Do you like Marquette?" she asked.

"So far, but I've only been here a couple days. I thought this picnic would be a good chance to meet people. I will say that Marquette girls are prettier than the ones we have back in the Sault."

Thelma blushed. He thought of her as a girl, although she thought of herself as an old maid. Somehow, she had always suspected she was so pretty that she looked younger than her age. "I'm actually from Calumet," she corrected the only inaccuracy she had heard in his statement, "but when my father died I came here to live with my aunt and uncle."

"I'm grieved to hear of your father's death," Vincent replied. "Such sadness reminds me of my own poor family."

"Why, what happened to them?" she asked, while munching on an overly chewy celery stick.

He set his plate on the grass and reached for his handkerchief as his eyes misted.

"I'm sorry," said Thelma. "Tell me what's wrong?"

"I just haven't gotten used to it yet," he said. "My beautiful wife and our twin girls — they were just babies. They died last winter. Double pneumonia.

All within two weeks. I couldn't stay in the Sault after that; not when everything there reminded me of them."

"Oh, how awful," said Thelma. "I'm so very sorry."

"I probably wouldn't get so upset," he replied, returning his handkerchief to his pocket, "except that you remind me of my dear Honey."

"Your wife?"

"Yes," he said, looking her in the eye. "She had a soft voice just like you."

Thelma's heart skipped a beat. She had always feared her voice a bit sharp. Honey must have been a wonderful woman to have made such a handsome man love her, and now to have him mourn her so. Thelma felt honored to be compared with her.

"I'm so sorry if I'm making you uncomfortable," he said.

"No, it's all right," she replied, placing a consoling hand on his wrist. "It must be a relief for you to talk about it."

"You're so kind. Meeting nice people like you does help."

Thelma imagined how lonely he must be, not knowing a single soul in Marquette. She was lonely too. She knew what it was to lose a family. She still missed her father.

"The worst part is," he said, "they might have lived if I'd taken them to the hospital, but we were so poor my wife refused to go. When I saw the situation was desperate, I called the doctor, but he said it was too late by then. He still charged me outrageously, and then there were the funeral expenses. I had already been laid off from my job, so the funerals wiped out all my savings. I suppose I'm no worse off than lots of other people during these hard times, but it's rough to take so many blows at once."

"How terribly unfair!" said Thelma. "I wish I had known you then. I would have loaned you the money. I have more than I know what to do with."

"No, the bills were tremendous," said Vincent. "No one has that kind of money anymore."

"I do. My father was a lumber baron. He left me comfortable for the rest of my life, but it's not much use if I can't help people with it. I wish I could have used it to save your family."

But Thelma was only being polite. She realized if his family had lived, she would not now be enjoying the pleasure of his company.

"You're too kind," he said. "I'm glad you don't have to worry about money like the rest of us."

Thelma knew many of her neighbors were struggling these days. She often felt guilty to have so much. She wanted to compensate for it by being kind to him.

"You must be lonely not knowing anyone in Marquette. I could show you around," she said. "I'm not doing anything tomorrow. I could tell you everything you want to know about the town."

"Oh, I couldn't impose."

"It's no imposition. I'd be happy to. I know what it's like to move to a town where you hardly know anyone."

They set a meeting time. By then, the picnic was breaking up. Vincent excused himself, saying that speaking of his dead wife and children had upset him and he felt he needed to go back to his little rented room and lie down. However, he promised to meet her downtown the next day.

Once Vincent left, Thelma found her aunt and uncle sitting with Hilda and Ernestine.

"Thelma, who was that young man you were with?" asked the old spinsters.

"Is he your beau?" Ernestine teased.

"Have you been keeping secrets from us?" Hilda giggled.

Everyone laughed. No one expected Thelma to have a beau.

Uncle Patrick said, "I don't think Thelma will ever marry. She's content keeping her aunt and I company."

Thelma was infuriated. Who were they to say whether she could have a beau, or how she should spend her life? She would not tell them one thing about Vincent. She would keep it all a secret. That night, she found it much sweeter to think about him because it was a secret.

When Henry and Roy arrived at the McCarey house, they were unsure how to proceed. Thelma was a grown woman; if she wanted to keep her approaching marriage a secret, Henry did not know that they should interfere. Roy also had doubts. He could not imagine the Vince he had known doing such a thing — he remembered the fellow had been crazy in love with Honey, the girl he intended to marry. Could it be the same fellow? Or could Vince's wife have died and now he was free? Henry said they had to find out the truth; he would not have any man going around making up stories about any member of his future wife's family.

Henry intended to ask whether he could speak to Thelma in private, but instead, he and Roy found the McCarey family, minus Thelma, sitting down to supper.

"Come in, Henry; there's plenty," said Kathy, resolved to be kind despite Henry's determination to marry her daughter. "Thelma has a headache and isn't eating, so we have more than enough. Who's your friend?"

"This is my brother, Roy," he said. "He just came home."

"Hello, Roy. Welcome back," Beth smiled at him. He was to be best man at her wedding; his homecoming made her hopeful the happy day was approaching.

"Patrick, could I speak to you in private?" asked Henry, finding Thelma's headache mighty suspicious.

Patrick feared the worst when he saw Henry's troubled look. Had Margaret Whitman finally brainwashed her son enough to break off the engagement? He wished Kathy and Mrs. Whitman would come to their senses. The children had suffered enough from this silly religious bickering — things never changed; religious disputes were one reason why he had left Ireland, and now religious prejudice was interfering in his daughter's happiness.

He followed Henry into the front room, silently preparing to lecture him about how to stand up as a man and cut his mother's apron strings.

"I've come about Thelma," said Henry, completely perplexing Patrick.

"Thelma? Should I go fetch her?" he asked.

"No, first I want to know whether she's engaged to be married."

"No, of course not. Why?"

Henry repeated what his father had said. Without a word, Patrick went back into the dining room.

"Beth, go tell Thelma to come downstairs," he said.

Beth, seeing the intensity of her father's look, instantly obeyed.

"What's wrong?" Kathy asked. She could read lips, but not men's anxious faces.

Within a minute, Beth ran downstairs, clutching a piece of paper.

"She's gone! Her room's a mess. Her dresser drawers are empty. And look at this!"

She thrust the note at her father. He scanned it while Henry peered over his shoulder.

"What's wrong? What's wrong?" Kathy repeated.

Patrick passed the note to his wife. While she read, the rest stared in stupefied horror.

Dear Aunt Kathy, Uncle Patrick, and Beth,

I know you will be surprised to find this letter, but it will be all the more fun if it is a surprise. I wish I could see the looks on your faces. I am sorry I lied about having a headache, but I needed an excuse to go upstairs so I could climb out the window to run away with my new husband. That's right, I got married today at the courthouse. By the time you read this, we'll be on a train to Mackinac Island to spend our honeymoon. What do you think of me now? You all thought I would be an old maid, but I guess now you'll admit you were wrong. I suppose you wonder who my husband is — his name is Vincent Smiley and he's handsome and wonderful, and best of all, madly in love with me, so how could I resist him? I'll write later to let you know when I'll be back.

All my love, Thelma

"Father," said Beth, slowly recovering from the shock. "Thelma couldn't have left more than an hour ago. If we hurry, we might — "

"Right," said Henry. "Come on, Roy."

Henry ran to his car, Roy close behind. Beth and her parents followed.

"Let me go too," said Beth.

"No, Beth," said Kathy. "It'll be dark soon. You'll be gone overnight. It won't be proper."

"Mother, it's for Thelma's sake. It's because — "

"No!" Kathy stamped her foot. "I won't have both my niece and daughter disgraced!"

"It's all right, Beth," Henry said. "We'll bring her back."

"Hurry," said Patrick as the brothers jumped into the car.

"Oh, Henry, the expense," said Beth. "We'll pay you back."

"Don't worry about it," he said. "We'll find them if we have to go all the way to Mackinac Island and even get the police involved."

"Thank you," said Beth. She waved as the car rolled away.

Henry and Roy were too intent on their mission to speak until they were well out of Marquette. Then Henry asked, "What else do you know about this fellow, Vince? Was he always a scoundrel?"

"Seemed like a nice fellow when I knew him," said Roy. "Back then he was crazy about this girl he was going to marry."

"Then what's he want with Thelma?"

"I don't know. Maybe he's not married anymore."

"He wants her money is what it is," said Henry.

Roy knew Vince had come from a rather poor family, but so had he, and he did not chase after rich young ladies.

"He's a big fellow," Roy laughed to ease the mood, "so you're lucky you have a tough cowpuncher like me to help you out."

"What does he — "

POP!

Henry clutched the wheel, trying to pull the car toward the side of the road. They were five miles from Munising, and they had a flat tire.

"I'll help you put on the spare," said Roy.

"That was the spare."

"What?"

"I was waiting to buy another spare when I got paid on Friday."

"Well, it's just past ten o'clock. You're not going to find anyone to sell you a tire at this hour."

"We have to try," said Henry.

"It's too late," said Roy. "By the time we reach Mackinac Island, he'll have — "

"I know," Henry grumbled, "but I can't not try."

Henry walked into town while Roy remained behind to protect the car. It was nearly two in the morning when Henry returned, lugging a tire. Roy jumped out of the car and helped his brother change it. By then, Henry was so exhausted, he needed to rest. He fell into a fitful sleep while Roy drove.

They reached Lake Michigan's shore as dawn broke. Henry woke. They were both starved, but there were no restaurants along the way.

Then the radiator started smoking. Roy pulled over the car to let it cool down. The brothers leaned against the bumper and stared out at the lake.

"Why does the radiator have to go," Henry grumbled. "As if we don't have enough troubles now."

"Look at it this way; you'll be in the family's good graces for your efforts. That'll give them more reason to consent to you marrying Beth."

"I don't want to profit from someone else's misfortune," said Henry.

The day was beautiful. The sun shone brilliantly on the beach. Lake Michigan's waves glistened as they rolled into shore. Seagulls circled overhead. Roy marveled how the world could be so at peace when people's lives were falling apart.

They climbed back into the car and drove to St. Ignace. Roy looked out at the lake all the way, until he caught a glimpse of the Straits, and then across the water, of Mackinac Island. He had been to San Francisco, New Orleans, Chicago, but nowhere had he seen any place so pretty as that little island.

When they drove into St. Ignace, they found a telephone booth so they could call Beth. In two minutes — the longest long distance call they could afford — Beth told them she had contacted the Michigan State Police, who said Vincent Smiley had been listed as a missing person for three weeks. His wife in Sault Sainte Marie had no idea what had become of him. Henry explained he and Roy were about to cross on the ferry to Mackinac Island and then he rung off.

"The bastard!" he cursed.

"I just knew he was still married," said Roy. "He wasn't too smart not to change his name."

"Let's be glad he isn't smart," said Henry. "I don't imagine too many bigamists are."

As they crossed on the ferry, Henry roamed up and down the deck, too nervous to sit still. Roy, rather than getting worked up before knowing what they would find, sat down and enjoyed the view of the Mackinac Straits, where the Great Lakes met and separated Michigan's two magnificent peninsulas. As the brothers approached the island, first only tall pine trees were visible, but then the boat curved around the shoreline to the small village's harbor; there rose the bluff whose mansions were among the Midwest's most exclusive summer homes; there was the Grand Hotel, featuring the world's longest sunporch; in the distance surged up church steeples, and in the center hill, Fort Mackinac, staunchly proclaiming the island's role in its nation's history.

Roy was not quite prepared to find himself stepping back into time. Years before, when the first automobile had come to Mackinac, it had frightened the horses, and since then, all automotive contraptions had been banned from the island. People only walked, bicycled, or went by horse and buggy around the island. Henry and Roy felt sudden nostalgia for an earlier time they only dimly remembered from earliest childhood; the island recalled years before there were even streetcars, the quiet world of the Victorians, even of the old French voyageurs.

"If we were smart," said Roy, overwhelmed by tranquility, "we would never leave here."

"Where should we start looking?" Henry asked.

"If Thelma's going to blow her fortune on Vince," said Roy, "chances are they checked into the island's best hotel, that big white one we saw from the boat."

The brothers left the little downtown area of the island and walked east to where the Grand Hotel dominated the landscape.

As they started up a small hill, into view came the island's enormous, alabaster temple of leisure. From the hotel's white columns, American flags flapped in the breeze, declaring the hotel as part of the American dream. "Make a million dollars and you may stay here with America's socially elite." Here was a sunporch filled with rich men in leisure suits, ladies in evening gowns, the well-to-do sipping tea as violins played, the beautiful people swimming in a pool where movie stars might be glimpsed. The Great Depression was at its worst — the hotel was facing the hardest year in its history, yet enough millionaires were present to keep Roy and Henry in awe.

The brothers were feeling bewildered by all this grandeur when the doorman approached them.

"Are you guests of the hotel?" he asked.

"No, but we need to speak to someone staying here," said Henry. "We're her cousins." It was not quite a lie — Thelma would be his cousin when he married Beth.

While the man looked them over, Roy watched dainty women in satin dresses, gentlemen with silk ties and silver buttons, pass up and down stairs draped with red carpet. He was ashamed of his denim pants and the cap he had worn for two years. In later years, he would be ashamed that he had felt less than these people because he did not have a share of what he would call their "dirty money."

"Please," said Henry, "we need to speak to her. It's a family emergency."

"Follow me," said the doorman, leading them through a side entrance. They passed up a few stairs, then down a tremendous hallway, past numerous groupings of chairs and tables, vacant save for the few elderly women who were playing bridge, or waiting for their husbands to take them shopping.

After walking several hundred feet, they reached the hotel's front desk.

"Ralph, these gentlemen want to know whether their cousin is a guest here."

"What's her name?" asked Ralph.

"Thelma Bergmann," Henry replied.

"It might be under Vincent Smiley," said Roy, "or Mr. and Mrs. Smiley."

While Ralph looked, the doorman hovered menacingly beside them. He appeared ready at any moment to pitch them from the property.

"I see a Mr. Smiley. I'll call his room to notify him of your presence," said Ralph.

"That's not necessary. Tell us the room number and we'll go up," said Henry.

"Our guests are entitled to privacy," the doorman said.

Roy clutched Henry's shirtsleeve. "There they are."

Turning, Henry saw Thelma walking toward the sunporch, her arm wrapped around that of a tall man in a tuxedo.

"Who wears a tuxedo at noon?" Roy muttered, but Henry had already raced across the lobby and placed his hand on the man's shoulder.

Vincent Smiley turned around in surprise. He did not understand until Thelma said, "Henry, what are you doing here?"

Then Vincent cringed and tried to shake off Henry's grip.

"Is there a problem?" asked the doorman.

"I don't know," said Henry. "It depends on this gentleman."

"Who are you?" Vincent asked.

"I apologize, Mr. Smiley," said Ralph, stepping forward. "He said he was the lady's cousin."

"Henry, did you come after me?" Thelma asked. "Were they surprised at home? I wish I had seen their faces. Did Beth come? I imagine you came to take me back, but I won't go. Oh, this is your brother, Roy, isn't it? I won't go, you know. I'm Mrs. Smiley now."

"No you're not," said Henry, staring Vincent in the eye. "I'm sorry, Thelma, but your so-called husband already has a wife."

"Sir, we cannot have any trouble in the hotel. You're creating a scene," the doorman said. "I must ask you to leave."

Roy looked about. A dozen people stared at him. Thelma looked around, then smiled to see herself the center of so much attention.

"You don't know what you're talking about," Vince quivered, nervously stroking his eyebrows.

"I tell you, Thelma. He has a wife and children in the Sault," Henry said.

"They're dead," she said, but she knew better when Vince would not look at her.

"It's true, Thelma," said Roy. "I know Vince; he's been married seven years."

"We've talked to the police," Henry said. "They've been looking for him. Apparently he abandoned his family a few weeks ago. Roy, go find a policeman."

Beads of sweat formed on Vincent Smiley's forehead.

"Please, you're creating a scene," pled the doorman.

But Henry refused to leave now. The group stood awkwardly, Henry's hand still gripping the back of Vince's tuxedo. In a few minutes, Roy returned with a security guard and the hotel manager.

"Please, let's go to a private room," the manager requested, calmly leading them into an office. Henry shoved Vincent along, indifferent to the cowardly man being three inches taller and forty pounds heavier than him.

The situation was quickly explained. Vincent's guilty face and Thelma's silly chattering verified the story. The manager, disgusted that such a scandal should erupt in his hotel, called the island police. Roy and the hotel security guard stood watch over Vince until he could be taken into custody.

Henry meanwhile persuaded Thelma to go with him up to her room to collect her belongings.

"I loved you, Vince," she sobbed as she was led away. "How could you do this to me? I loved you!"

Vincent Smiley only stared at the expensive, polished shoes Thelma had bought him, just as she had bought the expensive suit on his back, and paid for the expensive room in this most exclusive hotel.

Roy felt sorry for the fluttery-headed Thelma, but he also pitied the dejected young man before him. Positioning a chair in front of the door, he asked, "Why'd you do it, Vince?"

"What do you mean, why?" Vince asked. "You'd have done the same thing if you had any guts."

"I don't understand."

"All my life I've struggled to get ahead in this world. I thought I'd have a good job someday, a future, you know. Now I'm out of work, and all my wife does is throw that up in my face. I've got two little girls who cry every night because they're hungry. I couldn't take listening to them anymore. I was just one more mouth to feed so I left. I was heading out West and only intended to stay in Marquette one night. Went to the church picnic to get a free meal, but then I met Thelma and my plans changed."

"And you figured you could just take her money as your own," said Roy.

"Well, no, not totally. She seemed real nice. First person who'd been nice to me in a long time. I didn't want to take her money, just have her share it with me."

"That's a diplomatic way to put it," said Roy.

"I just wanted something nice in my life," Vince said. "Just not to have to worry for a little while. Thelma wanted the same thing, only she wanted the security of having someone love her. I figured I could do that for her, and she could give me money. She clung to me as if she were desperate for love. I kinda liked it. My wife hasn't loved me like that in a long time."

"Didn't you figure you'd get caught?" Roy asked.

"I didn't think about that. I guess I just wanted to see how long it would last and enjoy it while I could. Can you blame me? Isn't being rich what everyone wants?"

"No," said Roy, but the security guard chimed in, "Yeah."

"Money's not worth committing a crime for," said Roy.

"Maybe not, but it sure makes life easier," Vince replied. "Last night was the first time I ever slept under satin sheets. First time too I ever wore silk pajamas. First time I was ever treated respectful, like I was a somebody. Do you know what that's like? I bet you don't. But now I do, and I won't never forget it."

The police arrived with the hotel manager.

"Not in handcuffs," pled the manager. "I don't want a scene."

"We'll take him out the employee entrance," said one of the policemen, leading Vincent back into the lobby, then into the dining room and finally into the kitchen where they handcuffed him.

Roy shook his head. It was a shame. He did not understand how any man could abandon his wife and children, but he reminded himself he had never been a husband or father. He did understand what it was to want nice things. His parents had struggled for years, and his mother would have loved all those things Vince had mentioned. Thelma had the money to buy all those things, yet she would give them all up for someone to love. Roy did not see how a person could win either way.

When Thelma and Henry returned with her suitcases, Roy saw her eyes were bloodshot, despite the veiled hat she wore. He took her suitcase from her. When she muttered, "Thank you," he replied, "It'll be all right."

They stepped onto the sunporch. Henry hailed a carriage to take them back to the harbor. A Negro in finer clothes than Henry could ever afford drove up with a cab for them to ride in. Henry handed Thelma in. She ended up having to pay for the carriage fare to the dock. Henry only had enough money for gasoline to get them back to Marquette. Fifteen minutes later, they were on a ferry returning to the mainland.

Roy watched as the fairy island faded in the distance. In the brief time he had been on it, he understood why it was called the gem of the Great Lakes. Removed from the hectic modern horror, its old world elegance was comforting, but Roy also realized it was illusory. As Vincent and Thelma had just proven, having money to escape to an expensive hotel on a beautiful island did not solve any problems.

❧   ❧   ❧

Thelma remained brokenhearted for weeks after her marriage was declared null and void. She refused to believe Vincent had not loved her. He had been so kind, so appreciative toward her, even for the smallest things she had given him. And on their wedding night, after he had hurt her and made her cry, he had spent the longest time holding her, promising it would not hurt next time, explaining that she was so beautiful he had been unable to control himself, and explaining that a man can become sick from the yearnings if he is not with a woman. Now, when he was gone, she told herself she understood him, that despite the pain, he had thrilled her like nothing before. She wished she could have spent one more night with him just so she could have done more to please him. Instead, she was left with lonely cravings that only intensified when she spent her evenings in the dull front room while her uncle dozed in his chair and her aunt clicked her knitting needles.

Now a week later, she lay on her bed in the summer evening's humid heat. Henry had come over for supper; she could hear him and Beth talking on the front porch. She paid no attention to their words until she heard Beth mention her.

"Mother is so thankful you helped us find Thelma."

Thelma thought she would have been happier if Henry had not found her.

"I think," said Beth, "that it's made Mother soften toward you. I don't think she'll oppose our marriage much longer."

"Good," said Henry. "I'll keep working on my mother. I think we've waited long enough now."

Thelma jumped up to slam her window shut. She did not care whether they heard her. She hated them. Henry had thwarted her chance for happiness, and now his interference was working to his and Beth's benefit. She was sick of watching them spooning over each other and being too stupid to do anything about it. She had tried to help them, but they were too afraid to elope as she had. If they truly loved each other, they would have married by now. She did not care whether they ever married, and she bet they would have ugly children when they did. And if Beth even dared ask her to be maid of honor, especially after Henry had ruined her own marriage, well, she would tell Beth a thing or two, including the fact that she was no longer a maid.

1934

That year, even Roy was reluctant to move far from home. Money was hard to come by, despite President Roosevelt's attempts to turn around the economy. Most people who had blamed President Hoover for the Depression now claimed his Democratic successor had only exasperated the matter. The Depression's causes were largely beyond the understanding of Marquettians. All they understood was that money, work, and food were becoming harder to find. Henry and Beth, whether or not their parents softened, agreed to postpone their marriage. They did not see how they could maintain their own household separate from those of their parents. They were frustrated but steadfast in their love.

One spring morning, Harriet Dalrymple appeared at the Whitmans' door. She never knocked since she considered herself part of the family. She walked through the living room Margaret had not dusted all week, then into the kitchen where laundry was draped about since it was not warm enough yet to hang clothes outside to dry. From the top of the basement stairs, she bellowed, "Margaret, are you down there?"

"Damn," Margaret said, trying to balance the half-dozen preserve jars she had just carried downstairs. No matter how much she worked, she never seemed to catch up, and having to deal with Harriet would not help matters.

"I'll be up in a minute," she hollered back. She hated making preserves, but what could you do when you had five nearly grown yet hungry children all living at home? These days she could not allow one ounce of fruit to spoil and go to waste.

"Hurry up, I have news," Harriet screeched back.

"If it's so important, you could come down here," Margaret mumbled to herself.

When she came upstairs, Margaret found Harriet sitting at her kitchen table, already having helped herself to a cup of coffee, and no doubt, a few teaspoonfuls of sugar. Margaret looked in the sugarbowl, trying to remember how much had been there. She had hoped to save enough to make Easter cookies as a special treat since sugar was so expensive these days.

"What is it?" Margaret asked, immediately running dishwater to make it clear she had no time to chat.

"Did you get a letter from Sarah?"

"No. I'm sure she's far too busy to write to me."

Margaret's last letter from Sarah had described how she and the senator were remodeling their Washington home. Margaret had not mentioned the letter to anyone because it had irritated her so much.

"She wrote that she was mailing you a letter the same day as me," said Harriet.

"Well, you know what the postal system is like. It'll probably come tomorrow."

"She had something important to tell you, but perhaps she would want you to read it in her letter rather than have me tell you."

"It doesn't matter." Margaret was annoyed that her sister would give Harriet as much consideration as herself. "If she told you, it can't be a secret."

"Then here. I brought the letter with me. I'll read it to you."

Harriet pulled an envelope from her dress pocket. Margaret hated the way Harriet's voice droned on as she read.

"I'm so busy today, Harriet. I can't listen to the entire letter right now. Just tell me what it says."

Margaret industriously scrubbed the frying pan. If she did not keep up with the housework, she knew Harriet would comment. Not that Harriet's house was spotless, and Harriet only had one son, not five children, to keep an eye on.

"Theo is getting married."

"Married?" Margaret was surprised enough to stop scrubbing. "Well, I guess it's time. He's twenty-six now, I think."

"Twenty-five."

Margaret ignored the correction. "Who's the girl?"

"Some social climbing heiress from New York."

"How did Theo meet her?"

"Some party in college apparently. They've gone out for a few months and now they've gotten engaged."

"When's the wedding?"

"They're not sure yet, but listen, Sarah wants us to come out. She says she'll pay for all four of us, Charles, Will, you, and me to come to San Francisco for it."

Margaret had never imagined she would see San Francisco. Immediately, she thought, "I'll get to see my parents. They're getting old so it might be the last time." She asked, "What did Charles say?"

"He's at work so he doesn't know yet."

"I'll have to ask Will, but I would love to go." She would not ask Will. She would convince him. She had a right to see her parents, especially if Sarah paid for the trip.

"It'll be such a treat for us," said Harriet. "I've always wanted to see California; maybe we'll meet some movie stars."

"Not in San Francisco — it's hundreds of miles from Hollywood," Margaret said, scornful of her sister-in-law's ignorance.

"Think what the girls at church will say about us going to California, the guests of a U.S. Senator at a big society wedding — "

Margaret quit listening to Harriet's prattle. She had the same thoughts — that she would be aunt to the groom at this important wedding. She would be respected in California as a senator's sister-in-law, not like here in Marquette where few remembered she was anything but a housewife. In California, no one would know how poor she was or how dull her life had been. She would be pampered, treated as she deserved. She knew Will would let her go.

Margaret planned to tell Will the news at supper. Henry brought Beth over that afternoon to see his nearly finished house. The lovers had not yet set a wedding date, but Margaret knew she could not make them hold off forever; if times were not so hard, they would have already been married. Henry insisted Beth stay for supper. Margaret did not like Beth, but she figured the girl's presence might make Will less argumentative. And perhaps when Beth heard Henry's parents would be guests at a society wedding, the girl might realize she was not in the same class as her fiancee so a marriage between them would not work. Fortunately for Margaret, Beth did not know her own well-to-do grandmother had been the midwife at Margaret's birth in a boarding house.

"Will," Margaret began as she poured gravy on her potatoes. "Harriet got a letter today from Sarah."

"Ma, you're dripping gravy all over the table!" said Bill.

Margaret felt ever thwarted in her attempts to be elegant. She was so nervous that not only had she dripped on the table, but somehow her sleeve had gotten into the potatoes. She wiped up the gravy, then tried again, "As I was saying — "

"Pass the rolls," Bill told Roy.

"Just a minute," said Roy, taking one for himself.

"Roy, give me one too before you pass them," said Ada.

"I'm trying to tell your father something," Margaret snapped. In her day, children were seen and not heard; they did not constantly interrupt their parents; it did not matter that they were grown now.

"What is it, Maggie?" asked Will; he always used her nickname to soothe her when she was irritated.

"Sarah," she began, then turned to address Beth, "That's my sister who is married to a U.S. Senator."

"And Ma's only sister," said Henry.

"As if we could ever forget it," laughed Ada.

Margaret frowned. Had she been such a bad mother that her children should mock her like this? She better say it all before they interrupted her again. "Sarah wrote to say that Theo is getting married and we're invited to the wedding."

"Theo's getting married!" said Roy. "I don't believe it! I can't imagine what girl would want him; he's so prissy and fussy."

"Roy, don't talk like that. He's our cousin," said Eleanor.

"Well," Roy replied, "he's a swell enough guy; he just doesn't strike me as the type females are attracted to."

"I'm happy for him," said Will, "but he'll have to settle for a card from us."

"No," said Margaret. "I want to go to the wedding. Harriet and Charles are going, and it's probably the last time I'll ever get to see my parents."

"Maggie, you know we don't have the money."

"Sarah's offered to pay for you and me and Charles and Harriet to come out."

"Since she's so rich, why doesn't she invite us all?" asked Ada. "We're the groom's cousins."

"My sister is very rich," Margaret told Beth. Beth, however, was not listening but having a silent poking game with Bill. Henry adored how playful Beth was with his siblings. Margaret thought Beth decidedly unladylike. "But Sarah can't invite us all. She has so many important people who will have to come. I wouldn't be surprised if President Roosevelt came, or at least the Governor of California."

"Maggie," said Will, "you know we can't take her money, or should I say her husband's money? I'm sorry, but we're not going."

Margaret was angry, but she would not lose her temper in front of Beth. Calmly, she repeated, "I want to see my parents. Whether or not you go, I shall."

"We'll talk about it later," Will replied.

"There's nothing to talk about. I'm going. I never get anything else I want, so I should at least be allowed to visit my family."

She could hear the whining in her voice. She realized everyone was staring at her. She went into the kitchen to dish out the apple cobbler.

Everyone grew silent and concentrated on their beans and potatoes. After a minute, Henry said, "Pa, you should go. You both deserve a break."

"No, I'd like to see your grandparents, but not on Sarah or her husband's money."

"Then let Ma go," said Eleanor. "She works so hard, and Ada and I can look after the house while she's gone."

"As long as Ada's not doing the cooking," said Bill.

Ada did not like her services being offered, but she said nothing.

"I'll think about it," Will said. "Pass me some more mashed potatoes."

Eleanor and Henry exchanged smiles. "I'll think about it" was always their father's way of agreeing without making it look as if he had backed down.

By bedtime, Will had given his consent for Margaret to go to California alone. She felt triumphant, especially when Charles refused to go. Harriet ruled the roost, but for once Charles put his foot down; he insisted he could not afford to lose his wages to go to California, and they could not go without their son, who was only fourteen and had not been invited. Harriet laughed off her disappointment by telling Margaret, "Oh well, we'd just stick out like sore thumbs around all those la-di-da millionaires Sarah rubs elbows with. You probably won't even enjoy yourself, Margaret."

But Margaret had no qualms as to whether she would fit into elegant San Francisco society. Was she not of the Scottish blood royal? She knew her own worth, and the sophisticated people of California would recognize it more easily than the yokels of Marquette. And she was glad Harriet was not going — she could use a break from her sister-in-law. She would wear her finest dress to the wedding; the one she had bought last year for Ada's high school graduation. She had never felt so excited.

The night after Margaret left on the train, Beth went to bed early with a bad cold. Her nose was plugged up, making it difficult for her to breathe. That night she dreamt she and Henry had eloped and gone to live in California. She woke at three in the morning, startled but feeling happy. She realized she must have dreamt such a thing because Margaret had gone to California, and perhaps also because with Margaret gone, she thought she and Henry had more freedom. Soon she drifted back asleep.

Then a sudden jolt roared through her body — she felt as if someone had pounded her chest, as if she had been hit by an automobile. She bolted into a sitting position and tried to regain her senses. Then she heard her father shouting her name.

Terrified, she ran to her parents' room. Later, she would have no memory of how she got there, only of wrapping her arms around her father, crumpled up on the floor beside the bed. At first, she thought he was the one suffering.

Then she heard a moan from the bed. Her mother's face was constricted, and she was clutching her stomach.

"I don't know what to do for her," Patrick cried.

"What's wrong?" asked Thelma, appearing in the doorway.

"I don't know. She's in too much pain to tell me," said Patrick.

"Thelma, go call the doctor. Hurry," Beth ordered.

Kathy gasped for breath. Her forehead and pillow were soaked with sweat.

"Maybe she caught my cold," Beth thought.

"Get her some water," said Patrick.

Beth ran to the bathroom and waited for the faucet to chug out a glass of cold water. When Beth returned, her mother tried to sit up to drink, but her fingers would not bend around the glass. She dropped it, spilling water all over the bed. Then she let out an agonizing shriek and began to tremble.

"Oh God! Oh God!" Patrick cried.

Beth froze, unsure what to do. Then she went back into the bathroom to get a damp washcloth for her mother's forehead. When she returned, her mother was lying back down, looking as if the pain had passed.

"The doctor's on his way," said Thelma, appearing back in the doorway.

"What should we do?" asked Patrick, turning to Beth for instructions.

"Thelma, go downstairs and wait for the doctor. Turn on the porch light so he knows which house it is."

Thelma gladly went, relieved to escape major responsibility in a crisis.

"Kathy, how do you feel?" asked Patrick, taking her hand. He forgot that since she had closed her eyes, she could not know he was speaking to her.

Beth took her mother's other hand. She squeezed it without response.

After a couple silent minutes, Thelma hollered, "The doctor's here." Just as Beth heard his footsteps on the stairs, she felt her mother's hand go limp. The doctor was startled when he entered. He was just in time to see Kathy's body relax as the breath passed through her, releasing her spirit.

"I'm sorry," he said, searching for the patient's absent pulse.

For a moment, Beth thought she would go into shock, but then she heard her father sob. Fearing she would lose him as well, she grabbed him by the shoulders and guided him downstairs to the parlor. They sat down on the sofa and she held him. Thelma glumly settled into a chair. The doctor came down and spoke for a few minutes to Beth, stating it was heart failure. Thelma disappeared into the kitchen. Patrick, tears streaming down his face, was oblivious to everything.

When the doctor left, Thelma brought her uncle a plate of eggs, toast, and coffee. He did not feel like eating, but his daughter and niece insisted. Thelma practically spoon-fed him while Beth went upstairs to dress. She knew she would have a busy day planning the funeral.

Upstairs, she sat down on her bed and stared into her closet, unable to choose a dress to wear. She was less horrified for herself than for her father. She imagined his pain was greater, as would be hers if she were to lose Henry. She did not know whether losing a spouse or a parent were worse, but she did not want to lose any more time with the man she loved. Beth was sure religious conflicts could not exist in Heaven, and her mother, who was now there, would finally understand her daughter's love for a Protestant.

Even after the funeral, a steady stream of visitors came to pay their respects to the McCarey family. Henry spent every free minute with the family, and Beth was grateful for his strength. Michael returned home to say his mother's funeral Mass and stay for a week. His presence in the house made Beth nervous because of her intention to marry Henry. When she overheard her mother's friends, Ernestine and Hilda, tell her brother, "Your mother was so proud you became a priest. She considered it the greatest blessing of her life," Beth could not help being annoyed. She felt she had been a more dutiful child than her brother; she had been the one to care for her parents all these years. She knew her brother had a higher calling, that he was a comfort to a great many people. Still, it irked her that her own sacrifice to care for her parents should go unnoticed. Now she would have to care for her father, a task that would become more difficult as he grew older, and she knew she would get little help from Thelma.

The Monday after the funeral was the first day of respite from frequent guests. Even Henry did not come over for supper that night because his mother was returning from California and he had to meet her at the train station. Michael took his father out for a ride that afternoon so he could get some fresh air. Beth used her father's absence from the house as an opportunity to go through her mother's clothes and donate them to the poor. Thelma helped by adopting half her aunt's wardrobe for herself.

After supper that evening, Thelma played the piano for her uncle. Michael offered to help Beth wash the dishes. Michael told her how their father had spent the afternoon telling him about the old days, how he had first met their mother, how beautiful she had been, and how bravely she had fought for them to be married, despite their grandmother's opposition, and finally how their grandmother had warmed toward him. "He said," Michael concluded, "that he was in utter despair when he met Mother; he attributes her with saving his life and bringing him all his happiness. I don't think I ever met two people who were so much in love as our parents. I think all the adversity they faced just made their love stronger."

"Maybe," said Beth. Since the day Michael left for the seminary, she and her brother had not spent a moment alone. Now she felt awkward around him. Sometimes she nearly forgot she had a brother who was a priest; he had left when she was a little girl, and then her other brothers had gone off to war, so that she had often felt like an only child. Because Michael was a priest, she imagined he would disapprove of her relationship with Henry. She did not know what to say to him. She was afraid to tell him she was contemplating what he might consider a sin. She was trying to think how to broach the subject with him.

"When are you going to marry your young man?" he asked.

Beth stiffened. Here was the battle she had expected.

"I don't know."

"Why not? You've been going out with him long enough, and it's clear he loves you. I don't think you could find a better man than Henry."

She did not know what to say. How could Michael even discuss it with her? He knew Henry was not a Catholic.

When she did not answer, Michael added, "Mother is gone now."

"Henry's mother doesn't like Catholics," Beth replied, laying the blame on Henry's family rather than her own.

"She'll come around."

"Think what people will say, me marrying a Baptist when my brother is a priest."

"God isn't a Catholic or a Baptist; He's too loving to discriminate."

Beth had never thought of it that way.

"But I thought it was a sin to marry a heretic."

"Henry's a good man, and he loves you. The two of you will express Christ's love to one another. That's what matters."

Beth could not believe this! Her brother was a priest, a voice of authority. His vocation should make him strictly adhere to the rules of the church. She did not know how to respond to such unexpected words.

"But Father and Thelma — "

"They both like Henry."

"No, I mean, I need to look after them. Father's old, and Thelma, well, she — "

"You're a good caretaker, Beth, but you also deserve to be happy. Thelma can take care of herself, and I bet Henry would let Father stay with you and him. You can always find ways to do your duty and still find happiness."

Beth was astounded by this unforeseen support. She would have hugged her brother if soapsuds were not all over her hands. He was a blessing from God.

Now if Henry's mother would just come around.

Margaret was relieved to be home. She had never before been away from Marquette more than a day, and then always with Will. Even with her parents, she had felt lonely in California.

When her family asked how her trip had been, she replied, "It was wonderful." When asked to elaborate, she described her sister's impressive mansion, the wedding decorations, the bridesmaids' dresses, the cake, and the beautiful bride. She found that most people outside the family forgot to ask how her trip had been, and she was relieved not to discuss it.

Her parents had met her at the San Francisco train station. She had been thrilled to see them, but equally shocked to see how they had aged; her father had lost nearly all his hair, her mother's face was a mass of wrinkles embedded with two sparkling eyes. They were now seventy-eight and seventy-two, having lived beyond the average lifespan. She found she wanted to spend every minute with them, and she was glad when they said she would stay with them, although she was a bit disappointed not to be a guest in the senator's mansion.

She had found San Francisco to be amazing. The high hills reminded her of several of Marquette's streets, and peeking between the city's tall buildings was the ocean, just as back home, Lake Superior was visible between banks and stores on Front Street. She had always loved streetcars and mourned the recent dissolution of them in Marquette, so she was delighted to ride them all over the city with her parents as they went sightseeing. They had their fill of shopping in Market Street, treating themselves to seafood at Fisherman's Wharf, and they even ventured into the exotic streets of Chinatown.

Then two nights before the wedding, Sarah came over to see what her sister would wear to the ceremony. Margaret brought out her dress to show.

"Isn't it rather old-fashioned," Sarah frowned.

"I just bought it last year for Ada's graduation," Margaret replied.

"I'm sure it's okay for Marquette," said Sarah. "Back there, they're always ten years behind the rest of the country, but I can't have you come to the wedding dressed in that."

Margaret's feelings were hurt, but she did not wish to embarrass her sister before the leaders of San Francisco society. Sarah coerced her into shopping the next day; feeling terribly guilty, Margaret bought a new dress that cost an entire week of Will's salary, and which she knew she would never wear again. Margaret thought she would cry when the snooty shopkeeper rang up the purchase, then looked down her nose to state, "All sales are final."

The wedding itself was fine enough. As for the reception — well, Margaret told herself she could not expect the bride and groom to pay attention to her when they had five hundred guests to entertain. Theo did smile at her, said he was glad she had come, and asked after his cousins, but the bride, Melinda, with her ash-blonde hair, and her nasal New England accent, only muttered, "It's nice to meet you," then pushed Margaret out of her way to greet Mr. Upton Sinclair.

Margaret noticed her parents were equally ignored. Her father had always been able to talk to anyone, but these socialites ignored his attempts to converse. She felt she and her parents were dismissed as "poor relatives." She had to admit Harriet had been right. She did not belong among these "la-di-da" rich people.

Margaret cried when she said goodbye to her parents at the train station, but she had no intention of ever visiting California again. Will had expected she would come home, depressed to be back in humble Marquette after all the grandeur she had experienced, but that night, she snuggled against his chest contentedly, and he understood how much she had missed him.

❦   ❦   ❦

Beth took Michael's words to heart. Henry was the only man she could ever love; either she married him, or she spent her old age as a spinster with Thelma, filling their empty lives with a collection of old tabby cats. The thought made her shudder.

"Henry, I'm ready to marry you."

She made the declaration the next night when they sat alone on her front porch.

"I don't see any reason to wait now," she said. "Mother is gone, and Father isn't particular about religion. I know your mother doesn't want you to convert, and I wouldn't feel right getting married in a Baptist church, but I'm willing to go with you to the courthouse."

Thelma had been eavesdropping inside the screen door. Now she butted in, "The judge who married me at the courthouse was real nice."

Ignoring Thelma, Henry asked, "Are you sure?"

"Yes."

"When will you do it?" Thelma asked. "Beth, I'll help you write the invitations and pick out the dress."

"No, I don't want a big wedding," said Beth. "Just a little private one."

Henry kissed her forehead. He did not want a showy wedding; they could not afford one anyway. He imagined his mother, just back from his cousin's high society wedding, would want them to have an elaborate ceremony, but he did not care what his mother wanted. This would be Beth's day.

"When?" he asked.

"How about Friday?"

"That doesn't give you time to buy a dress," Thelma said.

"I'll wear my blue dress with the little pink roses on it."

"I'll loan you the new hat I just bought. That way you'll have something borrowed and something new to go with your dress that's old and blue."

"All right." Beth felt so happy she could even be gracious to Thelma.

When told of the wedding, Margaret refused to attend. When Patrick heard this, he decided he would not go either. Henry dropped his future father-in-law off at the Whitman house so the parents could get acquainted while their children were married.

Then Henry and Beth drove to the Marquette County Courthouse. Of course, Roy was best man. Thelma was maid of honor — Beth had no way not to ask her — and somehow Thelma had gotten over Vincent Smiley enough not to tell off her cousin, even if she were to be an old maid — well, not quite — she would always have that night at the Grand Hotel to remember.

The ceremony was short and simple. No violins played. No rice was thrown. Just one happy, heartswelling half hour took place. After the marriage vows were said, and rings and kisses exchanged, the couple returned to the Whitman house. Beth braved giving Margaret a hug, then took a flower from her bouquet and pinned it to her mother-law's dress. "You'll have to be my mother now," she said. Beth's brown eyes were so sincere that for that day at least, Margaret's sternness vanished.

Henry and Beth planned to move into the house Henry had built beside his parents' home. Patrick had agreed to come live with them.

"I'm glad you and Henry will live next door," Margaret told Beth. "I better go see about supper. Ada and Eleanor baked you a wedding cake."

"Your father and I," Will told Beth, "are looking forward to being neighbors. I imagine we'll have many fine talks, sitting on the front porch, drinking coffee, and remembering the good old days."

"Only if I can add a little whiskey to my coffee," Patrick said. Luckily, Margaret had gone into the kitchen before this remark was made.

At supper, Eleanor asked, "Thelma, will you also live with Henry and Beth?"

"No. I have my own life."

"But then what will you do?" asked Ada.

"I'm buying Uncle Patrick and Aunt Kathy's house, and I've advertised in *The Mining Journal* to give piano lessons."

Ada and Eleanor exchanged amused glances, but Roy said, "Thelma is an extremely talented pianist. Thelma, why don't you play something for us while we eat our cake."

Margaret had a clanking old piano tucked away in the corner of the dining room. Her mother had owned it, but decided not to take it to California. No one in the family knew how to play it. Recipe books and knickknacks covered the lid over the keys and the piano bench, but Roy quickly cleared it so Thelma could play.

Thelma sat down on the bench. The piano had remained in tune despite years of neglect, so she made good on her declaration, "Let me show you what music is."

A loud rendition of the wedding march filled the room, the first time it had been heard on this felicitous occasion.

"Better late than never," Henry said as he squeezed Beth's hand. The lovers had waited a long time, but now they were together — forever.

1937

Henry and Beth's marriage started a trend among the Whitmans. Within two years, Eleanor and Ada found handsome, prosperous young husbands. Ada married Louis Lowell, a Marquette salesman who had managed to keep the company he worked for afloat despite the Depression; his employers expected yet greater things from him, and someday he dreamt of being head of the company. Eleanor married Ronald Goldman, a science professor at what had been the Normal School, now upgraded to the Northern State Teachers College. Ronald was from Lower Michigan; he had heard tales of the frigid land above the Mackinac Straits, but could not have been prepared for Marquette's enormous snowbanks. He claimed that only Eleanor's love kept him warm on a winter night.

In Margaret's eyes, a professor and a prosperous businessman for son-in-laws far surpassed a Catholic daughter-in-law. After Eleanor and Ada moved across town with their husbands, Margaret found Beth's next-door presence mundane while her daughters' weekly visits were treats. Even when Beth presented Margaret with her first grandchild, James "Jimmy" Whitman, Ada and Eleanor quickly regained their mother's devotion by presenting baby girls for Grandma to coo over. Almost as bad, Bill was seventeen and dating several pretty girls; Beth suspected Margaret would soon have another daughter-in-law for her to compete with.

Meanwhile, Roy wondered whether he would ever be so lucky as to find a wife. He did not even know how to talk to the opposite sex. At the Huron Mountain Club, the girls had always seemed to mock him — perhaps it had only been good-natured teasing and flirting, but it had made him uncomfortable. Out West, he had worked on the land where women were few and men's talk about women was coarse. He had listened with amusement to the other men boast of their escapades, while he remembered what Henry had told him

— that men tend to exaggerate their female conquests. Roy made up a few of his own stories, all in good fun, but only to fit in. He suspected he was the least experienced of the men, but he felt no strong desire to gain experience. Not that he did not notice a pretty face or a female figure, but he felt he was intended for something beyond the ordinary life of marriage and children. How he conceived this belief, or why he believed it, he could not say. Occasionally he dismissed it as his own inflated ego inflicted on him by his preposterously regal name. Then he told himself he just wanted to be normal — to have a family — yet he felt called, almost cursed, by a sense of personal destiny that seldom left his thoughts.

Work relieved Roy from his consuming dreams. By the summer of 1937, all the Whitmans had regular work again. Henry had continuous carpentry jobs, and Bill, to his parents' displeasure, dropped out of high school that year to work with his oldest brother. Will found work with the Civilian Corps, one of the new programs President Roosevelt had initiated. And that summer, Roy returned to the Huron Mountain Club as a guide and custodian. He was surprised to find his old roommate also there.

Lex Weidner had left Marquette years before to work in Green Bay. There he had married, then decided the big city was not for him. Against his wife's wishes, he had insisted they move back to the Marquette area. Along the Big Bay Road, they had built a little house, close enough for Lex to drive to the Club. Roy admitted Lex was as handsome and strong as ever. By contrast, Roy bemoaned that he was fast approaching thirty and his hairline was quickly receding. He envied Lex his looks, but since his old roommate had always been one of the Club's hardest workers, he and Roy now developed a mutual respect and cordiality toward one another.

Initially, Roy was excited to be back at the Club, but after a couple weeks, he found himself going into Marquette every chance he could, even if only to attend church and have Sunday dinner with his parents. Since all Roy's siblings except Bill had now moved out, his parents were too pleased by his visits to ask why they were so frequent. Had they asked, they would have been surprised by the answer.

Roy was actually depressed. One Saturday he came into town, relieved to get away from the Club. The day before, Lex had bragged to him about what he and his wife would be up to all weekend. Roy thought his coworker vulgar, but he still envied him. He wondered how someone so obnoxious could have a loving wife, while someone like himself, smarter and kinder, even if not good-looking, should be alone. When he reached his parents' house, he found

Henry and Beth holding hands on the sofa, their eyes adoring little Jimmy, who was taking his first steps. Roy thought Jimmy a screaming holy terror, but his parents and grandparents only laughed and spoiled him. As Roy walked in, Henry kissed Beth's cheek and told her, "You sure do make beautiful babies."

Roy envied the bond between them. He wondered whether he would ever have such a relationship. What was wrong with him? Everyone else in the family had someone. His mother was always bursting into songs of love and singing them to his father. And look at Grandpa and Grandma Dalrymple. Grandpa had died last winter, and a month later, Grandma had also died. Everyone said, "Grandma died of a broken heart. She could not live without Grandpa." Roy could not imagine such love. Even Aunt Harriet and Uncle Charles occasionally exchanged an affectionate word. Yet Roy was alone. He wondered whether any girl would ever want him; what woman would ever tolerate his need for solitude, his moodiness, his absorption in his work and his books? He could not love a woman who did not believe in his capacity for greatness, and so he was alone at twenty-nine.

That afternoon, Patrick came over to visit the Whitmans. He was growing forgetful; at times he could be a bit burdensome to Henry and Beth. Trying not to be in his daughter and son-in-law's way, he often walked next door to visit. He chatted incessantly about the old days; Will had been delighted when Patrick mentioned he had known Will's mother, and Margaret was astounded to learn he had been present the night she was born in the Whitmans' boarding house. But what struck Roy was the way Patrick spoke about his departed wife, especially when he explained that by the time she had gone deaf, they no longer needed words because they knew each other so well. Old Mr. McCarey, Roy noted, was nothing to look at; his liver was rotted from drinking too much whiskey, his back was hunched over, half the time he forgot to shave, yet even he had once known a great love.

The next morning, Roy was in a foul mood, but he still went to church with his parents and Bill. Henry and Beth tried to keep peace between their families by not attending church. Roy could not understand why God had given them such happiness when they avoided church, while he never missed a Sunday, yet had nothing. He was further disgusted when he noted that almost everyone in the congregation had a spouse.

As the opening hymn was sung, a pretty girl entered the church. She had on a pink skirt, white hat, and white gloves. Roy would have noticed her even without the nice clothes. She looked to be in her early twenties; her hair was long and gold and looked like silk. She stepped into the pew in front of him. He could not take his eyes from her. The curve of her back was so enticing. He bowed his head in prayer, telling himself not to think sinful thoughts, but bowing his head only focused his eyes on her behind. He realized church was the perfect place for the most lustful thoughts. He could stare at this beauty for an hour without anyone noticing because everyone pretended to be intent on the preacher's words.

Roy had not yet glimpsed her face. He wished she would turn around. Would he be disappointed? He told himself she must be ugly; otherwise, she would have come to church with a husband. She probably had buckteeth, or worse, a mustache, and then he would be so revolted he would forget about her.

When the service ended, he waited a moment for her to turn and leave.

"Roy, move. What are you waiting for?" Bill barked.

Roy turned around to scowl at his brother, then stepped into the aisle and nearly collided with the beauty.

"Please, after you," he said. She stepped past him, but not before he caught a glimpse of her face, a glimpse that told him she was perfect: lips red, nose pink, complexion flawless, eyelashes long, neck white, everything delectable. She was the finest woman he had ever seen.

Roy went home with his family for Sunday dinner. In the afternoon, Ada and Louis stopped by. They were another happily married couple, but Roy did not let their happiness depress him. He now knew he wanted that kind of happiness for himself, and he would see about acquiring it. When he left that evening, he told his parents, "I'll come again for church next weekend."

The following Sunday, he found himself again sitting behind the beautiful girl. Adult Sunday school followed the service that week; then he was able to sit across from her and directly admire her. No words were yet exchanged, but Roy imagined what he would say and how she would respond. He wanted to ask her out; he tried to persuade himself she would accept. He imagined being with her, holding her hand, whispering her name, but he did not yet know her name, and he liked her too well to make up one for his fantasies. He would wait until she told it to him.

The next weekend, he was needed at the Club so he could not go to Marquette.

"I'd ask Lex to work this weekend," his boss told him, "but you know, he has a wife while you don't have anyone expecting you to be home."

Roy said nothing. He could not protest that he had to see a pretty girl at church. He felt it unfair to be discriminated against for being single. He stayed and worked, but all the next week, his yearning to see the pretty girl was near unbearable.

And then the next week, the pretty girl was not at church. Roy was enraged. Two weeks without seeing her! But he dared not tell anyone. He stayed overnight with his parents that weekend, and Monday morning, he went out for coffee with Henry and Bill before he had to pick up some supplies for the Club and head back.

The brothers went to a downtown restaurant that morning. While they waited for the waitress, Henry regaled his brothers with tales of Jimmy's adorable exploits. Roy listened politely. Bill peered out the window and inserted remarks about each "skirt" that walked by.

"Bill, if you start whistling at girls," Roy said, "I'll walk out of here."

"Oh, let him have his fun," Henry said.

"What do you think of that one behind the counter?" Bill elbowed Roy. "Only reason I eat here is to look at her."

Roy frowned, but turned his head to look. The waitress had her back to him, but after a few seconds, she turned enough for him to discern ample breasts, a well curved figure, long beautiful legs. He knew it was her — the girl from church. Before he could prepare himself, she came over to take their order.

"Hi, sugar," said Bill. "I'll have scrambled eggs, toast, a piece of ham, and coffee." Henry ordered the same. Roy fumbled. He could not remember the word to describe how he wanted his eggs cooked. She smiled patiently. He gave up and requested scrambled as well. He felt retarded. When she finished jotting down the order, he said, "Thank you," and she smiled.

"Hey, sugar, could we get some cream?" Bill shouted after her.

When she brought it, Roy again said, "Thank you," and she smiled at him again.

The brothers ate breakfast. Roy could not stop himself from glancing at her. She caught him looking once. He blushed. She kept smiling.

Henry soon jumped up. "Come on, Bill, or we'll be late." He handed Roy a couple dollars and asked him to pay the check. Bill grabbed his hat and followed Henry out the door. The waitress came over to offer Roy more coffee. He also had to get going, but he let her pour him another cup.

Roy sipped his coffee and tried to watch her when she would not notice him. She returned with the coffee pot. He had another cup. This time he noticed her name tag. CHLOE. A beautiful name.

"Thank you, Chloe," he said.

"You're welcome," she smiled. "What's your name?"

"Royal," he said. Then he realized she knew he had stared at her breast to discover her name. And what was he trying to prove by using his full name? He waited for her to laugh at him.

"What a great name," she said. "It's so proud and strong."

"Thank you," he said. "I've always been partial to the name Chloe myself."

He had never before given the name a thought. That did not matter. He was flirting with her. It was easier than he had imagined.

"Chuck, I'm taking a break!" Chloe called back to the kitchen.

"Ten minutes!" Chuck shouted back.

"Do you mind?" she asked, sliding into the booth across from Roy.

"No, please, sit down."

"I'm not interrupting, am I?"

"No, I'm in no hurry. I have the day off," he said.

"That's nice," she said. "Were those your brothers in here with you?"

"Yeah."

"I thought so. They come in pretty often. You're from a good looking family."

"Do you think so?" He was surprised. He knew Bill had a cocky way about him that appealed to the girls, but Henry was not particularly handsome.

"Oh yes, I always thought your younger brother really cute, until I saw you."

He could not believe any girl, let alone Chloe, would say such a thing to him.

"Are you from around here?" he asked for lack of a better question.

"No, Wisconsin. I've only lived here a few months. People are nice here, but it's been kind of lonely. I don't really know anyone yet."

"Not even at church?"

"What?" she asked, confused.

"I'm sorry. I mean, I've noticed you at church a few times."

"You go to church. That's nice. Not a lot of young men do anymore. I thought I had seen your younger brother there, but I don't remember seeing you. I'm surprised I don't remember because you seem like you would stand out in a crowd."

"Why do you say that?" he blushed.

"You just seem different from most guys. Better spoken maybe, or smart, like you've been to college or something."

"I only went for a semester. That's all I could afford."

Why had he said that? Had he hurt his chances with her by leaving college?

"I don't know what it is," she said. "You just seem more polite, or maybe more wise. You have intelligent eyes."

Roy was flattered. She must like him if she said that. He sure liked her. She seemed to notice something about him that he felt about himself, something other people missed. He felt he could be his true, hidden self with her.

"I would have finished college, but I needed to work to help out my family," he said. It was not quite true, but if he let her know he cared about family, she might think him a good catch.

"That's noble of you," she said. "Family should come first. Usually, women are the only ones who understand that; that must be why I like you; you're more sensitive than most men."

Roy knew Henry had sacrificed for the family far more than he had. He had practically abandoned the family while for years he wandered aimlessly about the country. But if he had a good woman like Chloe, he would settle down. He wanted to be responsible, to care for someone.

"I get off at noon," she said, then hesitated. "Um, like I said, I don't really know anyone in Marquette. Would you maybe want to go for a walk or something? I mean, since you have the day off, you could show me around."

The offer was more than he had expected. He let out a meek, "Yes." She smiled again. He thought her absolutely charming.

"I'll meet you at the corner a couple minutes after twelve," she said. "Don't come in 'cause we'll be busy for lunch. I'll sneak out the back door."

"All right," he said. "I'll see you then." He picked up his cap and stumbled out the door. He could not believe such a woman was interested in him. He had better hurry and pick up the supplies for the Club. He did not want to come back late after weeks of dreaming about this moment.

He met her at noon on the restaurant's corner. He wanted to hold her hand but did not dare. They walked toward the lake, then turned onto Lakeshore Boulevard and walked to McCarty's Cove, past Picnic Rocks, and out to Presque Isle. They walked all around the island and back. They talked all the way, neither complaining of being tired although the walk was several miles. Roy told her the full reason why he had left college — that he sought to understand life and people, and those things could not be understood simply by reading books. She listened silently, then said she admired him for his quest to be more than ordinary. She told him of her childhood on a Wisconsin farm, a childhood similar to his own. Neither mentioned much about the present; they were too busy comparing their pasts that seemed to make them compatible.

By late afternoon, they returned to the restaurant corner. Roy had to get back to the Club. Chloe thanked him for the offer of a ride home, but her car was parked behind the restaurant. No promise was made to see each other again. Roy was too nervous to ask, but he intended to go back to the restaurant or to church to see her. He told himself a serious relationship had to be built gradually; to hasten it might destroy his chances. And if nothing else, he would always remember this lovely day.

Henry and Beth went over to his parents' house for supper that night. They brought little Jimmy, but Patrick said he would stay home and lie down. Beth wanted to stay with her father; she worried he was ill, and she did not relish an evening with her mother-in-law, but Patrick insisted he would be fine.

"I think he was out in the sun too much," Beth told her in-laws. "He worked in the garden most of the afternoon. I keep reminding him to wear a hat, but he's forgetful. He probably just needs a little rest."

"Keep an eye on him and make sure he doesn't get dehydrated," Margaret said in her most patronizing tone.

After supper, Beth helped with the dishes. She tried to tolerate Margaret's idiosyncratic method of washing, rinsing, and drying the glasses and silverware. Bill left to go out with his friends. Henry turned on the radio he had bought his parents at Christmas. Then he and his father smoked cigars and shuffled the playing cards until the women joined them for a game of rummy.

At eight o'clock, Beth said, "I better go over and check on Dad."

"Why don't you just call him?" said Will.

Beth let the phone ring a dozen times without an answer.

"I better go over," she repeated.

"I'll go," said Henry. Jimmy had been napping for over an hour, and Henry expected him to wake any minute. He would rather check on his father-in-law than deal with Jimmy's crying and the inevitable diaper changing.

"No, honey, you stay and rest," said Beth. "You had a long day."

"Tell your father to come over for some cake," said Margaret. "There's plenty left from supper."

Beth found her father in bed. He had changed into his nightshirt and was sleeping peacefully. He was a heavy sleeper so she was not surprised he had not heard the telephone. She felt his forehead without waking him. He seemed fine. Rather than disturb him, she went back to her in-laws' house. She could always bring him a piece of cake later. She stayed and played cards with her in-laws until ten o'clock; then Henry, Beth, and Jimmy returned home.

"I better go check on Father," said Beth, heading for her father's room.

Henry sat down to rock Jimmy so he would stay asleep.

"Henry," said Beth, nervously returning to the living room, "Dad isn't in his bed, and it doesn't look as if he got dressed. His nightshirt and bedroom slippers are gone so he must be wearing them. Where could he have gone?"

"Check the bathroom or the basement," said Henry, although he handed the baby to Beth and went to look for himself.

"Where would he have gone?" Beth fretted when Henry returned without success. "He should have told me if he were going somewhere. He's getting so forgetful it worries me."

"I'll look outside," said Henry, putting back on his shoes. "He couldn't have gone far in his night clothes."

"He should have at least left me a note," said Beth.

"I'm sure he's fine," said Henry. "I'll just walk down the street and be back in five minutes."

"I'll go with you."

"No, you stay here with the baby."

But Beth was stubborn. Carrying Jimmy, she followed her husband outside. Henry briskly walked up one end of the street while Beth went down the other.

She could hear Henry shouting Patrick's name. She wanted to find her father, but she didn't want the whole neighborhood woken, or worse, to have everyone think what she already suspected — that her father was losing his mind.

Patrick had gone out. He had gone farther than would be expected from a man in a nightshirt and bedroom slippers. He had left the house only a few minutes before Henry and Beth came home. Had she known to look when she left Will and Margaret's house, Beth would have seen her father disappear around the street corner.

Patrick heard his name being called, but that only caused him to run. He knew if the English soldiers caught him, he would be imprisoned, or worse, shot. He knew if they killed him, his nation would bless him as a martyr, but he did not want to die yet.

He had to hide. But where? He did not recognize this town. He had thought he was in Dublin, but now nothing looked familiar. This was not his home village back in County Leitrim. He wondered whether the bomb he set off had knocked him unconscious for a while and now he was just confused. If he could find a church, he could claim sanctuary — if those British bastards would respect a Catholic church — he doubted they would. He remembered his grandfather telling him stories of how that tyrant Cromwell had turned St.

Patrick's Cathedral into a horse barn. His grandfather had told him many tales of Ireland's woes. The Irish would never forgive the English for their crimes. Not even once Ireland was free could those crimes be forgotten because they could never be allowed to happen again.

He had to keep running if he would live to fight another day. He would have to lose himself in the back streets until the soldiers quit looking for him.

Henry caught a glimpse of white, moving like a ghost, until it reached a picket fence, and then the way it climbed over the fence, actually fell over, showed it was clearly a man. "Patrick!" he shouted again. The figure looked back, then picked himself up from the ground and started running again. Patrick crossed Presque Isle Avenue. Fortunately, no cars were passing. Then he entered the woods. Henry could not believe how nimble the old man was. "I've spotted him Beth," he shouted, then ran across the street and broke into the woods in hot pursuit. He would have to stop Patrick before he reached the lake.

Patrick ran faster, valuing his life. But what was that roaring sound? God save him, it was the Irish sea. If he jumped in, he could swim along the shore, maybe find some bushes or reeds to hide in until the soldiers gave up the search. Then he could walk home to County Leitrim and wait until things settled down. He could make bombs there and carry them back to Dublin to plant in the British government buildings.

Henry forged his way through scratching branches and headed toward the beach. He had lost sight of Patrick in the dark woods, but when the forest broke into the sandy beach, he spotted him again. Somehow, despite a nightshirt and slippers, the old man had managed not to trip or tangle his clothes in the tree branches.

"Patrick!" Henry shouted, trying to run only to stumble along the beach.

Patrick ran, but lost his balance in the sand. When he fell forward, he knew he was a dead man. He struggled to get up, every second expecting to be shot in the back. He would not let them take him prisoner. He would not be a trophy in a British prison. He got to his feet, but after a couple steps, slipped back down.

Henry wrapped his arms around the old man.

"Patrick, come home. Beth is worried sick."

"I'll kill you!" Patrick screamed, his mad fists flailing in the air. "You pig! You son of a British whore! I'll kill you!"

Henry grabbed Patrick's left arm and held it behind his back while trying to grasp the other. The two men wrestled, Patrick twisting about, being a formidable opponent despite his age. But Henry soon secured both arms, then clasped the old man about the chest so he could not hurt either of them.

"Patrick, it's Henry. Calm down. It's okay. Let's go home."

"I spit on you, you British pig! I spit on your whole bloody nation of bloody British pigs!"

"Patrick," Henry kept repeating. Slowly, his father-in-law quit struggling and accepted defeat. Henry relaxed his hold and turned Patrick around to look him in the eye. Then he received a wad of spit in his face.

"Patrick," he said, while wiping his face on his sleeve. "It's Henry, Beth's husband. Your son-in-law. Look at me."

Patrick's face shook. He blinked his eyes as he started to wake from his confusion.

"Henry? Beth. Where's Beth? Is she with Kathy? Kathy!" he called.

"Let me take you home to Beth."

"Oh, Kathy. Beth. You're Beth's husband. What's your name?"

"Henry. You live with me and Beth. Do you remember?"

"Yes — I — yes, I remember. Henry, why are we on the beach? It's cold here."

"You had some sort of spell. I think you lost your memory for a moment. You ran from the house."

"Oh." He was embarrassed, exhausted. He remembered feeling angry for some reason. "I think I was running and — was I shouting? What did I say?"

Henry did not know what to reply. Patrick never talked about Ireland. Henry feared that to repeat his father-in-law's words would only upset the old man.

"You said you wanted to go swimming. That must be why you ran down to the lake. Come on; let's go home so Beth won't worry."

Henry guided Patrick, his arm around his shoulder. They skirted around the woods to reach the street, then walked across Presque Isle Avenue. Beth saw them when they were a block away. She ran to them, Jimmy still in her arms. Henry took the baby while Beth put her arm around her father's shoulders.

"You scared me, Dad. Why did you do it?"

"I don't know," he shook his head.

"He was just a little confused," said Henry. "Let's get him inside."

Beth saw the bewilderment on her father's face and decided it was best not to question him now. The family walked home.

Once Patrick was asleep in his bed, and Jimmy in his crib, having peacefully dozed through the crisis, Henry and Beth whispered from their pillows.

"What did he say when you found him?" asked Beth.

"Nothing, he was just confused," said Henry. He did not want Beth to know her father had nearly gone into the lake in such a state. "I found him on Presque Isle Avenue. He wasn't sure how he got there."

"I'll never leave him alone again," said Beth.

"No, I wouldn't either," said Henry.

"But how can I keep an eye on him all the time?"

"Maybe Ma and Pa can help you watch him."

"I'm afraid even to go to sleep. What if he sneaks out during the night?"

"I locked the door. We'll hear him if he gets up. Get some rest now."

Henry kissed her cheek and stroked her hair. The crisis had so exhausted her that she was soon asleep.

Henry stayed awake. He could not tell Beth how her father had been violent, or that he had been forced to restrain him. Henry felt frightened. Patrick had always been congenial, but what if he should become dangerous? Should Beth be left alone with him? Would he hurt her or Jimmy if he had another spell? Maybe they could get some pills from a doctor, or lock Patrick in his room at night for his own protection?

Henry worried for several days, but Patrick did not have a relapse. Soon, the family nearly forgot the episode.

Roy had no more free weekends that summer to spend in Marquette. The Club's summer season was at its height, and as a reliable and hardworking employee, Roy constantly had one task after another. Still, he thought of Chloe constantly.

One day, Lex asked whether Roy would like to come over to his house for supper.

"Come on," Lex insisted. "You can meet my little woman. She's a good cook."

Having no other plans, Roy found it hard to refuse.

It was a beautiful evening, and although he had little in common with his host, Roy enjoyed the drive to Lex's house, hidden a mile off the Big Bay Road.

"Here we are," said Lex, pulling the car up to a little red cottage. They got out of the car, and Lex led the way up the steps.

"Honey, I'm home!" he shouted, opening the door. "I brought a dinner guest!"

When his wife did not answer, Lex went into the bedroom. Roy stood in the kitchen, hoping he was not intruding.

He heard mumbling — a female voice. "I thought . . . just have sandwiches and go for a ride into town . . . Well, I didn't know — "

"You'll have to cook something," Lex said. "I can't turn my friend away."

"All right . . . it'll take a little while . . . if you had told me."

"Don't argue, woman. Get out there and make something decent to eat."

Roy felt uncomfortable. He did not want to impose. He had not really wanted to come anyway. He did not like the tone Lex took with his wife.

Lex came back into the kitchen. "Let's have a couple drinks and sit out on the porch while my wife makes us supper," he said. "I hope you're not in a hurry to eat. She's got to make herself presentable first."

"That's fine," said Roy, wishing he had not come.

"How about I take you for a walk around the property. I've got six acres here."

Roy let Lex lead him through the wooded land. He made polite comments about the trees, the scenery, the house. All the while, he pitied the poor girl forced to make a meal for a stranger she had not expected. Besides the insinuations Lex had made about his wife, he had told Roy she was pretty, a good cook, and madly in love with him. Roy suspected Lex had exaggerated a little.

After half an hour, they returned to the porch. Roy sat down while Lex poured them drinks and checked on supper's progress. Roy wondered how he would get through the meal. He hoped Lex's wife would not be angry with him for showing up unannounced. He did not want to cause her any trouble.

Lex soon returned, complaining about the heat. He sat down, unbuttoned his shirt, and held a cold bottle against his bare chest. Roy could not help noticing that Lex was developing the start of a middle age spread. He grinned to himself.

They smoked cigarettes and drank a couple beers, with their feet resting on the porch railing. When the sun started to go down, the mosquitoes came out. Lex then went inside, but Roy did not want to go in until he was called for supper. He wondered whether he should apologize to Lex's wife for coming, or if he should just praise the food as being delicious — whether or not it was.

But when he was called inside, he found himself speechless.

Mrs. Lex Weidner stood at the counter, slicing a tomato. She laid the knife down and turned to shake her guest's hand. A muttered "Hello" was all that escaped either her or Roy's lips. Mrs. Lex Weidner was Chloe.

"Roy, you look surprised," said Lex. "Have you two met before, or are you just stunned by how gorgeous she is?"

"Um, both," Roy tried to laugh.

"We've seen each other at church," Chloe said. "It's nice to meet you finally, Roy."

"You too," he replied.

"Roy, you sit here," said Lex, ushering him to the table. "Take the comfortable chair since you're the guest."

Roy should have been pleased by this attention, but he felt the evening was ruined. He was not too fond of Lex, but here the man was being generous toward him, all the while not knowing how his guest lusted for his wife.

Chloe set the food on the table while Lex grabbed more beer from the refrigerator. Roy was no drinker, but tonight he took what was offered. They seated themselves and Chloe said the blessing.

Remembering his manners, Roy said, "Everything looks delicious."

Chloe smiled. He remembered she had made the meal on short notice. It was not a difficult meal — spaghetti, green beans, sliced tomatoes, and bread — but Roy appreciated it. He would have appreciated anything Chloe did for him. Lex began to praise Chloe, wanting Roy to believe she was the best wife in the universe. He even mentioned that she worked part time; he did not like his wife working, but he appreciated that she wanted to help with the finances. "But once we have children," he said, "she won't work."

Chloe smiled. Roy felt nauseous; the mention of children reminded him that Lex and Chloe had been together as man and wife, the way he dreamed of being with Chloe. Now because he knew she was married, he should no longer think of her that way.

Chloe asked Roy about his family. How many siblings did he have? What did his parents do? Did he like Marquette? He had already answered all these questions during their long walk together so he found it awkward to repeat the answers now. Lex mentioned that Roy had been all over the West. Chloe asked to hear about his travels, then listened with a concentration Roy had never known anyone else give to his words. Her attention flattered him, yet he felt flustered by the intense way she looked at him. She only turned her gaze from him when Lex asked her to pass the salt or get him another beer.

Roy tried to imagine this couple being together. Chloe seemed more sophisticated than her husband, who had not even bothered to button his shirt when he came to the table. Roy thought Lex a total lout, lacking in respect toward his wife, despite how he praised her. When Lex belched during the meal, Roy could see Chloe was embarrassed; she seemed ashamed that Roy should know what an uncouth man she had married.

"I gotta take a piss," said Lex when the meal was over. "Honey, why don't you fix us some dessert?"

"I'll see what we have," she said, getting up.

Lex stepped outside.

"We have an outhouse," Chloe explained to Roy. "But we're hoping to build a bathroom onto the house next year. I'll go see what we have for dessert."

"Let me help you," said Roy.

"No. I can manage."

He followed her into the kitchen anyway. Through the window, he could see Lex walking to the outhouse. They would have a couple minutes alone.

Chloe dug in the icebox for some leftover chocolate pie. Only a couple pieces were left. She said that was all right; she did not want any. She apologized she had nothing better, but she could add a scoop of vanilla ice cream to it.

"Why didn't you tell me you were married?" Roy asked her. "How could you lead me along like that, asking me to go for a walk?"

"Don't be angry," she whispered.

"What am I to think?"

"I didn't know you were Lex's friend."

"That doesn't matter. You're a married woman."

She cut the pie while he waited for an answer.

"You — it's just — you wouldn't understand," she said. "Let me be, or you'll make me cry. Don't upset me when Lex'll be back in a minute."

Roy glared at her.

"I'm sorry," she said.

He felt like a beast. He had no right to reprimand her. Why had he built her up in his mind as someone significant to him when he did not even know her?

"It's just — I'm lonely," she said. "I only work a few days a week. The rest of the time I'm cooped up in this little house without any neighbors nearby. I just wanted to talk to someone."

"What would Lex say if I told him we went for a walk?" Roy threatened. He was being a beast. He did not want to hurt her, but he felt deceived. He knew it was his fault for presuming, but what married woman goes for a walk with a strange man?

"We had a pleasant afternoon together," she said. "Please don't spoil that for me. You don't know what it's like being married to him."

Roy saw Lex come out of the outhouse, then pause to zip his fly and adjust himself. He would be inside in a minute. Roy returned to his chair.

"Give me a kiss, honey. That was a fine meal you made for us tonight," said Lex as he came inside. Roy watched him put his hand on the small of Chloe's back, then sensuously lower it. "If Roy wasn't here right now, I'd — "

"Please, Lex, you're embarrassing me."

Lex laughed, then sat down at the table. "I didn't lie, did I, Roy? I told you my wife could cook. And she's pretty like I said too, isn't she?"

"Yes," said Roy. "You're a lucky man, Lex."

Chloe blushed as she set the pie on the table. Roy wished he could apologize to her. He hoped she understood he would keep their secret.

Once he was back at the Club, Roy vowed he would not think about Chloe anymore. She was Lex's wife. Lex did not deserve her, but Roy could not help that. He did not intend to accept any more dinner invitations from them.

After Henry and Beth married, Thelma lived alone in her aunt and uncle's house. She filled her days with giving piano lessons. She did not need the money, but she soon discovered the loneliness of living alone, so she kept herself occupied. At first she had difficulty finding pupils, but soon one proud mother spread the word to another that Thelma Bergmann was turning her daughter into a talented pianist. Thelma's teaching abilities may not have been great, but mothers are apt to exaggerate their children's minor triumphs, and they rarely listen to their children play the piano except when they have visitors, who are then forced to sit through banging renditions of "When Irish Eyes Are Smiling" and politely compliment the young pseudo-Mozarts before them.

By the fall of '37, Thelma had thirty-one students — twenty-five girls, five boys, and one middle-aged housewife. Each student came once a week for a half hour lesson. Thelma soon realized few of her students had any talent and not one had the discipline to become a great pianist, but she was content that her services were appreciated, for whatever affected reasons they were sought out. Her students became her main contact with the outside world through the bits of gossip that dropped from their mouths. Occasionally, she did get out of the house to visit Henry and Beth and play the overindulgent aunt to little Jimmy. But she still felt lonely, and in her weakest moments, she fantasized about Vincent Smiley, fruitless as she knew it to be.

Then Jessie Hopewell entered Thelma's life. The girl was eleven, and the piano seemed all the world to her. Jessie came from a poor family who had fallen on hard times because of the Depression and an absent father. Jessie's mother struggled to provide for two daughters by cleaning houses. Mrs. Hopewell wanted her daughters to know a better life, but she saw no way to accomplish this goal. When Jessie's teacher at school suggested the girl had musical talent and should take piano lessons, Mrs. Hopewell was pleased. She could scarcely afford to pay for lessons, but she picked up extra work, scraped together some money, and told Jessie if she worked hard, playing the piano might help her advance in life.

Mrs. Hopewell invited Thelma over for tea so they could discuss the terms of Jessie's lessons. She mentioned over the phone what she could pay, which was only half what Thelma usually charged, but Thelma would not turn away someone with true musical talent. She accepted the invitation to tea, hoping finally to have found a serious student.

At the Hopewell house, Thelma was shone into a clean and cheerful, if rather decrepit kitchen. When she was seated at the kitchen table, she realized there was no dining room. Mrs. Hopewell poured the tea while Thelma looked about. She had always lived in spacious rooms, so such poverty — even the Whitmans were comparably more comfortable — appalled her. She was glad Mrs. Hopewell had not come to her house — she would have been embarrassed by the lace curtains, the grand piano, the elegant parlor. As she spoke to Mrs. Hopewell, she learned the woman had once known better times; Mrs. Hopewell spoke of attending concerts and operas as a girl. She hoped her daughter would learn to love Schubert as she had.

"We never had a piano at home," Mrs. Hopewell said, "but Papa encouraged us to be musically minded. We had a large collection of Victrola records." Thelma wondered how the woman had sunk to such poverty. She wanted to ask about Mr. Hopewell. She assumed he had died and left his wife penniless. Feeling almost guilty about taking payment for Jessie's piano lessons, she said that the first two lessons were free to make sure the child was interested.

While the women talked, Jessie came home from school. Thelma got a good look at the girl as she kissed her mother's cheek. She was tall, with a hint of freckles and sandy blonde hair. Her dress was faded, but neat and clean. She smiled pleasantly when Thelma was introduced as her new piano teacher.

"I can't wait to begin playing," she said, her whole face lifting. "My teacher thinks I'll be good at it; music has always been my favorite subject."

"That's sounds promising," said Thelma. "Do you know your scales?"

"Oh yes. I can sing a little, and I've learned how to play a couple simple songs on the piano at school, but of course, no one has had time to teach me more."

"Well, it sounds as if you're off to a good start," said Thelma. "I'm looking forward to your showing me what you already know."

"Jessie," her mother said. "I hear your sister shouting in the yard. Will you go make sure she's all right?"

"Yes, Mama."

"She seems like a good girl," said Thelma when Jessie went outside. "She must be a great help to you."

"That's observant of you," said Mrs. Hopewell. "Most people say she's a tall girl, or that she's cute, but a good girl best describes her. I don't know how I'd get along without her. I wish her sister took after her more."

Thelma finished her tea and was ready to depart, but her kind remark made Mrs. Hopewell want to chat further.

"I sure do appreciate your teaching her like this, Miss Bergmann. She's always wanted to play the piano, so I hope it'll make her happy. She has too many worries for such a young girl."

"Is she unhappy now?" asked Thelma, fearful of moody pupils. Last year a little boy had thrown a temper tantrum during his lesson and pounded his fists on Thelma's precious piano. When his mother came for him, Thelma had told her the piano lessons were over.

"She's not carefree like other children," said Mrs. Hopewell. "Her younger sister, Lyla, constantly wants my attention, but Jessie doesn't demand anything from me. I think she better understands her father's leaving so she tries not to worry me. Still, she hasn't been the same since her father left."

"When did your husband pass away?" asked Thelma, as she allowed Mrs. Hopewell to pour her another cup of tea.

"Oh, he's not dead."

Most people would have been hesitant to press further, but Thelma bluntly asked, "Did he abandon you?"

"No, I wouldn't say that. At least, he didn't intend to. We've just never heard from him since he left."

"I don't understand," said Thelma.

"I'm sorry. I thought everyone in Marquette must know," said Mrs. Hopewell. "Even though I took back my maiden name to protect the girls, I know how people talk."

"My," said Thelma, eager to hear a scandalous tale.

"I hope it won't make any difference in your giving Jessie lessons," said Mrs. Hopewell. "There are some who discriminate against Finns, you know."

"Finns!" said Thelma.

"Yes, my husband was Finnish — the girls get their blonde hair from him."

"I'm half-Finnish myself," Thelma said.

"Oh, I thought your name must be German?"

"My father was half-German and half-Irish," said Thelma, "but my mother was full Finn, so I'm half through her. She died when I was five, and then my father raised me so I didn't grow up knowing many Finnish people."

"Well, I don't mean to speak ill of your people," said Mrs. Hopewell, "but some of them like my Heiki, they sure did a foolish thing in leaving this country."

"What do you mean by 'leaving this country'?"

"Lots of Finns have — they've gone to Russia because the Depression made them decide communism is better than democracy."

"Oh," said Thelma. She felt ashamed by her ignorance about her own Finnish people.

"Heiki went to Karelia, in Russia, somewhere near the border of Finland. Lots of Finns in America have gone there. He left four years ago. We couldn't afford for all of us to go, so he said when he found work, he'd send for us."

"And he never did?"

"We only got two letters from him. The first when he reached New York, and the second he said he wrote on the boat, so I figure he must have mailed it when he reached Karelia. There hasn't been a word since."

"Are you sure he didn't intend to desert you?" Thelma asked.

"No, I don't think the Soviets let him mail letters to the United States. I knew it was a mistake for him to go, but a woman has to support her husband's decisions. After we didn't hear from him for a year, I became ashamed of what people must think, so I changed my and the girls' name back to my maiden name. I don't think they'll ever see their father again. I imagine the Russians put him in a prison or a labor camp, if he's even still alive. You never know with communists."

"True," said Thelma.

"Anyway, I appreciate your not holding her father's mistakes against Jessie," said Mrs. Hopewell. "Do you want some more tea?"

"No, thank you." Thelma could not bring herself to drink another cup of the weak stuff. "I'll look forward to seeing Jessie this week."

"I do appreciate it, Miss Bergmann. We can't pay much, but it means so much to her."

Thelma was about to say the money did not matter, but then she stopped herself, not wanting to patronize the poor woman.

"I'm just thankful to have a student who wants to learn," she said.

"There ought to be more teachers like you, Miss Bergmann," Mrs. Hopewell replied. "I can tell you really care about your students."

Thelma went home, feeling how lucky she was. She had been lonely since her father died, nearly ten years ago now, but he had always loved and provided for her while alive. She hoped that by giving Jessie piano lessons, perhaps the girl would find some solace from the pain of a father whom Thelma was sure had intentionally abandoned his family.

Late that autumn, Roy left the Huron Mountain Club to spend the winter in town with his parents. Then through the winter, he found occasional carpentry work with Henry and Bill or just did some snow removal. By Christmas, he had not seen Lex for a couple months. He thought about Chloe everyday. A few times, he went down to the restaurant where she worked, but it was always so busy, she could only take his order and smile. He thought her eyes showed she longed to speak with him, but he would not have known what to say. Once, in a desperate moment, he scribbled on a napkin, "Have a wonderful day, Roy." Then he went outside, walked a block, and returned to peer through the window. He felt exuberant when he saw her pick up the napkin, read his note, and smile. He replayed this moment — and each time he had seen her — over and over in his mind.

Sometimes he thought he was exaggerating the feelings she must have for him, but usually, he ignored these qualms to fantasize about how he would confess his love to her, and then how she would agree to leave Lex to be with him. He fantasized about her telling him she was getting a divorce to be with him, or of Lex dying in a tragic accident — not that he really wished ill upon his coworker, but he wanted Chloe free to be with him. Sometimes, his longings for her became so intense he wanted to cry or scream. He skipped church two consecutive Sundays because he could not bear to see and not speak to her, not touch her. His mother grew angry with him, but he could bear her anger better than the sight of the woman he could not hold.

On Christmas Day, however, he could not avoid attending church.

The First Baptist Church was packed Christmas morning. When the Whitmans arrived, the only half-empty pew had Chloe and Lex sitting in it. Apparently Lex had decided to join his wife for the holiday. Roy could not object when his mother entered the pew, followed by his father and Bill. Roy went in last, placing himself the farthest from Chloe. On this day the Savior of the World had been born, but Roy's thoughts fixated on Chloe's singing, only occasionally drowned out by her husband's slurred words. Lex must have started celebrating Christmas early that morning. Roy was angered by Lex's disrespect for his wife at Christmas, the day he should be the best of husbands. When communion came, Chloe turned around enough for Roy to see her left arm was in a sling. He instantly believed Lex was responsible. His rage could barely be contained. Save for the respect he owed God, he would have leapt across the pew to thrash the bastard. He was determined to speak to Chloe as soon as the service ended.

But by the time he got out of the church, Chloe was already in the car. On the church steps, Roy found his way blocked by Lex.

"Merry Christmas, Roy!" he said.

Margaret was surprised her son should know the odd man she had sat beside. She and Will passed on to speak to the Boardmans.

"Merry Christmas," Roy replied, but his hand remained in his pocket. He was unwilling to give the sign of peace to the scoundrel.

"Do you have any big plans for today?" asked Lex.

"Just dinner with the family. My brothers, sisters, nephews, and nieces will all be over."

"Oh, I was going to invite you over to our place, but since it's late notice, I understand if you have other plans."

"Well," said Roy, "I do have to spend time with my family."

"Come over later this evening then," said Lex. "Don't tell me it's too far to drive. It's not supposed to snow tonight."

Roy could tell Lex had already had a few drinks. His breath reeked. Roy pitied Chloe for having to spend the day with her own husband. He wanted to see her, just to make sure she was okay. To ask her how she had hurt her arm.

"Maybe I could come around eight or nine," Roy said.

"Sounds like a plan," said Lex, patting him on the shoulder.

Roy mustered up a smile.

"Why don't you tell Henry to come too. How is he? I didn't see him in church."

"He doesn't go to church anymore," said Roy.

"Not go to church! Henry! I thought he was as straitlaced as they come."

"His wife's Catholic, so he doesn't go to church to avoid causing family problems."

"Hmm," said Lex. "I never thought he would have married one of that kind. Anyway, Chloe must be getting cold in the car. I better go warm her up; she hasn't given me my Christmas present yet." Lex laughed.

Roy turned away, hiding his disgust. He was further annoyed that Lex would refer to Beth as "one of that kind." Who was he to talk when he came to church on Christmas Day smelling like a tavern? Roy did not mention Lex's invitation as he rode home with his parents. He told himself he might not go, but he knew he would.

Once home, Margaret prepared dinner. Soon Eleanor, Ada, Henry and all their families filled the Whitman house. Even Thelma was invited, having no other family than Beth and her Uncle Patrick. Christmas dinner was crowded but merry. People grew irritated as the dishes were passed and repassed around the table, people wanting gravy on one end while the potatoes were on the other. "Pass the butter. Pass the cream. Where are the cranberries? Did everyone get sweet potatoes? Mother, quit worrying about everyone and sit down. Everything looks so good, Maggie. I didn't know whether I put enough salt in the turnips. Is someone going to pass me the butter? Hold your horses. Don't be crabby; it's Christmas." How could anyone eat with all these dishes circulating, and all these women jumping up to wait on the men? But it was all this bustling and fussing that gave a sense of family belonging, and if all their stomachs rumbled while they waited for the blessing to be said and their plates to be filled, no one would go home hungry, and later everyone would be grateful for the good company.

After the meal, the women wanted to wash the dishes, but the men insisted the dishes could wait. The children wanted to open their presents. The little toddling grandchildren were set down on the floor around the tree while the adults squeezed onto the couch and into chairs. Then began the great tearing, the ripping of the wrapping paper, the screeching with delight, the "Thank you so much," and "You shouldn't have," and "It's exactly what I wanted," and "If it doesn't fit you, I kept the receipt so you can bring it back."

Against Margaret's better judgment, Will's gift to Patrick was a flask of whiskey.

"I know you always need a shot of that stuff before bed," said Will.

"That I do," said Patrick. "I wouldn't be a good Irishman otherwise."

"Just don't end up smelling like that fellow I sat next to in church," said Margaret.

"Who did you sit next to?" asked Ada.

"I don't know who he was," Margaret said, "but he stank of liquor. His poor wife, married to a drunk like that."

"Roy, isn't he the fellow who spoke to you after church?" asked Will.

"Yes, that's Lex. He works up at the Club with me," said Roy. "Henry went to school with him."

"Lex? I didn't know he was married," said Henry.

"Yes, his wife is that pretty waitress where you and Bill go for breakfast."

"Really?" said Bill. "Here I was hoping she was single."

"She wouldn't look at you anyway," Henry laughed.

"She's a pretty girl," said Margaret, "but she deserves better than a husband who shows up to church drunk on Christmas morning."

"Lots of people deserve better," said Thelma, thinking of poor Mrs. Hopewell, abandoned by her husband.

"Maggie," said Will, "you haven't opened your present from me."

More gifts to unwrap. Stockings for the children. Candy canes distributed to everyone. Bubble lights gurgling on the Christmas tree. Margaret yelling at Will to take his spittoon out of the room before the children stepped in it. Ada and Eleanor's dull husbands discussing their careers. Henry and Bill talking about carpentry. Neither set of men remotely interested in the occupations of the other two. Babies fell asleep on the couch and were carried into the bedroom. Boxes of chocolates were passed, the men grabbing up two or three at a time, while the women hesitated to take one, then lied to themselves that their New Year's resolutions would be to go on diets. The radio tuned to Christmas music. Roy felt it was all so perfect, except that he could not be with the woman he loved. He glanced constantly at the clock, waiting until he could see her, frustrated that when he was with her tonight, the person he despised most would also be present.

At eight o'clock, the coats were put on, the children were bundled into their mittens, hats, scarves, and baby blankets. The men went outside to warm up the cars. The women offered once more to stay and help with the dishes. Final wishes of "Merry Christmas" were made. Thelma was last to leave. Roy could see she did not relish leaving all the festivity for her empty house. The last guest gone, Margaret went to combine the remains of four pies into one pan so she could fit them all in the icebox. Will collapsed into his chair and reached for his already half-empty box of chocolates.

"I'm going out for some air," said Roy.

"All right. Don't be late," Will replied.

Roy had waited to leave until his mother was in the other room so he would not have to answer her half-dozen questions about where he was going. Now he quickly grabbed his coat and car keys and went outside. Down a dark, empty road he drove. All the way, he felt guilty to be a guest whose host would hate him if he knew his motives.

When Roy reached the house, he pounded heavily on the door, then shivered for two full minutes before it was opened. Lex stood in the doorway, his belt undone, his shirt half-buttoned.

"Roy!" he bellowed. "Chloe, Roy is here! We were starting to wonder whether you'd show that mug of yours. Come on in. I'll get you a cup of Christmas cheer."

Chloe did not answer her husband, but Roy could hear her shuffling around in the bedroom. He imagined how difficult it was for her to have her lover arrive after she had just been intimate with her husband. Then he reprimanded himself. He was not her lover; he only wished to be.

He stood in the kitchen while Lex mixed him a drink. Then they sat down on the couch. Lex put his feet up on the coffee table.

"You coming out, Chloe?" Lex yelled just as she appeared.

"Hello, Roy, Merry Christmas," she said, perching on a chair arm. Roy again noticed the sling around her arm. She saw him staring at it so she got up to fetch a sweater to cover it.

No one said anything for a minute. Roy swiveled the drink in his glass. Lex burped, then said, "That's what happens when you have turkey for Christmas."

The mention of food recalled to Chloe her role as hostess.

"Roy, could I get you something to eat? We have some Christmas cookies."

"Oh no," he said. "I'm still stuffed from my mother's cooking."

"Oh," she said.

Another minute of silence. Roy wished he had accepted the cookies. He tried to think what to say.

"It's a beautiful tree."

"Yeah," said Lex. "I cut it down off the property here."

"You did a beautiful job decorating it," said Roy.

"Chloe did that," said Lex.

Roy pretended deep interest in the tree. Its multicolored bulbs cast a festive, almost romantic glow through the room. He had often imagined himself with a girl in such a dark setting. He wished Lex were not here. He had a momentary glimpse of what it would be like if Chloe came to sit on his lap, if she wrapped her arms around his shoulders. He cast a guilty glance at her. With that sling, she could not wrap her arms around him, even if she wanted.

"Chloe, what did you do to your arm?" he asked. He had to know. He doubted she would tell the truth, but he felt he would know if she lied.

She turned slightly pale. Lex laughed. "The silly girl was trying to put the star on the Christmas tree, but she fell off the stepstool and hit her arm on the coffee table."

"Did you break it?" Roy asked.

"No, just hurt the rotating cuff," Chloe said.

"The doctor said it'll heal in a couple weeks," said Lex. "It didn't stop her from making me a fine Christmas dinner."

Roy wanted to slug Lex. The lout was more concerned about his dinner than his wife. Roy knew if he were just a little bigger, stronger, then he would

—

"You finding any work in town for the winter?" Lex asked.

"Just a few odd jobs with my brother."

"We might need a hand up at the Club in a week or so. One of the members' cabins looks as if its roof is starting to sink in. I could use some help shoveling off the roof and maybe putting up some poles inside to bolster it up."

"Sure," said Roy.

"I'll give you a call when I'm ready."

"Why don't I put on some Christmas records," said Chloe.

"Oh God," Lex groaned, "didn't you hear enough of that at church?"

Chloe had stood up, but now she sat down again.

"I wouldn't mind some Christmas music," Roy said to vex his host.

Lex rolled his eyes, but nodded to give Chloe permission.

She went to the record player. Soon "Silent Night" filled the room.

"That song's enough to make the angels themselves need a drink," said Lex, downing what was left in his glass, then going into the kitchen for another.

"It must be lonely for you," Roy dared say to Chloe. "I mean, being away from your family during the holidays."

"Yes," said Chloe, "but Lex says we can visit them this spring. We don't want to travel that far in winter."

"No, you never know in winter," said Roy. "You wouldn't want to get caught on the road in a blizzard."

"I don't know what she misses in Wisconsin," said Lex, slouching back onto the couch. "Just a bunch of cows and tractors and cheese. I'd rather be up here in the peace and quiet of the woods than be some redneck farmer."

"Yeah, in the woods, no one can hear your wife's cries when you beat her."

Roy only thought it; he wished he had the guts to say it.

His drink was almost gone. He quickly drained the glass. He felt gloomy, as if the Christmas tree lights had been extinguished, leaving him in utter black-ness, without relief from either this darkest, coldest time of year, or his own somber life.

"Roy, do you have plans for New Year's Eve?" asked Chloe.

"No," said Roy. "I'm not much for going out."

"The bars overcharge for drinks at New Year's anyway, especially since Prohibition ended," said Lex. "I prefer to drink in the peace of my own home. You should come over for New Year's, Roy. Maybe Chloe can fix you up with one of her girlfriends from work. What do you say?"

"I don't know," said Roy. He looked at his watch. He had been here half an hour, the longest half hour of his life. "Well," he said, "they're saying we might get a storm tonight so I better head back to town."

He stood up to leave.

"Hey, you can't drink and run!" said Lex. "Don't you like our company?"

Roy let out a nervous laugh. "I'm just tired. My little nephew and two nieces wear me out with all their demands for attention."

"Oh, I bet they're adorable," said Chloe.

"Chloe wants to have a couple brats," said Lex, standing up next to Roy. Roy again wished he could deck him, but he noticed how much broader in the shoulders, and thicker in the chest Lex was. "I don't know what she wants kids for. She's got enough to do looking after me."

Roy tried to smile, wondering whether Lex would let him make an exit. He was relieved when Chloe said, "Thanks for coming over, Roy. Merry Christmas."

"Thank you," Roy replied.

"Don't be a stranger," said Lex.

"No, I won't," said Roy to be polite.

"I'll call you about that work at the Club."

"Okay," said Roy. "Thanks for having me over. Merry Christmas."

"Merry Christmas," said Lex, practically slobbering as he grabbed Roy in a bear hug. "Happy New Year."

Roy smelled liquor breath, but he was touched by the pathetic embrace of his enemy. Was Lex so desperate for a friend?

Roy stumbled out the door and down the porch. He climbed into his car, then cast a look back at the Christmas tree in the window. He could see Lex already wrapping his arms around Chloe.

"You bastard!" Roy shouted as he backed his car out of the yard and swerved onto the road. He was so angry he thought he might just smash his car into a tree before he got home. He wanted to curse the entire world, he was so ticked off.

Why did the only girl he had ever loved have to be married to a man he despised? Why was his life this way? He had never gotten anything he wanted, but Chloe was the hardest blow of all. He was so angry about the way Lex treated her. It should not even matter that she was married when that bastard treated her as just a pleasure toy! A beautiful, sweet girl like Chloe deserved to be loved. Roy knew he could love her. He already did. He ached for her.

But how was he any better than that bastard husband of hers? He would never hit her, but he wanted to possess her. He felt he was nothing better than an adulterer. He was so full of carnal thoughts; he had such intense dreams about her — and then he would wake up and nearly cry from frustration and try to force himself back into sleep's oblivion, so preferable to the daytime world.

When he got home, he wanted to go straight to bed, but he dreaded going inside because the lights were still on. He did not want to talk to anyone, and least of all, to explain to his mother where he had been. But when he opened the door, he found his parents asleep in their chairs, their quilts over them, while the radio played "Silent Night." The same song had been played at Lex's house, but in his parents' house, it was a silent and holy night. His father puffed out snores, with his glasses half falling off his face. Roy reached over and carefully removed the glasses, folded them and placed them on the side table. He was surprised by how round his father looked with a blanket tucked around him. He was definitely plump now — Roy's own future no doubt. Yet his mother never made a derogatory comment about his father's weight. His mother lay peacefully in her chair. She was exhausted from the day's work, but Roy knew she rested in the glory of pulling off another sumptuous meal.

Roy smiled. He loved them both. The radio kept reminding him it was Christmas. He told himself he should be thankful for what he had. He turned off the Christmas tree lights. He would have to quit thinking about Chloe; he could not have her, and thinking about her only upset him. A New Year was coming; he resolved to find someone else to love, someone who could return his love. If Henry, his sisters, and his parents could find love, so could he. He would only be thirty in the coming year. He still had time.

1938

Monday, January 24, 1938 began as a typical winter day. Henry and Bill were working indoors installing cabinets at a house in Negaunee. Roy had gone up to the Huron Mountain Club to help Lex with some repairs. Thelma spent the day alone, reading her movie magazines, listening to the radio, and waiting for her piano students to arrive once school let out. Margaret should have been cleaning house — she did run the dustcloth over the living room furniture, then turned on the radio and hummed as she crocheted. Beth and Patrick sat quietly at home. Patrick kept nodding off in his chair. Beth tried to keep Jimmy occupied while baking a cake for supper. About the time Beth put Jimmy down for his afternoon nap, the snow began to fall. Beth remarked on the heavy snowflakes to her father, but he simply grunted and dozed off. When he awoke an hour later, he wanted to go for a walk; it was only January, but he already had cabin fever. Beth, seeing that the snow was picking up, refused to let him go out. Instead, she found a jigsaw puzzle for him to work at the table, while she read the paper aloud to him. As the snow began to fall more heavily, she could not concentrate on the news stories and began to worry about Henry getting home safely.

Shortly after five, Will stopped in. He often checked on his son's family after work before going next door to his own house.

"How are the roads?" Beth asked him.

"Not good, but I was only on side roads. The main ones are probably plowed."

"I wonder whether it's snowing this hard in Negaunee," Beth worried.

"Negaunee usually gets more snow than Marquette," said Patrick.

"Don't worry about Henry," said Will, attune to Beth's concerns. "He knows how to drive in this weather."

"I hope he gets home soon. The radio said we're getting a big blizzard tonight."

"What did you do all day, Will?" asked Patrick, tired of his daughter's fretting.

Will described his day's work at the Teachers College. That winter he had started doing carpentry work there, including building desks at a cheaper rate than if the school had bought them from a factory. Will described the lab tables he was making while Patrick listened intently. When Will finished his descriptions, he asked Patrick the same question.

"Just been sitting home all day. Beth thinks she's my mother these days, so she won't let me go out."

"Say, why don't you both come over for supper?" said Will. "We can all weather this storm together."

"No," said Beth. "Henry might call, and I just put a roast in the oven."

"Bring it over with you. I doubt Margaret's even thought about supper yet." Will was all too familiar with his wife's procrastination about cooking. "Henry will know if he can't get ahold of you to call our place, and if this snow keeps up, he and Bill might just decide to stay in Negaunee tonight."

Beth hesitated, but Patrick was tired of being snowed in all day.

"Come on, Beth. We'll get ourselves up a card game," said Patrick. "It's best to keep each other company during these bleak winter nights."

"No, I think I would rather stay home," she said.

"I'd feel better if you came over," Will replied. "The wind's really picking up; I wouldn't be surprised if the power and telephone lines get knocked out, and then we won't know if you need anything. You'll have your hands full with Jimmy if you don't have power. Let Maggie and me help you."

"It's not even fifty feet to your house if we need you," Beth argued. "I think we can manage."

"Fifty feet's a long way if the snow is three feet deep," said Will.

Beth listened to the wind roar down the chimney. She had already seen a tree branch break during a strong gust. She hated not to wait for Henry to get home, but finally, she gave in. Will telephoned Margaret, who was delighted to hear Beth would be bringing over a roast. Beth had planned to have leftovers from the roast for sandwiches, but now the meal intended for three would have to feed six. Still, she appreciated her father-in-law's concern.

They waited until five-thirty before leaving. By then, the roast was cooked and could be served as soon as they reached next door. Just as Beth took the pan from the oven, Henry called. Will wrapped up Jimmy, and Patrick put on his coat while Beth talked to her husband.

"Henry won't be home tonight," she said after hanging up the phone. "The snow is so bad it took him an hour to drive from Negaunee. He got into Marquette, but the roads are so slick, the truck won't make it up the hills so Bill and him got a room at the Janzen Hotel."

"They're okay though? No real car trouble?" asked Will.

"No, he said not to worry, and to say thank you for having us over for supper."

"You're welcome," said Will. "We can try calling him later if you like. I think you and Patrick better plan on spending the night at our place. There's three or four inches of snow out there already and more to come. You won't want to walk back in this storm in the dark, especially not trying to carry Jimmy."

Beth tried to be brave, but during a crisis, she only felt safe when Henry was near. She told herself it was just a little snowstorm, that she had lived through a hundred of them, that there was nothing to worry about. She went to find a suitcase, then threw in nightclothes for herself and her father, some extra underwear, and a change of clothes and extra diapers for Jimmy. She was ready in ten minutes.

When they opened the door, the snow blew into the kitchen, and already there were several inches piled up on the steps for them to wade through. Just to walk next door, they had to go down the driveway to the road and then up the other driveway because that winter's snowbanks were already higher than their knees, and it was still only January.

The wind blew so hard none of them could speak as they walked. Once Patrick nearly stumbled into the snowbank, but Will managed to grab his arm and still not drop the pot roast. Beth stepped gingerly, trying to balance herself while carrying the little suitcase and the waking Jimmy, whom she was terrified of dropping. When they reached the house, Will had to push the snow away from the screen door with his foot before the door would swing out. Once inside the screened in porch, Beth brushed the snow off herself and Jimmy while Margaret told them all to hurry inside before they let in the cold air. She took the pot roast from Will, and then he found the broom and brushed off his and Patrick's long coats.

"I've never seen a storm like this in my life," said Patrick, finally able to step in the house. "Not in all the years I've lived in Marquette."

"How many years has that been?" asked Will, panting from the cold air that had seeped into his lungs.

"I moved here in 1884."

"That's about as far back as I remember. I was four that year," said Will, "and I think this storm ranks right up there, especially since it came up so sudden."

"It looks like the end of the world outside," said Beth, "only with snow and wind instead of fire and brimstone."

In the growing darkness, the city lights illuminated the blowing gusts of snow so they looked like white, swooping angels of death. The howling wind reached forty miles an hour, and already, drifts were filling in what an hour before had been plowed driveways. Beth felt exhausted just from the short walk next door. Jimmy had woken while out in the cold; now he wiggled to get out of his winter clothes and run about. Margaret had on a comfortable knitted sweater. She quickly found another for Beth, whose dress had gotten wet in the snow and now was thawing, ice chunks still clinging to the bottom of it. Beth went to stand by the radiator, while Will opened the suitcase to fetch out Patrick's bedroom slippers. Margaret went to finish setting the table, while trying to keep Jimmy calm with promises of cookies for dessert.

Once everyone could again feel his or her toes, Patrick and Will settled down to listen to the weather reports on the radio and shout constant updates to the women in the kitchen. Beth helped Margaret finish the potatoes and gravy she had made to go with the roast. In fifteen minutes, a warm meal cheered all their spirits. Then after they ate and the dishes were washed, the adults started a game of cards, except for Will, who got down on the floor to build block castles with Jimmy.

"I almost forgot about Roy," said Margaret, playing her Queen of Spades. "I hope he's all right."

"I imagine he'll stay at the Club," said Will. "I'm not sure if they have a phone there for him to call us."

"It would be a long distance call anyway," said Margaret, "so I don't expect him to spend the money. I just hope he stays there until the storm's over."

"Roy is one I never worry about," said Will. "I think he can handle just about anything, despite how sensitive he is."

The great North Wind Kewadin continued to roar, to send its chill into every Marquette home, to spread snow to isolate everyone. The havoc it would yet wreak that night would far surpass the typical blizzard.

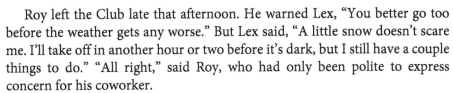

Roy left the Club late that afternoon. He warned Lex, "You better go too before the weather gets any worse." But Lex said, "A little snow doesn't scare me. I'll take off in another hour or two before it's dark, but I still have a couple things to do." "All right," said Roy, who had only been polite to express concern for his coworker.

Roy started his car and set out into the storm. The heavy woods between the Club and Marquette helped block much of the drifting snow, but the volume of snow still made the driving terrible. Already an inch of snow was on the road to sludge through, and it was bound to get worse. Roy crept along at thirty miles an hour, even then feeling nervous on the twisting, curving road. Once, his car started to slide, then fishtail, and he nearly lost control. Pumping his brake, he slowed down enough to avoid getting stuck in a snowbank, then put the car in reverse and backed up until he could straighten out on the road. His heart now pounding with delayed panic, he continued yet more cautiously. He told himself if he did get stuck, he always had a shovel in his trunk — only a fool would drive through an Upper Michigan winter without a shovel — but he did not want to dig himself out of a ditch with this fury of snow pelting down.

"Lex will never get home in this mess," he muttered. Then he thought, "Poor Chloe will be alone tonight." And finally he thought, "Now would be a chance to see her privately since Lex won't be able to get home for at least an hour more."

He came to Lex and Chloe's long driveway off the Big Bay Road. The snow was packed heavy and deep on the side road, so he floored down his gas pedal to plow his way over the snow. He wondered whether he would even be able to get his car back out to the main road. He knew he was a fool to stop there; if he got stuck in the driveway, he would never get away before Lex came home. But he could always tell Lex he was just checking to make sure Chloe was okay, or that he did not think he could make it home, and he figured that because Lex was such a good friend, he would put him up for the night. Whatever happened, he would deal with it then. Right now, he had an overpowering need to speak with Chloe, perhaps to tell her he loved her. He might be making a mistake, but aching swelled his chest until he felt he would burst if he did not proclaim his love.

When he stopped his car in front of the house, he felt stupid, like an animal controlled by his passions. But he got out of the car anyway. He shivered as he stumbled up the snow-covered steps. His balding forehead was freezing as the wet snow struck it. His heart pounded as he knocked on the front door.

"Roy? What are you doing here? Are you all right?" asked Chloe, holding open the door.

He did not answer, just stepped inside.

"Roy, what is it? Is Lex okay?"

"Yes," he said. "I just wanted to let you know Lex is going to be late. I didn't want you to be worried about him."

"Oh," said Chloe. "I appreciate it, but you nearly froze out there just to tell me."

"That's all right," he said. "Well — I better get going. I have to drive into town."

"You can't in this weather," she said.

"I have to. I can't stay. Anyway, Lex will be home soon."

He hoped she knew what he meant. That he cared about her, but that he could not stay. It had been stupid of him to come at all.

"At least let me fix you some coffee to warm you up before you go."

"No, the storm's getting worse," Roy said. "I better go now."

"Well, I appreciate your coming," Chloe repeated.

The phone rang.

"Wait a minute." She ran to pick up the line.

Roy heard her say, "Hi, honey."

He knew he should not listen to a woman's private conversation with her husband, but it was a small cottage, so he could not help hearing every word she said.

"All right, but what will you eat? Is there any food there? . . Yes, the snow is coming down like mad here . . . Don't worry about me. I'll be fine. I've been alone all day and it hasn't hurt me . . . Call me in the morning? . . . Yes, be sure to let me know when you're coming home . . . I love you too . . . Goodbye."

She hung up the phone and returned to where Roy stood, his pants wet because they had started to thaw.

"Lex is going to sleep at the Club and come home tomorrow."

"How can you lie like that?" asked Roy.

She looked puzzled.

"What do you mean?"

"How can you lie and say you love him when you know you don't?"

"He's my husband," said Chloe. "It would be worse if I didn't pretend to love him. Sometimes I almost convince myself I do."

"I better go," Roy said. He felt disgusted, angry.

"Lex worries about me being alone, but I told him I'd be fine," said Chloe.

"You will be," said Roy, his hand on the doorknob.

"He won't be home tonight." She stared at the floor as she added, "He'll call before he comes home in the morning. You can stay."

Roy knew he should open the door. His hand clung to the knob, but he did not turn it. He felt a bead of sweat on his forehead — or was it just a melting snowflake? He stared at Chloe. Each one's face gave answer to the other's fearful question. He let go of the doorknob.

After Henry called home, he and Bill went to find somewhere to eat before every restaurant closed and the hotel's only exit would be climbing out the second floor window onto a snowbank. Throughout the meal, Henry was glum, worrying about Beth and the family. Bill's energy increased with the storm's fury and the effort of walking a couple blocks to a restaurant on Front Street. The snow was accumulating at such a record speed that most of the city was already closed down, but the brothers managed to find a quick meal. Then they struggled back to the hotel in the blowing drifts, relieved they would not have to go back out that night. At the restaurant, they had heard predictions of twenty more inches over night. They would be lucky if the road were even plowed so they could go home tomorrow.

"I'd walk home if I had my snowshoes," said Bill. He was thoroughly enjoying the raging winds and trying not to think of all the shoveling he would have to do when the storm ended. Once back in their room, Henry read a copy of *The Mining Journal* he found in the hotel lobby. Bill pulled out the girly magazine he had been hiding in his lunch box. Henry scolded him, then to keep his brother from the path of evil, he suggested they play cards, even though he had to go fetch them out of his truck's glove compartment. As they played, Henry said they would have to call their employer in the morning to explain they would be late since they had to go home first to change clothes and check on the family. Bill replied, "I don't think we'll be going to Negaunee tomorrow with all this snow." Henry did not want to hear that; he did not like to lose a day's wages, and he hated to be idle while waiting for the weather to let up.

At ten o'clock, Henry said goodnight, determined to get up early to ensure he got to work on time tomorrow. Bill crawled into bed and waited until his brother began to snore. Then he turned on the bedside lamp and looked at his girly magazine.

The card game was in full swing at the Whitman house. They played late into the evening, the wind and cracking tree branches making them all too nervous to sleep. Even Jimmy was excited by the weather, and only after repeated attempts by his mother and all three grandparents to get him to sleep, did he fall into a restless doze. Then to Beth's irritation, the telephone rang and Jimmy woke up crying. Eleanor had called to check on her parents and give the latest storm developments from her house on Crescent Street. She was dismayed to hear Henry and Bill were staying in a hotel when they could have walked to her house, which was only half as far as the Whitmans' house in North Marquette, and only a half dozen blocks beyond the top of the hill the truck refused to climb.

"Oh, the wind is blowing so hard," said Beth, who had answered the phone, "they probably didn't want to walk even that far." She was too polite to say Henry would not spend a night at his sister's house because he disliked her husband. She changed the subject by saying they had not heard from Roy.

"I wouldn't worry about him," said Eleanor. "He's traveled all over this country, so I'm sure he can handle one Upper Michigan blizzard. He's probably staying overnight at the Club."

Fortunately, Jimmy fell back asleep right after the phone call. Margaret suggested she make ovaltine and they all play one more hand before bedtime. Beth felt sleepy, but she did not want to destroy the festive air the storm had brought out in the older generation. She was a poor card player tonight from worrying so much about Henry; she was surprised Margaret did not complain when she played the wrong card.

When Patrick said he was too tired to play anymore, Beth went upstairs with him to lay out her father's things for bed while he used the bathroom. Margaret rinsed and piled the dishes in the kitchen sink. Will collected and put a rubberband around the playing cards. Then he turned on the porch light and saw the snow had drifted up to the windowsill. After a minute, Margaret joined him to look out the window.

"I've never seen anything like it," said Will.

"I hope Roy is all right," Margaret replied.

"He'll be fine. I hope Beth can sleep. She sure does worry."

"All wives and mothers do," said Margaret.

"I'm afraid to think what it will look like in the morning. I may have to dig a tunnel just for us to get out of the house."

Margaret gave him a little squeeze. Then they climbed the stairs to bed.

Chloe rubbed his chest, then slid her hand between his shirt buttons.

"It isn't right," said Roy. He was still standing by the door.

"We love each other, and Lex doesn't need to know. He's so rough and selfish. I need just once to be with a man who'll be gentle with me."

"I — " He could not speak. He was breathless from wanting this.

She put her lips to his; he leaned forward. He felt her hair tickle his eyes. She smelled of strawberries even in January.

He took off his jacket. She unbuttoned his shirt.

"I don't — I — "

"Please," she said. Then her mouth caressed his cheeks, nose, again his lips.

"Yes, but I — I never before — "

She pulled back and gazed into his eyes.

"I know," she said. "You've been waiting for the right one. This might be our only chance."

He knew sexual sin was never to be engaged in before marriage. His mother had never told him so, but it was an unspoken understanding in their home. He had always obeyed, perhaps as much from lack of opportunity as moral righteousness; or perhaps he had purposely avoided situations that might give him the opportunity.

But this was different, he told himself. This act was based on love. Chloe needed him. Lex did not love her, except to fulfill his selfish needs. She deserved better; she deserved to be loved. Even though Lex was more experienced, Roy believed he could make Chloe happy. He would do whatever she asked. He let her take his hand and pull him into the bedroom. She sat on the bed. He stood before her. She unbuckled his pants. He let her pull him down on top of her.

Then guilt, fear, resistance all vanished. He was overcome with the desire to satisfy himself, to take desperate revenge upon Lex for making him feel inferior. His sudden fierce brutality surprised and excited him, and was only constrained when Chloe stroked his back and confessed over and over, "I love you."

His entire body screamed in response, his actions too intense for him to speak. He heard roaring in his ears, the gusting storm shaking the house, its power seeming to surge through his very veins. For once, he had overthrown his priggish self to know what it was to be completely human, completely a man. This moment relieved all the aching, the hurt, the needs he had repressed for years. He had found a woman. He loved her and she felt the same about him. He was her man. They would share a bond forever. His whole existence had pointed toward this moment with her.

No one would ever know precisely how it happened, whether it was intentional or an accident, but in twenty-four hours, downtown Marquette permanently changed.

In the early morning hours, the blizzard was keeping the employees at *The Mining Journal* working at a furious pace. Fearing the storm might cause a blackout, a rush was on to finish the paper in time for morning delivery. Whether the paper could be delivered in the blizzard mattered little until the paper was printed.

At 4:50 a.m., the mailroom employees noticed a red glow down the street. A minute later, Marquette's streetlights went out. The feared blackout had happened, and the darkness made clear that the red glow down the street was a raging fire. At first, no one believed a fire could blaze amid the torrential snowstorm, but the powerful winds only fanned the flames, spreading them to several buildings before the firetrucks could arrive.

Residents near downtown Marquette were rudely woken by the fire brigade's sirens. People peered out their windows to see an eerie conglomeration of smoke, bright red flames, and hurling white snow. The fire had begun in the Masonic Building. How it began or how long it had already raged would not be determined until much later. For now, the fire must be stopped before the entire downtown crumbled to cinders, before history repeated itself — several residents recalled their grandparents' stories of another great downtown fire seventy years earlier. By the time the firetrucks arrived, the Masonic Building was counted as lost, including inside it, the Peter White Insurance Agency and the much-loved Opera House. Already the fire had spread along the street, engulfing Jean's Jewelry, the Nightingale Cafe, the Scott and Woolworth stores, De Hass Builder's Supply, and the Marquette County law library.

Had electricity been required to pump water, the fire's destruction would have been inestimable. Fortunately, the waterworks was powered by gas engines run on batteries. Hoses were quickly unrolled along Washington Street to fight the formidable fire. The bravest men struggled with feelings of panic and loss to see buildings that had stood since before their childhood, where they had spent countless joyful hours — the Opera House, the theatres, the stores — all at the mercy of the raging flames. No one had ever seen such a firestorm, much less been asked to fight it. Firemen dug their footholds into snowbanks and aimed their hoses at the flames, only to have the wind whip the waterstreams straight back into their faces, where ice formed on their noses while smoke choked their lungs. Yet they dared not back down.

Across Marquette, children slept contentedly, believing school would be canceled tomorrow; adults tried to get a good rest to deal with the next day's laborious shoveling, and many moaned to think that even when this storm was over, two more months of winter would have to be faced. But none could imagine waking to hear of this winter holocaust.

Far from the fire, at the city's northernmost end, one of Marquette's oldest residents opened his eyes in a state of confused panic. Patrick McCarey looked about him; this was not his bed; these were not his blankets. Where was he? How had he gotten here? Where was his family? This wasn't his parents' house. Was he in prison? Had they caught him after all? He remembered the soldiers breaking into the room, then he and his friend getting out, realizing their three companions were being slaughtered. He remembered seeing — his friend — he had been shot in the back as they ran! And he had run around a corner, and — but he could not remember beyond that. Had he blocked it all out? He remembered anger; he still felt anger; he wanted to kill those bastards who had hurt his friend and imprisoned him. But if this were prison, where were the bars on the window?

He got up to look outside. The ground was covered in snow. He had never seen such a storm. You could barely see that tree over there. This was the perfect opportunity to escape! The damn Brits would never catch him in this weather. Not with the snow burying his footprints.

He went to try the door, but before he got there, he discovered his shoes and an overcoat on a chair. Why had the guards left those for him? This was the most comfortable prison he had ever heard of — nothing like what they had in

Ireland. The bastards must have taken him to an English prison. He would have to figure out how to get out of their bloody country once he escaped. He sure the hell wasn't going to let them ship him to Australia like some common convict. All he had done was fight for the rights of his people. These damn English would have done the same if the situation were reversed.

He grabbed his shoes and sat down to put them on. His poor family. They must be worried sick over him. He could just imagine his mother down on her knees, praying the rosary for his safe return. He had to let his family know he was all right, but first he had to get out of here. What a strange prison, to have a little room rather than a cell with bars. Solitary confinement — that must be it. They were trying to break him down by isolating him, hoping he would confess and turn on his conspirators. He threw on his coat. He would never confess. He was too proud to turn traitor against his brother patriots.

He tried the doorknob. The stupid jailer had left it unlocked. If all the English were this stupid, he would have no trouble getting back to Ireland. He poked his head out the door. The hallway was dark and quiet. No guards. They must be on their rounds. Now was his chance. He tiptoed down the corridor. He was surprised to see the stairs were not blocked. He stole down them and came into a little parlor.

"I must be a political prisoner," he thought. "Maybe I'm not in England; maybe I'm under house arrest in Dublin. Doesn't matter. I still have to get out of here."

He made his way across the parlor to the front door.

"The cowardly Brits must have been afraid of the storm and gone home." The door was unlocked. He opened it. Whirling snow flew into the building. The wind howled like a banshee. He did not hesitate; better risk his life in the storm than stay here to await life imprisonment or being shot; better get frostbite, even lose a couple toes or a finger, and live to fight another day.

He stumbled out into the blizzard, itself as fierce a foe as any British pig of a soldier. He hoped to find a little Irish village nearby. He started down the street. He could scarcely see. It looked like there were some cottages along the road, but he could not quite tell. He pushed on. The farther he went the better. His ungloved hands were growing numb from the cold. The snow blew up his coatsleeves and down his neck, even though he clutched the coat around his throat. He could not run, barely even walk in the heavy, wet snow. But he kept moving.

Ow! He slipped on a patch of ice and fell on his back. He lay there, dazed for a moment, glad he had not cracked his head. Then he forgot how he had fallen. What was that pain in his spine? Had he been caught? Had he been shot in the back by the soldiers? He felt so hot. He was sweating madly from the exertion of walking against the wind, but now the snow falling on his face felt cool, refreshing. If he had been shot, it would be pleasant to die here in the snow, before the soldiers reached him. Everything was so white! He imagined Heaven looked like this, if Heaven existed. He hoped if anything the priests said was true, it was that Heaven existed. They could keep Purgatory — people suffered enough in this lifetime without needing Purgatory to suffer in. He had suffered enough, and watched all those he loved suffer — but he had done his best. Now he was in God's hands. "May St. Patrick bless old Ireland!" His grandfather used to say that. He hoped to see Grandpa in Heaven. Everything was so white, he almost believed himself already there.

Chloe rose from the bed.

"Where are you going?" Roy asked. His hand brushed her thigh as she got up.

"I'm thirsty. I thought I'd get us some drinks."

She walked out of the bedroom to the kitchen. He could see her down the hall. He was surprised she had not put on her clothes when she got up. He had never before seen a naked woman. He had just held a naked woman, but that was different from looking at one; in his mind, he caressed her every curve, every spot of her beautiful, soft flesh. A moment before, he had been satisfied, but now came a new arousing urge. Embarrassed by how easily his body betrayed his feelings, he covered his waist with a blanket. He marveled at Chloe's lack of self-consciousness; did she always walk about naked or was it a show just for him? He was sure she would not do the same for her husband; she could probably just barely tolerate Lex's touch. Roy continued to gaze at her as she poured and mixed the drinks. When he had seen other men look at girly magazines, he had turned away in disgust and personal shame to have caught a glance at such pictures, but this was different. This display was solely for him; he was free to look and appreciate. But when she returned, he shyly cast down his eyes. She smiled when she handed him his glass. He knew she had seen his eyes pay her homage.

"I've never been so thirsty in my life," she said, crawling back into bed.

Roy felt the words were a compliment to him. His heart pounded.

She quickly swallowed her wine, then crawled back beneath the blankets, her leg crossing over his. She lay her head on his chest and wound her fingers in the hair around his nipple while he tried to sip his drink. Roy set the glass on the bedside table. Then he stroked her hair, and she moaned with desire. He lowered his head to kiss her lips.

The first time had been a bit awkward for him, but now that their love had been urgently consummated, they could spend the night slowly pleasing one another until they fell asleep, exhausted, completed, in each other's arms.

Henry and Bill were woken by blasting horns. They heard people rushing about in the hotel hallway. For a moment, they feared the building was on fire. Bill grabbed his pants. Henry, a bit more calmly, stuck his head out the door to learn what had happened.

"The whole downtown is on fire!" shouted a man, rushing to the stairs. "They need as many men as possible to fight the flames."

"A fire in this weather!" cried a woman, popping her head out from across the hall.

"Everything's on fire! The Opera House! The Woolworth building! Everything!" the man shouted back as he bolted down the stairs.

In a minute, Henry and Bill were dressed. They joined the crowd rushing into the storm to help save what remained of Washington Street. Blowing winds, drifting snow, freezing temperatures would not stop them from performing their civic duty.

The baby woke at seven in the morning. That meant everyone in the Whitman house woke. Everyone except Patrick McCarey who had already left. An hour passed before anyone noticed his absence. No one wanted to disturb his rest. They had all had a rough night's sleep because of the howling wind. Waking with a headache, Margaret went to make coffee so they could all get through an expectedly difficult day.

Beth changed Jimmy's wet diaper that had caused his cries. Will dressed, then considered shoveling the steps while Margaret made breakfast. When he opened the door, there was a four-foot drift on the steps. He could not even walk out the door. And still the wind was whipping snow up against the house, blowing it in furious circles and dumping it randomly upon the entire city. He retreated inside. The shoveling could wait until the snow stopped. He was a little worried that if there were an emergency, they would not be able to get out of the house, but he would risk that rather than go out into the storm. He needed to eat breakfast before he moved all that snow.

When Will stepped into the dining room, Beth handed him the baby, then went to help Margaret.

"I can't believe it's still snowing," said Margaret as she cracked the eggs.

"I hope Henry calls soon," said Beth.

"I hope the phone lines aren't down," Margaret replied.

This possibility made Beth more nervous. She wanted to check the telephone, but she did not want to look foolish by worrying too much. She made the toast, buttered it, and placed it on the table. Then she poured coffee for everyone. Margaret divided the eggs from the frying pan onto their plates. They ate quietly, staring out the window at the whiteness barely visible from the blocked sun. They could scarcely see the house across the street.

"I think you should just wait until it's over to shovel," Margaret told Will. "I don't want you out in this weather. It's not good for your lungs."

"I'll help shovel," said Beth.

By the time breakfast was finished, Beth thought her father was sleeping rather late. She was glad the baby had not woken him, but he was usually up by this time.

"Let him sleep," said Margaret. "He's probably overtired from the storm waking him up."

Beth got up anyway. Since her mother's death, she always feared losing her father. She went upstairs to where Patrick had spent the night in Bill's room.

The bed was empty. She stepped across the hall to look in the bathroom, but the door was open and the room vacant. Where could he have gone? He could not have gotten up while they were awake or they would have heard him. She peered into the other bedrooms. He was nowhere upstairs. She knew he was not downstairs. He could not be in the basement because he would have had to pass through the dining room to reach the basement door in the kitchen — unless he went down there before they had all woken. She told herself not to panic, but she nearly leapt back downstairs. Ignoring Margaret's questions, she went into the kitchen, and down the basement stairs, but when she turned on the lights, she could see the basement was empty.

"Beth, what's wrong!" Will shouted. Slowly, frightened, she climbed back upstairs.

"I can't find my father. He's not in his room or anywhere upstairs or down here."

That was all she needed to say. Will and Margaret knew Patrick sometimes became confused, and once before, he had run away.

"Let's go upstairs again. Maybe he's hiding in a closet or under a bed," Margaret said, trying not to be unduly alarmed.

As soon as the women left the room, Will looked out the windows, searching for footprints, but the snow was coming down so fast, and drifting so swiftly, that within an hour, any footprints would have been filled in. He went down into the basement and opened the back door just in case footsteps were on the back steps. Nothing, except more snow crammed up against the door. He went back upstairs and met the women in the dining room.

"His shoes and coat are gone," said Beth. "They were on the chair beside his bed last night."

Jimmy, confused by all the rushing about, chose to bang his spoon on his high chair and scream "pannycakes," although at breakfast, he had obstinately refused to eat. Margaret calmed him while Will and Beth debated what to do.

"Beth, you better call the police," said Will. "I'll go out and look for him."

"I'll go too," said Beth.

Margaret said she would call the police. Beth put on her coat. Margaret picked up the phone, only to get dead silence. The storm had knocked out the phone lines. Beth burst into tears. Will said nothing, just put on his boots and headed outside, leaving Margaret to console their daughter-in-law. Margaret was as worried about Will being out in the storm as she was about Patrick, but she did not stop her husband. She fumbled for comforting words, but after a minute, Beth wiped her eyes and said, "I have to go look too." Margaret sat helplessly while Beth put on her boots. "I'll watch Jimmy," she said as Beth went out the door.

Will had trudged next door, wondering whether Patrick had gone home. Beth saw her father-in-law's three-foot deep footprints and struggled along in them, praying her boots would not get stuck while the hem of her dress became drenched and little snowballs formed on the lace edge of her slip.

By the time Beth reached her own front porch, Will came out the door, shaking his head. Silently, they struggled to the street. Despite the blinding fury of the storm, they crawled up the neighbor's snowfilled driveways, asking whether anyone had seen Patrick.

Margaret, meanwhile, brewed another pot of coffee; everyone would need something warm when they came back inside. But the pot was only half-brewed when the power went out, leaving the house in cold darkness. Jimmy was startled by the sudden outage. Margaret picked him up to comfort him as she dug with her free hand through the kitchen drawers to find candles and matches. She prayed the storm would end before anything worse happened.

Nobody could guess how much snow had already fallen, and it kept falling, as it would throughout this day and the next. Downtown, people were so worried about the fire that they did not even take time to marvel over the storm's power and fury. Most of the city had four to six feet of fresh snow piled on it, and drifts as high as twelve feet were being reported. In North Marquette, residents were ignorant about the fire because power outages had cut off communication. As word of mouth slowly spread the news, people braved the storm to come downtown to watch, and then be enlisted to fight the fire. Volunteers were paid twenty-five cents an hour for their help, but few gave the money a thought when their hometown was in peril.

Henry was aghast at the conflagration. His heart sank when he saw the Opera House on fire; he remembered the night he and Beth — and Thelma — had sat in its balcony, the night he had proposed to his wife. Thoughts of that happy night made him worry now for Beth's safety. Had she heard about the fire on the radio? Was she worried that the fire would prevent him from reaching home? He was thankful she did not know he was here fighting the flames; then she would be really worried. He wished he were home with her, waking safely in their bed to see her smiling face, then eating the breakfast she would make him, and giving Jimmy a bounce on his knee before he headed off for work. But if he could not be with his family, he would fight to save his town, to prevent the fire from spreading to the residential district and wreaking havoc on the lives of other families.

He had never seen such a night before. The high winds exacerbated the flames. As fire destroyed a building, the wind whipped the structure's remains into the air. Henry watched plate glass windows from the Masonic building soar through the sky, then shatter in the street. Chunks of wood sailed through the air as though it were Judgment Day. Burning cinders drifted on the wind to land on buildings blocks away, creating the potential for several smaller fires.

Bill, although large and strong for his seventeen years, had to use all his might to brace against the frigid winds and direct the hoses so the water struck the flames. Much of the water froze on powerlines and building fronts just seconds after it spurted from hoses. Heroic efforts appeared ineffective against the blazing furnace that had once been Washington Street. At times, the slush in the street was up to Bill's hips, making him feel more like he was fishing in the Dead River than fighting a blazing fire. A firetruck froze in the slush and could not be moved. Henry waded through the watery mess to help dig out the truck so it could hose down the bank buildings on the corner of Washington and Front before the fire spread downhill toward the lake.

As morning broke, Mr. Donckers opened his cafe to provide hot coffee for the firemen and volunteers. Bill and Henry took a quick, welcomed breakfast break after learning the Kresge store was no longer in danger. They emerged from breakfast, refreshed and ready to fight again, just as the west wall of the Masonic building tumbled down. Even though the wall fell inward, glass shot out from its windows, injuring a traffic officer and three firemen, while bricks struck two other men. None were seriously injured, but even the witnesses felt shaken. The accident made everyone fight with greater determination to prevent worse accidents. Curses and prayers were muttered in hopes the blizzard would end so only the fire had to be fought. There would be many more hours of frustrating toil.

They lay in each other's arms until morning broke. Then they made love once again, the surging, rhythmic winds stirring their animal instincts. When this final moment of passion ended, they felt a calm in the storm of their hearts, a belief their bond was permanent.

Finally, they rose from the bed and had breakfast together. They listened to records and talked. Chloe dreaded the phone would ring, warning that Lex was on his way home. Roy wanted to ask how and when they would see each other again, but he feared such a question would ruin the moment, and he did not want to admit the future might separate them.

By afternoon, the storm was slowly letting up. Roy sighed and said, "It's time I head home. For all we know, the telephone lines might be knocked out, so Lex won't call but just come home."

Chloe said nothing as her lover put on his coat and dug for his car keys.

When he was ready to leave, she came to him and put her arms around his waist.

"I love you."

"I love you too."

He kissed her one last time.

Then he had to ask, "What will we do now?"

"I don't know," she said. "Let's not spoil the day by discussing it. We'll see each other soon and figure it out."

She looked as if she would cry. He would not be able to bear her tears. He gave her a brave smile, feeling at ease because her love made all other cares seem insignificant. He went out the door, shutting it behind him so she would not follow.

The storm had reached one of those stunning conclusions when the snow stops instantly, the clouds lift, and the sun envelops everything. Roy was blinded by the dazzling light. The sun reflected off the snow crystals, creating so much glare he could barely open his eyes. He felt he had stepped into a white world of nothingness, where right or wrong did not exist, only an awesome sense of well-being. Despite the cold, he felt warm from his inner glow of content.

He trudged his way through the snow to his car. He used his hands to brush snow off his trunk, then unlocked it and reached in for his shovel. He shoveled behind him for a good hour just to make a path to back his car out to the road. In all that time, he dared not look toward the house for fear he would see Chloe watching him, and then he would be tempted to go back inside. Before he finished, the snow began to fall again. He was thankful for it. He hoped it would keep falling until it covered his tracks so Lex would never know he had been there. But he would not forget he had been here, and he was certain Chloe would not forget.

The gray, dark clouds returned. The sun hid behind them. Night was approaching, but the blinding light of an hour ago continued to glow inside him. Yesterday, he had groped about blindly, but now he had found Chloe. The whole glory of life had seemed to flash upon him. He was in love. Love was everything. To him, Chloe was everything.

He hated to leave her now, but by the next time he saw her, he was determined to have found a way for them to be together.

Beth was beside herself. How would they ever get him home? He was such a big man. Not even two strong men could carry him when the snowdrifts were up to their waists.

They had found Patrick a block away on Norwood Street. He was sitting up against a telephone pole, his legs already covered by a drift. At the same time, a neighbor, Mr. Rushmore, glimpsed them through the storm; he came out and offered up his overcoat to keep Patrick warm while Will checked Patrick's pulse. Beth stood, feeling numb more from fear than the windchill.

"He's still alive," said Will, "but I'm worried he has frostbite."

He tried to wake Patrick by lightly slapping his cheek; the only response was a slight groan and a fluttering of snowcrusted eyelids.

"How can we get him home?" cried Beth.

"I'll get my kids' toboggan," said Mr. Rushmore. He set off, urgently climbing over the snowbank to reach his garage before anyone could reply. While they waited, Beth rubbed her father's cheeks and hands and Will stood with his back to the wind to provide some shelter for the sick man. Mr. Rushmore soon returned, pulling a toboggan over the snowbank.

The two men managed to lift Patrick onto the toboggan; then with the effort of draft horses, they pulled him back toward the Whitman house. Beth followed alongside the toboggan, steadying her father's shoulder so he would not fall. He was sitting up, but hardly conscious, and as placid as a sleeping babe. It was a five-minute trip, but a physically and emotionally exhausting one. When they came into the yard, Margaret ran outside with a quilt to throw around Patrick. Then Mr. Rushmore helped Will lift Patrick up the front steps while Beth stood behind in case he toppled backward. Once Patrick was laid on the downstairs bed, Margaret went to get the still warm coffee to pour down his throat.

Since the telephone lines were down and the streets unplowed, Mr. Rushmore offered to walk the half dozen blocks to St. Luke's Hospital, but Beth and Will both refused from fear he would likewise be lost in a snowdrift. He went home but promised to check back later that day. Margaret sought out her medical book and read up on what to do for frostbite. Beth found a bucket and filled it with what little hot water could still be drained from the pipes since the power went out. She soaked her father's hands in the bucket so the blood in his fingers would start to circulate again. Will pulled off Patrick's frozen socks and wrapped his toes in towels Margaret had heated over the still warm radiator, despite the recent power outage. The Whitmans lived in a completely modern home without a fireplace so the only heat and light they could now garnish was from the several candles Margaret had lit.

Patrick remained in a half conscious state throughout the morning; then at noon, he fell into a restful sleep. Margaret insisted Beth eat a sandwich and take a little rest while she kept an eye on Patrick and Jimmy. Will braved the storm to shovel a path to the street, in case, once the roads were plowed, Patrick needed to be taken to the hospital.

All afternoon, they were without power. Unable to listen to the radio, they remained completely ignorant of the disaster downtown. The snow continued to fall, but people were coming out of their homes now, taking pictures of the storm's impact. As the Whitmans sat down to eat a cold supper of cereal, for Margaret could not cook anything without electricity, Mr. Rushmore returned to tell them the roads to St. Luke's Hospital had been plowed. He had heard that several frostbite cases had already been checked into the hospital. He had also heard about the terrible fire downtown. They were all shocked by the news. Beth, already worried about her father, knew Henry and Bill would have lent a hand fighting the fire, so she only worried more. Since Patrick was resting peacefully, they decided not to bring him to the hospital. Jimmy now fell asleep, so Beth brought him upstairs to lay down with her, while she waited to hear from Henry.

Will and Margaret sat down in their chairs to rest for the first time that day. They had nearly dozed off when the front door opened. In came Roy, looking like a frozen polar bear because so much snow clung to his coat and hat.

"Roy, where have you been?" asked Margaret, jumping up to take off his coat.

"I stayed overnight at the Club," he said. "I waited to head home until there was a lull in the storm, but even so, it took me over two hours to get here."

"Did you go off the road at all?" asked Will.

"No, but I clutched the steering wheel so hard my knuckles are still white," Roy said. "Every minute I was afraid of getting stuck. Quite a few cars were in the ditch, but they looked empty as I passed them. I sure hope they were."

"Well, we're glad you're home," said Margaret, carrying his coat into the bathroom so it would thaw over the tub rather than on her carpet. "I'd make you some hot chocolate or coffee but the electricity's out."

"That's all right, Ma," he said, collapsing into a chair. He felt dizzy from concentrating so intensely on the road while the snow had blared at his eyes. He had scarcely dared blink as he drove home; now his eyelids were heavy from the effort.

"Did you hear the news about downtown?" asked Will. "There's a big fire on Washington Street. The Opera House has burnt down."

"No, really?" said Roy, too tired now to let the news upset him.

"Hello, Roy," said Beth, coming into the room. "I thought I heard a voice."

"Henry and Bill didn't come home," Will told her, knowing she had hoped it was her husband. He explained to Roy, "Your brothers couldn't get the truck up the hill from downtown so they stayed at the Janzen last night. We can't hear from them now that the telephone lines are down. We suspect they're helping fight the fire."

"I don't know how any fire could burn in this weather," said Roy.

"Mr. Rushmore said the heavy winds are only making it worse by fanning the flames," Beth replied.

"Oh, dear, that candle's dripping wax on the table," Margaret cried, wiping up the spill with a handkerchief.

"How long has the power been out?" asked Roy.

"Since this morning," said Will. "They say the downtown fire is worse than the one that burnt down the cathedral three years ago."

"Oh, that was a horrible fire," said Beth. "One of the priests almost died in it."

"I never heard that," said Margaret.

"Yes, Monsignor Bucholtz wanted to rescue the Blessed Sacrament so he and two priests went in to get the key to the sacristy and — "

"What is the blessed sacrament?" asked Margaret.

"The Eucharistic hosts. You know, the body of Christ."

"You mean the communion wafers," Margaret corrected.

"Why would he run into the church just to rescue the bread?" asked Roy.

"It isn't just bread," said Beth. "It's the body of Christ. It's the mystery of transubstantiation."

"Mystery of what?" laughed Margaret.

Beth realized she had been mistaken to mention the mystery before her Baptist mother-in-law, but she did her best to explain. "During the Mass, the bread is transformed into the body of Christ."

"You mean, it symbolizes the body of Christ."

"No, it actually turns into Christ's body," said Beth. After the day she had been through, Beth felt irritable enough to argue when Margaret pulled her anti-Catholic attitude.

"That's ridiculous," said Margaret. "How could bread become the real body of Christ?"

"It's a miracle," said Beth.

"You Catholics and your miracles," said Margaret.

"Did the priest save the bread?" Will asked to prevent an argument.

"Yes, the firemen tied the custodian and the priest together by a rope and then held onto it so they would not be lost in the smoke. They got to the altar and retrieved the Eucharistic hosts. Then, just as they came back outside, the cathedral roof caved in."

"They were lucky," said Roy.

"I guess God looks out even for the crazies," said Margaret.

Beth bit her tongue. She reminded herself that her mother-in-law had been good to her and her father today, but she would never understand Margaret's unchristian attitude toward Catholics.

Will again changed the subject. "I guess several downtown buildings have burnt down."

Beth was too angry to say more, and Roy too tired. Margaret sat, looking smug. Then from the bedroom, a raucous voice sang out,

I met with Napper Tandy, and he tuk me by the hand,
And said he, "How's poor old Ireland, and how does she stand?"
"She's the most distressful country that ever yet was seen;
They're hanging men and women there for wearin' of the green."

Everyone jumped with surprise at the angry voice ringing through the house. Beth ran to check on her father. Jimmy screamed from being woken by the song.

"Poor Beth," Will told Roy, "her father ran out into the storm last night and none of us knew it. We found him half-buried in a drift. We're afraid he may have frostbite. As soon as the storm's over, we'll take him to the hospital."

"He must be delirious," said Margaret, following Beth into the bedroom. A minute later, she shouted, "Will, get some ice and a wash basin." Patrick had a fever.

Will left his son alone in the living room. Roy stared out the window at the persistently falling snow. What a strange storm this was. Poor Patrick. Poor Beth to have such a worry. He wondered whether Lex had made it home yet; he wished he had not left Chloe. The storm was still so bad that Lex might not get home; then Chloe would be alone tonight, and if so, he might have spent another night with her. Well, that could not be helped now. He just hoped the drifting snow had wiped away any evidence of his tire tracks in Lex's yard.

When it was all over, Henry could scarcely believe thirty-six hours had passed battling the fire. With all the blowing snow, the difference between

night and day had been scarcely discernible. Once the flames were finally extinguished, one and a half million gallons of water had been used, and an entire block of Washington Street was in ruins. The damage was estimated at four hundred thousand dollars. Even the handful of elderly residents who remembered the great fire of 1868 declared they had never seen anything like this winter blaze. People now came out of hibernation; in droves, they photographed the downtown area with its mountains of snow in the middle of the streets, and the bizarre icicles hanging from power lines where water sprayed from hoses had instantly froze. Not a few eyes teared up when viewing the remains of the once magnificent Marquette Opera House.

Later, Henry would be saddened by the destruction, but at the moment, he was too exhausted to feel anything except a desire to go home. The main streets were now plowed enough to allow slow passage through, but it would be days before the road crews made every street accessible. Henry and Bill finally got the truck to climb uphill and head toward North Marquette. They had to park on the street because only a small path, already shoveled and drifted in twice, led to the front door of their parents' home. Henry's house was completely blocked in by snow, so he went next door, assuming Beth was there. He and Bill found their mother on the floor, playing with Jimmy. She immediately got up to greet them.

"I was so worried," said Margaret, clutching Henry to her.

"Hello, Ma," he replied, then picked up Jimmy while she hugged Bill. "Where's Beth?"

Margaret told how the family had weathered the storm, including that Will, Roy, and Beth had brought Patrick to the hospital that morning, and just half an hour ago, Will had called her — Margaret's first indication that the telephone lines were up again. Patrick had died from a combination of frostbite, pneumonia, and heart failure.

Henry was sick at the news. He wanted to go up to the hospital, but Margaret was afraid he would only miss Will, Roy, and Beth on their way home. Unsure what to do, he looked out the window to see his house was still buried in a snowdrift.

"I'm going to clean out my yard," he said. He was exhausted from battling the fire, but he felt too restless to sit and wait. When Margaret looked at him in astonishment, he said, "Beth will want to stay in her own house tonight."

He went outside, picked up a shovel, and worked off his frustration against Mother Nature for all the damage done to so many people's lives. Bill was equally exhausted, but at his mother's urging, he joined his brother. By the time, Will, Roy, and Beth returned, the path to Henry's front door was cleared, and his truck was parked in the yard. The steps still needed to be shoveled, and the roof would need to be cleaned off so it did not collapse, but for now, Henry put down his shovel, put his arm around his wife and led her into their house to console her in private. Margaret and Will agreed to watch Jimmy that night so Beth could grieve. Beth then repeated to Henry how Patrick had disappeared in the night, how they had found him, but been unable to bring him to the hospital, then how he had slept peacefully until they thought he was out of harm's way, only to have a relapse overnight. By the time they got him to the hospital, it had been too late.

Henry shared his wife's sorrow, but he also knew Patrick's dementia would have become a worse strain for them if he had lived much longer. When Beth mentioned her father's delirious song about Irishmen being hung, Henry merely said Patrick must have been delusional. Whatever Patrick's secret past had been, it had now gone with him to his grave.

While the blizzard had raged, Thelma Bergmann's heart had disputed with itself over her favorite pupil, Jessie Hopewell. She had only taught Jessie for a couple months, but she believed the girl had extraordinary talent. At first, she despaired that Jessie would never get far because the Hopewells had no piano, nor could they afford one, but a neighbor had agreed to let Jessie practice at her house, hoping Jessie's interest would rub off on her own indolent daughter. Jessie's first lesson proved she was a fast learner, but Thelma had seen intelligent students quickly lose interest and make little progress. By the second lesson, Jessie played the simple pieces assigned with ease and without fingering errors; she had even forged ahead on her own in the piano book. By the sixth lesson, Jessie had mastered every song in the beginner's book and was prepared for more advanced pieces. Thelma knew Mrs. Hopewell could not afford to buy additional music books, so Thelma lent several of her own to the girl. Then Jessie missed her seventh lesson because Mrs. Hopewell had pneumonia and she had to stay home to watch her little sister.

A couple days later, Thelma learned Mrs. Hopewell had died unexpectedly, having been unable to afford sending for a doctor. A neighbor had taken in Jessie and her sister until their mother's family could be contacted. Jessie's piano lessons were apparently over.

That night, the blizzard struck. Thelma remained at home, without pupils for two evenings; the radio's updates on the blizzard and the downtown fire did little to interest her. Neither did she feel alarmed when the electricity went out. Wednesday morning, the snow was so deep she could not get out of her house so she missed Mrs. Hopewell's funeral. She did not know whether she would ever see Jessie again.

Then early Thursday morning, Jessie trudged through the snowbank to her piano teacher's house.

"I came to return your book," she said, when Thelma opened the door.

"Oh." Thelma was pleased to see the girl. "Come in, Jessie. I want to speak with you. I can't tell you how bad I felt to hear about your mother."

"Thank you," said Jessie. She hesitated, then stepped inside.

"I have some cake, and I'll make us some tea. Let's talk for a minute," Thelma said, tempting the girl to sit down at the table.

Thelma set the kettle on to boil and cut the cake, but she could think of nothing to say. Jessie stared at the piano she believed she would never play again.

"I won't be able to come for lessons any longer," Jessie said when the tea and cake were placed before her. She was too sad even to say, "Thank you."

"That's why I wanted to talk to you," Thelma replied. "I know you won't have money for lessons, but Jessie, you have such talent that it would be a shame for you to quit playing. You're my best student, so I'm willing to give you free lessons for as long as you wish."

Thelma expected the girl's face would light up, but Jessie only frowned. "I can't come for lessons. I'm moving away."

"To where?" asked Thelma.

"My mother has a cousin in Minneapolis. He wired that my sister and I have to go live with him."

"Oh." Thelma tried not to show her disappointment. "That'll be exciting for you. Does this cousin have children to be playmates for you and your sister?"

"No, he doesn't have any children. He doesn't even have a wife. He's all alone, and we've never even met him. My mother didn't even like him, but he's our only family now."

"I'm sorry," said Thelma, sipping her tea in embarrassment over the girl's obvious sadness. "But Minneapolis is a large city. I'm sure you'll make lots of friends, and you'll probably find a good piano teacher there."

"No I won't," said Jessie. "I'll hate it there! I won't know anyone, and our cousin obviously doesn't want us! He won't even come to get us. We have to go by ourselves on the train!"

Jessie began to sob. Thelma felt helpless; she had rarely cried as a child, but she had never truly wanted for anything. Jessie's destitution was unimaginable to her.

"My goodness," she said, handing the girl her handkerchief. "How do you know you'll hate it there until you've tried it?"

"I know. Especially since our cousin's going to stick us in a boarding school."

"Boarding school!" Thelma shivered at the thought. Later, she could not remember what she said following this announcement. She knew she tried to cheer the girl, but it was impossible when she could not cheer herself. She cut two more slices of cake for Jessie to bring home and share with her sister. Then she made Jessie promise to return on Saturday for a final piano lesson before leaving on the train to Minneapolis on Monday.

"Will, look at this?" said Margaret, calling her husband's attention to the guest book. They were in the vestibule of Tonella's Funeral Home during Patrick McCarey's visitation.

"Come sit down, Maggie. They're going to begin the rosary."

Margaret frowned. She and Will had already had an argument about staying while the rosary was recited. She hated these Catholic superstitions, but he insisted they stay out of respect for Beth.

"Come, look at this," she repeated.

"What?" asked Will. He stepped over to see where she pointed in the guest book. Written among the visitors was, "Harry Cumming Jr."

"What is he doing here?" asked Margaret.

As they looked at each other in surprise, the first words of "The Apostles Creed" began the rosary. A tall young man brushed against Will's coat, muttered, "Pardon me," and headed toward the door.

But not before Will saw his face.

"Will, do you know which one — "

Ignoring his wife, Will went after the man, following him out to the sidewalk. "Harry!"

Harry Jr. turned. He was stunned to see who had called his name.

"Uncle Will?"

"Yes," said Will, offering his hand. "How are you?"

"I'm fine. How are you?"

"It's been a long time," said Will.

"Yes." Harry felt he had to acknowledge his uncle despite the awkwardness, despite years of family division for reasons he had never fully understood.

"What are you doing here?" asked Will. "Did you know Patrick?"

"Yes," said Harry. "He was a guard when I was in prison."

Will had almost forgotten his nephew's shady past. He was surprised by the admission. Most people would be too ashamed to mention time in prison. He did not know what to say.

"How did you know Patrick?" Harry asked.

"My son — your cousin, Henry, married Patrick's daughter, Beth."

"Then, we're kind of like relatives — Patrick and me I mean," said Harry. "He was a good man."

"Yes," said Will. "Did you meet Beth inside?"

"No, I just wanted to pay my respects. Patrick was kind to me once; he convinced the warden to let me out for my sister's funeral."

Will's thoughts flashed back twenty years to the parade where he had met Harry's sister, Serena, the only time he had ever met her. What a loss he had felt when she died, his own niece, whom he had never known. He remembered how Serena had resembled Sylvia in her youth. And now, as he scanned Harry's face, he thought he saw his brother Clarence's eyes looking at him.

"Why don't you come inside to meet Beth," said Will. "I'm sure it would mean a lot to her to hear you speak well of her father."

Harry watched the cars pass by on Third Street. He wanted to escape.

"I don't want to disturb the family."

Will faltered a moment, then said, "Well, maybe you could come over to visit sometime, or for Sunday dinner?"

"I don't know," said Harry. "I'll have to check with my wife."

"I didn't know you were married," Will smiled.

"Yes. I have two boys."

"Bring all of them," said Will, remembering the warmth he had once felt for two little boys, his nephews.

"We'll see," said Harry.

"My number's in the phone book," said Will.

"All right," said Harry. He was surprised by how Uncle Will had aged. He must be almost sixty now — so different from the young man who had bounced him on his knee, who had gone to the Buffalo Bill Wild West Show with him as a child.

"Your cousins will want to meet you," said Will.

"I'd like that," said Harry. "Thank you."

"And give your mother my love. How is she?"

"She's fine. I'll tell her I saw you."

Will realized nothing more was left to say. He extended his hand again. "It's good to see you, Harry. Take care."

"You too, Uncle Will. Goodbye."

Will watched his nephew start down the street; then he went back inside the funeral home. Margaret stood in the doorway. She had watched the meeting and understood whom Will had spoken with.

"He's going to come over on Sunday," said Will. Harry had not promised, but Will intended to call his nephew on Saturday to remind him, maybe even talk to Harry's wife to convince her if necessary.

"We better stay out here until the rosary is over. We don't want to interrupt," Margaret said. She told herself that would give Will time to regain his composure. He seemed shaken by the unexpected meeting with his nephew, but she could see he was pleased.

Thelma was deeply grieved over her Uncle Patrick's death. Ten years had passed since her father's death and five since Aunt Kathy's. She felt she was losing all her family. Only her cousins, Beth and Michael, remained. She rarely saw Michael. She visited Henry and Beth every couple weeks, but they were usually occupied with the baby and Henry's family. Uncle Patrick seemed to Thelma to be the last of that strong generation she could depend on. He had welcomed her into his home and looked after her like a second father. Now no one was left to look out for her. She mourned him so deeply she could scarcely find words to console Beth when she sat beside her at the funeral luncheon.

"I'm so sorry," she kept repeating.

"It's all right. He's at peace now, with my mother and your father and Grandma," said Beth. "I'm happy for him, just sad for myself. I guess we're both orphans now, Thelma."

"Ye-es," said Thelma; at her age, she hardly thought of herself as an orphan; she was reminded of someone who better fit the description.

"How do you bear being without your parents the rest of your life?" Beth asked.

"You surround yourself with the people you love," said Thelma, remembering her aunt and uncle's kindness when her father died.

"It's so hard," said Beth, "but I imagine it was worse for you. You were even younger when you lost your father, and you were a little girl when your mother died."

"Yes." Thelma knew only her mother's photograph; she had no actual memory of her mother's face, but she could still hear her singing in Finnish. "I miss them both, but it gets easier with time."

Eleanor and her husband, Ronald, came over to express their sympathies. Beth thanked them for coming. Thelma politely said hello; she had liked Eleanor ever since they had conspired to keep Henry and Beth together. But Ronald, like all good-looking men, intimidated her, and worse, because he was a college professor, she was afraid he thought her stupid. Eleanor sat down to chat. Ronald sat beside his wife, nibbled a brownie and looked bored. Ada's husband, Louis, sat down beside his brother-in-law. He clapped Ronald on the shoulder and asked, "How's it going there, Professor?"

"Fine, how's it with you?"

"All right, now that I've finished shoveling out my driveway," laughed Louis.

"I'll never understand," Ronald replied, "what possessed me to move to this frozen tundra. Downstate we never had more than a foot of snow on the ground all winter."

Thelma quit listening to the men's conversation. She already knew they rarely spoke to anyone in the family except each other. They were obviously Whitman in-laws because Will and Margaret's sons were never unfriendly. Bill liked to flirt with her, even though she could almost be his mother, and Roy was so nice — he deserved a good woman — if she ever dared to ask him —

"I hear some Finlander's suspected of starting the fire," said Louis, instantly regaining Thelma's attention.

"Wouldn't surprise me," said Ronald. "Most of them are dumb as logs. My Finlander students sure aren't bright, and this old guy who's a janitor at the college — he's been living in this country fifty years, yet I still can't understand a word he says. I say if you're not going to learn our language, go back where you came from."

"Most of them are too damn lazy to work anyway," said Louis, "and then they complain about how the American way doesn't work. I wish they'd all go to Russia; most of them are Communists anyway."

"Louis," Thelma seethed, "I'm half-Finnish, and I'm neither lazy nor a Communist."

"Well, your other half must have won out then," Ronald laughed. He had barely ever exchanged a word with Thelma. He was not even sure how she was related to his wife's family.

"My mother migrated to this country when she was a little girl, and she worked just as hard as anyone else," Thelma said.

"Well, I suppose there are exceptions," Louis said, "but you can't deny that lots of those Finlanders who came to America are a bunch of Reds."

"If they have turned into Communists," said Thelma, thinking of Jessie's father, "it's only because this country has let them down."

"Ha!" said Ronald. "That sounds like a Communist speech to me. You better watch your mouth, or people will quit sending their kids to you for piano lessons."

"Oh, honey," said Eleanor, ashamed of her husband's behavior.

"Now, Thelma," said Beth to make peace, "you know you don't really count as being Finnish."

"And why not?" Thelma asked. "My mother was Finnish."

"But you barely remember her," said Beth, "and it's not as if you were raised around Finnish people."

"I'm as much one of them as I am anything else," said Thelma.

"But it's not as if you were raised among them," said Beth.

"Excuse me," said Thelma before she could say something worse.

She stood up and headed toward the coffee pot, then felt so angry she grabbed her coat to leave. She had paid her respects to her uncle, so she need not go back and sit beside those ignorant men. How could anyone be so narrow-minded? How could you lump an entire group of people together because a small number of them went to Russia? The Finnish had come to America for a better life, the same as Ronald and Louis's ancestors, whatever country they had come from, and if the Finnish had then sought a better life in Russia, well, was not America built on the right to pursue happiness? She had always thought Louis was ignorant, but Ronald surprised her. How could a college professor be such a bigot? If she ran that college, she would not let him teach in any classroom where he might poison young people's minds. Why Jessie Hopewell, Finnish or not, had more brains in her talented fingers than that man had in his lump of a head.

As Thelma walked home, she knew what she must do. Her mind was moving faster than her feet. She carefully stepped over patches of ice and skirted around seven foot snowbanks left from the blizzard. Once home, she went into the kitchen to put the kettle on for tea, then took off her coat. She sat down at the piano and played until she heard the water boil. Then she poured a cup of tea and collapsed in her rocking chair; she thought so furiously that the tea grew cold before she tasted it.

Yes, it was what she should do, what she wanted to do. But what did she know about raising a child? And to do it on her own, when she had no husband! But it was not as if she really needed help. Jessie was twelve, not a little girl, almost a grown woman. She would only have to feed and clothe her for a few years until she finished school. But what about Jessie's sister, a whiny, runny-nosed little thing? What was her name? Lola? Awful name, but fitting for such a nasty girl. She did not have to adopt both of them — maybe she could find a home for the other one. Someone at church might take the girl if she asked around. Jessie was calm and well-mannered and more deserving anyway. To take in one child was more than doing her duty.

Of course, she would have to find out whether Jessie would want to be her daughter. She liked the idea better the more she thought about it. She would no longer have to be alone. She would have someone to talk with during the long evenings when the radio failed to be sufficient company. She would have someone to cook for. Jessie would be a friend to tell her troubles to, a daughter to spend time with and buy pretty dresses for. She would make Jessie Hopewell happy, and in doing so, maybe gain a smidgeon of happiness, even love, in return.

Her heart was so set upon it that she went to the phone and rang the neighbor's house where the Hopewell girls were staying. A dry throated "Hello" came from Jessie when she answered the phone. Thelma suspected the girl had been sobbing for her lost mother, but soon now, for both her and Jessie, everything would be well.

Beth wondered whether Thelma had really thought through what she was doing by adopting a girl, even one nearly grown. She suspected Thelma was lonely, but that was why she had suggested Thelma hire a housekeeper — she could easily afford it, and her house always seemed covered in dust. Or Thelma could rent out a room, maybe get a live-in companion to share the housework and keep her company. But to adopt a girl and raise her alone? Thelma had never had much common sense; Beth doubted she would make a responsible mother.

"She has no idea how much work it is to raise a child," Beth said one morning when Roy was over for breakfast. "She'll have all that extra laundry to do, and she'll have to keep after the girl to do her homework, and she'll have to cook decent meals. You should see what she eats now, she's getting so fat. I don't think she has any idea of the responsibility she's taking on."

"Even if her life is a little unusual," said Roy, "don't you think the girl will be better off with Thelma than going to an orphanage or living with strangers?"

"I don't know," said Beth. "If she went to the orphanage, someone might adopt her and her sister together. I understand why Thelma feels she can't handle two children, but it's not fair to break up sisters."

"I think that's rather unreasonable myself," Henry agreed.

"It's better one child have a good life than both children suffer," said Roy.

"Well, it's not right to break up families," Beth repeated. "And Thelma doesn't know anything about raising children."

"Seems to me," said Roy, standing up, "that you didn't know anything about raising children until you had Jimmy."

Beth was too surprised by the comment to reply.

"Thanks for breakfast," said Roy. "I have to get going."

He left quickly. Beth realized she must have offended him, but she did not know how. Henry said nothing. Roy had been moody ever since the blizzard, but he obviously did not want to discuss why.

As soon as Roy walked down Henry's front steps, he regretted his harsh words to his sister-in-law. Beth was a sweet girl, and she made Henry happy; he should not have snapped at her. But he could not understand why people fussed about other people's lives. Thelma should do as she chose, and in this case, her intentions were good. Just because she was not married and knew nothing about raising children did not mean she would not be a good mother.

And just because Chloe was married, although Roy could already hear all his family's objections on this point, that did not mean she should stay with an abusive lout when she could be with a man who truly loved her.

Roy had thought of nothing but Chloe since the storm. He had considered all the possibilities for them, and all the consequences. Finally, he accepted he could not plan their future, only act and hope for the best. He knew they would have to move away; to remain in Marquette would create an unbearable scandal. He would hurt his family enough by leaving, especially leaving with a married woman, but to remain would constantly remind his parents of the disgrace he had brought upon them. He did not think Chloe would object to leaving. She had no family here, and any life would be better for her than remaining with Lex.

Roy had told Henry he had work to do up at the Club today. That was his excuse. Lex would be at the Club today, so Roy knew he would be free to visit Chloe that afternoon. He would wait until she returned home from the restaurant. They would still have several hours to pack and plan their escape before Lex came home.

He had already secretly slipped his suitcase into the backseat of his car before going to Henry's for breakfast. No one suspected anything of his plan. He hated to make his family worry, but he would call them the next day, when he and Chloe were far enough away, in Duluth or Minneapolis or maybe past the Sault and into Canada, wherever Chloe wanted to go, just so they could get far enough away to hide from Lex's wrath until the divorce was final. They would live together until then — it did not matter when they married because their love was true.

During the morning, Roy drove around town, saying goodbye to all the familiar landmarks, unsure when he would see them again. He stayed occupied to keep from second-guessing his decision. He loved Chloe; that was his only consideration now. And she loved him. That was why he had to rescue her. His intentions were no more wrong than Thelma's were in adopting that girl.

Chloe came home from work just minutes before Roy appeared at her house. Since the night she had been with Roy, not a waking hour had passed without her yearning for him. She knew he would come to her again; everyday she debated what she would say when she saw him. When she heard his car pull into the yard, she knew it was Roy before she looked out the window. Despite all the speeches she had rehearsed in her head, she remained petrified. She did not answer the door until he knocked for the third time.

"Chloe, I'm sorry I didn't come sooner," he said when she opened the door. He stepped inside and put his hands on her arms. "I've done a lot of thinking, and I have to be with you, and I know you feel the same way. Nothing should keep us apart, not Lex, or society, or anything. I know it's scary to think of getting a divorce, but it's the only way we can be together, and — "

He was rambling, his words excitedly pouring out. He knew she would have to be convinced, so he flooded her with arguments. But after the first couple sentences, she ceased to listen. When he finally stopped talking, he let go of her, went into her room, opened her dresser, and pulled out her clothes to pack them.

"Roy, stop," she said. "Listen to me. I can't go with you."

"Yes, you can. You can't stay with him. He doesn't love you, and we were meant to be together — I'm sorry it's so difficult, but this is the only way we — "

"I do love you, Roy, but I can't be with you."

He dropped her clothes on the bed and stared at her. He saw this would be more difficult than he had thought.

"If you love me, that's all that matters," he said. "What does Lex matter?"

"He doesn't," she said, "but the baby does. I'm having his baby."

Roy's eyes bulged. His heart dropped. His head ached. Then, he went nearly crazy. "Are you sure? Maybe it's really mine. That would be wonderful if it were."

Chloe pitied him. He was so naive. How could she possibly know whether she were pregnant by him after less than two weeks? He was sweet but so innocent. She truly wished the baby were his.

"No, it's Lex's," she said. "I already knew the night we were together."

Roy sat down on the bed. She sat down beside him and took his hand.

"Even that night with me," he said, "you were pregnant with his child?"

"Roy, I'm so sorry to hurt you like this, but you don't know how awful it is. I had just found out I was pregnant a couple days before, and the thought of having his child — I had thought about leaving him so many times before, but once I became pregnant, I knew I couldn't. At first I thought I would hate this child, but I can't; it deserves a mother and father to love it."

"It doesn't mean we can't still go. I'll raise your child as my own. I — "

"No, Roy. Lex knows I'm pregnant. I can't take his child from him. I'm hoping once I have the baby, he'll treat me better."

"You know that won't happen."

"It might," said Chloe. "He was real nice when I first met him. I thought he'd be a good husband. I — "

"You married him because he's good looking and you let that turn your head," Roy accused. "You never would have looked at me except that he's abusive to you, and you realize I would treat you well. You women are all the same."

"Don't be angry, Roy. I don't want us to part this way."

"I love you," he said, his anger turning to desperation. "I would never hurt you. I would treat you like a queen. I would be your slave. I — "

"Roy, please stop," she said. "I would go with you if I could. I almost wish Lex would beat me so I would lose the baby, but I can't abandon him. He's been nicer to me since I told him he's going to be a father. There's nothing I can do."

"Yes, there is. You can be with me. I know you love me, but you're afraid ."

He jumped up, not knowing what more to say. He started from the room, but she went after him, grabbing him around the waist. He felt the pain disappear at her loving touch.

"It hurts so much," she cried, as he turned around. She buried her face in his chest. "You're the lucky one. You'll forget me. You'll find yourself a better girl who can love you without exception, while all I'll have is memories of our love."

"No," said Roy. "I'll never look at another woman. I'll wait until you're free, until you're brave enough to leave him. I'll wait until he dies if I have to."

"You're talking crazy," Chloe wailed. "Don't punish yourself, Roy. Forget me."

"I never can." He loathed himself for being stupid enough to love a married woman, but he had gone too far to change it now. To punish his own stupidity, he laid a curse upon himself to love her forever while always separated from her. He hated himself for ever thinking he could deserve or possess such a woman.

"Do you really love me, Chloe?"

"God forgive me," she said, "but yes, I love you."

"Then I'll wait forever," he vowed.

She buried her face in his chest again. He held her as she trembled. He wanted to make love to her one last time, to comfort them both, to relieve, if only momentarily, this unbearable pain. He put his hand under her chin and raised her lips to his.

"You damn asshole!"

Before they could turn around, they knew Lex had caught them. In shock, Roy watched Chloe yanked from him and flung on the bed. Then Lex shoved him up against a wall. Roy had never felt such fear. He had never been in a fight, not even with his own brothers. His mother had told him only lower class boys fought. He had thought he was lower class, but with a name like Royal, he did not know where he belonged. Now he wished he had learned to fight. He wished he had learned to kill. He could have killed Lex right then, but instead, Lex's fist repeatedly pounded his jaw. Roy raised his arm to block the blows, but Lex brushed away his arm as though it were made of straw.

"Stop it!" Chloe cried. She tried to drag Lex away from his victim. Roy collapsed on the floor; he reached up to rub his jaw. He was surprised Lex had not broken his head open — it felt like he had. He had always been intimidated by Lex; he considered himself lucky he was not dead. Then Lex grabbed his shirt. Roy saw Chloe lying on the floor where she had been shoved. Roy was yanked to his feet, then lifted up until his head banged the ceiling. Then he was dropped, flung half on top of the dresser.

"You bastard, I'm going to kill you!" Lex shouted.

Roy was as terrorized by the words as the violence. No one in his home spoke such vulgar words. He did not care what pretense of friendship had existed between them. Such a brute did not deserve a woman like Chloe.

"Let him go, Lex. It's all my fault!" Chloe cried, pulling herself from the floor and up onto the bed.

"You're my wife!" Lex roared. "No man touches you."

"Please, Lex," Chloe shrieked, balancing herself, then grabbing her husband around the chest. "Roy, go! Please, run!"

Roy struggled to walk while Lex loomed like a mad ape, lightly bound by his wife's arms, but able to break loose any moment.

Roy had only reached the living room when Lex tore after him.

"I hate you!" Lex yelled. He grabbed the back of Roy's neck with one powerful claw while the other yanked open the house door. "Don't you ever come back! You were supposed to be my friend. You betrayer! You piece of shit."

He muscled Roy onto the porch, then flung him down the stairs into the snow. Roy collapsed, thankful to feel the cool snow against his burning neck where Lex had gripped him. But Lex grabbed him again, jumped on top of him, pounded his face into the snow. His hand was on Roy's throat, pushing him down into a chunk of ice until Roy thought his spine would snap. He struggled to free himself from Lex's iron arm.

"How could my wife ever want you?" Lex asked. "You're no man. You're just a scrawny piece of chicken shit!" He climbed off Roy, then spit in his face as the final insult.

Roy lay in the snow, wondering where his assailant had gone. He tried to open his eyes, but the blows to his head had upset his vision.

"Roy, are you all right?" Chloe cried from the porch, but Lex pushed her back inside and shut the door after them.

Roy tried to regain his feet. He grabbed the porch railing so he could stand while he dug in his pocket for his car key. He feared his enemy watched from the window, like a cobra playing with a mouse, enjoying its victim's fear. Pain made movement difficult, but Roy managed to stumble to his car. His hand was bleeding, or was it blood from when he had rubbed his chin? He felt covered in blood. He crawled into the car. He wanted to cry, but he would not give Lex the satisfaction. He would wait until he was safe.

He got in his car and locked the door for protection. He despised himself for not being man enough to protect Chloe. He shook so much he could barely get the key into the ignition. As the car backed out of the yard, he looked at the house. Chloe stood in the window, looking over Lex's shoulder. Lex stood leering, waiting for an excuse to finish Roy off.

Roy stopped the car. He rolled down the window and shouted, "Don't forget, Chloe. I'll wait for you. We'll be together yet!"

He did not know whether she heard. He was afraid to find out. He floored the gas and backed the car all the way to the road.

As he drove home, he dug his handkerchief from his pocket and sopped it with his blood. He did not want his parents to know about this. He hoped that bastard did not brag around town that he had thrashed him. If he did, Roy would tell everyone he had slept with Chloe — it would serve the bastard right, and Roy no longer cared what it did to his reputation. Except that it would hurt his parents. He discovered his pants were ripped, his shirt sleeve torn. He could not go home like this. Maybe he could go to Henry's house. But Henry would not be home; would Beth keep his secret and bandage him up? Would she loan him some of Henry's clothes to go home in so his parents need not know? He wished he had not been rude to Beth this morning. He had nowhere else to go; his sisters would tell his parents if he went to them.

He pulled into the yard. He hoped to run over to Beth's house before his parents saw him. But the second he was out of his car, his parents' front door opened. A tall man came down the steps and walked toward him before he could escape.

"You must be Roy," said the man. "I'm glad I caught you before I left."

Roy did not know who he was. He managed a shaky hello.

The man was close enough to see his battered condition. "You've been fighting," he said.

"Who are you?" Roy asked.

"I'm your cousin, Harry Cumming."

"Oh."

"Your father asked me to come visit. I finally got the chance this afternoon."

"Glad you could come," said Roy, trying to brush past him.

"You don't look too happy to see me. I'm guessing you don't want anyone to see you, the way you look."

"It's none of your business."

"Your mother'll be upset to see you like this," said Harry. "Come over to my place. We'll wash you up and get you some clean clothes so your folks will never know."

Roy felt he was being treated like a child, but he was tempted by the offer. He did not know this cousin, who looked so strong and capable. Where had he been when Roy could have used him in a fight? Roy knew his mother often complained about the Cummings, but he sure needed a friend right now.

"Come on," said Harry. "I want to get to know all my cousins, and it looks as if you could use a strong drink."

He put his hand on Roy's shoulder, gently pushing him down the driveway to his car. Roy winced, only then realizing his shoulder hurt, but he let himself be led like a child.

He got into Harry's car, anxiously glancing toward the house to make sure his parents did not see him. He would have to think of an explanation later as to why his car was left in the yard, and Harry would have to give him a ride back home.

"My wife and kids have gone over to her mother's house for the evening," said Harry. "Lucky thing for you. They won't be back for hours so we've plenty of time to patch you up. Maybe I can find us some supper too."

Harry took Roy's silence for consent. Once at his house, Harry washed and bandaged Roy's bleeding chin. "We'll just leave the bandage on until the bleeding stops. I'm sure you don't want to wear it home," said Harry. Then he found some clothes for Roy to wear, even though they were baggy on his skinny cousin.

When Roy tried to take off his shirt, his shoulder hurt so badly, he could not reach over to unbutton it. Harry helped him. Then Roy let out a screech of pain as the shirt was pulled off his arm.

"I'm going to be sick," he said. He fell down in front of the toilet. Harry remained with him as he vomited.

"I hope she was worth all this," said Harry, sitting down on the edge of the bathtub as Roy wiped his mouth.

"What?"

"I hope she was worth taking such a beating," said Harry. "No guy would let himself be beaten like that except for a woman."

"Yeah, it's something like that," said Roy.

"Someone trying to steal your girl?" Harry asked.

"No," said Roy. "Her husband beats her. I was trying to get her to leave him." Roy thought he sounded heroic, noble.

Harry said, "And get her to be with you instead? It never works that way."

"What do you know about it?" He was angry that Harry had guessed the truth — that he was an adulterer.

"I've been in lots of fights, even been in prison," said Harry. "I've had lots of girls too, but one thing I can tell you is never to interfere in someone's marriage."

"She loves me," Roy defended himself, "and she's afraid of him."

"Do they have any kids?" asked Harry.

"She's pregnant with his child."

"You just stay away from her then," said Harry. "There are other women. You be patient and you'll find the right one. I'll tell you this, no married woman will ever be the right one for you. Now let's get you dressed."

Roy let Harry pull a clean shirt on over his aching shoulder. He hoped he could trust Harry. He felt he could. He had no one else to talk to. He was too ashamed to talk to his father, and Bill was too young and foolish, and Henry too perfect to do anything wrong. Harry was not judgmental; how could he be after being in prison? He spoke from common sense and experience.

Once Roy was cleaned up, Harry got him a drink, then made them supper. They spent a long time talking. Roy felt a lot better when Harry drove him home. He told Harry he would try to forget Chloe. He was glad his face was not very bruised; the mark would probably go unnoticed if he avoided his parents for the next couple days or just did not shave to hide the bruise.

Love knows no reason. In the morning, Roy woke with the all-consuming ache of love still tormenting him. He struggled against it for several days, but he knew eventually he would try to see Chloe again. After a week, he gave in and went to the restaurant. He sat down in a booth and waited to see her, but after half an hour, she never appeared. Finally he asked one of the other waitresses about her.

"She quit," said the girl. "Her husband got a job in Wisconsin. They left town yesterday."

Roy was dumbfounded. He left his breakfast unfinished and tossed some money on the table for the bill. Then he drove to Lex's house, not caring if it meant another beating. He had to know. There stood the house, silent, the driveway unplowed. Roy trudged through the snow to the porch. He peered through the windows. It was empty inside.

Chloe was gone.

Thelma had no regrets. She had written to Jessie's cousin, who had been fine with her adopting the girl, and then he decided he would not take Lyla either. Thelma had tried to find Jessie's sister a home, but without success. The

girl had finally been sent to the Holy Family Orphanage. The Hopewells had not been Catholic, but the orphanage took her anyway. Thelma told herself this way Jessie could at least see her sister and the girl would be cared for, and someone might still adopt her. Jessie did not seem to mind being parted from Lyla. She had felt a great strain in first caring for her mother during her illness, and then in looking after her younger sister. She saw her own adoption as a chance to be free from worry. Rather than complain for her sister's sake, Jessie was thankful to Miss Bergmann for taking her in and letting her continue her music lessons.

"Follow me. I'll show you your bedroom," said Thelma when she brought Jessie home. They climbed upstairs, and Thelma opened a door at the top of the landing. Inside was a room freshly wallpapered with a new lilac pattern. Some of the finest furniture in the house had been placed inside, furniture that had been Thelma's own as a girl growing up in her father's Calumet mansion.

Jessie could not have been more pleased if she were a princess in a palace. The dazzling winter sunshine lit up the room so that it looked like spring.

"It's beautiful, and I never had my own room before," said Jessie, smiling. "I love you. I'll do anything to make you glad you took me in."

"You'll make me glad by being happy," Thelma replied.

Jessie squeezed her new mother so hard Thelma's fat rolls became bruised with love.

"We'll always be together now," said Thelma, stroking the girl's hair. They held each other a moment. Then Thelma said, "Look what else I bought you." She opened a closet filled with dresses. She showed Jessie the desk and bookshelf filled with dolls and books and even a phonograph. Jessie felt spoiled but grateful.

When Thelma went to bed that night, she felt like a child again. This experience was like playing house with the little sister she had never had, only the sister had turned out to be a daughter. Both girls slept soundly that night, certain they would have a happy future together.

1944

"I'm sorry, Henry, but the U.S. Army isn't going to take you."

The doctor watched Henry's face droop. He had seen his share of men who did not want to go to the war. He had seen a few rejoice when told the army would not take them. But Henry Whitman was from that rare breed of dutiful men.

"Should I try again later?" Henry asked.

"No, this is your third time down here. Your lungs aren't going to get any stronger. I don't understand why you're so keen to go. You have a wife and two children to look after. What would they do if you were killed?"

"What would all the wives and children overseas do if the men there found excuses not to fight?"

"I'm sure the army appreciates your willingness," said the doctor, "but I can't let you go. If you got sick, it would cost the government more to hospitalize you than it would gain by having you as a soldier. I'm sorry, but that's the truth."

"I've got two brothers who've gone," said Henry. "How can I live with myself if anything happens to them while I stay home? I just want to do my duty."

"You'll do your duty by living a normal life. That's why we're fighting this war — to make the world safe so people can live normal lives. Make your brothers' efforts worthwhile by going home and being with your family rather than adding to their worries."

Henry frowned. "I'm sorry to have wasted your time, Doctor."

The doctor dismissed the apology with a wave of his hand. Henry clutched his cap and headed out to his truck.

He was disappointed, but it was no one's fault. He drove home, wondering why the government would draft mere boys, forcing them to go to the battlefield when willing men like himself were kept behind. He knew the doctor was right, but all his life he had taken care of his family, and now it was hard to be told he could not continue to do so by fighting to protect them.

Since Japan had bombed Pearl Harbor on December 7, 1941, the United States had been embroiled in World War II. Marquette's citizens, just like other men and women across the nation, were shocked and outraged, and then they enlisted to serve their country. For many Marquette natives, military service would mean their first journey overseas, for some even their first journey outside the Upper Peninsula. But when the nation called them, when all that is good and right was in danger of being destroyed, conscientious people stepped up to fight for democracy, to ensure basic human rights and to preserve freedom, just as their ancestors had done before them.

As in past conflicts, the good people of Marquette sent their sons, brothers, fathers, and husbands, and this time they also sent their daughters, sisters, wives, and even mothers to aid in the war effort. When rationing went into effect, those few who grumbled were patriotic enough to blame the Nazis for bringing such deprivations to their country. By contrast, Marquette's economy, after years of being hampered by the Depression, was now accelerated. As early as Germany's 1939 invasion of Poland, fear of war had stimulated Upper Michigan's mines to quadruple production, placing the iron and steel industry, as during the Civil War and World War I, at the backbone of the war effort. And for the first time since colonial days, Upper Michigan feared an attack upon its very own soil. The importance of the region's mineral and timber resources caused concern that the Germans might bomb the Soo Locks to destroy shipping on the Upper Great Lakes. The enemy might even attack Marquette County as a major harbor and outlet for the iron mines. The Marquette County Aircraft Warning Service was formed by volunteers who would watch the skies and send up the alarm in case of attack. Inmates of the Marquette Prison watched from the prison's spotting tower while in Ishpeming, a watchtower was established on the roof of the Road Commission's offices. In Marquette, Graveraet High School's roof became a lookout. Over the course of the war, two hundred sixty-two local men and women would watch the skies to ensure the community's protection from foreign planes.

Despite fear of attack, the war was fought quietly in Upper Michigan. Victory gardens were planted within the city; Henry planted one with the help of Jimmy, telling his son how he had planted a similar one as a boy during the last war. In 1942, celebrities Abbott and Costello came to town to promote war bonds; they posed at the Marquette prison for photographs and performed for the inmates. Children dug into their piggy banks, wives gave up buying a new dress or apron, husbands forsook having an extra drink to pool their money, hoping that with each war bond purchased, they might help brother Mike or cousin Joe come home sooner. Dances were held to raise funds, and church and ladies groups made up care packages to send the troops. Letter after letter was written to the men overseas, reminding them that mother and father loved them, or that a special girl waited for her soldier boy to return.

The number of Marquette's sons who went to the war are too numerous to mention in full. Each one gave Marquette reason to be proud of its steadfast residents. David McClintock became a submarine commander at the Battle of Leyte Gulf. Otto Hultgren would be wounded three times, yet live to be Marquette's most decorated hero. Many families made multiple sacrifices: William White would serve with the airforce in England, while his brother Roland served in France and Germany, and his brother Frank was stationed in the Pacific. The U.S. Naval Air Base in Illinois was flooded with soldiers from Northern State Teachers College who became known as the "U.P. Wildcats," after the college's team name; several accomplished pilots would spring from this group. Michigan's long winters forged the talents of many in the 10th Mountain Infantry Division, a skiing combat unit sent to the Italian Alps where it would achieve victories at Riva Ridge and Mount Belvedere. So many heroic exploits, too many to tell, but each a reason for gratitude.

For those who stayed home, the chores were less dramatic, but still stressful. Families struggled to carry on from day to day; mothers held in their tears so they would not frighten their children, and children tried to behave so they would not make mother cry when she was already worried about father or big brother. Everyone prayed the separations would not be permanent.

That noon, Beth was terribly anxious when Henry walked in the door. She did not even notice when two-year old Ellen tipped over her glass of milk. Beth stood, staring at her husband, waiting for the verdict. Henry shook his head in response to her stare. Then he wiped up the spilled milk.

Beth paused to say a silent prayer of thanks that her husband could not go to the war. She had never believed he would, but she had still been fearful. She was proud Henry wanted to go, but she could not forget her brother, Frank, who had not returned from the last war. If she lost Henry, she knew she would never bear it, yet she sympathetically placed a hand on his shoulder as he stooped to wipe the floor.

"It's all right, Henry. No one thinks less of you because you can't go."

Henry said nothing. He was too furious with his physical defects, his constant bouts of pneumonia, his scrawny frame. He worked harder, and for longer hours than anyone else. He could pound a hundred nails in half the time it would take any twenty-year old in the U.S. Army. A man felt useless when he was not thought good enough to serve his country in its hour of need.

"Can I help you with anything?" he asked to change the subject.

"No, I have lunch ready. Just pour Ellen some more milk."

Henry wiped his daughter's hands; not content simply to spill her milk, Ellen had enjoyed splashing her fingers in what had puddled up on her high chair tray. He poured her a new cup of milk and set it out of her reach. Beth set the bologna sandwiches, liver sausage, and cookies on the table.

They said little as they ate. Beth knew she could not console her husband. Henry knew she was relieved he could not go, and he did not blame her, but it was hard to be the man who had to stay home with the women and children.

"I thought I'd make a pot roast for supper," said Beth.

"That's fine."

"I told Jimmy he could go over to his friend's house after school. I didn't think you needed him to help you with anything."

"No."

She tried to think what else to say.

"Oh, a Robert O'Neill called. His porch is starting to sink in; I guess the boards are rotting from all the snow last winter. He wants to know whether you would look at it?"

Henry had plenty of carpentry work to do since his brothers were not around to help him, and his father was busy working at the college. This afternoon, however, he was free, so it would be a good chance to go give an estimate on the potential job.

"Did you get his phone number?"

"It's on the counter."

Henry finished his sandwich and swallowed down his coffee. Then he went into the other room to dial the telephone.

Beth did not listen to the conversation. She thought she would make a chocolate cake for supper. That might cheer Henry up.

"I'm going over to look at that porch," said Henry, returning into the kitchen to grab a couple cookies to eat on the way.

"Have a good afternoon," said Beth, giving him her cheek to kiss goodbye.

When the door slammed, she sighed, then cajoled Ellen into finishing her milk. As she got up to clear the table, the door opened again. She had heard the truck drive away, so she knew it had to be Margaret.

"Hello," said Beth as she ran the dishwater.

"What did he say?" asked her mother-in-law.

"They won't take him. I knew they wouldn't."

"I'm glad," said Margaret, collapsing into a chair with relief.

"So am I, but he's disappointed."

"Men. They all want to be heroes," said Margaret. "They never understand they're most heroic as good husbands and fathers."

"I know," said Beth.

"It's hard enough for me to have Roy in France and Bill in the Pacific. Every minute I wonder whether they're still alive. I don't think I could bear to have Henry go too."

"I know, Mother," said Beth. She and Margaret had their differences, but they both loved Henry.

"Henry's my most responsible son," said Margaret, wiping away Ellen's milk mustache, "but this war makes him act like a little boy who wants to prove he's tough and brave."

"It's not that," said Beth. "He just wants to do his duty."

"A man's first duty is to his family," said Margaret.

Robert O'Neill was a Marquette resident, yet his name was not unknown across the nation. In his early twenties, he had published his first novel, and every couple years since, a successive work had appeared until his books would now fill half a library shelf. He had begun his literary career by writing novels of social criticism, works with a philosophical and intellectual base. Then he had lost his wife, suffered like everyone else through the Great Depression, and remarried. During the Depression, many writers used their pens to criticize the government or to reminisce about a golden American past they believed would never return. Robert O'Neill had stayed levelheaded enough to write about the struggles of everyday people who by self-reliance, love of family, and faith in God, succeeded. His characters did not gain sudden fortune like those of Horatio Alger, or sink into sin and despair like those of Nathaniel Hawthorne, or lose themselves in the world of alcohol and beautiful women like those of F. Scott Fitzgerald. His characters simply struggled and survived. Robert

O'Neill's writings had their humorous moments, but he was not Mark Twain; he had his moments of pathos, his sympathy for human nature, not unlike his contemporary Steinbeck, but he was not as prone to depict life's tragedies. His novels were not overwhelmingly popular, but they received critical respect, and if they were not the cocktail conversation of the New York intelligentsia, they were taken to heart by hardworking Midwesterners.

But today Robert O'Neill's pen was dry. The words would not flow, so when Henry returned his phone call, he felt a vague hope Henry might let him help rip up boards and pound nails as a breather from his writing. Robert was delighted with all sorts of people, and a carpenter like Henry was no exception. Just before the war, Robert had been invited to a literary dinner in New York, where he had been privileged enough to sit beside Willa Cather, whom he admired most of America's living writers. He had felt honored when she said she had enjoyed his last book. Their conversation drifted from books to bookshelves. Robert mentioned that in his youth, he had done carpentry work with his father, including building several bookshelves. Miss Cather had replied, "Any man who can build a good bookshelf I respect just as much as a man who can write a novel. Art exists in many simple works we fail to notice in our self-indulged quest for intellectualism." Robert had never forgotten the remark. He understood that each person, each task can be interesting and give insight into life's experiences. So this day, Robert O'Neill greeted Henry Whitman with as much enthusiasm as if he were meeting President Roosevelt or E.M. Forster.

"Hello, Henry. I'm Robert," he said, shaking Henry's hand at the front door and instantly appreciating the honest face of a fellow hardworker. Then he showed Henry the work he needed done.

"It looks like an awful mess to me," said Robert, as they walked along the side of the house to survey the porch. "Lots of the boards have rotted and need to be replaced. The house is about seventy-five years old now, and I think some of the boards must be that old. I used to do some carpentry work myself, but this porch is a bigger mess than I think I can handle, so I asked around for who was the best carpenter in Marquette."

"Good," said Henry, pleased by the compliment.

Robert smiled. "But the best carpenter was too busy, so I was told you were second best."

"Oh," said Henry, amused by the joke. "Just who is said to be the best?"

"Lester White," Robert replied.

"Well, I won't argue with that," said Henry. "He gives me some real competition, and he does fine work, but I think you'll be pleased with the work I do for you."

"I'm sure I will," Robert replied. "Can you give me an estimate of the cost?"

Henry explained the price of lumber, the type of wood required, and the charge for labor. Robert thought the estimate surprisingly low and accepted it without pause. A date was set for the work to begin. Henry started to say goodbye, but Robert said, "I'd like you to see the rest of the house. I think it's a real treasure, and then you'll better understand why the porches are so important to me."

The O'Neill home was a great, Victorian sandstone structure on Ridge Street. Built in 1868, its tower and extravagant side porches, not to mention its internal treasures, were intended as its mistress's declaration that she was the leader of Marquette society. Now, in 1944, it was derided as representative of America's worst architectural period, terribly old fashioned, even beside its wooden Victorian neighbors. Yet Robert O'Neill thought it the finest home ever built.

Robert's possession of the house had resulted from several strange twists of events. The original owners, the Hennings, had sold the house and returned East in 1876, shortly after their daughter had drowned. The house had been sold to a young lawyer and his Southern bride. The latter was Carolina Smith, Robert O'Neill's great-aunt. Carolina had died during the First World War, leaving the home to her grandson, Mark Hampton. The new owner never moved in, being in the service at the time, and soon after dying in the war. The house then passed to his young bride, Eliza, who during the Depression, married her deceased husband's second cousin, Robert O'Neill. Since that time, Robert and Eliza had lived in the house and loved it thoroughly. Neither would succumb to the cries of their friends to redecorate the Victorian Gothic monstrosity they had inherited. The house was updated to include mid-twentieth century comforts, but its Victorian splendor, as they considered it, was preserved.

Robert gave Henry a little tour of the downstairs, ending with the room Robert considered the heart of the house — the library. Here, the blue William Morris wallpaper set the room's tone, while richly carved bookshelves extended halfway up the walls with Pre-Raphaelite paintings hanging above. At the far end was a small solarium with bay windows and Boston ferns. Extravagant Persian rugs were spread along the floor, adding to the colorful collage of paintings and novels with gilded bindings. Here were the complete works of the Victorian geniuses: Dickens, Trollope, Bulwer-Lytton, Wilkie Collins, George Eliot, the Brontes, Matthew Arnold, Tennyson, the Brownings, Emerson, Mark Twain, Nathaniel Hawthorne, Robert Louis Stevenson, and Rudyard Kipling. Carolina Smith had bought the volumes more for their splendid covers than their contents, but Robert and Eliza found the books a perpetual delight. In this splendid room, Robert O'Neill sat each day, writing in longhand, at the large cherry colored table, which he fantasized might someday be as revered as Charles Dickens's desk.

Henry was awed by the library's elegance. He saw the beauty of the paintings, the gilded books, and the Oriental rugs, but the bookshelves especially attracted him. He ran his hands lovingly over the carved wood, the perfectly rounded corners, and the fine stain.

"I could never hope to make anything finer than these," he said.

Robert smiled. "You don't see many bookshelves this size; they're perfect because they exhibit the books, yet rather than dominating the room, they are small enough to leave room for paintings above them."

"They're brilliant," Henry said.

"Books make a library, but there's no reason why they can't be displayed to their greatest advantage rather than be stockpiled on shelves."

"I'd give up fishing to make such shelves," said Henry.

"Do you fish? Where do you go?"

"Usually Pickerel Lake or the Chocolay River," said Henry. "I grew up in Cherry Creek and the Chocolay bordered our farm. I don't get to go as much as I'd like, however."

"I bet you know all the best fishing holes," said Robert. "Maybe you could show me one someday."

"I'd be happy too," said Henry, "but I get up awful early when I go."

"That's no problem," said Robert. "I'm a light sleeper. The morning is good for me because I write best in the afternoon."

"Oh, do you write for *The Mining Journal*?" asked Henry.

Before Robert could explain his profession, the library door opened and in walked a tall, middle-aged man with a slight limp that made many a female think he looked like a distinguished hero.

"Don't you ever knock?" Robert joked.

"Hello," said the intruder, surprised to see Robert had company.

"Henry," Robert made introductions, "this is my friend, Eric Hobson. Eric, this is Henry Whitman. Henry is going to repair the porches for me."

"Then what are you doing in the library?" asked Eric, sitting down to take the pressure off his leg. "Trying to impress people again with how many books you've written?"

"You write books?" asked Henry, turning to Robert with surprise.

"Yes," said Robert.

"Oh, you're Robert O'Neill, the novelist," Henry realized. "I'm sorry. I didn't make the connection at first."

"That's all right," said Robert. "Most people don't recognize my name."

"I guess you're not much of a reader, Henry," smiled Eric.

"I mostly just read the newspaper," said Henry. "I've only read a few books, except *The Autobiography of Buffalo Bill.* I've read that four times."

Eric chuckled. "That hardly counts as literature in Robert's opinion. Only Shakespeare and Dickens are good enough for him."

"Shakespeare is overrated," Robert replied, "but I am partial to Dickens. Ignore Eric's abrupt manners, Henry. We're old friends who like to give each other a hard time. I've actually read *The Autobiography of Buffalo Bill* myself."

"Henry, you aren't related to Bill Whitman are you?" asked Eric.

"He's my younger brother," said Henry. "Do you know him?"

"I was his history teacher in school. How is he?"

"Well, he's gone to the war," said Henry.

"Oh, where's he stationed?"

"He's in the navy, somewhere out in the Pacific."

"I'm glad I don't have any sons or brothers to worry about," said Robert.

"Same here," said Eric. "My boys are both too young to go."

"Both my brothers, Bill and Roy, have gone," said Henry, "and my cousin, Joe Dalrymple."

"I taught Joe too," said Eric.

"I'd go myself," said Henry, "if they'd take me, but the doctor says I'm too old and my lungs aren't that strong."

"Be thankful for it," Eric said. "War is a horrible thing. The last one is what gave me this limp."

Henry looked at Eric's slightly twisted leg and wondered how the man could endure his pain.

"Do you wish you had never gone?" he asked Eric.

"No, it was horrible, but I'd do it again if necessary. Sad thing is we fought the last war to prevent future ones, but this one is worse than the last."

"The war must be almost over now that they landed at Normandy the other day," said Robert. "Let's hope this is the war to end all wars."

"I don't know," said Eric. "As a history teacher, whose studied the patterns of humanity, I've become rather a pessimist. But the last war made the world safe for twenty years at least. So Henry, what do you think of this old house? Can you help keep it from falling over?"

"It's a fine, solid house," said Henry. "I've worked on lots of large homes, including Granot Loma, but this one looks to be the sturdiest I've ever seen."

"I've been told it was the finest home in Marquette in its day," said Robert, "but most people today think it too old fashioned."

"It's an amazing house when you consider it was built when this town was little more than a settlement in the wilderness," said Eric. "We fight these wars to preserve homes like these; they represent the American spirit and the strength of family in the face of adversity. The people who built houses like this had the gumption to succeed; if we have half the character they had, the world will end up just fine, even with pessimists like me in it."

"Home is where the heart is," Robert smiled.

"Well, I better get going," said Henry. "I'll get the necessary supplies for the job and then start on it Monday morning."

"Sounds good," said Robert. "Only, I won't let you work too hard. I expect you to take me fishing some morning next week. I get lonely sitting all day with just my pen and paper."

"Maybe I'll tag along," said Eric. "Now that school's out, I'll have time to dig for worms and try to get a few bites."

"Sounds good," said Henry, delighted to have met two interesting, yet everyday sort of fellows. And he was proud to work at the O'Neill house, the oldest home he had ever done work on. Less skilled carpenters might feel overwhelmed to work on such an ornate old mansion, even if it were just to fix the porches, but Henry was thrilled by the opportunity. As he drove down Ridge Street, gazing at the neighborhood's other fine old homes, he recalled his mother once saying something about a relative of theirs who had lived on this street. He wished he knew in which house. He intended to ask his parents, but he soon forgot because he was busy remembering Eric's words — if he could not go to the war, Henry decided he would stay home and do his patriotic duty by preserving a fine American home that was part of his country's history and spirit.

❦   ❦   ❦

While the war was actively waged on the battlefields of Europe and in the Pacific, another quieter war was waged in Marquette by two women, one middle-aged, the other barely a girl. Thelma Bergmann never guessed what a blessing she would receive when she adopted Jessie Hopewell. Nor had Jessie realized how well she would keep her promise to work hard and be worthy of Miss Bergmann's love. For six years, their mother-daughter bond had strengthened. Now they found themselves as allies against a war they fought daily on an emotional and mental level, a war against human frailty. That spring, Thelma began to complain constantly about being tired, yet she refused to go to the doctor. She became irritable; she blamed Jessie for creating extra work for her around the house and declared that her piano students were so lazy they were exhausting her. Jessie, knowing her mother's complaints were not legitimate, became concerned, but did not know what to do. Then one morning, Thelma was in so much pain, she had to holler for Jessie to help her get out of bed. When the aspirins Jessie gave her failed to relieve her pain, she finally admitted she had been feeling miserable for months but had been afraid to say anything. Jessie immediately took her to the doctor.

After several tests, the problem was diagnosed. Thelma insisted Jessie be with her when the doctor told her the news.

"It's multiple sclerosis," he said. "If we had caught it at an earlier stage, it would have been better, but it looks as if it's been growing for a couple years now."

Thelma remained stolid, not even blinking at the words, but Jessie took her mother's hand, visibly shaken.

"Tell me the worst and get it over with," said Thelma.

"It's hard to say just how bad it is," the doctor replied. "It's been developing for a couple years, but its progress appears to have been slow."

"Come to the point, Doctor," said Thelma. "Will I die from it?"

"Eventually, yes, but you may live another twenty years first."

"Will it develop faster as it goes along?"

"Yes, but we can give you medication to ease some of the pain. It may be several years before it affects your everyday life. But in time, you'll have trouble getting around, and in the end, you'll be bedridden."

"I see," said Thelma. "Do you have any questions, Jessie?"

Jessie had stopped listening. She was so shocked she could not concentrate on the doctor's words. She had already lost one mother; to lose another was an unbearable thought. Watching her daughter's face, Thelma felt only regret for how her disease would affect Jessie. The girl's entire future could be altered because of her illness; Jessie only had her to depend on, so Thelma was resolved to live for her daughter's sake.

"What can I do to help my mother?" Jessie asked. Thelma began to cry. She wanted to take care of Jessie, not to have the situation reversed.

"You can help her keep track of the pills and drugs she'll take for her pain. We can set up some exercises for her to slow the spreading of the disease. Most importantly, you can help keep up her spirits. It's never pleasant to receive this kind of news, but I've seen people with multiple sclerosis live normal lives for years, even reaching ages of sixty or seventy. If you both stay hopeful, you'll win half the battle."

"Thank you, Doctor," said Thelma.

Once home, Thelma went to take a nap. Jessie worried that her mother would be depressed, but she also realized her mother needed time to accept the situation. She went upstairs with Thelma, pulled back the bedcovers for her, then promised to make her a cup of tea when she got up. Thelma replied she was not an invalid yet; she would make her own tea. Jessie returned downstairs. She wanted to relieve her anxiety by playing the piano, but she would not disturb her mother. She tried to read, but she could not concentrate. Then she thought she should call Beth, but her mother would want to tell her cousin herself. All Jessie could do was sit and worry how their lives would change.

When Thelma came downstairs an hour later, she found Jessie lying on the couch in a half-slumber, her eyes wet with tears.

"Do you want some tea now, Mother?" Jessie asked, embarrassed to be discovered in such a lazy posture.

"I'll get it," said Thelma. "You look tired."

Jessie followed her into the kitchen.

"This won't be easy for either of us," said Thelma.

"I know," said Jessie. "Everything will change now."

"But it will happen slowly. We'll adjust."

"I've decided I won't go to school in the fall," said Jessie.

"What do you mean?" Until that moment, Thelma had forgotten to consider the girl was going away to college.

"I'll stay home to care for you."

Thelma grimaced. Jessie was a good girl to make such a sacrifice. For years, Thelma had yearned for a man's love, but her daughter had become more to her than any husband could have been.

"No," said Thelma. "You heard the doctor; it'll be years before I can't get around. You go to school. You can always come home for holidays or in the summer."

"I can just go to Northern," said Jessie. "Then I can be here with you."

The girl felt her doom descend upon her as she spoke the words. Her foster mother had a natural gift for music, but no intellectual desire to study it. Thelma could not even remember how many symphonies Beethoven wrote, and she constantly confused Handel with Bach and Schubert with Chopin. In Marquette, any talent was appreciated; any person who could bang out a tune received a standing ovation, but Jessie knew a greater musical world awaited her entrance. Why must she now be forbidden to enter that world to care for someone who was going to die, but not die until it was too late for her own future? She loved her mother, but to have to make such a choice — even though she knew she would stay, was unfair.

"No, Jessie. I want the best for you," said Thelma. "Go to Juilliard. Then when you finish school, you can come home and look after me."

Thelma had already felt it hard that her daughter would go away to college, but now it was almost unbearable when she most needed her. But she had wanted to give the girl a better life, and make her into a lady, unlike her unruly mannish sister, Lyla, whom no one had ever wanted to adopt. If nothing else, with Jessie gone to school, Thelma would be relieved of inviting Lyla over from the orphanage once a month for dinner. She wanted Jessie to have the best, so she would not let her own weakness interfere.

"Are you sure? I don't really mind not going," Jessie fibbed.

"Yes, now get that leftover cake out of the icebox," Thelma said, while pouring their tea. "I think after we have our little snack, I'll call Beth to tell her what the doctor said."

"All right," said Jessie. She would go to college, but she vowed she would come home to care for her mother whenever she was needed.

Margaret woke up early to start the coffee. Christmas Day was just about the longest day of the year for her because of all the work she had to do. But it was also the only day she had the entire family gathered under one roof — well, almost all the family. Roy would not be home — he was somewhere in France she believed. And Bill — she had no idea where he was, only that he was sailing on the U.S.S. — -; she imagined the ship was somewhere in the Pacific. She hoped it would not be too melancholy a holiday for her boys; this was the third Christmas they would be away from home. Even the joy of her grandchildren could not remove the worry from her heart. She hoped next year this damn war would finally be over. For a moment, she chided herself for thinking the word "damn," but then she told the kitchen stove, "It is a damn war," and for the thousandth time, she wondered why God allowed it.

The kitchen clock said it was seven-thirty. Henry's family would be over for breakfast in an hour. She wished she had stayed in bed another half hour — she could use the extra sleep, especially after being at church late last night, and then staying up to finish wrapping all the packages. But she was up now. She turned the radio on to keep her awake, then started the coffee. She hoped some Christmas music would get her in the spirit, and then she would go get dressed. She would have preferred to get dressed first, but that would have woken Will, and then he would have been cranky if the coffee were not made when he came downstairs.

Her heart lightened a bit as "White Christmas" came over the radio; she had first heard the song last year. It always reminded her of when her parents had been alive and living in California and writing home that they missed the snow in Marquette. That was two more people — her mother and father — who would not be here for Christmas dinner. Six years now they had been gone, yet she still missed them everyday.

Twelve cups should be enough for breakfast. She could always make another pot later. Before getting dressed, she had better put the children's presents under the tree in case they arrived early — she hoped she had not forgotten anything. She had presents hidden all over the house, but trying to remember where, and how many she had bought, and who was to get what was becoming a problem. She would have to plan better next year, especially if she kept having more grandchildren.

She put the coffee pot on the stove, wiped her hands on the dishtowel and headed toward the stairs.

Then the radio stopped her.

"This just in. The U.S.S. — - has been sunk in the Pacific by a German submarine. Further details will be forthcoming."

Margaret froze. She must have heard wrong. It couldn't be. Didn't they notify families before broadcasting this kind of news? Maybe she had heard the ship's name wrong. Why didn't they repeat it? No, instead they were playing "Silent Night" and at this hour of the morning! Oh Bill. And she had just been wondering how he would spend today, all the while not knowing the truth. It had probably happened hours ago, and now the news was just broadcasting it. Imagine, to have slept soundly all night, not knowing. How could a mother not have felt it?

She caught sight of the Christmas tree. She should turn on its lights before Henry's family arrived. She would turn on the lights in a minute, but she felt too dizzy right now. She told herself not to faint. No, better stay seated and take it in. If it were true, she would have felt it. She knew she would have. She would have woken up in the middle of the night feeling upset or odd at least. It must be a mistake. Not her Bill. And why today, Christmas — what timing. She must have heard wrong. Why didn't they quit playing that damn "Silent Night" and broadcast more news? If she hadn't heard wrong — she'd have to tell Will. How could she? But she would have to. And then Henry and Beth would have to be told, and then Eleanor and Ada and — oh, the poor grandchildren — they were all too young to understand — they scarcely remembered Uncle Bill from before he left for the war, and now their Christmas was ruined.

She just couldn't tell everyone. Not today. She would keep it to herself — so everyone could still have a Merry Christmas — if Bill were gone, what difference would it make to tell them tomorrow?

The radio paused. She waited for another announcement. She could hear the water on the stove boiling. The coffee must be almost done. Another Christmas song started to play. Coffee would help her nerves, distract her attention and give her another minute to compose herself before going upstairs. She trembled as she walked back into the kitchen. She found a cup and filled it, putting in a teaspoon of sugar and a drop of milk, then another spoonful of sugar, too distracted to remember the first one; then she sat back down at the dining room table. She tried to listen to the radio, but instead, she heard Will coming downstairs. What would she say? How could she possibly tell him?

"Maggie, I thought you'd wake me up. It's eight o'clock already."

"I'm sorry, I didn't realize how late it was. I was just enjoying the Christmas music. I better go put the rest of the presents under the tree. Grab your cup of coffee and then you better get dressed before Henry's family arrives."

"Yeah, all right," muttered Will, not much of a talker before his morning coffee.

The radio kept playing Christmas music. Margaret went upstairs to find the children's presents. What if the radio repeated the announcement while she were gone? Then Will would hear it. What a way for him to find out, but at least then she would not have to tell him. She did not know if she could. Bill was his namesake — the baby of the family.

"I can't obsess about it now," she said, opening the bedroom closet and digging into its hidden recesses to discover where she had stuffed away her grandchildren's gifts. As she found them, she piled them on the bed. Then she took off her nightgown and quickly put on her slip and dress. As she buttoned the dress, a weakness overcame her and she sat down. Then the tears came. She grabbed a pillow and covered her face so Will would not hear her sobbing. After a couple minutes, she still ached, but the sobs had helped her regain her self-control.

She was still not sure whether what she had heard was true, or whether she had heard it right. If it were true, wouldn't she have received a telegram? Didn't the government always notify the family before making a public announcement? But maybe the telegram was lost, or maybe the government accidentally forgot to send one. She might have been overlooked — after all, there must have been hundreds of men on that ship, and the ship might have sunk days ago, and its loss was only now being announced after the families were contacted. But that she had not received a telegram might also be a sign that she had heard the news wrong.

She heard Will's step coming upstairs; quickly she jumped up, set down the pillow and started to make the bed. His step sounded slow — had he heard the news? Her heart nearly stopped as he entered the room. But his face looked composed — he must not have heard anything.

"You better get dressed," she told him. "Henry's family will be here any minute."

Will said nothing to her as she left the room — that seemed strange — could he have heard, and not knowing she already knew, he did not know how to tell her? But after forty years of marriage, they often did not speak to each other — what was there left to say when they understood each other so well? Will had never been talkative, the direct opposite of her, but even she did not talk that much around him anymore. Funny, none of the children seemed very talkative. They must all take after their father that way. Roy was so moody and quiet, and Henry always seemed just silently content. And Bill was —

Poor Bill — how could she even for a few seconds be thinking of something so stupid as how much people talked when her son might be dead? But for those seconds, there had been no fear in her heart. She would have to think of other things if she were to get through this day — she could not tell Will yet, not moments before the family came over. She did not want the family depressed on Christmas morning.

She went downstairs and arranged the presents under the tree. Then she flipped on the tree lights. They were so pretty, especially so early in the morning when it was not quite daylight. How her grandchildren would love it! And she was certain she had done extra well at buying their presents this year. What a wonderful Christmas she had thought it would be until —

Through the window she saw the front door of Henry's house open — Jimmy came down the steps, followed by his mother carrying little Ellen, and Henry last, shutting the door behind him. This was it. Too late to tell anyone now. She would not ruin everyone's Christmas even if hers were ruined. Hers and Bill's.

"Will! Henry and the family are here," she shouted, then went to open the door.

Henry's family practically rolled inside, they were so full of life. Beth had gotten so chunky since the children were born that she filled the room like a Mrs. Santa Claus, and here was Jimmy, by proportion, nearly as round as his mother, with those adorable curls. Ellen immediately wanted Grandma's attention, and Henry supervised Jimmy taking off his boots so he would not track snow on Grandma's carpet.

Will came downstairs. Chitchat began about the weather, the beautiful tree, whether they should have sausage or bacon for breakfast. Margaret's attention was in such demand she had no choice but to listen to everyone rather than think of poor Bill.

Once the coats were removed, the boots off, and more presents placed under the tree, the family went into the dining room, the men and children sitting down at the table. Beth went into the kitchen to help Margaret with breakfast. She poured Henry and Will coffee while they waited. Then the pot was nearly empty.

"Would you like me to make more coffee?" Beth asked her mother-in-law.

"Um — " said Margaret, remembering she had heard the bad news right after making the first pot. It took her a moment, then she said, "Um, sure, go ahead."

"Are you feeling all right?" Beth asked, noticing Margaret seemed distracted.

"Yes, of course," said Margaret, turning her face away as she cracked the eggs.

"You look upset. Is something wrong?"

"Wrong? No. I suppose I'm just tired."

"Holidays are tiring," Beth agreed. "I'll be glad when the day's over. But don't you overdo it. Eleanor, Ada, and I can do all the cooking. Maybe you should go lay down a little after breakfast before everyone comes over for dinner."

"Oh, no, I won't let anyone else take over my kitchen."

Beth could not understand why. Margaret was a terrible cook. But she was a stubborn woman, never budging an inch to make room for the Catholic girl who had dared to marry her son.

Beth bit her tongue and made the coffee.

Ellen now escaped from her seat and charged into the kitchen, demanding attention. Since she had learned to walk, she seized every opportunity to go wherever her inquisitive mind demanded. Today she was especially enthusiastic; it was the first Christmas she had some understanding of what the fuss was all about, and she had barely slept last night because she was so excited. She grabbed her mother's hand, trying to pull her toward the Christmas tree.

"Ellen, go sit down at the table. Mother is busy right now."

Ellen began screeching and running in circles around the kitchen until Henry had to fetch his daughter if he ever wanted his breakfast cooked. By that point, the eggs were almost finished, so Beth had to hurry to make the toast and butter it. Margaret left the eggs in the frying pan on a back burner to stay warm; then she flipped over the sausage one last time. She thought Beth very unorganized not to get the toast made on time. Here she had Bill to worry about, yet she was not the one holding up breakfast. She must not think of Bill anymore. Beth already suspected something was wrong. Christmas would not be ruined for everyone.

All through breakfast, Ellen would not eat; she kept wanting to run away to touch the pretty ornaments on the tree. Beth's eggs were cold before she got two bites into Ellen's mouth. Jimmy kept repeating, "I sure hope Santa brought me that train set I want. I sure hope I get that train set." Margaret sure hoped he got it too; she was sick of hearing about it. She noticed that the only one who seemed to enjoy breakfast was Will, who gobbled down his eggs, food taking priority over grandchildren.

Margaret knew Will's appetite would not be so good if he knew about Bill. For a second, she stared out the window, thinking of her missing son, but then Henry saved her from more tears by asking her to pass the jam, and already Beth was up and clearing away the dishes. Margaret gulped down the last of her coffee, then started to clear as well; she wanted to get in the kitchen before Beth went and put all the juice glasses in the sink where they would only get knocked over and broken.

"Is everyone ready to open presents?" asked Will, letting Beth take his plate.

"Can we open all of them, Grandpa?" Jimmy asked.

"No," said Margaret, "just the ones your parents brought over. You can't open the ones from Grandpa and me until your cousins come over."

"Darn it!" said Jimmy.

"Jimmy, be polite to your grandmother," said Beth.

But Jimmy had already run into the living room, followed by his sister and a father nearly as excited as his children on Christmas morning.

In a minute, they were all sitting around the tree, wrapping paper scattered all over, despite Beth's efforts to bring order to the chaos. Jimmy opened one of his sister's presents, and when the error was discovered, she broke into tears until she realized the present was a baby doll, and then her brother's mistake was forgotten.

Margaret opened a present from Will — a Bing Crosby record, featuring "White Christmas." That was the last song she had heard before — and the radio was still on! What if there were another announcement about the ship? Someone else might hear it. She excused herself and went into the kitchen, claiming she had forgotten to take her vitamins. The radio could barely be heard in the living room, so she turned it off, hoping no one would notice.

By the time she was back in the living room, Jimmy had found his much desired train. He was already ripping the box open while Henry warned him to be careful so he did not lose any pieces. Then Ellen abandoned her doll because Jimmy's train looked more interesting. She grabbed the train engine, but Jimmy yanked it back, and then she slapped him, and he slapped her, and Ellen started wailing.

"It's just too much excitement for her," said Beth, trying to soothe Ellen.

Henry scolded Jimmy for slapping his sister.

Margaret did not mind the children's tantrums. Christmas was always this way. She remembered her own children had fought like that thirty years before. She and her sister had fought that way fifty years ago. People never changed. Even with Bill gone, Christmas had not changed. Life went on. That was why she would be able to carry on without her son, she told herself. Then the next moment she wondered how she dared think she could live without him. She had lived on after her parents' deaths. But that was different — people were supposed to outlive their parents, not their children. Stop it, she warned herself. You can't cry in front of everyone. "Ellen," she said quickly, "come to Grandma. We'll get you some water. Your throat must be sore from all that sobbing."

She carried Ellen into the kitchen and gave her a glass of water and one of Will's sugar cookies, even though it was barely ten o'clock. Ellen was excited enough already, but she had scarcely eaten any breakfast. Beth would not approve; sugar would only make Ellen more energetic, and Ellen knew cookies were forbidden between meals so she took the cookie willingly when Grandma told her she must eat it in the kitchen and not tell her mother. What was a grandmother for if not to give out forbidden treats? And how better to make a child behave than to bribe her with sweets? Content, Ellen returned to the living room, picked up her doll, and cuddled into the couch corner, talking baby talk to her new little friend until she drifted asleep.

"Thank goodness," said Will, who loved Ellen, but had had enough screaming for one morning.

"Jimmy, why don't we set up your train," said Henry.

"Yeah!" shouted Jimmy.

"Shush," said Margaret. "You'll wake your sister."

"Henry," said Beth, "there isn't that much space on the floor for those train tracks, and when the other kids come over, they'll probably break it from running around. Why don't you wait until this evening, so we can set it up at home?"

"It won't take long to set up," said Henry. "We can always take it back apart before the others come. We've got a couple hours."

Beth looked irritated, but she did not contradict her husband from fear of her disapproving mother-in-law's eyes striking her.

"I think I'll have another cup of coffee," said Will.

"I'll get it for you," said Beth, needing a momentary break from her family.

"I'd like one too," said Margaret. "Do you want one Henry?"

"Sure."

"Can I have one too, Daddy?" asked Jimmy.

"No."

"Please."

"Jimmy, your father said 'No,'" Beth replied.

"Oh come on, Daddy."

"It is Christmas," said Margaret. "One cup won't hurt him. We just won't put much sugar in it."

"I want lots of cream and sugar!" Jimmy said.

"How do you know how you like it?" asked his mother. "You don't drink coffee."

"I do so. Grandpa and Grandma give it to me when they babysit me."

Grandpa and Grandma exchanged guilty glances, but Beth was too tired to fight with her in-laws today.

"All right," she gave in, "but just half a teaspoon of sugar, and only one cup. You're only eight, so you don't want to stunt your growth."

"I'll help you," said Margaret, following her daughter-in-law into the kitchen.

"The Christmas tree is so beautiful, Margaret," said Beth. Margaret knew Beth only said it to show she was not mad that she had let Jimmy drink coffee, but to keep her mind occupied, Margaret replied, "Thank you. Will helped me put on the lights, but I did most of the work."

"We women usually do," said Beth.

But Margaret was not listening. She had again started wondering how something so awful could happen, and on Christmas day. And again, had it even happened? Had she heard right? She wished Beth would go in the other room so she could turn on the radio low enough that no one else would hear it — just in case there might be an update.

"Should we start dinner?" Beth asked, once the coffee was all poured and sugar and cream generously added.

"It's still early, isn't it?"

"It's ten-thirty. Do you have the ham in the oven?"

"The ham? Oh no, I forgot all about it. Oh dear."

"It's okay," said Beth. "Nobody will notice if we don't eat on time. Let me help, and we'll have it in the oven in a jiffy."

"No, I'll take care of it," said Margaret. "Just bring the men their coffee."

Beth saw Margaret was becoming irritable; she collected the coffee cups on a tray and fled the kitchen.

"Damn it!" thought Margaret. How could she have forgotten the ham? Well, she knew why she had forgotten it, but she could not think about that now. She hoped everyone would not be starving when they came. How could anyone expect her to carry on this holiday farce, considering — but they did not know so she would have to carry on.

In a few minutes, Beth returned to peel potatoes. "Ellen's still asleep," she said, "so I'm free to help. Henry can watch her if she wakes." Margaret was thankful; Beth really was helpful, but when she thanked Beth, she was ashamed to hear herself only sound coldly polite. Politeness was all she could muster today.

"Ellen sure did like her doll," Margaret said to make conversation.

"Yes, I hope so," said Beth. "I remember one Christmas when I was a girl that my mother and father each bought me a doll. Two dolls for Christmas. I thought that was the best thing that could ever happen to me."

Margaret smiled. She remembered Christmases from her own childhood when she and Sarah would go downstairs to open their presents and hope baby Charles would not touch anything of theirs before they got to it.

Sharing more memories of happy Christmases past helped the two women get the ham in the oven, the potatoes peeled, the rutabagas chopped, the cheese sliced, the pickles and olives placed in little appetizer plates, the rolls buttered, the gravy heated until it bubbled, the table set for dinner.

Then the rest of the family arrived.

"Eleanor's here with the girls!" Will hollered into the kitchen.

Beth and Margaret went into the living room and looked out the window. Both of Eleanor's little girls were struggling to walk through the snow. Poor Lucy and Maud, all their lives to be known as "the girls" by the family, even when well past the age when they could have had their own girls. But today they were only seven and three, and it was Christmas at Grandpa and Grandma's house, so all the world was wonderful for them.

Eleanor came in the door, surprised by the tight hug from her mother. Then Margaret collected herself and vowed to keep her secret.

"Merry Christmas, Ronald!" Will greeted his son-in-law, who brought up the rear of the family party.

"Merry Christmas," he replied as he stamped snow from his boots. "Hello, Beth, Henry, Margaret."

Then a loud thump startled everyone as Ellen rolled off the couch onto the floor. The arrival of aunt, uncle, and cousins had woken her. In a minute, she was running around with "the girls." She distinctly felt the disadvantage of having an older brother and no sisters, but girl cousins were the next best thing.

"Do you need help in the kitchen, Ma?" asked Eleanor.

"No, dear. Beth and I have it under control. You sit down and relax."

Beth wondered why Eleanor should relax. Beth had been on her feet all morning, and the potatoes must still be cooked and mashed and the ham sliced. But she would not complain about any of her in-laws. She went back into the kitchen; as she mashed the potatoes, she missed her parents and brothers, Grandma, and Uncle Karl and all the holidays spent with them.

"Maud! Quit running around!" Eleanor yelled. Beth cringed; she never would understand how anyone could name a precious little girl "Maud." What a ghastly name! But "Lucy" was not so bad. Ronald must have decided on Maud. Beth had long ago decided he had no taste, even if he were a college professor. She was becoming irritable; she realized the holiday must be getting to her; she mashed the potatoes harder to work off her frustration, and she told herself the day would be over before she knew it — already it was past noon.

Margaret returned to supervise her daughter-in-law. Then Jimmy ran into the kitchen, full of tears.

"Mom, Daddy and Aunt Eleanor won't let me play with my train!"

"Well, Jimmy, Daddy better put it away so it doesn't get broken. You can play with it tomorrow."

"No, they're playing with it instead of me."

"Who is?"

"Daddy and Aunt Eleanor!" Jimmy yelled. "They're just like kids. They don't know they're grownups yet, and it's my train, not theirs."

Margaret laughed, "At least they're still young at heart."

"We'll go tell Daddy to put the train away," said Beth. "You don't want all your cousins running around and breaking it."

They left Margaret alone in the kitchen. How could she have just laughed? She hesitated until she could hear Beth chiding, "Really, Henry, you're as bad as the children." Then, thinking she was safe for a minute, she turned on the radio.

The news was on. "President and Mrs. Roosevelt will be spending Christmas at — " As if she cared — that blasted Democratic president was the one who had declared war, and as a result, her son had been killed. Oh why didn't they shut up with these stupid commercials to buy war bonds? It was more than a mother could bear. Where was the news about the U.S.S. — -? Now they were back to playing "White Christmas" again. She was getting so sick of that song.

"Margaret, I never even thought about Christmas music. What a good idea," said Beth, reentering the kitchen.

Margaret had not heard Beth returning; now she could not switch off the radio without it seeming strange. She felt greater agony than before. If Beth heard the terrible news — Christmas would be ruined for everyone.

The rest of the family arrived. First came Ada and Louis and their daughter Judy. Could Margaret foresee the future, she would have woken that morning feeling depressed that this was Ada's last Christmas at home; in a few months,

Louis would receive a job offer in Louisiana and the family would move across the country. But Margaret already had enough to worry about today. After Ada's family came the neighbors, Mr. and Mrs. Rushmore, and they were quickly followed by Margaret's brother Charles and his wife Harriet; Margaret did not know how she would deal with Harriet's tongue today, but she reminded herself that her nephew, Joseph, had also gone to the war, so she should be tolerant of her sister-in-law. Next appeared Harry Cumming Jr. with his wife and kids. Margaret still thought the Cummings were white trash, but she kept the opinion to herself because Will was so happy to have his nephew around; still, she did not know why Harry Jr. could not spend the day with his own parents. Last came Thelma and Jessie. Everyone asked Jessie how she had enjoyed her first semester at college. Thelma was blabbing about all the A's Jessie got. Then Thelma complained she felt tired — Margaret realized she had a debilitating disease, but the woman would not be so tired if her mouth did not run constantly — Beth, of course, immediately went to get her cousin a glass of wine. In Margaret's opinion, Thelma had always thought she deserved preferential treatment, even before the multiple sclerosis hit her.

And so the house was full, and so loud with all the talk, the children running around, requests for handkerchiefs to wipe runny noses, lazy men demanding to know when dinner would be ready, people discussing the weather forecast, and no one listening to anyone else. Margaret asked how she had gotten herself into this mess? Why did she always have to feed everyone? Half these people were not even her relatives! Damn, that pot was going to boil over. She tried to pull it off the burner, only to have it start to boil over anyway and burn her finger. Then she nearly lost it. She wanted to scream, "Bill is dead! I can't take it anymore!" What would it matter if she did scream? The house was so noisy no one would hear her. Yet she held it all inside.

"The ham looks done," said Beth. "I think we can eat now."

Beth complimented her mother-in-law on how good all the food looked, although she had done half the work. She always tried to stay in Margaret's good graces, not that she expected Margaret would ever appreciate her.

Margaret began to buck up, telling herself not to cry into the potatoes. She hollered for Will to come slice the ham; of course, she had to supervise the operation so he did not hack it apart. Will might be head of the house, but it was her kitchen.

Once the ham was sliced, everyone sat down at the table. When no one was looking, Margaret turned the radio off again. Will asked that all heads be bowed while he said the blessing. Margaret did not listen — she had mixed feelings toward God at the moment. After all the years she had gone to church, helped with the bazaars, raised her children to be God-fearing Christians, how could He have taken her son? She peeked at the bowed heads, at her grandchildren seated around the card table, trying to sit still for the blessing. Everyone looked happy to be together. She had to stay calm for them. She loved them all, even if they did aggravate her.

"The ham looks terrific, Margaret," said Louis.

"Thank you," she said, knowing full well Ada had told Louis to compliment her.

A flurry of voices rose in agreement, until Margaret blushed with pleasure, even though the pleasure was tainted by knowing what no one else did.

"I think it's the finest Christmas dinner we've ever had," said Will.

"Well, Beth did help," said Margaret.

"So what did everyone get for Christmas?" asked Mrs. Rushmore. The children piped up to describe all their new toy treasures. The adults then recalled the wonderful presents of their own childhoods when Christmas was for them as magical as it now was for Lucy, Maud, Judy, Ellen, Jimmy, and the Cumming children.

"Christmas is still wonderful," said Mrs. Rushmore, "but it's not what it was. Seems as if all this commercialism has spoiled it. Even with the war on, people spend more time fussing over buying gifts than remembering the reason for today."

"Yes, Christ came into the world to save us, but we're too busy killing each other to notice," said Thelma.

"I haven't heard the news," said Henry, "but I hope the fighting stopped at least for today."

"I just hope all we love are safe," said Eleanor. Everyone was silent for a moment. They all worried for their soldier boys, but none would mention it from fear of upsetting everyone else.

"Our church sure was decorated beautifully this year," said Ada.

"Church is the most important part of the holiday," said Thelma. "Of course, the children should have their presents, but otherwise, everything should be cut back."

"I think the music is what makes Christmas," said Jessie.

"And the blasted tree," smiled Henry.

"Poor Henry, Beth gives him a hard time with that tree," laughed Eleanor.

Beth frowned but Henry smiled. "Yes," he said. "She has me trimming off branches, then drilling holes in the trunk so I can stick back in the branches I just trimmed off."

"I just want the tree to look full without any bare spots," said Beth.

"You have a beautiful tree," said Harry's wife Jean. "I could see it through your window when we arrived."

"Trees, presents, all those things make Christmas special," said Will, "but when I was a boy, what I loved best about Christmas were the ghost stories."

"Ghost stories?" said Jessie. "At Christmas?"

"Yes, people don't tell them as they used to," said Will, "but the Victorians loved them. My father always told us ghost stories at Christmas."

"Do you remember any of them?" asked Mr. Rushmore.

"Oh sure," Will smiled.

"Tell us one, Grandpa," said Jimmy.

"No, Will, you'll give the children nightmares," said Margaret.

"Children are braver than that," said Will.

"I like ghosts," said Jimmy.

"So do I," said Barry, son of Harry, who at thirteen feared nothing.

"I don't," said Maud.

"Will you be scared, Maud?" asked her grandfather.

"No. I just don't want no ole story. I want to open my presents now!"

"Maud!" said her mother. "Be polite to Grandpa."

"Let Will tell his story and then we'll open the presents," said Mrs. Rushmore.

"Well, we haven't had dessert yet," said Margaret. "Will can tell his story, and then we'll have dessert. You can't open presents before dessert, can you, Lucy?"

"No," said Lucy, realizing Grandma wanted her to set a good example for her little sister. "I always eat my dessert first because I'm not naughty like Maud."

"Me too," said Ellen, also not wanting to be grouped with Maud.

"All right, then," said Will, winking at his granddaughters. "This story was first told to me by my father many years ago, but it's completely true because I saw the ghost myself."

"Really?" asked Jimmy.

"Yes, it all began back when Marquette was just a little town, newly settled. There were only a few buildings surrounded by large, scary forests."

"What year was it?" Jimmy asked.

"Oh, it was way back in the 1800s — the 1850s I think."

"Almost a hundred years ago!" Jimmy gasped.

"Yes, but first I have to tell you about when I was a boy, just a few years older than you. Back then, I lived on the farm with my father and my brother and my sisters."

"Barry's grandma is your sister, right Grandpa?" said Jimmy.

"Yes," said Will. "We all lived on the farm with my father, a few miles out of town, but my grandparents lived in town. They lived up on top of the hill. Sometimes I would go visit them on the way home from school. My brother Clarence would usually go with me, but that day he had been too sick to go to school so I had to walk home by myself. That was partly why I went to visit my grandparents. They didn't know Clarence was sick so I wanted to let them know — that, and I wanted to ask them what I should buy my pa for Christmas.

"I wasn't going to stay long, but my grandmother, like all good grandmothers, insisted I have some cake, and my grandfather started telling me one of his stories. He was always full of stories and could talk for hours."

"Sounds like someone I know," laughed Ronald.

"We're all big storytellers in our family, I guess," said Will, "my father was the same too. So anyway, by the time I left my grandparents' house, it was getting dark. It was also starting to snow. Now that I think back on it, I'm surprised my grandparents even let me leave because it looked like a storm was brewing, but back in those days, hardly anyone had a telephone so I couldn't call my father, and I didn't want him to worry if I didn't make it home.

"Just as I set off for our farm, the snow picked up. I only walked a couple blocks before I was huffing and puffing as I struggled against the blowing wind and tried to see where I was going. When I reached Park Cemetery, I decided to take a short cut through it. By then, the snow was up to my knees and — "

"Oh come on, Pa, within three blocks of walking the snow was up to your knees!" laughed Ada.

"You don't know how bad the winters were back then," said Will. "Anyway, I got into the cemetery, but the snow was so high by then I was walking on top of the gravestones."

Jimmy looked alarmed at the thought of walking over the dead.

"Then I tripped on a stone sticking up out of the snow. I remember falling forward and my face landing in the snow. That's all I remember. I think I passed out from exhaustion. When I woke, I found myself huddled up inside the door of a crypt where I was sheltered from the wind. For a second I was confused, but then I looked out into the storm. There was a young girl, about my age, walking away from me.

"At first, I thought she was also lost in the storm. I called to her, but she only looked back and smiled. I remember thinking it was odd I could see her smile so clearly when the snow was coming down so hard I couldn't see anything else. A sort of glow about her made her stand out despite the storm. Then, all of a sudden, she just disappeared. I couldn't believe it. I sat there, wondering whether I had ever really seen her, or whether the storm just made it look as if she had disappeared. At that very second, the snow stopped, so I got up and looked for her footsteps. I tried to follow them, only to discover they disappeared at a gravestone sticking up out of the snow."

"The snow probably drifted and covered the rest of her footprints," said Louis.

"And the snow can play tricks when the wind whips it around," said Thelma. "You probably never saw an actual girl. Why, I've often seen gusts of snow that looked like angels floating over the earth."

"Now listen," said Will. "I can't explain it, but let me tell the rest."

The grownups smiled good-naturedly, but the children's eyes widened as he finished his tale.

"When I got home, I told my father what had happened, and then he told me the story of Annabella Stonegate."

"Who's she?" asked Lucy.

"Just listen and you'll find out," said Will.

"Annabella's a dumb name," said Jimmy. "And why does it have to be a girl ghost?"

"Well, Jimmy, I'm sorry," said Will, "but since I'm telling you what really happened to me, I don't have any control over it being a boy or a girl ghost."

"So what did your father tell you?" asked Jessie.

"He told me Annabella Stonegate is buried in Park Cemetery. She met an early death as a little girl, and several people have seen her ghost since then."

"How did she die?" asked Jimmy, hoping for a gruesome death to make up for a girl ghost.

"Well," said Will, "Marquette was so small during the first few years when it was founded that Annabella had no other little girls to play with, and she was very lonely. Her parents lived outside of town, but sometimes they let her walk a mile to a nearby farm to go visit some other little girls. Her mother made her always promise to be home before dark."

"How far did she have to walk?" asked Lucy.

"About a mile I said," Will replied.

"How far is a mile?" Jimmy wanted to know.

"About halfway from here to downtown," said Will.

"That's far," said Jimmy. "She might get lost."

"Not if she followed the road," said Lucy.

"Will you let me tell the story?" asked their grandfather, thinking he never would have started to tell one if he had known it would mean so many interruptions.

"Well, Pa, they just want to understand better," said Eleanor.

"Well, they can ask questions after I finish," said Will. "Now, one day, just before Christmas — since this is a Christmas ghost story you know," he said, winking at Ellen, "Annabella went to bring Christmas presents to her friends, Virginia and Georgianna Ridge. She stayed a couple hours at the house while she opened her present from the Ridges, and they had a little tea party like little girls love to have."

Lucy smiled; she loved playing tea party with her dolls.

"When it started to get dark, Mrs. Ridge told Annabella she had better head home. Mrs. Ridge was sorry her husband was not home to drive Annabella back, but Annabella was a brave girl, as little girls growing up in the Northwoods have to be, so she put on her winter coat, and picked up the Christmas present she had gotten from her friends, and she was — "

"What was the Christmas present?" asked Maud.

"Ah, I was just coming to that," said Will. "She had gotten a lovely new doll for Christmas, a doll the likes of which had never before been seen in Marquette in those early days. And Annabella loved it. She carried it beneath her coat because it had a china face, and she didn't want to drop and break it or even for the cold weather to crack it. But she had barely left the house when a snowstorm started up, and as it got darker out, and the snow got fiercer, she lost her way. She wasn't sure which direction she was going, but she just kept walking, hoping to see the light from her parents' window. Instead, she saw an Indian. Now all the Indians around Marquette were friendly to the settlers, but Annabella was just a little girl, and the boys at school had told her that Indians like to scalp little girls."

"Sound like typical boys," laughed Ada.

"What's scalp?" asked Maud.

"To cut off your hair," said Will, giving a mild description that relieved Eleanor, who did not want her girls to have nightmares.

"What's so bad about getting a haircut?" asked Maud.

"Maybe she had really beautiful hair, so she didn't want it cut off," said Judy.

"So," said Will, "when Annabella saw the Indian, she was so scared she ran out into the storm and never was seen alive again."

"Did the Indian get her?" asked Jimmy.

"No, but the Indian tried to find her because he was a good Indian, and he knew she was going the wrong way. Only he couldn't see her footsteps because of the blowing, drifting snow. Finally he went to her parents' house to tell them he had seen her. Then her father walked to the Ridges' farm to try and find her. He and Mr. Ridge searched for Annabella all night, but it was an Indian who found her and brought her home, frozen to death."

"Oh no," squeaked Ellen.

"Yes. It was very sad," said Will. "She was such a sweet little girl that everyone in Marquette cried when they heard she had died."

Beth could not help shedding a tear, as she remembered how her own father had died from being caught in a blizzard.

"Is that the end?" asked Jimmy.

"Almost," said Will. "Annabella was such a good girl that people say God blessed her by letting her come back to earth to help people who are lost in blizzards. That's why I saw her ghost in Park Cemetery. She must have pulled me from where I fell over in the snow and laid me in the doorway of the crypt where I would stay warm."

"So she's not really so much a ghost as an angel," said Jessie.

"I guess so," said Will. "They say good people tend to become angels."

Most of the grownups smiled, appreciating the story's moral ending, but Henry only laughed.

"Pa, you told me that story when I was little, and I remember going to Park Cemetery to look for Annabella's gravestone, but I never could find it."

"You must not have looked hard enough," said Will.

Henry laughed again, but Jimmy, despite his initial dislike for a girl ghost, said, "There are lots of gravestones in the cemetery, Daddy. You probably missed it. We should go look again."

"Why do you even need to look?" asked Will. "Don't you trust your grandpa?"

"If he's smart, he won't," Henry smiled.

"Well, the gravestone is there," said Will. "And furthermore, I went to school with one of the Stonegate boys. He told me about Annabella — she was his father's older sister — and when I told him the next day at school that I had seen her ghost, he verified it was her."

"You're too much, Pa," said Henry.

"Can we open our presents now?" asked Maud.

"Mother, are you okay?" asked Eleanor. Margaret had been silent during the story. "You look pale."

"No — I — well," said Margaret, trying to cover her confusion, "I'm probably pale because — well, they say when you speak of the dead, they live again, and for a moment, I thought I saw Annabella Stonegate looking into the dining room window."

"Did she look scary?" Jimmy asked while Lucy jumped up to stare outside.

"Oh no," said Margaret, standing up to clear the table. "I think she just wanted to see whether we were having a happy Christmas since she missed her own Christmas so many years ago. She looked happy to see there were children here."

"Can we bring her some Christmas cookies?" asked Maud.

Everyone laughed.

"Ghosts don't eat cookies, silly," said Lucy.

Margaret excused herself to fetch dessert. She had a couple seconds alone in the kitchen to regain her composure. She felt lucky to have covered her emotions by pretending to have seen a ghost. She laughed at herself now — Will's story was silly, but she had thought about how Annabella's parents must have grieved, just as she was now. She was determined to stay silent about Bill today, but she did not know how long she would carry on now that one of her children was dead. Would she end up in the grave from grief?

Beth came into the kitchen just as Margaret opened a bottle of aspirins.

"Do you have a headache, Mother?"

"Just a little one."

"You do look pale. Why don't you go lie down while we have dessert? Eleanor and I can clean up." Beth did not volunteer Ada's help. She figured Ada was lazy because her husband had recently gotten her a cleaning lady. What did a woman who was home all day need with a cleaning lady?

"No, I'm fine," said Margaret after swallowing the aspirins with a glass of water. "The children will be disappointed if I'm not there when they open their gifts."

Eleanor carried in more plates, then told her mother about the housedress Ronald had given her for Christmas while they rinsed and stacked the dishes. She now seemed oblivious to her mother's pale face. Beth went to finish clearing the table.

Dessert was served without any greater trouble than Harriet feeling the need to point out to Margaret what was wrong with her piecrust. Margaret asked Harriet for her piecrust recipe just to get her to shut up. The children only ate half their pie before the grownups finally gave in and let them open their presents.

"Ooh" and "Ah" and "Thank you" filled the room as the packages revealed trucks and balls, dolls and hair ribbons, unwanted socks, and toy soldiers, storybooks, blocks, crayons, and of course the candy — all that delights the childhood heart. The adults got shoes, sweaters, flannel shirts, dishes, tools, and other useful, unmagical items, but each present still added to the Christmas cheer.

Once everything was opened, the gifts were restacked in bags to be carried home, and the wrapping paper was carefully folded to be used again next year — for the war had come on the heel of the Great Depression, so not a scrap of paper could be wasted. Less had been bought this year than for some holidays past, but Christmas was still merry, and what money had been saved on presents had been used to purchase war bonds or to fund care packages for the soldiers overseas.

Then came that awkward moment when the Christmas activities are over, but the cheerfulness lingers. No one yet wanted the day to end, so they sat around talking, having another drink, and maybe one more piece of pie. Margaret had remained in silent agony all this time. She now wished everyone would just go home so she could listen to the radio. She would have to tell Will soon. But perhaps she could wait until the morning. Then again, she did not want to wake tomorrow morning with the painful words still waiting to be said. She knew she would not sleep tonight if she did not have Will to comfort her, and she would comfort him. But she would wait until tomorrow to tell the rest of the family.

"Beth," said Thelma, "did you hear from your brother today?"

"No, Michael called me yesterday because he's too busy with church today."

"Isn't your brother a minister or something?" asked Jean.

"He's a priest," said Beth. She was a bit perturbed that Thelma had even mentioned Michael; Beth tried to avoid religious subjects with her husband's family.

"Oh, I didn't know you were Catholic," said Jean.

"She's not," said Margaret. "When she married Henry, she quit going to church."

"Was your brother upset about that?" asked Jean.

"No," Thelma answered for Beth. "He doesn't mind so long as Beth doesn't become a Protestant."

"Is it true that Catholics worship statues?" asked Jean.

"No," said Beth.

"My mother always told me you Catholics had weird practices."

"Not any worse," said Thelma, "than you Protestants.

"What do you mean by that?" Eleanor asked.

"Well," said Thelma, "look at that scandal in the Episcopal church a few years ago."

"What scandal?" asked Jessie, too young to have paid attention when it happened.

"Back during the big blizzard in '38 when the Opera House burnt down," said Henry. "The Episcopalian Bishop was involved in it."

"The bishop didn't start the fire," said Jean.

"No, but someone did who was trying to cover up his activities."

"What activities?" asked Jessie.

"He was out in Chicago nightclubs fooling around with licentious women," Thelma said.

"Thelma, not in front of the children," said Eleanor.

"I'm sorry," said Thelma, "but you can't pick on the Catholics when the Protestants act like that."

Beth might avoid the subject of religion, but she was rather glad Thelma stuck up for the Catholic Church. She had not forgotten how shocked everyone had been about the Episcopalian bishop. The full scandalous details had spread nationwide in the pages of *True* magazine, and several copies had been sold in Marquette, despite the efforts of St. Paul's Women's Auxiliary to buy up all the copies. Of course, Harriet had gotten ahold of a copy, which she showed to Margaret, who then showed it to Will, who showed it to Henry, who showed it to Beth, who then showed it to Thelma. Before long, everyone in Marquette was shocked by what had happened.

True magazine revealed Marquette's Episcopalian Diocese had been having financial problems. Mr. Miller, responsible for the church funds, had embezzled church money, then lost it in the stock market. He went to the bishop for help, threatening that if the bishop exposed him, he would commit suicide. In desperation, Bishop Ablewhite sought out an investment counselor named Lyons to help rebuild the church's lost savings. Mr. Lyons suggested nightclubs would be a good investment, he being a frequent visitor to them since he had quite the eye for showgirls. Soon, Bishop Ablewhite had decided to buy his own little nightclub, the income from which would be used to replace the missing church funds. Gradually, the secret leaked out to the bishop's congregation.

Mr. Miller's office had been in the Masonic building, which also housed the Marquette Opera House. Speculations would never be confirmed regarding whether Mr. Miller had started the fire while burning the incriminating documents of his embezzlement, or whether the fire had just serendipitously destroyed them. People became suspicious when after the fire, Mr. Miller's safe was found open and everything burned inside it. Within a year, the congregation realized money was missing from several church funds until a legal investigation was deemed necessary. John Voelker, Marquette County's prosecuting attorney, ordered a grand-jury investigation into the case. By October, Bishop Ablewhite was found guilty as an accessory to the embezzlement of church funds and sentenced to ten years in prison, although he got off after nine months in the Jackson state prison. Upon the bishop's release, his friend Henry Ford, gave him a position as director of personnel in his River Rouge plant. Mr. Miller got off far more easily; he died of a heart attack before the embezzlement was discovered.

"Nothing like that would ever happen in our church," said Thelma, defiantly staring at Margaret, whom she had heard from Beth, held such ridiculous notions as that Catholics only built large cathedrals because they were in a secret alliance with the mafia and were storing arsenals in the cathedral basements.

"Neither would it happen in a Baptist church," said Eleanor.

"Or in a Methodist one," said Jean.

Margaret made no reply. She was not listening. Instead, she was hoping her son had died in good faith with the Lord. She tried to comfort herself with the thought that one day she would see Bill in Paradise.

"You can't blame all Episcopalians because of one bishop's mistake," said Henry.

"That's right," said Will. "One bad apple doesn't spoil the bushel."

"It looks as if it's going to snow again," said Ronald, who had little interest in Marquette events other than the miserable weather. "I don't know why we live here."

"I love the snow," Eleanor laughed, "but Ronald's from downstate where they only get a few inches."

"It wouldn't be Christmas without snow," said Mrs. Rushmore.

"It's been a fine Christmas," said Harriet. "If it wasn't for the war, it would have been perfect."

Leave it to Harriet, thought Margaret, to spoil the mood by reminding everyone of the war.

"I got a card from my son a couple days ago," said Mrs. Rushmore. "So I know he was safe at least up until he wrote it. He thinks the war won't last much longer."

"I hope this is the last Christmas we'll have to worry about it," said Eleanor.

"Has anyone heard the latest?" asked Harry. "I didn't see the paper yesterday."

Margaret trembled. What if someone had heard Bill's ship had sunk, but just forgotten he had been on that ship? If someone had heard a ship had sunk, she was sure to be asked what ship Bill was on. Then she would have to confess, in front of all these people, what she had kept secret all day.

"Grandma, my dolly's dress keeps falling down. Will you fix it?" asked Maud.

Margaret took the doll, scarcely knowing what she was doing as she rearranged the dress. Her mind was spinning. She tried to listen to the conversation but words were blurring, "Germany, France, Blitzkrieg, Churchill, Roosevelt, Hitler, Stalin, Japan, Pacific, MacArthur, shooting, bombing, killing, prisoners, wounded, missing in action, dead." She felt so hot. Why not just tell and get it over with? Why did it have to happen at Christmas? She would have gone to the war and died in Bill's place to change it. She felt so hot. She started to see black spots. She was going to faint.

"Grandma, not like that," Maud said. "You'll ruin my dolly's dress."

RING! RING! RING!

Margaret jumped. She woke from her engulfing fear.

"Who could that be?" asked Will, but Margaret had already tossed the doll aside and run for the phone. It would be the U.S. Government, calling to tell her about Bill.

"Hello," she gasped.

"Hello, Ma. Merry Christmas."

"Royal? Where are you?"

"It's Bill, Ma."

It took her a moment to understand.

"What — how — I?"

"Did you hear about my ship?" asked Bill. "They're reporting that it sunk, but it's a mistake. The news named the wrong ship. I thought I'd call so you wouldn't worry. I guess maybe you didn't hear but anyway I'm safe. I only got a minute 'cause all the other guys wanna call their families, but I wanted you and Pa to know I'm okay. How are you?"

"Fine, we're all fine," said Margaret, trying not to cry. "We're all here. Just a minute. Will! It's Bill. Come talk to your son."

"I only got a minute, Ma. But I didn't want you to worry. How's your Christmas?"

"Fine. We're all together. Henry and Beth, Eleanor, Ada — oh, all of us. We're fine."

"Give them all my love."

"You're sure you're safe?"

She didn't know what else to ask. It was Bill. Her son. He was alive.

"I'm fine, Ma. I love you."

"I — I love you too."

"It's good hearing your voice but I gotta go. The other men wanna call their families too so they're not worried. Put Pa on for a minute, will ya?"

Will was at her side. She handed him the phone. Then she collapsed in a chair. The tears sprang to her eyes. She wiped them with her apron. She knew Will was talking, but she could not listen. Thank God. Thank you, God. Thank you, God. I know the war isn't over and it could still happen, but thank you that at least today my little boy is still alive!

"Maggie, why are you crying?" asked Will. He had only talked a minute, then hung up the phone.

"I don't know," she said, wiping her eyes on her sleeve. "I just miss him is all."

"Come on back with the family. Everyone will want to know what Bill said. Too bad Roy didn't call also."

"He only called because — ." But Will had already left the kitchen to tell everyone what Bill had said. She got up and went into the living room.

"How nice that he called," said Harriet. "I hope my Joseph calls me."

"He only called because the news reported that his ship had sunk," said Will. "He said it was a mistake and didn't want us to worry."

"Oh," said Eleanor, "funny, we didn't hear about it. But I'm glad he's safe."

"Oh, Mother," said Beth, "how horrible if you had heard that news on the radio, and especially since it's Christmas."

Margaret stared at her daughter-in-law, wondering whether Beth suspected she had known all day. She sat down next to Will. He handed her his handkerchief.

"I think that knowing Bill is safe," said Henry, "is the best Christmas present I could receive."

"Me too," said Ada.

"Nothing is worse than losing someone in a war," said Beth. "I know it broke my mother's heart when my brother Frank died in the last one."

"Grandma, you still didn't fix my dolly's dress," said Maud. Margaret picked up the doll and quickly pulled the dress into place.

"We better get going," said Harry Jr. "My parents want us to stop over this evening."

"Give your mother my love," Will told his nephew.

"We better be going too," Mr. Rushmore said. "Are you ready, honey?"

"Yes," said his wife.

Coats were sought out. People exchanged goodbyes. The Cummings left, then the Rushmores, then Thelma and Jessie. After Eleanor's family departed, Ada's family said goodbye. Soon only Henry, Beth, Ellen, and Jimmy remained.

"Let me help with the dishes," said Beth. She was surprised Ada and Eleanor had not offered, but then, their husbands ran their lives. Henry did not mind sitting with his father an extra hour so his wife could help his mother.

"All right," said Margaret, too exhausted to refuse.

"Do you want me to help too?" asked Will.

"No," said Margaret. "I don't want all my dishes broken."

She realized it was the first joke she had made all day.

After all the dishes were done, they decided to have a light snack for supper. Then Beth, Henry, and the children went home. Margaret and Will were left to sit together on the couch, listening to her new Bing Crosby record. Margaret remembered how everyone had said the war would be over by this time next year. Bill had not been able to tell them exactly where he was, probably somewhere warm, but God willing, next year, he would be home for a white Christmas.

1945

The war had finally ended. Victory was declared in Europe before it was declared in Japan. But for the mothers, the wives, and the children, the real victory was not that the war had ended, but that the men were coming home. Perhaps the women had guessed there would be some awkwardness when their loved ones returned, but they could not be prepared for the strangers who had once been their sons, husbands, or brothers.

One late October afternoon, Sergeant Royal Whitman, having achieved respect and status in the army, came home. He had scarcely known when he left how much he had loved the haunts of his old town. Years away — not by choice as in his earlier youth when he had gone out West, but by forced necessity for his nation's good — had made him appreciate the simpler joys of life. He had done his duty overseas. Now he was thankful it was over.

When being trained for the army, when crossing the great Atlantic, when fighting in France, when liberating concentration camp victims in Germany, he had told himself how lucky he was to have a family back home who loved him and awaited his return. He had told himself he would ask for no other happiness if only he were allowed to return home. He missed his mother's prattling tongue, his father spitting in his spittoon, his brothers and sisters bickering, the laughter of his nephews and nieces. He missed watching the snowflakes fall, the springtime buds turn into massive leaf-covered summer forests, the white capped waves of Lake Superior. Missed everything that had once seemed monotonous to him, but now were affirmed as familiar comforts.

As the train entered his hometown, his eyes sought out each sight, St. Peter's Cathedral, the massive Marquette County Courthouse, the new Post Office on Washington Street that Henry had helped to build, the City Hall with its bizarre rotunda roof. But he had remembered Marquette in summer when all was green, or in early fall when the autumn leaves enhanced Marquette's beauty, or in deepest winter when the snow lent a peaceful look to the northern town. Today the autumn leaves had already fallen. The trees were bare. It was drizzling. The city was wet, the buildings dark and damp from rain; everything appeared dead and ugly. He felt disappointed. The buildings looked badly in need of painting. The people hurried down the streets, anxious to escape the rain, not at all showing the smiling faces he remembered. In the distance, he could see fierce waves pounding on the lake. What he remembered as grand landmarks looked small compared to the magnificent structures he had seen in London and Paris. When in those cities, he had sworn not all the glories of Europe equaled the distinct beauty of his Marquette. Now he felt he had lied to himself, and as a result, he felt disappointed.

He had not told anyone what day he would arrive. He did not want a crowd to greet him at the depot. He had thought too many loving greetings, so much happiness would overwhelm him after his lonely army years. Now he wished his parents, his sisters, someone had come to meet him. He could use some cheer. But he also felt awkward to be home, unsure how people would react to him. The rain made him think he should take a taxi home, but he decided to walk, to get used to the idea of being back here before he had to see anyone. He had marched through many a downpour during the war, so a little rain would not hurt him now. He only had one small bag, so it would take little effort to carry it home.

He stepped off the train and brushed past the small crowd waiting in the depot. He did not recognize one face. How, in his hometown, could he not know one person present? Marquette had changed while he was gone, or else, it had always been changing even when he lived here, but he had never noticed it then. It was no longer the small town of his childhood where everyone knew everyone else. But then, maybe he had been gone so long he just did not recognize the faces. He bet the war had also aged him so he would not be recognized. He did not like to think about it. He was glad to stretch his legs after they had cramped up in the train. He walked down Main Street, then turned up Third to Washington, then trudged West until he came to Fourth Street, then headed up the hill.

When he reached the top, he stopped to catch his breath; he could see the Peter White Library, and a glimpse of the Methodist and Baptist churches as he looked down Ridge Street. Then he turned around to look about him, down into the valley, where he saw the glowing dome of the courthouse, and St. Peter's Cathedral, rising up, as high as the hill he had just climbed. He was momentarily surprised, having forgotten the cathedral had been rebuilt after it had caught fire back in '35. The reconstruction had been finished before he left for the war, but perhaps because he was not Catholic, he had given it little attention. Now he was struck by the majesty of its new towers, its immense stained glass windows, its complete domination of the skyline and everything below it. Even though his own Baptist church was visible, even though St. John the Baptist's Catholic Church was closer with its tall belltower, St. Peter's Cathedral attracted him, reminded him of that other magnificent cathedral he had seen in Paris.

Notre Dame de Paris. Roy had known about Catholics since childhood, seen St. Peter's Cathedral all his life, heard his mother's disparaging comments about Catholics, then witnessed religious conflict when Henry married Beth. But he had never been inside a Catholic church until he visited Notre Dame. One of his army buddies had asked him to go to Mass one morning, and Roy, impressed by the outer appearance of the medieval church, and not wanting to hurt his friend's feelings, despite his mother having warned him about Catholics, agreed to accompany him. He found himself overwhelmed. How could a small town boy be otherwise? He could scarcely imagine the devotion, the faith of the builders, the centuries of prayers raised to Heaven in this sacred place, the constant reminder in sculptured saints and storied stained glass windows of man's relationship with God through the centuries.

The modern day atheists declared that religion belittled man, that man had created God out of his own mind, then allowed that fictional God to degrade man as vile, sinful, deserving of punishment. The atheists ignored the glorious proclamation that man was made in God's own image. That God loved man enough to make the ultimate sacrifice. That the greatest story ever told was an unending love story between God and His creation. The atheists were too caught up in their intellectual gymnastics to accept something so simple, so beautiful, so true.

Roy had not understood the Latin he heard at Notre Dame that day. He scarcely understood French. He certainly did not understand the mysteries of Catholicism. But he need not understand to believe that what made old ladies kneel on aching knees, great men humbly bow their heads, and children long to be like the saints, had to be truth. The human spirit always rallied, and in these desperate times of war, the belief that good would triumph over evil, that God would defeat Death, remained unquenchable.

It was the middle of the twentieth century. Man had learned to fly in machines. Science was curing diseases. Homes were heated as if by magic with coal or gas or electricity. Radio provided live communication to all parts of the world. What were these wonders when still no one had found a better explanation for the existence of life than those ancient Israelites who believed God was their protector? On that day in Notre Dame, just after the liberation of Paris, Roy had vowed that like those biblical people, he would never forget how God had used him as one of thousands of soldiers to free the world from its wicked oppressors.

From the top of Fourth Street, in the drizzling rain, the sight of St. Peter's Cathedral reminded Roy of that day in Paris when he had felt strong in his faith and his belief in humanity's ultimate goodness. He wished now he could have reveled in that false comfort. False because it could not compensate for the horrors he had seen soon after. Horrors that had made him completely reject the comforting old Christianity as nothing but a manmade dream designed to comfort.

Roy turned from St. Peter's Cathedral, his nose twitching with sadness. He started walking home, too tired to think anymore. Home was all he had now. He just wanted to be with his family, to rest. He hoped Ma and Pa would see him coming down the street — then they would run out the front door, down the steps, his mother shouting his name, his father close behind, waiting while his mother hugged him, then shaking his hand and patting him on the back. Henry and Beth would hear the commotion and come outside to join in the jubilation. His mother would pull him inside the house, never taking her eyes off him, insisting she call his sisters right away — well, call Eleanor anyway — he remembered Ada had moved down South while he was away. He could not think beyond that moment of his homecoming.

But Roy reached his block and his parents' house without being seen. He walked slowly, hoping to be spotted. He noticed the apple tree in the front yard was gone — Pa must have chopped it down. He climbed the front steps. He stood there, listening for voices. In the past, he would have opened the door and stepped in. But he felt like a stranger now. The screen door was locked. He pounded on the wall. He pounded several times without any answer. Then his mother looked out, her face dim behind the screen.

"Royal." It was barely a whisper. She struggled with the handle, then pushed the door open. A smile broke on her face. She pulled him inside and hugged him. Then his father appeared. Roy saw tears in his eyes. A minute later, Henry happened to stop by, not knowing Roy was there. He clapped his brother on the back. Margaret told Henry to bring Beth and the kids over for supper so they could greet Royal properly. But it was still early for supper. A strange sense of "What do we do now?" came over everyone. Everything was awkward.

Roy told himself he would have to adjust, that it would take time after he had been gone so long. Beth came over and said, "Welcome home." The children looked shy and kept their distance. Roy realized he was a stranger to them.

He wanted to tell his family everything he had seen, the cathedrals and towns, the strange customs of the French, the sadness of the defeated Germans, the horrors experienced by the Jews, cities destroyed by bombs, his comrades killed on battlefields, the beautiful countries filled with strange birds, trees, flowers, languages he had never heard before. Instead, he listened to his mother chatter about some neighbor he could not remember who had just had a baby, and then she told him about the church bazaar, and about a new store downtown. She talked nonstop, updating him on everything in her everyday life of dishes, shopping, cooking, cleaning, and church. He began to realize that what the war had done to him, his mother, father, brother, all his family would never understand. The war had been distant for them, save for the food rationing and the newspaper reports. They did not know what to ask him. He felt it would be frustrating to explain to them what they could not understand. His lips began to lock — the family did not want to hear about the war — they wanted to forget he had ever been gone and to pick up with him where they had left off. But he was not that same man who had left. Still, he loved them, so he refused to bring them pain by telling them what he had suffered while away.

In the days that followed, the Whitmans adjusted to Roy's return. When they referred to the war, it was in veiled expressions, as when Ronald greeted him with "Here's our returned hero." The words rankled in Roy's ears. He had only served his country.

One evening when Henry's family was over for supper, Margaret said, "Bill sent me a letter. He should be home soon now that the war with Japan is over."

"Good," said Will. "Then both our boys will be safe."

"Uncle Roy," Jimmy asked, "how many Germans did you kill?"

Roy stared at his nephew, stunned by his enthusiastic voice.

"I didn't count," said Roy. He had shot a few men, most of them nameless human beings he had tried to forget as quickly as possible. Killing people had disturbed him, but he had done it to defend himself and his comrades.

"You mean you killed so many you lost count?" Jimmy asked.

Roy opened his mouth, but he did not know how to respond.

"Jimmy," Beth said, "don't bother your uncle. We don't want to hear stories of bloodshed."

"I do!" said Jimmy.

"Shh," Beth warned, and Henry glared until the boy slouched back in his chair.

That was the problem, Roy thought. None of them wanted to hear the truth about the war. If they had to hear about it, they wanted tales of heroism. He had witnessed few acts of heroism. Most of what he had seen was motivated by fear, frustration, and hate. He knew his war service had helped to save lives, but he felt little pride in what he had done, especially when the Americans had come too late to save hundreds of thousands of people. How could he feel pride after the horrors he had seen? He could never tell anyone what he had witnessed in those concentration camps. He had thought he knew poverty as a child and during the Depression. He had had no concept of real poverty, of hunger that drove one mad, of fear, degradation, the humiliation of forced nakedness, being denied human necessities, basic respect. Thousands had died in those camps, never knowing an army was coming to liberate them, never knowing anyone cared about them. For most, the army came too late.

Roy Whitman had arrived in Europe, an ignorant young man from Upper Michigan, knowing scarcely a word of French or German, unable even to pronounce the name of the nearest village. He had once thought himself knowledgeable, well-read, intelligent. Now he felt he had lived in a narrow little world, controlled by the beliefs of his family and neighbors. He had been raised to believe the United States was the best country in the world, but he never truly knew it until he traveled overseas. He had been told Baptists were the best Christians, but he had nothing to compare their Christianity with until he understood the great gap between good and evil, and the simple naiveté of his mother's beliefs. He did not even know one of the handful of Negroes, much less Jews in Marquette. Now he did not believe any person was better than another. Everyone had to suffer from the absurdity, the cruelty of the human condition. His sympathy was far more Christian than his mother's often religious bigotry, but he could not claim to be Christian now when he ceased to believe in God's existence. All those theological arguments about how sin came into the world, how Christ was the key to salvation — they no longer seemed logical to Roy. People should be kind because everyone suffered; that was just common sense as far as he was concerned.

"How many Germans did you kill?" Jimmy had asked him.

What hope did humanity have when children asked such ignorant questions?

Roy had not seen much action during the war. Normandy, Paris, Germany and its concentration camps — he had come to all those places after the fighting was over. Only in a couple small skirmishes had he used his gun. Only once had he killed maliciously for the sake of killing.

The day after he arrived in Paris, he had walked down a deserted boulevard. Hearing a woman's desperate scream from inside a building, he instinctively ran in to help. He rushed up a dilapidated flight of stairs, following the screams, until he found, lying on the floor at the top of the landing, a Frenchwoman with a German soldier trying to mount her. Later, Roy would realize the soldier must be a deserter hiding from the allied forces, perhaps having held this poor girl captive for days while he used her to satisfy his lusts. For a moment, Roy watched in disgust as the German took his fist and bashed it against the Frenchwoman's skull to stop her wailing. Her head collapsed. Then the soldier, grunting loudly, performed his violent deed.

Roy was overcome with rage; he remembered another man hurting a woman — a man he had been helpless to stop. This time he would have his revenge. His hand clutched his gun. He raised it and aimed at the German's skull. He remembered the enemy falling forward, blood flowing through his hair, red, wet and sticky. Roy had grabbed the German's mane and yanked the man from the woman's body. She was unconscious. No, dead. The man's furious lust had made him crush her skull. When Roy brushed her hair from her face, he went into shock. Then he bolted, running from the building, into the street, crying out for help. Too late. He had witnessed the scene he most feared. The act of war that men inflicted upon women.

Roy woke in his bed in his parents' house having dreamt the nightmare again. He knew the woman he loved was not really dead, but he had never seen that Frenchwoman's real face because Chloe's face had intruded into his mind. He went sometimes days or weeks without thinking of Chloe, but now this morning he woke, aching for her.

"Roy, breakfast is almost ready!" his mother shouted from downstairs.

She had insisted on cooking him breakfast every morning since he had come home. He grumbled, then reminded himself it was not his mother's fault that he wished a different woman could cook his meals.

He pulled himself out of bed and got dressed. As he fumbled with his shirt buttons, he felt a moment of overpowering despair. Would it be better if he had died in the war? Then he would be free from this pain. Love hurt worse than death. But he still hoped to possess that love, to be with the girl he believed still wanted to be with him, and that small hope was enough for him to continue on. He would try to get through today, and if he could do that, he could get through tomorrow. He had promised to help Henry today. That would help; it would get him out of the house, away from his mother's constant fussing. But it would not free him from this aching.

Mrs. Eric Hobson, having seen the work Henry Whitman had done on Robert O'Neill's porches, ordered her husband to hire Henry to build her new kitchen cabinets. Henry recruited Roy to assist him. Roy recalled Mrs. Hobson had once been Mary Lawson, an obnoxious little girl close to his age. She had grown up to be an exacting taskmaster, who knew what she wanted and would not compromise. Henry had made the appropriate measurements, then built the cabinets in his workshop. Today, he and Roy were delivering the cabinets to install them.

Mary Hobson went to her mother's house for lunch that day; she instructed her husband to "keep an eye on those workmen." If keeping an eye on them was making them coffee and offering them his mother-in-law's cookies, Eric obeyed his wife's dictates. Henry did not like to take breaks, but Roy politely agreed to a cup of coffee.

"So, Roy," said Eric as they soaked their cookies in coffee, "Henry tells me you're just home from the war."

"Yes," said Roy, who wished less and less to discuss his military service.

"Where were you stationed?"

"France and Germany mostly."

"I was over there during the last war," said Eric. "In the trenches too. Nearly lost my leg. I've limped ever since."

Roy frowned sympathetically.

"I imagine," said Eric, "that it must have been even worse for you with all the new weapons they've invented."

"I imagine," said Roy.

"We feared gas then," said Eric, "but at least there weren't atomic bombs."

"Was it hard for you when you got back home?" Roy trembled as he asked.

"A little. I was in the hospital in Washington D.C. for many weeks. My mother came out to stay with me. I grew up on Mackinac Island, but after the war, I came to Marquette to go to Northern. That made it easier; people in Marquette didn't know me; it would have been harder to face everyone on Mackinac Island, all of them pitying me because of my war wound. In Marquette, people didn't always know I was in the war, so it was easier starting over."

"I don't know whether I can start over," said Roy. "I don't mind helping Henry, but I don't feel the desire to work as I used to. All I can do is keep thinking about the war."

Roy was surprised to make such confessions to a stranger; had he said such a thing to his family, they would have driven him crazy with worrying questions.

"I bet you've had an awful time of it," Eric replied, "but it's over now. Be proud of what you did and try to forget the horrors. You did what you had to do, and you can't change the past, only the future."

"Are you coming back to work?" Henry poked in his head.

Roy went back to helping his brother, but he thought that if Eric could barely walk without a cane, yet had married a beautiful, if not congenial wife, had children, and found a good job, he could also have a normal life. Still, he doubted the adjustment would be easy.

After the cabinets were installed and they left the Hobsons' house, Henry stopped for groceries. Roy went into the store with Henry. There he met one of the men he had known up at the Huron Mountain Club.

"Glad to see you're back, Roy."

"Thanks, it's good to see you," said Roy, although he felt like ducking down another aisle to avoid everyone he knew. He waited to be asked about the war.

"We could have used you at the Club this year. Why don't you come up next season? I'm sure we can find you a place."

Roy did not know what he wanted for his future. Nothing he had ever wanted had seemed to work out, not college, not an adventurous life in the West, not love. Working at the Club was just something he had done while waiting for something else. He was still waiting.

"I'd like that," said Roy.

"I'll call you in the spring then," said his old coworker.

Roy felt his spirits rise as he left the grocery store. At least someone still appreciated him. And he had several months until spring to decide whether he really would go up to the Club; he had known some good times up there, and he needed a break from being around his family, who looked sad around him, knowing he was depressed, but not knowing how to cheer him. Maybe they did not want to upset him with questions about the war, but just as likely they did not want to upset themselves with his answers to their questions.

No one wanted to hear about the war — except Jimmy. Only Eric Hobson could even guess what Roy had experienced, but Eric had said to forget about it and concentrate on the future. Maybe in the silence of the Club's great forests, alone in the Huron Mountains, there among the giant trees and the great sky, he might find peace at last.

But the thought of the Club also reminded him of Lex, and of the woman he loved. The first year he and Chloe had been apart, he had written her several letters after finding out Lex's new address from a friend at the Club. She had answered him a couple times, sending letters that suggested only friendship, but Roy believed she would have professed more if she did not fear her husband finding the letters. Sometimes, Roy feared Chloe was too kindhearted to say she did not want to hear from him. Sometimes, he thought her foolish to receive his letters and risk Lex's anger. But Roy wrote anyway, never putting his name on the letters or envelopes. Chloe knew only one man could write her such letters.

That evening, he wrote to her again. They were both prisoners, she of her husband, he of the loneliness of his separation from her. He would always love her, but now he wanted her to know his love had changed because of how the war had changed him. He wanted her to know that even alienated from her love, he was finding freedom, and until they were together, he wanted her to have the same freedom.

November 15, 1945
Dear Chloe,

   I'm sorry I have not written for so long. You know I have not forgotten you. That could never happen. I love you and will wait for you, despite how much pain I feel over our separation. I know you understand. My feelings for you have not changed. They never can.

   When I last wrote, I could not tell you where I was stationed. Now I am back home from the war, still in one piece. I served in England, France, and Germany. I didn't see much fighting — I guess I was lucky there — but I saw plenty of horror. I hope you did not worry about me, or imagine me dead because I did not write. There were many days I would have wished I were dead except for your saving love that keeps me determined to go on until the day I can be with you.

Chloe, you would not believe the horrors I saw: men killing men, the seats of Western culture destroyed, and worst of all, the concentration camps where the Germans imprisoned the Jews — I saw there what brutalities men commit against one another: starving, beating, killing, experimenting on human beings as if they were animals. I cannot begin to describe these horrors; I am glad you need never see them. Those people suffered so much they have forgotten what it is to be loved. I at least had my family and my memories of you to help me carry on — they had nothing. Even the terrible pain of being separated from you was nothing compared to the miseries those prisoners endured.

I do not write so you will feel sorry for what I have gone through. The war was awful, but I think I am a better person for having experienced it. I learned so much while in the army. I learned to speak French and German. I saw great cities, castles, and cathedrals. But most importantly, I learned about life, and how insignificant each of us is, yet what a difference each one of us can make. Those wretched camps were set up by men who sought to take away all human freedom, to restrict people from movement, to deny them food, love, even clothing. Yet those people, once we rescued them, told us how they survived by little acts of kindness to each other, and even their oppressors occasionally had weak moments when they showed charity. Seeing their spirits stay alive taught me about true freedom. They survived and had hope for the future despite their bondage. You and I share the bondage of separation, but we also hold onto hope until we can be together. Until that time, I want you to accept our separation, even by being a good wife to Lex until you are freed from him. And if we can never be together, we can still love one another. That we are not together matters little in reality. I would love to be with you, but life has no meaning, so ultimately, our separation is a small thing.

I don't know whether you will understand what I am trying to say — my words are probably just making a mess of it. I love you and want to be with you, but I also realize how trivial our longings are. I came to understand this while I was in Paris before returning home. A Frenchman there gave me a book to read that changed my life. It is called *La Nausee* or *Nausea* in English and is by a French writer and philosopher named Sartre. I don't know whether it's been translated into English, but I managed to read it in French, and if you can find a copy, you should read it too. I was overwhelmed with what it had to say. Sartre is the greatest thinker of our time — he is an atheist who says there is no meaning or purpose in our world, and consequently, we are free because we are not tied down by anything. I am doing a poor job of describing his philosophy, and I'm afraid I can't completely grasp it, but I think the answers lie within it. After the miseries

I saw during the war, and the pain of separation from you, I gave up believing in the Christian God. I cannot believe God would allow the suffering I saw. The beautiful artistry and design of this world could not have happened by accident, but if God exists, He does not care about the human race. I think once this world was created, God quit taking an interest in it. That is why I admire Sartre — he preaches human freedom. He says I am free to be whomever I want because there are no gods to appoint rules about life. I can do whatever I want during this life without fear of anything in the next. It is like Christian Free Will, only that doctrine was never true freedom. Religion says we can do whatever we want, but if what we want is not what God wants, we will be punished in the end. My belief is that we are free to do anything on earth because this is the only life, and if there is no life after this one, we need fear nothing. Many are frightened by Sartre's beliefs because it places responsibility on man, but such people are only cowards who refuse to live fully.

What I am trying to say, Chloe, is that after all these years of unhappiness, of missing you, I am free from pain and regret. I love you, but I will not be hurt by that pain any longer, nor feel guilt because I love you. It is confusing to believe all this — I do not know what it means for my future, or what I will do next, but I feel liberated. I want you to feel liberated as well. I highly recommend you read Sartre. He can explain it better than I can. I have now started to read another of his books I bought in France called *L'Etre et le neant*. It will take me a long time to read it because it is in French and it is so deeply thoughtful. I think there is more truth in it than in the Bible.

I love you, Chloe. I'll always love you. I hope we'll be together someday; maybe someday you will even shake away your own fear and leave Lex so you can be free to do what you wish. I know you wish to be with me. But I want you to know I understand why you stay enslaved to him, and that I will always love and wait for you.

Forever, Roy

When the letter was written, Roy felt how greatly it failed to express his feelings, but he trusted Chloe would understand what he meant, and that someday she would find the courage to be with him. He also understood that freedom meant being responsible for your actions. Chloe had children so she had a responsibility toward them. Maybe when the children were grown — that was many years away, but he would wait. He would endure.

He sealed the envelope and hid it under a book. He would mail it at the post office tomorrow. He could not mail it from home because his parents would not approve of his loving a married woman, and they were bound to ask why he was writing to one. He loved his parents, but he saw his own weakness, his own self-imprisonment in his fear of their opinions. He needed to be strong and free, even if it meant severing family ties so he could live fully. He had now begun a quest for self-knowledge that he believed would yet bring him happiness.

1948

"Roy, are you deaf?"

Roy turned his head. Henry had been trying to get his attention for the last two minutes. Every Saturday night, Henry's family came over to his parents' house for supper. Roy was growing tired of these loud family evenings; his thoughts had drifted to when he would finish building his cabin so he could live by himself.

"I'm sorry. What did you say?"

"When are we going fishing?" asked Henry. "The summer's almost over and once it starts turning colder, these old people here won't want to go."

Will, ignoring the jab at his and Margaret's age, added, "It's been a long time since the entire family went on a fishing trip."

"How about next Saturday," said Margaret. She did not like to fish, but she enjoyed a day out of the house.

"We'll ask Eleanor's family to come," said Beth, "and maybe Thelma and Jessie. They won't fish, but they'll enjoy the picnic. Poor Thelma doesn't get out much anymore."

"And we'll get Bill to bring his new dame so we can meet her," said Roy.

"If he really does have a girlfriend and isn't just pulling our legs," said Henry. "I never can believe a woman is crazy enough to go out with Bill until I see her. And then I'm just surprised by how many crazy women are in this town."

"Good, it's settled then," said Will.

"Maybe for you," said Beth. "All you men have to do is grab your fishing poles. We women need to arrange a time and place and make all the food."

"That's not true," said Will. "I'll make my famous sugar cookies. Ellen will help me, won't you, Ellen?"

"Sure, Grandpa," said Ellen.

"See, there you go shoving your work on a woman," Beth grinned. "Ellen's only seven, but you men are already training her to take care of you."

Will laughed but could not think of a good comeback. He and Beth enjoyed giving each other a hard time.

Margaret, however, thought her daughter-in-law's comment disrespectful; a woman was supposed to take care of her men. But the family matriarch bit her tongue and went to telephone Eleanor and Thelma about the fishing picnic.

Pickerel Lake. August. Those most precious last days of summer when the trees take on that deep forest green that forewarns they will soon turn color, that summer is almost over, and soon winter will arrive, so each remaining warm day must be lived to the fullest. The family drove to the lake that Saturday in their trucks and cars, down a dusty dirt path off the Big Bay Road to their favorite fishing hole. The Whitmans came, all in one vehicle, Henry and Beth, with Ellen in the middle, Henry's parents in the backseat with Jimmy squashed between them. Eleanor came with her girls, and picked up Jessie and Thelma to fill her back seat since Ronald claimed he was too busy preparing for the fall semester to go fishing, even on a Saturday. Eleanor was relieved he did not come; she knew he thought no one in her family sufficiently intelligent enough to talk with except her brother-in-law, Louis, who lived down South now. Roy drove up from his cabin in the woods bordering the Huron Mountain Club; he had just moved in two nights ago, as soon as its roof was on. Bill and his latest flame had also been invited, but they had given an indefinite answer regarding their attendance.

Everyone drove into the woods, parked their cars, then hauled out picnic baskets, folding chairs, fishing poles, tackle boxes, blankets to sit on, a first aid kit for the children at least one of whom was sure to hurt him or herself, bottles of soda pop and thermoses of coffee, and coolers that reflected an optimistic belief that many a fish would be caught. The girls — Ellen, Lucy, and Maud — leapt from the cars, their dollies in hand despite their mothers' insistence they would only muddy their toys or lose them in the lake. Jimmy crawled out of the car, looking scornfully at all these girls; he was the only boy, and he was too grown up to play with little girls; he intended only to fish and act like a grownup. The blankets were laid, the picnic baskets unpacked, the folding chairs unfolded, and the fishing reels cast out over the lake. Beth fussed over Thelma to make sure she was comfortable because she always complained of back pain due to her multiple sclerosis. Lawn chairs were arranged around her so she would not be isolated from the group; Jessie took a seat beside her mother, and Eleanor, who did not care to fish, set up a card table so they could have a game of rummy. The girls found their own amusement by running along the lake. The adults, Jimmy included, tied their flies and cast their poles. Perhaps more fish would be caught if the family spread out more, but Margaret was less interested in fishing than chatting, so she sat beside her husband. Henry was content to stand beside his father, and Beth wanted to be at her husband's side. Only Roy felt the desire to go off on his own down the lakeshore, promising to return in an hour for lunch. Jimmy awkwardly looked after his uncle. When Roy looked back, he saw the boy and nodded. Then Jimmy trotted after Uncle Roy; the boy was at the age when an uncle seemed a better companion than a father. Uncle Roy had killed Germans in the war, and even if he would not talk about it, it was exciting to be with him.

Half an hour after everyone was settled, in roared an automobile bearing Bill and his latest female fancy.

"It's about time you got here," Thelma yelled when Bill opened the car door. But either he did not hear her, or he chose to ignore the remark. He walked around the car to open his girlfriend's door. No one in the family could believe her when she stepped out. Bill had found himself a little lady to bring to a fishing party. A blonde in high heels, face encased in powder, dainty hat perched on her head, and white gloves to testify she would never soil her hands to touch a slimy fish.

She took Bill's arm, fearful her heels would trip her on the rocky dirt path. She and Bill sauntered to the table where Eleanor, Jessie, and Thelma were busy building their runs of cards, unaware that until now the Queen of Hearts had been absent from the pack.

"Linda," said Bill, "this is my sister, Eleanor, and this is Thelma and her daughter Jessie."

"Pleased to meet you," said Linda.

"It's nice to meet you," said Eleanor, trying not to stare at the girl's enormous breasts. Linda was only perhaps a year older than Jessie, who had just graduated from college, yet Jessie felt like a little girl beside this paragon of womanhood. Thelma smiled, then complained, "Bill, you're blocking my light. I can't tell whether I'm holding a spade or a club."

Linda felt uncomfortable. Thelma did not seem very tactful — could Bill's family be less couth than her own? Had Bill thought to inform her that Eleanor's husband was a college professor, and that Thelma's savings account had more money in it than Linda would see in a lifetime, her first impressions would have been better.

"Bill, why are you so late?" Eleanor asked.

"I'm sorry," Linda replied. "I took too long putting on my makeup. I wanted to look my best when I met Bill's family, especially when he's so good looking himself."

Bill smiled. Thelma rolled her eyes. Jessie put down the two of spades, as if giving a score to Linda's witty comment.

"Let me introduce you to my folks," said Bill, pulling his lady friend away from the card party.

Thelma and Eleanor exchanged meaningful glances. Jessie tried not to giggle. Then the three women returned to playing rummy.

"Ma, Pa," said Bill, "this is Linda."

Margaret turned around in her seat. Will finished reeling in his line before looking at his son's latest flame.

"It's nice to meet you," said Linda, giving Margaret her hand.

Margaret brushed her hand on her coat, then extended it to Linda, impressed that the girl had worn white gloves to meet her boyfriend's mother.

"Hello," said Will, shaking hands.

"And this is my brother, Henry, and his wife, Beth," said Bill. Henry and Beth nodded at Linda, smiled politely, looked her up and down, and wondered whether Bill had told her she was going fishing and not to a dinner party.

"Bill, where's your fishing pole?" Henry asked.

"Oh, I didn't bring it," said Bill. "Linda doesn't like the smell of fish."

"Henry, I think you've got a nibble," said Beth as she saw his pole jerk. He turned to reel in his line.

"Oh," squeaked Linda, upset by the sight of the slimy wiggling fish Henry reeled in.

"Come over here, baby," said Bill, pulling Linda away. He shouted back over his shoulder, "Pa, where's Roy?"

"He went down the lakeshore with Jimmy."

"Linda and I'll just go for a little walk and find 'em," said Bill, leading Linda into the woods.

"They're going to go make out," Will snickered.

"Will," Margaret frowned, "Linda seems like a proper young lady. I don't think she'd do that."

"You never know with the girls today," said Will.

"That's true," said Beth. "Some of them wear as much makeup as dance hall hussies."

"Well," said Margaret, "Linda seems like a nice girl to me."

"Nice girls don't go out with Bill," said Henry. "And what's up with all their fancy doodads?"

Beth smiled. Bill had on a white shirt and vest with his best cap, while his father and brothers were wearing flannel shirts and had fishing lures stuck in their hats.

"We should have told them to be back in time for lunch," said Margaret.

"I don't think they're hungry for cold cuts and potato salad," Will laughed, causing his wife to glare at him.

Bill and Linda started down the path Roy and Jimmy had taken, but before they went a hundred feet, the heel of Linda's shoe got twisted on a rock, and she let out a little cry. Bill steadied her from toppling over, then helped her to a log. He placed his handkerchief over the fallen tree so she would not dirty her dress when she sat down.

"Thank you, Bill," she said, after he checked her shoe and assured her the heel was still stable. "I guess I'm not cut out for the country, am I?"

"That's all right," he said.

"I'm glad you put up with me," she said, patting his sleeve. She let her fingers revel in his firm forearm.

The reader can imagine the rest of the conversation. Their speech did not last long before their lips were locked together.

Roy and Jimmy never noticed Bill and Linda's absence. They were too frustrated in their failure to catch any fish.

"Sometimes, fishing is just too boring!" said Jimmy.

"Never complain about boring things," Roy replied. "It's been my experience that things are better off boring."

"I can't help it. I keep wanting something exciting to happen. Do you think there'll be a war when I'm eighteen?"

"I hope not."

"But nothing ever happens around here. I want to do something important like you did."

"War isn't the kind of change you want," Roy replied.

Jimmy wished Uncle Roy would talk about the war, but he always refused. Yet Jimmy could not complain; he was relieved to be with someone who did not talk too much. He was usually surrounded by women — his mother, sister, grandmother, aunts, cousins — too many women who chattered nonstop until they gave him a headache. It was good to be alone with a man who did not expect you to yack all day. Only today Jimmy wanted to talk. There was a girl at school he had not seen all summer, but he could not get her out of his thoughts.

The feeling had begun the last week of school one day during recess. Everyone knew girls could not play football, but Tina had insisted she wanted to play. Finally, the boys had agreed, figuring if she got clobbered and went crying to the teacher, Tina would quit annoying them. But when Jimmy went running for a touchdown, she ran faster than a girl should, tackled him, knocked the ball from his hands, then straddled him and pinned his arms to the ground. Jimmy had been too surprised to fight back. Later, when his friends teased him about being tackled by a girl, he told them he had been afraid to hurt her. What he did not tell them was the strange feeling he had experienced when she leaned over him, her long hair tickling his face as her hands gripped his wrists. He had replayed that scene ever since and discovered he had enjoyed being tackled by Tina. Then after two months, it dawned on Jimmy that he might be in love. But to talk to his parents about it would be awkward.

"Uncle Roy," he broached the subject.

"Hmm?" asked Roy. He would have preferred to be alone, but he was too generous to turn away his nephew who clearly wanted to spend time with him.

"Have you ever been in love?"

Roy was surprised by the question. He tried to stall before answering. He stared at his fishing line, praying a fish would bite and distract his attention.

"Why do you ask?"

"I just wondered," said Jimmy. "I mean, you're forty now, right?"

"Yeah."

"But you've never had a girlfriend?"

"No."

"You never kissed a girl even?"

"I didn't say that," Roy sighed.

"Who did you kiss?"

"That's none of your business."

"Does my dad know?" Jimmy asked.

"No, it's none of his business either."

Roy was annoyed, both by the question and by the foolish sound of his answer. He had kissed a few girls, gone out several times with girls, especially when he lived out West, even been lonely enough to dance with a couple girls while he was in the army. But only one girl had ever meant anything to him.

Jimmy wanted to ask his uncle what it was like to kiss a girl. He wanted to ask whether his uncle had ever had tingling feelings like those he had known the day Tina had tackled and straddled him. He remembered how he had almost wanted to protest when she crawled off him, despite the jeering of his friends.

"Uncle Roy, I guess what I'm trying to ask is — well, have you ever been in love?"

"Yes," said Roy, unwilling to lie despite his fear of admitting his feelings.

"Will you tell me about it?"

"No."

Jimmy stared. His eyes scrunched up in anger. His question had been so difficult to ask. He had come to Uncle Roy for help, and he received nothing in return. He struggled to his feet, knocking his fishing pole into the lake.

"Jimmy, what are you doing?"

"You're so mean. I only wanted — I — "

Jimmy felt like a fool. He thought of reaching into the lake to get his pole, but he was too upset to care about it.

"Jimmy, what's the matter? I only — "

"Why can't you tell me?" Jimmy yelled, but before Roy could reply, his nephew ran back down the path.

Roy felt unable to breathe. He was sorry to upset his nephew, but how could he tell his love story, especially so a twelve-year old boy would understand it? Why didn't Jimmy go to his father with these questions? Henry would know what to tell him. Henry had had normal relationships with women.

Jimmy ran down the trail until he was out of his uncle's sight. Then he slowed to a walk, hoping Uncle Roy would come after him; when after a minute, he heard no footsteps, no shouting of his name, he started to stomp down the trail. All he wanted was to understand the feelings he had, to know what it was like to be with a girl. He wanted to kiss Tina, to ask her whether she liked him, but he was afraid. Then he heard laughter from across the lake. His sister and female cousins were laughing; he felt as if they were laughing at him although they could not see him. He felt oafish, ignorant of love. He cringed and told himself he hated all girls although he knew that was a lie.

When he turned a bend in the trail, he came upon Uncle Bill, sitting on a log, his hands all over a beautiful woman. Their lips were pressed together; Uncle Bill's hand was up the woman's blouse. She was not resisting. She was rubbing her hand up the back of his shirt. Jimmy was ashamed, afraid to be seen. He could not go forward and be noticed. He quickly turned and walked quietly back to Uncle Roy.

He found his oldest uncle reeling in his fishing line. Roy caught sight of his nephew and raised his eyebrows, not knowing what to say.

"I think it's almost time to eat," Jimmy muttered.

"Probably," said Roy. "Let's go see."

Jimmy waited for his uncle to walk up to him. Roy put his arm around his nephew's shoulder. Jimmy flinched, but Roy left his arm there. Jimmy wanted to warn Uncle Roy about Uncle Bill, but when they reached the log, Uncle Bill and the woman were gone.

Back at the picnic site, Thelma had won the rummy game.

"Mother, should we start setting up the table to eat?" Eleanor asked as the playing cards were put away.

"All right," said Margaret, leaving the lakeside to supervise lunch.

Just then another car pulled up. "Oh Mother, did you have to invite them?" said Eleanor. "I don't mind Uncle Charles so much, but Aunt Harriet can be such a crab."

"I know," said Margaret, "but her feelings would have been hurt if she found out we had a picnic without her."

"You didn't invite Joe and his wife too, I hope," said Eleanor. Her cousin had come home from the war to marry an obnoxious woman who had given birth to two obnoxious twin boys who would continue the Dalrymple name.

"Not unless Harriet mentioned it to him," said Margaret, twisting her face into a fake smile of greeting for her brother and sister-in-law.

"Yoo-hoo, everyone," said Harriet, walking over to the table while calling over her shoulder, "Charles, get the lawn chairs out of the trunk!"

Eleanor brushed past her aunt to help her uncle collect the chairs.

"I made my potato salad," said Harriet, setting it on the table as though it were the crown jewels.

"Mmm," said Thelma, "A picnic's not a picnic without potato salad."

"Or without one of Beth's wonderful spaghetti dishes," said Jessie, pulling out the giant pot of pasta made by her mother's cousin. If nothing else, the family loved Beth for her Italian cooking. She had learned to cook pasta from her mother, who in turn had learned from her mother, who had learned from an Italian sister-in-law that good cooking can protect a woman from a man. The Italian sister-in-law had long since been forgotten, but her influence on family meals continued.

When Beth heard her name mentioned, she joined the other women in laying out the food. Ten minutes later, the men were called to eat; despite vanquished hopes of fried fish for lunch, neither Henry nor Will grumbled when they saw the spread before them. Potato salad and spaghetti headed a table that included jello salad, pineapple brownies, liverwurst, baked beans, cold cuts, dinner rolls, cheese slices, pickles, koolaid and coffee, everything to fill the fisherman's stomach. And THREE BLUEBERRY PIES to top it all off!

The adults filled their plates, then returned to their chairs, balancing dishes upon their laps while the children sat on the picnic blankets. Roy and Jimmy emerged from the woods to join the end of the food line, completing the family-get-together.

Little girls who had run about the lakeshore, now tired and a tad bit crabby, were rejuvenated by sugary koolaid. Grandpas, sadly in need of a cup of coffee, began to crack jokes. Married couples fell in love again as husbands complimented their wives' dishes — even sophisticated Linda had brought a box of candy mints — she feared she would need them if Bill were to kiss her after they ate. And an adolescent boy, deeply troubled by thoughts of girls, forgot his worries in the ecstasy of a good potato salad that can always make a boy feel like a man. Faces were stuffed and barely a word spoken except those complimentary to the cuisine. Then spoke Harriet.

"So, since summer's almost over, I guess Ada won't be coming home to visit."

"No," said Margaret.

"She says they can't afford to visit right now," said Eleanor, "but maybe they'll come for Christmas."

"No, I don't think they will," Margaret replied, "probably not until next summer."

"They better come next summer," said Will. "It'll be Marquette's centennial year. They won't want to miss the celebrations. I hear the city is planning to —"

"Margaret," Harriet intruded, "I thought you said Louis got Ada a maid. If they can afford a maid, they should be able to afford a trip home to visit her parents."

"Well, I think the Mexicans down there are cheap labor," said Margaret, although she could not understand herself why Ada had not come home that summer.

"I wouldn't trust a Mexican in my house," said Harriet.

Thelma frowned. She had heard similar comments made about Finns. But she said nothing; the comment was typical of Harriet, who was probably just jealous not to have a maid herself. Thelma doubted any self-respecting Mexican woman would clean house for Harriet Dalrymple.

"I hope Ada does come home," said Will. "We still haven't seen our grandson, and he'll be two years old soon."

"And I want to see Judy," said Lucy. "She was my best friend until she left."

Jimmy did not miss Judy. She was the cousin closest to his age; when he was five, she had pushed him down and hit him with a stick; he had hated her ever since. Then he thought of when Tina had tackled him — but that was different — Judy was too freckled, and only eleven and had probably not started to develop yet like Tina. Besides, Judy was his cousin and — ick!

"Jessie," said Beth. "What are you going to do now that you've finished college? I haven't had a chance to ask you all summer."

"For now I'm just going to give piano lessons and maybe substitute teach."

"Where would you do that?" asked Eleanor.

"At Bishop Baraga," Jessie replied, "maybe also at J.D. Pierce or Graveraet."

"I go to J.D. Pierce," said Ellen. "So does Jimmy."

"So do Maud and me," said Lucy.

"Do you think you'll find a full-time teaching position?" asked Beth.

"I hope so," said Jessie, "but if not, that's all right. Mother needs me at home."

"You're a good girl the way you care for your mother," Margaret said.

"Yes, I'm lucky to have her," Thelma replied.

Roy had not been listening to the conversation; he had started to feel depressed, watching his brothers with their women. But he looked up when Thelma remarked how lucky she was. He wondered how she could say those words. He had always been fond of Thelma; when he first met her, he had thought her rather tactless, but as the years passed, he had realized they both lacked for love; he often thought the way the war had affected him was not unlike the merciless spreading of Thelma's disease; Beth said Thelma rarely complained about pain, but Roy guessed she bore her pain silently, as he bore his recurring mental anguish. He believed those who could not speak their pain were the ones who suffered the most. Thelma was lucky to have Jessie, and she deserved her because she had given of herself. Roy would have given of himself for Chloe, but the sacrifice had been denied him. He wished Jimmy had not asked him about love. Why couldn't the boy ask his father such questions? At forty, Roy felt he still had no answers.

Shaking off his melancholy, he asked, "Thelma, how have you been feeling?"

"I'm here, ain't I?" she laughed. "If everyday were as nice and sunny as this one, I'd be better in no time."

Beth smiled, proud of her cousin's spirit. She remembered a time before she married Henry when she feared she would be stuck taking care of Thelma, but her cousin had proven herself self-reliant, and even capable of taking care of others.

A buzzing overhead interrupted the conversation.

"It's an airplane!" said Maud.

"Yes, it is," said Will, craning back his neck to look.

"I don't know how anyone can go up in one of those," said Margaret. "I don't think they're safe at all."

"I'd fly in one if given a chance," Charles replied.

"Not while you're married to me, you won't," said Harriet.

"They're perfectly safe, Aunt Harriet," said Bill. "I flew in lots of planes over the Pacific during the war."

"You're just lucky you never crashed into the ocean," she replied.

"Or got shot down by the Japs," said Charles.

"Oh," gasped Linda, grasping her lover's arm at the horrid thought.

Bill laughed. "I saw lots of Japs get shot down, but hardly an American plane."

"They all deserved to be shot down after what they did at Pearl Harbor," said Charles.

"Oh, let's not talk about the war," said Margaret, but everyone ignored her. Bill could always tell an entertaining, if unbelievable story. He soon filled everyone's ears with stories of being shot at when landing on beaches, of tales of corpses piled into trucks, of Japanese ships destroyed by American submarines. The lurid tales delighted Jimmy, made Will and Henry proud of Bill, and caused the women to shake their heads sadly.

"Roy, did you see things like that?" asked Henry.

"Yes," Roy replied, wishing he had not been asked.

"What was it like?" asked Eleanor. "You never talk about the war."

"Awful," he said. "I wouldn't wish such horrors on my worst enemy."

"Not even the dirty Germans?" Jimmy asked.

"Hush, Jimmy," said Beth. She saw how Roy's eyes flashed at memories of the war. Eleanor lowered her eyes as Roy's face trembled. She would never again ask him about the war.

Margaret changed the subject. "Charles, I got a letter from Sarah yesterday."

"Oh, what did she say?"

"Everyone's fine. She said this is the last term Joseph will run for." Margaret turned to Linda to explain, "My brother-in-law is a U.S. Senator from California."

"Oh," said Linda, suitably awed by her lover's illustrious relation.

"Ma, Linda here's a singer," Bill said.

"Oh," said Margaret. "What kind of music do you sing?"

"I just sing in our church choir, but I've always wanted to be an opera singer. I think opera is so romantic. Bill doesn't like it though."

"Gives me a headache," chuckled Bill.

Roy had heard lots of opera music in France and Germany. He had even bought some opera records when he came home, but he made no comment.

"I love opera," said Margaret, "especially Victor Herbert and Sigmund Romberg. But Gilbert and Sullivan are good too."

Roy wondered whether his mother had ever heard of Wagner, Verdi, or Puccini.

"I don't know anything about opera," said Linda. "I just like the sound of it. I don't know whether I could ever sing it — I guess I'd have to learn Italian first."

"Mom, can we go play now?" Maud asked.

"Don't you want blueberry pie first?" Eleanor asked.

"Yes," said Maud. "I almost forgot about the pie, although I don't know how I could forget the best part of the meal."

The grownups laughed. The musical conversation was forgotten, allowing Margaret and Linda to hide their ignorance from one another. Pie was passed out. Despite tight belts and buttons ready to pop, no one turned down a piece.

After eating, Linda took out two breath mints and gave one to Bill. When she offered to help clean up, Margaret said, "Oh no, you're our guest."

"How about we go for another walk?" Bill said. In a minute, he and Linda had disappeared into the woods.

"She seems like a nice girl," said Margaret, "very elegant."

Eleanor rolled her eyes at Beth. "Wearing gloves doesn't make a lady, especially not when a girl will wander alone in the woods with a young man."

Beth resisted giggling by insisting Henry eat the last spoonful of spaghetti.

"Henry, I don't know how you keep from getting fat with Beth cooking for you," said Thelma.

"Henry doesn't gain a pound no matter what he eats," said Will. "He's been like that since he was a little boy. Not like the rest of us, hey, Beth?"

Beth was well over two hundred pounds, but nothing Will said ever riled her. He had been a good friend to her father in his last years, and not a few times, he had proven himself her ally against Margaret.

"Well, Pa," said Henry. "Are we going to sit around with the women, or are we going to fish some more?"

"After all that eating," Will replied, "I think I need to take a little walk first."

"Can I come, Grandpa?" asked Ellen.

"Me too?" asked Maud.

"Can I go too, Grandpa?" asked Lucy.

"Of course," said Will.

The three girls followed Grandpa down the trail in the opposite direction Bill and Linda had gone; Will knew it would be a mistake for three little girls to follow their amorous uncle and his girlfriend, no matter how ladylike Margaret thought Linda.

"This is where we were playing before, Grandpa," said Ellen as the trail curved into a little cove along the lake. "I was pretending to be that Indian princess buried at Presque Isle, and Lucy and Maud were young ladies coming to Marquette way back in the 1800s."

Will laughed. Way back in the 1800s. Was that century he remembered so vividly really "way back"?

"You mean you were pretending to be Charlotte Kawbawgam?" he asked.

"Yes," said Ellen. "My daddy told me she was an Indian princess."

"Did I ever tell you I knew Charles and Charlotte Kawbawgam?" asked Will. "It was Charlotte's father, Chief Marji Gesick, who led the white men to where the iron ore was. If it hadn't been for that, there might never have been the city of Marquette, and none of us would live here today."

But the girls' interest in history was limited to a princess having once lived in the area.

"Did the princess have a palace, Grandpa?" Maud asked.

"No, the Kawbawgams lived like most Indians, in a lodgehouse, and later in a little cabin at Presque Isle."

"Oh," said Ellen. She was not sure what a lodgehouse was, but it must have been disappointing to live there when other princesses had palaces.

"Maybe when the princess was a little girl," said Maud, "she had a dollhouse shaped like a palace. Grandpa, do you think anyone made her a dollhouse like the one you made me and Lucy?"

"Maud, shh!" exclaimed her sister. "You weren't supposed to say anything."

"You made them a dollhouse, Grandpa?" asked Ellen, feeling she would cry.

"Yes, dear," Will said, "but I'm making you one too. It was supposed to be a surprise."

"Oh," said Ellen.

"You should see ours, Ellen. It's beautiful. It's got — " Maud began, not thinking to apologize for failing to keep her grandfather's secret.

"Can mine be two stories?" Ellen asked. "Our house is only one story, but yours and grandma's is two, and I like two better."

"Of course," said Will.

"Will you make it tomorrow?" Ellen asked.

"It'll take me a while I imagine," said Will. "I have lots of other work to do, but I promise you'll have it for Christmas."

"I'm not worried," said Ellen. "I always wanted a dollhouse and now I'm going to get one. I just wish Christmas wasn't so far off." She was so excited she skipped down the trail.

"Here, girls," Will said, digging in his fishing jacket's pocket to retrieve a handful of Hershey's chocolate kisses. Lunch had been delicious, but Will believed meals should end with chocolate. "Listen to your grandpa now. These are the only kinds of kisses you should ever accept because they're the only kind that'll never get you in trouble."

Lucy laughed as she took hers; Ellen and Maud needed her to explain the joke to them.

"Actually," said Will, "it's not completely true that these kisses won't bring you trouble. Your grandma would be furious with me if she knew I had them. I always hide candy from her in my coat pockets. She's convinced all the sugar will kill me, but I can't help that us Whitmans have always had sweet tooths."

"Is that why you make such good sugar cookies, Grandpa?" asked Lucy.

"Yes, my grandmother taught me to make those when I was a boy. And you should have seen the sweets my Grandpa Whitman would eat. We used to joke that he liked a little coffee with his sugar."

Grandpa had had a grandpa and grandma! The girls found that hard to imagine. He seemed so old they could not picture him as anything but a grandfather.

But Grandpa could remember many family picnics when he had been no older than his granddaughters, picnics with his father, grandparents, brother and sisters. Will found it hard to believe they were all gone now — except Sylvia. A niece in Chicago he had never met had written that spring that his sister Mary had died. He and Mary had never been close, but he had felt troubled by her death. He wondered whether the niece had written to Sylvia.

He knew he should call his sister — his nephew had told him last week that Harry Cumming was not in the best of health.

The girls were becoming bored with their walk, and Will itched to fish some more. He could still remember the first time he had gone fishing, when he was only four, and his father had taken him down to the Chocolay River. How his father would have liked to be here today! Jacob Whitman would have been pleased to see how well his son had done for himself — perhaps Will was not as prosperous as his father had been — but there had been reasons for that, too long ago to worry about now. His large, happy family had more than compensated for a few disappointments. Life had been good to him.

A cool Canadian breeze blew off the lake, a sure sign that another of Upper Michigan's shortlived summers was nearing its end. Another season had passed but glorious autumn and a beautiful white winter would follow. Will hoped it would not be too cold to go ice fishing this winter. He picked up his pace, forcing his granddaughters to trot along beside him. He wanted to catch at least one fish before the day was over.

As he came back into the clearing, he heard Margaret singing.

"Do you know this one?" Margaret asked before launching into "After the Ball." Linda was smiling good-naturedly. She professed to be impressed with Mrs. Whitman's superb voice.

The granddaughters stared at Grandma, always surprised by her quaint old songs. Will found his chair and fishing pole.

Henry rolled his eyes in his mother's direction.

Will sang out, "Shut up, Maggie! You're scaring the fish!"

Margaret giggled. She knew Will was only kidding, but she hoped the remark did not make Linda think they were vulgar people.

"Well, Ma, Linda and I ought to head out," said Bill.

"Where are you kids going?" Will called over his shoulder.

"Linda wants me to take her to a dance in Escanaba tonight," Bill replied.

"Escanaba?" said Margaret. "That's so far away. Drive carefully and watch for deer."

"Can you imagine, Margaret," said Harriet after everyone waved goodbye to the young couple. "When I was a girl I never would have expected a boy to take me to Escanaba. The horse never would have pulled the wagon that far."

"Times sure have changed," said Thelma.

"I think you got one, Beth!" Henry shouted as his wife's fishing pole started to wiggle. Everyone watched Beth reel in her great catch. In another minute, Henry shouted he also had a bite.

"Look at that," said Will. "No catches all day, and then two within a couple minutes."

Once the luck had started, it seemed destined to last. Beth caught another. Then Will got two bites in a row. Then Roy, who had been fishing off a rock farther down the shore, came back with three. Finally, Jimmy caught one. Now everyone was content.

"It looks like rain," said Harriet.

Across the lake, storm clouds could be seen moving in.

"You can tell autumn is coming," said Thelma.

"It was a beautiful day while it lasted," said Jessie.

"Yes, it was," Margaret replied.

"Let's pack up before we all get drenched," said Beth, closing her and Henry's tackle boxes.

"Mama, can Ellen sleep over tonight?" asked Maud.

Beth and Eleanor discussed it, then agreed it would be all right. Ellen piled into the car with her aunt and cousins while Henry promised to stop by later to drop off his daughter's pajamas.

Jimmy sulked. He did not want to go home with his parents while Ellen got to have more fun. He wished Uncle Roy had married; then he might have had boy cousins to have a sleep over with.

Everyone departed with goodwill — well, maybe the poor fish were not so happy — but everyone who could be expected to be happy was — even Harriet whose potato salad had been such a hit. But for Ellen, the best part of the day was yet to come. At her first all girl slumber party, she saw her cousins' beautiful dollhouse. Then she went to sleep dreaming of the equally magnificent dollhouse her grandfather would build her.

Roy was the only one who went home by himself. He would spend his second night alone in his cabin. He was anticipating delicious reclusive isolation. The cabin was within walking distance of the Huron Mountain Club, where he continued to work, yet in the midst of the great northern forests, far enough from civilization to make him feel safe from mankind.

Roy had isolated himself into a rut by obsessing over a war he could not change and moping over a woman he could not have. A psychologist might have told him to forget the past and participate in social activities, but Roy felt that to go on with life's normal activities would be a charade. He still saw his family, still worked at the Club to earn a few extra dollars, but most days, he sought isolation and escape from the confines he thought society had inflicted upon him. Feeling the agonizing truth of Thoreau's words: "The mass of men lead lives of quiet desperation," he had followed Thoreau's example: "I went to the woods because I wished to live deliberately, to front only the essential facts of life, and see if I could not learn what it had to teach, and not, when I came to die, discover that I had not lived."

He wanted to live by understanding his life. He wanted to understand why he was not happy, if happiness mattered, and if he could transcend his pain. In isolation, he intended to learn to live with himself, to free himself from fear, disappointment, and personal flaws. After he had seen the brutalities of a concentration camp and how its victims had endured, he wondered what truths if any existed, and why some people despair while others triumph over distress. He had many questions, and in the silence of his own solitude, he now sought answers to an understanding of all he had experienced in life.

Tonight he told himself he should celebrate the beginning of his experiment, his quest for self-knowledge. He poured himself a glass of wine from a bottle sitting on a bookshelf Henry had built for him. Then he turned on his Victrola. He had no electricity in his little cabin; he wanted his life to be as simple as possible, but he had given into having an old crankup Victrola found in his parents' attic. Then he had bought a number of old opera records he had learned to love while in Europe. Placing *Rigoletto* on the turntable, he crossed his one nearly bare room, picked up his wine glass, and slouched onto his bed while Verdi drowned the atmosphere and floated out into the forests.

Perhaps the forest animals paused, the squirrels and chipmunks rising on their forelegs better to hear the musical air; the birds perhaps acknowledged their music was surpassed by the lovely human voice. Eternal love was vowed by the young Gilda to her handsome Walter Malde. Only, for Roy, the names should have been his and Chloe's, for his heart was equally promised.

> Dear name, within this breast,
> Thy mem'ry will remain!
> My love for thee confess'd,
> No power can restrain!

Did Chloe still feel that way for him? He hoped so. He could not stop thinking about her, especially today after Jimmy had asked him whether he had ever been in love. For ten years, never seeing her once in that time, he had loved Chloe. He wondered whether Jimmy suspected his secret, had a glimmer of understanding. He hoped the boy would never suffer such blissful agony.

The soprano's voice made Roy feel a tickling in his nose, then a misting up of his eyes. No, he would not let himself become depressed again. He jumped up from the bed, set his wine glass on the table and yanked the needle off the record. But it was too late. He went to the bookshelf, pulled down the volume of Matthew Arnold's poetry, and turned to the words,

> Ah, love, let us be true
> To one another! . . .

Just below them, squeezed between the pages of the book, was his only photograph of Chloe. She had mailed it to him in the first letter she had written after she moved away. Years had passed now since he had received a letter from her. He was being foolish still to care so deeply for a woman who had probably forgotten him. Why did he let himself remain in this agony? Before he could stop himself, before he could change his mind, he tossed the book on the bed. Then he tore Chloe's photograph into four pieces and threw it in the garbage can outside his door.

"She never even writes to me!" he shouted into the forest. He returned into the cabin and tossed himself on the bed. He gave way to the tears that overcame him. Ten years. Ten wasted years. The pain was still so terrible. Day after day he hoped Fate would be kind and either let him die or bring him together with her. During the war, the pain had been so intense he had often wished to be killed. So many men, better than he, had died in that war. Why had his pathetic life been spared? He cried until exhausted, until all the pain of that day, of seeing his brothers with women, of his nephew's questions, of his loneliness, of all the love lacking in the world, were whispered from his dry, aching throat. Then in the humid heat of evening, he slept a restless sleep.

He awoke, disoriented, surprised to find himself alone in his small cabin. The humidity broke with a sudden crash of thunder. Rain pounded on the cabin roof. Then he remembered what he had done. Scrambling up from the bed, he ran to the door; straining his eyes in the gathering dusk, he dug through the open garbage can to rescue the photograph pieces before the rain could damage them.

"I'll buy some scotch tape next time I go into town," he thought. He placed the photograph pieces on the kitchen cupboard to dry. Then he watched the rain, and love rose up in him again, until long after dark.

❦   ❦   ❦

What Will had thought a pleasant Canadian breeze turned into a terrific thunderstorm. When Henry went to his sister's house to bring Ellen her pajamas, he was caught in a downpour. Although only outside a few minutes, exposure to the rain gave him a severe cold; within a week, he was bedridden with bronchitis and pneumonia.

Since childhood, Henry had suffered frequent bouts of illness. His weak lungs had never quite recovered from his premature birth. That September, Henry spent more days in bed than at work. When the doctor started to make house calls, Ellen began to cry, convinced the doctor's presence meant her father was dying.

After diagnosing his patient, the doctor took Beth aside. "I know this may not be possible, but I really believe it would be best for Henry to move to a warmer climate."

"Oh," said Beth, "we could never leave Marquette. All our family is here."

"Well, if he continues to live here, he's only going to keep getting sicker and weaker," the doctor replied.

Beth thanked the doctor and promised to consider his suggestion, but she had no intention of moving. She worried about her husband's health, yet she laughed when she told Henry the doctor's recommendation.

"Oh, I'll be fine," said Henry. "I'm stronger than the doctor knows. I just happened to catch an extra strong bug this time. We can't leave Marquette. Ma was so upset when Ada moved away that I couldn't put her through that again."

A couple days later, on one of those stunningly warm days in early October, which trick a person into half-believing winter will never come, Beth was outside, hanging her laundry on the clothesline. Mrs. Rushmore happened to be passing by, and spotting Beth in the backyard, she stopped to inquire how Henry was feeling.

"He went to work today," said Beth, "although I wanted him to stay home and rest another day. He's just a stubborn workaholic. We don't need money so bad he has to kill himself."

And then, Beth felt the need to relieve what preyed on her mind. She would not mention it to any of the family, but Mrs. Rushmore was safe to tell what the doctor had suggested.

"But where would you go if you did move?" Mrs. Rushmore asked.

"I don't know," said Beth, although she had already thought it over. "California, I imagine. Henry has relatives out there."

"Oh yes, the Senator," said Mrs. Rushmore, nodding her head.

"He has a cousin close to his age there," Beth said. She had never met Theo Rodman, but she had heard plenty about him. She had no desire to be near the California relatives, but the only other people they knew in a warm climate were Ada's family; Beth did not want to go to Louisiana — the climate would be too humid.

"My nephew lives in California," said Mrs. Rushmore. "He does construction work and makes good money. California is growing in such leaps and bounds that you'd probably be rich in no time with all the building Henry could do out there."

"I don't know," Beth replied, then stuck clothespins in her mouth to prevent further discussion.

But when Henry came home, Beth saw how exhausted he was. She knew he was still not fully recovered from his illness. She started to think they should move, then rejected the idea by the time she had supper on the table, but when Henry started to cough, she considered it again. When she kissed the children goodnight, she told herself she could not take them from their grandparents; then she considered that moving would relieve the constant strain she felt of being around Margaret. Still, Henry would sorely miss his father and brothers. But when he complained of being cold, and when he began to shiver, she feared he would have a relapse.

Once they had crawled into bed, Beth said, "Henry, I think we should reconsider whether we should move. Mrs. Rushmore told me her nephew in California is doing really well in construction, and you do have family out there. The climate would be so much better, and the opportunities for the children might — "

Henry coughed. Beth handed him a cough drop from the bedside table.

"It's not that I want to move," she said, "but your health — I mean, I'm sure you're fine, but what would I do if I lost you? I can't raise the children alone. And it's not like we couldn't ever come home to visit."

Henry sat up, sucked on his cough drop and said nothing. He felt miserable. His head was congested, his chest had ached for a month. Sometimes he found it hard to breathe. He was always so cold. And it was not even winter yet; he dreaded being sick again. But he said nothing. When he finished his cough drop, he lay back down. Beth knew he did not want to talk about it. She put her arm around him; he placed his hand on hers and fell asleep although he would wheeze all night. Beth could not believe how hot his hand felt. She pulled away her own hand and rolled over, but she lay awake debating their choices.

❧   ❧   ❧

The next morning, Henry insisted on going to work. When he left, Beth watched out the window as he walked over to his parents' house rather than heading straight for his truck.

"Maybe Bill is working with him," Beth thought. "Funny he didn't mention it."

But she had no time to think further on it; she had to get the children off to school. She did not notice when Henry left, or if Bill went with him. But five minutes after the children had gone to school, Margaret and Harriet appeared at the back door.

"We thought we'd come over and have morning coffee with you," said Margaret. "I made us muffins."

"We women need to keep up with one another's lives," said Harriet. As usual, she had come empty-handed.

Beth let them inside, although she had plenty of work to do. She made coffee while her guests sat down at the table.

"Henry tells me," said Margaret, "that you're trying to make him move to California."

"Beth, why would you want to move out there?" Harriet asked.

So that was why Henry had gone over to his parents' house! Beth felt betrayed; she knew Henry did not blame her, that was Margaret's interpretation, but he should not have mentioned it to his parents until they had made a decision together. And now Margaret was playing dirty by bringing Harriet over to take her side. When her mother-in-law acted in this manner, Beth felt no qualms about moving away.

"The doctor," Beth carefully chose her words, "suggested we move to a warmer climate for Henry's health. We're considering California because Henry has family there."

"You'll never fit in with Sarah's family," said Harriet. "Ask Margaret. She knows what they're like. She went to Theo's wedding, remember?"

Margaret wanted Harriet to take her side, but she did not need to be reminded of how she had been ignored as a poor relation at Theo's wedding.

"It's not that we want to go to California," said Beth, "but we have to think of Henry's health."

"But all his family is here," said Margaret. "I know you don't have much family left, Beth, but you can't expect Henry to leave, and how can you take our grandchildren away from Will and me?"

Beth thought she would say a few choice words to Henry about leaking their personal business to his mother, but for now, she tried to stay calm.

"We haven't decided anything yet," she replied. "We probably won't go at all. We just talked about it because the doctor suggested we move."

"Half those doctors are just quacks," Harriet stated.

"Henry will feel worse if he moves away because he'll be homesick and lonely out there," said Margaret.

"Excuse me," said Beth. She disappeared into the bathroom before she lost her temper. Margaret blamed her for everything, no matter how hard she tried to make everyone happy. She did more for Margaret than Margaret's own daughters, and she took care of Margaret's son like no other woman would have. For nearly fifteen years she had lived next door to her mother-in-law. She had given up her first house so Henry's parents could live in it. She had waited years for the family to accept her before she married Henry. She had even quit going to church because Margaret hated Catholics. But there was a limit; she and Henry had a right to their own lives, and if they wanted to move away, they would. Margaret was not going to run the show anymore. And if they moved, it would be for Henry's health. Why could Margaret not understand that?

"Beth, are you all right in there?" Harriet knocked on the bathroom door.

"Yes, I just don't feel very good," Beth lied. If she came out right now, she felt there would be bigger family problems. After a couple more minutes, Harriet called, "We'll be going now, Beth. We only stopped for a minute. Charles is taking us to the market. Do you need anything?"

"No, thank you," Beth hollered back.

"Goodbye," called Harriet.

Margaret said nothing.

Beth heard the kitchen chairs scrape on the floor. A few words were spoken in a low tone. Then the back door opened and closed. Beth waited another minute, then emerged to wash her guests' dishes. She hoped they would not come back today.

🍁   🍁   🍁

"I've been thinking about California," Henry said at supper. "I think I'd like to see the place. Not that we have to move there, but maybe just go for a year to see whether my health improves."

"California!" said Jimmy. "I'd love to go to California."

"Isn't that where Mickey Mouse lives?" asked Ellen.

"Finish your pie, Ellen," Beth said.

"Can we swim in the ocean there?" asked Jimmy. "I'd like to take a boat out to look for whales."

"Jimmy, go do your homework. Your father and I need to talk," said Beth.

"I can do it later," he said.

"No, do it now. I'll check on you in an hour to make sure you did it."

Jimmy went to his room. Ellen went to hers once Henry confirmed that Mickey Mouse lived in Hollywood. Ellen dug out her Disney coloring book, then contentedly spent the evening with her crayons.

Beth cleared the table while Henry finished his dessert.

"Henry, you're not serious are you?"

"Why not?" he said. "My grandparents used to write in their letters about how beautiful California is."

"They have earthquakes there," Beth said.

"I could use a change of scenery," Henry replied. "All these years I've worked hard here. Maybe things would be easier for us there. I want us to have a better life."

Beth thought, "It'll be a better life if I don't have to deal with your mother." But she was surprised; Henry had never talked this way before; he was not the roaming type like Roy; his recent illness must have scared him more than she had thought.

"I'm just saying we should think about it," he said, carrying his plate to the counter. "I'm going to take a little nap. I don't think I'm quite over my cold yet."

"That's fine."

She was pleased when he kissed her cheek and said, "Doesn't much matter where we live, so long as we're together, right?"

"No, I guess not," she replied, but she began to run the dishwater so the noise would discourage him from saying more.

Henry went to lie down. After Beth finished the dishes, she went to check on him and found him fast asleep. The children joined her in the living room to listen to the radio. She told them not to be noisy because Daddy still did not feel well. When they asked her about California, she told them to hush so she could hear the radio program. She did not listen to a word, however, because her mind was racing. What if they did move to California? She had not told Henry how angry Margaret had made her that morning; he had looked so tired when he came home from work that she did not want to upset him. If they did move, Margaret would be furious, but neither would Margaret be around to tell her how to cook or how to raise her children. She saw no reason to stay. Her only family here was Thelma. Of course, there was Michael, but she rarely saw him; he had forsaken his family for the Church.

That thought gave Beth another concern.

After she put the children to bed, Henry called to her for some water and aspirin.

"I'm so cold," he complained.

"Well, it's a cold night," said Beth. "I wouldn't be surprised if it snows."

"If we lived in California," he coughed, "we wouldn't worry about snow."

"We can't make the trip in winter," said Beth. "If we went, it would have to be soon."

"I could build us a trailer. It wouldn't take more than a few weeks. We could leave within a month."

"Are you serious about this, Henry?"

"I don't know. We can think about it a few more days. I just hate feeling sick and helpless like this," he moaned. "I don't know how many more winters I can take this weather. I don't want to leave you and the children all alone anytime soon."

"Your family will be upset if we move away," said Beth, sitting down on the bed.

"I know. I'll miss them too, but they'll have to understand." He handed her back the glass of water, then lay down on his pillow. "Are you coming to bed now?"

"Yes, I'll go get ready." She went to the kitchen to put his glass in the sink. Then she went in the bathroom to put in her hair curlers. She wanted to talk further about California, but Henry was asleep when she returned to the bedroom.

The next morning, it snowed. Beth had always loved to watch the first snowfall with its intricate snowflakes gently floating to the ground; it excited her as much as a child who dreams of sledding and skating parties. But this year she dreaded winter. The cold air would only inflame Henry's lungs.

"Have you thought anymore about it, honey?" Henry asked at breakfast.

"About California? Yes, I'm willing to move, but on one condition."

He waited.

"I'm nervous about traveling across country. Anything could happen."

"It could," said Henry, "but I'm sure we'll be fine."

"Even so, I want to be safe," said Beth, taking a deep breath. "I won't go to California unless we have our marriage blessed by a priest and the children baptized in the Catholic Church."

Henry was not surprised, but he had to ask, "Why does it matter to you now after all these years?"

"It's always mattered to me. What do you expect when my brother is a priest? I always thought eventually when your mother — well, I've always wanted the children raised as Catholics, but now that they're half-grown, we're running out of time. I'm willing to move for your sake; can you do this for my sake?"

Henry thought it little to ask. Still, he said the obvious. "My mother won't like it."

"Your mother," Beth snapped, "has no business interfering in our marriage."

Henry guessed what a trial his mother was to Beth; he imagined there had been several difficult moments between the two women he had never been told about. Nor had he ever interceded in Beth's behalf.

"All right," he said. "If you want the marriage blessed and the children baptized, then it'll be done. We're a family after all."

Beth was grateful he had given in so easily.

"All right," she said. "I'll call St. Michael's tomorrow. It's the closest church. If I tell them my brother is a priest, I'm sure they'll do it."

Henry kissed her.

"I'm glad we're going to California," he said.

Every night during the week before Jimmy and Ellen were baptized, Beth explained to them what it meant to be a Catholic. She told them about the sacraments and the gifts of the Holy Spirit, the Beatitudes, the Stations of the Cross, the Mysteries of the Rosary, and everything else she could remember from her days at Bishop Baraga High School. She recited for them the "Our

Father," "Hail Mary," and the "Nicene Creed," hoping the beautiful words would inspire them. And she warned them under no circumstances to tell their grandparents they were becoming Catholics.

The evening of the baptism, Jimmy came inside for supper, stomped across the kitchen, slumped in his chair, and poked at his food.

"Jimmy, hurry and eat. We have to be to church in half an hour."

"I'm not going," he said. "I don't want to be a Catholic."

"Why not?" asked Henry. Beth looked dismayed.

"Just don't," he said.

"Jimmy, you're too young to know what you want," Henry told him. "Your mother and I know what is best for you."

"Grandma is older than me, and she doesn't think it's best for me," he mumbled, afraid to meet his parents' gaze.

Beth let out a little gasp. Henry coughed nervously. Ellen wondered what was wrong.

"Jimmy," Henry asked, "did you tell Grandma you're going to be baptized?"

"Not 'xactly," he grumbled.

"What do you mean, 'not exactly'?"

"I said I was going to become a Catholic, and — "

"Oh no!" Beth cried.

Ellen looked at her mother, still not understanding the problem.

"And what did she say?" Henry asked.

"She said if I become a Catholic, I'll never be allowed in her house again. I don't think it's fair at all that I have to become a Catholic. I like going over to Grandpa and Grandma's house, and none of my friends at school are Catholics, and I — "

"Jimmy," said Beth, "since you won't eat, go brush your teeth and put your good pants on. We have to leave in twenty minutes."

Jimmy looked at his father, but saw the same orders would come from him. He scraped his chair across the kitchen floor, then stomped off to the bathroom.

"Mama," asked Ellen, "can I still go to Grandpa and Grandma's house?"

"Of course," Henry replied.

"It hardly matters, Henry," said Beth, getting up to clear the table. "Once we move, the kids won't be going over there anyway."

"Do you think Ma took it seriously?" asked Henry.

"If she did, she'd be over here right now raising a fuss," said Beth. Then she scurried to get the kids out to the car before Margaret appeared on crusade to save her grandchildren's souls from popery.

❦   ❦   ❦

Mom had told them not to tell Grandma. But Jimmy had told Grandma anyway. Grandma was mad now. They would all be in trouble if she caught them. That was why they had to leave in the dark, to sneak to the church before Grandma saw them.

Ellen walked down the front steps of the house, looking next door to see whether Grandma would pull aside the curtains and catch them before they could escape.

"Hurry, Ellen, before you catch cold," said her mother, pushing her into the car.

What would Grandma do if she saw them leave? Would she know where they were going? Maybe Jimmy had not told her that. Jimmy was so stupid. She got in the car, and then Jimmy and Mom got in, and then Daddy. Daddy shut his door so loudly Grandma was sure to hear, and the engine was loud too. The car pulled out of the driveway. Even if Grandma ran down the street after them, she could not catch them now. They were safe.

It was only a few blocks to the church. Ellen knew where it was because it was across the street from her school, J.D. Pierce. She had never been in the church though. She had not even known it was a Catholic Church until her mother told her so a few days ago. She did not know what the difference was between being a Catholic and a Baptist, only that Grandma did not like Catholics. Maybe Grandma did not like that they would get baptized because Baptists do not get baptized. Did their name mean they were against being baptized? Ellen did not understand why a priest had to pour water over you. Mom said it was so the Holy Ghost would come into you, but Ellen did not think she wanted a ghost inside her.

Mom said she had always wanted Uncle Michael to baptize them, but yesterday Mom had said, "Uncle Michael spoke to Monsignor Zryd, who will do the baptism."

"What's a monseenyer?" Jimmy had asked.

"It's a priest," Mom had replied.

Ellen thought the priest's name sounded like "Monster Dread." The building he lived in looked scary enough to be a haunted house.

Until a few years ago, St. Michael's Church had been an abandoned college dormitory first built in 1900. The first president of the Normal School, Dwight D. Waldo, had lived there with his family and seventy college students. Eventually, the Diocese of Marquette had acquired the four story building, but they had only used it sporadically until World War II. The building had steadily disintegrated, so to turn it into a church during the war years, the top two floors had been removed and a church, convent, and school were established in the remainder of the building. Recently, a foundation had been laid to build a new Catholic school beside the old dormitory building. The new parish testified to the strength of religious faith in time of war and economic adversity, but to Ellen, the building was simply frightening.

Monsignor Zryd met the family at the church door. He welcomed Beth, remembering her from when she had attended St. Peter's Cathedral with her parents. Ellen felt nervous around the priest, but he smiled kindly, rather like Uncle Charles. Two altar boys were with Monsignor Zryd, both a couple years older than Jimmy. They were clad in black and white robes like the priest. Ellen did not know why they wore such strange clothes, but she thought them handsome as angels.

They walked through the church to the baptismal font. The priest asked Ellen and Jimmy whether they wanted to be baptized. Ellen looked at her mother, who nodded her head to tell her to say yes. Jimmy muttered, "Yeah." Ellen told the priest that she believed in God, Jesus, and the Holy Ghost. She was still afraid of the ghost, but she was more afraid to say she was afraid.

Finally, the holy water was poured over her head. She waited for something magical to happen, for her to feel like an angel, or else for the ghost to come get her because it had found out she was a naughty girl. But she only felt that the water was very cold. She watched Jimmy grimace when the priest made the sign of the cross on his forehead. Then Monsignor Zryd handed them their baptismal candles. Her parents never would have let her touch a candle. She did not think the priest very smart if he didn't know children weren't supposed to play with fire. She was relieved when he told her she could blow the candle out. Then she and Jimmy had to sit in one of the pews while they watched their parents' marriage be blessed. Ellen did not listen much. She looked over and saw Jimmy had shut his eyes. She felt sleepy, but she was afraid she would get in trouble if she closed her eyes.

As they drove home, Jimmy said, "I'm glad that's over. I don't want to go to church again."

"We'll be going to church regularly once we're settled in California," said their mother.

"Is Daddy going too?" asked Ellen.

"No, myself and the two of you."

"If Dad doesn't have to go, then I don't have to either," Jimmy said.

"When you're an adult," Henry replied, "you can decide for yourself whether you'll go to church, but until you're eighteen, you'll go with your mother."

"That stinks," said Jimmy.

"Don't you sass me, young man," Henry warned as they arrived home.

Jimmy knew when he was called "young man" he had better shut his mouth. They all went into the house. Ellen looked over at her grandparents' house to see whether they would be caught. But it was too late now. She was a Catholic.

"I suppose, Ellen," Jimmy said once they were inside, "that you'll grow up to be a nun. But you know what, nuns get none."

He roared with laughter, but Beth snapped, "Jimmy, I'll wash your mouth out with soap if I hear one more word from you tonight."

Ellen was stunned by her mother's anger. She did not know what Jimmy meant. She thought being a nun was a good thing. She thought being Catholic was supposed to make people good and holy, but everyone seemed angry now.

"Mom," she dared ask, "what do I say if Grandma asks me whether I'm a Catholic now? What if she won't let me in her house?"

"You tell her," Henry answered for his wife, "that if she has a problem, she can come talk with me. You don't discuss it with her, Ellen. Now go get ready for bed."

"All right," she said, but it was not all right. She did not like being Catholic, not if Grandpa and Grandma would not love her anymore.

Henry built a wooden trailer. By the first week of November, his family was ready to move. They loaded whatever they could into the trailer that would be their home for the next several months until they were out West and Henry found steady work. They sold or gave away any furniture or belongings they could not bring with them. The house was put up for sale. Will agreed to watch over it and wire the money when the house was sold.

While Henry built the trailer, Will worked to finish the dollhouse he had promised Ellen. She visited her grandfather in his woodshop everyday because she was worried the dollhouse would not be finished in time to take to California. But the morning the trailer was packed, and they were to leave, Henry and Beth decided the dollhouse was much too large to fit into the little trailer.

Ellen burst into tears. "Then I don't want to go to stupid California!"

When her father promised to build her another dollhouse once they reached California, she said, "It won't be as good as the one Grandpa built."

"Maybe I could mail the house to you once you get out there," said Will.

"Don't be silly," said Margaret. "It would cost a fortune to ship something that big across the country."

Then Margaret kissed Henry and her grandchildren and returned inside before she started to cry.

Beth remained glad they were going. Margaret knew the children were baptized, and although not a word had been spoken about it, she had been cold toward Beth ever since. Beth knew Margaret blamed her for everything, but she did not care. They had to go for Henry's health, and if Margaret could not understand that, nothing Beth said would change her mind.

"Don't worry. Everything will be fine," said Will as he hugged everyone goodbye. "We'll come visit you sometime."

"I hope so," said Beth.

Then the children were herded into the trailer. Soon the family was rolling down the street in their new portable home. They wondered when they would see Marquette again.

1949

Letters sent by Mrs. Henry Whitman to Marquette relatives.

January 2, 1949

Dear Thelma,

Happy New Year! I hope you and Jessie had a good Christmas. It was a lonely one for me. Henry and I only had money to buy the kids some candy, but fortunately we got some packages in the mail that Eleanor was kind enough to send. We are staying in Riverside now, but for Christmas we went to Los Angeles and spent the day with Henry's cousin, Theo Dalrymple, and his wife. Henry's aunt and uncle — the Senator — whom you've heard Margaret talk about constantly — live up in San Francisco so we haven't seen them yet, despite their telling Margaret they would visit and help us out if we needed anything. Henry found a job all on his own without any help, not that I think we would want help from his relatives. Christmas Day was a miserable experience. Theo tried to be friendly, but his wife looked down her nose at us through the entire visit. They have a son and daughter. The son, David, is Jimmy's age and the daughter, Rosalie, only two years older than Ellen. The girls tried to play together, but Rosalie is too spoiled to share her toys. The boys have nothing in common. Jimmy tried to talk about fishing, but David is lazy and not interested in doing anything except whining. It makes me thankful we are not rich because our children will grow up self-reliant. I for one don't care whether we ever go to visit Theo's family again, and I let Henry know that too.

Riverside is a bigger town than Marquette, but not at all as attractive. I did not know I would miss Lake Superior so much. I miss the snow too, although for Henry's health, I do not mind. It sure is lonely here without all my old friends and family. I want what is best for my family, but I'm not sure that living in California is for the best. I don't think Henry likes it here either, but he tries his best to be positive.

I am sorry to complain but I can't write as honestly to Henry's family, and I don't want to complain to Henry because he has a hard enough time of it just working. I'm sure everything will work out. I just need to get used to it. God would not have put it into our heads to go to California without a reason for it.

I hope you and Jessie are well. Write and tell me everything that is going on in Marquette.

Love, Beth

January 3, 1949

Dear Eleanor,

Now that we are settled, I can finally start to write some real letters. First of all, thank you so much for the Christmas presents you sent for Jimmy and Ellen. We did not at all expect them since we didn't think your parents would get the letter with our address in time even to send a Christmas card. The children will be sending you their own letters of thanks, but I wanted to thank you personally. It was a hard Christmas for all of us, our first away from the family. But I think we will soon adjust.

Henry has already found steady work. It is amazing to me all the building and construction that goes on even in the winter here since there is no snow and the temperatures are often in the 80s even for December and January.

The children are fine. Ellen does not like her school. I think she is just scared of all the Mexican children, but a few days ago, a new family came into the trailer park and they have a little girl. They are an American family, so now I hope Ellen will have a friend. There are lots of boys here, most a couple years older than Jimmy, but he seems to get along with them. I worry about him without the family's influence around him. He's at an age where he doesn't always want to listen to me and his father isn't always home to discipline him.

Henry's health has been fine since we got here. He insists he is glad we came, but he doesn't say much more than that. I am lonely for home myself, but I hope to make friends with some of the other ladies in the trailer park.

How is all the family? Do you think your mother is still angry with me? I know she is worried, but as a mother I felt baptizing the children was best for them. I know you are more understanding about it. How are Lucy and Maud? Ellen sure misses them. How is Ronald? I imagine he is busy with a new semester at the college.

Write soon as we miss you all.

Love, Beth

❧   ❧   ❧

Eleanor folded up her sister-in-law's letter. She was replacing it in its envelope when her husband came home for lunch.

"I have good news, honey," he said, kissing her on the cheek. "I've been offered a job at the University of Michigan for this fall."

Eleanor was startled. "But Ron, you never told me you applied for a job there."

"Because I didn't want to get your hopes up until I got the position."

"But," Eleanor fumbled for words, "we can't move there. It's so far from the family."

"Your family. What about mine?" he said.

"Your parents are gone. All you have is a brother in Lansing. That's miles from Ann Arbor. You'd hardly ever get to see him, and what about all our friends here, and the girls need to be near their grandparents and cousins, and — "

"It's a better job, Eleanor. It's more money," said Ronald, as if money were the only factor.

"I know, but — ." She did not know what to say. She slumped back in her chair.

"I thought you'd be happy about this," said Ronald. "I thought you'd be proud your husband is finally getting the recognition he deserves."

"I am proud of you," said Eleanor. "I'd be proud of you no matter what, but I don't want to move five hundred miles away at a moment's notice."

"Ann Arbor's a great city. There'll be more there for us. Better schools for the girls, better opportunities for them when they're older. I'll make contacts there who will help me rise even higher in my profession."

Eleanor noticed he did not mention what advantages Ann Arbor held for her.

"You're just being selfish," said Ronald, opening the cupboard to find a glass. He filled it at the sink, then quickly drank the water, as though his wife had drained all his energy.

"I just don't know why we have to go downstate," Eleanor said. "We have everything we need right here."

"Come on, Eleanor. There's nothing for us in this little town. Why are you making such a big deal over this? Ada and Louis moved all the way to Louisiana and Beth and Henry to California. We're only going downstate. We could still come back to Marquette to visit a couple times a year."

Eleanor remembered what Beth had said in her letter. 'It was a hard Christmas for all of us, our first away from the family.' Still Henry and Beth had moved. Everyone seemed to move these days.

"I don't know, Ron. I need some time to get used to the idea."

"I need to send my letter of acceptance."

"It's already Thursday," said Eleanor. "Will it make such a difference if you wait until Monday? The university will just think the letter was delayed in the mail."

"Why should I wait? So your mother can talk us out of it?"

Eleanor hated that he blamed her mother for everything. Trying to remain calm, she said, "I just think we need to consider all the pros and cons of moving and make the decision together."

"I don't see that there's much of a decision to make. We barely get by in this little house on my salary."

"Even if you made more money downstate, the cost of living is higher there," said Eleanor. "What advantage will that be? And my family — "

"Jesus Christ!" he shouted, banging his glass down on the counter. Then he stomped out of the house. Eleanor winced as the screen door slammed shut. Was he coming back for his lunch? She looked out the window and saw him walking back toward the college. Good, let him go without lunch. She wanted to call her mother, but it would only infuriate him more if her mother got involved.

Was she being selfish? They had lived here all these years, and Ron had hated it more each year. He constantly complained about all the hicks in the area, the stupid students, the lack of cultural activities beyond gutting a deer or falling into a river while ice fishing. He said the winters were mind numbing and the whole town lacked intellectual stimulation. Once he had even had the nerve to say all her relatives were mentally shallow. He had said he could breathe better in the freedom of a big city. Eleanor wondered how a person could breathe at all where it was so polluted. Twice she had been to visit Ron's mother in Detroit. All the while they were there, Eleanor had felt constricted by the giant, concrete-covered, filthy, crime-ridden city; only after crossing the Mackinac Straits into Upper Michigan did she feel able to breathe without chronic fear.

She remained at the kitchen table until her coffee grew cold. She should get up and do her chores, but she felt incredibly lethargic. "I always feel sleepy after lunch," she lied to herself. She had barely nibbled her sandwich. Her entire system seemed in shock, wanting to shut down rather than deal with the crisis.

She sat there for hours until she dozed off. Her fingers had been around the handle of her coffee cup, and now her arm fell, dropping the cup to the floor. It did not break, but the sound startled her awake. She looked at the clock. Quarter to three. The girls would be home soon. Coffee was all over the floor. She better clean it up before they asked how she had made such a mess. She got up and wiped the floor. Then she cleared the table. She quickly washed the dishes, but the girls came home before she finished. She tried to be cheerful; she asked them about school, their homework, and whether they were going out to play. She would not alarm them until a decision had been made.

"Hello," Ronald muttered when he came home. The girls were playing in their rooms by then, so he felt free to ask Eleanor, "Have you come to your senses yet?"

"It's just so sudden, Ron," she said, but that only made him grab the newspaper in a huff, and go into the living room.

Eleanor busied herself with making supper; she forgot to turn on the oven; then she nearly burnt the gravy. Her head was so addled. She could not even think about moving away when first she had to placate her husband.

After supper, Ronald said he was going to the library. Eleanor played monopoly with the girls; Lucy got mad at her for helping Maud. Then Maud won and Lucy pouted when she went up to bed. Eleanor tucked them both in, then returned downstairs to wait up for her husband. By that time, she knew the library was closed, yet Ron still did not come home. She suspected he was down at the Tip Top Cafe, hanging out with his idolizing students. He was always seeking to be worshiped for his mind.

At eleven, she went to bed. He did not come home until after midnight. She pretended to be asleep when he crawled into bed.

But he reached for her in the blackness. It was his way of making up. She did not pull away.

Afterward — she lay awake, upset, pleased, confused. He snored beside her. In the early morning hours, she drifted into such a heavy sleep she did not hear the alarm clock go off. Ronald got the girls off to school and himself off to work. When the first glimmer of daylight came through the bedroom curtains, Eleanor woke in confusion to find the bed empty. Then she remembered he had been with her during the night, and her heart instantly sang out that she loved that man. If he wanted to move, she would follow where he led her.

❦   ❦   ❦

Easter Sunday evening. The day had been filled with church, family, and Sunday dinner. Now that everyone had gone home, Margaret collapsed in her old rocking chair while Will lied down on the couch. She was exhausted, but a letter from Sarah had come yesterday, and she had still not had time to read it. Now she put on her glasses, tore open the envelope, unfolded the pages, and read aloud the passages she thought would interest Will, oblivious to his desire to nap.

"Listen to this," Margaret read, adding commentary inbetween. " 'I don't know how Henry and Beth can stay in that little trailer among all those poor people. It's not civilized' — Like it's any of Sarah's business — 'I know Joseph is sorry he wasn't reelected for another term, but at his age, it's probably for the best. Now we have time to do all the things we never could before. We're sailing for Hawaii in a couple weeks.' — Can you imagine! Hawaii! — 'We're going to redecorate the house when we return. It hasn't been done in nearly ten years now and it's looking decidedly out of date.' — She just laid a new floor last year! — 'President Hoover was here to visit. I can't imagine the Depression was his fault when he's such a charming man.'"

"I bet he is," Will sarcastically interrupted.

Margaret continued, " 'Spring here has been beautiful, not at all like those slushy springs back in Michigan. I imagine all your snow still hasn't melted. Theo got a promotion at work; he works so hard he deserves it.' "

The last comment made Margaret want to rip up the letter.

"Works so hard," she scoffed. "I never saw such a lazy young man. Henry works his fingers to the bone and scarcely has a dollar to show for it, yet he's worth two of Theo."

"Well, life isn't completely fair," said Will, "but I bet on any given day, Henry is happier than Theo."

"Sarah makes me so angry," said Margaret. "She always writes just to brag. As if I don't already know how filthy rich they are, how beautiful California is, or that they know all the famous people. And really, who ever heard of people their age going to Hawaii? I almost hope there's a hurricane while they're there."

"Maggie," Will moaned, "if reading her letters upsets you so much, then don't read them."

"If you're going to put your feet on the couch, then take off your shoes," Margaret replied. "She's my sister. How can I not read her letters, I'd like to know?"

Will kicked his shoes onto the floor.

"I just mean there's no reason to get upset. Nothing she says can make any real difference to us."

"It just bothers me when less deserving people have so much. We've worked hard all our lives, and Sarah's hardly worked a day. She just got lucky when she married Joseph. He's the only reason she has so much."

Will sighed. He wished he could have been rich for Margaret's sake. But he tried to console her with words that would have made Roy proud.

"What do they really have?" he asked. "Just a bunch of stuff. We have stuff too. Maybe not French silk sofas, maybe just an old couch with an afghan over it, but you can still sit down on it just like a French silk one. We've done all right for ourselves, Maggie. We've got children and grandchildren, and we all love each other. That's enough."

"At least Sarah's son is nearby," Margaret still complained, although she knew Will was right. "When Eleanor moves, Bill will be the only child we still have here. Roy hardly comes to see us so you can't count him. I love Bill, but he's not dependable like Henry or Eleanor. Bill is just — "

She did not need to say more. Bill had become the worry of his parents' old age. They had hoped he would return home from the war to settle down and raise a family. They had hoped the same of Roy, but his morose, hermit behavior was easier for them to take than Bill's running around. Of all Bill's girlfriends, Margaret had liked Linda the best. Linda was pretty, fashionable — any girl who still wore gloves had Margaret's approval — and Linda loved the opera. But last October, Bill had broken it off with her. Then there had been Marianne, but he broke up with her the week before Christmas. Next came Doreen, but while still with her, he started seeing Nadine on the side. Then at Easter dinner today, he had shown up with Rosalind — none of the family had even known she existed until she walked in the door. Apparently, Nadine was out of the picture. Margaret hoped Bill had at least told her it was over. Since he had moved out on his own last year, Margaret could not keep up with his girls, and when she tried, he just laughed and confessed, "I know I'm a bit of a bad boy, but that's the way I like it." He had even quit going to church. What was a mother to do?

"We did our best with Bill, just like with all our children," Will said. "He'll find his way eventually. You know the Bible says if you love a child and raise him in the right path, he won't stray from it when he's older."

"Maybe if we had more money, though," said Margaret, "we could have helped the children more so they would not have moved away and — "

"Henry left for his health, and Ada because of her husband. If Eleanor goes it will be because of Ronald. None of them left because we failed them in any way."

"I would just feel better if we had money to take care of them when we're gone. I don't want to leave this earth without knowing they'll be safe and secure."

"They will be," said Will. "We taught them to be self-reliant and to make good decisions. As for us having more money, all the money in the world would not have made this couch more comfortable to sleep on, or your cooking better, or my wife more beautiful. We can't understand life, Maggie. We just have to accept and be thankful for what we have."

Margaret took off her bifocals and laid Sarah's letter on the side table. She stood up and pushed Will's feet off the couch, then sat down beside him. He sat up, and they cuddled together.

"I'm thankful for you," he said.

"I don't know why," she replied. "I was never cut out to be a farmer's wife, and my house is a mess, and I never helped your career like Sarah did for Joseph."

"You've made me happy. Remember that day I was going to work at the Longyear house and it was snowing out. I was really depressed that day, and then I heard you coming down the street, singing at the top of your lungs. I knew then you were the girl who would make it easy for me to get by from day to day. Just coming home to you every night has made it all worthwhile."

"You're a good liar," she said, kissing his wrinkled old cheek. They sat together for an hour, scarcely saying anything, just basking in each other's company.

Will came down with pneumonia the following week. Considering how he had worried about Henry the autumn before, his sickness was cruelly ironic. In a couple days, the illness had developed into bronchitis. He was so weak, he had to be checked into the hospital. He had a high fever and a horrific cough that his chest and lungs could not bear. His third day in the hospital, in the early morning hours, Will passed away. Margaret was holding his hand when he left this world.

"Ma, you need your sleep," Bill said after he had brought her home from the hospital. "People will be coming over later, and there'll be plenty to do. Get some rest now."

Margaret went to her and Will's room, changed into her nightclothes and crawled into bed, despairing over the loneliness of Will not being beside her. She cried softly into her pillow. He had been her strength all these years, although he had always pretended she was his. She could not imagine life without him.

Bill called Eleanor to come stay with their mother. Then he drove up the Big Bay Road to tell Roy their father was gone.

Eleanor found her mother asleep when she arrived so she did not know what to do. She had been stunned when her father went to the hospital; he was a fighter who had scarcely been sick a day in his life. His death was a shock to her. Her first thought was to call Henry — he would know what to do. But California was hours behind Marquette. Henry was probably not out of bed yet. He and Beth would not be able to make it home for the funeral anyway. And even if they could, it would make more sense to call them once the funeral arrangements were made. Maybe she should call Ada first, but she doubted Ada would come home for the funeral either.

"I'll call the radio station and *The Mining Journal*," she decided. "Then when Mother wakes up and Bill gets back, we can go to the funeral home."

The death would need to be announced so people would know. Then they would come over to help console her mother. Eleanor did not know what to say to her mother right now, her own grief was so deep. Trying not to think about her father, she looked through the city directory until she found the number for the local radio station. Then she dialed the telephone.

"WDMJ Radio. How may I help you?"

"Hello, my father just died. I wanted to have you announce it over the radio, please."

"Uh, okay, um, just a minute," said the girlish sounding receptionist, scrambling on the other end, presumably to find a pencil. "Okay, what's the name of the — um — dead person?"

"Mr. William Whitman."

"Occupation?"

"He was a carpenter."

"Oh," said the woman. "We only read the obituaries of prominent people."

Eleanor hesitated a moment. It was only nine in the morning. Her day had already been trying enough. She had just lost her father, and her husband wanted her to move away, and now this woman was saying her father's life had been unimportant.

"My father was prominent," she stated. "Everyone in Marquette knew him. He built some of this city's finest homes."

"I'm sorry, ma'am. If he were a doctor or a lawyer, or — "

"My father built the doctors and lawyers' houses. He built beautiful homes for them, for Dr. Fisher and many others. He helped to build the First National Bank and the Post Office on Washington Street. He helped to dismantle the Longyear Mansion when they moved it out East, and he helped to build Granot Loma for the Kaufmans, and — "

"All right," huffed the radio chit. "What year was he born?"

"1880."

"Place of birth?"

"Marquette."

"Parents' names?"

"Jacob Whitman and Agnes Henning."

"And he died when?"

"This morning."

"Any survivors?"

"His wife, Mrs. Margaret Dalrymple Whitman, and five children."

Eleanor gave her siblings and their spouses' names. Then as an afterthought, she added, "Oh yes, and a sister, Mrs. Harry Cumming." She doubted she would even recognize her aunt if she saw her, but Eleanor knew her father would want Aunt Sylvia included.

"All right, ma'am," said the radio chit.

"Thank you. I'll be listening to hear it read during the next news broadcast."

"Good day, ma'am."

"Thank you. Goodbye."

Eleanor hung up the phone, then sat down at the dining room table, rankled by the phone confrontation. How dare that snooty girl suggest her father was unimportant! As if every human life were not of the greatest importance? And her father had been prominent. He came from one of the oldest and finest families in Marquette. If he had not lived a more important life, that was only because he had given selflessly to take care of his brother and sister, his wife, his children, and grandchildren, and he had been loved by them all.

Wasn't that the most important thing a person could do, love and be loved?
Her father had known hundreds of people in this city. Had probably built a
hundred homes. Those houses were his memorial; they would be standing long
after that snooty radio girl was dead and buried.

Eleanor had a horrible headache. She felt so alone, so helpless. Coffee would
help; she made a pot and while she waited for it to brew, she decided she would
call Henry. It would be six o'clock in California now. Henry had always been
an early riser, up and ready to work at dawn. She hated to give him the bad
news, but her mother was too upset to do it, and Bill had already been burdened with telling her and Roy. She had always felt closest to Henry of all her
siblings. He would want to hear it from her.

"Hello," Beth answered the phone.

"Is Henry there?" Eleanor asked. She was afraid to say who she was; then
they would know immediately something was wrong because she was calling
long distance.

"Just a moment."

Beth sounded tired. The telephone must have woken her.

"Hello," said Henry.

"Henry, it's Eleanor. I have some bad news."

Eleanor started to cry. She wanted to be strong for her brother, but instead,
she found she needed him to be strong for her.

"What's wrong?" he asked.

She tried to speak but sobs constricted her throat.

"Eleanor, what's wrong? Has Ronald been mean to you?"

She was surprised by the question. Did the family suspect what her husband
was like?

"No," she said, "it's Pa. He's been sick with pneumonia and bronchitis. He
died this morning."

Silence. Then in the background, she heard Beth ask, "What's wrong,
Henry?"

"Henry, are you okay?" Eleanor asked.

"Yes, it's just — I don't know what to say. It's — how is mother taking it?"

That was Henry, always worried about others.

"What's wrong?" Eleanor heard Beth ask again.

"Ma's pretty shaken up," said Eleanor, "but she's sleeping now. She stayed
with him all night. She was holding his hand when he went."

"I can't believe it," Henry said. Then she heard him tell Beth, "Pa died."

Ellen could be heard crying. Eleanor imagined Beth was trying to comfort her. She realized she had not told her own girls yet. They had left for school just before Bill called her.

"I'm so sorry, Henry," Eleanor said. "I thought I should be the one to tell you. I know you won't be able to come for the funeral, but — "

"When is it?"

"We don't know yet. We're going to the funeral home this afternoon to arrange everything."

"I don't know whether I can come, but — "

"Don't worry. We don't expect you to come. I'm sure Ada won't."

"Did you tell her yet?"

"No, I'm going to call her next."

"How are you taking it?"

"I'm okay," she said. "I have to look after Ma; that'll keep me busy."

"I'm sorry, Eleanor. I wish I were there. I wish I had never come out here. We never would have if we thought Pa would — I just can't believe it."

"I know," she said.

Then neither knew what to say.

"Well, you probably have to go to work, Henry. I'll let you go."

"Okay. Tell Ma how sorry I am. Maybe I'll call her tonight."

"She'd like that," said Eleanor. "Give my love to Beth and the kids."

"I will. Thanks, Eleanor. Goodbye."

Eleanor hung up the phone, then dug for her handkerchief. Her mother always said a lady is never without her handkerchief. She did not have hers today; she had been in too much of a rush after Bill called with the shocking news. She wiped her eyes on her sleeve, too upset to care. Ada would have to wait. She did not have it in her to give bad news to anyone else right now. She swallowed down her entire cup of coffee, then poured another. She carried it into the living room and sat down in her mother's chair. Catching sight of an old photograph album in the corner, she pulled it out and slowly flipped through the pages. Most of the pictures were taken when she was a girl — during the First World War and the '20s. She remembered her father so well from those years. He looked so strong and capable in the pictures.

She heard her mother's feet shuffling about upstairs. She shut the album and hid it away, as if ashamed to have found an outlet for her grief. Then she sat stiffly in the chair until her mother came downstairs. She wondered what they would say to one another.

Despite Eleanor's confrontation with the radio chit, Sylvia Cumming learned of her brother's death from *The Mining Journal* obituary the next day. She did not tell her husband until after she had fed him supper and helped him out of his wheelchair to use the bathroom. Harry Cumming had consumed so much alcohol during his life that his liver was rotted, and he could scarcely walk. Despite her own seventy-seven years, Sylvia was his sole caretaker.

"Harry, my brother Will died," she said, showing him the newspaper, although he could not see well enough to read it. "The funeral's the day after tomorrow. I want to go."

All afternoon, she had rehearsed how she would tell him and how he would respond. She should have known whatever she did, the result would be the same, an abrupt, snarling, "No."

"Please, Harry. It's my brother. I want to go."

"I said 'No.'"

"I missed Clarence and Mary's funerals. Please let me go to Will's."

"You know I don't want you having anything to do with those people."

"He's not one of 'those people.' He's my brother."

"I said 'NO!' and I don't want to hear another word about it!"

She turned away and carried the newspaper into the kitchen. Then she washed the supper dishes until rage made her nearly blind. Picking up a plate, she found herself slamming it against the counter and bellowing, "I'm going to my brother's funeral!"

Before Harry knew what was happening, Sylvia stormed into the living room and stood menacingly over him. She felt stunned, yet exhilarated by the rage that for years had simmered up in her until it now exploded.

"Don't you backtalk me, woman!"

"What will you do about it?" she replied. "You can't even get out of that chair. You'd pee your pants without my help."

"Don't you talk like that to me!"

"You're just an ornery, hateful old man. There's nothing you can do to stop me. I'm going to Will's funeral!"

Then she retreated to her kitchen. For the moment, she was winning, but she feared if she remained near him, she might yet cower.

As she scraped leftovers off his plate, she thought, "He's damn lucky I just don't stop feeding him. The world would be better off if he starved to death."

She knew tomorrow he would treat her like crap, and she would put up with it as she always did, but for tonight, she had won a victory.

When she put him to bed, they only said necessary words. Then they slept side by side with their backs to one another. All the next day, neither mentioned the argument over the funeral. Harry had not liked his wife's mouthiness, but when she did not mention it further, he thought she had come to her senses. The following day, after Sylvia had finished the breakfast dishes, she came into the living room where he was listening to the radio. She had on her good dress and shoes.

"Where are you going, all dolled up like that?" he asked.

"To my brother's funeral," she said as naturally as she could.

Harry's face scrunched into a prune shape that made his beady eyes bug out of his bald head.

"If you go," he hissed, "don't you ever set foot in my house again."

"I think," Sylvia replied, surprised by the composure in her voice as she trembled inside, "that while I'm gone, you should use the time to reflect upon how you became such a miserable creature."

Harry began to whine. "You'll kill me, you know. You can't go and leave me alone. What if I have an accident? I might die while you're gone."

"I should be so lucky," she said. Then she picked up her purse and went out the front door. She did not know how to drive. She had not thought to ask Harry Jr. if he were going to the funeral. Sheer determination made her old legs carry her ten blocks to the funeral home.

"He looks so good," said Thelma, standing between Margaret and Eleanor to look in the casket, "just like he's at peace."

"I hope so," said Margaret.

Eleanor turned away. So many people had told her how good her father looked. How could anyone look good when he was dead?

"Who's that, Mother?" asked Maud, pointing toward the funeral home door.

An elderly woman entered. Her face was indented with wrinkles, her hair salt and pepper colored. Her clothes were worn and outdated, despite an obvious attempt to come well-dressed. Eleanor did not recognize her until Harry Jr. greeted her.

"That's Grandpa's sister," she told Maud, "your Great-Aunt Sylvia."

Maud stared. "I didn't know I had another aunt."

Eleanor did not stay to explain. She crossed the room.

"Hello, you must be Aunt Sylvia. I'm Eleanor."

"I knew you were Eleanor the minute I entered the room," said Sylvia. "You look like my sister Mary. She was a beautiful woman."

Eleanor did not know how to respond. She had never met Aunt Mary. She smiled and said, "I'm glad you could come."

"Too late, I'm afraid," said Sylvia, her eyes speaking her sorrow. "I should have come years ago. But your father understood why I didn't."

"Come meet my mother," Eleanor said, taking Sylvia's hand. Harry Jr. nodded to assure his mother it would be all right; then he went to give his sympathies to Roy and Bill.

Sylvia was introduced to Margaret beside the casket. These two women had been such important parts of Will's life, but they only met now at his death. Sylvia had come to pay respects to her brother, but she barely cast a glance at his lifeless form before Margaret led her away to meet the rest of the family. Since her wedding day, Margaret had not liked the Cummings, and she had begrudged the dollars Will had slipped his unfortunate sister, but now she clung to Sylvia as if she were her own sister. Sylvia was introduced to Margaret's children and grandchildren, then Margaret's side of the family, then every neighbor and friend of Will.

When the funeral began, Sylvia found a seat in the back of the room with Harry Jr. and his wife. She looked over a sea of heads, each belonging to someone who had been a part of her brother's life. She knew she would not have so many people at her funeral. Everyone seemed so kind, so glad to meet Will's sister. Had she stayed part of her brother's life, she probably would have known most of them, maybe even been friends with many of them. She had waited so long, until it was too late for her and Will, and now the only person she could ever depend on was gone. She had her sons, but Harry Jr. had his own family to concern him, and Doug wanted nothing to do with the family. She felt more alone in the funeral parlor than at home with her husband, yet she was glad she had come. As she wept through the service, she condemned herself as weak and stupid to have let anyone come between her and her family.

"I'm worried about Ma," Eleanor confided to Roy at the funeral luncheon. "She's so quiet, as if she's scared of going on without him."

"Quiet" hardly described Margaret's reaction to her husband's death. She had known plenty of troubles, but never deep, overwhelming sorrow. Until the funeral, she had wondered whether she could go on, but now she suspected someone else hurt more because of Will's death, and so she sat with Sylvia at the luncheon.

"Your brother cared a great deal about you," Margaret told Will's sister. "He always felt bad that the two of you could not spend more time together."

"It was all my fault," said Sylvia.

"He never blamed you," Margaret replied.

"No, he wouldn't, but it was my fault. I shouldn't have let someone else control me. But we didn't have all this women's rights stuff back then. By the time Will and Clarence moved out of our house, I was in a rut, and I didn't know how to pull myself out. I'm so sorry for all the grief I must have given him."

"He understood. He wouldn't want you to feel bad."

Harry Jr. came to ask his mother whether she needed a ride home.

"No, I'd like to stay a little longer," Sylvia replied.

"How did you get here if not with Harry?" Margaret asked, after he had left.

"I walked."

"Well, one of my children can drive you home when you're ready," said Margaret.

Lucy and Maud came to say goodbye to Grandma. Their father then took them home while their mother stayed to help clean up. Eleanor had her own car so when all the dishes were washed, she offered to drive Aunt Sylvia home. Roy brought his mother home, and he agreed to stay with her a few days until she adjusted to the enormous change in her life. Eleanor had asked Bill to stay with their mother, but he had confessed he had just moved in with his girlfriend, who would not appreciate his absence from home. Eleanor was too tired to argue about her brother's immoral lifestyle, especially in the Baptist Church's kitchen. She said goodbye to her mother and brothers, then sought out Aunt Sylvia, who was being regaled by descriptions of Thelma's multiple sclerosis.

As Eleanor walked her aunt to the car, she did not know what to say. They had never spoken a word until today. She had nearly forgotten her father had a sister. She found herself stunned to notice her aunt shared several of her father's mannerisms and facial expressions.

"I'm the last of four children now," said Sylvia once they were in the car. Eleanor did not know what to reply — she hoped she would not outlive her own siblings; she could not imagine such loneliness. To make conversation, she asked her aunt what her father had been like when he was young. Sylvia told anecdotes from Will's boyhood — how she used to babysit him, the troubles he got into, his secret kindnesses to her when she was married — and then why a distance had grown up between them.

When Eleanor pulled into the Cummings' driveway, Sylvia hesitated to get out of the car.

"I just need a moment," she said. "I never fully realized until today how that man in there took everything from me. I'm not sure how I'm going to face him."

"Is he violent, Aunt?" Eleanor asked.

"He used to be, but not anymore. He's in a wheelchair now, but he still has a nasty mouth."

"I'm sorry," said Eleanor, thinking of her own marriage difficulties.

Sylvia breathed deeply, then opened the car door.

"Aunt Sylvia, you'll come to visit us from now on, won't you? Mother and I would both like it."

"Ye-es, I'd like it too," said Sylvia. "I'll find a way."

She got out of the car and closed the door. Slowly she walked up the driveway, then up the front steps, fighting her urge not to go inside. Eleanor felt she should go in with her aunt, but it was not her place when they had only just met. She drove home, thinking it a shame her father and aunt had been separated until it was too late. She never wanted such distance between herself and her family.

Once inside, Sylvia gently shut the house door. She stepped into the living room and found Harry staring at her.

"Hello," she quaked as she removed her coat. "Were you all right while I was gone?"

"What do you care?" he spluttered.

Sylvia dug into her pocketbook. "I brought you a couple brownies from the luncheon. You wouldn't believe how much food they had there. I'm sorry I was gone so long. I'll make your dinner right away."

"Who drove you home?" Harry asked.

Sylvia hesitated but saw no harm in answering.

"My niece, Eleanor."

"Don't you think you'll be going out riding with her all the time," said Harry.

"Now Harry," Sylvia tried to pacify him, "you're just a little cranky because you haven't had your dinner yet. I'm sure you'll love these delicious brownies." She held them up close to his eyes so he could see them.

His feeble paw struck them from her hand.

Sylvia turned and walked from the room. She refused to pick up the brownies, and Harry could not.

"I guess you're not hungry today," she said. She went upstairs where he could not follow her in the wheelchair. She entered Serena's old room and shut the door so she would not hear him yell. She sat down and told herself she must not give in to him. She would call Harry Jr.; he would have to help her. She could not deal with her husband any longer. Fifty-six years was long enough.

When Eleanor returned home, the first thing Ronald said was, "The semester will be over in a few days. Then we can go downstate to look for a house. The girls can stay with your mother. That will give the two of us a nice little vacation. I was thinking — "

Eleanor walked past him without a word. He had scarcely said a consoling word to her since her father's death.

"Did you hear me?" asked Ronald, following her upstairs into their bedroom.

"I heard you."

"Well, what do you think? I figure the sooner we move the sooner we can get used to the area and get the girls feeling comfortable before school starts in the fall."

Eleanor had her back to him. She took off her jewelry. He knew she was not listening.

"Eleanor, just because your father died doesn't mean you can ignore me."

"I'm not ignoring you, it's just that — " She did not know how to say it.

"Don't start that crap again about our not moving. I already told the University of Michigan we're coming. You know they've found a replacement here for me."

Still she said nothing.

"Damn it, Eleanor, I — "

"I can't go, Ron. I've tried to convince myself I could. Maybe if my father hadn't died, but I can't now. My mother needs me. You don't understand because your family isn't close like mine, but I — "

"Your mother doesn't need you. I'm your husband. You're following me. We can't stay in this hick town with all this damn snow. What kind of a wife and mother are you? Don't you want the girls to have better lives? Don't you want — "

Through the window, Eleanor saw her girls playing in the backyard. She was thankful they could not hear their parents arguing. She sat down on the bed and buried her face in her hands.

"Eleanor, please, understand," said Ronald, stepping toward her. He felt he should touch her shoulder, but he could not make the gesture.

"I can't go, Ron," she repeated.

"I have to go, Eleanor. It's my big chance. I'll have more money there to do my research, maybe to make a significant breakthrough, and we'll have a better life there; things will be easier for us."

"We've discussed all this before," Eleanor sighed. "It's no good. I can't go, and I am thinking of the girls. Maybe there are more opportunities for them downstate, but I think they're happier here. We can't uproot them from all their friends and family."

"You know what you're saying, don't you?"

"Yes. I'm sorry, Ron. I've always tried to make our marriage work, but how many years do we keep trying? It's not just about moving; we both know things have been wrong between us for a long time."

"You haven't tried hard enough," he said. "You're the one making this decision, not me."

"You can't blame me. It's neither of our faults if we're incompatible."

"If I go, I won't be coming back."

She spent a second absorbing this fact, then said, "I'll go with you to file the divorce papers. We'll figure out a way for you to visit the girls, and — "

"I don't care about seeing the girls so long as I can get the hell away from you."

"But Ron, they're your daughters!"

"No, they're your daughters. You never let them be mine. You turned them against me a long time ago. They're more Whitman than Goldman."

"That's not true. I — "

"This is all your fault, Eleanor!"

He stomped downstairs. She heard the front door slam shut.

She had feared his anger. She had feared he might cry and that would have made her give in. But his indifference, especially to his children — how could she be prepared for that? She had hoped it would not come to divorce, yet she had always felt their separation was inevitable. What would people think of her now? And her poor girls would be from a broken home. She would have to love the girls even more to make up for their uncaring father. How could he say she had turned the girls against him? They were closer to her because he was never home. He might be a great scholar and scientist — although she had her doubts about that — but he was a lousy husband and father.

These difficult days for the Whitman family were marked by one happy event. The day after Ronald left her, Eleanor received a postcard from California.

> Hi Eleanor,
>   We're moving back home. Should be there in early June. We'll call when we know the exact date. Homesick and longing to see you all. Please tell everyone.
>   Love, Henry

A couple weeks later, good as his word, Henry Whitman and his family returned to Marquette. When they left behind the heat of California, the deserts of the Southwest, and the flatness of the barren Great Plains, they thanked God to be in the North again. When they crossed the Mississippi River into Wisconsin, they began to marvel at all the trees; when they crossed the Menominee River into Upper Michigan, their hearts began to pound; they had barely stopped, even to sleep overnight, so anxious were they to return. At half-past midnight, they arrived in Marquette. It being too late to disturb the family, they parked near Picnic Rocks along Lake Superior and closed their eyes to the soothing roar of the waves. They woke to a cold summer morning, with dew on the grass and the beach sand cold to bare feet.

"I wish we were back in California," said Jimmy, when he stepped out of the trailer. "The beaches are always warm there." He put his hand in Lake Superior, but quickly drew it back; the water was still freezing although the ice had melted a month ago. The lake never grew warm in summer.

"I never knew I could miss a place so much," said Beth.

Henry wrapped his arm around her in agreement.

Ellen had missed Marquette, but she had missed her relatives more. "When will we see Grandpa and Grandma?"

"We'll go over right now," said Beth. She had explained to Ellen that Grandpa had died, but she was not quite sure whether Ellen did not understand yet or whether she said 'Grandpa and Grandma' out of habit. Beth was thankful Jimmy did not reply, "Grandpa's dead, stupid!" He had been irritable and smart-mouthed all the way home. He now trudged back into the trailer, unhappy to have left California, but having no choice but to stick with his family.

Henry drove the trailer to what was now his mother's house. When the vehicle pulled into the yard, Beth felt an urge to get out and walk next door, but that house was no longer hers. It had been sold, so they would have to find a new house. They would no longer live next door to Henry's mother, for which Beth was thankful, but until Henry built another house, they would stay with Margaret.

Before anyone could step outside, Roy opened the trailer door to greet them. Everyone was startled to see he had grown a bushy beard.

"Oh Lord, he looks like a mountain man," thought Beth, wondering whether living secluded up on the Big Bay Road had affected Roy's mind.

"Those are quite some whiskers," said Henry, patting his brother on the back. Jimmy shook hands with his uncle, and Beth hugged Roy, but Ellen stepped back, looking at her bearded uncle with trepidation.

"Hello," called Margaret, coming down her front steps as everyone poured out of the trailer. More hugs followed, then expressions of sympathy for Margaret's loss.

"We should have been here," Beth told her.

"We never should have left," said Henry.

"Oh, you didn't need to come back for my sake," Margaret replied.

"Yes, we did," said Beth. "I told Henry we needed to move home and be near the family. We were wrong to go in the first place."

"Good health isn't worth it if the people you love aren't around," Henry smiled.

"In a few days," Roy laughed, "you'll be so sick of us you'll want to go back to California. Welcome home."

"I wish we still were in California," Jimmy grumbled. "It's too cold here."

"Cold? It's a beautiful day," said Margaret. "It's going to be seventy today." Jimmy shivered. "In California it would be ninety."

"Anyone who likes weather that hot is just plain nuts," said Margaret. "Come on inside."

As they climbed up the front steps, Beth remembered that Margaret had told Jimmy if he became a Catholic, he would never be allowed in her house again. Beth had nearly forgotten about the religious dispute until that moment, but now she feared an inevitable argument would arise. Henry had promised her the children would be raised as Catholics. She would not let him go back on his word — not even if they were living with Margaret until he built them a house. "God give me strength," she silently prayed.

Margaret insisted she would make breakfast for everyone. She would not even let Beth help. "That's a change," Beth thought. As they sat down to eat, a strange bearded man appeared at the door.

"Who's that?" asked Henry.

"Your brother," laughed Roy.

Bill entered and beamed at his family.

Henry found himself wrapped in a bear hug.

"Stop it!" said Henry. "Your whiskers are scratching me. What's up with all these beards?"

"You better grow one yourself and fast," said Bill. "Otherwise, you'll be thrown in the clink."

"Would someone please explain," said Beth.

"Marquette's celebrating its one hundredth birthday," said Margaret. "The festivities include a beard growing contest. Any man without a beard will be arrested."

"You're in serious trouble, brother," said Bill, rubbing Henry's hairless chin.

"I'll grow one in a jiffy and beat both of you in the contest," Henry boasted.

Jimmy glared at the three brothers. No one in California had wild beards like that, and no one there would be caught in cheap flannel shirts. People knew how to dress in California.

"How's my girl?" asked Bill, grabbing Ellen around the waist and picking her up before she had time to be squeamish about his beard.

"Fine," she laughed, feeling more at home now that she was back in her grandmother's living room.

Everyone settled around the dining room table except Margaret, who disappeared into the kitchen.

"Tell us about California," said Bill.

"First you tell us how everyone back here has been," Beth replied in a low voice. "How is your mother handling things?"

"It's been hard on her," said Roy. "She doesn't say much. But she's been better since she knew you were coming home."

"She misses Pa," said Bill, "but she's too worried about Eleanor to spend time grieving."

"What's wrong with Eleanor?" asked Henry.

"That bastard is divorcing her."

"Divorcing her!" said Henry.

He and Beth were too surprised to reprimand Bill's use of rough language before the children.

Roy and Bill gave the update on Eleanor's situation.

"Strangest part, in my opinion," said Roy, "is that Aunt Sylvia came to Pa's funeral. Then she went home and told our cousin Harry Jr. he had better see about putting his father in a nursing home because she wouldn't put up with him any longer. Next thing I know, Eleanor's telling me Aunt Sylvia's going to live with her. I guess they're going to cope together without their husbands."

"I thought no one spoke to Aunt Sylvia," said Beth.

"Right," said Roy. "Believe me, we were just as surprised as you."

Margaret returned now with eggs, toast, sausage, and coffee.

"I'm glad," she said when asked about Aunt Sylvia. "Eleanor is happy to have some help with the girls and you should see how Sylvia dotes on them. And you can't blame Sylvia for putting Harry Cumming in the nursing home. He can't even get out of his wheelchair so it was becoming too hard for her to take care of him. She's done more than her share for him all these years. She deserves some happiness now."

After breakfast, Jimmy went into the trailer to sulk away the morning. Ellen went into the backyard to reacquaint herself with her grandmother's flower garden, her grandpa's old shed, and the tree in the backyard where grandpa had hung a swing for her. Her mother had told her not to go into their old backyard, but she looked longingly across the picket fence. Coming home was sad when you could not play in your own backyard.

"Ellen!" shouted Maud, running behind the house.

"Maud, she's probably inside," Lucy called after her.

But already Maud had found her cousin, flung her arms around her, buried her face in Ellen's cheek, and declared she had missed her best friend. Ellen had not thought she and Maud were so close, but now her heart thumped within her. She liked both her cousins, but Maud was her age. Maud was her best friend too.

"Mom'll want us to go inside and see Aunt Beth and Uncle Henry," said Lucy.

"No, not until we've had a good swing first," Maud exclaimed, grabbing Ellen's hand and running with her to the backyard swing. The girls sat together on the same swing and began to pump their legs in unison.

"Someone's happy to be home," smiled Margaret, watching her grand-daughters through the kitchen window.

"The girls really missed Ellen," said Eleanor, helping her mother carry dirty dishes into the kitchen. Sylvia, who had come over with Eleanor and the girls, sat down at the dining room table and became acquainted with Henry and Beth.

Margaret whispered to Eleanor, "For a few weeks there, I didn't know how I was going to make it, but now all the family's together again, except Ada of course."

"I know," said Eleanor. "I just wish Henry and Beth had been here when Pa died."

"Maybe it's better this way. They'll remember him in his prime, not sick and frail as we last saw him. And it seems as if Sylvia came into our lives now to ease the pain. I can't get over how much she resembles Will."

"Neither can I," said Eleanor. "She's an old dear."

"A woman would have to be dear to put up with the husband she's had," said Margaret.

"I wish Pa could know she's happier now."

"Yes," said Margaret. "He would want you to be happy too."

Eleanor did not feel brave enough to be happy. "I wish I could feel as little stigmatized by my divorce as Aunt Sylvia feels about being separated from her husband."

"You did nothing wrong," said Margaret. "Ronald is the one with his values mixed up. In time, the pain will heal, and you'll find you're better off without him."

And now a page turned in the Whitmans' history. They had suffered many trials, but good days seemed finally to have come. Henry and Beth had returned at the most opportune time; their hometown was celebrating its hundredth birthday, and they were thankful not to miss the festivities marking this momentous occasion in Marquette's history.

Centennial birthdays happen only once. In the life of a city, they are a time of civic pride for the residents and the many native sons and daughters who return to celebrate. Marquette's birthday party would be the finest imaginable.

On July 1st, an adult costume ball was held at the college's Lee Hall. Eleanor normally would have gone with Ronald, not from any love of such events, but as her duty to network for her ambitious husband. This costume party, however, she attended with Bill, who forsook his many girlfriends that evening out of loyalty to his sister. Eleanor wore a mask she did not remove all evening; then made fearless by her anonymity, she mingled with faculty members. She found the opportunity to make not a few disparaging remarks about her husband to Dr. Luther West, head of the science department, to Don H. Bottum, Dean of Men, and to President Henry Tape, who, to Eleanor's delight, declared he did not know who Professor Goldman was. Eleanor went home that evening, feeling a bit guilty for her secret revenge, but also feeling a tremendous sense of vindication.

The next morning, a special children's parade was held, although postponed nearly an hour until Governor Williams could arrive to participate. Henry, Beth, Eleanor, and Margaret took the children, all of whom had a fine time, except Jimmy, who claimed he was too old for "such childish things." Later that afternoon, a huge treasure hunt was held at Shiras Park for the children. Two thousand scoops of ice cream, four hundred gifts and seven hundred fifty bags of candy were handed out to please Marquette's children, the hope of the city's next hundred years.

On the same day, a pistol shooting match was held at the prison range. Roy and Bill both attended, Roy acquitting himself nobly as he demonstrated his expertise learned from his war days. He had been reluctant at first to attend; he did not like to use a gun, although he frequently carried one for protection while living in the woods. Bill, however, had convinced Roy it was a harmless contest. The family interpreted Roy's participation as a sign he was coming out of his reclusive hermit attitude. They naively believed he was still troubled by the war; none of them tried to understand the deeper thoughts brewing within him.

The highlight of the celebrations was the Fourth of July parade, which Roy did not attend, thinking it all "too much fussing." People all over the city dug through their attics and their grandmothers' old trunks for historical costumes. Margaret pulled from the closet Will's wedding suit for Henry to wear to the parade. A pair of Henry's old knickers was offered to Jimmy, but he refused to wear anything that looked so "lousy." Margaret decked herself out in one of her old dresses from forty years ago. Beth found her mother's old wedding dress, but only Jessie was thin enough in the family to wear the petite thing, and she had to let the hem down. Others found clothing that at least looked old fashioned. They all felt a tad ridiculous, but that was part of the fun. They traipsed to the parade, women lifting hoop skirts or twirling flappers' beads, while men raised Victorian top hats to twentieth century ladies.

Marquette would never again see such a parade. Automobiles from every decade of the last half century rolled down the street. Horses, carriages, and buggies represented an even earlier period of Marquette's history. And then there were the floats — over one hundred. *The Mining Journal*'s float was designed as a barbershop with the Pitch Pipe Peers singing in harmony. The Duluth, South Shore, and Atlantic Railway placed an old M.H.&O. locomotive and caboose on a truck, and the engine spread steam throughout the streets to the children's delight. The Schneider Bros. Lumber Co. had an immense float depicting a family lawn party. These grand floats were separated in the procession by city and high school bands blaring out John Philip Sousa marches and patriotic hymns.

After the parade, the Whitman clan went home to change into modern clothes before reassembling at Margaret's house for a huge family picnic that evening.

When Henry drove his family home, Margaret and Beth went inside the house while Jimmy and Ellen helped their father remove the ribbons and streamers he had used to decorate the car for the holiday. Had the children gone inside the house, they would have interrupted, but Beth and Margaret's entrance was not heard by the two men deeply engrossed in conversation at the dining room table. The women were surprised to see Beth's brother the priest sharing a cup of coffee with Roy, the avowed atheist. Roy's tongue was running quickly, more words flowing from his mouth than his family had heard him speak in a month.

". . . and who can say if I had gone to college, if all my dreams had been fulfilled, that I would have been any happier? If I had been successful, or rich and important, and had power — the ability to hire or to fire, to teach, to fail or pass a student, what happiness would there be in that? Not that such people are not needed, or that the wisest people should not make such decisions, and it's not that I feel myself lacking in wisdom — it's just that I realize such a life would not make me happy, such decisions would agonize me. I saw too much suffering during the war for me to hurt anyone, even if the person deserved punishment. And some of the world's wisest people, politicians and scientists, have done some of the stupidest and cruelest things — like what the Germans did to the Jews, the Gypsies, and the Catholics — people essentially no different from them. What good did power do the Nazis? They misused it so it was taken from them. Even if I should not make such huge mistakes, I could never bear to be so madly involved in the world. My whole life has taught me that the only thing I want is simplicity, peace, and satisfaction with the humble person I try to be."

"You seem," Father Michael replied, "to understand more than many who go to Mass every week. I don't think God judges you for not attending church. I wish you could believe in Him, but He loves you all the more for struggling and searching your heart for understanding. I don't think — "

"I do want to believe in Him," Roy broke in. "The idea of God is beautiful, but after all the horrors I've seen and all life's frustrations, I can't believe He is a good god. If it means I'll go to Hell — if Hell exists — at least I'll be true to myself until the end."

"I believe," said Michael, "and I know this is against many of the beliefs of my Catholic brethren, but I do believe everyone goes to Heaven. Only God is our judge and can know how truly hard we strive to be good. That's why I also believe in Purgatory. Despite God's anger toward the Israelites whenever they did wrong, He always showed mercy in the end. When you and He are ready, you will feel His love again."

"Whether I believe," said Roy, "matters less than finding the truth."

Michael reached for his coffee cup as he sought words to respond. Then he saw his sister from the corner of his eye.

"Beth," he said, quickly crossing the room to wrap his arms around her.

"Michael, what are you doing here?" she asked when he released her.

"I haven't seen you since you came back from California, and I had to come celebrate Marquette's Centennial year and Bishop Baraga Days."

"Oh, Monsignor," said Margaret, "I hope Roy hasn't been impudent. I did my best to raise him as a Christian, but now that he's grown he has such odd ideas."

Beth was surprised by Margaret's reverent tone toward her brother.

"On the contrary," Father Michael replied, "I've greatly enjoyed our conversation. I wish my own parishioners sought for knowledge and understanding so painstakingly."

Henry and the kids now entered, followed by Bill and his latest playmate and roommate, Sally.

"Hello, Sally," said Margaret. "Let me introduce you to Beth's brother. This is Monsignor McCarey. We're all so proud to have a monsignor in the family."

Sally smiled; she had no idea what a monsignor was; her parents were Lutherans. But Margaret hoped to impress upon Sally that Bill came from a religious family, so Sally would be dissuaded from being a naughty girl.

Beth now understood her mother-in-law's sudden fussing over Michael. While in California, she had received a letter from her brother, informing her he had been honored by being named a monsignor by the Catholic Church. Eleanor had written to Beth that when Margaret had heard the news, she had said, "My, isn't that almost like being a bishop? Just think, a monsignor in the family!"

Beth had never guessed Margaret's religious discriminations could be overridden by her love of rank, but she was glad the honor given her brother might bring some peace between her and her mother-in-law.

While Henry and the children visited with Michael, Beth helped Margaret get ready for the family picnic.

"Do you think Eleanor enjoyed herself at the parade?" Margaret asked.

"Yes," said Beth. "She's been much more cheerful the last few days."

"I hope so. I've been so worried about her, but I think having you and Henry back home has helped raise her spirits."

"We're glad to be home," said Beth. "When Will died, I told Henry we belonged back here. It took some convincing, but he finally agreed."

"I guess you can never tell about people," said Margaret. "I thought a college professor would make a good husband, but Eleanor probably would have been happier married to a miner or a sailor. Beth, of the three people who married one of my children, you're the one I least thought would make a good spouse, yet you've turned out to be the best one. You're as much my daughter as Ada or Eleanor."

Beth blushed. The compliment was unexpected, all the more because she could tell Margaret was sincere.

"Thank you, Mother," she replied. "Do you want me to butter all the buns, or should we leave some unbuttered?"

"Go ahead and butter them all," said Margaret. "I hope we have enough."

They needed no more words. Twenty-one years of conflict between the two women had ended.

Soon Whitmans, Cummings, Dalrymples, Bergmanns, McCareys, and Goldmans swarmed across the backyard. Dish after dish of jello salad and baked beans, potato salad and apple pie were carried to the backyard picnic table. If there were one thing the Whitman clan knew how to do, it was to eat; they enjoyed the activity second only to each other's company. Family events can be trying — someone in the family always annoys someone else. A family picnic may even be nothing more than a group of strangers, tied together by blood, who get together from a sense of obligation, and every moment, each one asks him or herself how soon before the ordeal can be escaped. The young especially think they would rather be with their friends than their dull family members. But while the friends abandon you and the lovers cheat, you keep attending the same dull family get-togethers with the same familiar faces. And then you begin to feel fond of even the distant cousins. Blood becomes thick. Kinship ties strengthen. Today the Whitmans bonded over the recent death of the beloved family patriarch, and they supported each other, to praise the accomplishments of some, to wish for the presence of others, to be thankful for one another's company.

In small towns, people depend on each other. In Upper Michigan, through long, harsh winters and economic woes, people form bonds even without blood ties. On this day of civic pride, an entire city became one family, a city filled with people descended from a handful of brave pioneers who came to Iron Bay a century before to build a community which still prospered. Even Jimmy Whitman, who today would rather be in California, and as an adult would live miles from Marquette, would in later years look back on this day with fondness.

The picnic broke up all too soon as everyone looked at their watches and realized it would soon be time for the fireworks. People went their separate ways. Bill wanted to be alone with Sally. Thelma was tired so Jessie brought her home. Harry Jr. had promised to take his children over to a friend's house. Some decided to go home rather than attend the fireworks, but Sylvia insisted on seeing the finale of the city's celebrations, and Eleanor, finding her daughters' enthusiasm matched that of her aunt, agreed to take them all. Margaret told Roy he had no choice but to drive her to Memorial Field for the fireworks. "It won't hurt you to take me and then stay at your mother's house another night before going back to that old cabin of yours," she insisted. Roy knew better than to argue. Henry and Beth talked Michael into piling into their car with the children. Then they followed Roy's vehicle while Eleanor and company brought up the rear. Once the three automobiles reached Memorial Field, the Whitman clan found thousands of people crowded together, eagerly awaiting the finale to the centennial celebrations.

The Boy Scouts of Racine, Wisconsin entertained the crowd with their drum and bugle corps. Then a Vaudeville show made the crowd laugh and join in singing.

Gazing at the crowd, Sylvia felt overwhelmed. "I never saw so many people in my life. Everyone in Marquette must be here."

"Yes, this city sure has grown," said Margaret, remembering as a girl how she had thought Marquette much too small. Now amid a sea of jubilant faces, she scarcely recognized anyone. Proudly, she said to Sylvia, "Unlike us, most of these people don't have their names in *The Mining Journal* as Marquette residents for over fifty years."

"No, I guess not," said Sylvia. "I've lived here my whole life, that's seventy-seven years. I was born in Marquette's twenty-third year, so I feel as if I belong more to the little village of a hundred years ago than to this big modern city."

As they found a place to set up chairs and lay a blanket for the children to sit on, Margaret asked her sister-in-law, "Do you remember the day they unveiled the statue of Father Marquette? There was a big crowd that day, but nothing like this."

"Yes," said Sylvia, "I remember that, and I remember when the streetcars were put in; we were all so excited to have them, and now they've been ripped out for I don't know how many years. I can even remember when we first got electricity."

"I can remember the days before electricity," said Margaret. "I'm sure glad those days are over."

"Life was harder then," said Sylvia. "But back then, since we had no idea there would one day be electricity, and automobiles, and movie theatres, we didn't miss them. I don't think people are as polite and courteous as before the wars either. I do miss that."

"People don't have the class they had back then," Margaret agreed. "All these young girls running around with skirts above their knees."

Eleanor and Beth chuckled, knowing this comment was pointed toward Bill's girl Sally, who had come to the picnic with her knobby knees on full display.

"And this modern architecture," sighed Sylvia. "Houses look like boxes now, and each one is painted a dull white. Houses had more color when I was a girl. I remember my grandparents' house on Ridge Street — my grandparents moved away when I was only four, so maybe my memories aren't exact, but my parents often told me what a beautiful house it was. Inside there was ornate woodwork and elaborate colored wallpaper and stenciling on the walls and borders along the ceiling. It was so beautiful you never wanted to leave it. Now we have these puffy sofas and metallic kitchen tables with pop-up leafs and —"

Sylvia could not finish her sentence but just shook her head.

"Which grandparents' house are you talking about?" asked Henry. "Your Grandpa and Grandma Whitman?"

"No, they had a boarding house when I was a girl," said Sylvia. "Not that their house wasn't nice, but the house I'm talking about was my Grandpa and Grandma Henning's house. They built one of the first and finest homes on Ridge Street, but they only lived there a few years before they moved away. I wonder what happened to all their money. I never saw any of it. I bet Grandma Henning left it all to Aunt Edna."

"You mean that big sandstone house, don't you?" said Margaret. "I remember Will pointed it out to me one time."

"Is the house still there?" asked Henry, his carpenter instincts awakening.

"Oh, yes." Sylvia described it until Henry suspected it was the same as Robert O'Neill's house, where he had fixed the porches during the war.

"Aunt Sylvia, why did your grandparents move away?" Lucy asked.

"Well, their daughter, my Aunt Madeleine, drowned in the lake. I can't really remember how; I was just a little girl then, but my grandparents were so upset they sold their house and moved back East. I never saw them again except once when my grandpa came to visit just after I was married. I don't remember much about him either. I wish now I knew more, but my mother died when I was just a girl and my father died when I was in my twenties, so I guess I was too young to think about asking them many questions then."

"I know what you mean," said Margaret. "My grandfather always said the Dalrymples were related to the royal family of Scotland, but I was too lazy to ask exactly how and write it down. Just think, I might've been a Scottish princess."

"I do remember," said Sylvia, ignoring Margaret's pretentious claim to the Scottish throne, "that my father said my mother's family came to Marquette the year the city was founded."

"You know," said Michael, "my Grandma Bergmann used to tell me she came to Marquette during its first year. How odd. I bet our families have known each other a long time."

"They have," said Sylvia, taking his hand. "I remember being at your parents' wedding when St. Peter's Cathedral was just being built. I must have been about twelve then."

"Someone," said Roy, "should write all this down. Marquette is the finest city ever, and since our family is part of its history, neither should be forgotten."

Everyone nodded in agreement, but writing Marquette's history seemed too daunting a task for any of them. Not one felt confident with pen and paper.

"Hello, Roy," said a young man passing by. "How are you?"

"Hi, Fred. Everyone, this here is Fred Rydholm," Roy introduced. "He works with me up at the Club. He drove the Club's car in the parade today."

Everyone greeted Fred. Introductions were made and remarks exchanged about how impressive the parade had been. Then Fred said goodbye and walked away. One day, Fred Rydholm would pen two mammoth volumes detailing the history of the iron ore industry, the founding of Marquette and the Huron Mountain Club, and the Upper Peninsula's important role in American history.

"How long before the fireworks start?" asked Ellen.

"Can't we go home?" Jimmy complained. "It's cold out here, and fireworks are boring anyway."

"Don't be a creampuff," his grandmother teased. "The fireworks will be marvelous. This has been the best Fourth in the North."

At that moment, the first loud cracking thunder broke. Memorial Field was packed with thousands of city residents and visitors who lifted their eyes to the glorious explosions in the night sky. Pink blazing sparks spread in every direction. Then a burst of blue, an explosion of green, a shot of white, a spray of orange, then yellow, then blue again, and red, and green, and blue, and orange, and yellow, and pink, and white. Burst after burst, straight firing white lines, kaleidoscopic green, pink, purple, all at once. One separate firework to mark each year of Marquette's history. Up into the sky they shot in shimmering streaks like a hundred candles blazing on a bombastic birthday cake. Ellen covered her ears; the fireworks were so delightfully loud.

Henry leaned over to kiss his wife's cheek.

"Ouch, that tickles," Beth giggled. "When will you shave off that silly beard?"

"First thing tomorrow morning," he promised, "but you have to admit it looks pretty good for having been grown so quickly."

"Shh, Daddy, you're missing the fireworks," Ellen scolded.

Henry and Beth both chuckled, glad to see their daughter happy. They were happy themselves. They were back where they belonged, in their hometown for its centennial, which they would not have missed for anything. Henry thought back on all of Marquette's remarkable history, the raising of the courthouse, the library, the banks, the houses, the bravery of its people, the struggles through fires and blizzards, economic woes and wars. He thought of the ore docks, those formidable giants of the iron industry, stretching out into the world's greatest lake as emissaries to distant lands. For a hundred years, from Iron Bay, the Upper Peninsula's riches had been shipped out to bolster a nation, yet Marquette had scarcely received mention in a history book. Many people could not even pronounce its name, much less find it on a map. But its Northern sons and daughters knew the great privilege they shared in living here. They knew Nature had blessed them by giving them this land of pristine beauty, mighty forests, fresh air, and remarkable weather. Henry and Beth were grateful to have been born here, and thankful they had been wise enough to return. Thousands that night felt in their hearts what Henry spoke as he turned to Beth.

"We truly do live in THE QUEEN CITY OF THE NORTH."

BE SURE TO READ THE REST OF THE MARQUETTE TRILOGY!

Iron Pioneers
The Marquette Trilogy: Book One

When iron ore is discovered in Michigan's Upper Peninsula in the 1840s, newlyweds Gerald Henning and his beautiful socialite wife Clara travel from Boston to the little village of Marquette on the shores of Lake Superior. They and their companions, Irish and German immigrants, French Canadians, and fellow New Englanders face blizzards and near starvation, devastating fires and financial hardships. Yet these iron pioneers persevere until their wilderness village becomes integral to the Union cause in the Civil War and then a prosperous modern city. Meticulously researched, warmly written, and spanning half a century, *Iron Pioneers* is a testament to the spirit that forged America.

SUPERIOR HERITAGE
The Marquette Trilogy: Book Three

The Marquette Trilogy comes to a satisfying conclusion as it brings together characters and plots from the earlier novels and culminates with Marquette's sesquicentennial celebrations in 1999. What happened to Madeleine Henning is finally revealed as secrets from the past shed light upon the present. Marquette's residents struggle with a difficult local economy, yet remain optimistic for the future. The novel's main character, John Vandelaare, is descended from all the early Marquette families in *Iron Pioneers* and *The Queen City*. While he cherishes his family's past, he questions whether he should remain in his hometown. Then an event happens that will change his life forever.

To learn more about Tyler R. Tichelaar's novels and to order autographed copies, visit: **www.MarquetteFiction.com**